BROKEN WINGS

&

MIDNIGHT FLIGHT

V.C. Andrews® Books

The Dollanganger Family Series
Flowers in the Attic
Petals on the Wind
If There Be Thorns
Seeds of Yesterday
Garden of Shadows

The Casteel Family Series
Heaven
Dark Angel
Fallen Hearts
Gates of Paradise
Web of Dreams

The Cutler Family Series
Dawn
Secrets of the Morning
Twilight's Child
Midnight Whispers
Darkest Hour

The Landry Family Series
Ruby
Pearl in the Mist
All That Glitters
Hidden Jewel
Tarnished Gold

The Logan Family Series
Melody
Heart Song
Unfinished Symphony
Music in the Night
Olivia

The Orphans Miniseries
Butterfly
Crystal
Brooke
Raven
Runaways (full-length novel)

The Wildflowers Miniseries
Misty
Star
Jade
Cat
Into the Garden (full-length novel)

The Hudson Family Series
Rain
Lightning Strikes
Eye of the Storm
The End of the Rainbow

The Shooting Stars Series
Cinnamon
Ice
Rose
Honey
Falling Stars

The De Beers Family Series
Willow
Wicked Forest
Twisted Roots
Into the Woods
Hidden Leaves

My Sweet Audrina
(does not belong to a series)

Published by POCKET BOOKS

V.C. ANDREWS®

BROKEN WINGS

&

MIDNIGHT FLIGHT

POCKET **STAR** BOOKS

New York London Toronto Sydney Singapore

An *Original* Publication of POCKET BOOKS

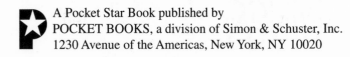 A Pocket Star Book published by
POCKET BOOKS, a division of Simon & Schuster, Inc.
1230 Avenue of the Americas, New York, NY 10020

ISBN: 0-7394-3757-7

First Pocket Books paperback printing May 2003 for Broken Wings,
October 2003 for Midnight Flight

Contents

Broken Wings   1

Midnight Flight   323

BROKEN WINGS

Contents

Prologue   5

Part One: ROBIN   7

Part Two: TEAL   121

Part Three: PHOEBE   227

Prologue

Once when we all had a quiet moment, when no one was demanding anything of us and our punitive chores were completed, we sat and watched the sky turn from deep blue to mauve and turquoise.

A sparrow landed on the top rail of the horse corral and tapped about for a moment before settling and staring at the three of us. Teal was the first to notice.

"I wonder," she said, "if birds who live in cages ever wonder why they are in cages."

Robin looked at her as if she were going to say something sarcastic to her and then she looked at the bird and her face softened.

"I suppose we could pretend to be confused about that ourselves," Robin said. "Couldn't we, Phoebe?"

"What do you mean?" I asked. "I'm not confused. I know I don't belong here."

"Phoebe, we're all so good at lying to everyone else, we're even good at lying to ourselves," Robin replied.

Teal smiled.

"She's right, you know."

"No, I don't know."

"Well, I'm telling you, Phoebe. We don't need to be told or shown why we're like caged birds. We each know why we're here."

"I know why I am. Let me tell you," Robin said.

And then she began . . .

PART ONE

ROBIN

1

Jerked into the Night

"**W**ake up, Robin!" I heard my mother say. I felt myself being rocked hard.

At first I thought the rocking was in my dream, a dream so deep I had to swim up to consciousness like a diver from the ocean floor. Each time my mother shook my shoulder, I drew closer and closer to the surface, moaning.

"Quiet!" she ordered. "You'll wake Grandpa and Grandma and I'll have my hands full of spilt milk. Darn it, Robin. I told you what time we were headin' outta here. You haven't even finished packin'," she said.

My suitcase was open on the floor, some of my clothes still beside it. Mother darling had insisted I not begin until after I supposedly went to bed last night. My mother said I couldn't bring but one suitcase of my things, and it was hard to decide what to take and not to take. She needed everything of hers because she was going to be a country singing star and had to have her outfits and all her boots and every hat as well as half a suitcase of homemade audiotapes she thought would win the admiration of an important record producer in Nashville.

I sat up and pressed my palms over my cheeks, patting them like Grandpa always did when he put on aftershave lotion. The skin on my face was still asleep and felt numb. My mother stood back and looked at me with her small nose scrunched, which was something she always did when she was very annoyed. She also twisted her full lips into her cheek. She had the smallest mouth for someone who could sing as loudly as she could, but most women envied her lips. I know that some of her friends went for collagen shots to get theirs like hers.

Everyone said we looked like sisters because I had the same petite features, the same rust-colored hair, and the same soft blue eyes. Nothing she heard pleased her more. The last thing she wanted to be known as was my mother, or anyone's mother for that matter. She was thirty-two years old this week, and she was convinced she had absolutely her last chance to become a singing star. She said she had to pass me off as her younger sister or she wouldn't be taken seriously. I was sixteen last month, and she wanted everyone, especially people in show business, to believe she was just in her mid-twenties.

Although I was closer to one of her idols, Dolly Parton, than she was when it came to breasts, we did have similar figures, both being a shade more than five feet five. She always looked taller because she hardly ever wore anything but boots. She wore hip-hugging tight jeans most of the time, and when she went out to sing at what she called another honky-tonk, she usually tied the bottom of her blouse so there was a little midriff showing. Grandpa would swell up with anger, his face nearly breaking out in hives, or just blow out his lips and explode with biblical references.

"We taught you the ways of the righteous, brought you up to be a churchgoing girl, and you still dress like a street tramp. Even after . . . after . . . your Fall," he told her, and swung his eyes my way.

That's what I was in his way of thinking: the Fall, the result of "the grand sin of fornication." Mother darling had been sexually active at the age of fifteen and had me when she was only sixteen. Grandpa, despite despising the situation as much as he did, would not permit even talk of an abortion.

"You abide by your actions and pay for your sins. It's the only path toward redemption," he preached then, according to Mother darling, and preached now.

I remember the first time I was arrested for shoplifting. The policewoman knew my grandparents and asked me how I could behave so badly coming from a solid, religious, and loving home. Wasn't I just a self-centered ingrate?

I fixed my eyes on her and said, "My mother didn't want me. My grandparents forced me down her throat, and she never stops throwing that back at them. How would you like living in such a solid, religious, and loving home?"

She blinked as if she had soot in her eyes and then grunted and went off mumbling about teenagers. I was just barely one. It was two days after my thirteenth birthday and the first time I was arrested. I had shoplifted a number of times before, but I was never caught. It amazed me how really easy it was. Half the time, if not more, those machines that are supposed to ring don't; and the employees, especially of the department stores, don't seem to care enough to watch for it. I practically waved whatever it was I was taking in front of their faces. Many times I threw away whatever I took almost immediately afterward. I couldn't chance bringing it home.

Grandpa placed all the blame on Mother darling, telling her she was setting a very bad example for me by dressing the way she dressed and singing in places "the devil himself won't enter." He would rant at her, waving his thick right forefinger in the air like an evangelist in one of those prayer meetings in large tents. He made me attend them with him when I was younger, claiming he had to work extra hard on me since I was spawned from sin. Anyway, he would bellow at Mother darling so loudly, the walls of the old farmhouse shook.

Grandma would try to calm him down, but he would sputter and stammer like one of his old tractors, usually concluding with "Thank goodness she took on your mother's maiden name, Kay Jackson. When she goes singing in those bars, I can pretend I don't know who she is."

"You don't have to pretend. You don't know who I am, Daddy," my mother would fire back at him. "Never did, never will. I'm writin' a song about it."

"Lord, save us," Grandpa would finally say and retreat. He was close to sixty-five but looked more like fifty, with a full head of light brown hair with just a touch of gray here and there, and thick, powerful-looking shoulders and arms. He could easily lift a fully grown Dorset Horn sheep and carry it a mile. Despite his strength and his rage, I never saw him lift his hand to strike my mother or me. I think he was afraid of his own strength.

My grandparents owned a sheep farm about ten miles east of Columbus, just outside the village of Granville. The farm was no longer active, although Grandpa kept a dozen Olde English Babydoll sheep that he raised and sold.

Before she went anywhere, Mother darling would practically bathe herself in cologne, claiming the stench of sheep and pigs permeated the house. "It sinks into your very soul," she claimed, which was another thing that set Grandpa on fire, the farm being his way of life and his living. Mother darling had the ability to ignite him like a stick of dynamite. Sometimes, I thought she was doing it on purpose, just to see how far he would go. The most I saw him do was slam his fist down on the kitchen table and make the dishes jump so high, one fell off and shattered.

"That," he said, pointing to it and then to her, "gets added to your rent."

Ever since Mother darling quit high school and worked in the supermarket and then began to sing nights with one pair of musicians or another, Grandpa insisted she pay rent for her and for me. It wasn't much, but it took most of her supermarket salary, which was another justification she used for her singing, not that she needed any. She was convinced she could be a big star.

I knew she was saving up for something big. Suddenly, she was willing to work overtime at the supermarket and she took any singing gig she and her partners at the time could get, from private parties to singing for an hour or so in the malls in Columbus.

Then one night, she slipped into my room, closing the door softly behind her. She stood with her back against the door and looked like she had won the lottery. Her face was that bright, her eyes seemed full of fireflies.

"We're leavin' this trap tomorrow night," she said in a voice just above a whisper.

"What? To where?"

"I've got a job in Nashville with a three-piece band my old boyfriend from high school, Cory Lewis, runs. He's the drummer and they lost their singer. She ran off with a car salesman to live in Beverly Hills, which I'm sure was just an old tire which will go flat before they get close. Not that I care. It's become an opportunity for me. We're going to play in places where real record producers go to listen for new talent."

"Nashville?"

"You don't make it in country music if you don't make it in Nashville, Robin. Now here's what I want you to do. Quietly pack one suitcase. It's all I got room for in the Beetle."

Mother darling had an old yellow Volkswagen Beetle that looked like someone with a tantrum had kicked and punched it for hours. The car was rusted out in places so badly, you could see through to the road beneath, and it had a cracked window on the passenger's side.

"But isn't Nashville very far away?"

"If you attended class more often, you'd know it's only a little over four hundred miles from here, Robin. Four hundred in actual distance, but a million in dreams," she added.

"That lawn mower you drive won't make it."

"Just shut your sewer mouth and pack," she ordered, losing her patience. "We're leavin' at two this mornin'. Very quietly. I don't want him on my tail," she said, nodding toward Grandpa and Grandma's room.

"How long are we gonna be there?" I asked, and she shook her head.

"Girl, don't you get it? We're leavin' here for good. I can't leave you with Grandpa and Grandma, Robin. Believe me, I wish I could, but they're too old to be watchin' after you, bailin' you out of trouble every week. And it's now or never for me. I'm gettin' nowhere singin' in the honky-tonks here. It's nothing for you to leave the school, so don't make like it is," she warned. "You've been suspended a half-dozen times for one thing or another. They won't miss you when the new year begins and you're not there," she reminded me.

"And don't try tellin' me you'll miss your friends, Robin. Those no-bodies you hang out with just get you into more trouble. I might be savin' your life the same time I save my own. Be sure you're quiet," she said.

Despite her bravado, Mother darling was still frightened of Grandpa.

"If we're lucky, he won't realize we're gone until it comes time for him to collect his rent. In his mind that was a way of imposin' penance on me for havin' you. Pack," she ordered, then opened the door quietly and slipped out as fast as a shadow caught in the light.

I couldn't help but admit surprise at her courage. For as long as I could remember, she talked about picking up and leaving Granville. But it was certainly one thing to talk about it and another to actually do it. Despite Grandpa's monthly rent and his ranting and raving about saving our souls, we had a home. Grandma cooked our meals, and even though Mother darling and I were supposed to do our share of the household chores, Grandma usually did them for us. She had them to baby-sit for me when I was younger so she could pursue her music career, even though Grandpa thought it was "coddling the devil" to perform "half-naked" in "slime pits." He talked so much about the devil and hell that I used to believe he had been there and back. One of these days, I thought, he will bring out some pictures to show me tortured souls.

When the farm was active, he tried to get Mother darling to work, feeding and caring for the variety of sheep he raised, as well as miniature Hereford cattle. On purpose or not, she was more trouble than value to him, always wasteful when she was shearing. He finally gave up on her, which couldn't have pleased her more. By the time I was old enough to be of any use, he was retreating from the business and there wasn't much to do. He let all his help go.

Anyway, after she had awoken me, I splashed some cold water on my face and finished packing. Of course, she had promised to buy me a whole new wardrobe when we got to Nashville and she had earned big money in the music business. I couldn't deny she had a nice voice and looked pretty up on a stage, but it just seemed so unreal to think of her as actually making records and being on television or singing in front of thousands of people. I didn't tell her that. Nothing would set her off as much as being told she didn't have what it takes. Actually, I envied her for having some sort of dream at least. The only thing I looked forward to when we left was a cup of strong coffee.

She was at the door fifteen minutes later.

"Ready?" she asked.

I had the suitcase packed and closed and I was sitting on my bed with my eyes closed. I was falling asleep again, hoping it was just a dream.

"I've already got all my things in the car," she whispered. "C'mon, wake up, Robin."

Impatient, she picked up my suitcase. It was obviously heavier than she expected.

"What did you take?"

"Just what I needed," I said.

She grimaced and led the way. Grandpa always kept his hallway lights low to save on electricity. The weak illumination, the heavy thick shadows following along the wall, all made me feel it was still a dream. It was mid-July, but nights and mornings were cold to me. I shuddered, wrapped my arms around myself, and followed Mother darling down the fieldstone walkway to the car. A partially overcast night sky provided minimum starlight. The whole world looked asleep. I felt like I was sneaking into a painting.

The car doors complained when we opened them, metal shrieking. Mother darling started the engine without putting on the lights and drove slowly down the long driveway. I was still in a state of disbelief, groggy, my eyes half closed.

"Good riddance to this," she muttered. "I'm gettin' out. I'm gettin' away, finally."

I turned and cuddled up as best I could with my head against the window and the top of the seat. I couldn't crawl into the rear because she had her guitar there resting on a pillow she wouldn't let me use. Nevertheless, despite the bumps and turns, I fell asleep.

I woke up to the screaming shrill sound of a tractor trailer as it passed us by on the highway. We were already on I-71 South heading toward Louisville. The driver in the tractor trailer sounded his horn again.

"Donkey," Mother darling called him. I groaned and sat up straighter, stretching my arms.

Suddenly, it all came back to me.

"I thought I was dreaming," I told her.

She laughed.

"No more, Robin. Dreams turn into reality now," she vowed.

I saw the road signs.

"I don't see why we have to go to a place where people call people Bubba and Sissy," I complained. Mother darling knew how much I disliked country music. I told her it was soapy and full of tears.

"I told you—it's where you have to go to make it in country music," she said.

"Country music. You've got to chew on straw and be barefoot most of the time to like it."

She practically pulled off the highway, jerking herself around to yell at me.

"You'd better keep that stupid opinion to yourself when we get there, Robin. People in Nashville have been known to hang rock-and-rollers like you by their ears for less."

"Yeah, yeah, right," I said.

"I don't see how you can afford to make fun of anyone anyway, Robin. You're sixteen and you've already got a criminal record. You should be happy I'm takin' you to a place no one knows you. You'll have a chance to start new, make new friends."

"Friends. You never liked any of my friends and probably never will, no matter where we live. In fact, you never liked anything I've done."

"What are you talking about now?"

"When I was in that school play in seventh grade, everybody else's mother or father was there, but not my mother darling. My mother darling was strumming a guitar in some sawdust-floor saloon instead."

"Damn, you never let me forget that, do you? I do the best I can, Robin. It's not easy bein' a single mother, and my parents never helped us all that much. You know Grandpa took my money, even though he condemned me for the way I earned it. You know what he says, 'There's no such thing as dirty money, only dirty people.' He's been punishin' me ever since I got pregnant with you," she reminded me.

"You should have run off and had an abortion. I wish I wasn't born anyway."

"Yeah, right. That's easy for you to say now. Bein' a girl out there alone in the world is no picnic with or without a baby, and it's not been a picnic for me livin' with my parents and hearin' Grandpa complain about you all the time, blamin' me for every stupid thing you do."

"Don't worry, Mother darling. I'm not complaining about your not leaving me back there with them. I'd probably have run off anyway."

"I don't doubt it. I know I'm savin' your life takin' you with me, Robin. The least you could do is be a little grateful and very cooperative. And another thing, I don't want you callin' me Mother darlin' anymore. I know you're just bein' sarcastic 'cause of that book *Mommie Dearest*. Besides," she said, "I told you how I have to present myself as bein' younger. From the day we get to Nashville, until I say otherwise, you're my younger sister. Always call me Kay."

"That won't be hard," I said. "It takes more than just calling someone Mother for her to be a mother."

"Oh, you're so smart." She thought a moment. "Actually, I like that. It's a great first line for a new song: It takes more than calling someone Mother for her to be a mother," she sang. She looked at me. "Thanks."

I shook my head and stared at the floor. She turned on one of her country music stations and began to sing along. The happier she was, the angrier and more depressed I became. This wasn't my dream life; it was hers. I was like a piece of paper stuck to the bottom of her boots. She couldn't shake me off, and I couldn't pull away.

The road streamed ahead. She saw only promise and glory. I just saw a strip of highway going to nowhere, which was where I had been.

Why did she ever name me Robin? I thought. She should have called me Canary.

I'm just like one: trapped in a cage.

All I had to do was tell her and she would turn it into another song.

2

Getting to Glory

I fell asleep again, despite Mother darling's singing. When I woke this time, I had to go to the bathroom. She moaned about it.

"We're almost to I-65. Can't you put a plug in it?" she whined.

"I have to go now!" I screamed.

Reluctantly, she turned into the first road stop, complaining about the time we were going to lose. I didn't understand why she had to get to Nashville so fast.

"Where are we going to live when we get there anyway?" I wanted to know.

"We're going to live with Cory. He has a two-bedroom apartment, and it's not far from where you go to school," she told me.

Two bedrooms? I thought. She and I weren't going to share one. That was for sure.

"How do you just go and pick up again with someone you haven't seen in years?" I asked her.

She stared ahead, looking for a place to park. I thought she wasn't going to answer.

Then, when we stopped, she turned to me and with steely eyes said, "You do what you have to do to move ahead in the business, Robin. Cory knows people now and besides, what are you worrying about? I'm the one sleeping with him, not you."

"Who don't you sleep with?" I mumbled. "That's why you never could tell who my father was."

It was the only explanation I knew. From what I could put together, she had been at some wild party and actually had gone to bed with three different boys. She was either so drunk or hopped up on something, she didn't know who was first and who was last. Some wild sperm had seized upon one of her eggs and brought me into this world. Like Grandpa paraphrased, "The sins of the mother rest on the head of the daughter."

"I heard what you mumbled, Robin. Don't be so smart," she said, turning off the engine.

I got out, slammed the door behind me, and went into the restaurant and to the bathroom. I heard her follow me into the bathroom. I could never mistake the clip-clop of those boots on tile.

"Thought you could wait until the precious exit," I said to the closed stall on my way out. She didn't reply.

I went to the shop. As I stood there looking at newspapers, magazines, candy, and other things, I remember feeling like I was floating in space. I didn't think I'd miss Grandpa and Grandma, but at least I had a home with them. Where were we really going? Did Mother darling really believe I would be better off in Nashville, or was I just like some old suit of clothes, stuffed in a bag and dragged along? She had made it crystal clear to me that she didn't want me to call her Mother. How much easier would it be if she could just drop me off on her way to a new life.

Back in the car, after we drove off and were on the highway again, I pulled the entertainment magazine out from between the sections of newspaper. She watched me do it and nearly turned off the highway again, jerking the car and hitting the brakes.

"Did you steal that? Did you? Did you put that magazine in the newspaper first and then just pay for the newspaper? I know your tricks."

"No," I said, but she fixed her eyes on me like two small spotlights and scrunched her nose.

"You're lyin', Robin. I can always tell when you do. Are you ever goin' to stop stealin'? Don't you know you could have gotten me in trouble, too, back there? And me on the way to Nashville. How do you think I would be able to explain that? Sorry, I couldn't make the audition because my daughter shoplifted a magazine and we were arrested on the way."

She continued to drive.

"Why do you do these things?" she asked, but mostly of herself. "Maybe my father is right. Maybe people do inherit evil."

"Who did you inherit it from then?" I fired at her.

She glared at me for a moment.

"I don't think of what I did as so evil, at least not as evil as my father does. I was young and into stupid things like drugs and alcohol and I was very frustrated livin' in that house and bein' told that everythin' I liked and everythin' I wanted to do was bein' inspired by Satan."

She turned back to me, glancing at the magazine again.

"I'm warnin' you, Robin. If you get into trouble in Nashville the way you did back home, I'm not goin' to come to your rescue. I won't want anyone, especially people in the business, to know I gave birth to a petty thief. Do you understand me?"

"You already told me you're going to pretend you're my older sister, didn't you? No one will blame you for giving birth to anything."

"Don't be so smart. Oh damn," she said, grimacing. "I was hopin' we would have a nice trip and you would be as excited about all this as I am. We're startin' a new life!"

"You're starting a new life," I corrected.

She sighed and shook her head again.

After a moment I took out a pack of cigarettes and lit one. She spun around even faster than before.

"Where did you get those?"

I shrugged.

"You stole them, too, probably. My God, the trouble we just missed. Didn't I tell you I don't want you smokin' around me? Didn't I tell you how bad it was for my throat, my voice? I can't chance strainin' it, not now. Stop makin' me shout!"

"I'm not making you," I said.

"Throw that cigarette out the window!"

I took one more defiant puff, rolled down the window, and flipped the cigarette out.

"Throw out the whole pack," she ordered.

"The whole pack? But—"

"Throw it out, Robin. Now," she said, and I did.

Then I sat back with my arms folded and pouted, until we both heard the police siren and she looked in the rearview mirror and exclaimed, "Oh no!"

As she slowed down to pull over, my heart began to pound. Had I been seen back at the store?

"Now you've gone and done it," she wailed. "I'm ruined before I even begin."

The state trooper got out of his vehicle and sauntered over to my side, moving his hand in a circle to indicate I should roll the window all the way down.

"Let me see your license and registration," he ordered Mother darling. He looked ten feet tall to me and broader than Grandpa.

Mother darling hurried to dig it all out of the glove compartment and her purse. It took a while, and all that time, he stood there glaring at me. I'm caught again, I thought sadly.

He took the license and the registration.

"Where are you going?" he asked as he read it.

"To Nashville, Officer. I'm a singer and I have an opportunity to improve my career. My daughter and I are goin' to start a whole new life," she continued. I thought she was pathetic, trying to sound so sweet and innocent.

He didn't smile.

"Do you realize," he began, looking more at me, "that you could start a serious fire tossing lit cigarettes out of the window and into the dry grass back there?"

"Oh," Mother darling said, obviously relieved I wasn't being arrested for shoplifting. "Yes. I mean, no. I didn't realize she had thrown a lit cigarette out the window. I thought she had snuffed it out. Didn't I tell you to do that first, Robin?" she demanded with a face full of steam.

I looked at her without answering. He would have to be a very stupid policeman to buy that, I thought.

"We've had some serious fires here recently, and with the drought and all . . ."

"Oh yes, Officer. You're absolutely right. We weren't thinkin'. You know how two young women can git sometimes. We were listenin' to music and talkin' because we're so excited about startin' a new life."

"Umm," he said. "I really should cite you for this."

"We don't have much money," she wailed. "Just enough to get ourselves goin'. I swear we won't do anythin' like that again. Will we, Robin?"

"No," I said dryly. "Never again."

He nodded.

"All right. You watch it, and watch your speed. I notice your right rear tire is too worn. You had better get that changed soon."

"Oh. It's so like me to neglect my car. But," she said, flicking her eyelids, "I never neglect my men."

He finally laughed.

"I'll bet," he said. "Have a good trip."

"Thank you kindly, Officer," she told him.

I could have puked, but I swallowed hard, closed my eyes, and pressed my lips shut.

"Okay. Good luck in your career. What's your name in case I hear about you later?"

"Kay Jackson," she said. "And you will hear about me."

He broke a smile, tipped his hat, and returned to his car.

Mother darling released a hot, trapped breath.

"There," she said, satisfied with herself. "Let that be a lesson to you. If you're nice to people, they'll be nice to you. Especially men," she added, and started away.

"If you're so nice to them, how come you never had one ask you to marry him?" I asked.

In my heart of hearts, I thought the reason was really me. Most men didn't want to marry a woman who had a child to raise, and as I grew older, that became more and more a problem. I used to have night-mares in which Mother darling did decide to marry someone, but only if I remained with Grandpa and Grandma. She would come to me in the dark dream and say, "You can't expect another man to take on the responsibilities of raisin' someone else's child, now can you, Robin? I'm sure you understand." I'd wake up as she was leaving the house, and for a long moment, I would wonder if it hadn't happened. The dream was usually that vivid.

"What makes you think no man has asked?"

"You never talked about any," I said.

"Plenty have, but I can't pursue a singin' career and keep house, can I? And what if he wanted more children, huh? What would I do, hold a baby in my arms and record songs? I don't need a marriage. I need a break in the business," she declared.

She looked at me.

"I'm not sayin' marriage is bad or nothin', Robin. It's right for al-most all other women. Someday, I hope you find a good man. It's just not for me," she said. "Remember that song I wrote: 'I'm not the mar-ryin' kind, so don't go bendin' your knee for me,' " she sang.

"I remember. I'm just trying to forget it," I muttered.

"You're goin' to be sorry you said all those mean things to me, Robin. Someday, you're goin' to be lookin' at me up on the stage of the Grand Ole Opry and be sorry you ever made fun of me and coun-try music. At least it's honest; at least it's from the heart and not like that rap talk or bangin' and screamin' you think's music."

I closed my eyes and tried to sleep again. She was quiet and then, as we drew closer to Nashville, she began to get very excited. She found some new radio stations and sang along whenever she could.

I opened my eyes and looked at the beautiful day, one of those days when there are just a few scattered soft puffs of cloud against the aqua blue sky. An air force jet began to trail a line from one horizon toward the other. I imagined I was in it, just sailing toward something blue.

"Oh, I can feel it," Mother darling cried. "I can feel the changes comin', Robin. Can't you?"

"No," I said, but I said it sadly. I really wished I could feel what she felt. She was glowing with expectation. Would I ever be that radiant with happiness?

She ignored me because she was concentrating hard now on the directions Cory Lewis had given her to a section called Madison. Either he had left out something or she was confused and I wasn't much help. Finally, she pulled into a gas station and got better directions. About a half hour or so later, we made a turn down a residential street and came upon Garden Apartments.

"We're here!" she declared, pulling into the parking area. Cars were parked under carports. She found Cory Lewis's apartment number and pulled in behind what I imagined was his red pickup truck. For a moment she just sat there, smiling. "We made it," she said. She took a deep breath and added, "The rest will be easy."

I raised my eyebrows. Maybe it wasn't so good to have high hopes and dreams, I thought. Without them, there's no disappointment, and if there was one thing that described my life, it was disappointment with a capital D.

We got out of the Beetle. She said we should find Cory first and then bring along our things.

"He'll help," she told me.

The apartments looked seedy to me. The stucco was stained and discolored after years of rain. On some of the balconies, I saw old furniture, rusted exercise equipment, and sick-looking plants. The walkway through the complex was cracked and chipped and, at one point, gouged, with a chunk of the cement gone. There was a swimming pool, but it was empty and there wasn't anyone around it. As we passed it, I looked down and saw all sorts of garbage at the bottom, including what looked like a little child's tricycle.

Cory Lewis's apartment was on the second floor, number 202. Mother darling, still smiling from ear to ear with excitement and expectation, pushed the buzzer. I didn't hear anything. She pushed it again.

"Maybe it doesn't work," I suggested.

"Oh." She knocked, but there was still no sound from within. I knocked harder, practically pounding the door.

"Robin!"

"Well, maybe he has the radio on. Doesn't everyone in Nashville have the radio on?"

She scrunched her nose and then the door finally opened and we looked in at a tall, lean man with a thin nose and thin lips. He had what looked like a two- or three-day beard, stiff enough to sand off paint. His light brown hair hung listlessly down the sides of his head to his shoulders, where the split ends curled. Dressed in a black T-shirt with the faded words Bulls Are Always Horny and a pair of jeans, he stood barefoot and looked like he had just woken up. His blue eyes were glassy. I saw he had a small scar just under his right eye. It had tiny spots in it like it had been created with a dinner fork.

"Cory, it's us!" Mother darling was forced to declare because his face hadn't recorded any recognition yet.

"Whaa . . ." He ran his hands over his eyes and blinked. Then he smiled. "I'll be damned. So it is. Kay Jackson herself," he cried. "Never thought you'd do it, Kay. We was just thinkin' about lookin' for another singer."

"You'd better not," Mother darling said. "I told you I'd be here, and I'm here."

"Yeah, but you been tellin' me that for some time now." He turned to me. "And this is . . ."

"Robin Lyn."

"I like to be called just Robin," I said quickly.

"Whatever you like, sweet thing. Well, I'm sorry to say the place ain't exactly in prime condition, Kay. I had the boys here last night playin' cards until three in the mornin'. I didn't get a chance to clean up or fix up the other bedroom yet."

He stepped back and we gazed in at the small living room. The coffee table was covered with empty beer cans and a pizza box in which two dried pieces remained. There was a bowl with cigarette butts in it and various articles of clothing scattered over the sofa and the two easy chairs, each with thick arms and what looked like holes burned into them by dropped ashes. Pieces of newspaper were scattered about, and I saw what looked like a racetrack form under the table.

"What the place needs badly is a woman's touch," he said. Before Mother darling could say it, he flipped his forefinger at her like a pistol and added, "Make a good song."

She laughed.

"Still the same old Cory. Well," she said philosophically. "We didn't expect it would be a picnic right from the start, now did we, Robin?"

"Never that," I said dryly.

"Why don't you go back to the car and start getting our things," she told me. "I'll help Cory get organized and then maybe he can come out and get the heavier pieces."

"That's a good suggestion," he said. "It's been a while since I was organized."

I started away.

"Oh," he said, looking out the door after me. "I forgot. Welcome to Nashville."

"Thanks," I said, and walked on.

I wished I could just keep going and never stop.

3

Settling into Nowhere

If ever I felt lost or out of place at Grandpa and Grandma's in Granville, it was nothing compared to how I felt at Cory Lewis's apartment. At least at my grandparents' home, I could find space for myself, escape to my own music, into my own little world. Living in this apartment, I knew what bees must feel like in a hive, I thought. Nothing was mine. Nothing was truly private, and everyone's conversation was buzzing in everyone's ears whether he or she wanted it or not.

Besides the fact that my room was about one-third as big as the room I had at the farm, the real problem was, there was only one bathroom and because it wasn't very big either, I had to keep most of my things in my room. I could see that the only time I would have any real privacy was when Mother darling and Cory had to go to the garage owned by Del Thomas, one of the other musicians, to practice and prepare their music. At least for a good part of those days, I would have the apartment to myself, not that there was much to do in it. There was only one television set and Cory wouldn't pay for any cable or satellite reception, so the set was able to show only local stations pulled out of the air by a rabbit-ear antenna. Some improvement to the life we had, I thought. At least Grandpa had cable and I had my own television set there.

Mother darling saw it in my eyes.

"This is just a temporary residence for us, Robin. As soon as I start makin' big money, we're gonna have a place of our own."

"By then I'll be on social security," I said, and she came as close to slapping me as ever.

"It would help," she said, standing in front of me with her hands on her hips, "if you would be a little more encouragin'. I'm doin' this for both of us."

"Right," I said.

Cory watched our little arguments with a wide, stupid grin on his face. Most of the time he wouldn't say much. He would just shake his head and go, "Robin Lyn."

"I'm Robin," I shouted at him. "Not Robin Lyn."

"Heck, girl, most of the girls I know here got two first names."

"I'm not from here."

"Right. You're from a bigger, more sophisticated town," he said, and laughed. Mother darling laughed too. It wasn't long before I felt like it was me against them. She sided with almost anything he said or did.

For my part, I couldn't see where he was so connected and important in the music business. If he knew so many influential people, why was he living like this and why didn't he have another singer, one with more experience or fame than Mother darling? I couldn't believe how much hope and faith my mother was putting in him. From what I could see, he didn't even seem as successful as the musicians Mother darling played with back in Granville. It was as if she was blind or just didn't want to see. I actually felt sorry for her, but it wouldn't be long before I would feel sorrier for myself.

In fact, I felt sorry for her the very first night there. Cory called his two other band members and told them to come over, supposedly to talk about their music and hear Mother darling sing and play her guitar. She got as nervous as a hen. It was as if she was already auditioning to play the Grand Ole Opry.

"What songs should I choose? Which ones do I do best?" she asked, more of herself than to me as she flitted about the small apartment, going from the room she was sharing with Cory to the bathroom and back, barely concerned at all about my room and how I was adjusting to this.

She paused once to say, "Oh, you have a view of the street from here. That's more interestin'. We're lookin' out on the courtyard."

"Right. I'll spend my time watching cars go by," I said.

"There's nothin' to stop you from fixin' this room up any way you want," she said. "Cory said that would be just fine. He was only usin' it to store things and occasionally let someone sleep over when he had too much to drink or somethin'. I'm not sure what shirt to wear. I've got that one that sparkles like the Electric Horseman. Bet that would be good, huh?"

I didn't answer. I just continued to take my things out of my suitcase and put them in the drawers of the rickety, old, chipped, and faded dresser. After I cleaned out the spilled tobacco and gum and other junk, that is. The closet was crowded with Cory's clothing, cartons of sheet music, six pairs of old boots, and a guitar with broken strings.

"Where am I supposed to hang things?" I asked.

"Oh, hell," Cory said, overhearing me. He rushed in, scooped up clothes, lifted them off the rack, and threw them in the far left corner of the room. "Don't matter if this stuff's hangin' or not. The closet is yours completely, Robin Lyn," he said with an exaggerated stage bow.

"Robin," I said sharply, and he laughed. He had already opened a bottle of beer. It seemed he didn't move without one in his hand. I noticed a tattoo on his right forearm. It was a picture of a heart split in two with tears dripping from it and the words My Heart Cries for You underneath. He saw me staring at it.

"You can read it better like this," he said, turning his arm so I'd have a better view.

"Why would you put that on your arm?" I asked, grimacing.

"Oh, didn't your mother . . ."

"Sister," Mother darling corrected from the bathroom where she was fixing her hair. He laughed.

"Sister, I mean, tell you I once had a song on the charts called 'Broken Heart'?"

"No, she left out that little detail," I said.

"Kay Jackson. You never told her the important guy you're working with?"

"Oh yes, she told me that," I said. He sucked on his beer bottle and then smiled.

"You want to see the rest of the song?"

I didn't, but I could see it was important to him.

"Sure."

He opened his shirt and there were two lines tattooed on his chest with that broken heart between them.

Each time it beats a beat,
My heart will cry for you.

He took his shirt off completely and showed me his back, where there were two more lines tattooed.

Each time I see your face,
My heart will cry for you.

He turned back to me, undid his jeans, and lowered them and his briefs almost to his private place. Another two lines were on his abdomen.

When I see your hand in someone else's hand,
My heart will cry for you.

Then he turned around and dropped his pants and briefs to his knees. There across his buttocks was tattooed:

Until the very end of time,
My heart will cry for you.

He pulled up his clothes and turned around to sing some more of his song.

"So take me back and hold me tight and never let me go.
Please mend a heart that's torn in two,
A heart that loves you so."

He laughed.

"I couldn't get the whole first verse on me. Well, what'cha think?"

For a moment I had to convince myself I had seen what I had seen.

"What I was thinkin'," he continued, gulping some more of his beer and not waiting for me to respond, "is I might have the woman I love tattooed with the rest of it. Then, whenever we stood naked together, we would have the whole song between us. Huh?"

He looked at Mother darling and then at me and burst into laughter.

"Look at her face, Kay."

Mother darling did, and then she laughed, too.

"Let's call the boys and tell them to come over earlier. We want to get this thing goin'."

He looked at me again and sang, "My heart will cry for you."

Then he put his arm around Mother darling and went out to the living room to call his fellow musicians.

If anyone's heart's crying, I thought, it's mine.

Before the musicians arrived, I left the apartment to explore what looked like it would be my new neighborhood for some time to come.

Down on the lower level, in front of the apartment closest to the street, I saw a girl who looked about my age, with licorice black hair tied in a ponytail. She was sitting on a lawn chair and seemed to be singing to whatever was coming through her earphones. She wore a T-shirt with the sleeves torn off to her shoulders and jeans. I thought the T-shirt was splattered with red paint, until I drew closer and saw the red dots were all connected to form a pair of lips. Underneath it read, Don't Give Me Any Lip.

When we made eye contact, she took off her earphones.

"Quién está usted?"

"Excuse me?"

"I asked you who you were in Spanish. That's what I'm doing with these earphones, learning Spanish."

"Oh."

"So?"

"What?"

"So who are you, or is that a secret?"

"My name's Robin Taylor," I said, making sure to leave out the Lyn. "My mo . . . sister and I are staying with a friend for a while."

"Quién?"

"What?"

"I thought you might have figured it out by now. Who? Quién? Get it?"

"I don't speak Spanish," I said sharply. I was just going to keep going, but she leaped out of her chair.

"Neither do I. That's why I'm studying it."

"Why?"

"I'm going to run off to Mexico and live on a beach and drink tequila and not care what time it is, ever," she vowed. I guess I looked pretty skeptical. "I am!" she insisted. She looked back at the front door of her apartment. "I'm tired of my stepmother telling me what to do, what to wear, what to eat. My father never says anything. She's got him wrapped around her you-know-what."

This time I smiled.

"Quién está usted?" I asked, and she broke into a wide smile.

She had a round face that made her dark brown eyes look too small. Heavy boned, she looked a good twenty pounds overweight. It gave her a more matronly look, especially with her big bosom and wide hips. I imagined that when she said her stepmother was telling her what to eat, she was trying to get her to lose weight.

"Mi nombre es Kathy Ann Potter. And I'm warning you now, don't call me Pothead," she said with a face bracing for a fight. Then she smiled again. "So, who is your friend?"

"Friend?"

"Who are you and your sister living with?"

"Oh. Cory Lewis."

"The vampire? That's what my stepmother calls him because he's out all night and sleeps all day."

"Musicians usually do," I said, "and so do singers. My sister is a singer in his band, or will be."

"Peachy keen," she quipped. "Where are you going?"

"I don't know. Just for a walk."

"Forget it. There's no place to go around here. You've got to get into the city. You wanna go to Stumpin' Jumpin' with me and my friend Charlotte Lily tonight?"

"What's that?"

"A dance club. You got to be twenty-one, but we can get in. Lots of college boys go there."

"Twenty-one? How are we going to pass for that?"

"Charlotte Lily's sister's boyfriend is one of the security guards. Lots of kids under twenty-one get in." She glanced at her watch.

"Can you meet me here in about an hour? We'll take the bus and meet my best friend, Charlotte Lily, downtown by the Tennessee Fox Trot."

I smiled in amazement. Talk about someone making friends fast, I thought. For all she could know, I was a serial killer.

"Well?"

"An hour?"

"You need more time to dress?" she asked. "You're not going out in just a pair of jeans and a shirt like that with sneakers, are you?"

"Oh, no. What do you wear to this, what did you call it, Somethin' Jumpin'?"

"*Stumpin'* Jumpin'." She smiled. "Something sexier," she replied. "It's very hot."

"What's the other place? What did you call it, Tennessee Fox Trot?"

"Oh, the carousel at Riverfront Park." She tilted her head with suspicion. "For people coming here to be in music, you sound like you don't know anything about Nashville."

"I don't," I said. "Except it's the home of the Grand Ole Opry, where my sister intends to sing."

"Oh, sure, her and about two million others," Kathy Ann said.

"She might make it," I muttered. Funnily enough, I could be critical and skeptical about Mother darling's chances of becoming successful, but I didn't like anyone else being that way.

"I hope she does," she said without much emotion. "Well, you going or not? I have to call Charlotte Lily and let her know, make sure it's all right with her, too."

"What kind of a place is this?"

"Fun with a capital F," she replied. "Are you afraid of fun?"

"Terrified," I said dryly. "Okay, I'll see you in an hour."

I went back up to the apartment. Mother darling was dressed in one of her outfits and was picking on her guitar. The bathroom door was closed with Cory obviously in there.

"I'm going out with a friend," I told her.

"What? You have a friend already? How could you do that? You just walked in and out of the apartment."

"She lives here, too. She was just downstairs."

"Great. Where are you goin'?"

"Riverfront Park. They have a carousel."

"That's it?"

"I'll just learn about the city and then I'll know where to go myself," I told her, and went to pick out something to wear from my meager wardrobe. In the end I decided to borrow one of her western blouses and do what she did, tie it at the bottom and show some midriff. Cory was still in the bathroom.

"I want to fix my hair and put on some makeup, but I don't have a mirror. What's he doing in there?" I asked loud enough for him to hear. Just then there was a knock on the door and Mother darling let in Del Thomas and the third musician, a man named Ernie Farwell, who was way over six feet tall, with long arms and a long neck. He had dirty blond hair as messy as Cory's and dull brown eyes with lids that looked poised to shut. Del was the neatest of the three, with well-trimmed dark brown hair and a trim beard. I thought he had an intelligent look, and I would soon see that he was the most serious of the three when it came to their music.

Mother darling introduced herself and then me. Cory finally emerged from the bathroom. While they talked, I fixed my hair and put on some makeup.

"Where's she goin'?" Cory asked Mother darling. She told him. "Who'd you meet?" he demanded as if he had become my legal guardian.

"Her name's Kathy Ann Potter."

"That fat girl? Didn't know she did anything but listen on her earphones and eat and smoke dope, I bet. Mother's a looker," he told Del.

"Thanks for the rundown on the neighborhood. Let's get busy. We've got a lot to do," Del said dryly.

"Sure." Cory turned to Mother darling. "You gonna let her go out lookin' like that?"

She looked at me hard, turning her eyes into two steel balls of cold threat.

"Don't you get into any trouble here, Robin. We don't know a soul, except Cory."

"Who says he has a soul?" I quipped, and the three men laughed. "I need some money," I added.

She got up, went to her purse, and gave me a twenty-dollar bill.

"We have to watch our budget, you know," she said. "Be home by eleven, and I better not hear about you smokin' no dope, Robin."

"Right," I said.

"Robin Lyn," she called after me. She always added my middle name when she wanted to emphasize something.

"Robin Lyn," Cory chorused. "Don't you sin."

I shut the door on the laughter behind me and hurried down to Kathy Ann's apartment. She was already out and waiting.

"Don't you look killer," she remarked. She herself wore a silk ruffled sleeveless blouse with a collar deep enough to show the cavernous promise of her cleavage. I thought she had gone hog-wild with makeup, too heavy on the eye shadow and thick on the lipstick. Her skirt was nearly a mini, and she didn't have the legs for it. They were short and stubby, with bony knees. She reminded me of a young girl who had snuck into her mother's bedroom to play grown-up.

"C'mon," she said, grabbing my hand and tugging me toward the street. "I told Charlotte Lily about you, and she's anxious to meet you."

We started toward the bus stop and then broke into a run when a bus pulled up. Kathy Ann didn't seem to notice the way other passengers looked at her.

"Here," she said, handing me a college ID. "Tonight, you're Parker Carson and you're twenty-one."

"Why do we need this? I thought you said we could get in."

"Just in case," she said. "You have to flash something so Charlotte Lily's sister's boyfriend doesn't get into trouble."

I shrugged and put it in my shirt pocket.

"Now tell me all about yourself," she said, sitting back and looking like a five-year-old about to hear a bedtime story, "and don't leave out the sad parts."

I made up a story, claiming Mother darling, who was now known as my older sister, and I had lost our parents in a plane crash. The more elaborate and far-fetched I was, the more Kathy Ann believed and enjoyed the story. I went into how we had to live with our grandparents, who were both old and feeble, with no memories, and how Grandma had set the house on fire accidentally in the kitchen one night. They were both now in homes, and we had left to start a new life in Nashville.

"Wow," she said with envy, "you have had an exciting life already. You're going to love Nashville," she added when I had mentioned my concern about moving here. "You'll see," she promised.

With all the lights, people, and music, downtown was more interesting than I had anticipated. We went directly to the park and to the carousel where Charlotte Lily was waiting for us. She was quite the contrast to Kathy Ann. Tall and stylish in her cowgirl's hat, red fringed-sleeved shirt, and laminated black jeans and black boots, I thought she was pretty enough to be a model. She had long, light brown hair parted in the middle and brushed down, hazel green eyes, and features as petite as mine and Mother darling's, only with a dimple added to her right cheek. She looked me over quickly.

"Hi," she said, and glared angrily at Kathy Ann. "You're nearly twenty minutes late."

"We left when I said we would," Kathy Ann whined. "I can't help it how long the bus takes."

"C'mon," she ordered, and marched ahead of us.

We caught up, and she looked at me again.

"Where are you from?"

"Granville, near Columbus, Ohio."

"Why did you come here?"

"Her sister's in a band and someday will be singing in the Grand Ole Opry," Kathy Ann bellowed.

Charlotte Lily smirked.

"What about your parents?"

"Her parents were killed in a plane crash when she was only five."

"What did you do, Kathy Ann, get her whole life story in ten minutes? Be careful," she warned me. "Her picture's next to the word *gossip* in the dictionary."

"It is not!"

"What's it next to then, Pothead?" Charlotte said, laughed, and impulsively crossed the street.

"I thought you said she was your best friend," I told Kathy Ann as we caught up.

"She is. She's very popular and she can get us into Stumpin' Jumpin'," Kathy Ann reminded me.

"Maybe it's not worth it," I told her.

She looked at me as if I was crazy.

"Give me a cigarette," Charlotte ordered.

"Oh, I left them home," Kathy Ann said. Charlotte stopped walking and glared at her.

"What? I told you not to forget."

"I know," she said mournfully.

"You smoke?" she asked me.

"Yes, but I don't have any cigarettes on me at the moment."

"Terrific."

I looked at the drugstore just down the walk.

"Give me five minutes," I said, and headed for it.

"Five minutes?"

They followed me in. I located the cigarettes quickly, but picked up a box of tampons I actually did need. I checked out the mirrors, watched the clerk behind the counter, and then picked up a pack of my favorite menthol cigarettes, shoving it into my blouse. Then I paid for the tampons and walked out, the two of them standing at the door.

Charlotte watched me take it out of my blouse.

"Here."

"I thought something would ring if you did that," Kathy Ann said.

"Obviously not," I said.

"Why did you steal them? I saw you have enough money to buy them," Charlotte asked.

I shrugged.

"I'll save my money for something I can't steal," I told her, and she smiled.

"C'mon," she said. "I think we're going to have a lot of fun tonight."

Kathy Ann's face brightened.

"She likes you," she said, as if the queen had just granted me permission to live in Nashville.

If it's that easy to win friends here, I thought, maybe I'll have a good time tonight.

Charlotte Lily offered me one of the cigarettes from the pack I stole for her. I took it.

"I want one too," Kathy Ann said.

"You don't get any. Punishment for forgetting," she told her, smiled at me, and continued on. Like a whipped puppy, Kathy Ann remained a few steps behind us all the way to Stumpin' Jumpin'.

I was in Nashville and if Grandpa saw me now, I thought, he'd have me at a prayer meeting in the morning.

Too late for that, I told the voices inside me.

Maybe too late for a lot of things.

4

Getting into a
New Groove

On the exterior Stumpin' Jumpin' looked almost like another one of Mother darling's honky-tonks. There was a blazing red neon sign over the two large black metal doors, at either side of which stood two human bulldogs. Each looked like a football linebacker, with thick necks and shoulders that made Grandpa's look puny. Charlotte Lily exchanged some sort of greeting and message with her sister's boyfriend through their own eye and head signals and then turned to us and said, "It's a little too early. We have to go in when there's a good crowd. We're less conspicuous if we do it that way," she explained. "C'mon, we'll visit Keefer for a while."

"Who's Keefer?" I asked when I saw that Kathy Ann was very pleased by the suggestion.

"An old boyfriend of mine I toy with from time to time. He works in an auto body shop."

"His father threw him out of the house," Kathy Ann said.

"I believe it was by mutual consent," Charlotte Lily told her.

"His father beat him up, didn't he?"

"I swear, Kathy Ann, you still don't know anything about men, do you?"

"Why?" she wailed as we turned a corner into a side street.

"Why? You don't remind a man of a time when he looked a fool or lost a fight. Sometimes I wonder if you learn anything being in my company. She's still a virgin," she told me.

"So am I," I said.

"Sure, right. And there really is a Santa Claus. Oh, good, Keefer's at work," she announced. "The light's on in the shop, and he's the only one who would be working now."

We entered through a side door. A young man was working on a car fender, the sparks flying from his welding torch. There was a radio blasting country rock music. The shop was lit by a half-dozen white neon lights. Next to the car that the young man worked on was a vehicle with its rear end bashed in, a taillight hanging by wires as if the accident had just occurred.

"He hates it when I sneak up on him," Charlotte Lily told me with an impish grin. Then she did just that. She walked up beside him, waited a moment, looked back at us, and with her hands around her mouth, shouted, "Keefer!"

He jumped to the side, the torch nearly turning at Charlotte Lily, who then screamed.

"Damn you, Charlotte Lily," Keefer shouted at her after lifting his mask off his face. There was a streak of grease down his right cheek. "I told you a hundred times that's dangerous. You nearly got fried."

Charlotte Lily regained her composure.

"Oh, fiddlesticks, Keefer. You've become an old fuddy-duddy at the ripe old age of nineteen."

"Right," he said. He still hadn't noticed either Kathy Ann or me. "What's up?"

"I wanted you to meet our new friend. She just moved here from . . . where you from, Robin?"

"Granville, Ohio," I said.

Keefer turned to me, and for a long moment, we just gazed at each other. He had a strong, square jaw with firm lips, dark eyes, and hair the color of a crow. Although his hair wasn't really long, it looked wild and untrimmed, but somehow, it wasn't unattractive. There was something very natural about it.

"Like what you see?" Charlotte Lily asked, and followed her question with her short, thin laugh.

He tilted his head and looked at her, the side of his mouth lifting just slightly as he squinted.

"What are you up to now, Charlotte Lily?"

"Nothing. We're going to Stumpin' Jumpin' and thought we'd stop by and see how you were doin' first, Keefer," she said with a voice dripping maple syrup.

"Right," he said, and wiped his hands on a rag before walking toward me and Kathy Ann. "You really her new friend?" he asked.

"We just met about twenty minutes ago," I replied. He smiled at my honest and exact reply.

"I'm Keefer Dawson."

"Robin Taylor," I said.

He held out his hand, looked at it, and then pulled it back because it was thick with grime.

"You don't want to shake that if you're going to Stumpin' Jumpin'."

"You wanna go with us?" Charlotte Lily asked him. "We can wait for him to clean up, can't we, girls?"

"Oh yes," Kathy Ann said quickly.

"You'd even take him along dirty," Charlotte Lily told her, and she withered quickly, even stepping back.

"No, thanks. I've got to finish this car tonight. Promised Izzy I'd have it ready for paint in the morning. You here for good or what?" he asked me.

"I think both," I said, and he laughed. "I'm with my sister, who came here to be in a band. She sings."

"Parents let you move off?"

"They were killed in an airplane crash," Kathy Ann volunteered.

"Oh. Sorry."

"It's okay. It was a long time ago. We're all the family we have now."

"I know the feeling," Keefer said. "It's like my parents went down in a plane."

"Keefer lives here," Charlotte Lily said, obviously enjoying our warm conversation.

"Here?"

"In the back," he said. "I have a small apartment Izzy lets me have. It's all one room, nothing special."

"I'm going to the bathroom," Charlotte Lily declared.

"Don't do nothin' bad in there," Keefer warned. He looked serious. I waited until she went in and then asked him what he meant by that.

"She's been known to light up a joint or two or sniff some snow. All I need is Izzy to think I let something like that happen in his place. Ain't that right, Kathy Ann?"

"Yes," she said obediently.

"Where do you live?"

"She lives in my complex, upstairs, in Cory Lewis's apartment," Kathy Ann answered for me.

He shrugged.

"I don't know him. So, are you a singer, too?"

"Hardly," I said.

He laughed.

"You're probably the only one in Nashville who would admit it."

Charlotte Lily emerged from the bathroom, apparently having gone in only to check on her makeup.

"Don't worry," she said when he glared at her. "I didn't do anything that would get you in trouble."

"That's a surprise. Well, I gotta get back to this car," he said, more to me than to Kathy Ann and Charlotte Lily.

"Sad when a young man like that is more interested in working on a car than being with us, isn't it, girls?" Charlotte Lily teased.

He looked back.

"I don't get many arguments from my cars," he told her. "And they appreciate what I do for them."

"Oh, you poor sad boy. Someone done your heart in good. Put that torch to work and mend it," she told him, laughed again, and sauntered back to the door. "Let's go, girls, unless you'd rather stand there and watch Keefer make love to a fender bender."

I glanced back at him. He had his mask on and turned the torch back on. The sparks were flying again.

Not sure myself why I was so reluctant about it, I followed Charlotte Lily and Kathy Ann out of the shop.

"You don't want to get yourself involved with him," Charlotte Lily lectured as we started back toward Stumpin' Jumpin'. "He's a loser from the get-go. Quit school, has no family anymore, and never does anything with his old friends. That's one boy you look at and know that what you see is what you get. Now," she said, turning toward the dance club, "let's see if we can entice a few of those college boys. They know what fun is. After all, what's the point of being young if you're going to waste it on being responsible, huh?"

She laughed at herself and looked at Kathy Ann, who smiled widely and then glanced at me for approval. I shrugged.

"I don't know if I'll ever be considered responsible," I said, "young or old."

She liked that.

"Yes, we're going to have a good ole time of it tonight. If you listen to us and watch us carefully, Kathy Ann, you might even lose your virginity," she said, and laughed again.

Kathy Ann looked to me, but I walked ahead, still thinking about the way the sparks flew around Keefer Dawson.

There was a long line at the entrance of Stumpin' Jumpin', but Charlotte Lily took us around on the inside of the crowd, and when we approached, her sister's boyfriend glanced at our fake IDs and just stepped out of the way. Kathy Ann looked excited enough to explode.

The moment we entered, the music washed over us like an ocean

wave. The dance hall itself was a long, dark room with sofas and tables and drapes, giving the impression you were in someone's house,
except that there was a large dance floor and to the right a long bar
with a half-dozen bartenders, all with black cowboy hats, black sus-
penders holding up jeans, and no shirts. They were all well-built,
good-looking men. The bar was already jammed, mostly with what
looked to me like college-age women flirting with the bartenders.
Small spotlights combed through the dancers as the beat grew quicker
and the volume of the music was turned up another notch or two. It
was very hard to hear anyone talk, but no one cared, even though people sitting side by side at the bar were literally shouting at each other.

Waitresses in cowgirl outfits and fancy, glittering boots took orders
from those seated on the sofas. We were just standing, drinking it all
in, when suddenly Charlotte Lily saw someone she recognized.

"C'mon," she screamed, pulling at my arm. "There's Wyatt Baxter.
He goes to Tennessee State."

I didn't know how she could see anyone through the thick jungle of
swinging bodies. We wove our way through to three young men sitting
and drinking at one of the sofa and coffee table setups. One of them
recognized Charlotte as we approached and broke into a wide smile.

"Hey, Charlotte Lily, I was hoping you'd be here tonight," he cried,
standing.

"I haven't seen you here in a while," she said.

"Busy, busy in summer school session," he said, shaking his head.
"Who are your friends?" he asked, focusing mainly on me.

"This is Robin. She's new to Nashville. Surely you remember
Kathy Ann?"

"Oh," he said, looking at her. "Yeah, yeah. How ya doin', Kathy
Ann?"

"Just fine, thanks," she said.

"I'm Wyatt," he told me, and extended his hand. He was a little less
than six feet tall, with an athletic build and dirty-blond hair, the
strands of which lay trim over the top of his forehead.

I shook his hand, but he didn't let go of mine. Instead, he pulled me
a bit closer because of the loud music and screamed, "This is Axel
Farmer." He pointed to the stout boy in the middle with dull brown
eyes and a military-style haircut. He looked as big as the security
guards at the door. "Axel's a linebacker on the football team. And that
there is Birdy Williams," he said, pointing to the third boy, who was
lean and had an interesting, sensitive-looking face. "He plays trumpet
in the marching band, and he's in a jazz band on the side, thus we call

him Birdy, after Bird, the famous jazz musician. Hey, make some room, Birdy," he ordered.

Birdy shifted to the left. Charlotte Lily moved quickly to the open seat.

"You wanna dance?" Wyatt asked me.

The music changed to something more rock than western. I looked at Charlotte Lily, who seemed already interested in Birdy Williams. Grandma would say she had "wandering eyes" and was never satisfied.

"I guess," I said.

"Hey, Axel, order a round of drinks for everyone, will ya," Wyatt ordered. "What do you want?"

I wasn't sure what to order.

Charlotte Lily piped up with, "Get us three Saddle Soaps."

"You heard her, Axel," Wyatt said, and pulled me toward the dance floor. When I looked back, I saw the waitress taking the drink orders and then Axel asking Kathy Ann to dance.

The truth was, I had never been to a dance club before this. I had gone to some of the honky-tonks Mother darling sang in, and most had a dance floor, but there was nothing that compared to this. The frenzy, the loud music, the exciting lights were all hypnotizing. Wyatt was a good dancer, too. I copied some of his moves and we danced into the next song, which was more country western. I wasn't into the beat as well and unsure of my steps, so he leaned over and shouted, "Let's get a drink."

I found out Saddle Soap was some kind of draft beer. It tasted very good, and after working up a sweat dancing, I found it very enjoyable. I drank it fast. Wyatt saw that and hooked a waitress to bring me another.

"You go to school with Charlotte Lily?" Wyatt asked.

I shook my head.

"No. I just moved here from Ohio. We just met, actually."

"Great. You'll love it," he promised. "We're all having a good time." He howled something which Axel mimicked and then we were all out on the dance floor. Nearly an hour later, and two more rounds of drinks, Charlotte Lily announced she had her house empty. Her parents had gone away for a few days and her sister was at a friend's until very late.

I saw that it was approaching ten and knew that Mother darling would be upset if I didn't get back by eleven, but I wasn't even sure which bus to take. Before I could express any of my concerns, everyone was up and moving toward the entrance. When we burst out on the

street, my ears were ringing and my throat felt like I had swallowed
sandpaper because of how much shouting I had done to be heard while
we were dancing. The beer had just enough alcohol to give me a buzz,
and for a moment, I felt a little unsteady.

"Whoa," Wyatt said, taking me around the waist. "You all right?"

"Yes," I said quickly.

"Hurry," Charlotte Lily screamed, "we can catch this bus."

Everyone ran, Wyatt pulling me along. When we got on the bus, I
wasn't able to talk to Charlotte Lily because we sat boy-girl. The bus
trip only took about five minutes, but as soon as we got off, I pulled
Charlotte Lily aside.

"This is my first night here," I told her. "My sister wanted me back
by eleven."

"Why? You don't have any school to go to tomorrow. It's summer.
We're not college students taking a summer session. We're free, like
we're supposed to be."

"I know, but my sister and I just arrived and . . ."

"She'll be happy you made new friends so fast. That way you won't
be in her hair," Charlotte Lily assured me. I started to shake my head.
"C'mon. My house is just ahead. We've got to do it for Kathy Ann.
Axel looks serious."

I gazed back at them. He had his arm around her. Together, I
thought, they would sink a rowboat. He looked like he weighed two
hundred and fifty pounds. Charlotte Lily giggled and moved back under Birdy's long arm. Wyatt seized my hand and began to ask me
questions about where I had lived, what interested me. I was nervous
because he was the oldest boy I had ever been with and yet he didn't
seem to care about my age. He told me he was going to get a B.A. in
public administration, but he might go on to law school. When he
asked me what my interests were, I didn't know what to say. I didn't
want to sound young and stupid, so I said I was still thinking about it.

"Smart," he told me. "Don't make a decision too fast. Explore.
That's the fun of being young, you know, discovery. If you don't have
fun now, when will you, I always say. What do you think?"

I shrugged.

"I guess," I said.

"You guess right," he said.

Charlotte Lily's house was a large, two-story colonial-style home,
all gated.

"We can't drink too much of Daddy's booze," she said before opening the door. "He measures the bottles."

"Just put in some water and he'll never know the difference," Wyatt suggested.

Charlotte Lily laughed.

"I've done that already," she said.

The house was as impressive inside as it was outside. She wanted us to stay in the living room–den area and immediately put on some music that came through speakers in every room. Then she and Birdy prepared drinks, measuring the vodka and gin carefully and replacing it with water.

"It's too bright in here," Wyatt told Charlotte Lily. "Can't you do something about that?"

"Sure," she said, and turned the lights down very low.

"Dance?" Wyatt asked me when the music became slower. I looked over at Axel and Kathy Ann. They were already kissing. "C'mon, show me those Ohio moves," Wyatt teased, getting up and pulling on my hand.

"I don't have any moves," I said. He put his arm around my waist and tightened it so that I was practically attached to his hip. Then I felt his lips on my neck. I jerked back, but he held on firmly.

"Easy," he said. "We're just getting to know each other."

"I know enough," I said sharply.

"What you need is a little more to drink. You've got to loosen up," he advised, and handed me the drink that had been prepared for me. He tried to lift my hand to bring the glass to my mouth as if he was feeding a child.

"No," I said. "I don't need it."

"You need it," he retorted sharply.

Axel and Kathy Ann got up and went into the den. Charlotte Lily had already taken Birdy out and up to her bedroom, I imagined. Everything was happening so fast.

"C'mon," Wyatt urged, "get with it."

He put his arm around me and sat me on the sofa, bringing his lips to my neck while he fumbled with the buttons of my blouse so he could slip his hand under it to cup my breast while he pressed his lips to mine and then put his weight against me, driving me back.

"Now, that's better," he whispered, his breath reeking with the odor of his alcohol.

His hands were like spider legs, going everywhere. He had my jeans undone with his right hand while his left went over my hip. In a matter of seconds, he would have me half naked, I realized, and panic set in. I wasn't going to end up like Mother darling.

"No," I insisted, and pushed him so hard, he spun and fell to the floor.

"Whaaa," he cried.

I leaped up, zipped my pants closed, and rushed to the front door.

"Hey!" he called after me. "Where are you going?"

I didn't know where I was going, only out. Once on the street, I ran for half a block and then walked quickly to where we had gotten off the bus. Confused and lost, I realized I was sobbing. I clutched at the money Mother darling had given me and I hoped to see a taxicab. Maybe I had enough to get back to Cory's apartment.

The streets here looked empty, however, and I walked and walked for some time before I recognized the downtown area where we had been. Then I saw the side street we had taken to go to see Keefer Dawson. I strolled down it and saw the lights were still lit in the shop. Maybe he could give me directions on how to get back, I thought.

When I entered, I didn't see him or anyone else for a few moments. Then I heard, "Hey?"

He was sitting back on what was once an easy chair but now had no legs. Its stuffing leaked out of the torn arms.

"What are you doing here? Where's Charlotte Lily?" he asked.

"She's home. I was hoping you could tell me how I can get back to my apartment."

He sat up quickly.

"You just left her."

"You can say that," I said, and he smiled.

"What happened?"

"One of her college boyfriends thought I was going to be his good time tonight."

His smile widened.

"C'mon," he said, standing. "I'll take you back in Izzy's pickup."

"You don't have to do that," I said.

"I'm not doing it because I have to," he replied.

5

Sinking Deeper into the Dark

I hate being dishonest with someone who bares his soul so willingly and is so trusting with his emotions, but Mother darling's fears and dreams weighed heavily on my mind, and I was afraid she would think I had betrayed her if I told the truth. Keefer just started to talk frankly about himself. It was as if he had not found anyone to talk to before he met me.

"My daddy drinks a lot," he began. "And he gets real mean when he's drunk. I have a scar on my right leg from the time he hit me with the broken end of a beer bottle. He threw it across the room. I was about seven."

"What about your mother?"

"She's what they call a manic depressive. Ever hear of that?"

I shook my head.

"She goes up and down. Sometimes she gets so depressed she won't come out of her bedroom all day, not even to eat. Can't blame her, being married to him."

"Do you have any brothers or sisters?"

"I have a sister, Sally Jean, but she ran off with her boyfriend about two years ago. She had good reason to get away from my father, even better reason than I have," he said, his eyes growing small and dark. "She's out in Texas and once in a while, she sends me a postcard. One of these days, I might join her," he added wistfully. Then he turned to me and said, "I'm one who knows it's not easy to be on your own, so I can appreciate what you and your sister have been going through. I hope she does well here."

"Thank you," I said in a small voice. Guilt made me feel like I was taking a bath in dirty old engine oil.

"But just know that Nashville's so full of people dreaming of stardom, you can smell fantasy in the air," he warned.

We were both quiet until he turned into the apartment complex.

"The apartment seemed farther by bus," I said.

"Yeah, with the stops and all, it would."

"Thank you very much," I told him after opening the door.

"No problem. Next time you're downtown, stop by if you want. I'll show you how to pull a ding out of a car door."

I laughed and got out slowly. He waved and then shifted and backed up. I watched him drive off before heading for the stairs to the upstairs apartments. It was nearly twelve-thirty and I was anticipating Mother darling's rage. Instead, I was surprised to find no one home and even more surprised to find the door unlocked. Was it just that there was nothing here anyone would want to steal?

At least I had the bathroom to myself for a while. Afterward, I got into bed and realized the sheets and the blanket smelled like they'd been made in a cigarette factory. The stench nearly choked me. I decided to put my clothes back on and not use the blanket. I put one of my skirts over the pillow and finally, after tossing and turning for an hour, fell asleep, only to be awakened by the sound of laughter. It was just Mother darling and Cory, but they made enough noise for a half-dozen people. I heard Cory say, "Told you this would be easier here."

"I'd better check on Robin and be sure she's come home," Mother darling told him.

I decided to pretend I was in a deep sleep. She opened the door and stood there so long, I thought she didn't believe I was asleep. Finally, she closed it. I heard them giggling and then, a little while later, I heard them in his bedroom. It wasn't hard to realize what they were doing. Mother darling kept trying to get him to be quieter.

"What for? Robin Lyn surely knows what it's all about, and if she don't, it's time she did," he said.

I tried burying my head in the pillow, but the odor of cigarettes was too much to endure. It wasn't until they fell asleep that I did. I was up ahead of them in the morning, which suited me fine because I was able to take a shower and get dressed before Mother darling and Cory woke. At least, that was what I had hoped.

I was positive I had pushed in the little button on the doorknob that would lock it, but just a few seconds after I had gotten under the water in the tub shower, I heard the door opening and screamed at the sight of Cory, naked himself, stumbling his way toward the toilet. For a moment I thought he didn't even realize I was there, despite the sound of the shower and my scream. He just began to urinate.

I pulled the flimsy shower curtain around me.

"I'm taking a shower!" I screamed.

"You gotta go when you gotta go," he mumbled.

When he was finished, he turned to go, but paused at the door and said, "Don't forget to wash behind your ears." He closed the door on his laughter.

Flushed with embarrassment and anger, I turned off the shower and dried myself. As soon as I was dressed, I charged out of the bathroom. They were both still in bed.

"Mother!" I called at the closed door. There was a long moment of silence and then I heard, "Call me Kay, damn it."

"Kay, I need to see you right now."

I heard her groan. I waited and waited until she finally opened the door and peered out at me.

"What?"

"I was in the bathroom. I had the door shut and I thought locked and he just came in while I was in the shower and . . . and went to the bathroom."

"Next time be sure you lock the door," she said.

"It doesn't work and he saw it was closed and I had the shower running. He had to know I was in there."

"He had to go," she told me. "Don't make a big deal of it," she said. "We have to get some sleep. We've already gotten a job and we start tonight," she added, and closed the door.

My face felt like my blood was boiling just under my skin. I started toward their bedroom door again and then stopped and returned to my room to fume. After a few minutes, I came out and saw that Cory and she had been quite wild and drunk last night. Clothes were strewn everywhere in the already disheveled-looking living room. I thought for a moment, and then I went to his pants and pulled out his wallet. There were three twenties, a ten, a five, and five singles in it. I took the three twenties and put the wallet back.

"That's your fine for being disrespectful," I muttered at the door, and left the apartment.

I didn't get too far before I heard a door open and my name called. Kathy Ann was standing in the doorway of her family's apartment. She was dressed in a robe, and her hair looked like a family of rats had run through it. I debated just ignoring her, but she kept beckoning. As I approached, she stepped out of her apartment and closed the door most of the way.

"What happened to you last night? I didn't even know you had left. How did you get home? I had a great time," she told me before I could offer a single answer.

"Good for you," I said.

"Axel can speak a little Spanish. His family has a Spanish maid. He was impressed with what I already knew."

"Sounds like a match made in heaven," I said dryly, but she was on a happy roll and either ignored or didn't see my disinterest.

She looked at me with a smile smeared across her lips like cake frosting.

"What?" I finally asked.

"We did it," she said. "I mean, I did it."

"It's not like running the four-minute mile or something, Kathy Ann. You don't get a medal."

Her smile faded.

"Don't you want to hear about it?" She looked like she was going to burst into tears.

"All right," I said with great effort. "What happened?"

"He was very gentle and considerate and first announced and showed me he had protection."

"I'm glad of that," I said.

"Still, I was afraid. He told me he understood, that it was like the first time he had to be a linebacker on a college football team and had to bang heads with a guy just as big as he was if not bigger. He said it was like knowing you were going to run into a wall, but you had to go ahead anyway."

"Yeah, that sounds just like making love," I muttered.

"He meant every time you do something new, you are nervous. I thought that was sweet, his sharing his fear with me. He's so big and strong, it was hard to believe anything could frighten him."

"It is hard to believe," I said.

"Anyway, I closed my eyes and held my breath and it was just as wonderful as Charlotte Lily told me it would be. After a little pain, I mean. Axel said he would call me every time he comes into the city." She leaned toward me to add in a whisper, "He's really not supposed to be so wild and active. He's in training."

"It's nice of him to put you before football."

"I thought so," she said.

I stared at her. Are we all like this at one time or another? I wondered. Do we all wear blinders, deliberately ignore the truth just to hold on to one of our fantasies? Is that what was happening to Mother darling, still happening? What can be the final result? Only a great fall, I thought, great disappointment, and from that, bitterness and cynicism. We would be like the fox in the story one of my teachers told, the fox who couldn't reach the grapes and then said they were probably sour anyway. Sincere happy smiles would become so rare, we would wonder if it was our faces we saw reflected.

"Where are you going?" Kathy Ann asked.

"I'm going shopping," I said. "I need some new clothes."

"Can you wait? I'll go with you. I love shopping, even when it's someone else doing it."

I'm not sure what department store to go to anyway, I thought. She would know.

"Okay, but don't take too long."

She hurried back into her apartment and I went to the faded brown bench that was near the empty swimming pool. I heard another door close and saw a woman holding the hand of a little boy and a little girl. They looked close enough in age to be twins. The woman paused to fix the little boy's collar, and then she kissed him on the cheek and he smiled. As if she could sense her daughter's envy, she turned, brushed her hair, and kissed her as well. Then the three walked to the parking lot, an aura of happiness and contentment surrounding them.

That's what love really is, I thought, a thick cocoon that helps you feel safe, secure, and most of all, cherished.

For a moment I actually missed Grandpa and Grandma. Despite his hard, critical eyes, there were moments when the three of us sat and watched television or ate a meal together and I felt like I belonged to a family. Grandma was so gentle and loving that she softened him, and he would go on about some adventure he had when he was about my age. For just a little while, a door had been opened and I could look in and see enough to make me understand what it was that connected me to him, to Grandma, to this idea of family.

But then Mother darling would come home or say something and the door would slam shut again.

I heard a door slam shut and looked up to see Kathy Ann practically bouncing toward me.

"Let's go," she said. "I want to buy something for Axel, something to give him the next time he calls."

"Where should we go?"

"Let's go to Dillards," she suggested. "C'mon, we'll catch the bus. So, why did you leave Charlotte Lily's house like that?"

"I had to be home by eleven, and it was already close to midnight," I said.

"Oh. How did you get home?"

"I took a taxicab," I said, instinctively deciding not to reveal Keefer Dawson.

She believed me and then spent the rest of our travel time talking about Axel. From the way she spoke about him, I thought it wasn't only the first time she had made love, it was the first time she had been with anyone. She went on and on about the promises he had made to her concerning their future, how he was going to make sure she had tickets to all the home games, and how he would take her to dances and parties.

"Promises can be like balloons," I told her. "They look and feel good when they're pumped up, but they all leak and eventually fall to earth."

"Not my promises," she vowed. "And when my daddy makes my stepmother a promise, he always keeps it."

"Goody goody for her," I said.

"And he keeps the promises he makes to me most of the time. Didn't your father do that, before he was killed in the plane crash, I mean?"

I gazed out the window without replying.

"I'm sorry," she said. "I know it's painful for you to think about it. Let's just think about good things. I know, I'll practice my Spanish. How's that?"

"Whatever," I said, and she began a catalogue of Spanish words for common things.

After a while I didn't hear her anymore. I felt tight inside, like my stomach had been tied into a knot and everything in it and around it was being squeezed. No, I didn't have a father to even break his promises to me, and now, now I wasn't permitted to have a mother. I was the balloon I spoke about. My life was just full of hot air, and I was leaking badly. Soon, I would fall to earth.

When we arrived at the department store, Kathy Ann went to the men's department to search for a gift for Axel. I went to the women's clothing area, and after a while, I found a young-miss skirt and blouse I really liked. I thought about Keefer Dawson and how he would appreciate seeing me in the outfit. The skirt was nearly sixty dollars, however, and the blouse was another thirty. One wouldn't be good without the other.

The saleslady was a little overwhelmed, which gave me the opportunity to take the skirt and the blouse into the fitting room together. I had done this before, so I felt confident about it. I put the blouse on under my blouse and made sure it was well hidden. Then I came out with the skirt and told the saleslady I wanted to buy it.

She glanced at me quickly and asked me to wait until she was finished with the customer ahead of me or else go to another register. That was even better, so I went toward the front of the store and placed the skirt on the counter. The cashier ran it through the register, and I paid her with Cory's money. Now that I had what I wanted, I wanted very much to get out of the store and away, but I didn't see Kathy Ann anywhere. Nevertheless, I thought it would be wiser to leave, so I did.

Not more than a minute after I left the store, a tall, dark-haired man in a suit and tie seized my left elbow, squeezing it hard enough to make me wince.

"Hey!" I snapped at him. "What do you think—"

"Where do you think you're going, young lady?"

"I'm going home. Who are you?" I demanded.

Some customers going in and out paused to watch the exchange, and I thought I would start to scream any moment to draw more attention and frighten whoever he was away, but he surprised me by opening his wallet and showing me a badge.

"I'm the store security man, and you, young lady, are under arrest for shoplifting. Now, turn around and head back into the department store," he ordered.

"I paid for this!" I cried, and showed him the slip.

He smiled.

"What about what you're wearing underneath your blouse?"

How could he know that unless they had some sort of camera or peep hole in the changing room? I wondered.

"Do you want me to make you take it off out here, or what?" he asked.

I thought about running, but the small crowd of onlookers had built considerably and was now surrounding us.

"Well?" he demanded.

I turned and headed back toward the entrance of the store. As we approached, Kathy Ann came out.

"Where were you? I've been looking all over for you. Why did you go out without telling me?"

"Step aside," the security man told her.

"What?"

"Go home, Kathy Ann," I said, "and tell my sister I'm in trouble."

"For what?" she asked, looking at the security man.

"For shoplifting," he said.

Her mouth dropped open. The security man put his hand on my back and pushed me toward the store entrance.

He took me to an office at the rear of the store where the store manager waited. He was a small, baldheaded man with deep wrinkles under his eyes and thick, wet lips. I could see from the way he was nodding and smiling that his day had been made.

"You juvenile delinquents think you can come in here anytime you want and just rip me off," he said. "This time you were fooled, eh."

I didn't say anything.

"Well? What's your excuse? C'mon, let's hear it. Maybe you have something new."

"I just forgot," I said.

"Oh," he groaned, and sat hard in his seat. "She's not even a little original. I've already called the police. We're going to press charges against you to set an example. We know you kids have been coming in here and pulling these stunts all year long, and we've grown sick and tired of it. The only way to stop it is to see to it that when you're caught, you pay the price, and I don't mean the price of what you stole, either."

I was hoping he was saying that just to frighten me. I was afraid, but something in me kept me from milking it. I couldn't even cry. The rage and tightness I had felt on my way here were still strong.

"What's your name?" he demanded.

"Puddin' Tame," I said.

"Oh, I see, a smart-ass. All right, we'll leave it all to the police and the courts. Sit," he commanded, pointing to a chair.

I looked at it, at the security man and the door, and then sat.

"She had a friend with her," the security man told the manager.

"And?"

"She was clean, as far as I could tell."

"Sure, they come in pairs. One distracts while the other pilfers."

"That's not true," I said. "She has nothing to do with this. She wasn't even with me in that department."

"What's her name?" he asked.

"Pippi Longstocking," I said.

He sat back and rubbed his hands together like someone anticipating a great feast.

A few moments later, the door opened and a policeman entered.

"This is our thief," the manager said. "She's wearing the stolen item under her blouse. You've got your evidence. Book her," he told them.

"Stand up," the policeman told me. He took out a pair of handcuffs. This had never happened to me in Ohio. The sight of them did stab me with a cold blade of fear. I know my arms trembled as he snapped the cuffs around my wrists.

"Let's go," he said firmly.

Marching through the store again, this time with a policeman right behind me and me wearing handcuffs, I drew more curious faces, some heads shaking with disgust. When we emerged, I looked for Kathy Ann, but I didn't see her anywhere.

"Move," the policeman said, poking me toward the patrol car. There was a policewoman waiting beside it. She held the rear door open.

"Watch your head," she said, putting her hand on top of my head as I leaned in to sit on the caged rear seat. "What do we have?" she asked the policeman.

"She's wearing a blouse under her blouse."

The policewoman smiled and shook her head at me.

"Honey," she said, "you just put yourself in a whole can of worms."

They got into the patrol car and we started away. I looked back at the people watching from the entrance.

At least I made someone's news of the day, I thought.

6

Strike One

I had been in a police station before, but I was two years younger then, and although everyone had been serious, I'd had the sense that my youth would provide a parachute. This time when they brought me into the station, I saw no one remotely close to my age. All of the other prisoners looked hardened and experienced.

The policewoman took me into a private room, where I removed the blouse I had taken. She folded it and then brought me back to the desk sergeant, where they took down my name and address. I had a picture ID from my school back in Ohio. Then I was fingerprinted and put in a holding cell with two other women. One looked like she was still coming down from a drug she had taken. The other was talking to her, but I didn't think she heard a word. I gathered they had been arrested for soliciting sex on the street. I was actually happy they showed no interest in me.

I sat on the bench and waited nearly three hours before Mother darling appeared.

"Robin Taylor," I heard, and stood up. The policeman unlocked the door. "Come with me," he said. I looked back at the two women, who were both asleep now, one leaning on the other. In the lobby Mother darling and Cory were standing and talking with the policewoman who had brought me to the station.

They all turned to me as I was brought along.

"I don't even want to hear your excuses, Robin," Mother darling said. "Cory and I have guaranteed your appearance in court. Just walk," she said.

I glanced at Cory, who had a twisted smile on his face.

"Told you not to sin, Robin Lyn," he quipped as they followed me out of the station.

"Don't joke with her, Cory. She knows she's in deep trouble with me. The whole Nashville world can find out I'm really her mother and not her sister," she said, and I spun on her.

"That's what bothers you the most?"

"No, what bothers me the most is your not keepin' your promise not to get into any trouble here. I told you this was a strange, new place. Luckily, Cory knows one of the policemen, and he helped arrange your release, but now we got to think about gettin' you a lawyer and that costs money. How could you do this?"

I got into Mother darling's Beetle and sat in the rear. Cory was driving.

"When that girl, Kathy Ann, came huffin' and puffin' up the stairs to tell me you were arrested for shopliftin', I nearly fainted with disappointment. They said you paid for this," she added, showing me the bag that contained the skirt. "Where'd you get the money for it, Robin, or did you somehow fool 'em?"

"I had some saved," I lied.

"I don't want you goin' anywhere until I say it's okay, hear me? You stay right around the apartment complex. Hopefully, you can't get into any more trouble doin' that. You know they could send you to jail for this? They do send sixteen-year-olds to jail, Robin. You're just lucky they don't know about your record in Ohio."

"They keep the juvenile records secret," she told Cory.

"How many times did she get in trouble like this?" he asked.

"Enough to have her called a kleptomaniac. I had her see a therapist, too."

"That did a lot of good, I see," he said.

"Now you see how hard it is to work on building a career and bring up a child," she told him.

"I'm not a child."

"You sure behave like you are," Cory said.

"At least I don't bust in on people when they're taking a shower."

"Oh, save me," he said. "Next time I'll do my business in a beer bottle. No, maybe I better not do that. Del might drink it by mistake," he said, and laughed.

Mother darling laughed, too.

"Oh, Robin," she said, shaking her head, "with me startin' work in a real club tonight, too. Don't you realize how good our lives could be?"

I folded my arms under my breasts and stared out the window. It was always Mother darling who was disappointed, always Mother darling who had to be protected.

The moment we drove into the apartment complex, Kathy Ann, who was obviously sitting by her window waiting, came charging out of her apartment.

"What happened?" she asked.

"What happened? I'll tell you what happened," Mother darling replied. "She was booked, fingerprinted, and given a court date where she could be sentenced to jail. That's what happened. Go on upstairs, Robin. You sit and contemplate what you've done."

I hurried ahead and went into my bedroom, slamming the door closed behind me. Then I threw myself on the bed, became aware of the stench in the sheet and blanket again, and sat up quickly. I thought for a moment and went to the door. They were sitting in the living room, feeling sorry for themselves. Cory was saying how grateful he was that he never got married and had any children. The ones who should be grateful are the children, I thought, who never had him as a father.

"Can I go down to the laundry room and wash something at least?" I asked.

"What?" Mother darling wanted to know.

"The smelly old sheet on this bed and the blanket and the pillowcase. I can't sleep on it! It all stinks from cigarette smoke," I moaned.

"It's better than what you'll have in jail," Cory called back.

"Can I?"

"Just the laundry and back, Robin, and I mean it. You better not run off."

"Unless you want to keep going," Cory added, and then laughed.

"I wish I could," I muttered, returning to the bed to strip it and roll up the sheet, blanket, and pillowcase. Then I started out.

"Don't you need money for that washing machine and dryer?" Mother darling asked Cory.

"Yeah, you have any change?" he asked me.

"No."

He reached into his pocket and then he pulled out his wallet.

"You can get change for a dollar. They have a change machine," he said, and froze, his eyes blinking rapidly as he fingered the bills. "Hey." He looked up at Mother darling and then at me. "I had eighty dollars in here. Now I have only twenty."

"Robin, did you take Cory's money?"

"No," I said.

"She's lying. You can see it in her face."

"Robin?"

"No," I said. She shook her head.

"I'm so sorry, Cory. I'll give it to you," she told him.

"I didn't take it. You don't have to give it to him."

"You see what I've been livin' with," she told him.

"I have some money left over from what you gave me," I told her. "I don't need anything from him."

Before either of them could say another word, I left the apartment and went down to the laundry. All I could think was Kathy Ann spent her whole time at that front window because she saw me and came over to the laundry a second or two after I began to load in the sheet and blanket.

"Tell me what really happened," she said.

"Just what my sister said."

"Why did you do it?"

"I wanted it and I didn't have enough money for it. You never stole anything?"

"Not like that," she replied, shaking her head. "I'd be too scared. I was amazed at how you stole those cigarettes last night. Were you ever caught before?"

"Not often," I told her. "I should have kept some of those cigarettes. You have any?"

"Sure," she said, and dug one out of her shirt pocket. She lit one for herself too, and we sat there watching the washing machine churn away. "How is your sister punishing you?" she wanted to know.

"I'm not supposed to leave the apartment complex until she says it's all right."

"Oh. That's too bad."

"But she's going to be busy nights, singing with the band. They have a job or a gig, as they call it."

"So you'll sneak out anyway?"

"What do you think?"

"Wow," she said, and looked at me as if I was some sort of celebrity myself. "Where are you going to go?"

"I have to have a dent in my head fixed."

"Huh?"

"I didn't tell you the truth when you asked me how I had gotten home last night. I went to see Keefer Dawson and he drove me here."

"You didn't?"

"All right, I didn't."

"Wow," she said again.

Yes, I thought. Wow.

She sat with me until I was finished with my sheet and blanket and pillowcase. Now that she knew more about what had happened, she had a laundry list of questions to ask about my life in Ohio. I told her as much as I could. I wanted her to think I was taking her into my confidence because I had a favor I needed from her.

"You weren't going anywhere tonight, were you?" I asked her.

"No. Why?"

"Can you do me a little favor?"

"Sure," she said, excited that I was taking her into my confidence.

"Come up to my apartment to hang out."

"Oh, sure. I'd like that."

"And when my sister calls to see if I'm there, if she should, tell her I'm in the bathroom. As long as you answer the phone, she'll believe it."

"You mean you won't be there?"

"No, silly," I said. "I'll be fixing my dent."

She made an O with her mouth and nodded, and then she smiled at me.

"Wow," she said.

Maybe that would become my new name, I thought. Wow.

After I made the bed with the fresh sheet, pillowcase, and blanket, I joined Mother darling and Cory, who were eating take-out Chinese Cory had had delivered. Mother darling was not much of a cook. I was a better cook than she was, in fact, because I was around Grandma more when she made our meals, and she taught me. "Your mother was never interested in learning any of this," she said. "All she wanted to do was sing and hang out with nobodies."

I smiled to myself, remembering that.

"You better sit down and eat 'fore it gets cold, Robin," Mother darling told me.

I plopped onto a seat, petulantly. Cory was feeding his face as fast as he could scoop the noodles, chicken, and shrimp into his mouth.

"You're really in serious trouble now, Robin. I hope you appreciate the situation and behave."

I picked up a fork and started to serve myself some food. Cory glanced at me and then burped.

"What she needs is a job," he said, "but with her history, I don't know nobody who'd hire her, except a pickpocket."

"He's right, Robin. That's somethin' we should think about. You have weeks and weeks yet before school starts here."

"I can't look for work if I'm locked up in the apartment, now can I?"

She thought a moment.

"We'll buy a paper and see what sort of work's out there and then we'll see about how to apply."

"I won't hold my breath," I said.

"Damn girl, if you was my daughter . . ."

"I'd commit suicide," I finished, and he sat with his mouth open for a moment and then shook his head and got up.

"I'm gettin' ready to go," he told Mother darling.

"Why are you so mean to him?" Mother darling whispered. "Don't you realize we'd have nothin' and be nowhere if he wasn't helpin' me? The least you can do is show him some respect and appreciation, Robin."

"What? He—"

"Don't start," she snapped. "If you can't be nice, then just don't be anythin'. Just keep your mouth shut, hear?"

I pushed the food away and pouted.

"I don't have time to baby you now, Robin. I've got to make a career happen. You're just goin' to have to grow up or suffer the consequences. Meanwhile, you clean up," she declared, and left to follow Cory.

I sat fuming until I heard them come out of their bedroom.

"I'll be callin' you first break I get, Robin," Mother darling said. "Least you could do is wish me luck."

"Good luck," I spit back at her.

After they were gone, I cleared off the table and washed the silverware and dishes. I began to think Kathy Ann wasn't going to come up to the apartment, but she finally did appear.

"When are you coming back?" she asked.

"I'll be back before midnight," I said. "I won't forget this favor."

"Can't you be arrested for leaving the apartment?" she wanted to know.

"No. You're not guilty of anything until the court says."

"I was never in a courtroom," she told me, as if she had been denied some pleasure that all girls our age had already enjoyed.

"Lucky you," I said.

"Does Keefer know you're going to see him?"

"Not exactly," I said.

"I told Charlotte Lily about you. She was very interested."

"Like I care," I said.

"Bring me back a chocolate bar with nuts. My stepmother threw every piece of candy out of the house today."

"Axel will like you more if you lose weight."

"That's not what he said. He said he likes a woman with something to grab on her."

"Okay," I said. "One chocolate bar with nuts."

I was getting away cheaply, I thought, and after I put on the skirt I had bought with Cory's money and found a blouse that came close to the one I had stolen, I went to the bathroom to fix my hair and put on some lipstick. Then I started to leave before Kathy Ann could change her mind. Fortunately, she was already hooked on a television program.

"Call me," she said as I started toward the front door, "and let me know what's happening."

"Will do. Don't forget. I'm in the bathroom, and if she calls again, say I've got the runs. She'll believe that."

"I bet you've been lying all your life, haven't you?"

I thought a moment.

"No, my whole life's been a lie," I told her. She smiled in confusion.

"Huh?"

"Thanks, Kathy Ann. I owe you," I said, and left quickly.

I had to wait longer for the bus and at one point wondered if I should try hitching a ride. Finally, it came. I went directly to the shop, but stopped dead in my tracks when I turned the corner and looked at the building. There were no lights on like there had been the night before. Disappointment settled over me like a leaden cape. I felt like crying. Then I remembered Keefer saying he had an apartment behind the shop.

I went around the building and saw a small window with a light on behind it. What if he was with someone? I thought. It would be very embarrassing for both of us. I should have called him first. Feeling timid now, I went to the window and peeked through the flimsy curtain. I saw it was as he had described: a single room with a pullout sofa, a small stove and sink on the right, and a television set across from the sofa. There was a table with two chairs as well. The walls were bare. The truth was, it looked more like some sort of a storage room that had been converted into a living space. The floor was bare, and the only light came from two lamps. How depressing, I thought.

"See anything you like?" I heard, and nearly jumped out of my skin.

I turned, holding my breath. There was Keefer, a bag of groceries in his arms. When he saw it was me, he broke into a big smile.

"Robin, what the hell are you doin'?"

"I was just seeing if you were in, or if you had any company," I explained.

He nodded.

"Company? Here? It's just me, myself, and I," he told me. "What are you doin' here?"

"I had to get away from my place," I said. "I got into trouble today."

"Oh? C'mon inside then and tell me about it. I love to hear about trouble."

He opened the door, and I followed him into the one-room apartment. He had a very small refrigerator, actually more like a portable thing. He had to bend down to put his food in it. He took two quarts of beer out of his bag and put one in the refrigerator.

"Beer?" he asked.

"Sure."

Now that I was inside, I felt even more depressed. The walls seemed to close in, and I could hear what sounded like a leaking pipe in the wall.

"There's a couple of rats livin' here, too," he said, seeing how I was listening. "Friendly. I even put out some cheese for them."

"Keefer!"

"I'm just kiddin'. That's the hot water heater. So, tell me about your trouble," he said, pouring me a glass of beer. He sat beside me and I described it all. He went from a smile to a serious face and then a very pensive look.

"I doubt they'd send you to jail," he said, "but you will get some sort of probation. You don't need a lawyer. Tell your sister to just throw you on the mercy of the court."

"How do you know so much about it?"

He poured himself another glass of beer, filled mine again, and smiled.

"I wasn't exactly an Eagle Scout myself." He stopped smiling. "Only when I got home, my daddy didn't just tell me to stay put. He took his belt out and gave me welts that lasted for a month."

"What had you done?"

"Stole a car," he said nonchalantly. "Just for a joyride."

"Was that when you had your fight with your father?"

"Who told you about that?"

"Kathy Ann."

"Yeah, I had a real fistfight with my father. I didn't do well. He nearly broke my cheek bone, in fact, but I wouldn't stop until he backed off. He knew he had to kill me to get me to stop, and that's when he told me to get out and stay out, which is just what I did. He never wanted me anyway. I wasn't just an accident, I was a train wreck as far as my father was concerned."

He finished the beer in his glass and poured another. I stared at him long enough for him to widen his eyes and say, "What?"

"I'm living a lie here," I said.

"What do you mean?"

"I'm not here with my sister. I'm here with my mother. She makes me say she's my sister because she wants music people to think she's younger than she is."

"Oh. Then that story about the plane crash . . ."

"I just made that up on the spur of the moment to tell Kathy Ann something."

"Well, what about your father?"

"Your father could be my father for all I know," I said. His eyes widened more. "No, I'm kidding, but not as much as you think. My mother can't be sure who made me. She was high on something at a wild party, and she says she was with more than one man the same night."

"Wow," Keefer said.

"That seems to be a popular word around here, or maybe just around me."

"Huh?"

"Never mind," I said. I finished my beer. "I guess you and I are more alike than I first thought, only you're lucky. You got away."

"Got away? To this?" He looked around the room. "No, ma'am, this isn't luck. It's a stopover on the way to something better, I hope."

I held out my glass and he filled it again.

"What made you want to come to see me after all this?" he asked.

I shrugged.

"You mend things that are banged around, dented, and broken, don't you?"

He laughed, and then he looked at me long and hard before leaning over to do what I wished he would from the moment I saw him sitting in a pool of sparks.

He kissed me.

And I kissed him back, harder and longer than I had ever kissed anyone.

In my mind the sparks were flying all around us.

7

Honeymoon Fantasies
and Strike Two

"**Y**ou sure you want to get mixed up with the likes of me?" Keefer asked before he kissed me again.

"I could ask you the same question," I replied. He liked that.

"Girls like Charlotte Lily always make me feel small, feel like something disposable."

I saw how angry he became just thinking about it, so I leaned forward and kissed him softly on the lips.

"I'm not Charlotte Lily," I told him, and the smile returned to his face.

"You sure ain't," he said, put his beer glass down, and kissed me on the cheek, the neck, and the lips while he turned me in so he could embrace me more easily. I felt his hands move down to the zipper on my skirt.

"I don't want to get pregnant," I said.

"Don't worry, you won't," he promised. He paused, took out his wallet, and then took out a contraceptive. He held it up as if he was showing off a diamond in the lamplight. My heart was pounding. He thinks I've done this before, I thought. I was going to tell him I hadn't, but he kissed me again and then began to slowly undress me, kissing every naked part of me he uncovered until he stood up and undid his pants while he looked down at me and said, "You're really beautiful, Robin."

My heart was pounding so, I could barely breathe. When he was beside me, I finally confessed. He hesitated so long, I thought he was going to stop, but then he smiled and said, "You'll never forget me then. Women never forget the first man."

A part of me was disappointed in myself. When I had learned the facts of life, I used to fantasize my first lovemaking. It was always on some glamorous island during a wonderful honeymoon with music in the background and stars blazing above. Instead, here I was in some thrown-together, makeshift, dingy one-room apartment on a sofa that could have been rescued from a junkyard, both Keefer and I tasting the beer on our lips.

There were no shooting stars, no tinkling bells, no angels with magic wands around us. I was uncomfortable with my excitement, sensitive and nervous, moaning under his pleading to relax. Instead of being as soft and downy as a cloud, I was a tightening guitar string, stretched to the point of breaking, every nerve in my body cracking and snapping like a shorted electric wire.

"It gets better," Keefer assured me when we were finished. He lay there, catching his breath, his head against my naked breast, listening to the thumping of my heart. "Are you all right?"

"Yes," I managed.

He lifted his head and kissed each of my nipples before pushing himself away.

"Be right back," he said, and went to the bathroom.

I sat up and began to dress. When he came out, we heard the phone ringing in the shop.

"Who the hell is that?" he wondered aloud. "Be right back," he said, and went to the door that opened on the shop.

I continued to dress.

"Got a message for you," he said, returning. "That was Kathy Ann. She says your 'sister' called and said she was calling back in fifteen minutes and if you weren't there to answer, she was going to call the police herself and report you."

"She would, too, I bet," I moaned.

"C'mon," he said. "I can get you back there in fifteen minutes."

He pulled on his jeans, slipped into his shoes, and grabbed his shirt as we started out.

"Hold on," he told me after starting the engine. I had barely closed the door.

The rear wheels spun and kicked up gravel, and then he turned sharply into the street and accelerated. He wove in and out of traffic, cutting someone off at one point. The driver leaned on his horn. Keefer laughed and just accelerated again, turning abruptly down a side street.

"I know a little shortcut," he said, gunning the engine.

He went through a stop sign and then made some sharp turns again, throwing me from one side of the seat to another. I screamed and he laughed. I couldn't remember feeling more excited and afraid at the same time. Then, when he made a final turn into the street I knew brought us to my apartment complex, he sideswiped a small sedan we passed.

"Damn," he yelled. "I ain't stoppin'. I'm not supposed to be drivin' this truck. Izzy will throw me out."

The driver of the car laid on his horn and followed us as best he could, but Keefer outran him and then bounced into the parking lot of my complex. I caught my breath, not knowing whether to cry or laugh.

"Get movin'," he ordered.

I jumped out of the truck and ran up the stairs. Just as I reached the apartment door, I heard the phone ringing inside. I threw it open and charged in. Kathy Ann had just picked up the phone.

"Here she is," she said, a look of shock and surprise on her face.

I swallowed down a throat lump that would choke a horse, and as calmly as I could manage, said, "Hello."

"What's wrong with you now?" Mother darling asked.

"I think the Chinese food was bad."

"It didn't bother Cory or me."

"Maybe I just had a nervous stomach."

"Well, I'm glad you're listenin' to me for once at least. We're doin' real well here. The owner knows people who he says he's goin' to invite to hear us now that he has heard us more, especially me. I really think I'm goin' to make it, Robin."

"Good for you, Mother darling."

She was quiet.

"I was hopin' you'd change your tone and your ways."

"I am," I said. "That's a promise."

"Okay, Robin. I'll see you later."

"I'll be asleep, I'm sure," I said, and hung up.

Keefer was standing in the doorway. I nodded, and then I laughed and he laughed.

"How'd you get here so fast?" Kathy Ann asked.

"We took the bus," he said.

"The bus?" She looked at me and then at him. "You liars."

We laughed again, and then Keefer heard something and turned to look down at the parking lot.

"Oh, no," he said.

I stepped forward and looked down with him. There was a Nashville police car, its bubble light going, parked right behind Keefer's boss's truck. The two policemen got out, and one directed a large flashlight at the right front area of the truck. The other turned and looked up, so we backed into the apartment and closed the door quickly.

"What's happening?" Kathy Ann asked.

"Shut up," Keefer said. "Put out the lights, quick."

"Why?"

"Just do it," he said, and she and I went to every lamp and switch and turned off the lights.

We stood waiting, no one speaking, but the sound of my breathing and Keefer's loud enough for us all to hear. Moments later, we heard footsteps on the second-story landing. We held our breath.

"Who is it?" Kathy Ann asked.

"Shut up," Keefer snapped.

We waited.

There was a very loud rap on the door, a rap made with a police stick for sure, I thought.

"Open up, it's the police," we heard.

"Oh, my God," Kathy Ann whined.

"Jesus," Keefer said.

"We're going to have that truck towed and impounded if you don't open this door," the policeman threatened.

"Damn it," Keefer said. "Okay, put on the lights," he told Kathy Ann. She was too terrified to move, so I did it. Then he opened the door.

"That your truck below?" the policeman asked him immediately.

"No. It belongs to my boss," Keefer replied.

"Step outside, please," he said. He looked in at us. "You, too, ladies," he added.

"Why?" Kathy Ann whined.

The policeman just stepped aside for us to come out and we did. The three of us stood on the landing with both of the police officers.

"You were driving that truck a few minutes ago, then?"

"Yes," Keefer said.

"Which one of you was in the truck? C'mon," he said, "the man lodging the complaint saw two people."

Kathy Ann was actually trembling.

"I was," I confessed.

"You know it is a serious offense to leave the scene of an accident?" he asked Keefer.

"What accident?"

He smiled.

"You're not going to stand there and tell us you don't remember hitting another vehicle, are you? The other vehicle's paint is on the truck."

Keefer looked at me.

"I told you I thought I might have hit something," he said.

"I didn't think you had," I said.

The two policemen stared at us a moment.

"Let me see your license," the first policeman asked Keefer. He took out his wallet and produced it.

"This your apartment?" he asked Keefer.

"No."

"Whose is it then?"

"My sister's music partner," I said. "We're living here temporarily."

"Where are your parents?"

"They're dead," I said, glancing at Keefer, who tried to hide his eyes.

"And where is your sister now?"

"She's performing at a dance club."

"What's the occupant's name?" the second policeman asked.

"Cory Lewis," I said. I could feel cold tears coming into my eyes.

"And your name, miss?"

"Robin Taylor."

"All right. For now, we'll take Mr. Dawson here and you, Miss Taylor, to the police station."

"Can I bring the truck back?" Keefer asked.

"Not until the matter is settled," the policeman said.

"Well, why do you have to take her, too? I'm the one who was driving," he said.

"Procedure," the policeman replied. "She was a witness to the events. Maybe next time you'll think about all the ramifications that occur when you break the law. Let's go," he said. Then he paused. "How old are you, miss?"

"I'm sixteen," I said.

The second policeman took his cell phone off his belt.

"Where is your sister performing?"

I started to speak and then realized I didn't know. I really didn't know. They never had told me.

"I don't know," I said. "She forgot to tell me."

"I would think," the first policeman said, "that you would have realized by now how serious this situation is."

"I'm telling you the truth." I turned to Kathy Ann. "Did she tell you where she was working when she called earlier?"

She shook her head like someone who was incapable of speech.

"All right, come along," the policeman said.

Kathy Ann remained in the doorway.

"What should I do?" she called after us.

"Go home," the policeman told her.

She nodded and quickly closed the door behind her. She remained far behind us as we walked down to the parking lot.

"I won't go anywhere," Keefer told the first policeman. "At least let me take the truck back."

"You can do that later if you're not incarcerated," he said.

They put us into the patrol car. This was the second time within a twenty-four-hour period that I had been in a Nashville police car. The fact didn't escape me, nor would it escape Mother darling when she found out.

At the police station, Keefer confronted the owner of the vehicle he had hit. He was a short, plump man, a chef in one of the local restaurants. Keefer apologized and told him he was an auto body repairman and he would fix whatever damage he had done.

"I'll get on it immediately," he promised. He explained we were in a big rush, and he apologized again.

In the end he decided not to press charges against Keefer. We were there almost two and a half hours. I saw the policeman who had been talking to Mother darling and Cory. He looked at me for a long moment, went to the desk sergeant to find out what it was all about, and then shook his head and left.

The police brought us back to the apartment complex so Keefer could get his boss's truck. It was nearly two-thirty in the morning.

"You'd better keep your nose clean," the policeman told him when we got out.

We watched the patrol car leave.

"Sorry about all this," Keefer said. "Trouble just seems to enjoy my company."

"It was my fault. If you didn't have to rush me home, you wouldn't have hit that car."

He shrugged.

"I guess we're both good and screwed up," he said. "You were right. We're a pair."

We looked at each other and laughed. It was more a laugh of relief than anything else, but it felt good, and then we embraced and I started up to the apartment. I glanced at Kathy Ann's apartment and saw the lights were all out. At least she wasn't hovering at the front window this time, I thought.

As quickly as I could, I undressed and got into bed. Despite all the excitement, I was so exhausted, I fell into a deep sleep, almost a coma, moments after my head hit the pillow. I'll worry about everything tomorrow, I told myself. I'll be Scarlett O'Hara in *Gone With the Wind.*

But I wasn't that lucky. My life was a totally different movie.

A little after four in the morning, Mother darling threw open my bedroom door and screamed my name so loud, she surely woke everyone in the entire apartment complex.

I groaned and reluctantly forced my eyes to open. She was at the foot of the bed.

"Tell me it's a lie. Tell me it isn't true. Tell me they made a mistake and thought you were someone else."

"It's a lie. It isn't true. They made a mistake," I said, and dropped my head back to the pillow.

"You ain't gonna be able to do this, Kay," Cory said from behind. "You can't concentrate on making music, writing new songs, getting better and better if you have that lead weight around your neck."

"I know," she said sadly. I heard her sniff back some tears, but I kept my eyes closed and pretended I had fallen asleep again. "Let me think on it," she told him. "You're impossible, Robin Lyn," she threw back at me, and then she left and closed the door.

I slept into the next day almost as long as they did. I had just made some coffee and was sitting and sipping it in the kitchen when Mother darling shuffled in, her hair wild, her eyes bloodshot.

"I didn't sleep much last night, Robin." She poured herself a cup of coffee and looked at me. I was staring down at my own coffee cup. "Talk," she said. "Cory's policeman friend told us you were brought to the station, that you were involved in a hit-and-run accident. How could you be? I spoke to you here, didn't I? Well?"

"I went for a ride earlier," I said, "and we hit a car and didn't realize it was serious."

"Who's we? Who was drivin'?"

"A friend of mine," I said.

"How can you have so many friends so fast?" she asked.

I looked up.

"I guess I'm a naturally sociable person. Look, nothing happened. My friend is taking care of it all. No one was arrested. It was all settled."

"But didn't I tell you not to leave the apartment?"

"I can't stay cooped up in here. It's too small. The television set hardly gets anything. I hate it here!" I screamed.

"I really don't know what to do with you," she said.

"Trade me in for a new guitar," I shot back.

"Sometimes, I wish I could," she said.

"I always wish you could."

I got up and went back to the bedroom. I heard her bring Cory a cup of coffee.

"She's just a spoiled brat," I heard him tell her.

Yes, I'm a spoiled brat, I thought. I'm spoiled because I don't have any real parents or a real home or a real family. I'm spoiled because my mother sees me as a burden, and always did. I'm spoiled because my grandpa thought I had inherited sin. I'm so spoiled the angels close their eyes when they fly near me.

Later that afternoon, Keefer called.

"How are things?" he asked.

"Status quo. I'm as unwanted as ever, maybe a little more than ever."

"You won't believe it, but this guy I hit is my new best friend. I told him I would take out all of his dents and nicks and make his car look new. Izzy wasn't happy, but I can fix that too, and since it didn't cost him anything, he's just a little upset. He knows he's getting a day and a half and sometimes two days' work out of me a day, and for what he pays me, he's not about to throw me out. I'll be leaving under my own steam," Keefer vowed.

"Take me with you," I said half jokingly. He was silent.

"Maybe I will. I have a plan, and one of these days, I'll talk about it with you. If you're still interested in me after this, that is."

"I'm more interested, not less," I said, and he laughed.

"Okay. Tell you what. Tonight, I'll come to you. I have this extra work, but figure me for about ten. What time does your mother and Cory get home?"

"Sometime after two, I guess. I gather they calm down by having a few drinks and hanging around or going somewhere else."

"I'll be there."

"In Izzy's truck?"

"No. I'm layin' off it for a while. I have another customer's car at my disposal."

"Does he know?"

Keefer just laughed.

"What he doesn't know . . ."

"Won't hurt him. I know, I know," I said.

Knowing he was coming took the shadowy cobwebs of gloom out of my mind. Mother darling watched me with suspicion as I went about straightening up the apartment and doing some cleaning.

"What are you up to, Robin?" she asked finally.

"Nothing. I'm bored, that's all."

"Then you should get a job. If they don't send you to jail, that is. Cory and I will talk to some people tonight. He knows the manager of a supermarket. Maybe you can get a job as a packer."

"Right. That's sure to cure boredom."

She glared at me a moment, and then she shook her head and went off to fix her hair and prepare herself for another night of performing. She and Cory were going to eat out tonight. I told her not to worry about me. I had found some pasta that was less than a year old.

"You're always so smart, Robin, so quick to be sarcastic. Why don't you put that to good use and do somethin' constructive with yourself."

"I am. I'm writing a song for you," I told her.

"You are? What's it about?"

"About a girl like me who finds out her sister is her mother."

"Very funny."

"Wait," I said as she started away. "It gets better. She find out her brother is her father."

She slammed the door of her bedroom. Cory, who was reading a motorcycle magazine, looked up at me.

"Robin Lyn, what's your sin for today going to be?"

"Living with you," I shot back. His smile wilted as I strutted back to the kitchen to wash down the refrigerator. Grandma always said, "You can't be clean on the inside if you're not clean on the outside."

I wondered what she really meant.

8

Drifting Deeper
into the Abyss

Every night for the rest of the week, Keefer came to visit me. I really had little to do with anyone else. Kathy Ann's parents had heard about the truck accident, either from her own mouth or from some other gossips in the complex who witnessed it, and they told her to stay away from me or she would be grounded until school began again. She came into the laundry to tell me.

"Of course, I can meet you downtown sometimes," she said, "but I can't come up to Cory's apartment or anything like that."

"Don't worry about it. Oh," I said, "how's Axel?"

She looked down.

"Nothing bad happened to him, did it?"

"He hasn't called me since that night, and I went and bought something for him, too," she complained.

"Well, football players are like that," I said as if I had all the experience in the world with them. "Maybe he got hit in the head since then," I offered. "How's Charlotte Lily?"

"All right, I guess." Her face brightened. "I told her about you and Keefer and all and she sounded jealous."

"Why? She was the one who told me he wasn't worth her time."

Kathy Ann shrugged, glanced out the window nervously, and then said she would try to see me later. She hurried away.

Now, I thought, I'm like a leper here. Mother darling, if you're going to be a success, you'd better be one soon and get us somewhere nicer to live.

What Mother darling and Cory did manage to do was get me an interview for that job in the supermarket. She was excited enough about it to get herself up early so she could drive me to the supermarket to meet the manager, a man named Al Ritter. He was lean and dark, with a very black mustache and the deepest cleft chin I had ever seen. His office was cluttered with postings on the walls, and his desk was buried under forms and mailings.

He began by asking me to fill out an application. There was a question that asked if I, the applicant, had ever been arrested. Since my court date was coming up the following week and if I got the job, I would have to ask for time off to go to it, I decided to tell the truth and I checked yes. At first I thought it really didn't matter. He glanced over the application so quickly, I decided he had already told Cory or Mother darling he would hire me.

He began by telling me he usually hired only college-age kids because they needed the money desperately and were mostly reliable. Then he picked up the application again, perused it, and paused. His eyes lifted slowly.

"What were you arrested for?"

"Shoplifting," I admitted.

"Where?"

"Here in Nashville. I have to go to court next week," I said as casually as I could.

"I see," he said. "Well, why don't we wait until we hear what happens to you then."

"Whatever," I said, shrugged, and left the office. Mother darling was waiting in her car, her head back, her eyes closed, but one of her tapes playing.

As soon as I opened the door, she sat up and said, "Well?"

"He wants to wait to see what happens next week," I told her.

"Next week? Why next week? What's supposed to be happening?"

"My court appearance, remember?"

"Huh? Well, how did he . . . you told him you were arrested?"

"There was a question about that on the application. At the bottom of the form it says if you deliberately put in false information, you can be summarily dismissed, which I believe means fired on the spot."

She stared at me, her eyes small, dark.

"You did that deliberately, Robin. You made sure he wouldn't hire you, and after Cory had asked him to do us a favor, too."

"Did you want me to lie, Mother darling? That's no way to start a career in the supermarket."

"Oh you . . . you . . ." She mumbled under her breath and started the engine. "I half hope they do send you to jail next week," she said.

I didn't say anything. She looked like she was wiping away a tear before we returned to the apartment complex. Cory was still asleep.

"I don't know what you're going to do with yourself, Robin, except get into more and more trouble," she told me after we entered the apartment.

"I'll keep house here," I offered. "If you like, I'll make dinner whenever you can eat at home."

She studied me closely to see if I was serious and then nodded.

"We'll see," she said, and went quietly into the bedroom, closing the door softly behind her.

"Thanks for making a fool out of me," Cory said after he had heard the story and risen. He opened the refrigerator, took out the orange juice, and drank right from the bottle, making it far less appetizing for anyone else to drink from it now.

"That's something you can do easily yourself," I said.

He glared at me with such rage, I thought I had stepped over the line and he would lunge at me. I actually braced for it, but he calmed down when I added, "I didn't think I should lie to a friend of yours. It would make things even worse."

He frowned.

"If I was hired and I needed time off to go to court, don't you think he would be slightly suspicious and then annoyed that you never told him about me?"

"You coulda just called in sick."

"People gossip," I said.

"That's it," he said, raising his hands, palms to me. "I'm finished. You're not my responsibility."

"Who ever said I was?" I asked, not to be smart, but to see if Mother darling had somehow convinced him he had to look out for the both of us and not just her.

"Nobody, and I thank my lucky stars for that," he told me.

I rose and left him in the kitchen. Lucky stars, what do they look like? I wondered.

The following week Keefer offered to go to court with me, but I didn't think Mother darling would like that, and the truth was, I was a little embarrassed about it and how I would look there. I told him I'd much rather he didn't.

"Fine," he said. "If you need me for anything, you just call."

I thanked him. Despite my brave front, I was trembling inside the moment I awoke on the morning of the court date. Mother darling was complaining from the get-go about how she had to get up early after a hard night of singing.

"It's not easy looking fresh and young when you don't get any sleep," she whined.

"So don't go. I'll go myself," I said.

"Oh, sure. Lucky we were able to get you a public defender. You just dress neat and conservatively, Robin Lyn, and you keep that smart mouth shut, if you know what's good for you."

I was not the first defendant at court. In fact, we had to wait almost an hour to go in. The judge, Judge Babcock, was a woman with short salt-and-pepper hair. She looked like she had last smiled on her first birthday. Her thin lips were so tightly pressed together as she read the report on me, it looked like she had a zipper where her mouth should have been. When she finally lifted her eyes and looked my way, I felt like she was burning two holes in my face.

"Your client is pleading guilty?" she asked our public defender, a very plain-looking, light-haired man named Carson Meriweather, whose suit hung on his body the way it would hang on a clothes rack. It was as if he was all head with a skeleton beneath.

"Yes, Your Honor."

"Do you understand what this means, Miss Taylor?"

"I guess," I said.

"You guess? Either you understand that you are pleading guilty to shoplifting or you are not. This is not some game. Which is it?"

"Guilty," I said before my throat closed.

"Unfortunately, too many young people have reached your age with a warped sense of right and wrong. There was a time when morality was taught in the home, but," she said with a sigh, "it's becoming more and more the responsibility of the court."

She turned to Mother darling.

"Mrs. Taylor, how have you dealt with this situation in your own home?"

"I . . . we just moved here recently, Your Honor."

"Yes? So?" she asked when Mother darling apparently thought that was some sort of an answer.

"I told her she wasn't to leave the apartment complex. She was grounded."

"I see. Did you take the time to explain to her how people are working to make a living, how the employees of this department store depend on the department store succeeding, and how robbing and stealing hurts everyone, that if we didn't stop it, someone could rob her as well and we would have anarchy? Well?"

"I did, Your Honor. I've been asking her to behave herself for some time."

"Oh?"

"I've even had her see a therapist back in Ohio when we lived there."

"I see. And how long do you intend to remain in Nashville, Mrs. Taylor?"

"Oh, I'm here for good, Your Honor. I'm a singer and . . ."

"Then you had better be sure your daughter understands our laws and what we expect of our citizens," she snapped.

"Yes, Your Honor."

Judge Babcock sat up and tapped her pen on the documents before her. It was a long, nerve-wracking pause. She really looked like she was debating whether or not to send me to the gallows.

"My best instincts tell me I shouldn't do this. I should deal with you as severely as the law permits, but I am going to place you on two years' probation and return you to the custody of your mother in the hope that this experience has made an indelible impression on you. Understand, so you won't have to guess, that should you be brought in here for any other offense, I will not hesitate to send you directly to a juvenile detention center, unless," she said, leaning over her desk, "your new crime is so heinous as to have you tried as an adult. In such a case, you would not be sent to a juvenile center. A juvenile center would be like a nursery school compared to where you would be sent. Am I making myself clear, Miss Taylor? You don't look like you're listening."

"I'm listening," I said, a little too petulantly. I knew that the moment I uttered the words, and then I held my breath.

She glared hard at me for a long moment before she turned to Mother darling.

"You have a serious parental responsibility here, Mrs. Taylor. I hope you are impressed with this fact and you will devote more time and energy to your daughter's upbringing and behavior."

Mother darling nodded. She looked like she was going to burst out in tears any moment. I wanted to poke her with my elbow and make sure she didn't embarrass us both. She bit down on her lower lip and nodded again.

"Very well. The matter is resolved for now," Judge Babcock said.

The public defender, who had done little more than instruct me to plead guilty and be polite to the judge, smiled at us and indicated we could leave.

I heard another name called and saw a boy who didn't look much older than ten being brought in with a man who had his hand firmly around the back of the boy's neck. I thought, if that's his father, he would be better off being sent to a juvenile detention center.

"I hope you appreciate the break you just received, young lady," the public defender said.

"She doesn't, but I'll make sure she does," Mother darling told him.

"You don't want to come back here," he said. "That's one hard judge."

Mother darling thanked him, and then she hurried us out of the courthouse.

"I swear," she muttered as we drove back to Cory's apartment, "I don't know where you get that belligerent streak that's in you."

"Maybe from my mysterious father," I suggested. "Hey," I said, nearly bouncing on the seat, "that's how you can tell who my father was. Which of the dozen or so men you slept with that night was most like me?"

She looked at me as if she wasn't sure whether I was being serious or not, and then she smirked and shook her head.

"Keep it up, Robin. Keep punishing me for your own failin' and faults. See what it gets you in the end."

"You mean this isn't the end already?" I retorted.

She tightened her face and drove the rest of the way in silence. Inside, I felt like brittle china that had just been hit hard and was full of deep cracks. It would take only a small nudge to have it fall completely apart.

Cory seemed only vaguely interested in what had happened to me in court. He said, "Kids her age get away with murder these days." The judge's decision only reinforced his views. Anyway, he didn't want to spend any time talking about me. He had a big announcement to make to Mother darling.

"Bill Renner, a scout for Reliable Records, was at our club last night. I just got a call. He liked your song, 'Ridin' on a Dream.' He wants us to go down to the studio to talk to him about cuttin' a record. I already told Del and Ernie. You go in and put on your best outfit," he continued. "Fix yourself up real good, Kay. I want him to see the possibilities for photos, covers, advertisements immediately."

Mother darling squealed with delight and then ran into his arms. He spun her around. They looked like two happy kids. I couldn't prevent the soft smile that came to my lips, but then, thinking about where I had just been, I couldn't help feeling even more like the lead weight around Mother darling's ankles Cory accused me of being. This was their success, not mine, their dreams coming true. There was no room in that for me.

How I envied them both for the looks of joy and elation on their faces. Mother darling's eyes brightened like a little girl's. Her face blossomed before me, and Cory looked really satisfied with himself.

"Do I know what I'm talking about or don't I?" he asked her.

"You know, Cory, oh, boy, do you know."

She paused to look at me.

"Oh, be happy for us all, Robin. This is a very big opportunity, and it's one of my songs, my songs!"

"I'm happy," I said. "I'm so happy, I could turn into a bubble and burst."

Her smile froze. Cory curled his lip.

"Good luck," I said, and went to my bedroom.

"Forget about her," he said. "We've got to concentrate on this chance and put all our energy toward it."

I could hear their happy voices as they dressed and prepared themselves in the next room. I lay on the bed staring up at the pale white ceiling and tried to think of a dream for myself. Where would I go someday? What would ever make me that happy? Maybe people who are in limbo like me never have any dreams. We just float from one boring moment to another.

I must have dozed off for a while because when I opened my eyes, it looked like twilight. My bedroom door was open, but I heard no one. I listened hard, then I looked at my watch and saw it was already after five. They had to have left. Mother darling probably had stopped by to show me what she looked like and she found me asleep. I was sure she had dressed in that frilly short skirt and sequin-covered blouse that had a matching hat and boots. It was her favorite outfit, and I had to admit she looked like a star in those clothes.

There was a note on the refrigerator.

I left you some money on the kitchen table. Get yourself a pizza or something. I'll call later.

Kay

She couldn't even sign it "Mother." Was she really afraid someone would see this and know? I crumpled it up and threw it in the garbage. Then I scooped up the money and marched out of the apartment. When I walked out of the complex, I looked to the right and saw Kathy Ann peeking out between the curtains of her front window. Deliberately, I waved vigorously at her and the curtain closed instantly.

Laughing, I hurried down the street and took the bus downtown. All I could think of was Keefer. For now he was my dream and I was happy only when I was with him. The lights in the body shop window were like the lights of a lighthouse beaming protectively into the darkness of my world. The only safe harbor I had was within his embrace.

I entered the shop. Tools were out on the floor. The radio was blasting at its usual volume, but I didn't see him.

"Keefer?"

I looked at the small office, but it was dark. I walked around the cars that were there for repair and then I started toward the door to his apartment. Where else would he be? I thought, and realized he might have stepped out to buy some beer or something.

When I opened the door, I heard a groan. My first thought was that something terrible had happened to him. Either he had gotten hurt in the shop or his drunken father had come looking for him and beaten him up again.

Then I heard her laugh and saw her rise up on the sofa. She was half-naked, her breasts gleaming in the light from the small lamp. She saw me and cried out. A second later, Keefer appeared and they both looked at me. My surprise and shock had nailed my feet to the floor, even though all I could think of doing was turning and running.

"Why, look who's here, Keefer. Robin. You come to have Keefer fix somethin' for you, honey?" Charlotte Lily teased as she reached for her blouse and slipped it over her head.

Keefer pushed her off him, buckled his pants, and stood.

"No, looks like you're the one getting fixed tonight, Charlotte Lily," I said, the tears burning under my eyelids because I refused to let them emerge.

She laughed.

"I thought he wasn't worth the time of day," I said, my anger now replacing my shock. "Slummin' tonight?"

She laughed again, but with less confidence. Keefer glanced at her and then took a deep breath and started toward me.

"I'm sorry," he said.

"There's nothing to be sorry about, Keefer, unless she was a big disappointment. That's probably most likely," I added, threw her a cold smile, and then turned and left the apartment, closing the door hard behind me.

I heard her laugh again and then Keefer tell her to shut up.

When I was outside the shop and on the street, I permitted my tears to escape. I flicked them off my cheeks and walked quickly away.

I kept walking, at first in no particular direction, and then in the direction of the apartment. It was a long walk. Cars rushed by me, sometimes the drivers sounding their horns because I was too far in the street. Every once in a while, I felt like throwing myself in front of one, but the prospect of all that pain without being killed right off frightened me.

Somewhere in the city behind me, with all its lights blazing excitement, the music rolling out into the streets, people laughing and joking, enjoying their vacations or their evening with friends, somewhere out there, Mother darling was singing her heart out, reaching for her dream.

I was as far from her thoughts as I could be, so far, in fact, it was as if I had never been born.

Maybe I wasn't, I thought. Maybe this is all just a bad dream, and I'm still sleeping in that never-never land where souls exist until they are chosen to be born. I was like an orphan passed over time and time again. Not this one, she's not ready to be in the world, I heard the angels say.

"Just keep dreaming, honey. Just keep dreaming. We'll tell you when it's time to wake up."

Even promises in heaven are broken, I thought.

9

Always Us
Against Them

After marching along the highway for nearly half an hour, I felt a pair of headlights remain on me.

Here I go again, I thought. The police. Someone probably complained about a young girl walking on the highway. I heard the horn, and then I stepped aside and turned in anticipation.

It was Keefer in Izzy's truck.

"Get in, Robin," he said.

"No."

"Just get in. I need to talk to you. You've got a ways to go, and you're in the middle of all this traffic. Don't be stupid."

"Why should I change now?" I replied. "Seems all I do is stupid things."

"Stop it. Get in. I need to talk to you."

A car came up behind him, and the driver leaned hard and long on his horn.

I could see Keefer wasn't going to move and that might soon create even more trouble, so I got into the truck and he drove on.

"I'm sorry about what happened back there, but I never told you I was a saint, Robin. Did I?"

"No."

"And I never thought you were one, either," he said.

That made me laugh.

"There are a few people who would agree with that," I said.

"The truth is, I got drunk and she came in, teasing me like she always does. I feel bad about it because I know she did it because she was jealous and just wanted to hurt you, and I let her do it."

"You didn't even call to see what happened to me today," I fired back at him.

"I know. I was thinking of it, but I got drunk."

"Why did you get so drunk during the day?" I asked. From what I could see, Keefer was usually very reliable when he was working. He was good at what he did and he took pride in the results.

"Izzy gave me some bad news today. He's selling the shop. The new owner is going to take over in about a month, and I'm out. He said his wife was tired of them livin' here, and he was going to work with his brother in Florida."

"So? You were planning on leaving someday anyway, weren't you?"

"Yeah, but after I had some money saved. You don't just pick up and go without enough money. I might not get a job that quick, and you need to put down money for rent or a hotel, and you got to have travel money."

"What about your sister?"

"I can't ask her for anything. She's just getting by as it is. I can tell. Besides, I don't want to live off someone else. I want to be on my own."

"I don't have any money, or I'd give it to you," I said, and I meant it.

"Thanks. I believe that."

We were both quiet for a while, both staring ahead at the traffic.

"I'm really sorry about Charlotte Lily. We went together once. I always knew she was toying around with me. She can't be serious about anyone. Her family is well off and she lives in a nice house and all, but she's always unhappy and always out to make someone who is happy unhappy.

"Talk about being stupid, that's me. I let her manipulate me. She's like a devil or somethin', comin' in just when I'm feelin' sorry for myself," he said. "And then the luck of it all with you poppin' over just at that time. Damn."

"I guess I have no right to think I own you or anything, Keefer. We made no promises, and as to finding you with her, well, I'm not one to think she can judge someone else. However," I added after a short pause, "I will confess it hurt."

"I know. I'm sorry. Really," he said. "I ain't never gonna have anything to do with her again. She might have nice clothes and jewelry and all, but she's a tramp compared to you."

"I won't go that far," I said, and then shook my head, "but I'll let you."

He laughed.

"So, tell me what happened today. You're out on the street, so I guess they didn't sentence you to prison."

"I'm on two years' probation."

"Ah, that don't mean nothin'," he said. "Half the city is on probation. You hungry?"

"Starving," I said.

"Let me take you to a great place," he said, and whipped the truck down a street on the right. A few minutes later, we bounced over a gravel driveway to park at a restaurant with a pig lit up in pink lights. The place was called Porky's Hideaway. "Best ribs in town," he said.

The restaurant was one big room, with a band playing what I called hillbilly music, but which Keefer said was really more Cajun style. The food was out in a buffet, and for ten dollars you could eat all you wanted. Besides the ribs, there were Buffalo wings, chicken legs, fish sticks, potatoes, vegetables, all sorts of breads, and a variety of desserts. My stomach churned in anticipation.

We piled our plates high and found a table. The restaurant was nearly full and the good food, music, and party atmosphere drove away my doldrums.

"Before my mother got sick with depression, she used to tell me the only real cure to sadness is a good-tastin' dinner. That's why people serve so much food after a funeral," Keefer told me. The music was so loud we had to shout to hear each other even at the same table.

There must be some truth to that, I thought, because I ate way more than I usually did. Afterward, I sat back and watched some of the people dancing.

"Funny," Keefer said, "Nashville is a place full of music and good times, but I don't often see it. I guess you got to be happy with yourself first before you can go out and have a good time."

I felt sorry for him and wished there was something I could do. At least I had Mother darling. He had no one but himself, and that had to be pretty scary most of the time.

After we left and we were in the truck heading to Cory's apartment, Keefer asked me if I was really serious when I told him I wouldn't mind running off with him.

"Yes," I said.

"What about now? I mean, considerin' what you saw and all, are you still feelin' the same way about it?"

I thought a moment. I knew he was asking me to forgive him com-

pletely for being with Charlotte Lily. Neither of us is a saint, I concluded. If we can't forgive each other, no one will forgive us for anything we do.

"Yes," I told him, and he smiled.

"Great. I have a plan. My father threw me out of our house before I
could get to all my things. He never knew it, but I saved all the money
I received as birthday gifts from relatives and friends. I was a little
miser, in fact. I stuffed it all in this piggy bank my mother gave me
when I was about three, I think. It was a giveaway from some hog
farm she had been at one time or another. Anyway, I think I've got
over four hundred dollars in it, and I want it. It's mine. Only, I don't
think I can just walk up to the door and ring the bell."

"Why not? Your mother isn't mad at you, is she?"

"She's not going to go against him," he said. "Never did. Never
took my side, ever, or my sister's." He was quiet a moment. "My sister
was . . . I guess they call it abused nowadays. Softens it, I suppose, but
it ain't softened for her. I know she told Mama, but Mama thought she
made it up to get back at him. She just wouldn't believe it."

"Maybe she did, and that was what made her like she is, Keefer."

"Maybe. It's more reason for me to hate him. I just don't want to
see him."

He looked at his watch.

"There's a good chance he ain't home. I know how to get into my
house without going through the front door. I just want to get my
piggy bank and get out. Want to help?"

"What can I do?"

"You just stay in the truck and be the lookout," he said. "If a car
drives into the driveway, you sound the horn. Do it at least five, six
times, and I'll know to get out of there fast. No tellin' what would happen otherwise. He'd kill me or I'd somehow kill him. Okay?" he
asked.

"Okay," I said, but my heart was thumping like an old-fashioned
steam-engine train pounding the tracks.

"Good," he said. "It won't take long. Don't worry."

He turned the truck around and headed back toward the downtown
area, but before getting there, turned again and wove his way through
residential streets until we came to a house that looked hidden from
the road behind sprawling old oak trees and untrimmed bushes. With
the moonlight peeking through clouds, I could see the lawn was spotted with dry and bare patches. The house was completely dark.

"Usually there's a light on somewhere," he said after we pulled to
the curb. He sat there, looking worried.

"Can't you tell any other way if there's someone home or not?"

"He's not home. He doesn't park his truck in the garage. It's full of tools, his work bench, and a table saw. Okay," he said. "The window in my room has a broken lock. I'm going in that way. Get behind the wheel here and hit the horn if a truck pulls in."

"Be careful, Keefer."

How strange, I thought, to have to break into your own house.

He got out slowly, hesitating as if he expected his father to pop out from behind a tree or something, and then he hurried over the lawn and around the right corner of the house. A few minutes later, a light went on. I could see the glow of it on the bushes at the side of the house.

When a pair of headlights appeared ahead of me, I held my breath and placed my hand on the horn. It turned out to be a car, which passed by quickly. Once again, the street was dark. I looked toward the house. Why was he taking so long? Surely, he knew where his piggy bank was. Another set of headlights appeared, and again it was only a car going by. After it had, I looked toward the house and saw the light was out.

I spotted Keefer. This time he wasn't hurrying along. He was walking very slowly, his head up, his hands clutching something. I wished he would hurry. He came around the truck and I opened the door. He just stood there in the street looking in at me.

"What is it?" I asked.

He extended his hands. In them were the broken pieces of what I supposed was his piggy bank. I shook my head.

"I don't understand."

"He took my money. He took my savings, my birthday savings."

"Oh, no," I said.

Keefer spun on his heels and heaved the pieces at the driveway.

"That's not all," he said, moving to get in. I slid over on the bench seat.

"What else?"

"My mother wasn't there. I went looking for her to see if she was in bed, asleep."

"Maybe she was out with him."

"I doubt that." He started the engine. "The lamp beside her bed was on the floor. I put it upright, and then I turned it on, and there, on the floor in the bathroom, was . . ."

"What?" I asked, hardly able to breathe.

"Blood," he said. "Lots of blood."

"Blood?" I gasped.

He drove away. I felt like I had stopped breathing and I was leaving my body. That was how numb I had become.

We drove to the apartment complex, and Keefer came up with me.

"If something terrible happened, wouldn't someone tell you?" I asked him.

"It looked to me like whatever happened wasn't all that long ago," he said.

I stared at him. What could have happened? His eyes were filled with all the horrible possibilities, and my mind began to roam through Horror Hotel. Could his father have done something terrible to his mother and then taken her body off somewhere?

"Should we call the police?"

He thought for a moment. Then, he nodded and walked to the phone like someone who wanted desperately not to use it. I watched as he punched in 911 and then told the dispatcher his address and what he had found.

"I'm her son," he said.

"She's transferring me to someone who might know something."

I nodded and waited, embracing myself. Before I could say anything, he raised his hand.

"Yes," he said. "Yes, I'm her son. I was just at the house and . . ." He listened and as he did, his face lost color. "Okay," he said. "Thanks."

He hung up and stared at the phone a moment. Then he sucked in his breath and turned to me.

"She tried to commit suicide. She's in the hospital," he said.

"Oh, Keefer, I'm sorry."

"I'm gonna go."

"Should I go with you?"

He thought a moment, and then he nodded.

"Sure, that'd be great."

Mother darling wanted me home, of course. She might have already checked to see if I had listened to her, but that didn't matter to me now. None of that mattered to me, and maybe, it never had.

Besides, I thought as we charged down the stairs and to the truck, I'm sure Kathy Ann is watching and could tell Mother darling everything anyway.

After we parked at the hospital, we went to an information desk and found out where Keefer's mother was located. It turned out she was still in what they called an intensive care unit. Only the immediate family could go in, and only for a little while. I waited outside. I was very nervous because we didn't know if his father was in there already, and what sort of a scene he would make as soon as he set eyes on Keefer.

Fortunately, he wasn't. Keefer came out after ten minutes.

"She's still alive," he said, "but she's lost so much blood, she's in a coma. All the nurse would say is, 'We'll see.' "

He sat, and I held his hand.

"She looked so small in there. It was like she had shrunk or somethin' from losin' all that blood. I tried talkin' to her, but her eyelids didn't even twitch. It was like talkin' to a corpse."

"Oh, don't say that, Keefer. She can get better."

He nodded and looked around.

"I wonder where the hell he is. It doesn't surprise me that he's not here." .

"What do you want to do?"

"In an hour I can go back in again. You mind waitin'?"

"No, of course not," I said.

He leaned back against the sofa.

"You want a soda or somethin'?"

"No, I'm fine," I said. He nodded and closed his eyes.

I couldn't help wondering how I would feel if that was Mother darling in there instead of Keefer's mother. Would I be worrying about her or about myself? She was all I had now, all the family in the world to me. Most of my life, she did her best to pretend I wasn't there. Sometimes I thought that was what bothered her the most when Grandpa complained about me: he reminded her I was her daughter and her responsibility.

I supposed I had never made things easier for her. Not only didn't I think I should, but I resented her placing herself at the top of the list of who was important and what was important. Her career was the end-all. If it meant sacrificing my advantages, my time, my opportunities, that was all right. The excuse was always that she was doing it for both of us. All I could think was, if she ever did make it in the music business, I would fall even further down the list until I did what she wanted: disappeared.

And yet, imagining her in there like Keefer's mother with Death standing at the foot of her bed looking covetously at her thin grip on life, I couldn't help feeling sorry for her and sad. The few good times we had together returned to memory. I recalled once when she had sung successfully at a county fair and she had me dressed in a cowgirl outfit. She brought me on the stage with her and I sang a chorus. Everyone thought it was cute and she hugged me. Afterward, we had a good time on the rides. We ate cotton candy and had hot dogs and she won a stuffed puppy on the wheel of fortune game.

I left that back at the farm.

It was part of a dream now, something unreal.

"You got a helluva nerve bein' here," I heard, and opened my eyes to see a stocky, six-foot-three-inch man with the shoulders and arms of a logger standing before us. His black hair looked like it was in revolt, the untrimmed strands going every which way, some stuck on his sweaty forehead and looking like streaks of ink. He had big facial features, but I could see Keefer's jaw and eyes.

He wore a faded plaid shirt, the sleeves rolled over his thick forearms, back to his elbows, and a pair of greasy, stained jeans and black shoe boots.

"You're the reason she's in there," he said, pointing his thick forefinger down at Keefer. The rest of his hand was clutched in a fist, making it look like a pistol.

I looked at Keefer. He didn't move, but he didn't flinch or look frightened either.

"Me?" he said. "You got that backwards. You're the reason she's in there. What happened? What did you do to her to make her do this?" he fired up at him.

His father's face ripened like an apple in an instant.

"You ungrateful little bastard," he said, and reached down to seize Keefer, who pushed his hand away and shifted to his right.

I couldn't help it. I screamed. It seemed to snap his father out of his monomaniacal drive. He turned and looked at me.

"Who's this little tramp?" he asked.

"Shut your mouth," Keefer said. He moved farther to the right and stood up.

Now they were facing each other, and the one-sidedness of the pending battle was clearly evident. It looked like David against Goliath.

"Keefer, no!" I cried. "Don't get into any fights here!"

"You'd better listen to her and get out. Crawl back to whatever hole you're livin' in."

"I'm not the one who should be crawlin'," Keefer said. "You stole my money. You went and broke my piggy bank and took my money."

His father smiled coldly.

"Ain't nothin' in that house belongs to you, boy. You were livin' under my roof, and you owed me for all the things that got broke throwin' you out."

"You're just a common thief and a pervert," Keefer accused.

The rage rose like steam in his father's face, but before he could act, a nurse emerged from the intensive care unit and asked for Mr. Dawson.

They both turned to her.

"Yeah, that's me," Keefer's father said.

"I'm sorry," she said. "Your wife's heart just gave out. The doctor did everything he could."

The words hung in the air a moment, and then Keefer made a terrifying animal scream and charged at his father like a football tackler, hitting him in the right side with his shoulder and driving him back and onto his rear end. The nurse gasped and I screamed. Keefer looked at me and then charged down the hallway.

"Little bastard," his father said, getting to his feet.

"You can come in now," the nurse told him, her eyes still wide and her face still a bit white.

He looked in Keefer's direction, nodded, and followed her into the intensive care unit.

I went hurrying after Keefer. At first I didn't see him. He wasn't by the truck. Then I spotted him at the end of the parking lot, walking in a small circle and raving, his arms flying up. Slowly I approached.

"I'm sorry, Keefer," I said. He continued to circle and then stopped and looked at me.

"He killed her, you know. He should be arrested and tried for murder. He as good as did it himself."

"I know," I said.

"Someday . . ." His threat trailed off into the night.

I went to him and embraced him. I could feel his rage cooling down, and finally he held me and started to sob. He realized it and pulled back.

"I gotta get outta here," he said, marching toward the truck.

I ran after him.

"What are you going to do?"

"Just go back to my hole and maybe drink myself to sleep," he said. "C'mon. I'll take you home first."

I thought a moment.

"No," I said.

"What?"

"I want to be with you."

He stared for a moment.

"Are you sure?"

"Positive," I said, and I got into the truck before he did.

10

From the Frying Pan into the Fire

Most of the night, I was just a good listener. Keefer sat drinking hard liquor instead of beer. Izzy kept a bottle of bourbon in his office, and Keefer brought it back to his one-room apartment. I sat on the sofa bed, and he sat on the floor and talked about his early life, the happier days when he was too young to realize how bad things were for both his mother and his older sister.

"It wasn't until I was about nine," he continued, lying back on the floor and looking up at the cracked and pealed ceiling, "that I understood how horrible it was for Sally Jean. I came into her bedroom one night because I heard her sobbin'. My mother drank with my father often those days, and they were both sunk in a stupor. Only before he had collapsed, he had gone into Sally Jean's bedroom to tell her one of his bedtime stories. That's what she said he pretended to be doin'."

Keefer formed a wry smile.

"It began with that 'Three Little Pigs,' " he said. "You know, where he would run his fingers up her side to tickle her."

"Oh, Keefer," I said. It not only frightened me to hear such a sick story, it made me nauseated.

"He was still tellin' her the same story, only the pigs . . ."

"Keefer, stop!" I pleaded.

He looked at me.

"Yeah, it's better not to hear about it. No one wants to hear about it. I bet my mother put her fingers in her ears half the time. Well, she don't hafta do that anymore, huh? She's better off."

"No one's better off dead, Keefer."

"Right," he said, and took another long drink of the bourbon.

"Why don't you lie down here for a while," I suggested. "Get some sleep."

"Sleep," he said, as if it was an impossibility.

"C'mon," I said. "I'll hold you."

He looked up at me and then he rose slowly, put the bottle on the floor on his side of the sofa bed, pulled off his shirt, dropped his pants, and crawled under the blanket. I stroked his hair, kissed his cheek, and got undressed to lie beside him.

We kissed. I could feel his tears, the ones he couldn't stop, and I kissed them off his cheeks. We held on to each other and our passions grew. He made love to me with a desperation I welcomed. I never felt more giving, even when I sensed anger had slid alongside affection and actually had taken command. He was rough with me, and at times I tightened my arms around him to calm him down as much as to keep myself from screaming. He realized it and became more loving, whispering how sorry he was and how much he cared for me as he kissed and stroked my hair, all the while still inside me.

We made love longer than we ever had, and when he reached his climax, he cried out like someone falling. I brought my mouth to his and we kissed so hard, it was nearly impossible to breathe. When it was over, we rolled on our backs, gasped, and waited to speak.

"Are you all right?" he asked me.

"Yes," I said.

"Thanks for bein' with me," he said, and closed his eyes. I tried to stay awake a little longer, but the day's events took on their full weight and soon, I was just as deeply asleep as he was.

A very loud rapping on the rear door woke me first. Keefer groaned, but did not awaken. I had to shake him.

"Someone's at the door," I whispered.

He opened his eyes, but he was totally disoriented and confused.

"Whaaa."

"Keefer, you better wake up," I urged, looking for my blouse and jeans.

"Open up!" we heard. "It's the police!"

"Oh, no," I cried. The door was rattled hard, and I had just managed to slip my jeans on when it was thrown open, the lock giving way.

Because we had no lights on and the night was overcast, the policeman turned on a large flashlight and searched the room, washing the illumination over Keefer, who was sitting up and rubbing his face with his palms, and over me, who was standing at the side of the bed, barefoot, buttoning up my blouse.

"Put on a light," the policeman commanded.

"What is this?" Keefer asked.

"Put on the light!" the cop repeated in a louder, more demanding tone.

Keefer fumbled for the switch on the lamp and got it on.

Two policemen stood in the doorway, looking in at us.

"You," he said, pointing the flashlight at me even though there was enough light to see everything now. "You're Robin Taylor?"

"Yes."

"Your mother called 911 and reported you missing." He turned the flashlight toward Keefer. "You know how old this girl is?"

"It's not his fault!" I cried. "His mother died tonight. I stayed with him to comfort him."

"Comfort him?" the second policeman said, smiling. "That's a good way to put it. Get your things together and come along," he added.

"I'll go home myself," I said.

"Hey," the first patrolman said, stepping closer. "Don't you think we have better things to do than babysit some juvenile delinquent? I should take this guy down to the station and have him booked for corrupting the morals of a minor."

"You'd better go with them," Keefer urged.

"She didn't have to do this."

"No, she didn't. If you would behave, she wouldn't have to call us, now would she?" the second policeman asked.

I slipped on my shoes.

"I'll call you," I promised Keefer.

"If I were you, cowboy, I would tell her to stay away. This girl's mother might still press charges against you," the first patrolman told Keefer. "If she does, we'll be back. You can bet on that," he said.

Keefer looked at me and then urged me to go.

They put me in the rear of the patrol car, and I felt helplessly trapped again. Once we were on our way, the two policemen seemed to forget I was in the car, too. They got into a discussion about baseball and began to argue about the ability of a player. I didn't have to wonder how Mother darling had discovered my whereabouts. I was positive she had gone to Kathy Ann, who surely told her everything she knew.

That was confirmed for me when we drove into the parking lot and, despite the lateness of the hour, I saw her peering between the curtains. I knew she couldn't see my face, but I looked her way with contempt. I couldn't wait to tell her off.

Mother darling was in her bathrobe, waiting, when the police brought me up to the apartment. Cory was in bed.

"She was where you thought," the first patrolman told her. "Do you want to do anything more about that?"

I looked at her, terrified.

"No," she said. "Thanks so much."

"All right. You'd better behave yourself, young lady. You're on thin ice," he warned, and left.

"You're just determined to sink my ship, ain't you, Robin? You're just not goin' to be happy until we're both in so desperate a place, we got to call my father for help, huh?"

"No," I said. "You don't understand what happened."

"No, I don't understand. I guess I never will. Just go in and go to sleep. I'm exhausted, and so is Cory. We've been hired to play at a much more respected place. It's taken a big effort and a lot of concentration, but that's what responsible people do. They try their best. I'm warnin' you for the last time, Robin Lyn, you're not goin' to ruin my chances. Now go to bed."

"Don't you even want to hear anything?"

"No," she snapped. "But I will tell you this. The next time you disobey me, I'll call the police and I won't come to the courthouse with you."

She went into their bedroom and closed the door.

I was too tired to cry or to care. I went to bed and slept longer than they did. When I opened my eyes, I could hear them having their breakfast. The radio was on. I lay there, hoping they would get up and go out before I rose. Finally, she opened my door and stepped into the room. She was dressed.

"Well," she began, "I suppose you're proud of yourself."

"Are you going to listen to me?" I asked.

"You can't tell me anything that will justify your behavior since we arrived here, Robin. I told you when we left that I was goin' to need you to be a responsible person because I would be too busy to watch after you as if you was a child. I thought I was doin' you a favor takin' you away with me. I thought you'd want to be part of my life, not a burden."

"I'm not trying to be a burden, but I have this friend, Keefer Dawson, and . . ."

"I know all about him," she said.

"You don't know anything about him, Momma."

"Oh, I'm Momma now, not Mother darlin'?" she said, smiling.

"Will you just listen. He's a very nice person. It's not what you think or whatever that jealous Kathy Ann told you."

She sighed and looked at the ceiling.

"Okay, you listen," she said. "Cory went back to his friend at the supermarket, and he had a nice talk with him about you. His friend is willing to give you a chance, despite what you've done. This would help you a lot, too, Robin. The court will be pleased you're doin' somethin' worthwhile and respectable. You'll be able to have some expense money and you won't be idle and gettin' yourself in trouble.

"You go back there today and ask to see Mr. Ritter. We said you'd be there before two and you could start today. You better not screw this up, Robin. This is absolutely the last time anyone's gonna do somethin' to help you.

"We're goin' off to Del's garage to work on our music for tonight. I want you to come right home after work. If I hear you went back to that boy, I'll do what the policeman told me to do. I'll have him arrested. You understand me? Well? Don't just lay there glarin' up at me, Robin. Do you understand?"

"Yes," I said coldly. "I understand you real well, Mother darling."

She flared her eyes, spun on her heels, and walked out, closing the door sharply behind her. I remained in bed until I heard them leave the apartment. I was certainly in no mood to see Cory and hear his sarcasm.

As soon as I could, I called Keefer.

"I've been afraid to call you," he said. "What happened?"

I told him everything.

"We'd better be careful."

"Did you call your sister and tell her about your mother?" I asked.

"Yeah, but she doesn't want to come back for the funeral. She doesn't want to see him under any circumstances, and she can't do our mother any good anyway, she says. I guess I can't blame her. I told her I'd see her someday, and I will."

"You're not going to just pick up and go without telling me, are you, Keefer?"

He was silent.

"Keefer?"

"No. I have some things to plan out yet," he said.

"I'm going to see you no matter what my mother threatens. She won't do anything anyway, because that would expose her even more and she's too nervous about spoiling her chances to be a big country singing star."

"Well, be careful," he said.

I told him what they had arranged at the supermarket.

"Where's that market?" he asked. After I told him, he was silent again and then he said, "That might be good."

"Why?"

"I'll tell you later when I see you," he promised.

"When is your mother's funeral?"

"It looks like it's tomorrow. He's just tryin' to get it all over with fast as he can so he can get back to his miserable ways. I wouldn't a known anything if I didn't call my cousin Charlie. He's the only one on my father's side has anything at all to do with him and only because he's almost as much of a drunk."

"I'd like to be there with you," I said.

"I know, but maybe it's better you stay away for a few days. I'll find a way to get in touch. Sorry about all the new trouble I got you in," he added.

"You didn't get me into any trouble, Keefer. I get myself in trouble. That should be my middle name. My grandpa used to say he knew exactly who my father was. 'He's Old Scratch.' "

"Who's that?"

"The devil," I said, and laughed. "Maybe he was right."

"Well, if all his daughters are as pretty and as nice as you are, he's not so bad after all," Keefer said, and we both laughed. "Be seein' you," he said. His voice, small and hopeful, lingered in my ear after we hung up.

I didn't have much of an appetite, but I made some fresh coffee and then had some toast and jam. I really didn't want to go to work in a supermarket, but I had to agree that Mother darling was right about my earning some expense money, although I wasn't thinking of having it for incidentals and recreational expenses. I was thinking I would work awhile and save up enough to go off with Keefer some day, just as he dreamed. The idea became more and more exciting and possible. I couldn't wait until we were together again and we could make some real plans. I would convince him to find some other work here in the meantime. With the two of us earning, we could have enough to travel and find a new and happier life someplace. Why not? Mother darling would probably be grateful. She probably wouldn't even report my leaving to the police. As long as I wasn't around and couldn't hurt her reputation and spoil her chances, why would she care?

With new motivation and energy, I dressed and started out to make the best impression I could on Mr. Ritter at the supermarket. Before I left the complex, I stopped at Kathy Ann's apartment. For once, she wasn't planted in the window, watching for me or anyone else to fill her boring life with new gossip. But I was still fuming.

She opened the door, surprised and then immediately frightened by the look on my face.

"I'm not supposed to hang out with you, remember?" she said, and started to close the door. I put my foot in the way to stop it.

"I know you told where I would be last night. I know it was because of you that the police arrived."

"I couldn't help it," she wailed. "Your sister came down here and begged my mother to let her speak to me. It was so late and my mother was very upset. My father was still asleep, thank goodness, or it would have been worse."

"Why did you do it?"

"My mother called me out and she said if you know something to help this woman, you had better talk now, Kathy Ann, or I'll see to it you're punished for the rest of the summer."

"You were just jealous," I accused, my eyes fixed on her so firmly, she couldn't look at me. "Charlotte Lily said you had a crush on Keefer and you were just a bitch, weren't you?"

"No."

"You know what I'm going to do? I'm going to tell Charlotte Lily what you did so she can tell every person who knows you what a creep you are to betray someone. No one will ever trust you again," I vowed.

Her eyes filled with tears, and she shook her head.

"I couldn't help it."

"Me neither. I can't help it, either," I said. "Go have something else to eat. Maybe they'll take you in the circus some day," I spit at her and walked away.

She closed the door behind me. I was sure she would be trembling all day and what she would try to do now was call everyone she knew and explain what happened. That, I thought, would create more problems for her, because I really didn't intend to bother talking to Charlotte Lily. I couldn't care less if she had any friends or not, but once she started to talk about it, they would wonder why she was being so defensive and that would be just as effective.

I left for the supermarket and arrived there about twenty minutes later. Mr. Ritter made me wait for nearly as long and then finally called me into his office.

"Well," he said, "I try not to hire anyone with a history that would make me think twice about having them around money in my store, but I'm going to make an exception with you. You have a good friend in Cory Lewis," he added. "I hope you appreciate that."

It took all my effort to smile and swallow down the words I wanted to say, but I did and nodded.

"Even so, I want you to understand you're on probation here, a test of sorts. I don't expect you to ever, ever be late for work, understand? The floor manager, Tammy Carol Allen, will show you around, describe your exact duties, and tell you when you take a break and what's expected of you. Don't come here wearing makeup like a clown or wearing anything that might be inappropriate. You don't smoke in the store, and I don't want to see you chewing and cracking gum in your mouth, hear?"

"Yes, sir," I said.

"Always be clean-looking and neat. People expect to see the employees looking that way. We're handling food here. Never sass a customer, no matter what. You're always polite and helpful. We pride ourselves on service. Always be sure to ask if the customer wants assistance with his or her packages, hear?"

"Yes, sir."

"Okay, I have your information on the application you filled out. You go see Tammy Carol and she'll give you your assignment. Mind," he said when I stood up and turned to go, "you break any of my rules, there's no second chance. You're out. Hear?"

I wanted to say I hear fine, but I just gave him a plastic smile and nodded.

He kept his stern face, and I left.

Tammy Carol was a woman in her late twenties who looked ten to fifteen years older. She was the sort of person who enjoyed even an iota of authority. She let me know that on the floor, she was God, Jesus, and the Holy Ghost. She made me stand and observe other grocery packers for nearly half an hour before giving me a shopping center apron and assigning me to a cashier.

"You be sure to ask paper or plastic before you start," she emphasized. "And you smile until your face hurts."

I was tempted to say, "I guess yours never does, then," but I nodded again and put on the apron.

All the while I kept one thought at the top of my mind: You're doing this to be free. As soon as you can, you will be gone and this won't even be a memory.

I wished I could treat the rest of my past life the same way and yet still have a future. Those who saw no tomorrow for themselves, I realized, would be forever stuck in their yesterdays.

That wasn't going to happen to me.

11

The Best-Laid Plans

Whenever there was a lull in the supermarket, Tammy Carol was right behind me, assigning me to other duties, which included washing down the freezer areas, mopping floors, and stacking canned goods. Everything I was told to do, I was told as though it was as important as doing brain surgery. The cans had to be turned just so. The mop had to be moved from right to left in perfect squares. When I wiped down the glass cases, I had to use a circular motion, not making my circles too large or too small. I could feel her breathing over my shoulder, making sure I did it as she instructed, and from time to time, Mr. Ritter appeared to scrutinize my work.

It was constantly on the tip of my tongue to tell them where they could put this job, but I swallowed back the urge to scream and kept my plastic smile until it did exactly what Tammy Carol predicted it might: hurt.

Finally, it was quitting time. Mr. Ritter was there at the front door to watch me leave.

"You've passed muster this first day," he said. "If you behave yourself accordingly, we'll get along fine and you will work here for the remainder of the summer. If you're really good, I might consider you for weekend work once you return to school," he added as another incentive. He spoke down to me as if he was on a high throne and I was kneeling at his feet.

"Thank you," I said.

I didn't realize how tired I was until I was outside, walking to the bus stop. And then, as if my body wanted to take revenge on me for what I had put it through all day, I felt cramps beginning and realized I had forgotten the time of the month and I hadn't brought any protection along with me, not even thinking about it when I passed the sanitary napkins and tampons on the store shelves earlier. I was in a small panic that grew more and more intense as the bus made stop after stop on its way to my station. By the time I arrived, I felt the beginning of staining and hurried out, practically running down the aisle.

I was surprised that Mother darling and Cory were home. I didn't know that they weren't starting this gig at their new and better place until later in the evening. They were now the principal act, and that meant they wouldn't begin until about ten. When I came charging through the door, they both looked up in surprise.

"Well, at least she knows what come right home after work means now," Cory quipped.

"How did you do?" Mother darling asked.

"I gotta go to the bathroom," I said, and hurried on. When I got in there, I saw my tampons were gone, removed from the area under the sink where I had placed them. I opened the door and screamed, "Mother, where are my tampons?"

"You don't keep things like that in the bathroom," Cory replied for her. "I don't like looking at them."

"They were under the sink."

"Next to my stuff," he shouted back.

"Where are they?"

"They're in your room," Mother darling said. "Calm down, Robin."

She brought them to me. I took them from her and slammed the door. I could hear Cory's laughter.

"He's a sick person," I yelled.

"Yeah, right. I'm not the one stealin' and sleepin' around. I wouldn't be so quick to call anyone else a sick person. Besides," he said when I came out of the bathroom, "we just wanted to be sure you weren't pregnant, right, Kay?" He grinned at me.

I looked at Mother darling.

"That's all I'd need now," she said.

He kept grinning at me.

"Maybe you're not sick," I said. "Maybe you're just ignorant."

Before he could reply, I went into the bedroom and closed the door. I hate it here, I told myself. I hate it!

"That's a fine way for her to behave after I go and beg Al to give her this job. And you're eatin' and sleepin' in my home!" he shouted.

"Not for long," I said in a loud whisper. "Not for long."

After they had left, I called Keefer, but no one answered at the shop. There was an answering machine, so I left my name and told him I would be home. I didn't think he was going to call. It was nearly midnight and he hadn't. I fell asleep curled up on the sofa watching television on that small set of Cory's. Every once in a while, something would interfere with the reception. It sounded like someone on a two-way radio. Finally, the phone rang and I jumped up.

"Can you talk?" he began.

"Yes. They're at work," I said.

"I was with my cousin Charlie. He called to tell me my father had gotten dead drunk and he dropped him off at the house. I told him I wished he had dropped him off a bridge, and then he decided to come downtown and meet me at the Giddup Saloon. We sat and talked for hours about my mother. He's ten years older than me and remembers her as a young woman. He said she was quite a dancer. Imagine that," Keefer said. "I don't think I ever saw her dance."

"Are you all right?"

"Me? Yeah. So, how was your first day on the job?"

"Hard," I said. "They had me do everything but sweep the sidewalk outside, but I think that's coming."

"Don't you work with a cashier?" he asked quickly.

"Oh, yes, most of the time. But if it gets slow and they have enough packers, they put me on stacking goods or cleaning."

"When the cashiers are through with their shifts, they have to prove—check out—their registers, right?"

"Yes, why?"

"I have an idea. I'll talk about it when we see each other again, if we ever do," he added.

"Don't be stupid. I'm saving almost everything I make so we'll have money to get out of here together."

"You are? That's great," he said. "What time do you work tomorrow?"

"Tomorrow I'm twelve to eight."

"Okay. I'll stop by about eight."

"Let's meet outside," I said. "The manager is Cory's friend, and he might tell him he saw you."

"I'll be in a blue Chevy with a bashed-in right front."

"Keefer, how do you know these cars are safe to drive?" I asked, laughing.

"They're safe. Don't worry. The funeral's tomorrow morning," he added. "That's why he got dead drunk tonight."

"Oh. I could be there maybe."

"No. It's not going to be long."

"Don't get into any fights with him, Keefer."

"I won't. Charlie will keep him away from me. It'll be all right."

"I'm anxious to see you," I said.

"Same here. I'd better get some sleep. You too. Take care, Robin," he said.

I wanted to say more, but he hung up. I really was so tired and achy with cramps that I looked forward to falling asleep. It didn't take long. I was in such a deep sleep that I didn't hear Mother darling and Cory come home from their show. It surprised me to wake up with sunshine spilling over my face. At first I thought they had not yet returned. I imagined they had gone partying to celebrate their continued success, but when I stepped out of the room, I saw Mother darling's outfit on the sofa, her boots on the floor. I had slept until almost nine-thirty myself and I didn't hear a peep coming from their bedroom.

Taking care to make as little noise as possible, I made some coffee and had a small bowl of cereal. Afterward, I took a quick shower, dried myself and then went to change my tampon. I was so lost in thought about Keefer and his mother's funeral, I didn't at first realize the bathroom door had been opened. I looked up and saw Cory standing there, gaping at me, and I screamed, this time so shrilly and loud, he actually winced and jumped back, closing the door quickly.

I dressed as fast as I could, the rage keeping me hot and frantic. Cory had retreated to his and Mother darling's bedroom, but that didn't matter to me now. As soon as I was dressed, I opened their door and shouted, "That was disgusting. You knew I was in there."

Mother darling was still in bed, her eyes closed. She turned and her eyelids fluttered open. Cory was standing at his closet. He was in his underwear and choosing a pair of jeans to wear.

"Whaaa? What is it?" Mother darling asked.

"He did it again. He just burst in on me and after he saw I was in there, he didn't close the door. He just stood there gaping at me," I accused.

Cory smirked.

"That's a lot of crap. You didn't give me a chance to close the door. You just went hysterical."

"Did you enjoy the view? Are you interested in women's hygiene that much?"

Cory looked at Mother darling.

"Can you do something about her?"

"Robin," she began, sitting up and letting the blanket fall to her waist. Her nudity never shocked me, but her nudity with a man in the room did. I turned away. "I'm sure it was just an accident," she began.

"Right," I said. "An accident. That's exactly what he is, an accident. I bet his mother collected on collision insurance or something when he was born."

"Very funny."

"Robin."

"Forget it," I said. "I'm going to work."

I slammed their door and rushed out of the apartment, my steps pounding the stairway and clicking over the walk. There wasn't a bus for quite a while. I grew impatient and walked toward the next station. With the way my nerve endings were twanging and my stomach was churning, I couldn't just sit and wait with the other people. It was a mistake because the bus arrived only five minutes later and passed me up on my way to the next stop. I ran, but I didn't get there in time. Tired and disgusted, I flopped on the bench and waited again. This bus seemed to make more stops. By the time I arrived at the supermarket, I was just a minute or so late. Mr. Ritter jumped out at me the moment I entered.

He didn't speak. He pointed to his watch.

"I missed the bus," I began. "And the next one wasn't as fast and . . ."

"You have to anticipate such things, young lady. The trick is to start earlier, understand?"

"Yes, sir."

"My policy is if you're a minute late, you are still docked for an hour. My advice to you is be here early tomorrow to be sure you're not late. If you were a minute or so more, I'd fire you, so count your blessings."

I mouthed a thank you and went in to get my apron. Everything made my cramps more intense this particular morning. People thought I was smiling, when I was really grimacing in agony. My bad luck continued. It turned out to be one of the busiest days of the week. I never stopped until my break for lunch.

Instead of joining the other employees, I went outside and found a bench upon which to sit and eat one of the ready-made sandwiches the store sold. It was to be subtracted from my salary, of course. I ended up feeding most of it to the birds.

When a lull came in the afternoon, Tammy Carol had me working at the frozen food freezer. She wanted everything taken out and re-arranged neatly. It was hard because it was so cold my fingers became numb. If I paused too long, either she or Mr. Ritter was there to tell me I couldn't leave the items out of the freezer too long. Get with it.

My last shift as a packer was the hardest. I was so tired and cranky, I dropped a bottle of cranberry juice, which shattered at my feet.

"That will come out of your salary," Mr. Ritter told me instantly. "I want this cleaned up immediately. First, get our customer another bottle so she is not delayed another unnecessary second. Go!" he shouted.

I hurried, clinging to this bottle for dear life, and returned. Then I started to clean up the mess. I cut my finger on a piece of glass, which enraged him even more.

"Dropping blood everywhere now. Go in the back and use the first-aid kit. I should have my head examined. Cory owes me big time," he eagerly announced.

Finally, eight o'clock came and I punched out.

"Remember," Mr. Ritter said as I was leaving, "get here early tomorrow."

I nodded and left. I was in such a daze that for a moment, I had forgotten Keefer was going to be there. He actually had to sound his horn. I turned and saw him waving from the battered vehicle. Never so glad to see him, I ran to the car and he got out to embrace me.

"Hey," he said. "You look worse than me."

"I had a terrible day," I said, and rattled every moment off in minutes. Then I remembered what his day had to be like and asked him how it went.

"It was hard. My father was in a stupor, which was good. He actually looked like he didn't know who I was. Charlie was great. I stayed after everyone left and had my last conversation with her," he added, his eyes getting glassy. He took a deep breath.

I kissed his cheek and squeezed his arm gently. He shook his head.

"I can't stay here," he said. "I thought I could work it through, get another job for a while, but I just want to get away."

"Me, too," I said. "I'm miserable back at that apartment, and they really don't want me around." I told him what a creep Cory Lewis was and how I was devastated by my mother always taking his side no matter what.

"She's dependent on him now." He looked back at the supermarket. "You have an idea about how much money the cashier checks out when the shift is changed?"

"I don't know. I think about twenty-five hundred or so. Why?"

"I'd like to borrow it," he said.

"What?"

"It's an easy robbery. I thought about it even before you began to work for a supermarket."

"Really?" My heart began to thump.

He shrugged, and then he reached under the seat and brought out a pistol. I thought all the breath left my body. It was one thing to shoplift—some of my friends back in Ohio actually thought it was a game—but a gun!

"Where did you get that?"

"It's Izzy's, but he doesn't even remember he has it half the time. Don't worry. There are no bullets in it, but no one would know, of course. What I want to do is walk in just as the cashier finishes checking her receipts and do it and walk out. We'll leave right from there."

"But I can make enough money in a month or so and—"

"I don't want to wait," he said sharply.

"But didn't you say Izzy wasn't selling for a month and—"

"You don't have to be part of it if you don't want to, Robin. I'll understand. Just pretend you don't know who I am."

I stared at him for a moment, and then I looked at the gun and sat back. He waited as I thought.

Could I do this? Should I? What would life be like here after Keefer left? How long could I stand it, anyway? What was I leaving? Mother darling had a new family: her band and all the people who would be involved in her career. I would always be on the outside or sitting in some dark corner waiting for her to remember me, and when she did, it wouldn't be a memory of joy; it would be a memory of obligation. All I did was remind her of one of her big mistakes in life.

I nodded slowly and then turned to him.

"Okay, Keefer. Let's do it. Let's get as far away from here and everything that is here as we can."

He smiled.

"Okay, here's my plan. Don't cause any undo suspicion by packin' a bag or somethin'. Choose whatever is so important to you that you can't leave it behind and let's get it out tonight so you leave for work lookin' just like you did this morning. We'll have enough money to buy you whatever you need along the way."

"There's nothing I want," I told him, "nothing to get tonight."

"Same here," he said, nodding in understanding. Then he got excited again. "We've got this SUV that was in a multiple-car accident two days ago. The back end is smashed in so that the door can't be opened, but the taillights still work and there's nothin' wrong with the engine. It's perfect. The owner left for a meeting and a few days' vacation in Florida. We'll use it and dump it somewhere. I know exactly how to do all this, so don't worry," he assured me.

"But you've never robbed anyone, Keefer, have you? How do you know what to do?"

"It's not that hard, and it will only take a few minutes at the most. In and out, and then we're gone," he added, "gone for good. Believe me, it's easy."

"I believe you, but I don't think I'll sleep tonight just thinking about it," I said.

"Yeah. I know what you mean. I wish we could be together, but that would set off all sorts of alarms and make tomorrow impossible. I won't even take you all the way back now. I'll let you out about a block or so from the complex. Do exactly what they want you to do so you don't cause any suspicions or concern, okay?"

I nodded.

He kissed me and then we both looked at the supermarket a moment. Suddenly, the place I hated more than anywhere was the source of new hope.

"I guess you'll feel a little funny takin' their money, huh?" Keefer asked.

I laughed.

"Are you kidding? There's no one I'd rather rob from than that manager. I can't wait to see the look on his face."

Keefer smiled, started the engine, and drove off. We were both pensive until he reached the block where he thought I should get out and walk the rest of the way.

"All we need is Kathy Ann to see us together and blab," he said.

"She'll have plenty to blab about when it's over."

We looked at each other silently.

"If you change your mind for any reason . . ." he began.

"I won't. Don't worry about it." I leaned over to kiss him, and then I got out of the vehicle. He remained there looking after me as I walked away.

My heart wasn't pounding anymore, but it was acting strangely—ticking like a time bomb. My whole body felt strange, in fact. I thought I had lost all my weight and would soon start to rise off the sidewalk and float with the wind like some balloon that was released.

Off I would go into the distance, growing smaller and smaller until I became a thin memory, easily forgotten.

By now I was sure Grandpa had forgotten me. Good riddance to that child of sin, he probably thought, and went about his work with a sense of relief. He no longer had to worry about the devil moving in and out of his home, threatening his precious pure soul.

And Mother darling . . . she would surely turn my running away into a song.

Off she went into the night, thinking there was nowhere she
*   belonged,*
My accidental daughter who came and went like a dream to be
*   remembered only when dark clouds warned us of another*
*   storm.*
My accidental daughter.

That's not bad, I thought as I strolled slowly back to the apartment.

Maybe I'll just write it down and leave it for her so she would have something from me she could use.

It was already something of far more value than anything I would take from her.

12

Strike Three

As I had predicted, I couldn't sleep. First, I tried tiring myself further by watching television until nearly one in the morning. My eyes did close and open, close and open. I thought I had dulled my teeming brain enough and finally rose, turned off the set, and went to bed. For a few minutes, I actually did sleep, but then I woke with a twitch that nearly sent me flying off the bed. My eyes snapped open, and all the thoughts, plans, and words Keefer and I had exchanged came flooding back. My heart started to pound.

Hours later, I heard Mother darling and Cory return. They were both obviously drunk. They didn't seem to care how loudly they talked. I heard their great excitement. Mother darling's songs and the band had gone over exceedingly well, I gathered. I heard her keep saying, "Ten weeks! We have a guaranteed ten weeks there!"

"Next stop, the Grand Ole Opry," Cory cried, and they clinked bottles of beer. Then they broke out in one of Mother darling's songs:

"My heart is a prison and you've got the key,
But darlin' there's no prisoner I'd rather be."

I couldn't help lying there and envying Mother darling's happiness. Everything I heard her say was about her and Cory and the band. There was no mention of me. It was truly as if I wasn't there; I never existed. I buried my face in the pillow and tried to shut out their cries of joy. They were up celebrating for at least another hour or so before they finally collapsed in bed. Their laughter lingered in the silence. I fought harder to get some sleep, and some time just before the first glittering rays of morning, it came.

I woke up and groaned and turned over and fell asleep again, this time not waking until nearly eleven. Panic nearly froze me in bed. I leaped out and dressed as quickly as I could. It had been my intention to review all my possessions, despite what I had told Keefer, so I could decide if there was anything dear to me. Now, all I could do was throw some cold water on my face, run a brush through my hair, and hurry out to make the bus. If I was late today, Mr. Ritter would surely do what he threatened and fire me on the spot. That would mess up Keefer's whole plan.

For a moment or two, I hesitated at Mother darling's bedroom door. I was leaving without saying any sort of good-bye, any final words. We might not speak to each other for some time, I thought. How would she really react? Would she breathe a sigh of relief and go on happily with her developing music career? Would she spend a few hours worrying about me or regretting how I had been treated? I imagined Cory telling her not to waste any time thinking about me. I wasn't worth it, not after all they had done for me. Like that was anything significant.

Neither she nor I had called Grandma and Grandpa to tell them we were fine. I knew she believed they thought good riddance when they thought of us, but I couldn't believe that completely. Grandma surely worried, and despite his harsh, cold ways, Grandpa had to give us some thought. People, family people, surely just don't dispose of each other like empty milk cartons or something, do they?

Maybe they do, I thought. I couldn't be more confused when it came to all that. All that seemed concrete and sure to me at the moment was Keefer's devotion, Keefer's dreams and plans, because everything included me. I was made a big part of it. I was important to someone finally, someone who needed me about as much as I needed him. That's a gift, I thought. That's a stroke of luck that's come my way, and I can't just toss it aside. For what would I give it up, anyway? This?

I looked around the disheveled apartment with their clothes strewn about, the empty beer bottles on the table and floor, Mother darling's boots staring at me. That's it, I realized. I'll take those. At least, I'd have something of hers. I scooped them up and left the apartment, closing the door softly behind me.

Stay asleep, Mother darling. You're better off, I thought, and hurried down the stairs.

I was lucky with the bus and made it to the supermarket ten minutes early. Now came the hard part—working until the first cashier shift ended. I had to keep up that plastic smile, look calm and innocent. Despite that, I couldn't help but gaze out the window, anticipating Keefer's arrival. When I finally did see him pull up to the curb outside, I think my heart stopped and started. The blood drained from my face, and I fumbled with the groceries.

"You all right?" the cashier, Betty Blue Nickols, asked. I had worked with her before and found her to be pleasant. She was an older woman, close to fifty, I thought. The regular customers knew her by name and obviously liked her. Many exchanged small talk with her as she worked, talking about their children or their other family members as if she really knew them. It brought a warmth to an otherwise very cold and impersonal world, I thought.

"I'm fine," I said quickly.

My eyes went to the big clock on the left wall. In ten minutes, Betty Blue would be closing out her register. Keefer was sitting in the battered SUV, watching me through the window, waiting for my signal. Every minute that clicked off brought more blood to my face. My skin felt like it was on fire. Did I have a fever? The inside of my throat became dry as well. My hands trembled around the groceries I packed. At one point Mr. Ritter came around and looked hard at me, his eyebrows turning in like two annoyed caterpillars. I held my breath, and then he walked off to help a customer.

Betty Blue closed her register and put up her sign to indicate her aisle was shutting down. Then she opened her register again to begin to count her cash. I turned slowly, and looked out at Keefer. This was the moment of decision. If there was a good angel on one of my shoulders, he or she was asleep. I nodded emphatically and he got out of the SUV and strutted toward the supermarket entrance.

I was supposed to move over to the next cashier, but I hesitated long enough for Keefer to come in and approach Betty Blue, who looked up with surprise.

"I'm closed," she said, and then grimaced at the realization he had no grocery cart or groceries to check out anyway. Keefer glanced at me and then pulled the pistol out of his jacket.

Betty Blue gasped.

"Just put the cash into a paper bag."

Betty Blue froze. Keefer's eyes registered a sense of panic. I was afraid of what would happen next if she didn't move quickly, but she was in shock.

"Robin, do it," he said, and I pushed her back and began to take out the cash and drop it in a bag.

"It's all there," I said.

"Let's go," he snapped.

I knelt down and grabbed Mother darling's boots where I had hidden them under the counter.

"Hurry up, Robin," he ordered.

A customer coming up saw the gun in Keefer's hand and screamed. Mr. Ritter came around one of the aisles and dropped his jaw, his eyes nearly popping out.

Keefer and I ran to the exit and out, me clutching the bag with one hand and Mother darling's boots in the other. We got into the SUV and he started away. I didn't look back. I didn't think I could move my head. I was that frozen.

"Count the money!" Keefer screamed. "Let's see what we've got."

I nodded and then began. We had just a little over two thousand dollars. He was pleased.

"That's great. It'll be enough to start." Then he smiled. "It was easy, easier than I thought, huh?"

"Yes," I said.

"Hey, what's with those boots?" he asked. I was clutching them again. I hadn't even realized I was.

"They're my mother's," I said.

"You're the same size?"

"No," I replied.

He shook his head, his lips twisted in confusion.

"Then . . . why did you take them?"

"I don't know," I said. I looked at them. "I don't know."

"Forget about it. You'll have a nice new pair that fit you soon."

"I don't care about boots."

He laughed and shook his head. We were driving fast, slipping under streetlights before they turned red and weaving around slower traffic.

"Do you know where you're going?" I asked.

"Absolutely," he said. "I've been planning carefully on this getaway."

He let out a whoop.

"We're outta here!" he cried.

I tried to smile. Were we? I looked ahead and relaxed a little. Maybe it would be wonderful. Maybe it would be great, I thought, and closed my eyes to wish hard.

Then I heard Keefer's guttural cry and I opened my eyes to see a police patrol car ahead. At first I thought it was just there, waiting for speeders, but suddenly, it pulled out and planted itself right in our way, its bubble light going. Keefer hit the brakes and turned to back up, but there behind us, coming up fast, was another police patrol car. He started to turn and then stopped. A third patrol car was coming too fast down the other lane.

He turned to me.

"Bad luck," he said, and shrugged. "They must have been just close enough to get the call and cut us off. And we were almost to the open highway. Damn."

Blood drained from my face at the sight of two policemen, their guns drawn and pointing at us. They were crouched behind the doors of their vehicle. Another policeman screamed through a bullhorn behind us, ordering us to come out of the truck with our hands raised high.

"I'm sorry," Keefer said.

I began to cry. With Mother darling's boots still in my hands, I stepped out of the truck when Keefer did. His hands were up and so were mine.

It occurred to me as the police drew closer that Mother darling might still be sleeping.

We were separated almost immediately at the police station. I thought I would be placed in a prison cell, but I was brought to a room with a long table and two chairs. There was a mirror on one wall. I sat there for a long time, staring at myself and wondering what was going to happen to me next. Finally, a woman with very short dark hair, wearing a gray skirt suit, entered. She looked about thirty or thirty-five to me. She didn't smile, but there was something warm about her soft brown eyes. She opened a briefcase and took out a long pad and a file.

"I'm Lou Ann Simmons from the district attorney's office," she began. "There is someone coming over from the public defender's office. I guess it's someone you know fairly well, Mr. Carson Meriweather. It's not all that long since you and he were in court," she added pointedly. Then she smiled and continued. "You can wait for him to arrive, if you like, or you can tell me your side of this."

"My side?"

"What was your role in the robbery exactly?"

I wasn't sure what she meant by exactly. I shrugged.

"I put the money in the paper bag. Is that what you mean?"

"You were in on the planning, too, weren't you?" she followed, obviously pleased I was responding.

"Yes."

"You were supposed to give a signal or something, which you did?"

"Yes."

The door opened and Mr. Meriweather entered quickly. He looked at Lou Ann Simmons.

"Have you been questioning my client?"

"She was asked if she wanted to wait for you," Lou Ann Simmons replied. The warmth in her eyes was gone. I had the feeling it was something she could turn on and off at will.

"She doesn't understand what's happening here. She's a minor."

"She was involved in an armed robbery. That status might be denied."

"All the more reason for you not to have gone ahead without me," he fired back.

I felt like I was an observer in an argument that involved someone else besides me.

"She's confessed to her active participation in the event. I can ask her the same questions with you present."

"I want to speak to my client alone," he said sharply.

"I think the best thing you can do and convince her to do is cooperate with me. Keefer Dawson will not be tried as a minor, and he is responsible for bringing her into the act. I hope you're not going to make this complicated," she added, put her notebook and the file back in her briefcase, and left.

"I would have thought you would know enough not to speak to anyone without your attorney present," Mr. Meriweather chastised before sitting in the seat she had taken.

"I didn't know what to do."

"With your past record, I would have thought you would," he said dryly. "Don't you realize how serious this situation is? You were on probation."

I tried to swallow, but couldn't. All I could do was nod.

"She's not bluffing. They could have you tried as an adult. You'll go to a hard penitentiary. And for years!" he emphasized.

"Was my mother called yet?"

"Your mother can't save you now," he muttered. "This man, Keefer Dawson, talked you into participating in this robbery, didn't he?"

"He didn't talk me into it."

"He talked you into it," Mr. Meriweather insisted. "You didn't have any idea he would have a gun?" he said, seemingly as a question, but more as an answer he wanted to shove down my throat.

"Yes, I did. I saw it before, but he told me there were no bullets in it."

"That would make no difference. How would anyone being held up

know there were no bullets in it, and how do you know for certain that
there were no bullets in it?"

"He told me," I said.

"Then you did not know for certain," he concluded. "You see how
complicated this can be and how much trouble you can be in?"

I nodded.

"All right. Just sit here and don't—don't—ever talk to anyone
about this without my being present."

He got up and left the room. To me it felt like nearly an hour had
gone by before the door was opened again. This time it was Mother
darling. She just stood there for a few moments and looked in at me. I
thought she was going to back up and close the door. Finally she entered. I saw her eyes were bloodshot from crying. She sucked in her
breath and sat.

"There were many times," she began, "when I thought my father
was right. I didn't know why it should be, but evil, like some pollu-
tion, seeped into me and then into you. That was a big reason why I
wanted to leave home. I wanted to get away from his eyes, from his
way of lookin' at us, remindin' me all the time of the mistakes I had
made."

"Me, especially," I said.

She stared.

"Yeah, I suppose I always thought of you that way, Robin. I'm not
denyin' it. It's no secret I never intended to be pregnant, but I really
believed that somehow, some way, because of my music or through it,
I'd make things right. I guess I never got that across to you, no matter
how many times I tried gettin' you to see it."

"It's your career, not mine," I snapped back at her. "You're the star,
Mother darling."

She shook her head.

"I don't blame you for hatin' me, I guess." She smiled. "Remember
that song I wrote years ago: 'I want to love you but I can't help hatin'
myself for wantin' that.' "

"I'm not the reason for a song, Mother darling. I'm a person," I told
her.

She nodded.

"Yep, I guess, but what sort of a person have you become? I'll take
as much blame as goes around, of course, but that's not goin' to help
us much now."

She turned and looked at me.

"Mr. Meriweather says Keefer Dawson is tellin' the district attorney that he talked you into this, that you didn't know he was goin' to have a real gun."

"It's not true!"

"It's somethin' that will help you, Robin. Mr. Meriweather sent me in here to convince you not to contradict Keefer. Keefer should do this. He had no business bringin' you into it."

"He didn't bring me into anything. I wanted to do it," I practically shouted back at her.

"You want to go to a real terrible prison where ugly things happen to girls your age and you want to go there for years and years? Is that what you want?"

"No, but—"

"But that's what's goin' to happen to you if you don't shut your trap, Robin. You nod when you're told to nod and you shake your head when you're told to shake it, understand? Otherwise, there's no tellin' what that judge is goin' to do to you. Mr. Meriweather is tryin' to work somethin' out with that assistant district attorney. If you will sign the statement agreeing with what Keefer Dawson is tellin' them, she'll consider a recommendation to the judge that will help you."

"I don't want Keefer taking all the blame," I said.

"He would have done somethin' like this with or without you, wouldn't he?" she asked.

I thought about it.

"Probably," I said. "His mother just died—committed suicide—and his father hates him and he lost his job."

"That's all for his lawyer to tell, Robin. There's no point tyin' yourself to someone else's troubles."

"It is if you care about him," I told her. "That's something you wouldn't understand, Mother darling. You never cared about anyone more than you cared about yourself."

"That's not fair, Robin. I did care about you. I do."

"Then how did you bring us—bring me—to live with that horrible Cory Lewis?" I cried.

She stared.

"I didn't just come to Cory with you because he was involved in the music business, Robin. There was a chance—there *is* a chance," she corrected, "that he is your real father."

I felt as if lightning had snapped over my head.

"No," I said. I shook my head vigorously to throw the words back out of my ears.

"As I told you, there was more than one, but he was there that night and we . . . we were lovers that night."

"No," I insisted.

"It doesn't matter. Cory wanted to do somethin' for us because he thought it might be true."

"If it is, I wish I was never born," I said. "Almost as much as you wish it."

"I don't wish it anymore, Robin, but I don't expect you to believe that. I really was hopin' you'd be part of my success and be happy."

"Good title for a new song. Start writing it," I snapped, and she bristled.

"I'm tellin' that lawyer you'll do what he says, Robin. If you don't, you're goin' to be one sorry girl."

She rose.

"You don't help him by hurtin' yourself," she added.

I looked up at her. It was the first thing she had said that I thought made any sense at all.

And something I wished she would turn into a song.

13

Caged Birds
Sing Sad Songs

"**T**his is the story," Mr. Meriweather said, with Mother darling sitting beside him. "We can keep you out of prison, keep you from being tried as an adult, even keep you out of a juvenile detention center."

I held my breath and looked from him to Mother darling and then back to him.

"How?"

"There is a special school for young girls who, shall we say, have exhausted all the traditional means of correcting their behavior, or rather, their misbehavior. Their parents are totally defeated, as is your mother."

I glanced at her, and she shifted her eyes guiltily away.

"What sort of special school?"

"It's a school run by a specialist in behavior modification, and for many, a school of last resort. Now before I go any further in my explanation, let me make clear to you that once you go there, you do not have the privilege of deciding you don't want to be there. You're there until it is decided you can return and behave in a reasonable manner, and you would still be on a term of strict probation. Should you attempt to escape or run away from this school, you would be immediately returned to court and sentenced to a real prison—sentenced, in your case, as an adult. It's part of the agreement we will sign."

"But how long am I at this school?"

"You can be there months; you can be there years. It's entirely up to you. That's the beauty of it, if we can say there is any beauty. You're in control of your own destiny. In a real prison, you're lucky to be in control of your own bowel movements," he said, his lips taut, his eyes ice-cold.

"It's just another school?"

"No, I'm not saying it's just another school. It's a special school. There are different rules, different activities. Its purpose is to change your behavior, change your miscreant ways, and make you a productive member of society. You sign a contract to turn yourself over to the school. Your mother signs as well," he added, looking at her.

Something in her face told me she wasn't happy to be doing it, even though Mr. Meriweather had made it sound like a way out of a horrible prison experience. It made my heart flutter.

"I don't know," I said.

"You can have a little while to discuss it with your mother. Then I have to inform the assistant district attorney, and together we will confer with the judge. This is the last breath of mercy you will find in this court," he added, and rose. "One more thing. It's normally very, very expensive to go to this special school. It's privately run, but an anonymous benefactor has provided what we can best describe as scholarships for girls whose families cannot afford it, but who need it desperately nevertheless. That, for you, is another stroke .of luck just when you need it the most."

He looked at Mother darling.

"I'll be back in a little while," he said, and left us.

"What is this all about?" I asked.

"Just what he said. I didn't even know it existed. Even though we said you would sign the statements, the judge was not persuaded to consider you a minor. The gun made all the difference. You're headin' for some hard time in a hard place with women who have done some terrible things and will see you as a ripe piece of fruit. Virgin fruit," she added in practically a whisper.

"Do you know anything about the school?"

"Just what you heard."

"Where is it?"

"I don't know."

"You don't know? What do you mean, you don't know?"

"They don't want the parents to know where it is. They don't want parents to change their minds and go fetch their children."

"But what if I call you and tell you where I am?"

"You can't call anyone, Robin."

"But . . . that's worse than jail, isn't it? Don't prisoners get the right to call people?"

"Not right away. I think you can call after a while. I don't know everything."

I stared at her.

"You don't know anything, do you, and you don't care. It's a way to get rid of me. That's all you know."

"That's not true. I don't want you goin' to a real prison and . . ."

"And what?"

"I haven't been a good mother, and I probably won't ever be," she admitted. "It's true what he said. I'm not capable of doin' what has to be done. I need help. Look at this," she said, unfolding a paper. "I was asked to check off what applies to you."

Does your teen struggle with basic family rules?

Has your teen ever been expelled? Been truant? Failed subjects?

Is your teen verbally abusive?

Does your teen associate with bad peers? Have problems with the law? Lack motivation?

Lack self-worth? Have problems with authority? Has your teen been sexually promiscuous? Been manipulative and/or deceitful? Stolen money or other valuables from your home?

No matter what rules and consequences are established, does your teen defy them?

When dealing with your teen, do you often feel powerless?

I put the paper down.

"You see, I had to check everythin', Robin."

"Big deal," I said.

"Yes, it is a big deal. I'm signin' the paper."

"I don't care," I said. "Sign it."

"You'll thank me someday."

"I can't wait," I said.

She rose and walked slowly to the door.

"They're goin' to take you directly from here, Robin. We won't have a chance to say good-bye."

"We said good-bye a long time ago, Mother darling," I told her. I said it firmly, but my eyes were clouded with tears.

She nodded.

"I'm sorry, honey. I'm sorry I hurt you. No matter what you think, I'll never stop lovin' you. I hope you come back."

"To what?"

"To me," she said, and opened the door. She hesitated, and then she closed it.

It wasn't a loud noise, but to me it was like a gunshot.

A few minutes later, a policewoman came in.

"You'd better go to the bathroom," she said. "You've got a long trip ahead of you."

I did what she suggested. When I came out, she was waiting for me.

She took me down a hallway to a door where a police vehicle was parked. A patrolman opened the rear door and I got in. It occurred to me that I had nothing but the clothes on my back. I was going to say something about it, but no one seemed interested in anything I had to say, so I kept my mouth shut.

I looked back when the car pulled away. I don't know why. Something made me do that.

I saw Mother darling standing on the walkway, clutching the boots I had taken.

She held them as close to her as I had held them to me.

It was all we shared at the moment.

But it was enough to free the tears locked in my heart.

PART TWO

TEAL

1

Suspended

As soon as our English teacher, Mr. Croft, took off his sports jacket and draped it over his desk chair in front of the classroom, I knew I was going to laugh. The laughter rose in my chest in waves, rolling freely upward. Mr. Croft turned to write the first grammar exercise sentence on the board, and I saw his shirt partially out of his pants. It really wasn't anything all that unusual. He was not a very neat dresser. However, everything had struck me as humorous this morning, from the security guard at the front entrance looking at me with grouchy, suspicious eyes, to the snob birds in the bathroom who nearly exploded with shock when I plucked my silver flask out of my purse and took a sip.

"What's that?" Evette Heckman asked.

"Orange juice and vodka," I replied, smiled, and drank some more. When I offered it to them, they fled as if I was offering them a drink of poison.

In class my laugh came out with a sound that resembled someone spitting up a drink first, and then I went into the giggles. Mr. Croft turned with confusion on his face and raked the room with his eyes, finally settling on me. His grimace of bewilderment changed to a smirk of annoyance, and that made me laugh even harder.

I knew the vodka I had taken from my parents' bar to mix with the orange juice had most to do with my inability to contain myself. This wasn't the first time, and something told me it wasn't going to be the last, no matter what happened this particular morning.

"What do you find so funny, Miss Sommers?" Mr. Croft asked.

"Surely not restrictive and nonrestrictive clauses, although the results of your quiz yesterday might suggest you're not taking this very seriously."

Everyone's eyes were on me. Some of the snob birds looked angrier than Mr. Croft, probably to win favor or maybe because they really did think I was interrupting their precious private-school educations. The idea was, if you paid more for it, you would take it more seriously. At least, that was the theory my parents believed or, should I say, hoped was true, especially for me. I had all but failed tenth grade the year before in public school. I had been suspended three times there and put in detention so often, there was a joke that I would get a degree in it. After I was caught vandalizing the girls' room, which cost my father nearly a thousand dollars, my parents thought a strategic retreat to a private school would be the solution. I would be less apt to be influenced by bad seeds. The truth was, I was the one doing the influencing.

Mr. Croft brought his hands to his wide waist and glared at me. His nostrils were as big as a cow's when they flared. He turned his lips inward, outlining his mouth in two thin white lines of rage, and clenched his teeth.

"Well?" he demanded, speaking through the wall of cigarette-stained enamel.

I laughed harder. I couldn't help it, even though my stomach was hurting and I was gasping for breath.

He sighed.

"I think it's best you get up and go to the principal's office, Miss Sommers," he said in a tighter voice.

I continued to laugh.

"Teal Sommers!" he screamed, stepping toward me. "Get up and get out this minute."

He pointed at the door so vigorously and sharply, the button on his cuff undid and his sleeve sagged like a torn curtain. Someone gasped, but that just widened my idiotic grin. He saw what happened and lowered his arm, pointing more gracefully with the other arm and hand toward the door.

"Go. I will intercom the office to let Mr. Bloomberg know you are coming," he assured me.

I caught my breath and let my head fall back a moment. I was looking up at the ceiling, watching the lines of the tiles wiggling. Mr. Croft walked all the way down the aisle to my desk. By this time his rage was building like milk boiling in a pot. Any moment he might seize my arm and pull me out of my seat, I thought.

"What is wrong with you, young lady?"

"Smell her breath," one of the snob birds cried out. I wasn't positive, but I thought it was most likely Ainsley Winslow. Always full of herself, she'd hated me from the moment I told her that her nose job was poorly done, was too pointed, and made her resemble a chicken.

Mr. Croft looked in her direction and then down at me with more intense scrutiny.

"Is that true, Teal? Have you drunk something you shouldn't?"

"No, sir," I said, and then I covered my mouth with both of my hands quickly because my stomach was starting to send up more than laughter. It took two hard swallows to keep it down, my eyes bulging with the effort.

"Go!" he commanded with a sense of panic as well as anger in his voice.

I rose much too quickly and awkwardly and fell against him. He jumped back as if I was on fire. As fast as I could, I scooped up my books and charged toward the door. Behind me I heard the rest of the classroom laughing. I fumbled with the knob and went out, closing the door behind me. The churning in my stomach stopped for a moment, but the corridor seemed to turn on its side and then right itself. I hiccuped so loudly, the sound bounced off the walls, echoing all the way to the end of the corridor. With one hand against the wall to steady myself, I started down the shiny tiled floor.

The librarian, Ms. Beachim, came out of the faculty room and paused to look at me. She lowered her glasses over the bridge of her bony nose and peered.

"Are you all right?" she asked.

"No," I said. "I feel like I'm inside out."

"Pardon?"

"Like a sock when you take it off," I told her. Then I laughed, and she stood there gaping at me with her hands pressed against the base of her throat.

I straightened my shoulders and tried to walk a straight line, but I guess I had drunk more orange juice and vodka than I normally did, especially in the morning. The world would not stop swaying. I was getting more and more seasick.

Finally, I reached the principal's office. When I stepped in, I paused, or at least I thought I had. Even though my feet were planted, somehow it was as if I was still moving.

Mrs. Tagler looked up from her desk. As soon as the principal's secretary set eyes on me, her eyebrows lifted and her lips went into a crooked smile. She had a hairdo and a face that reminded me of a praying mantis, especially with those long, thin arms she kept bent at the elbows and those hands with fingers curling inward.

"Now what?" she asked.

"I thought he was going to call and lodge a complaint," I said.

"Who?"

"Mr. Croft's shirt is out of his pants," I said.

"What?"

"He's a mess."

I giggled, and she let her jaw drop enough for me to see the gold crown in the back of her mouth.

"You were sent to see Mr. Bloomberg?"

"No, I was asked to pay him a friendly visit," I replied. "To see how things were going and if there is anything I can do to help improve the school," I added, and, before I could stop it, hiccuped.

She nodded knowingly.

"Sit down," she ordered as she rose like a gusher to her full six feet of height. Her husband, I was told, was only five feet five and had to be careful he didn't get poked in the eye by one of her breasts. She always wore those stiff pointy bras that looked like they had been borrowed from Madonna's costume closet.

Mrs. Tagler went into the principal's office, closing the door behind her. Only seconds afterward, the door was thrust open and Mr. Bloomberg stood there glaring out at me. Something in my face told him the whole story. His bushy rust eyebrows curved downward when I hiccuped again.

"I don't want to talk to you in the state you're in," he said. "Go directly to the nurse's office. I'm calling your mother." He turned to Mrs. Tagler. "See that she goes to Lila's office," he said, and she nodded.

"Come along, Teal," she said, her voice softer now.

I stood, remembered my books, and reached down, knocking them every which way.

"Oh, forget them," Mrs. Tagler said. The phone was ringing. Mr. Croft had finally gotten himself together enough to call, I thought. She picked up the receiver and listened.

"Yes, he knows," she said. "Thank you."

She considered me, wavering before her. She seemed to go in and out of focus, and that made me smile. Then came another hiccup, and another.

"Go on, Teal," she ordered. "I have more important things to do than baby-sit a sixteen-year-old girl who should know better."

I left the office and, with her walking beside me, went to the nurse's office, which fortunately was only two doors down.

Mrs. Miller looked up from her desk. She was completing one report or another. That's all she ever seemed to do in this place, I thought, complete reports or coddle one of the snob birds who was having a bad monthly, as she referred to it.

"What is it?" she asked, staring up at me, her eyes glittering with suspicion.

"Our Miss Sommers has had something alcoholic to drink, apparently. She needs to sleep it off until her mother arrives. She was sent to the office but Mr. Bloomberg doesn't want to see her in this condition."

Mrs. Miller was up and around her desk. She took a long look at me and then directed me to one of the small rooms in which she had a cot-size bed.

"How are you feeling now?"

My hiccuping had finally stopped, but that didn't help all that much.

"Nauseated," I said.

"Lie down. If you have the urge to regurgitate, use this," she said, putting a basin next to the bed. There wasn't any sympathy in her voice, just firmness. "Why do you do this?"

Instead of answering her, I closed my eyes. The question seemed to reverberate in my brain: Why do you do this? Why do you do any of these things, Teal? Who do you think you're hurting? Where is your appreciation for all the wonderful things you have and all the wonderful things we're doing for you? Blah blah, I thought. It was like a broken CD or like being locked into an echo chamber.

I felt my stomach settle down, and moments later, I was asleep.

"What have you done?" I heard someone shout through the walls of my pleasant cocoon. I groaned, opened my eyes reluctantly, and looked up at my mother.

I never fully appreciate how tall she is, I thought, or how bony her shoulders are, even through her stylish designer suit. My father accused her of being anorexic, but somewhere, at one of her spas, no doubt, someone told her if she stayed thin, she would never look old. To me, just the contrary was happening. She was in her late forties, but looked ten years older. Her skin seemed so taut over those high cheekbones she prized, and the effect of that was to emphasize her jawbone. In dim lighting, with just a glow on her face, she looked like a skeleton. I told her that once, and she nearly took off my head with a sharp slap. Despite the miles and miles of skin creams she had available on her vanity table, her hands were never soft to me. I couldn't remember them ever being soft, and of course, she had perfect nails always. She once missed an important gynecological exam because it conflicted with her manicure.

"Well?" she demanded. She swung her purse toward me in an aborted move to club me into attention. It hovered over my face a moment, and then she brought it back toward her.

I scrubbed my cheeks with my palms and, unfortunately, burped.

She stepped back as if I was truly going to explode.

"You're disgusting," she said, pulling the corners of her mouth down.

I sat up.

"Is it morning already?" I teased.

My mother's eyes were truly her best feature. They were normally big, luscious-looking hazel-green, with naturally long eyelashes. She could widen them to almost twice their size when she wanted to show her rage or surprise. For a moment she looked all eyes to me, like some sort of extraterrestrial creature.

"You're not funny, Teal. Do you know how much your father is spending to have you attend school here?" she asked.

I always thought it was odd how she referred to any expenditures the family had as purely my father's. She was obviously not one of those wives who believe half of everything their husbands own belongs to them. Sometimes, she gave me the feeling that she was as much a tenant in the home as my older brother, Carson, had been, and I still was.

"I forgot, Mother," I said.

"Fifty thousand dollars," she said, tapping her foot after each word for emphasis. To me she looked like she was keeping beat to music. "If we add that to all the money he's spent on psychotherapy, tutors, fixing the things you've broken, paying off people who have lodged complaints against you, and everything else I can't think of, he's spent as much as some third world countries spend over a year!"

"Maybe he should ask the UN for help, then," I said.

"Get up," she snapped. "You've embarrassed me again and again. Don't you have any concern for this family and its reputation? Oh, what have I done to deserve this?" she asked the ceiling.

"Forgot your birth control pills sixteen years ago?" I offered.

She turned a shade darker than blood red and looked out toward Mrs. Miller's desk. In front of other people, my mother was always stylish, elegant, and able to manage her rage. She rarely, if ever, had a strand of hair out of place, and when I was little, I used to believe that creases were terrified of forming in her clothing. She would have them ironed to oblivion.

"I suppose this is really all my fault," she said, not really sounding like she was taking the blame, "for having you so late in life."

I did actually agree with that diagnosis. My parents made me on a hot summer night after they had both had too much to drink. My father let that little detail out once when they were arguing over something stupid like how much of his money my mother spent on fresh flowers, especially in the winter. I happened to overhear it.

"Maybe I was just dying to be born, and there was nothing you could do about it," I offered dryly.

She pulled herself up, primping like a proud peacock. Then, as cool as a brain surgeon, she stepped out of the little comfort room and spoke to Mrs. Miller.

"Do you think she is in any sort of condition for a meeting with the principal?" she asked, hoping to hear no, of course.

Mrs. Miller rose and came to the room.

She grabbed my shoulders and turned me to her as I stood, and then she shook her head.

"What gets into you kids these days?" she asked.

"Aliens?" I responded. "Through our belly buttons, I think," I added.

Mrs. Miller nearly smiled.

"She's fine, Mrs. Sommers. She'll probably have a good headache all day. Give her some Advil at home."

"I think it would be better if she suffered all day and appreciated the damage she is doing to herself," my sweet, loving mother replied.

Mrs. Miller looked like she agreed.

"Come along, Teal," Mother said, and I started out.

"Your books," Mrs. Miller reminded me. "Mrs. Tagler brought them in after you arrived."

"Oh. Sorry," I said. I really meant sorry she had brought them in, but Mrs. Miller smiled and handed them to me.

I continued after Mother, who tapped the corridor floor tiles with the sharp heels of her shoes like some drum roll as she reluctantly led me back to the principal's office to be executed in red ink. I remained a good yard or so behind her, imagining an invisible rope tied to my neck, which was used to tug me through life itself.

"How is she doing?" Mrs. Tagler asked my mother when we entered.

"Rather badly, I would say, wouldn't you?" Mother replied, her lips slicing a thin red line in her face. I always thought that for an expert on cosmetics, Mother wore her lipstick too thick.

Mrs. Tagler rose without speaking and went into the principal's office. Mother turned to me, shaking her head.

"I was on my way to have lunch with Carson," she said. My brother, who was nearly fifteen years older than me, was already running the business affairs division of my father's real estate development company. He had his own townhouse and was practically engaged to the daughter of a wealthy banker.

Carson was everything they would want me to be, I thought. He is Mr. Briefcase, a suit and a tie with a perfectly designed manikin within, Mr. Perfect who uses a Waterpik after every meal. I called him my father's second shadow, especially when it came to business.

Our father specialized in malls and entertainment centers, and it had made him—us—very wealthy, millionaires a few times over. At the end of the fiscal year, Carson liked to break it down to how many dollars were made per minute. I suppose in my case it was how many dollars were wasted every minute.

We lived in a full-blown estate house with nearly twelve acres, an Olympic-size swimming pool, and a clay tennis court, which only Carson used occasionally. The property was walled in and gated.

"I'm sorry I spoiled your day," I told my mother. When Mr. Croft asked for examples of understatement once, I raised my hand and said, "My mother favors my brother over me." *Worships* would have been more like it.

"My day?" She laughed. "It's more than one day you've spoiled, Teal," she added.

I looked up at her sharply and felt tears trying to introduce themselves to my eyes. Only my own ever-present boil of rage kept that from happening.

The principal's door opened before I could say anything, and we were ushered in. Mr. Bloomberg did not get up when we entered, and I could see that bothered my mother. He was trying to make a point, however. The point was, this was definitely *not* a social occasion.

"Please have a seat," he said, nodding at the chairs Mrs. Tagler must have just placed directly in front of his marble-topped, immaculate-looking desk. Everything was so neatly organized, I felt like wiping my hands through the piles of papers and files before sitting and knocking them all about. Of course, I didn't.

"I am sure you realize, Mrs. Sommers, that this is Teal's fourth appearance before me generated by her misbehavior in three months."

"Yes, of course. I'm very, very upset about it, Mr. Bloomberg."

"We pride ourselves on how well run our classrooms are and how professional our staff is. To waste all that over this sort of thing is more than just a breach of our school rules; it's a veritable sin."

"Oh, I agree," Mother said. He could have said, "Let's hang her at dawn," and she would have nodded. As long as it didn't conflict with her hair appointment, of course.

"Alcoholic beverages, drugs of any kind, weapons of any sort, all those are grounds for expulsion after only one incident, Mrs. Sommers, much less three or four. I have," he continued, reaching for a document on his desk, "asked Mrs. Tagler to retrieve your contract with us. Both you and Teal signed the document when she entered the school, you will recall. I have underlined the stipulation that if and when Teal should be asked to leave the school as a result of repeated misbehavior, you forfeit your tuition."

He handed it to Mother, who pretended to read it with interest and then handed it back to him, nodding.

He then sighed deeply and looked at me.

"Is there any possibility you will change your behavior, Teal?" he asked.

Mother turned and glared through me.

I shrugged. He knitted his thick, dark brows together and leaned forward.

"That's not quite the response I was looking for," he said.

My mouth felt so dry. That was all I could think about, and I was on the verge of asking for a drink of water. He turned to Mother.

"If she is sent to this office again for any reason, no matter how small the violation, we will have to ask her to leave the school. For now, she is suspended for three days. I hope you and your husband will impress upon her how serious this has become, Mrs. Sommers. We're not a public school. We don't have the time or the inclination to reform disrespectful young people. Anyone who attends this school should know the value of the education he or she will receive."

I wanted to put my fingers in my ears, but I didn't dare. Most of the time, actually, I wanted to put my fingers in my ears. I guess drinking booze was just another way to do it, especially at this school for penguins and canaries, I thought.

"I understand," Mother said. She glared at me. "We'll have a good talk."

He nodded, firming his lips and looking at me skeptically. Our eyes met, and he knew the clock was ticking on my expulsion. He could also see how little importance I was placing on it.

"Very well," Mr. Bloomberg said in a tone that clearly indicated the meeting had ended.

Mother rose, and I followed her out. Mrs. Tagler looked up at us as we passed through the outer office. She and my mother exchanged looks of sympathy as if I was more like a disease than a child.

"Your father is going to go ballistic over this, Teal," she said as we left the building and headed toward Mother's big Mercedes.

I knew what was coming. Mother had a set lecture. I really believed she had written it all down and memorized it. It always began with how much my father had done for me. The lecture started as soon as we were in the car and she was driving out of the school parking lot. She should have recorded it and put it on a CD she could just play, I thought.

"Look at what you have, Teal. A beautiful home. Your own suite, your own telephone and a computer, clothes that rival any princess's wardrobe, clothes you don't wear, I might add. Any toy you wanted as you grew up, you got. You have servants waiting on you, a car and driver to take you wherever you want to go, and if you behaved, you would have your own car. Why, why are you like this? What do you want?" she asked, a little more hysteria in her voice than usual.

I looked out the window.

What did I want?

Should I tell her? Could I ever tell her? How do you tell your own mother that what you want the most is simply to be loved?

2

Grounded

It wasn't a surprise to me that I often imagined myself locked in some echo chamber. My big house was filled with words that bounced around me, repetitions of threats, lectures, and ever-changing rules. In other homes, I suspected the walls lovingly absorbed the words spoken between mothers and daughters, fathers and daughters, brothers and sisters, but not in mine. The warmth in our home came from central heating, not from smiles and kisses, hugs and loving caresses.

A few years ago, I sat and thumbed through the pile of family albums we had in the den. I was more fascinated with my brother when he was younger and his relationship to my mother and father than I was with anyone else. One of my therapists once accused me of being a little paranoid about it. He was referring to the way I described my mother smiling at Carson or holding Carson's hand, or the way my father held him when he was a little boy, and the way they held me or looked at me when I was his age.

First, there were three times more pictures of Carson than there were of me. Mother's explanation for that was my father became more successful during my early years and was far busier than he had been when Carson was growing up. Therefore, there wasn't as much time to recreate. As he became more important in the business world, they moved up the social ladder, and Mother had the added burden of presenting him and herself to the substantial world, as she liked to call it. She became a social bird who primped her feathers and held court at dinners and balls, making sure her face was pasted on the society pages and in the slick community magazines. If I even approached

what some might consider a complaint about how little we did together, I was told the sacrifices were all very important and good for
the family, which of course included me, so I shouldn't feel I was neglected.

I had three nannies in my first ten years, two of whom, according to
my father, demanded battle fatigue insurance. I suppose the worst
thing I did before I was nine was knock over the perfumed candle in
Mother's bedroom after she and my father had left for a dinner with
the mayor. It was my misfortune or my intention, depending on who
tells the story, that the candle remained burning. Its tiny flame managed to lick the sheer nightgown my mother had on a hanger by her
closet door. That triggered a bigger fire, which spread into the walk-in
closet.

We had a sprinkler system in the house. Naturally, we would,
Daddy being a developer and up on everything that was possible and
necessary. The flames set off the sprinkler, which then soaked
Mother's wardrobe, ruining, she claimed, one hundred fifty thousand
dollars' worth of clothing. My father actually fired the nanny I had at
the time. I knew that if he could have, he would have fired me.

"You're finished here as my daughter," he would have said. "Get
out. Go to some orphanage!"

I actually dreamed such a scene and woke up crying. Carson, who
was twenty-five at the time and still living at home, was the only one
to come to my bedroom to see what was going on. I told him I had a
nightmare.

"My advice to you," he said, "is to stuff it back into the pillow.
That's what Mother used to tell me to do when I had a bad dream, and
it works."

It was something she had told him when he was only four or five, I
was sure; but at least she had come to his room when he had cried. My
tears made her nervous because she was older and more apt to get nervous, and making her nervous was forbidden because "nervousness
leads to wrinkled brows and palpitating hearts."

"I didn't mean to start the fire," I said. Vaguely, I wondered if I did.
It was during the period I was seeing a therapist and was told that
sometimes we don't realize ourselves what we secretly want to do.
Now I know he meant subconsciously, but I was too young to understand that, so he called it my secret self. He had me so convinced I had
a secret self that I often paused quickly in front of a mirror to see if another me would be visible, perhaps caught unaware.

My brother Carson grunted after I protested my innocence. He has
my mother's nose and mouth, my mother's eyes, but my father's bulky

upper body and my father's dark brown hair. From the rear, especially from a distance or when there isn't much light, it's hard to distinguish who it is, Daddy or Carson.

"You know what Daddy says about apologies," he reminded me. "They are always too little too late and might as well not be uttered. Usually they serve only to remind the injured party he or she has been injured."

He stood there stiffly in the middle of the night and lectured me just the way our father would. I couldn't remember anyone speaking to me as an adult would speak to a child. We were all always adults in my house. Whether I liked it or not, I was never classified as an infant or an adolescent, or even a young adult.

"In my house we all take responsibility for our actions," my father preached. "You are told or shown what is right and what is wrong and you are in charge of your own behavior accordingly. No one can look after you better than you can yourself, and you shouldn't expect it or depend upon it."

Carson was the one who came up with the idea to keep a profit-and-loss statement in relation to me. Everything I broke, accidentally or not, every bit of damage that could be calculated, was placed on the loss side. Someday, I would do something to earn a living and he would then calculate the assets and work out the profit and loss. Daddy thought he was so clever and even suggested he submit his idea to some business magazines.

I told Carson it made me feel good to know I provided some amusement to them. He either didn't understand or deliberately mis-understood my sarcasm. I suppose I always felt like an outsider, and they had always treated me as one. It shouldn't have come as such a surprise to my mother that I was nothing like her.

Especially now, during what she saw as my debutante years, she puzzled over why I was such a mystery to her. Why didn't I want the same things she always wanted? Why did I insist on wearing torn jeans instead of the expensive designer jeans she bought for me? Why did I put a ring in my nose and on my belly button occasionally? Why did I listen to that terrible music, and especially, why did I still want to hang out with friends who were, in her words, "beneath us"?

There was never any doubt in my mind that if I, as I was, were not her daughter, I would be beneath her as well. She never really looks at me, never sees me for who I am, I thought. Maybe she is afraid of what she helped create. Maybe my father has the same fear. I just re-mind them of their biggest mistake.

My father wasn't even there for my birth. He was away on a business trip. My mother accused him of deliberately scheduling it for that time. Finally, she got him to admit that he felt my being born was chiefly her responsibility.

"How come?" she asked.

"The woman," he said, "is the one primarily responsible for preventing pregnancy, not the man."

The way he described it, the man was an innocent bystander.

And so Mother was to be in charge of my upbringing. When I had all that trouble in public school, I overheard them arguing about it.

"I know what we agreed," she told him, "but I'm too old for this sort of thing, Henderson. She's rushing me into old age. The stress shows. You don't have the full brunt of it. You're off doing your projects."

He was quick to remind her that those "projects" paid for the big home, the expensive cars, expensive vacations, miles of clothes in her walk-in closet, on and on.

That was when she convinced him to spend the money to send me to this wonderful private school.

"We've got to get her away from this crowd of juvenile delinquents," she argued.

"It seems to me," he replied, "their parents probably want to get them away from her. Maybe we could ask them to contribute to the tuition. They'd gladly do it to get her away," he muttered.

Nevertheless, he relented and wrote the check to get me into the private school. Now, I was being sent home from that one, as well.

"Go directly up to your room and remain there until your father returns," my mother ordered when we had arrived. "And I don't want to hear that music blasting. Just sit and contemplate what you've done and what you've become," she advised.

I marched up the stairway. I was still feeling tired and bored and actually looked forward to getting back into bed. I fell asleep pretty quickly and awoke only when pangs of hunger made me dream about food.

Mother was gone again, so there were only myself and the two maids at home. It took one just to look after mother's things, clean her suite, and do her errands. I could hear the vacuum cleaners roaring away, sucking up every particle of dust. I sauntered into the kitchen and made myself a cheese and tomato sandwich. I didn't realize how hungry I was, which was probably a result of the alcohol I had drunk. I ate two sandwiches and a chocolate-covered frozen vanilla yogurt bar.

Usually, young girls envy their mothers for one reason or another.

Most of my girlfriends at public school felt they weren't as pretty as their mothers. It was different at the private school. There, the snob birds I cared to talk to all had no problem with their egos. I don't have the same sort of bloated self-image, but I couldn't say I ever wanted to be just like my mother. There are things about her I like, but we do seem so different that I can understand someone wanting to double-check my birth certificate to have proof she gave birth to me.

For me the envy was reversed when it came to our figures. Mother could never understand how I could eat whatever I wanted, as much as I wanted, and not become a blimp. She was always on one diet or another, and she had a personal trainer. A new ounce of weight, a wrinkle, something sagging, whatever, put her into a panic. When I was very little and I walked with her, I noticed how she would often pause to look at her reflection in a store window. She would never pass a mirror. I first thought she was checking to see if anyone was following us. I'd turn to look back. It didn't take me long to realize I was right. Mother was being chased by age.

Now I often caught her looking at me. If envy could be translated into tears, she would be crying her eyes out. The only satisfaction she had was in telling me that if I didn't take better care of myself, I would regret it someday.

"One day you'll wake up and see fat where there wasn't any or that firm behind of yours will suddenly turn into marshmallow, Teal. You've got to do preventive things. You don't exercise like you should. You eat everything I tell you not to eat. I should know," she concluded. "I had your figure and I discovered how hard it was to maintain."

Sometimes, being spiteful, I would deliberately add another scoop of ice cream to my dessert or gorge myself on a bag of Kit Kat bars right in front of her. I knew she was dying to eat one.

"Who bought that?" she would cry. "I distinctly left orders not to buy that."

"I did," I said. "I love them."

She would practically flee from me, or from the desserts.

Go on. Run away. I'll never get like you, I vowed.

After my late lunch, I took my portable CD player and went for a walk. We had a telephone in the pool cabana, so I stopped there and called one of my so-called "beneath us" friends from public school, Shirley Number. I expected she would be home by now, and she was. I told her what I had done and what had happened to me. She thought it was funny, of course, and then went on to talk about some of the things she and the other girls I knew were doing. I really missed being with them.

"Do you see Del Grant?" I asked her. He was a senior I'd had a crush on since ninth grade.

"No," she said. "Don't you remember? Oh, I guess I didn't tell you," she added.

"What?"

"He dropped out of school when his father left them. You know what his mother is like, her drugs and all."

"Dropped out?"

"Yes, he works full-time at Diablo's Pizza in the mall. He says he has to help support his seven-year-old brother and five-year-old sister."

"Oh. Bummer," I said.

"He doesn't seem unhappy, but you know Del. You couldn't tell if he was unhappy anyway."

"Is he going with anyone?" I asked, and held my breath.

"Not that I know of. Selma Wisner has a mad crush on him and practically stalks him, but he doesn't seem terribly interested in her."

"I'll meet you at the mall this weekend," I said. "Saturday, okay?"

"Really? I thought you weren't allowed to hang out with us anymore."

"I'm not."

She laughed.

"Okay, we'll meet for lunch. Are they going to let you out on the weekend?" she asked.

"No, but that hasn't stopped me before," I said dryly.

She laughed again.

"I miss you," she squealed. "Everybody's so . . . everybody," she said. It brought a smile to my face.

"See you soon," I said, and hung up.

I walked some more, thinking mostly about Del Grant now. I suppose what I liked about him the most was that he was a loner. Probably because of his home situation, he avoided making friends with many people. He never had time to be in an extracurricular activity at school, and was absent so often, he barely got by. He kept to himself and wasn't very talkative in school, and whenever I saw him anywhere in the city, he smiled or nodded, but always looked like he was afraid to do much more.

Yet I never thought of him as shy. To me he looked like he knew more and was older than the other boys his age. I had the feeling he thought that the things that were important to them were childish or meaningless. He was clean and neat even though he was poor and didn't have much of a wardrobe, sometimes wearing the same thing for days. But he looked like he took care of what he had. Neal Sertner told me Del's mother cut his hair, when she wasn't drugged out on something or other. When he had it cut, he looked stylish. His mother worked on and off in a beauty parlor, but she had gone through so many, been fired from so many jobs, that people said she didn't only burn her bridges, she burned the roads to the bridges.

I liked Del's dark eyes, the way he tilted his head just slightly when he looked at someone, especially when he looked at me. I saw a strength in him I admired. He wasn't big by any means. He was just about five feet ten and about normal weight for his age. He didn't have big muscles or shoulders, but he looked tight, firm, hardened not by exercise but by life itself, and for me that added a note of maturity I respected.

His nose was perfect, and his lips weren't too thick or too thin. His jaw line was a bit sharp, perhaps, but he had a male model's cheekbones. He walked through the school not so much with confidence as with indifference. His eyes were always fixed straight ahead, and when he sat in the cafeteria or when I saw him sitting in a classroom, he stared down and looked up only when he had to, but he never appeared to be afraid of anything.

The other boys in the school simply kept clear of him. When he walked through a crowd, it was like Moses parting the sea. The other students would step back. They looked like they were afraid of touching him. They glanced at him and then quickly returned to their own conversations as if he wasn't really there. I loved the fact that Del didn't seem to care at all. Their indifference reinforced his.

We're alike, I thought. Someday he'll see that; he'll look at me a little longer, let me talk to him a little more, and he'll understand and he'll smile and he'll want to know me. That was my schoolgirl fantasy before I was abruptly ripped out of public school and sent to Snob Birdland. My biggest fear was that he would think I wanted to be there; he would think I was just some conceited little rich girl.

"Teal!" I heard Mother scream. "What are you doing outside? Didn't I tell you to stay in your room? Your father is on the way home from work. Get yourself in that house and up those stairs," she ordered.

She had just pulled up in her Mercedes, stepped out, and saw me sauntering along the edge of our gardens. I saw she had a bag with the name of one of her favorite boutiques printed on the outside.

"I needed some air," I said.

"You're going to need more than some air," she fired back. "Get in that house."

I did what she said and went up to my room, where I flopped on my bed and, with my earphones still on, folded my arms and pouted, staring at the door. Soon my father would be opening it, and I had to prepare myself for that scene.

Daddy could be the most dramatic man. I think it came from his business negotiations. He was good at posturing, and no one I knew could fix his eyes on you and burn a hole through you as well as my father. It was probably that and his quick mind that had made him so successful in the business world. Carson had inherited his math abilities. It was like I was completely passed over when it came time to distributing his genetics, as far as mental capacity went. Maybe that was why he and I never got along. If I didn't resemble him in other ways, I would bet he would have accused my mother of infidelity. Even now he often had a look on his face that suggested he thought I was created with a mixture of sperm, his and some lover's my mother must have taken. What else could explain me?

The door opened slowly, and he was standing there staring in at me.

My father never hit me, never so much as raised his hand. I know there are many people who would say I am the way I am because of that. Ironically, Carson says he did spank him and once slapped him so hard, he made his head spin.

I didn't take off the earphones for a long moment. I knew that was only adding fuel to the fire, but I was trying to postpone the inevitable. Finally, I did.

"Drunk? At school?"

I didn't answer.

"I don't even want to hear an excuse. You're so clever with your excuses, Teal. You really should think seriously of becoming a defense attorney. But that would mean taking school seriously and trying to become something, do something with your life other than ruin and destroy and bring static and havoc into everyone else's life.

"I don't want you leaving this house until I say so, understand?"

"Don't leave the house? I don't have to go to school?" I asked.

"You know what I mean, Teal. Of course, you have to go to school, although I don't imagine you will last there much longer. When they kick you out, you will be in a far worse situation, believe me, so if there is any advice you should heed, it's this: don't get into any more trouble. I mean it, Teal. I have reached the end of my patience."

I started to put the earphones back on.

"Just a minute, young lady. Before you withdraw into your own world as usual . . ." he said, and marched across my room to my phone. He unplugged it. "No more private line, and you will not be permitted to make any phone calls on the family lines or my line, understand?"

"Smoke signals still okay?"

He stared at me and for the first time, I did see something more than just impatience and disappointment. His eyes weren't hot with anger. They were cold, deadly, fixed on me like a snake fixes on its prey. It actually put a shudder down my spine. I had to look away quickly.

"You're not going to go on bringing this family down, Teal. Your mother has given up, and I don't have the time or the inclination to baby you and try to convince you how you are wasting your life. Don't push me on this," he warned.

"I hate the school I'm in," I whined. "It's full of snobby girls and boys who act like they're all God's gift to women. I haven't a single real friend!"

"That's not why you're there. You're there to get an education, not to socialize. It's an opportunity other girls your age don't have, and you should make the most of it."

"I hate it," I insisted.

"You're there because you couldn't go to a public school without getting into trouble."

"I got in trouble here, too," I said, and he straightened up.

"Don't do it again, Teal." His eyes were clouding like a sky being prepared for a fierce thunderstorm.

"Now," he said in a softer tone, "I want you to spend your time thinking about your future, thinking about what you've done with your blessings. You and I will sit and talk about what you want to do with yourself."

"When?" I asked, looking up quickly. He had never offered to do that before.

"As soon as you show me I won't be wasting my time," he said.

"Oh."

"No 'oh.' I'll do it when you prove to me you're worth it, Teal. I want to see an improvement in your school work as well as your behavior. I don't want to see you giving your mother any more aggravation. If you show me you're mature and you can behave like an adult, I'll treat you like an adult and talk to you like an adult."

When will you treat me like your daughter? I wanted to reply, but I bit down on my lip and trapped the words in my mouth.

He walked to the doorway, carrying my phone, and then turned back.

"You're grounded now. You don't go anywhere but school and back, Teal. Do you understand?"

Instead of replying, I put my earphones on again and lowered my-self to the pillow to stare up at the ceiling. I didn't know how much longer he stood there looking at me. All I knew was when I lifted my head some time later, he was gone and the door was closed.

I was just as alone as ever.

3

Drifting

My three-day suspension did not pass quickly. When you have so much time to spend by yourself with no responsibilities, the clock becomes arthritic, its hands creaking reluctantly along. One of our maids who also prepared our dinners used to tell me that a watched pot never boils. Every time I asked if dinner was ready, she would recite that. I suppose there was some truth to it. I found the more I looked at the clock, the slower it seemed to move.

Without any transportation, I really couldn't leave the house. I suppose I could have called for a taxi or snuck a ride in Mother's Lexus SUV when Mother wasn't around, but there was no place for me to go during the day anyway. All my real friends were in public school. Late the first day of my suspension, a taxicab did arrive, but that was because the driver had been hired to deliver my homework assignments. I could just see my brother Carson adding that cost to his profit-and-loss statement on me. I found out Mother had asked Mr. Bloomberg if I could be given the work so I didn't fall too far behind. I didn't know how to break the news to her that I was already far behind. My report card was sure to be in Christmas colors, with failures twinkling like holiday lights.

Out of boredom more than anything else, I diddled with the assignments, getting slightly interested in the history chapter on the American Civil War. Mr. Croft sent a pile of grammar exercises, more than he was giving the rest of the class, I felt sure. I knew he used homework as punishment or as a means of revenge.

On Friday, I was permitted to return to school. Even though the snob birds looked so self-satisfied about my punishment, I handed in the assignments and sat in class like a perfect little angel. There was a great temptation to chew off their feathers and wipe those gleeful smiles off their faces, but I was operating under the hope that if I didn't get in trouble right away, my father might grant me a reprieve.

At dinner that night, he cross-examined me on my day, and I tried to give him the answers I knew he would like. I had passed a science quiz with a seventy-eight and a history quiz with an eighty-two and showed them to him. He looked them over carefully, studying the grades to be sure I hadn't tampered with them. I had done that before, changing threes to eights and ones to nines.

"Well," he said, tapping the papers, "this is not terrific, but it is an improvement of sorts," he relented.

I threw Mother a mournful look.

"I'm trying," I declared. "The other kids have been attending this school for years. They're used to everything," I moaned. "It isn't fair to judge me the same way. You've got to get used to new teachers, get used to the building, everything."

He looked like he was softening, so I continued.

"It's always harder when you attend a school or do something you've never done before. It was probably hard for you when you first went to college, wasn't it?"

"No," he practically bellowed back at me. "I had good study habits and I had a determined purpose," he said, continuing to hold on to his steel spine. "Challenges weren't challenges if they weren't hard. You can't be proud of yourself for hitting soft balls, Teal. If you want to survive in this world, you have to toughen up."

"Well, I'm trying," I whined.

"See that it continues," he said, glancing at Mother, whose neck muscles were straining. They always did when there was any sort of tension, especially at the dinner table.

I lowered my head and returned to my seat. Then I looked up as if I had just remembered something.

"Can I go to the mall tomorrow? I'd like to do some shopping," I said. "I need some things."

He continued to eat without replying.

"I'll come right back."

Still he was silent.

"I can't be locked up here like a prisoner!"

"Oh, let her go to the mall," my mother said, acting as if she was now having trouble breathing.

My father glared at me.

"I shouldn't let you out of here. You haven't done enough yet to make up for all the trouble you've caused your mother and me," he said. He paused, shaking his head. "It's a mistake, something I'll regret, I'm sure. Okay, but I want you back here before five, understand?"

"Yes," I said quickly before he changed his mind.

"I mean it, Teal. If you don't get back here by five on the dot, I'll have you locked in your room."

"I will!" I cried even though I had no intention of doing so. I would come up with some plausible excuse. Like he had said, I was good at it. "Can I use the SUV?"

It was the vehicle Mother was supposed to use when she went shopping, but she was still favoring the Mercedes sedan.

He put down his fork sharply.

"I'm glad you asked that. I had forgotten that I just received a serious warning from the police department concerning seven parking tickets I never knew you had gotten when you did use it."

I shook my head.

"I don't remember any parking tickets," I said. I did, of course. I had merely torn them up and thrown them away. My friends at public school thought that was funny. "You know," I added before he could speak, "I heard that for a joke some kids were taking parking tickets off the cars before the owners could find them. I'm sure we're not the only ones the police are giving serious warnings. Call your friends at the mayor's office if you don't believe me. You'll see I'm right," I said.

"You didn't do that, too, did you—take parking tickets off people's cars, Teal?" he asked, his eyes narrowing with suspicion.

"No, Daddy. That's really juvenile."

"I'm glad something is below you," he muttered. "Speeding tickets aren't, however, are they?"

"I haven't had one since . . ."

"And you better not have another, young lady, or driving my vehicles will become prohibited forever, understand?"

"Yes," I said.

He picked up his fork again.

"You can take a cab both ways. You don't need to take the car."

"But—"

"I want you back by five," he repeated sternly, which I knew meant the conversation was over.

"Okay," I said in a small voice. It was never good to argue too much with him.

"We do want so much to give you things, honey," Mommy said,

reaching over to put her hand over mine. "We want you to be happy and to succeed in life, but you must improve your behavior."

"I know," I said, nearly whimpering. She patted my hand and smiled.

I could be so agreeable when I had to be. Inside, that second self my therapist used to talk about was laughing so hard, I thought she would break out and dance on the table.

"We have so much," Mother went on, "so much to give you if you will just be kind to yourself first."

I nodded.

"May I be excused?" I asked. "I want to soak in a bubble bath."

Mother smiled. Doing feminine things reinforced her lifestyle, validated it. If I could just be more like her and care about my hair, my skin, my fingernails and toenails, we could go off to the great beauty parlor in the sky together, mother and daughter choosing antioxidants and nail polish. Afterward, there was always lunch at the club with the ladies' auxiliary or some such charitable organization. What else could I possibly want out of life?

"Go on, go on," Daddy said, "but keep everything I've said here," he added, pointing to his temple.

Right, Daddy, I thought. I'll keep it there in your head, not mine.

Off I went, smiling to myself and thinking about Del Grant.

After my parents went to bed, I snuck out of my room and down to Daddy's office, where I called Shirley to determine a time and a place in the mall where we would meet.

"Why don't we just meet at Del's pizza parlor," she suggested, her voice full of giggles.

"Not a bad idea. That's what we'll do," I said, and hung up. I practically floated my way through the hall and up the stairs to my room, closing the door so softly, it was as if a breeze had passed through and nothing else. All the echoes, the lectures, and the threats were left outside.

Then I curled up in bed and dreamed the dreams I wanted.

I slept late and then, when I finally rose, I spent my time deciding what I should wear and how I should style my hair. Mother, passing by, was pleased I had put on the pair of designer jeans she had bought for me last month. They were hipster denim with a sash. They cost four hundred fifty dollars. If Mother hadn't seen the jeans advertised in *Vogue,* she would never have bought them for me. Normally, I wouldn't care, but I wanted to look outstanding and a little older so Del would notice me quickly. With my matching tight-fitting short-sleeved silk blouse, I thought I looked very sexy. I wore a bra because my father went into a small rage whenever I didn't, but as soon as I left the house, I would take it off.

I brushed my hair back and even put on a pair of earrings.

Someone else's mother might have questioned why her daughter was getting so dressed up just to go to a mall, but not mine. She would do the same thing just naturally. She wouldn't leave the house even to go to the post office unless she was prepared to have her picture taken for *Cosmopolitan* or some such magazine. As far as she was concerned, there was only one place where a woman should not have herself put together as perfectly as possible, and that was in her own bedroom. She shouldn't step out unless she was dressed well enough to meet the President of the United States.

I was only interested in meeting Del Grant.

Mother left the house before I did, and Daddy, of course, had long gone to his office. He worked six days a week, sometimes seven.

I started to call for a taxicab and then put the phone down and checked to see if the keys to the Lexus were where they usually were in Daddy's den. They were. I can be back before either of them return, I thought, and snatched them up. It would make more of an impression if Del saw me driving this.

Shirley was at the mall on time with Darcy Cohen, and Selma Wisner beside her.

"So how is life in the clouds?" Darcy asked immediately. She was a tall, thin redhead with patches of freckles on her cheeks and lips so orange, she never needed lipstick.

"I'd rather be in Philadelphia," I said.

"What?" Selma asked, grimacing like she had a toothache.

"That's something my father is always saying when he's unhappy. Someone named W. C. Fields had it written on his tombstone."

"In other words," Shirley told her, "Teal hates it."

"Oh. Well, why don't you just say you hate it?" Selma asked me.

"I did."

I looked through the window and saw Del preparing a pizza. He caught sight of me and paused. I smiled and he nodded. Darcy caught our exchange.

"You know they might take his brother and sister away from his mother," she said.

"Really? Why?"

"She's so drugged out most of the time, they don't even get fed," Darcy said. "His house is such a mess, even the rats are deserting it."

"I feel so sorry for Del," Selma moaned, looking at him. "It's ruining his life."

"I bet you feel sorry," Shirley told her, "so sorry you wished he would ruin yours."

"I do feel sorry, and not for those reasons!" she cried, but stole another quick glance at Del.

"Forget it," I said, pretending to have no interest. "What are you girls doing for fun these days besides painting your toenails and dreaming so hard of lovers you might get yourselves pregnant?"

Selma blanched and Darcy laughed.

"It's been very quiet since you left," she said. "Same old, same old."

"Why? What great things have you done at your precious private school where everyone is prim and proper?" Selma threw back at me.

"Actually, Teal was just suspended for being drunk in school," Shirley announced. The two looked at me.

"Really?" Darcy asked. "Suspended already?"

"Big deal," I said. "This place is so quiet," I added, looking around. I kept stealing glances at Del, who looked like he was stealing glances at me. "I tell you what. Let's play shoplifting."

"Oh, come on," Selma said.

"Scared?"

"No, it's just that we haven't done that since we were twelve, have we, Darcy?"

She shrugged.

I looked at my watch.

"Okay, here's the deal. In a half hour we return here and compare. Like always, whoever has the most expensive thing gets her every wish and command and the rest of us are her slaves for the remainder of the day."

"I hate this game," Selma said. She looked at Shirley and Darcy, who weren't agreeing with her, and then said, "Oh, all right."

"Go," I said, and they fanned out. I watched them for a moment, and then I went into the pizza parlor.

"Hey," Del said. "I thought you moved away or something."

"Something," I said, happy he had started the conversation. He laughed. "My parents forced me to attend this private school where everyone thinks she's better than anyone else."

"You don't have to go to a private school to meet people like that," he said, and returned to the pizza he was preparing.

"I heard you left school," I told him when he drew close again.

I didn't think he was going to respond. I stood there, waiting. He served another customer and then he returned to me.

"I left it years ago," he said, "only I was the only one who knew."

I smiled.

"Where are your friends?" he asked.

"Oh, doing my bidding as usual," I said. His smile widened.

"And what exactly is that?"

I told him our game, and he shook his head and walked off to serve some other customers.

He thinks I'm kidding, I thought. I decided to show him and hurried out. I went directly to Mazel's jewelry store because I had a good plan. Mother had bought a number of pieces there, including the bracelet I now wore on my wrist, and Mr. Mazel knew my father well. Everyone here did. Daddy had built the mall.

Mrs. Mazel was catering to a customer, and Mr. Mazel was in the rear working on repairing a watch.

"Oh, Teal," Mrs. Mazel said, "how are you?"

"I'm fine," I said, smiling. "I'm just thinking about what I'll buy my mother for her birthday this year."

"That's nice," she said, and called to her husband, who came out with a forced smile on his face.

"What can I do for you?" he asked.

"I'm just looking to see what would make a nice birthday present," I repeated.

He nodded and tightened his lips as he perused his own jewelry case.

"Bracelets are nice, especially with matching earrings," he suggested.

I looked into the case.

"Yes. Could I see a few?" I asked.

"Which?" he returned.

"This one, that one, and that one," I said, picking out three randomly.

They looked like they all weighed a ton as he put them on the counter.

"The ones you have chosen are expensive," he warned.

"Oh, and those earrings and those," I said, ignoring him and pointing.

He looked at his wife and then brought them out.

Another customer entered the store. I pretended to really be considering the bracelets, taking each and trying it on my own wrist, holding it up and studying it. To do so I removed the cheaper bracelet Mother had bought for me. When I had the opportunity, I put it in the box containing the one that most closely resembled it and kept the more expensive one on my wrist.

Mrs. Mazel had made her sale and was preparing to wrap the gift box. Mr. Mazel was very involved with his new customer now.

"Thank you," I called out to him. "I have a good idea. I'll talk it over with my father and be back."

"Okay," he said, now looking like he believed I would buy something.

"Thank you," I repeated at the door and left. I hurried back to the pizza parlor.

Darcy was waiting.

"How did you do?" she asked quickly.

"You'll see," I said. "Come on inside. Del wants to see what we've done. Where are the others?"

"There's Shirley," she said, and nodded to our left. She was hurrying along, a smile on her face.

"I'm going to win," she declared.

"We'll see," I said. "Come on inside."

We entered the pizza parlor. Del saw us and meandered over.

"You can be the judge of who has the most expensive thing," I told him. He squeezed his lips in the corners, still skeptical.

We all turned as Selma entered, her brow furled.

"I nearly got caught," she moaned. "I had to pretend I forgot and then I had to pay for this," she said, pulling a silk scarf out of a bag. "It took my whole allowance! Fifty dollars!"

"That beats me," Darcy said. She revealed a fountain pen. "This was only thirty-nine."

Shirley's smile went from ear to ear. I looked nervously at Del, who was shaking his head.

"Voilà!" Shirley said, and produced a PalmPilot from her jacket pocket. "Four hundred and ninety dollars. And it was on sale. It's worth a lot more. It's the newest model."

"Sorry," I said, raising my wrist slowly. Mouths dropped.

"How much was that?" Selma asked, breathlessly.

"Ten thousand dollars," I revealed as nonchalantly as I could while looking at Del.

"How did you do that?" he asked.

"I simply exchanged my cheaper one for this one in the box. There was a close enough resemblance so that Old Man Mazel won't notice until someone else looks at it. Maybe they'll buy it anyway and he won't lose a cent," I added.

They were all speechless.

"That's pretty serious shoplifting," Del said, impressed.

"It's not important," I said.

"It's beautiful," Shirley moaned, practically swooning.

"Big deal. It's just a bracelet," I said, and unfastened it. "Here. Consider it your birthday gift," I told her, and gave it to her.

She didn't move to take it. She looked from me to the other girls to Del and then at the bracelet.

"Really?"

"I'm not impressed by expensive things," I said, my eyes half on Del.

"I am!" she declared, and snatched it out of my hands.

"That doesn't matter," I said. "You've all still lost. Can I borrow a pen, Del?" I asked him.

"A pen, sure," he said, and handed me one.

I took a napkin and wrote a list of things I needed at the drugstore and at the department store, and a CD I wanted for the car.

"Here," I said. "Take this list and this money," I said, handing Shirley five twenties, "and get me these things. Bring them back here while I have a piece of pizza. And hurry," I ordered.

They left, Shirley practically hypnotized by the bracelet on her wrist.

Del laughed. He got me a piece of pizza, and I sat at the counter and picked at it. I really wasn't hungry.

"I guess you have them wrapped around your little finger," he said, standing back, his arms folded.

"I get bored, that's all," I said. I could see he was looking at me harder and with a lot more interest. "Don't you?"

"All the time. That's why I like to work. It keeps me from thinking."

"Sometimes I think I'm years older than all my friends. It takes so little to impress them."

He shook his head.

"That bracelet wasn't so little."

I shrugged.

"It was to me."

"I know a used car I could have bought with it."

"How do you get to work and home?" I asked.

"The bus and some walking," he said.

"I can take you home today. When are you off?"

"Oh, I have another four hours here yet," he said.

"No problem," I told him. "I have all the time in the world. I'm trying to avoid going home."

He smiled.

"You and me both," he said. He went back to work, and I thought he had forgotten what I offered. Later, after the girls had returned, he came over again and said, "Four-thirty."

"I'll be here," I told him, and left the parlor, the girls trailing along.

"What was that all about?" Selma asked.

"Nothing," I said. "I'm just giving him a ride home later. That's all."

"That's far from nothing!" she cried.

I stopped and looked at her.

"Never let a boy think anything is big or important to you. Always make them feel inadequate. That way, when you do show some appreciation or excitement, they will be so grateful. Your trouble, Selma," I added, "is you give it all away too easily and too quickly."

"Me! You just gave away a ten-thousand-dollar bracelet like it was bubble gum."

"That's all it is, Selma. It's just going to take you longer to find out than it took me," I said.

She stopped grimacing and looked at the others, who were looking at me.

Was I really so different after all?

Why, I wondered, do I feel like I'm drifting away from everyone, even the friends I thought I liked?

Where was I drifting to? Where was I going?

4

Pushing String Uphill

I left the girls a little after four o'clock and waited for Del outside the pizza parlor. He looked surprised I was still there when he was ready to leave.

"You really want to take me home?" he asked.

"Why not?"

"I don't live in the best of neighborhoods. I've seen your house from the outside."

"It's just a house," I said.

"A very big house."

"Forget about my house. Let's go," I said sharply. He pulled his head back as if I had slapped him, but he walked out of the mall with me, a small smile on his lips.

I paused outside the entrance and turned to him.

"I'm sorry I yelled at you. People think it's difficult being poor. Well, it can be difficult being rich, too. Everyone has so many expectations. You're supposed to act this way and do this and be this."

"So you're the original poor little rich girl, huh?" he said, not much moved to be sympathetic.

I glared at him, and then I started to laugh at myself.

"Okay, okay, forget it," I said, and led him to the SUV.

"Nice car. It looks brand-new," he said, getting in.

"It is. My father bought it for my mother to use for her daily errands, but she won't give up her Mercedes. She thinks it makes more of an impression when she pulls up to valet parking in a Mercedes and that's important, even when she's shopping at a department store."

He smiled and looked out the window.

"I always thought there was something about you that was different from the other girls at school," he said, still looking out the window. My heart began to thump harder and faster.

"What do you mean?"

He turned to look at me.

"You seemed . . . older, like you have had more experience, and I don't mean just the kinds of things rich people can do. I guess I'm not that good at explaining things," he concluded when I continued to look at him, keeping one eye on the road ahead. "Forget it," he tagged on, almost angrily.

"No, I like that. I know what you mean, too."

"Yeah? What do I mean?"

"You knew how much I hated being thought of as that poor little rich girl you just accused me of being."

He laughed.

"Maybe, but give me the chance to hate being rich," he said.

He followed that with more specific directions to his house. We drove into the city and to the very run-down neighborhoods. Many buildings looked like they had been condemned. They were obviously empty, their windows boarded or broken. Finally, in the midst of the garbage-laden empty lots, there was a small house with not much of a front lawn left, just some weeds and patches of wild grass. The driveway was broken and pitted. The house was a faded brown, with rust stains from the broken roof gutters streaking down the siding.

"Home sweet home," he said.

I pulled into the driveway. He sat there staring at the house's front windows.

"Looks like my mother's not home," he remarked, and then added, "Damn her."

He got out angrily, seemingly forgetting all about me. I shut the engine off and followed him.

"You oughta just go," he said at the door, waving behind himself as if he wanted to shoo me off. "Thanks."

"It's all right," I told him.

He hesitated, and then he opened the front door. I couldn't help grimacing at the smell. It was a combination of neglect, stale food, something that had burned in the stove, and cigarette smoke that was so embedded in the old, threadbare curtains and worn thin carpets and furniture, it would take a hurricane to wash it away.

There were toys scattered over the small entryway and hallway.

"Shawn," Del screamed. "Where are you?"

A thin, dark-haired seven-year-old boy with sad and frightened brown eyes appeared in the living room doorway. Evidence of a recently eaten chocolate donut was smeared about his lips. His shirt was out of his pants, his fly wide open.

"Where's Patty Girl?" Del asked him.

"In the bedroom playing with Cissy," Shawn replied.

Del turned to me.

"Cissy is her imaginary friend," he explained. "Ma's not here?"

Shawn shook his head.

"Didn't I ask you to clean up the house, get all your toys and Patty Girl's back in your toy chests before I got home from work every day?"

Shawn nodded.

"Forgot," he said.

"Well, get going," Del ordered. "C'mon, or I won't be buyin' you anything more."

Shawn began to gather the toy cars and little soldiers.

"Gotta check on Patty Girl," Del muttered, and I followed him to the first bedroom on the right.

There we found his sister sitting on the floor, her overly bleached pink dress spread around her, her feet shoeless, and her light brown hair hanging limply down the sides of her pretty little face. She had Del's hazel green eyes and petite facial features. The moment she saw him she lit up, and when she saw me, she became intrigued.

"Patty Girl, did you leave your toy teacups on the living room floor again?"

"Cissy did," she said.

He swung his eyes at me.

"Well, didn't I tell you to be sure to tell her to clean up every day?"

"She doesn't listen good," Patty Girl said.

"If she doesn't listen, you can't have the toys to share with her anymore."

Her face quickly saddened.

"Go help your brother clean up the hall and the living room and I'll start making your dinner."

"Can Cissy and I set the table?" she asked quickly.

"If you clean up," he told her and she jumped to her feet enthusiastically.

"Say hello to Teal first," he ordered.

She looked at me.

"Hello," she said.

"Hi."

"Are you a baby-sitter?"

"No," I said, laughing.

"I don't need a baby-sitter. I have Cissy," she informed me, but mostly informed Del, and then hurried out of the room, carrying a limp rag doll in her arms.

I looked at the small bedroom Patty Girl shared with Shawn. The wallpaper was peeling. The windowsill looked caked with dust, the windows cloudy. There was a wooden floor with a rug between the two beds, each bed unmade. Clothing was strewn about, over chairs, over the dresser, and on the bed. I could see there were garments dangling awkwardly from hangers in the closet.

"You don't have to hang around," Del said. "Thanks for the ride."

"I don't mind," I said, and he looked at me as if I had gone crazy. "What are you making them for dinner?"

"They love macaroni and cheese, and it's no big deal to make."

"Where's your mother?"

"Your guess is as good as mine," he said. "She'll come home and tell me she was looking for a job and lost track of time or something like that."

He went into the kitchen, and for a moment, I had trouble swallowing. Dishes were piled up beside the sink, which was filled with pots. There was a garbage can with paper, wrappers, stained napkins spilling over the edges and on the floor. Used silverware was on the yellow Formica table, the forks and knives caked with old food. One of the chairs had been pulled near the cabinet, obviously to be used as a ladder by Shawn. The cabinet door was opened, and the box of chocolate donuts was on its side.

"She was supposed to clean this place up this morning," he said, shaking his head. "She probably won't even remember the promise."

He sighed deeply.

"Well, let's get to it," I told him, and rolled up my sleeves.

He turned with surprise as I began to work on the pots and pans. I smiled back at him.

"Maybe if she sees how nice it can be, she'll keep it that way," I said.

"Right. Tell me another fairy tale," he muttered, and went to the cabinet to get the macaroni and cheese.

Two hours later, I was still working on the kitchen. I had to improvise when it came to cleansers and soaps. They had very little in the pantry. While Del prepared dinner for his little brother and sister, I organized their dishes, cleaned the silverware and put it away, and did my best to wash down the broken linoleum floor. I cleaned the front of the refrigerator and the front of the stove as well, scrubbing out the stains with pure elbow grease. Then I went to work on the cabinets, organizing what they had.

I never thought about the time. I saw Del looking at the clock on the counter and realized he was waiting anxiously for his mother's return.

"She doesn't even remember what time I come home from work on days when I go in earlier," he muttered after Shawn and Patty Girl had eaten and were sitting and watching television. "She couldn't be sure I'd be back to take care of them, and she's still not here."

"Where is she, Del? Don't you have any idea at all?"

"She has these friends, barflies. I'm sure she's drunk or high on something somewhere. Someone will dump her off tonight. Usually it's not a pleasant sight, Teal, so I wouldn't hang around much longer if I were you. Besides, don't you have to get home?"

"I'll just call," I said, seeing it was already well after six-thirty. Dinner at our house was promptly at seven. It was Saturday night, and my parents were going somewhere for sure, but by now my father surely must know I'm not home, I thought. He would see my empty place at the table and he would look for the Lexus and as my mother often said, he would "go ballistic."

"Can't use that phone," he said, nodding at the one on the wall. "Our service was shut off three days ago. I didn't know she hadn't paid the bills for months."

"Oh. Don't worry. I have a cell phone in the car," I said.

"Just go home," he said despondently.

"What are you going to eat tonight?"

"I don't know. Eggs," he said sharply. "Who's hungry?"

"I'm hungry. Where's the nearest supermarket?"

"Go home, Teal."

"I'm all right. Really," I said. "Besides, it's Saturday night."

"Some Saturday night," he muttered.

"I know. I'll get us one of those ready-made chickens or something. Where's the nearest place?"

He told me and gave me directions.

"You sure you want to do this?"

"Absolutely."

"Slumming, is that it?"

"What do you think?" I fired back at him, my eyes just as hot and fixed on him as his were on mine. He softened and shrugged.

"I don't think much anymore," he said.

"So don't. Just relax. I'll be right back," I said.

I rushed out and followed the directions he had given. I thought about calling home, but then thought that if I did, my father would just insist I come right home. I was in trouble as it was, I concluded. Why worry now about how much more I'd be in by not calling and not returning?

Instead, I went to the supermarket and bought the chicken, some easy-to-make frozen vegetables, bread, and a big chocolate cake I was sure Shawn and Patty Girl would like. When I drove back and pulled into Del's driveway, I knew something was very wrong. The front door was still wide open, and I could hear the kids crying.

Slowly and now nervously, I carried the groceries to the house and hesitated at the door.

"Del?" I called.

"Get outta here," I heard. "Just go, Teal." His voice was full of hysteria.

I stood there, shuddering, my feet nailed to the concrete step.

"What's wrong?" I cried.

I heard a terrible groan. Maybe I should have turned and run. Maybe my whole life would have been different if I had, but I didn't. I entered the house and looking down the hallway into the kitchen, I saw a woman's feet and legs on the floor. I hurried down and looked at Del trying to lift his mother, who had obviously passed out. Shawn and Patty Girl were in the corner, cowering and crying.

"What happened?" I gasped.

"She came home dead drunk and then passed out. She's done it before."

"I'll help you," I said, and put the bags of groceries on the kitchen table.

His mother was about five feet eight and stout so she was heavy to lift, especially as a dead weight. Her straggly brown hair was over her face. The blouse she wore was stained and missing buttons. Her breasts sagged beneath the flimsy material. We lifted her and together, practically dragging her, brought her to her bedroom, which, although larger than the bedroom Shawn and Patty Girl had, was almost as disheveled and dirty.

After we lowered her to her bed, she moaned. Her eyelids fluttered, her arm jerked up, and then she blew out her lips and went unconscious again.

"Shouldn't we get her to the hospital?"

"What for? They'd either laugh us out of there or commit her, which might not be a bad idea. Only then, they'd come and take the kids," he said. "She'll sleep it off and in the morning she won't remember any of it, believe me," he said with disgust. "C'mon."

We left the bedroom. I looked back. She did seem dead to the world. He closed the door and turned his attention to Shawn and Patty Girl.

"Stop crying!" he ordered. "She's just sleeping, just like you two have to be doing."

Shawn had his arm around Patty Girl, who clutched herself.

"Oh, Del, they're so scared."

"Tell me about it," he said.

I went to them and helped calm them down. Then he and I put them to bed.

"I've got a beautiful chocolate cake for you two," I told them. "To-morrow, you can eat it, okay?"

Shawn nodded.

"And Cissy, too," Patty Girl said.

"Of course," I told her. She smiled and then turned over to close her eyes.

One moment they were in abject terror and the next, they were clos-ing their eyes and hoping for a candy-cotton dream world.

Where were they drifting to? I wondered. We weren't all so unlike, despite the difference in wealth. However, there was no denying that this was a more serious case of neglect than any I could ascribe to my-self. It made me think I should stop wallowing in my own self-pity.

Del sat at the kitchen table, his body slumping in defeat.

"I don't know how much longer I can keep this up," he said. "They've been coming around threatening to take Shawn and Patty Girl away. Maybe they would be better off. Maybe I should stop push-ing string uphill, huh?"

"No, they need you," I told him.

He looked up at me, and then his face softened.

"Hey, thanks for all you did. You're tougher than I thought you were."

"What did you think I was?"

"A poor little rich girl being tortured with expensive clothes and private schools, forced to go on expensive vacations with her parents," he recited.

"You're exactly right, especially the tortured part."

He laughed and looked at the bags of groceries.

"You bought all this?"

"Yes, and I'm still hungry. Help me make dinner," I ordered. He saluted and we began. Somehow, despite the scene of horror we had just gone through, we had fun doing it, and I couldn't remember en-joying a meal more.

Afterward, he helped me clean up and then we sat in his living room and talked. He told me about his father and how he became so disgusted with his mother that he just upped and left them one day.

"I was only twelve when he did it the first time, but I remember thinking he was weak. He moaned and groaned about how she was killing him and how he couldn't stand it anymore. This last time, there was no doubt in my mind he wasn't coming back. 'Maybe after I leave and really stay away, she will see how serious it all has become and then she will straighten out,' he told me. He knew she wouldn't, but he didn't care. I hope he's just as unhappy wherever he is, and I hope it's hell."

What could I say? Could I tell him I often felt as alone? Looking around his home and seeing what he had to contend with, I couldn't imagine him understanding how someone who lived in what was practically a palace and had maids and servants and beautiful things could ever be discontented. In fact, suddenly, despite the warm time we had spent with each other, he glared at me angrily.

"So now you see how the other half lives," he muttered. "You can go home and be thankful."

"For your information, Del Grant, my life is not a bowl of cherries. My parents never wanted me and, despite themselves, can't keep it a secret. My mother and I have little in common, and my father favors my brother and treats me like a stepchild. I practically have to make an appointment to see him. The only thing that gets his attention is my getting into trouble."

"Is that why you do it?"

"Maybe. Maybe I'm just bored," I said.

He smiled.

"Okay. I'll pretend you're just as unlucky as I am," he said.

We stared at each other, and then we both broke into a laugh and he leaned over right in the middle of mine and planted a soft kiss on my lips. It took me completely by surprise, and I stopped laughing. His eyes were so close to mine, I thought we could look into each other's very souls. We kissed again, this time with his arms around my waist. It was a long, demanding kiss that seemed to reach into the center of my heart. A warm glow curled around me. When he lifted his lips, I brought mine back to them. After we parted, he stood up without speaking and took my hand so I would stand up.

We walked slowly to his bedroom. He didn't put on any lights. At the side of his bed, we kissed again and he began to undress me. I stood there like a princess who was dressed and undressed every day by her servant. I was totally nude before he undid a single button of his own. He lowered me to his bed and we lay side by side, kissing softly, his hands exploring my body, making it come alive and tingle until I thought I would go mad with my wet desire.

"Last chance to escape," he whispered.

"My last chance was out there in the living room," I told him, and he laughed and undressed.

Was it reckless to make love like that, to not think of any consequences?

Yes, but I wanted to be reckless. I think that not only surprised him, but frightened him a bit as well.

"Hey," he said. "You're not thinking about tomorrow."

"I thought it was tomorrow," I said with a smile.

He laughed, but he leaned over, opened a drawer, and prepared protection.

He came at me again and we made love and clung to each other just like the two drifting lost souls we were, finding safety only in our lovemaking, in the height of excitement we gave each other. Every cry of ecstasy, every explosion inside us reassured us we had a reason to be.

The darkness we lived in fell away like an old, rotted curtain and left us standing in the light, holding hands, waiting for that tomorrow full of promises to drown our disappointments.

Afterward, we fell asleep beside each other, his arm under my breasts, his face turned to me so that his breath warmed my neck.

I was unaware of how much time had spilled, but like milk, I didn't cry over it.

Of course, I was about to learn that I should have.

5

Brothers and Sisters

"It's two in the morning!" Del announced.

He had woken and turned on a lamp. The light blinded me for a few moments.

"What?"

"We fell asleep. I'm sorry. It's two in the morning. You're probably going to be in big trouble."

"I'm used to it," I said, sitting up and grinding the grogginess out of my eyes with balled fists. I looked about the room, trying to gather my wits. Then I smiled at him. "Hi," I said.

He laughed.

"You're crazy. C'mon. Get up and get dressed before the cavalry arrives."

"Don't worry about it. They would never do that. They couldn't stand the embarrassment of any bad publicity," I told him, but started to dress.

"You haven't done anything like this before, have you? I mean, stay over at a boy's house without their knowing?"

"No, I didn't stay, but I went to a party I shouldn't have gone to when I was in the ninth grade. It was a party for seniors and I got drunk. They found out I was with a senior boy that night, too."

"What happened?"

"I made love or let him. It was my first time, so I wasn't really in any sort of control. I think I was just trying to shock my mother. I even told her what I had done."

"You told her?"

I slipped my blouse over my head and pulled it down.

"Well, I came to her and I told her I thought I might be pregnant. She never paid more attention to me than she did those weeks. Almost every morning she was there to see if I had gotten my period."

"What happened?"

"She almost had a nervous breakdown, and she had me swear and promise that I would not tell my father anything. In the end she set up a secret appointment for me with her doctor and I had to confess I had gotten my period."

"You mean you had and you hadn't told her?"

"Like I said, as long as she was concerned, she was paying attention to me. She was so relieved when I told her. She didn't even care how I had been playing with her."

Del shook his head in disbelief.

"Most of the girls I have known would have done everything they could to keep such a thing from their mothers. They certainly wouldn't brag about being with an older boy and making love when they were only in the ninth grade."

He paused and thought a moment, nodding to himself.

"What?"

"You must really hate her," he said.

That made me pensive.

"I don't hate her," I said. "Just the opposite. I wish I had a mother."

"You and me both," Del said.

He walked me to the door, pausing at his mother's bedroom to listen. It was dead quiet.

"She'll sleep into the late morning and then tell me I'm lying about everything I said happened."

"I'm sorry about her," I said. I really meant I was sorry for him and his brother and sister. He nodded and followed me out to the car.

We kissed and I got in and started away. I was more than halfway home when I saw the police car behind me, its bubble light going. I checked my speedometer. I wasn't speeding. They pulled alongside and waved me off the highway. As soon as I stopped, I heard one of them through the loudspeaker on their vehicle.

"Get out of the vehicle with your hands up," he ordered.

"What?" I cried.

What was going on?

"Out of the vehicle now!"

Heart pounding, I stepped out and kept my hands up.

"Lie down on the road and put your arms straight up," I heard.

On the dirty road? I thought. I started to turn to argue when I saw one of the policemen was out of the vehicle and had his pistol drawn and pointed at me. I practically fainted. I went to my knees and then slowly did what they had asked. Moments later, I heard them beside me. One took my left arm and brought it around behind me, then took my right arm and did the same. The handcuffs were locked on my wrists, and I was told to stand.

"What is this?" I cried.

"This car was reported stolen," the officer who had put the handcuffs on me said.

"No, it's my car. It's my family's car. I'm—"

"Move," he ordered, turning me toward their vehicle.

"I'm not lying. Check my purse. Check the registration," I pleaded.

Without responding, he opened the patrol car's rear door and guided me into it, closing the door. I watched them search the SUV, and then they returned and got in.

"I'm Teal Sommers. That's my family's car!" I screamed when neither of them made any attempt to let me free. "Didn't you look at my license?"

"Just relax," the driver said. "The car was reported stolen, and that's all we know."

He drove off. I looked back at the Lexus and then slumped in the seat.

What was going on?

At the police station, they brought me to the desk and had me booked as a car thief. I was placed in a cell, and no matter how much I protested, no one stopped or seemed to care. Finally, because I remembered from watching movies, I asked to make my one phone call and I was led to a phone.

I dialed home. It rang and rang. I was calling Daddy's direct line. He always picked up when that line rang, but instead, I got his answering machine.

"Daddy!" I screamed. "I've been arrested for stealing our own car. I'm in jail. Come and get me."

The policewoman hung up the phone and led me back to the cell where I sat waiting. Hours went by and no one came. Finally, tired from screaming and protesting, I sprawled out on the hard wooden bench and fell asleep. I woke when I heard the door of the cell rattle. The policeman said my father had come to get me.

"Finally," I moaned, and walked out.

"Just get in the car," Daddy said when I saw him at the front desk. "Go out and get into the car. It's right in front."

"Why didn't you come earlier? Why didn't you call to tell them I didn't steal the car?" I asked.

He looked at the police dispatcher and then at me and said, "But you did steal the car, Teal. I told you that you couldn't have it and you took it. That's stealing. You don't own that car. I do. Now you're known as a car thief. Happy?" he asked. "Get in the car," he ordered before I could respond.

I went out and got into his sedan. When he got in, he said nothing until we had driven away from the police station and I asked him why he had let this happen.

"You let it happen, Teal. I am not going to coddle you any longer, young lady," he said. "From now on, whatever you do, you will pay the consequences that result, no matter what those consequences are, understand?"

I didn't say anything. I turned away and pressed my forehead to the window. Right now, I thought, I'd trade places with Del in a heartbeat.

Mother was waiting in the hallway when we arrived. She stood there with her arms crossed and her lips pursed.

"Well, what do you think of yourself now?" she asked as soon as I entered. Before I could respond, she cried, "Look at yourself, your hair, your expensive jeans. You're absolutely filthy. How could you want to be seen in public like this?"

"She wasn't in public, Amanda," Daddy reminded her. "She was in a jail cell."

"Oh, dear me, dear me," she wailed. "Will it get out, Henderson? Will it be in the newspapers?"

"No, she's still a minor," he said, and looked at me. "I'm afraid she will be a minor for a long, long time, the way she is going."

"Well, we can be grateful for that, I suppose," my mother said, and sighed. "Go up to your room, Teal, and sit and contemplate what you have done and what you are becoming. I have to get to an important luncheon," she added. She made it sound as if, otherwise, she would sit and talk with me.

"Get upstairs, young lady," Daddy ordered. "Don't even think of leaving this house."

I walked up the stairs slowly and just collapsed on my bed. All I wanted to do was sleep, sleep forever. Hours later, I woke, groaned, and stretched. I did feel terribly dirty and decided to take a bath. How would I contact Del? I wondered after remembering his phone had been turned off. I had to let him know what had happened to me. I thought he was the one person who would have any sympathy.

After I had gone down to get something to eat, it occurred to me that Del would be at work. I flipped through the yellow pages and found the number for his pizza parlor in the mall and then called. He answered the phone.

"It's me," I said. "Can you talk?"

"Yeah, there's a lull."

"You won't believe what happened to me," I began, and described it all without taking a breath.

"Your own father had you arrested and left you there?"

"You heard it," I replied.

"Well, you weren't actually convicted of anything," he said, sounding like an attorney, "so he wasn't right that you're labeled now as a car thief. Besides, you're still a minor in the eyes of the law, so no one can hold what happened against you or use it as evidence in any other court proceeding."

"I'm not in the least bit concerned about any of that, Del."

"You should be," he said.

"How are things at your house?"

"My mother was still sleeping when I left the house. I made her some coffee. She sipped it and passed out again. I got the kids up and dressed and came to work," he recited, "just like I do almost every day. I hope she will get up and give them lunch at least. I can't call the house to check on it, thanks to her."

"We should both just run off," I suggested. I was more than half serious, and he heard it in my voice because he was silent for a long moment.

"I wish I could," he said. "I'd hate to think what would happen to Shawn and Patty Girl if I left them with dear old Mom."

"I shouldn't have given away that diamond bracelet yesterday. You could have pawned it and used the money."

"No, I wouldn't have taken it, Teal. My brother and sister and me are in trouble enough. I go to jail, and they go to foster homes in a heartbeat."

"It's not fair," I said.

"I stopped thinking about what's fair and what isn't a long time ago. I got to get back to work. We just got a crowd of teenagers, and they all look hungry."

"I'll try to see you later," I promised. I had no idea how I would, but I felt I had to hold on to the hope.

"Good," he said, and hung up.

I sat in the kitchen, moping. I was still in a bit of a daze from the night before. I heard the vacuum cleaner go on in Daddy's office. The maid was permitted in there on Sundays only, which meant he wasn't home either. I was glad of that. I didn't want to have another lecture. Lately, that was the sole sum of all our one-sided conversations: sermons on behavior.

Moving like a sleepwalker, I went back upstairs and moped about my room. I had a pile of homework to do, but just starting it seemed like a monumental task. I flipped through some pages and then fell back on my bed and stared up at the ceiling. Prohibited from leaving the house, I felt just as trapped as I had the night before in the jail cell. I kept thinking about Del and our time together.

Suddenly, I heard the door slam downstairs and then heavy footsteps on the stairway. Moments later, there was a knock on my door.

"Who is it?" I called.

The door opened and Carson stepped in. He was wearing a sweater and sweat pants and looked like he had just come from his gym.

"Dad told me what you did last night and what happened," he began.

I sat up.

"He left me there all night."

"You're lucky he came to take you home at all," Carson said. "What is wrong with you, Teal? Why do you keep doing these things? What do you want?"

"I want to be left alone," I snapped back at him.

"You don't want to go to school? You don't want to achieve anything with your life? You just want to party, get drunk, screw around? What?" he shouted at me, his face red, his arms out.

For a moment Del's relationship to his siblings flashed across my mind. He was the older brother and he showed them so much love and affection. Carson and I rarely ever kissed each other, rarely held each other's hands, and rarely hugged each other, even on birthdays. He was so much older than I was in every way that it turned him into a stranger, not a brother. It wasn't hard to see that he really wasn't here this morning for me; he was here because he was upset for our father and mother.

"Just leave me alone," I said, falling back on the bed.

"Daddy thinks you might need some sort of military school, Teal."

"You mean prison, don't you?"

"The last step before it, yes," he said.

Out of the corner of my eye, I watched him wander over to the windows and stare out.

"I guess I should have done more with you," he said in a tone of voice that was softer than ever. It widened my eyes. "Your birth was quite a surprise."

"For me, too," I muttered. He nearly smiled when he turned to look at me.

"I used to resent you," he confessed. I looked up at him. "You came when I was a teenager, and for nearly fifteen years, I had been the center of all the attention."

"As it turned out, you had nothing to worry about, Carson. You still were and you still are," I fired back at him.

"That's not true, Teal."

"What do you know? You were out of this house by the time I was five."

"So that's why you're doing all these things? Just for spite?"

"I'm not doing anything. I needed the car yesterday and he wouldn't let me have it. He was doing that just for spite."

"You were sent home drunk from school! What was he supposed to do, reward you?"

"He loves punishing me. It helps him forget his mistake."

"What mistake?"

"Having me!"

"They're not sending you to the right therapist," Carson decided after a moment. "You do need real help."

"Right. You can go now, Carson. You did your duty. Go make your report to Daddy and tell him I haven't set the house on fire again."

He stared at me.

"I came to offer you help, Teal. I'm willing to listen to you and to give you advice."

"If you want to help me, tell him to stop punishing me so much and treating me like a common thief."

"Give him reason to have faith in you, and he will. You'll see," he promised.

I thought for a moment. There was a line I remembered from a story we had to read for English class. A grandmother told her granddaughter, "You can get more with honey than with vinegar."

"Thanks," I said, and looked up at him. "I really don't have anyone to talk to, Carson. Mother is so involved with her social events and Daddy's always so busy and you're hardly here. None of the friends I have at the new school are nice. They're all so snobby. They hold it against me because I was in public school all this time."

"Really? What creeps."

"Yes, I agree, so I don't try to make friends with them. I'm not happy in the private school. Maybe you can get Daddy to put me back in the public school. He'll save money."

"Um," Carson said, thinking.

"It's not any better. The teachers aren't so great. I heard they don't get paid as well, so the school doesn't get the best possible teachers."

"That's true. I attended a preparatory school, you'll remember, and that wasn't so terrific."

"You know, then."

"I'll talk with him," Carson said. "Obviously, some changes have to be made."

"Thank you, Carson. I feel so helpless sometimes."

He nodded. Honey was working, I thought.

"They took away my allowance. You know what it's like being around those snob birds and not having a cent in your pocket? They don't let me forget it. They flash their fifties and hundred-dollar bills in my face."

He grimaced.

"They do?"

"Oh, every chance they get. They don't buy things. They just carry it to show off or drive the cafeteria cashier crazy by handing her big bills. She doesn't have that sort of change, so their charges get put on a bill and sent to their parents anyway."

He nodded again. I felt like a fisherman pulling in a catch that nibbled, bit, and now was easing onto the hook.

"Can you imagine what it's like for me? And Daddy thinks I'm better off there."

"Okay, okay, I'll talk to him about it all."

"Could you do one more thing for me?"

"What?"

"Just loan me some money, just so I have it on me. I won't spend it," I said. "Daddy won't let me have any, but I dread returning to school tomorrow and looking like a pauper one more day."

He bit the inside of his cheek as he thought.

"It will be just between you and me, Carson. You and I have never had any brother-sister secrets between us. Can't we?"

"Okay," he said, "but you've got to promise not to spend it and not to let Daddy know what I've done, Teal."

"I swear," I said.

He reached into his back pocket and took out his wallet.

"If you have two fifties, it would be great," I said.

He hesitated, and then he gave them to me.

"This is an act of trust on my part, Teal. Don't disappoint me."

"I won't."

"And I want to see you work harder at school until we figure out what's best for you, okay?"

"Yes, I will," I said. "There's my homework waiting on the desk," I added, nodding at the books. "I'm getting right to it."

"Get your grades up. It will make it easier all around," he urged. "That way we can take another look at the situation after the midterm period. Any change would be easier. I know what it's like to be stuck somewhere you hate, believe me."

"Thank you, Carson. This is the first time I've really felt like you were my brother."

I got off the bed and stepped up to kiss him on the cheek. He turned a little red, but smiled.

"We'll get you on the right track," he said. "Dad will be glad we had this talk, too. I promised him I would try, and he was hoping it would help."

I smiled at him, and he went to the door. He stood there a moment and then suddenly smiled gleefully.

"What?" I asked.

"Since we're sharing secrets, I have one for you."

"You do?"

"I'm going to marry Ellery Taylor. I've bought an engagement ring and will be giving it to her this week, probably Wednesday," he said. "So, you will be a bridesmaid at a big wedding this June."

"Congratulations," I said. "I like Ellery."

I didn't. She always looked like she was constipated when she was around me, and she was such a good little audience for Mother, nodding and agreeing with every silly little pronouncement. I wanted to puke, and she saw it in my face and avoided me whenever she could. She would certainly hate the idea of my being one of her bridesmaids. She would be afraid I'd step on the train of her wedding dress or something. Maybe I would.

"I plan on telling Mother and Father on Sunday, so keep it locked up," Carson said.

"My lips are sealed," I told him.

The moment he left, I went downstairs to Daddy's den and called the pizza parlor. There was a great deal of noise in the background, so I knew Del couldn't stay on the phone long.

"I'm sending something over to you," I told him. "A surprise. It's for Shawn and Patty Girl."

"What is it?"

"It's a surprise. Just do what you have to with it," I told him.

After I hung up, I called Daddy's messenger service. Then I put the two fifties into an envelope and wrote "Del Grant" on the outside. The messenger arrived, and I gave him directions. By the time Daddy found out I had used his service, it would be too late anyway and I would have time to think of some excuse like I had to get homework from someone or something.

Then I went back to my room and started my homework.

Of course, I would do better in school, I thought.

Honey gets more than vinegar.

6

A Life of Rainbows

Del was angry about the money and called me from the mall before
he left for home. Fortunately, Daddy wasn't back from wherever he
had gone on business so I was able to take the phone call. I pleaded
with Del to keep the money.

"It's nothing, just pocket money for me. I'll waste it on some new
lipstick and such. Your brother and sister have real needs and it will
help you keep the dogs off," I reminded him. "If the social worker
comes around and sees they have what they need, they won't haunt
you."

"I don't like charity," he insisted.

"Okay, so consider it a loan. When you're rich and famous, you'll
pay me back."

"Right, me rich and famous. That's a good laugh."

"I'll try to see you this week," I said. Then I heard the front door
open and told him I had to go. It was Mother bursting in with all the
latest social gossip. She couldn't wait to get to her phone to pass it on.
In her world, whoever knew something someone else didn't was the
person to envy. She barely seemed to notice me and asked me nothing
about how I had spent my day. I almost felt like telling her about Carson's impending engagement just to see the shock on her face that I
knew something so socially important before she did, but I didn't want
to lose Carson's trust.

I went back to my room and returned to my homework instead.

The next day I discovered that despite the lesson Daddy tried to
teach me by having me arrested and kept in jail overnight, no one at

school knew anything about it. Del certainly wasn't going to gossip, and I wasn't about to tell anyone, either.

All that week I did as well as I could at school. I was even nice to Mr. Croft and stayed after class to apologize to him for my previous behavior. I knew he liked things that were dramatic, so I concocted a new story.

"Not that it makes what I did right," I told him, "but I had a bad shock at home. A cousin of mine whom"—I made a point of using the correct form, practically humming the *m*—"I was very close to was killed in a terrible car accident. No one wants to talk about it."

"Oh, I'm sorry," he said. "How horrible."

"No, I'm sorry for what I did," I repeated, and assured him I would behave in his class from now on. Then, I asked him about a grammar problem I really did understand, but I let him review it quickly, pretending to grasp it finally because of his extra help, and thanked him.

Every day thereafter, he gave me a nice hello before class began. I could see the looks of confusion, even anger, on the faces of the snob birds, and I smiled to myself. I was actually beginning to enjoy being good. People, I discovered, wanted you not to be a problem so much that they were more trusting and gullible. My grades improved, and then, unbeknown to me, Mr. Bloomberg had all my teachers fill out a behavior report. It was sent home by the end of the week, and at dinner that night, Daddy surprised me by bringing it to the table and announcing what it was.

Mother held her breath as he took it out of the envelope and unfolded it.

Daddy put on his glasses and sat back.

"Apparently," he began, "every one of your teachers has indicated a significant improvement in your classroom decorum and your work ethic."

He lowered his glasses on the bridge of his nose and peered over them at me.

Mother released a deeply held sigh of dread.

"Also apparently, your experience in the real world, namely a jail cell, has awoken you to the potential consequences of your misbehavior. I say 'apparently' because I've been disappointed in you many, many times before, Teal."

"Well, if all of her teachers have only good things to say," Mother interjected, "then certainly . . ."

Daddy held up his hand and she caught her next words in her throat.

"I need to see consistency. I want to see a report like this every week from now on."

He folded the paper and put it back into the envelope.

"I understand, however, that you and your brother had a good heart-to-heart talk about all this and about your future," he said.

"They did?" Mother asked, looking from me to him. I could see it coming. "Why wasn't I told about that?"

"Carson volunteered the assignment. You'd have to speak to him," Daddy replied.

I winced at hearing my talk with my brother referred to as an assignment. Didn't anyone in this family do anything because they really felt like doing it? Was everything a responsibility, an obligation? Was it the same for all families or just mine?

"Well," she said. "He didn't mention it to me when I saw him today. I'm just surprised, that's all."

"To return to my point," Daddy said clearly, showing he didn't like to be interrupted, "you complained about the private school and apparently won over your brother's support."

"She did? He did?"

"Amanda, please. I don't know if you realize the opportunities and advantages you have attending this school, Teal. Your classes are smaller, aren't they?"

"Some are," I said.

"As you can see from this report, your teachers give you more individualized attention," he added, waving the envelope. "And more to the point, your behavior and achievement at public school have been deplorable. There is nothing I would like more than saving money. I would love you to be able to attend public school and be successful, but you haven't been able to do that, and I can see you'll be watched over more closely here. However," he concluded, unfolding his napkin to indicate the conversation was ending and we were to concentrate on eating, "should you have a successful year and still wish to return to a public school, we'll discuss it. And," he added before I could protest, "you can thank your brother that you even have that. There are other places, not so pleasant, I was beginning to envision you in, Teal. Just continue to watch your step, young lady."

He turned to the maid, and she began to serve dinner. Mother, still upset about being out of the news loop, pouted.

"I just don't understand it," she said, "I just don't. Carson never keeps anything from me. We've always been so close. As close as any mother could be with any child," she added.

I couldn't help the tears that burned under my eyelids. We've never been close, I thought. And then it came. It just burst out of me, riding atop a magic carpet of pain and rage. I couldn't help it.

"He told me he's giving Ellery an engagement ring. Supposedly he gave it to her this past Wednesday," I said, sounding nonchalant about it.

Mother's mouth dropped open so wide, her yet to be chewed pieces of lettuce and tomatoes dripped over her lower lip. Daddy glanced at me, and I knew immediately that he had known. Carson had confided in him, and what he had told me was to be our special secret, our first brother-sister secret, was really not any such thing. It made me feel better about betraying him. I would have an answer when he learned about it.

"A formal engagement? A ring?" She turned to Daddy. "Did you know about this, Henderson?"

He shook his head and went back to his salad.

"First I've heard," he said, but anyone objective who heard him say it would know he was lying. Mother, of course, chose to believe him. She turned back to me.

"What did he say exactly?"

"I don't remember his exact words," I replied.

"Well, not exactly then. What?"

"He just said he was giving her a ring and would tell you at the end of this weekend. Oh," I said, making it sound like a small added detail, "and they would be married in June."

"June!" She threw down her fork. "There's not enough time between now and June to do a decent wedding."

"Maybe they'll elope," I offered, and she opened and closed her mouth.

"They will not. They most certainly will not. Henderson?"

He shrugged.

"I don't expect they would," he said. I was sure he already knew every detail of Carson's plans.

"This is . . . astounding," she muttered. She had turned a bit white and looked like she was going to have a panic attack. "I've got to get right on the phone with Waverly Taylor." She started to rise.

"Amanda," Daddy snapped. "How can you do that? Maybe Carson hasn't even given Ellery the ring yet. You will have to wait and hear it from him. Sit down," he ordered.

Mother froze and then, as if her body had turned to pudding, poured back into her chair.

"But . . . this is a crisis, Henderson, a true social crisis. Do you know how hard it is to book the club for a wedding, or any decent hall, with such short notice? These things are planned nearly a year in advance, maybe two. You don't know about such things," she lectured him. "You're too busy in the business world. This is my world."

"Nevertheless," Daddy said calmly, "you'll have to wait to see if the event is indeed going to take place. Right now all you have is Teal's report of a conversation she had with Carson."

Mother thought a moment and then turned to me.

"You are telling us the truth, aren't you, Teal? I mean, this isn't one of your terrible lies, is it? Please, be honest," she pleaded.

"It's what I remember," I said practically under my breath, and started to eat. I glanced at Daddy, who was looking at me angrily again. He was sure to run off and tell Carson what I had done.

Mother lost her appetite. Then she said she had a terrible migraine headache and went up to her room. Daddy pounced on me the moment she left us.

"Why did you do that? Why did you tell her Carson's plans?"

"I didn't see how it would matter," I said.

"Of course you knew it would matter. You can be very mean, Teal."

"I'm not mean," I said, my tears now clouding my eyes. "It just came out."

"Your brother obviously meant to present it as a surprise to her. He was wrong to confide in you, and all that you have done tonight is reinforce the belief that you cannot be trusted. Trust is something that has to be earned, and frankly, I can't see how you will have that with anyone," he lectured.

"You hate me!" I screamed back at him.

"Lower your voice."

"You've always hated me, right from the time I was born."

"Don't be ridiculous."

"I'm not being ridiculous, Daddy. You know it's true and I know it's true."

"I don't hate you. How can I hate my own flesh and blood?" he challenged.

"You can. You don't even believe I am your own flesh and blood."

"What? That's enough. You're walking on the edge of a cliff, Teal." He pointed his right forefinger at me like the barrel of a pistol. "If I ever hear such nonsense from your mouth again, I'll . . ."

"Have me burned at the stake. I know," I snapped, and rose.

"You haven't been excused, young lady," he shouted after me. "Teal Sommers."

I kept walking and then charged up the stairway to my room and slammed the door shut. For a few moments I stood there listening. Would he come up after me? I heard nothing and relaxed.

About two hours later, I went downstairs again. I had left in the middle of my dinner and I was still hungry, so I headed for the kitchen to get myself a snack. Daddy was in his den watching television. It was rare that he sat with Mother and me and watched television. He had his own set and liked to watch shows he said we wouldn't appreciate. To ensure his privacy, he actually locked his den door. More often than not, the three of us were like strangers in a hotel, each of us off doing his or her own thing, meeting in hallways, mumbling good night or good morning.

I made myself a sandwich with some of the chicken that had been put away and ate it at the breakfast table. It was nearly nine-thirty now. Del would be getting off work at the pizza parlor in a little over a half hour, I thought. I had spoken to him almost every day, but we hadn't seen each other since I was at his house. He told me that someone from the social services department had made another visit to his house and given his mother another stern warning.

Why was it such a battle to have a family, to be a family? Why did people who should love each other hurt each other so much? All that week I had been fantasizing about us, imagining Del and me together with his little brother and sister, imagining us running off and living happily somewhere by ourselves. We didn't need parents. They didn't want us anyway. We're too much of a burden. We're in the way of their selfish happiness, I thought.

It wasn't really such a fantasy, I told myself. He and I are strong enough to work, to support ourselves and two little children. We could go someplace where no one knew us and where no one would interfere. I was sure that in time I could convince him to do this.

As I made my way back to my room, pouting and hating being under house arrest, I saw Mother had left her purse on the entryway table. She often did when she came home excited about something and anxious to get on the telephone with her girlfriends.

After being sure no one was around, I opened her purse and sifted through it. As I expected, there was money folded, crushed, and crumpled. I took it out slowly and unfolded the bills. I had nearly four hundred dollars in hand. I knew I was taking a very big chance, but I had to see Del. I had to begin to convince him that my fantasy could be a reality for us.

I hurried around to the French doors that opened from the sitting room to the patio on the west side of the house and slipped out, taking care to keep the doors from locking behind me, but making sure they looked locked. Then I ran as fast as I could down the driveway. About a half mile or so down our street, there was a gas station and a quick-stop store. I used the pay phone and called a taxi. Fifteen minutes later it arrived and I had it take me to the mall. I arrived just as Del was finishing his cleanup and closing down the ovens.

"Hey," he said, seeing me, "I thought you were home in chains."

"I was," I said, "but I broke out."

He laughed.

"I'll just be a few more minutes," he said, and I waited for him outside. Because so many of the stores were closed or closing, the mall was nearly empty, with just a few stragglers here and there. I saw none of my old friends, but I wasn't upset about that. I didn't want anything to distract me and Del.

"So," he said, coming out, "how did you manage this?"

"I just snuck out," I told him.

"Oh, no. They're not going to have the police looking for you again, are they?"

"They won't discover I'm gone. My mother is having a social and emotional crisis, and my father is locked in his den. They rarely come to my room when I close the door. I got a cab and came here, so my father can't call the police and claim one of his vehicles has been stolen."

Del shook his head.

"I've got to get home," he said. "I'm worried. My mother was acting weird this morning. I can catch the bus in a few minutes."

"We'll just take a cab. I have money," I told him, and showed him.

"Wow."

"I can get more, Del. We can save it up as I get it until we have enough," I told him as we walked out of the mall.

"Enough for what?"

"Enough to run off together. With Shawn and Patty Girl," I quickly added.

He stopped and looked at me, a small, incredulous smile on his lips.

"Run off? To where?"

"I don't know. We'll plan it out. We can go almost anywhere we want if we have enough money, can't we?"

"If your father went ahead and sent the police after you when you were gone a few hours, what do you think he'll do if you left like that?"

"I don't care. Once I'm gone, he won't care, either."

Del shook his head.

"Here's a start," I said, showing him the money again. "I have nearly four hundred dollars here. Take it and hold it safe for us."

"I can't keep taking money from you, Teal. How are you getting it?"

"It's all around the house, like dust," I said. He stared at me. "My mother doesn't even know how much money she leaves about and doesn't worry about it in the least."

"It's still stealing, even if it's from your own mother, Teal, and if I take it, I'm an accessory to the crime."

"It's not a crime!" I insisted. "Oh, Del, don't you see? It's a real chance to be happy."

"You've been with me only once, and you're ready to spend your whole life with me and help me care for my brother and sister?"

"Yes," I said as firmly as I could. "And stop shaking your head. It's true, and it's a good idea."

He walked on, pensive.

"What did you buy Shawn and Patty Girl with the hundred dollars?" I asked.

"Clothes they needed."

"See? It was a good thing, then. Why shouldn't they have what they need? Why shouldn't all of us, you and me included?"

"I don't know," he said.

"Well, I do, Del. We should and we will."

He said nothing. We paused at the bus stop.

"We can take a taxicab," I reminded him.

"The bus is good enough."

"Don't be so afraid to use my money. You'll get home faster, Del. It's better that you get home faster, isn't it?"

He looked up the street. There was no sign of a bus yet, and the street looked desolate and dark. Then he turned back to me. I knew it was painful for him to say it, to admit it, but he did.

"Yes. It's better I get home faster."

I smiled.

"Good."

"But listen to me, Teal. You can't buy love. That's just something that happens on its own. It takes time sometimes."

"I'll wait," I said, smiling. "You're worth it. We're both worth it."

He shook his head again and then smiled.

"Okay, we'll see," he finally relented.

To me it was like being promised a life of rainbows.

We made our way to a taxi stand and left for his house. The moment we arrived, Del knew something was very wrong. The front door was wide open.

We paid the cab driver. Del hesitated after he got out.

"You should stay in the taxi and go right home," Del told me, his eyes fixed on the open door. "You don't want to get involved in anything now, not after all the trouble you got yourself in before."

"It's all right. Let me be sure you and the children are okay first."

Slowly, we both approached the front entrance. We heard some laughter and Del's shoulders relaxed.

"It's just her and her sick girlfriend LaShay Monroe. She's bad news," he told me. "She's connected to some Jamaican drug king and gets my mother smoking pot and doing other things," he revealed. Although he didn't go into detail, I could see from his face that the other things were better not mentioned in any detail.

We walked into the house and looked through the living room doorway. His mother and a tall, thin Jamaican woman were sprawled on the floor with their backs to the sofa. The room reeked of marijuana.

"What are you doing?" Del asked.

They both stopped laughing and looked up at us.

"Uh-oh, it's the voice of my conscience," his mother said, and they both laughed again.

"You're disgusting," Del spit at her. "Where's Shawn and Patty Girl?"

"They're sleeping. Stop being such a long face. You remind me of your father. Who are you?" she demanded, turning to me.

"None of your business," Del told her.

"She looks like someone's business, mon," LaShay said with a smirk, and Del's mother and she went into another fit of laughter.

"For your information, Ma, if you remembered half the stupid things you do, you would remember she helped me lift you off the floor and get you into bed the other night," he told her.

His mother stopped smiling.

"Watch your tongue, boy."

"Couldn't you at least close the front door? Does everyone walking by in this neighborhood hafta know what you are doing in here? You know that could bring more trouble down on us," he chastised.

How strange it was to see the son being more responsible than his mother, I thought.

"Who cares what this neighborhood thinks?"

"You'll care if they call social services," he said.

"See," she said to LaShay. "See what I put up with? Talk about ruining some expensive weed. Just like his father, he can mess up a good time."

LaShay nodded and glared back at us as if it was true that we were the bad ones.

Del shook his head and said, "You disgust me."

He went down to Shawn and Patty Girl's room. I followed, and when we looked in, we saw they were not asleep. They were together, holding each other.

"Hey," he said, moving in quickly. "What's the matter with you two?"

"Bad dream," Patty Girl said. "Screaming for Mommy, but she didn't come."

"Oh, the poor thing," I said.

"You have to go back into your own bed, Patty Girl, or neither of you will get any sleep. C'mon," he said, and tried to lift her away from Shawn, who just looked up at us wide-eyed and held on to his little sister for dear life.

Del turned to me.

"God knows what went on here before we arrived," he told me.

I knelt down and started to reassure Patty Girl.

"I'll stay with you until you fall asleep," I promised. That brought some hope into her little eyes. She loosened her grip on her brother, and Del got him to loosen his on her. I put her into her bed and sat beside her. "I have an older brother, too," I told her, "and he told me that when I have a bad dream, I should push it back into the pillow."

"How?" she asked.

"Just push your head hard into the pillow and then close your eyes and tell your bad dream to get out. Go on," I urged.

She looked at Del, and he nodded. Then she closed her eyes and pressed her head back.

"Say 'get out,' " I urged.

"Get out," she repeated.

"Good," I said. "Just a moment."

I took the pillow out and pretended to shake the dream onto the floor.

"There," I said. "It's gone. You can sleep now." I returned the pillow under her head and she smiled. "Close your eyes and try to sleep," I said.

Del and I sat in the room with his brother and sister and whispered to each other. Outside the door, we could hear his mother and her girl-friend LaShay continue to laugh and smoke.

"Maybe your idea about running off isn't so stupid after all," he said.

"It isn't. By doing what you've been doing, all you are accomplishing is keeping them in a bad situation, Del. I know you don't want to see them separated and sent off to foster homes."

He nodded.

"You're pretty good with her," he said, looking at Patty Girl, who was now asleep.

"I guess I just think about what I wish it had been like for me when I was her age," I said. "Maybe if I had a big sister like me . . ."

My voice and my wish drifted off like smoke.

He looked at his watch.

"You had better get home, Teal. It's getting late, and you could get into bigger trouble."

As quietly as we could, we slipped out of the bedroom. We paused in the hallway. His mother and LaShay had gone into her bedroom and were now talking very low.

"She's going to get her into something very bad," he predicted. "It's just a matter of time anyway."

"We can do something about this, Del. You'll see," I said.

He nodded and smiled hopefully. He looks desperate enough to believe in the tooth fairy tonight, I thought.

"It's not a fantasy," I assured him.

He walked me to where I could get a taxi home, and then we kissed good night.

"Thanks for helping with them," he said.

I felt so sorry for him, so sad when he closed the taxi door and we started away.

He stood there watching me drive off in the taxi and then put his hands in his pockets, lowered his head, and returned to a hell far worse than my own.

7

In a Reckless Mood

I was able to get back into my house and up into my room without being discovered. It reinforced my feeling that I could do anything I wanted if I was just careful and clever enough. I was so excited about the possibilities that loomed ahead for Del and me that it took me quite a while to fall asleep. I imagined us all heading west in my mother's SUV, looking forward like explorers out to discover new worlds, every experience fresh and promising. To live without rules and restrictions, curfews and punishments was truly to be free.

As usual on a weekend, I slept late into the morning. For a while when I was younger, my father tried to get me to rise earlier and take care of my personal chores, like make my bed and clean up my room, but Mommy never liked how I did it and was always afraid someone would look in and see.

"She's deliberately messy, Amanda, because she knows you'll have the maids do everything if she is," Daddy told her, but it was less stressful for her to have the maids take care of my things than oversee the way I did it. They just had to wait for me to rise and go down to breakfast, and that was that.

Actually, what woke me this particular morning was the sound of Mommy crying. I could hear her sobbing below in the sitting room because the window was open and the window in my room was open. At first I thought it was a baby bird that might have fallen out of its nest.

Seeing and hearing my mother cry was not very unusual. She could shed tears over the smallest, silliest things, such as getting a luncheon invitation days after a friend had gotten hers, or having her name left out of an article on the society pages. What, I wondered, would she ever do if she had even a tenth of the problems Del had? So I didn't rush down to see what was wrong. I showered, dressed, and by the time I got downstairs, she was sitting quietly in the living room and just staring out the window, dabbing her eyes with a handkerchief and jerking her shoulders up like someone with the hiccups.

"What is it now, Mother?" I asked from the doorway, my voice heavy with disgust.

She turned slowly. Then she sighed deeply, so deeply someone might think her heart had cracked in two.

"I confronted your brother this morning," she said, holding her hand to the base of her throat. "He has indeed gone ahead and proposed to Ellery, but what is worse is, everything has already been decided: where the wedding will be held, colors of the gowns, favors, even the menu!"

"Well, that should make you happy, Mother. Why are you crying? You don't have much to worry about now."

She paused and stared at me as if I had gone completely insane. Then she shook her head and looked out the window again. The sky was overcast and the day looked gloomy, which I was sure fitted her mood snugly.

"Leaving me out of what is the most important day in his mature life should make me happy?" she said. "I feel like my own son stabbed me in the back."

"Don't worry, Mother. I'll be sure to have you make all the arrangements for my wedding, especially the colors of the napkins," I said, and she spun around.

"This isn't funny, Teal. How do I face my friends when they ask about the wedding? Do you know the announcement has already been constructed and sent into the papers? To have accomplished all this so quickly, Waverly Taylor must have known this was coming for some time. My suspicion is your brother gave Ellery the engagement ring long before he even told you he was going to do it and certainly long before he planned on telling me."

That was a sour note for me. She was probably right, which meant I wasn't taken into his confidence to the extent I had thought. I was so desperate to believe my brother was finally treating me like his sister that I accepted it all without any doubt.

"I'm just sick over this, just sick," Mother said. "I have a good mind to just tell them to go ahead and plan the rehearsal dinner, too. That is supposed to be my—your father's and my responsibility. The worst thing about all this is, your father isn't a bit upset and probably wouldn't mind if I did tell them that."

"He's not upset because he knew it all," I blurted. Her eyes went into that wide mode that revived my memories of ET.

"What are you saying, Teal? I was the only one in this family kept in the dark? Your brother told your father everything, told you, had his future in-laws involved, but left me out?"

My perfect brother Carson, I thought, really messed up. It brought a smile to my lips, which my mother misinterpreted as my being happy she was excluded. She bristled.

"Well?"

"I'm not an experienced detective, Mother," I said, "but the clues seem to point in that direction," I added, and sauntered off to breakfast. Perhaps I shouldn't have been so gleeful, but I couldn't help it. For once, Mother might be thinking I'm not the worse of her two children, even if that thought lasted only a few hours.

To her credit, my mother wasn't one to wallow in her self-pity all day. She got herself together and decided firmly that she would not be left out of any more decisions concerning the wedding. She got on the phone and called Waverly Taylor, insisting they meet for lunch. Whether it would be true or not, she was determined to give the appearance of having been involved in the wedding arrangements right from the start.

In fact, Mother was soon talking and acting as if nothing contrary had occurred. She was on the phone with her friends, discussing all the details about the wedding as if she had been in on it even before Ellery, much less her mother. This, she claimed, was the way she wanted it to be; this was happening because of her suggestions. Soon the talk, the plans, the excitement all served as a big distraction. No one noticed my comings and goings. More importantly, I was able to add to what I now considered Del's and my escape money, pilfering periodically from Mother's purse.

So as not to create any more complications, I behaved like a little marionette in school and continued to improve in my studies, even to the extent that Mr. Bloomberg himself made it a point to stop me in the hallway one morning to tell me how happily surprised he was by my healthy new attitude.

"I never had any doubts you could do well, Teal," he said, "if you put your mind to it."

That remark almost shattered the mask of polite smiles I wore. Who did he think he was kidding? He probably had placed a bet on my impending expulsion.

I thanked him as politely and sickeningly sweetly as I could before I continued down the corridor. I was such a perfect young lady that I thought I would puke up my breakfast, lunch, and dinner.

The only one who was really upset with me these days was Carson, who cornered me in the house one night after he had a meeting with Daddy. I never had to try to avoid Carson. Usually he took little interest in me except to give me some warning or short lecture.

We hadn't spoken since the day he came to my bedroom and offered to help me, even giving me the money, which I gave immediately to Del.

"Just a minute, Teal," I heard after he had emerged from Daddy's office. I was halfway up the stairs. I paused and looked down at him. He stood there with his hands on his hips, shaking his head at me.

"You caused quite a mess for me, not keeping our secret," he began.

"Our secret?" I said, stepping down the stairs. "Our secret, Carson? You told Daddy long before you told me, didn't you? And you had already asked Ellery to marry you long before that, right?"

"I trusted you with the news," he countered.

"What news?" I shrugged. "Mother knows the Taylors knew before she did. She's putting on a good act now for her friends, but you and I know she was devastated, Carson, and for once it was you and not me who did the devastating."

"You're such a little bitch, Teal."

"Why, because I tell it like it is, because I'm honest?"

He choked back a laugh.

"You? Honest?" He stopped smiling. "Where's my hundred dollars?"

"I used it to buy bubble gum," I said, turned, and walked back up the stairs.

"You won't have any friends, Teal," he called after me. "When people can't trust you, they won't want you for a friend."

I didn't reply. I went into my room and shut the door. Maybe he was right. Maybe I would never have a real friend. Despite the brave front I put up and my toughness at times, I did fear that I had grown like a weed in a neglected garden. Even though I could claim it wasn't my fault, perhaps, I was still not a nice person, not someone anyone would want for a friend. When I was younger, I imagined my dolls weren't happy being with me. I didn't take especially good care of them, maybe because they were tossed my way like so much pablum designed to keep me quiet in my cage.

I would show all of them finally, especially Carson, I thought, sulking in my room. Del and I would do it. We would run off and leave them standing with their mouths wide open. I counted the additional money I had stolen. It was nearly fifteen hundred dollars. I knew it wasn't nearly enough, and that made me feel sick. How long could I keep up this goody-goody girl behavior? What a fool I had been to give Shirley the diamond bracelet, I thought. I had done it to impress Del, but now it would have come in handy. Maybe I could get her to give it back to me.

I went back downstairs and waited for an opportunity to use the phone. As soon as Daddy left the house, I went into his office and closed the door softly. The phone rang and rang, but no one picked up at Shirley's house. Frustrated, I left and found Mother getting herself ready to meet someone at the golf club. I asked her to drop me off at the mall, claiming I had to buy a new pair of running shoes for physical education class. I even got her to give me two hundred dollars.

"Don't spend it all at the mall," she told me. "Keep something for a taxi home and come right home, Teal, as soon as you buy the shoes. I don't need your father chastising me for letting you run loose."

"I'm not running loose, Mother. I'm doing some important errands."

"I know that, but your father keeps talking about waiting for the second shoe to drop, whatever that means. He makes me very nervous. Just keep being good, please. What I don't need now, with all these plans to work out for the wedding, are any complications."

"I thought everything had been decided about the wedding, Mother," I said.

She smiled gleefully.

"Waverly Taylor is really not equipped to handle such an important social event. I've had to make a number of changes already," she said proudly. "She simply doesn't understand what goes with what, what is the proper etiquette, and what people of quality expect at such an event. She has money but no class," Mother added.

"She's lucky to have you, then," I said.

She looked at me, deciding whether to believe me or not. I tried to appear as innocent and as sincere as I could, and she nodded.

"Yes, she is lucky," she concluded.

As soon as I arrived at the mall, I rushed to the pizza parlor to see Del. Luckily, he was on a break. His face brightened the moment he saw me.

"I was hoping you'd find a way here today," he said. "I've got some good news."

"What?"

I sat beside him quickly. Had he come up with some money, too?

Had he found a way for us to leave sooner? We had spent so much time talking about it since I first introduced the possibility. We would lie side by side in his bed after making love and talk until it was late and I had to get home. Someone else might think we were romanticizing, but he or she wouldn't know how serious we were and how desperate we were. Desperate people do desperate things, Del told me, and I could see he had come to believe in us. It had given him new hope, and when he had hope, I had hope.

"My mother got a good job," he said, and I felt my body sink as if all my bones had turned to soft clay. That was what made him so happy?

"What do you mean? What job?"

"Hairdresser, and in a very good and busy salon, too. She's going to make some decent money. She's been clean for nearly a week now, no drugs, no booze. She's even given up smoking, realizing it's damaging her complexion."

"Oh," I said, not hiding my disappointment that well.

"And it all hasn't come a moment too soon, either. We had another visit from the social services department. When she was able to show she had gainful employment, they backed off. Maybe they'll leave us be now. Isn't that great?"

"Yes," I said, but not with as much enthusiasm as he would have liked, I know. "But hasn't she done this before, Del?"

"She has, but not with as much enthusiasm. Something woke her up. Maybe she saw something, someone go bad or something. I don't know. LaShay hasn't been around either, so that's a good sign. My constant nagging finally paid off. The kids are happier, too."

I nodded. In my closed fist, I had the money Mother had given me. Del looked at it.

"What's that?"

"What? Oh. Something more to add to our fund," I told him, and unfolded my hand to show him the four fifty-dollar bills. He stared at it.

"You have to quit doing this, Teal. It's going to become very serious and you'll get into big trouble. I can't take any more of your money," he said. "Absolutely cannot."

"Why not? I thought we had decided that—"

"Don't you see?" he cried, his face in a vivid grimace. "Now more than ever, I have to be very careful for my family, Teal. I have to continue to set an example for my mother to follow. I know it should be the other way around, but it's not, and that's just the way it is."

I closed my fist around the money and pulled my arm back.

"What about our plans?" I asked.

He shook his head and sipped his soda.

"I'm just trying to get by each day for now. Thinking about the future is a luxury."

"Not to me," I said sharply, and stood up. "I'm not going to hang around here forever. With or without you, I'm going to do something."

"Don't do anything stupid," he warned. "You've kept out of trouble this long. Don't mess up, Teal."

"Thanks," I said, and walked away. I heard him call after me, but I didn't turn around.

He's the one who's doing something stupid, I told myself. He'll see. He'll be sorry. I was his best chance and the best chance for his little brother and sister. He'll regret not taking the money, I muttered under my breath, but before I left the mall, my anger turned to sadness and depression. I felt my eyes well up with tears. Even though it was a bright day with the sky a deep, rich blue and the few clouds looking soft and cotton white, I felt a heavy dreariness.

Instead of going to a taxi stand, I just walked and walked. Every once in a while, I felt another tear trickling down my cheek and flicked it off. I wasn't even thinking about direction, so it surprised me to find myself on a street corner near a gas station, at least a good mile or so from the mall.

A young mechanic, his dark brown hair looking as greasy as his hands, bounced a tire on the garage floor and then rolled it over to the side. When he looked up, he saw me standing nearby. He smiled, wiped his hands on a rag, and brushed back the strands of hair that lay over his forehead. I should have just turned and walked away, but I was in a reckless mood. I smiled back, and he strutted out.

"What, ya lost?" he asked, looking around and seeing I hadn't driven up and wasn't with anyone.

"Maybe," I said, and he widened his smile.

In the bright sunlight, the skin on his cheeks looked like gauze because of tiny pock marks. He was dressed in faded gray overalls and was about six feet tall. He wasn't handsome by any means. His nose was too thick and his mouth too wide, but he had nice brown eyes that were fixed with interest on me. I smiled at how easy it was to capture and hold his attention.

"This your garage?" I asked him.

"Might as well be. It belongs to Benny Dodge, but he's away more than he's here. Where are you going?"

"Nowhere," I said.

"Well, you're there," he replied, and laughed. "Wanna soda?"

"Sure," I said, and followed him back into the garage. He took a can of Coke out of an ice chest, pulled the tab, and handed it to me.

I took a sip. With his mouth slightly open, he stood there watching me as if I was doing something very special.

"It's warmer than I thought," I said, and undid the top button on my blouse. His eyes traced every move I made.

"How old are you?" he asked.

"Why?"

He shrugged.

"I don't want nobody sayin' I corrupted a minor."

"By giving me a Coke? Some corruption. Is that all you have to offer?" I challenged, and he laughed harder.

"Wow." He shook his head. "What else did you have in mind?"

"I don't know," I said, and picked up the air hose. I pressed it and blew some dust around the floor. "What are you working on?"

"Rotating tires. Why? You wanna learn how to be a mechanic?" he teased.

I stared at him and drank some more of my Coke. His eyes went from side to side and he fidgeted nervously.

"Who are you?" he asked.

"Nobody," I replied.

"Nobody going nowhere?"

I dropped the air hose and walked closer to him.

"Thanks for the Coke," I said, and kissed him quickly on the lips.

His eyes nearly exploded.

"Since I'm nobody and this is nowhere, that didn't happen," I said. I smiled and started out, but he reached for my arm and seized me at the elbow.

"What are you, crazy?" he asked. He pulled me closer. "You're a tease."

"Let go," I said, but he held on and then he kissed me hard and moved his hands over my shoulders and down over my breasts. I squirmed until I broke loose.

He looked like he was going to come after me again, but a car pulled up to the pumps and he hesitated.

"Stick around," he pleaded. "I'd like to talk to you."

"Sure," I said. "I bet you'd like to just talk."

I left quickly, my heart pounding. What's wrong with you, Teal? I asked myself. That was like playing with matches. You want to start another fire, one that can't be put out with a sprinkler system?

I hated myself for being so self-destructive, so angry that I would take it out on myself. Maybe I needed to go back to the therapist.

Maybe I should be on some kind of medication. Before I knew it, I was crying. I felt the tears streaming down my cheeks as I thought about what lay ahead for me. At home it was all about Carson's wedding. My mother had some purpose. And Del was filling himself with hope and treating our plans and dreams like children's fantasies.

Why was it that I couldn't hold on to anything, care about anything?

My father is right about me, I thought. He's right to ignore me, to try to forget I exist. Maybe I could forget I exist.

I walked on and on. Cars whizzed by me, but I didn't care. At one point a driver leaned on his horn because I had stepped too far into the road, but I didn't move and he screamed something nasty at me as he went by. Finally, I reached a familiar shopping area and called myself a taxicab. It was getting very late in the afternoon, and I was sure Mother would be home by now and upset that I wasn't. She was probably on pins and needles, hoping I would get there before my father.

The moment the taxicab turned into the driveway, I wished I hadn't. I wished I hadn't come home at all.

There was a police car parked in front of the house, and without knowing why, I knew that it had something to do with me. I got out of the cab slowly and paid him. For a long moment, I just stood there, dreading going into the house. I even contemplated turning around and running off.

But to where?

Del wouldn't want me, and as Carson said, I had no friends.

What difference did it make anyway? I thought. Even if I escaped from bad news here, it was sure to be waiting for me out there.

It was just part of who and what I was. Why that should be, I really didn't know. All I knew was, it was true. Curses float around us and attach themselves to someone, I thought. It could be as simple as that. Born lucky, born rich, born poor, born sickly, whatever, it was just the way it was and would always be. Fighting it was futile.

Surrender, Teal, I told myself.

Give up.

Be who you are.

8

A Disaster Heading
for Disaster

Carson, Daddy, and two policemen turned to look my way the moment I opened the door and entered the house.

"There she is," Carson said, and shook his head.

Daddy stepped forward, the two policemen now on either side of him. One carried a clipboard. They all looked like they were poised to charge at me.

"What?" I cried, my hands out.

"Your mother," Daddy began, "actually fainted when she heard about all this. She's upstairs in the bedroom. I have called Doctor Stein, who wants me to bring her into the office to check her blood pressure." He paused, glanced at Carson, and then added in a louder voice, "She could have a stroke, Teal. That's how people get strokes."

"What did I do?" I wailed.

"Tell her," Daddy ordered the two policemen. The taller and darker-haired man on his left stepped forward. He lifted the clipboard higher and peeled away the top page.

"Do you know a Shirley Number?" he asked.

"Of course she does," Daddy answered for me.

"Dad," Carson said softly. "Maybe you shouldn't have her say anything until you call Gerald Gladstone."

"I'm not wasting good money on any attorney," my father practically screamed.

Carson pulled his lips in and stepped back.

"I would like you to answer the questions," the policeman said. "Not your father. Well, do you know her?"

"Yes, I know Shirley. So what?" I snapped back at the policeman.

Daddy's face reddened until he resembled an overly ripe tomato. I thought he was the one who would get the stroke, not Mommy.

He pointed his right forefinger at me.

"I'd advise you to be contrite, Teal. Your only hope here is that people who don't know you will take pity on you," he said.

I looked away so the policemen wouldn't see the tears in my eyes. There was more love between Del and his estranged father who deserted the family than there was between me and my father, I thought. How many nights had he lain awake wishing my mother had gotten an abortion?

"Shirley Number had a diamond bracelet in her possession. What do you know about it?" the policeman asked. I could see from the look on his face that he already knew the answer.

So that was it. I felt the blood drain from my face. Shirley had given me up. Why couldn't she come up with a story? Say she had found it, anything? Some friend she was. She had obviously led the police to me. She didn't even qualify as a mere acquaintance.

When I glanced at Daddy, I saw that by the expression on my face and my silence, I was confirming whatever he had been told. He nodded as if he had expected no less.

"She knows everything about it, don't you, Teal?" he asked me.

I looked away again. Should I lie? Should I pretend I don't know anything? I could switch things around, maybe. I could put all the blame on Shirley. I could deny, deny, deny. Why should I do anything to protect her? I thought.

"Shirley Number's father contacted the police department and we questioned her. She claims you gave her the bracelet," the policeman continued. "She said you were all playing some sort of a shoplifting game, a contest to see who could steal the most expensive thing at the mall. Is that true?"

What didn't she leave out? What a coward, I thought.

"For God's sake, Teal, at least tell the truth when you have no other option," Daddy said, grimacing.

"Yes," I admitted. "It's true. It was just a game," I added to make it seem innocuous.

"Then you admit that you took the bracelet from Mazel's jewelry store?" the policeman continued, now sounding like a prosecutor.

I didn't respond. I had told him enough. Let him do some work, I thought. The policeman turned to Daddy.

"Once we heard the story, we went to see Mr. Mazel. He checked the bracelet case in question and discovered it wasn't the right bracelet that was in it. He recalled your daughter coming in to shop for a present. He said the bracelet she switched was less than half the value."

"You switched a bracelet? What bracelet was that, Teal?" Daddy asked me.

I folded my arms and stared at the floor.

"Well?" he shouted.

"The one Mommy bought me for my fifteenth birthday," I blurted.

Daddy's head was bobbing like the heads of those toy dogs people put in the rear of their cars.

"I knew it. Buy her expensive gifts. See what it gets you," he recited as if Mother was standing right there.

"Then you admit you switched bracelets?" the policeman asked me.

"Dad," Carson said, caution filling his voice.

"No, we're not protecting her, Carson. Let her pay the price," he told my brother.

I could see it in his face. My brother wasn't worrying about me so much as he was about the family name, especially now that he was engaged to the daughter of a well-respected and influential father. Newspaper headlines flashed across his eyes, filling them with shame.

"Yes," I screamed at the policeman. "I exchanged the bracelets! Are you all happy now?"

"We'll have to take her downtown," the policeman told my father. "This is a pretty serious crime. It might be considered a felony," he said, fixing his cold blue eyes on me.

He's just trying to scare me, I thought, but Carson looked like he was turning paler and paler every passing moment. Most of the time he tried to ignore that he even had me as his sister. Now, he might try to deny it. Maybe he would tell his friends I was really adopted.

"A felony?" he said under his breath.

"The bracelet sells for ten thousand dollars," the policeman told him. "It's a serious theft."

Daddy kept nodding as if he was enjoying the policeman's evaluation. The more he nodded, the tighter the knot became in my stomach. I felt the ache spreading up my chest. He looked so self-satisfied, as if he could predict my whole life and had predicted this scene in detail.

"Take her and do what you have to do," he told the police. He turned away as though he could no longer look at me.

I turned to Carson. He really looked sad for me now, the sadness overcoming any disgust.

"Come along," the policeman ordered.

The two of them stepped between me and my father and brother.

"I want to see Mommy first," I cried.

She doesn't want to see you," Daddy muttered.

"No. I won't go until I see her," I insisted. She would make him help me.

"You're not seeing her, Teal. She's taken one of her tranquilizers and she is resting quietly," Daddy said. "I won't permit you to risk her health another moment."

"I thought you said you were going to take her to the doctor."

"Later. Right now, no one feels like stepping a foot out of this house," he added. "The disgrace is so thick we can feel it in the air."

He nodded at the policemen, and the one with the clipboard seized my elbow and physically turned me toward the door.

"Mommy!" I screamed at the stairway.

"Dad," Carson cried.

"Leave it be!" my father insisted.

I don't know why I was so surprised, so shocked at my father's attitude. After all, he was the one who had me picked up for stealing our car.

I was led out of the house and quickly down to the patrol car, where I was placed in the rear behind the cage, a place growing more and more familiar to me. The door slammed on me again, and moments later we were moving away from the house. I sank back in the seat, first cursing Shirley and then cursing myself for being so stupid as to trust someone like her.

When we arrived at the police station, the desk sergeant looked at me as though I was a career criminal.

"What happened, you missed your holding cell and just had to get back to it?" he asked through the right corner of his mouth. Then he grinned at the other policemen.

Once again I was put through the booking process and led back to the Spartan cell where there was now a woolen blanket on the bench. A man who looked like a homeless man was sleeping on the floor of a cell across the way. After I was locked in, I realized there was no point in asking for my one phone call this time. Who would I call who could help me? My father wouldn't let me speak with my mother.

I crawled over the bench, put my head on the folded blanket, and closed my eyes. Maybe, if I'm lucky, I thought, I'll fall into a permanent sleep like Rip Van Winkle or Sleeping Beauty and I won't wake up until Del decided I had been right and had come to kiss me and take me away just like the fairy-tale prince. And of course, we would live happily ever after.

I spent all night and half the following day there before Carson came to get me. Daddy had sent him like some gofer to do some unpleasant chore.

"What's going to happen to me, Carson?" I asked. I was stiff from being so uncomfortable, and very tired.

"Lucky for you, Daddy calmed down enough to realize nothing would be gained for the family to have you convicted of a crime and sent to prison," he told me as we left the station. "He went over to see Mr. Mazel and got him to drop the charges."

"He did?"

"Yeah," Carson said, pausing at the car. "Do you know how he did?"

I shook my head.

"By buying the necklace. That's right, Teal, it cost him ten thousand dollars to fix the mess you created this time, ten thousand dollars! And Mother doesn't want to wear it. She says it will only remind her of the terrible thing you did."

"You going to add this to the profit-and-loss sheet you and Daddy are keeping on me?"

"Go on, be a smart aleck and see how much more it will get you now," he said, getting into the car.

For a moment I actually considered just turning and running off, even without a cent to my name. I'd be better off living in the streets, I thought.

"Get in, Teal. We have a lot to do yet," Carson ordered.

I got in and folded my arms around myself defiantly.

"He didn't pay the ten thousand for me," I said. "He did it for himself and for you, to keep things quiet."

"Same thing," Carson said, driving away from the police station. "We're a family."

"We're supposed to be a family. We're not a family, Carson, not by a long shot."

"Oh, boy. What are we going to hear now, the poor neglected me song?"

"No. You won't hear another word," I said, and pressed my lips shut.

He rattled on and on about the sacrifices our parents had made for both of us, especially me, describing the great efforts they had made and were making to find a way to get me to behave, be mature and responsible, and have a decent future. As I sat there and his words went in one ear and out the other, I thought how much like each other my mother, father, and brother sounded whenever any of them spoke to me. Never before did I feel it was me on one side and them on the other as much as I did this particular morning.

"Dad said you should remain in your room until he gets home today," Carson told me when we reached the house.

"What happened with Mommy?" I asked him.

"She went to the doctor and he put her on a new tranquilizer, but she had a meeting with Waverly Taylor and a wedding planner this morning and hasn't taken any of her medication yet."

"What a trooper," I muttered.

"You know what, Teal," Carson said, his eyes narrowed and dark, "I really don't think anything Dad does will make a difference with you. You're a disaster heading for disaster. It's just a matter of time, a matter of what you will do next to destroy yourself, and frankly, I'm not going to get myself sick over it."

"Like you ever did," I said, and got out, slamming the car door closed behind me.

He drove off before I reached the front door.

I watched his car disappear down the driveway. I've always felt like an only child, I thought. This just confirmed it. I wanted to be glad. I wanted to be defiant and hateful and not care, but the tears still came into my eyes. Why were Carson and I so different from each other? Was it just because I was born so much later? It was truly as though we had two different sets of parents. Why was he the lucky one? Why was he born first, born when they wanted a child more, when they had more time to give and to love?

It's so easy for Carson to look down at me from his mountaintop. He had been brought through all the valleys and over all the difficult terrain comfortably, with loving care, and gently placed in a seat of substantial success. I was still struggling to get a foothold, to hold on to anything that gave me even the semblance of meaning and self-worth. Was it really all my fault?

I went inside and up to my room. The experience of being arrested and held without the prospect of hope had been far more exhausting mentally and emotionally than I had imagined it would be this time. The moment I lay down, I was asleep. Hours later, I felt the bed shake and opened my eyes. Daddy was standing there staring down at me.

"Did you enjoy your second night in jail, Teal?"

I didn't answer. Instead, I turned away and stared out the window at the gray sky.

"Okay," he said, "this is how it will be until further notice. I've hired a driver who will take you to school in the morning and bring you home at the end of the day. He will take you nowhere else, so do not ask him to do so. You will come home, do your homework, have your dinner, and go directly to your room. You will speak to no one outside of this house, accept no invitations, even to go shopping, which to you means stealing anyway. You will be permitted to go with your mother to shop for the things you will need for Carson's wedding. Other than that, you will spend your weekends confined to this house and these grounds. You will invite no one here and accept no invitations."

"I would have been better off in jail," I moaned.

"Maybe I should have let you be tried and convicted and go to jail, Teal. Perhaps that would have been the only way you would know for sure that you would *not* be better off there. However, there are other people to consider here, other people who would be hurt more than you, in fact, and you can be thankful for that. Otherwise, believe me, I would not have hesitated to leave you there. Nothing else I've done or tried to do has had any success with you.

"Let me assure you," he continued, "that if you get into any more trouble at school, if your grades take a dive, this confinement will continue. Your therapist calls this tough love. As hard as it is for you to believe, it is tougher on your mother and me than it is on you. I try not to worry about her and about you at work, but it's not easy to do."

"Maybe I'll die and you'll be happy," I said.

"Self-pity won't work with me, Teal. Don't waste your time on tears and threats and moans. You'll behave yourself. One way or another, I'll make that happen."

He started for the door and then paused and turned back to me.

"The only thing going for you is the fact that you committed this disgusting deed before you were repairing yourself at school. I'm hoping that you did turn a corner and you will do a lot of soul-searching and continue on that track. If you do, we'll ease up on the restrictions. How you live and how you enjoy your life from this moment on is therefore solely up to you."

"It's always been up to me," I muttered under my breath. If he heard me, he didn't care to react. He stared a few moments more and then left, closing the door behind him.

To me it sounded like the door of the police cell, clanking and rattling.

When Mother came home, she looked at me as if I was someone suffering from a terminal illness. Her face was full of pity, her eyes gray with sorrow.

"Teal," she said, pronouncing my name like she would if she were standing over my grave, "Teal. I feel so sorry for you, so helpless. Forget about your father, your brother, and me for a moment. When you do bad things to people, do you ever think about the pain you cause them? Can you imagine how poor Mr. Mazel must have been suffering when he discovered his loss? His is a small, family-owned store. Do you ever think of such things?"

I didn't answer, but I knew the short answer was no. Whatever I did, I did on the spur of the moment. Consequences for myself and for the people involved never played on my thinking or my actions. I was truly like some hysterical person, flailing about, casting myself every which way, looking for some relief from my own unhappiness. The therapists at least got me to see and believe this.

But I didn't even know how to begin to explain that to my mother, so I continued to avoid her eyes. She sighed as deeply as ever and then added, "I guess I have to turn you over completely to your father, Teal. I can't interfere anymore. I can't plead for you anymore. I've failed you," she said, and then I looked up at her.

Oh, Mother, I thought, you don't know the half of it. You have no idea how long you have been failing me: all my life. Maybe she saw that in my eyes, for she turned briskly and walked away, returning to her favorite topics, Carson's wedding and other social events.

Daddy wasn't kidding about the driver. Apparently, he hired a former gangster hit man, I thought, because the man, a stout, dark-haired man with beady eyes and a neck that looked like it belonged on a young bull, gazed at me with a no-nonsense expression that shouted, "Don't give me any grief." He didn't introduce himself or even say good morning. He just grunted at me and started the car. Daddy had at least told me his name was Tomkins, but I didn't know if that was his first or last name.

At the end of the day he was there standing by the car, looking like a secret service agent. I saw the curiosity on the faces of the other students. To be sure, there were some others who had cars and drivers taking them back and forth to the private school, but most, like me, had been forced to ride the bus.

As I approached the car that first day, Tomkins looked at his watch. "You're ten minutes late," he chided.

"One of my teachers kept me to explain something. Sometimes, I have to stay after an hour or so for remedial work," I told him.

"This is the time I know to pick you up," he said firmly, tapping his watch. He looked like he could lunge at me and tear off my head. "If there are any changes to be made, it has to come from your father. Otherwise, I'm instructed to go in there and get you. One way or another, I will do that," he added, leaving little to my imagination. He opened the rear door and growled, "Get in."

I didn't know who I was more angry with at the moment: myself for getting into this situation, Del for backing away from our dream plan, or my father, who was like a prison warden. The ride home was dreary—no music, no conversation. When we arrived, Tomkins remained for a while to be sure I went into the house. I expected he would be out there, parked on the street, waiting to see if I would break my father's rule and try to leave the grounds.

I got my second shock after I changed my clothes and went downstairs to call Del at the pizza parlor to see how things were going for him. The phone on the kitchen wall was gone, and the phone in the sitting room was gone. Daddy's office-den door was locked. There wasn't a phone for me to use downstairs. I spun around in the hallway as if I had just gotten off a merry-go-round. I am truly in prison, I thought. It's even worse. It's solitary confinement.

Angry and even in something of a panic, I hurried down the corridor to the stairway and ran up. There were two phones in my parents' bedroom, but to my disappointment, I found that door locked as well. I rattled it angrily.

"You can't do this to me!" I screamed.

One of the maids downstairs called back to see if there was something wrong. I didn't answer her. I went into my bedroom and slammed the door. Daddy's strategy was to put the phones back when he returned at the end of the day. Mother was strictly forbidden to permit me to use their phones. I felt like I was being choked.

I will run away, I thought. I will.

The next day, I managed to talk Lisa Hardwick into letting me use her cell phone during lunch. Del had just arrived at work in the pizza parlor. I hurriedly told him all that had happened to me so that he wouldn't think I was avoiding him or had decided not to see or speak with him ever again.

"I had a feeling something like that might happen, Teal. You went too far when you took that bracelet, and it was stupid to give it to someone like Shirley."

"I know. I was just trying to impress you," I confessed.

That softened him.

"Yeah, well, just be yourself, Teal, the way you are with my little brother and sister. That's enough to impress me."

"I'm glad, Del. I miss them. I miss you. How are things?"

"My mother is still holding on to her job and doing well. I'm holding my breath, of course, but it looks good."

"I'm happy for you, Del."

"Don't do anything to get yourself in any more trouble," he said. "Maybe your father will ease up."

"I doubt it, Del, and I hate my driver. He's like a prison guard! You still want to see me, don't you?"

"Sure," he said.

I wanted to say so much more, but Lisa was standing over me, eager to get back her phone.

"I'll call you again. I'll figure something out."

"Whatever," he said. "Be careful," he added, and told me he had to get back to work.

I closed the phone and handed it to Lisa.

"Thanks," I said. "Could I use it again tomorrow?"

"It's expensive," she replied, grimacing through her braces.

"I'll give you ten dollars for five minutes, okay?"

She shrugged.

"Maybe," she said, enjoying her power over me and my desperation. "I'll see."

How I hated these snob birds and wished I could somehow pull out their feathers and keep them from flitting about, so contemptuous of everyone below them.

My day will come, I told myself. It will come.

9

Ten Thousand Dollars

I managed to steal twenty dollars from Mommy's purse that night. The next day at lunch, Lisa lorded it over me, practically making me beg her for her phone in front of the other girls. I swallowed my pride and did so. Finally, just before the bell was going to ring and make it impossible for me to use the phone, she relented and I gave her the ten dollars.

"Frozen custard for us after school today," she announced, waving my ten dollars like a flag, "on Teal Sommers."

The girls laughed.

I turned and called Del, but was disappointed to learn he wasn't at work.

"He's coming in at four today," the other counterman said, and hung up.

"That was an easy ten dollars," Ainsley Winslow cried when Lisa took the phone back. The girls laughed again, all smiling gleefully.

I hurried away, never feeling more helpless. I won't let this go on, I vowed. I won't.

With my driver herding me into the car and watching my every move, and with the house locked up like a penal institution, I boiled over with frustration. I couldn't call Del and I couldn't leave school and go to see him. After I was brought home at the end of the school day, I thought about breaking the lock on Daddy's den-office door so I could get to his telephone and actually went down to the kitchen and got a butter knife out of the silverware drawer. What more could Daddy do to me anyway? I decided.

Just as I was at the door, however, I heard the front door open and Daddy and Carson speaking as they entered. Why were they here this early? Was Daddy coming to check on me?

Panicking, I retreated to the powder room across the way. I heard them laughing, and then I peeked out and saw Daddy unlock his door.

"What a pain in the rear this is," he told Carson, "locking and unlocking my own office in my house, but for a while, I have to be sure she doesn't disobey me. And there's no doubt in my mind that she would if she could."

"I know, Dad. I'm sorry," Carson said as if he bore some responsibility for my behavior.

They entered his office, leaving the door open. Maybe they would forget and leave it that way, I hoped, and waited, watching them and listening.

"It was easy for Broderick to pay us the retainer in cash," Daddy told Carson. "We're saving him a ton of money and he knows it."

I saw Daddy put a stack of bills on the desk, open his top desk drawer, take out a key, and then go to his wall safe and take out a metal cash box. Neatly, he put the money into the box.

"Ten thousand tax-free dollars!" Daddy declared. Carson laughed. "I hope you're learning how to handle some of these clients of mine," Daddy continued. "Someday, you'll be in charge of the company, son."

"You're not retiring for a long, long time, Dad," Carson told him, and Daddy smiled at him with such love and pride, I felt my heart ache. Paranoia or no paranoia, I thought, I never felt him look at me like that.

Daddy put the cash box back into his wall safe and put the key to the safe in his top drawer. Then they sat and began to talk about another project.

Boring, I thought, and slipped out and up the stairs. I'd wait to see if Daddy would leave and forget to lock the door. Hours later, Carson left, but Daddy didn't. I heard him come up and go to his bedroom. When I went down to check the office, the door was locked again. Disappointed, but too frightened to attempt anything with the butter knife now, I retreated to my bedroom.

Later, dinner was conducted in the usual fashion it was conducted these days: a cross-examination of my activities, my school work, and my behavior. Mother sat looking as if she was the one being questioned and prodded. She kept her eyes down, held her breath, and nibbled on her food like a squirrel.

"Remember," Daddy ended as he did every night since I had been arrested for the bracelet theft, "I hear that you so much as look at one of your teachers cross-eyed, and I'll tighten the walls around you even more."

What else could you do, lock me in a closet? I wanted to fire back at him, but I didn't say a word.

Instead, I waited like some predator for an opportunity, which came when he went upstairs to change into more relaxing clothes. This time he had left the office door unlocked. I snuck away from Mommy, who was on the phone, and I slipped into the office, but I didn't call Del. I was too terrified Daddy might come down and find me in his office. Instead, I went to his window and undid the lock so it could be opened from the outside. Then I retreated to my room for the night, working on my homework, more to occupy myself and pass away the time than any interest I had in the material.

Close to eleven, Daddy came up to bed. I heard him go to his bedroom. Mommy was already there, after having given herself a foot treatment. I heard their muffled voices behind the closed door and as quietly as I could, tiptoed down the stairs and out the French doors in the sitting room.

It was a cool, overcast night, with just the ground lighting and some illumination from the house helping me to find my way around to Daddy's office. I worried that he had found the window unlocked and had locked it, but when I went to it and tried, it opened and I was able to climb into the room. I dared not put on the lights. Carefully, I picked up the phone and punched out the number of the pizza parlor. If Del had come in at four in the afternoon today, he would still be there to close up, I thought. It rang and rang until finally someone picked up and I asked for Del.

"Who?"

I was afraid to raise my voice too loudly, but I took a chance.

"Del Grant," I said.

"Del Grant?" I heard a voice I didn't recognize ask.

"Yes."

What other Del would be there? I wanted to snap at him.

"He couldn't come in today. He had problems," the man said.

"What kind of problems?"

"Family problems."

"What do you mean? Anything happen to his little brother or sister?"

"What do I look like, the Albany newspaper?" he griped, and hung up.

Couldn't come in? Family problems? What could have happened?

How was I supposed to go back up to my room and sleep? The very thought of having to beg Lisa for use of her phone again tomorrow sickened me. I've had enough of this, I thought. I don't care what happens to me now.

I went back into the house and found the SUV keys where they always were. Daddy didn't hide them. He couldn't even imagine my taking that car again, I thought. He was so confident I was too afraid. Well, I was, but this was more important to me. I wasn't going to let my fear stop me.

Our house was so big and my parents' bedroom was at the far end in the rear, so there was little chance of their hearing the SUV being started. Nevertheless, I drove out very slowly and kept the headlights off until I was out of our driveway and had turned onto the road. Then I gunned the engine and drove as quickly as I could to Del's house.

All the lights were out when I arrived. It was late now, close to midnight, so I shouldn't have been surprised, but after hearing what the man at the pizza parlor had said, darkness frightened me. I wasn't sure what I should do. What if it wasn't as serious a situation as the man had made it sound? Wouldn't I cause more trouble by appearing at Del's front door now? His mother might become very angry, and I might be responsible for bringing unpleasantness just when things were going well for Del and his little brother and sister.

I sat there, trying to decide, and finally concluded that since I had come this far and taken this great a chance, I had to do something. I couldn't just drive off and forget about it. As quietly as I could, I got out and approached the front door. Hopefully, Del will wake first and come to the door, I thought, and tapped lightly. No lights went on, and I didn't hear any sounds from within. I knocked harder and waited. Still, no light went on and no one came.

"Del!" I called. "It's me."

A dog began barking next door. I heard someone scream, "Be quiet!"

Disappointed, I turned away and started back to the car, but just before I reached it, a taxicab pulled up behind it and Del stepped out of the rear, holding Patty Girl in his arms. Shawn got out after him and immediately took hold of his jacket.

"What are you doing here?" he asked, the moment he saw me.

"I called the pizza parlor and some man told me you had family problems."

"You could say that," he remarked, and paid the taxi driver.

"Hi, Shawn," I said. "Can I take your hand?"

He looked at Del, and then he offered his hand to me.

"What's happening? What's wrong?" I asked.

"I'll tell you all about it after we get them to bed," Del told me.

They were both so exhausted, it didn't take long. The expressions on their little faces told me the exhaustion wasn't only physical. They were overwhelmed with fear and emotional trauma as well. As soon as we closed the door on their room, Del lowered his head.

"She overdosed," he muttered.

"What?"

"She's in the hospital, still in a coma. I stayed as long as I could with the kids." He shook his head. "I'm disgusted with her. I don't even feel sorry for her. She went off with that LaShay after work and she mixed a few things, including a lot of cocaine. I got the call just before I was supposed to leave for work myself and she was supposed to be home to watch the kids."

"Oh, Del, I'm so sorry."

"Yeah. It's just a matter of time now before the social service worker will be back at that door, this time to tell me they're going to foster homes," he said sadly, and flopped onto the chair at the kitchen table.

"You want me to make you something to eat?"

"No. I had a cheese sandwich at the hospital, and my stomach regrets even that," he replied. He stared so coldly at the wall, I felt my heart ache for him. "I don't know why I let myself believe her."

"Because you wanted it to be true so much, Del. Don't blame yourself for trying to be hopeful."

He nodded.

"You're right. I guess when you're desperate, you're most vulnerable to fairy tales," he said, and then widened his eyes with curiosity. "How did you get out to come here? What's happening with you now?"

"It's terrible," I said, flopping in the seat across from him. "I bet people in prison have more freedom than I have."

"But you're here," he noted.

"I snuck out, stole the keys, and came when I heard you were having troubles."

"Oh, no, not that again. The police will be at my door and that will bring the social workers here faster," he complained. "You had better get back."

"I don't want to go home again, Del."

"What are you talking about? Where are you going to go? What would you do?"

"What we decided. This is the best time to do it," I told him, my excitement returning.

"Oh. And how are we supposed to do that, Teal? You and I haven't enough money to travel and settle in somewhere else with two young children."

I stared at him and then smiled.

"What?" he said, his lips softening.

"I can get us thousands of dollars," I said. "And tonight, right now."

"Thousands? How?"

"I just know where there is a lot of money, and the beauty of it is, no one wants anyone else to know about it."

He shook his head.

"You're not making any sense, Teal."

"Never mind. If I return with ten thousand dollars, will you leave with me now? Will you, Del?"

The reality of what I was saying sank slowly but firmly into his consciousness. I could see his eyes changing, hope replacing defeat and sadness, as what we thought of as dreams and illusion suddenly began to slide into possibility.

"But where would we go?"

"There's that cousin of yours you mentioned in California, the one you've spoken with about your going out there."

"Yeah, but that was to be by myself, not with two little kids."

"It won't matter. He'll help you, help us. You'll get work right away and I'll look after Shawn and Patty Girl until we get them into a school."

"You just don't enroll kids in a school, Teal. There are legal papers, guardianships, all that."

"We'll figure all that out when we get there, Del. The main thing is, we don't want to stay here. For you it means losing them anyway, and for me it means walking about in shackles soon."

He smiled, and then he shook his head.

"It sounds great, but I don't know."

"Money will make the difference, Del. It always does," I said firmly. "The only thing is, we have to decide immediately. I have to do all this now, before they realize I've taken it and the car and I'm gone. We need the head start," I urged.

"I don't know," he said, but I could see his resistance weakening.

"It's a fresh start for both of us, for all of us, Del. We can make it work. Together, we can."

He looked at me.

"I don't understand about the money. Why do you say no one wants anyone to know about it?" he asked, and I told him what I had heard Carson and Daddy discuss.

"So they won't be so quick to report it missing," I emphasized.

He was thoughtful again.

"We're not incapable of doing this, Del. We'll get to California. We'll do it," I urged.

He lifted his eyes to me. I could see it was on the tip of his tongue. He was going to do it. My heart was pounding so hard, I thought that was what was making the noise, until we both realized, someone was at his front door. The pounding grew louder. For a moment neither of us could move, and then he rose and looked through the front windows.

"It's the police!" he said.

"Oh, no. My father."

"Oh, great," Del said. "I knew it. I just knew it, Teal. You weren't thinking."

"I'm sorry, Del," I moaned.

"Right, you're sorry," he said angrily, and went to the door.

A patrolman stood there gazing in at us. The thought of my being arrested again sickened me. I felt like I would actually faint.

"Del Grant?"

"Yes?"

"The hospital has been trying to reach you. No phone?"

"No, we lost service and I haven't restored it yet. What is it?"

"Your mother," he said, and shook his head. "I'm sorry."

It felt like a bullet had passed through Del into me. Cold and then numbed, I moved up beside him. He was just standing there, nodding.

"You'll have to contact the hospital as soon as possible," the policeman said.

Del continued to nod.

"Is there anything we can do for you, get in touch with anyone else?"

"No," Del said. "Thank you."

"I'm sorry," the policeman muttered. It was easy to see he hated the assignment and wanted to get it over with as quickly as he could. He turned and walked back to the patrol car. Del stood there looking out at the street, unmoving.

Despite how angry he is at his mother almost all the time, she is still his mother, I thought, and she's gone. Surely, he was also thinking about the impact it would all have on Shawn and Patty Girl. I felt so bad for all of them. Any thoughts about my own misery were forgotten.

"Del," I said gently, touching his arm.

When he turned to me, I was expecting to see tears, but instead I saw a face so stone cold, it chilled my heart.

"Go get the money," he said.

"Del?"

"Go on. We'll leave tonight. I'll start packing what I want to take."

He turned away. I stood there for a moment and then hurried out to the SUV.

All the way back to the house, I thought about Del's reaction to hearing his mother had died. How would I have reacted to such news? What did running away like this mean anyway, if not a total break with my family? What did I expect them to do once they had discovered what I had done? Forgive me? Wish me luck? Tell me they understood? Once I left the house with Daddy's money, it would be the same as hearing they had died. I'm sure it will be similar for them in relation to me, I thought.

I had been dreaming and fantasizing about this for so long that now that the reality of our actually going ahead and doing it was here, it still seemed like an illusion. It wasn't until I pulled into our driveway and confronted our big home that I began to feel afraid. Could I pull this off? Could I really do this? Was I a terrible person for giving Del such assurances, such hope?

I sat for a moment in the SUV with the engine off and the lights off, my body trembling. I almost wished I would be discovered, but no lights went on in the house and no one came to the front door.

Back in his house, Del was packing, getting ready to start a new life with me. His grief was being smothered with the fresh new prospects I had given him. I had to succeed now. I had to do what I had promised. I got out quietly and scurried around the house to the window of Daddy's den. There, I took a deep breath and then climbed back through it into his office. For a long moment I stood listening, half expecting to hear the sound of footsteps on the stairs, but I heard nothing. The maids were in their rooms. It was eerily quiet.

I went to Daddy's desk drawer and felt for the safe key. When I had it, I paused again to listen. There was just the sound of something creaking in the walls, a pipe or maybe just the house itself settling into a cozy rest for the evening. My heart started to thump so hard, I could actually feel the blood being rushed through my body when I opened the safe and felt inside for the cash box.

If there was any chance of Daddy forgiving me for my past actions, it was soon to end, I thought, but I had long gone past that moment. I had to harden myself against him, Mommy, and Carson in order to continue. I thought about the way Daddy looked at me now. I thought about Carson's washing his hands of me, and I thought about Mommy telling me I was too far gone for her to interfere. As far as they're concerned, I rationalized, I'm no longer part of the family anyway. What am I risking?

I opened the cash box, took out the money, and stuffed it into a manila envelope on Daddy's desk. Then I closed the box and put it back in the safe. I locked the safe and replaced the key in the top drawer. Once again, I paused to listen and heard nothing.

Good-bye Daddy, I thought as I stepped up to the window. Good-bye to seeing all the disappointment in your face, to hearing your voice harden with threats and the imposition of new punishments. In the end you will be happy I'm doing this. Think of all the relief I will bring you.

And good-bye to you, Mommy. I'm sure you'll be upset for a while, but some new social event will come up, and then you will have all the pressure of Carson's wedding. That will take your mind off me, won't it? It seems to do it for you now, to the extent that I'd just as well not be here.

And Carson, my reluctant brother, how happy you will be. Just think, you no longer will have to make up any excuses for me or try to avoid me. You can go on and believe you were an only child after all. Your sister was a fiction. What sister? Never heard of her.

You're all going to be happier, and there is no question in my mind that I will be, so good-bye, good-bye, good-bye, I thought, and went out through the window. I closed it behind me and walked slowly around the house and back to the SUV. For a moment I stood by it, looking up at the darkened windows and thinking about Mommy dreaming her happy dreams and Daddy feeling safe and contented beside her. I wondered just how long it would take them to realize I was gone.

I even imagined the scene at breakfast.

"Henderson," Mommy would say after sitting awhile and discovering I hadn't come down to breakfast. I hadn't even made a sound: no shower going, nothing.

Daddy would lower his *Wall Street Journal.*

"What?"

"Teal hasn't come to breakfast, and she has to get to school."

Daddy would sigh in annoyance and call to the maid to tell her to knock on my bedroom door. She would, and then she would return to tell them there was no response. Now, infuriated, Daddy would get up and pound up the stairs to my bedroom. He would thrust open the door and stare with confusion at my still-made bed.

"Teal?"

He would look into the bathroom and see I wasn't there. Confused, but more angry than worried, surely, he would come flying down the stairs and announce I wasn't in my bedroom. The bed, in fact, looked unused.

"What?" Mommy would say. "That's impossible. She didn't leave the house, and she certainly wouldn't make her bed."

Daddy would stand there a moment thinking, and then he would turn and march out to look for the SUV. When he saw it was gone, he would come stomping in, screaming about me. He would go to the phone, vowing to have me arrested again and this time, put into jail for years if he could.

Mommy would try to calm him, but soon she would feel she was getting too stressed over it and retreat. After all, she had to be ready for some luncheon or another and she couldn't very well go looking like a ragtag woman.

Daddy would call Carson and they would console each other and repeat to each other how terrible I was, how utterly hopeless I was.

"Don't get sick over her," Carson would advise.

"I won't do that," Daddy would vow, and he would gather his wits, call the police, and then go to work.

I played this whole scenario in my mind as I drove back to Del's house. In a way it made me feel good about what I was doing, and in a way, it made me feel even sadder.

Whatever, I told myself. It doesn't matter now. It doesn't matter anymore.

It's too late to turn back, and it's too late for regrets.

When I arrived at Del's house, I saw the lights were on and at the door, I saw two old suitcases. It wasn't until then that I realized I had nothing but what I was wearing and the money in the manila envelope.

He stepped out and looked at me.

"Get what you need?" he asked.

"I just got the money," I said.

"Wasn't there something important to you, something you had to have?" he asked. "Pictures, dolls, anything you wanted to take with you?"

I thought for a moment and shook my head.

"No," I said.

And finally, I had a reason to cry.

10

Following the Sun

$\mathbf{F}$ortunately, Shawn and Patty Girl were so exhausted and groggy, they didn't realize we were putting them into the rear of the SUV along with some of their things. We set up pillows and blankets for them and finally started out. Once we left the city streets and got onto highway I-90 toward Buffalo, I remarked how asleep the world looked this late at night. My excitement had kept the adrenaline flowing, but now that we were gassed up, packed, and on our way, my body began to soften.

Del said very little besides dictating the directions. The route west was something he had long ago committed to memory. I remember someone in history class in my public school asking our teacher why it was that people always seemed to head west to start new lives, explore, and make discoveries. He thought for a moment, nodding and smiling at the question, which was apparently a good question to him, something that gave him a chance to leave the prescribed curriculum for a moment, to be philosophical and original.

"I don't know exactly," he replied, "but if you think about it, the sun rises in the east and sets in the west. Maybe we all just follow the sun. Maybe we all believe it knows where it's going," he added with an impish smile. It was one of those rare moments when something was said or done in a classroom that stuck with me.

Do we really know where we're going? I wondered.

As we drove into the night, the darkness, interrupted now with only oncoming or passing vehicles, grew thicker. I know it was just my imagination, but it seemed as if the SUV was battling harder to move forward. I felt like we were inside a balloon, pressing harder and harder against the unexpectedly thick walls, stretching them and waiting to finally pop out and be free.

"How are you doing?" Del asked.

"Okay," I said in a voice smaller than I wanted it to sound.

I wanted him to be assured of my confidence and my determination. I wanted to fill him with courage and resolve, to believe that we could overcome whatever obstacles awaited us and solve any problem simply because we were young and free and bold. We could shut the door on our pasts firmly and finally. We could forget everything and live only in the present.

I remembered another thing from a classroom discussion, this one in science class. My teacher was telling us that one thing that distinguished man from the lower forms of life was his ability to draw upon memory and to foresee. And I remember thinking, but what if your memories were full of pain and what if you saw only danger and trouble in the future? What was the benefit of that? I almost asked him, but I anticipated some scientific, textbook answer that wouldn't really address my thoughts, so I didn't. I simply left class thinking the stupid ant or worm was better off. At least, better off than I was.

"We can't drive all night, although it's probably better. Less chance of being tracked and spotted," Del said. "I'll take over when you feel you're too tired, okay?"

"Yes, fine. I can drive a little more," I assured him.

He turned the radio on but kept it very low so as not to disturb Shawn and Patty Girl. In the rearview mirror, I saw how they were sleeping in a sweet embrace, safely surrounded by their childhood dreams. I envied them.

Del didn't look tired, but he was quiet.

"We're doing the best thing," I said. "You're probably right in thinking the social services people would be at the house in the morning."

"I know," he said.

"Count the money," I told him to help build his confidence. I pushed the manila envelope over, and he opened it and took out the bills.

"They're all hundreds," he commented. "There's so many, they don't look real."

"They're real, believe me," I told him.

He started to count.

"I thought you said something about ten thousand dollars," he said. I saw he wasn't finished yet.

"That's what I overheard. Why?" I asked, afraid I hadn't taken enough.

"I've already reached ten thousand and there's more, a lot more, maybe another ten."

"That's good for us!" I cried.

"I don't know," he said, wavering. The sight of so much money frightened him. "Your father might not want to write off this much."

"Don't worry about it, Del."

"Maybe your parents won't be as happy to see you gone as you think, Teal."

"Trust me, they will."

He continued to count.

"Twenty-two thousand," he reported, took a deep breath, and put it all back into the envelope.

"That should get us where we want to go and help us get started, don't you think?"

"Yeah," he said.

"I'm tired now," I told him. "You can drive."

If he was at the wheel, he would think less about it all, I thought. I slowed down and pulled to the side of the road. Cars whizzed by. More people than I thought traveled late at night. Maybe they were all running from something, too.

Del got out, went around the SUV, and got behind the wheel. I slid over to the passenger's seat. He adjusted the driver's seat, and we were off again. When we drew closer to Buffalo, Del decided we should pull into a motel.

"It will be daylight soon, and I'll feel better if we're off the highway, resting."

"Sure," I said. "Whatever you want to do."

Del wasn't happy with the first two motels we found off the exit. He thought they were too busy and too close to the highway. He drove on until we found a motel that looked out of business. Its sign had some blown letters, and there were only two other cars parked in front of units. The office was small and very dimly lit.

"I'll check us in," he said, taking out one of the hundred-dollar bills from the envelope. "Watch the kids."

He got out and went into the office. I saw he was standing at the desk for quite a while before a short, bald-headed man in a white undershirt came out of a back room. He scratched his head and looked past Del at the SUV. For a moment I thought there would be a problem, but then Del showed him the money, and he nodded and turned around to fetch a key.

"That's Norman Bates's older brother," Del muttered, getting back in. Norman Bates was the name of the psychotic killer in the movie *Psycho*. I laughed nervously.

We pulled in front of unit twelve, and Del handed me the unit key.

"Open the door first, and then we'll bring in the kids," he said.

Calling Shawn and Patty Girl the kids really made me feel that we were a family now. I hurried to do it and prepare one of the double beds for them. He carried the two of them in his arms, neither really waking up. I took Patty Girl and gently placed her in the bed. He put Shawn in, and we tucked the blanket in around them.

"I wish I could sleep like that," Del said.

"Me, too."

"We'll bring in what we need for them tomorrow," he said, and went into the bathroom. I fixed the bed for us and took off my sneakers, jeans, and blouse.

"I'm exhausted," he said, coming out. "I hope they sleep late."

I went to the bathroom and washed up. When I came out, Del was already asleep. I crawled in beside him, bringing myself as close to his warm body as I could without waking him. Then I closed my eyes and wished that Shawn's and Patty Girl's dreams would make their way over to me, even for a few minutes. I underestimated my own fatigue. Moments after I closed my eyes and snuggled up to Del, I was asleep.

The drapes were heavy enough to keep the morning light from jolting us awake. Shawn and Patty Girl were exhausted enough from the emotional trauma and all to sleep late into the morning, too, but when I awoke, I found Del was up. I turned and saw him sitting there, all dressed, staring at me.

"What's wrong?" I asked, grinding the sleep out of my eyes with my small balled fists. He didn't respond, so I opened them and sat up. "What is it, Del?"

"We can't do this," he said. "I don't know what got into me. I was so angry, so frustrated, I didn't give it all real thought."

"Why not? We have so much money. You said so yourself last night."

"It's going to take more than money, Teal, a lot more."

"Why?"

"Why?" He shook his head. "Look at them," he said, nodding at Shawn and Patty Girl. "We've taken on full responsibility for two infants. They have all sorts of needs, Teal, health needs, schooling, everything."

"But the money . . ."

"It's not going to last us forever, and we have to have some legal means, some proof of guardianship. Eventually, the law will catch up with us even if your father and mother are not coming after us. Then what do we do?"

"We can make it work. Somehow, we can, Del," I pleaded.

He lowered his head.

"I haven't even attended to her funeral," he said. "I know I should hate her like crazy, but she's lying back there in some cold hospital morgue, and there's no one going to come around to see about her. They'll dump her in some pauper's grave, and I won't even know where it is. Who knows what they'll do? They might just cremate her and scatter her ashes in a junkyard."

I stared at him.

"Del," I said, shaking my head, struggling to come up with more reasons, more hope.

"I'm sorry, Teal. I was too impulsive. I know I got you into more trouble and you have enough of your own. You don't need to take on ours as well. I'm sorry."

"You didn't get me into anything I didn't want to get into myself," I said petulantly.

Just then Shawn sat up and looked around, confused.

"Hey," Del said, standing and going over to him.

"Where are we? Where's Mama?"

"We took a little car ride for fun," Del told him. "We'll have breakfast in a restaurant soon, too."

Shawn looked at me.

"Hi," I said, and he smiled.

He looked down at Patty Girl and then at Del. Del glanced at me. Shawn wasn't as young and trusting as I thought, and Del knew it, too.

"Where's Mama?" he asked.

"We'll go home," Del said as an answer, and looked at me with an expression that shouted, *"See! See what I mean and why it's going to be so hard!"*

I fell back against my pillow and stared up at the ceiling. Del went out and got Shawn's and Patty Girl's clothing. By the time he returned, she was up and I was helping to get them together. Before we had pulled into the motel, we saw a roadside restaurant that looked like an old-fashioned diner. Shawn and Patty Girl were excited about being there and having pancakes.

I was so nervous about them, about how they were going to take the news of their mother's death, that I didn't think about my own situation until we were a good half hour on the road back home. We bought Shawn and Patty Girl some coloring books and small toys to amuse them for the trip. Del kept apologizing and blaming himself. I was terribly disappointed but kept my tears behind my lids. They fell inside me.

We didn't stop for anything but gas. Del got the kids some candy, and we were driving back into Albany proper by two-thirty.

"Where do you want to go first?" I asked him.

"We'll go home and I'll get their things back into the house. Then I'll contact the hospital and see what I have to do."

"I'll stay with you as long as I can," I said.

"Thanks, Teal."

The look of relief on his face made me sadder still. I was hoping to see that look grow stronger and brighter as we drove farther and farther away from here, not as we drove back here. Was I being too selfish? Was it true that I've always been?

As it turned out, neither Del nor I had much time to ponder these questions. We drove up to his home and got the children out first, but before we reached the front door, car doors slammed around us and we turned to see four men in suits marching toward us, followed by a woman Del recognized.

He groaned.

"Child welfare department," he muttered. "They must have been staked out and waiting for us."

"Just hold it right there, son," one of the men ordered.

Del put up his hand.

"Wait," he said. They all paused, the woman stepping a little farther forward. Del looked at Shawn and Patty Girl, who were now terrified and holding on to him. "They don't know anything yet, Mrs. Fromm," he told the woman.

"Something has to be done for them now," she insisted.

Del nodded.

"Okay. Just give me a few minutes, please."

She firmed up her mouth, glanced at me, and then said, "We've been here quite a while. Where did you take them? I know you weren't at the hospital."

Patty Girl, thinking she had something important to offer, piped up with, "We had pancakes."

None of them smiled.

"Ten minutes," Mrs. Fromm told Del, and he turned and took the kids into the house. I started after them.

"Are you Teal Sommers?" I heard, and looked at the man closest to me.

"Yes."

"Do you know that there is an all points bulletin out on you?"

"There always has been," I replied, and walked into the house.

I'm not very old, of course, and I have been well protected all my life, but just when I thought I had seen the saddest things I could see, there's always something sadder, something that wrings your heart more and tears at your very being. The sight of Del sitting Shawn and Patty Girl quietly on the sofa and then kneeling down before them to tell them their mother was dead and gone was something I will never forget.

I suppose when we're young, as young as the two of them were, we have built-in walls of skepticism to keep us from believing in such a thing as death. The finality of it is not easily understood and accepted when you're still young enough to believe in fairy tales and magic. Sick people always get better; they always come home out of the hospital.

"Mommy's not coming home anymore," Del began. "She was too sick to get better."

"Why?" Shawn asked quickly.

"Her body became too weak," he said. "The people out there, Mrs. Fromm, who you know, are worried you and Patty Girl won't be safe here anymore. I can't be with you all the time and work. They want to be sure you're all right, so you will have to go with them to live where people can take care of you for a while. Someday," he said, "I'll come for you and we'll be back together."

I suppose it did Del no good that I was standing there in the doorway with tears streaming down my face. Oh, why did he get cold feet? I cried. Why didn't we just go on and on? We would have made it. Anything would have been better than this, wouldn't it?

Del shook his head as if he could hear my thoughts.

"I don't want you two to cry about it," Del told them. "It will just make it harder for everyone, including yourselves. Be a big boy and a big girl. I'll see you soon. I promise," he said.

"Will we go to a restaurant again?" Patty Girl asked.

"Absolutely, yes," he told her.

He took her hand and then he took Shawn's and they stood up.

"Del."

"There's nothing I can do," he said, close to tears himself.

I lowered my head and stood back so he could walk them out. I was a coward. I didn't go out with him. I remained in the house and waited. Finally, curious as to why it was taking so long, I opened the door just as Del was waving good-bye to the kids. My body felt like it had turned to stone. He lowered his head and then, instead of returning to the house, he started down the street.

"Del!" I cried after him. He did not turn back. He kept walking.

I started after him, but when I reached the sidewalk, a police car pulled up and two patrolmen and Tomkins stepped out. Tomkins, without so much as glancing at me, went directly to the SUV and got in.

"Teal Sommers?" the policeman who had been driving asked.

Tomkins started the SUV and drove off.

"I said, Teal Sommers?" the policeman repeated with annoyance.

Here we go again, I thought.

"What if I say no?" I asked. "Will you leave me alone?"

"Believe me, young lady, we have a great deal more important things to do than chase after a spoiled brat. Get in the car," he ordered.

I looked down the street.

Del turned the corner and was gone.

I didn't know it then, but as far as I was concerned, he was gone forever.

11

The Court
of Last Resort

To my surprise, the police did not take me to the police station this time. They took me directly home. Now I understood what the driver meant when he said they had more important things to do than chase after a spoiled brat. Daddy had used his political influence to arrange all this.

I saw the SUV parked in front, but no sign of Tomkins. It was only then that I remembered the manila envelope containing all the money had been between the driver's and passenger's front seats. I wondered if it was still there. If it was, I might be able to get it back in his safe and have my father believe I had done nothing wrong, but only taken the car without his permission again.

Carson opened the front door for us as we stepped up to it.

"My father wanted me to thank you for him," he told the policemen without looking at me. It was almost as if I wasn't there.

"No problem," the driver said. He glanced at me, and then the two of them returned to their car.

"Just go to Dad's office," Carson ordered. He stood back for me to enter.

"Where's Mommy?" I asked.

"Just go to Dad's office," he repeated.

"Thanks, Carson," I muttered, and walked down the corridor.

I noticed that the maids weren't working. I heard no vacuum cleaner going, no dishes being washed, no sounds of anyone in any of the rooms. Daddy's den door was opened slightly. I hesitated, took a deep breath, set my mind on how I would act and plead, and then entered.

He was sitting with his back to the door, gazing out the window.

"Daddy?" I said.

At first I thought he wasn't going to turn around at all, but finally, he did, very slowly. He looked at me for the longest time without speaking. His face was oddly complacent, calm. His eyes did not have their usual red rage shining on me.

"When you were little and you misbehaved, we told ourselves it was normal growing pains, adjustments. My and your mother's only real experience with children had been with Carson. He has an entirely different personality, different nature, some of that because he is a male, I suppose.

"Other people, friends, used to tell me all the time that little girls were harder to bring up than little boys. In stories, movies, little boys are always made out to be the ruffians, miscreants, handfuls of trouble. Girls were supposed to be dainty, fragile; but in reality, everyone assured me, that was simply not so.

"And so, we accepted you as you were and tried to teach you, contain you every which way we knew, and even people who were supposed experts knew.

"When you were older, a preteen and then a teen, and you got into trouble, it clearly became more serious. Your mother, mainly, decided we should turn to child psychologists and even a psychiatrist. We sent you to the people we were told were the best, but there wasn't the dramatic turnaround we were expecting, hoping, to see.

"I took a more forceful position, especially after the more recent episodes. I thought okay, you're self-centered. Eventually you'll realize you can't do well for yourself and enjoy yourself if you continue to get in trouble and do poorly in school and you'll change solely to make yourself happier, but that didn't happen, either.

"Your mother—once again, more than me—hoped that if you were placed in a more controlled, richer, more advantageous environment where you would get more individualized attention, you would come around, but you didn't.

"In my heart I hoped you would care about this family, care about us at least enough not to really do us harm. That would be sort of the bottom of the barrel, the last straw, so to speak, wouldn't it?

"Then, you did this," he said, and held up the manila envelope. "You knew what this was, didn't you, Teal? You must have, because you knew where it was. You must have spied on me or something, right?"

I didn't care to answer. The truth was, I was having trouble forming words. My throat was closing up tightly. I looked away.

"Actually, I'm glad you're not speaking. All I'd get from you right now are lies, fabrications, excuses. Don't say anything."

He sat back.

"I'm going to do one more thing for you. You will realize that it's the last thing I'll do, I'm sure. I have, through some influential friends, been introduced to what we can call the court of last resort when it comes to you and kids your age who are like you."

I looked up. What was he talking about now?

"I'm sending you to another school. This one is away from home, Teal, so you won't have to answer to me for a while."

"What school?"

"The name doesn't matter. What it can do for you is all that matters. If you fail there . . . well, you fail. At least I will know that we did the best we could for you."

"I don't want to go to any new school," I said.

"What you want and what you don't want have no bearing on the matter anymore. It never should have had any bearing. That might have been one of my mistakes—caring about what you wanted."

"I want to talk to Mommy," I said.

"She's not here."

"Where is she?"

"She's gone to her sister's, your aunt Clare, for some very much needed R and R."

"I want to talk to her," I whined. "Call her on the telephone."

"She won't speak to you. She didn't want to be here when you were returned this time, Teal. She couldn't stand the idea of it."

"No."

"Yes," he said. "It's true."

He leaned forward on his elbows, folded his hands together, and glanced at his watch.

"There's a car outside, a limousine, waiting for you."

"What are you talking about, Daddy? Now?"

"Now is almost too late for you, Teal. Yes, right now."

"But my things."

"Everything you need is already in the automobile."

I shook my head.

"I'm not going anywhere, Daddy."

"I pulled some strings and, believe me, paid a lot of money, twice as much as your private school costs, to get you a spot right now, Teal. Someday, I hope, you will appreciate it. I realize you won't for a while, but that's a bitter pill I'll swallow."

I kept shaking my head.

"Where is this school?" I asked, seeing how determined he was.

"It's wherever your last chance resides," he said.

Instinctively, I backed up and suddenly hit what felt like a stone wall. I turned to see Tomkins smiling down at me.

"Tomkins will handle your transportation," Daddy said.

Panic swirled around me.

"Where's Carson?"

"He's gone home."

"I've got to go up to my room and see if there is anything I need that you didn't put in the car, Daddy," I said, playing for time.

"You didn't think about any of that when you ran off with your mother's car and my money earlier, Teal, did you? Why would anything matter to you now?"

"Please, let me call Mommy?"

"I don't understand all this interest in us suddenly, Teal. You didn't speak to your mother before you ran off, did you? You didn't speak to me or Carson. I'm giving you some of what you want—an escape from us," he said.

That wasn't what I wanted from my family, I was about to tell him. I wanted love and concern. I wanted attention and I wanted to feel wanted, but I said nothing. We were like oil and water, Daddy and me. For the moment, I was too angry and stubborn to do any more pleading. Send me to another school, I thought. See if it matters.

"Good-bye, Daddy," I said.

"Good luck to you, Teal. I really mean that," he said.

I turned and marched out of the office. Tomkins was right behind me. As we went by the stairway, I glanced up at it. Tomkins thought I might make a mad dash up to my room, I guess. He sped up so that he clearly blocked any such move on my part. He opened the front door.

There it was, as Daddy had described, a long stretch limousine.

At least I'm going in style to wherever I'm going, I thought.

What surprised me was that there was another driver. What was Tomkins here for, then? This driver was in a chauffeur's uniform. He got out as soon as we appeared and opened the rear door for me. To my further surprise, Tomkins followed me into the limousine and sat across from me.

"Are you going to a new school, too?" I asked him.

He stared coldly at me. What was Daddy doing, making sure I didn't have the driver stop and jump out somewhere? This is getting ridiculous, I thought.

The chauffeur got in, and we started away. It was funny how I didn't look back at the house with any sort of sadness the last time I had left it, but for some reason, perhaps because of Daddy's tone of voice and his strangely calm, almost defeated demeanor, I did now.

When I glanced at Tomkins, I saw a smirk on his face.

"That's a lot to throw away," he muttered.

"You don't know anything," I spit back at him.

"Of course not. No one but you knows anything," he replied.

We drove on, and I quickly realized we were heading for the airport. Daddy hadn't been kidding when he said far away. The limousine was permitted to go through a special gate and directly to a small plane.

"What is this?" I asked.

"This is an airport and this is a plane," Tomkins said.

"Very funny. Why am I going on a private plane?"

"You're so special," he replied with that same small cold smile on his lips.

The plane's engines were started as we approached. The door was opened as we pulled alongside. Tomkins got out quickly and held the limousine door open. The chauffeur sat staring ahead. I hesitated, my body feeling like it had sunk into the car seat.

"Let's go. I have other things to do today," Tomkins snapped. When I still hesitated, he leaned in. "Do you want me to embarrass you and pull you out of the limousine?"

"Where am I going?"

"Hey, my job was to bring you here. The guy in the pilot's seat knows where you're going. Move," he ordered.

I had no doubt he would pull me out, so I stepped out of the limousine. The wind whipped around us. Tomkins took my left arm, pinching it at the elbow with his thick fingers and directing me up the small stairway. I lowered my head and got into the plane. There was no one else there.

The door was slammed shut.

"Buckle yourself in," I heard. I felt the plane begin to move.

I looked out the window. Tomkins was getting back into the limousine. It sped off as the plane turned and the engines were revved up.

What about my things? I realized. I hadn't seen anything taken from the limousine and put onto the plane.

"Wait!" I shouted at the door between me and the cockpit.

The roar of the engines drowned out my voice.

"Where am I going?"

The plane began to roll faster and faster and soon lifted into the air.

I looked out the window.

"Mommy," I whispered.

The sun went in behind a cloud as we rose higher.

Across the way, I saw my face reflected in the opposite seat's window.

I was crying.

"Poor little rich girl," I heard myself say.

The sun went in behind a cloud as we ...
... laps she was. I will try ... face ... in the opposite
door ...

Poor little rich girl. I used to ... she ...

PART THREE

PHOEBE

1

Mama's Gone

"**W**ell, she's gone," Daddy announced at my bedroom door. "Your mother has really gone."

I turned slightly in bed and grunted, thinking, *why did he have to wake me so early just to tell me that?* Then, I peered at him through the slits of my barely opened eyes. He stood in my bedroom doorway, his head bowed and his hands on his hips. He was already dressed for work, wearing his gray suit and tie, looking as perfectly put together as a storefront manikin, as Mama would say.

"Right, Daddy, she's gone," I said, and pulled the cover over my head.

"No," he said, raising his voice. "I mean it. This time she's really gone, Phoebe."

I lowered the blanket again.

"What are you talking about, Daddy? She's really gone? Like this is the first morning you woke up and realized she didn't come home all night?"

In the beginning they would have loud arguments about that, Mama crying that he didn't consider how hard she worked and how she needed time to unwind. After a while Daddy gave up complaining and just ignored it, which was usually how he handled every crisis between them.

My mother worked as a waitress in a small jazz joint. Most of the time she spent what she made right there, or at least, that was what she claimed. Either that or she needed this and that for work: better shoes, nicer clothes, beautifying to make better tips. Whatever excuse she came up with, Daddy accepted.

With Daddy on the road selling tools to garages all around the Atlanta, Georgia, area, I was often home alone most of the night. Lately, he had to go even farther to bring in as much income as he had before. Because of that, he often had to sleep in a motel and I'd be alone all night, not realizing until morning that Mama hadn't come home.

"She didn't leave a good-bye letter for either you or me, but she's gone! She packed most of her things and took off."

I stared at him a moment and then sat up in bed. I was wearing one of his pajama tops, which was something I had done since I was four and was still doing at sixteen.

"What things? Her clothes?"

"That's what I said."

That was something she hadn't ever done, I thought. I ran my fingers through my hair before getting up and marching past him to his and Mama's bedroom.

Her closet door was wide open, and there were dozens of empty hangers dangling. Some of her less cherished garments had been tossed to the floor. There was only one pair of old shoes in the shoe rack. Now that the closet was almost empty, the gobs of dust were more visible. I stared at it and shook my head.

"She took all that and left," I said in amazement, mostly to myself. Daddy was standing right beside me.

Mama was really on a fling this time. I was sure it was something she had just decided to do on the spur of the moment. She hadn't given me any hints. I think I felt more betrayed than Daddy, not that Mama and I were all that close these days. She didn't like being reminded she had a sixteen-year-old daughter. Instead, she preferred pretending she wasn't much older than that herself, especially in front of men. I was absolutely forbidden to go to the club to see her when she was working, and she warned me that if I ever did, she would act like she didn't know who I was.

"All her cosmetics, too," Daddy said, nodding at their bathroom. The counter had nothing on it, no jars of her creams, no shampoos, nothing.

"Wow," I said. "I guess she did take off for a while."

"What time did you get home last night that you didn't even know it, Phoebe, and didn't even hear her do all this?" he asked. "I'm sure she wasn't alone," he added in a lower voice.

Anger didn't darken his ebony eyes as much as it turned them into cold black marble.

"I was home early, but she was still at work and I was so tired I went right to sleep," I lied.

Once again I had violated my curfew and come home very late, but I just assumed she was still at the club. I didn't go to her room to look for her, and if I had and had woken her, she would have ripped into me good. The gin I had drunk at Toby Powell's house practically put me into a coma anyway. I didn't even hear my dreams.

"She was threatening me with leaving all the time, but I thought like you," Daddy said, staring at the empty closet. "She's always threatening. But this time, it's obviously more than just a threat, Phoebe. I should have known. I should have expected something like this. I heard rumors about her and that no-account Sammy Bitters."

"What kind of rumors?" I had heard them, too, stories about her being with him, but I made like I knew nothing.

"Not the kind I'd care to discuss," Daddy said. "Anyhow, I gotta go off until late tonight. I don't have any time to worry about this or care. I just wanted to be sure you knew to be home after school and all, Phoebe. No hanging out on any street corners or staying late at some friend's house, you hear? You gotta stay good. Remember what that judge told you," he warned.

Along with two of my friends, I had been arrested for shoplifting at a department store. Sylvia Abramson had one of those tools the cashiers use to take off the thing that sets off an alarm, and we used it to steal clothes a few times before we got caught this time. A saleswoman saw me go into the changing room with a blouse, and afterward she went in and realized I was wearing the blouse under my own. They let me walk out of the store before they stopped me. Meanwhile, Sylvia and Beneatha Lewis got caught stuffing panty hose into their jeans.

This was the second time I was caught shoplifting and brought before a judge within one year. If it wasn't for Daddy, I guess the judge would have done something more than just sentence me to probation and impose a curfew. Daddy kept thanking him. To me it looked like he was begging for mercy, apologizing, taking the blame onto himself, and promising to try to do better as a parent. Before the session was over, the judge did bawl him out more than he chastised me, but he did tag on the threat of having me removed from our home and placed in foster care the next time I got into any sort of trouble.

"It's easy to have children, but it's a real responsibility to raise them," he lectured from his high desk. Daddy just kept nodding. "Too many people have thrown and are throwing their obligations onto the state or society. The court isn't here to take the place of a parent."

"I know, Your Honor. I am sorry to have my troubles in public."

"Um," the judge said. He had asked where Mama was, and Daddy had told him she was at work and couldn't get free. The truth was, she was home sleeping off a hangover. The judge peered at him when he explained that, and Daddy shifted his eyes quickly. It was like he had a glass skull and you could see any attempted lies tangle up and crumble. He kept rubbing his hands together nervously.

I felt more embarrassed for him than I did for myself, even though Daddy always looks respectable and is always nicely dressed. He says it's part of his work as a tool salesman. He sells very expensive equipment and says he has to look like someone who would. He's always telling me a good presentation, a good image, is half the battle in this world. He does his best to get me to dress more conservatively. I tell him he's just too old-fashioned, but he says it doesn't have anything to do with fashion. It has to do with being decent.

I told him being decent is no fun.

"It's like eating sugar-free candy," I said. He didn't laugh. He was laughing less and less these days, and now I wondered if he would ever laugh again.

Anyway, without Daddy around and with Mama out and about, working and such, I often violated the curfew, and the evening before was just such an occasion. Daddy told me I was skidding on thin ice. I almost fell through the day Daddy told me Mama was gone. Now that I knew he wasn't going to be home for dinner, I went off with Sylvia and stayed too long at her house partying with her, Packy Morris, and Newton James, two boys whom the principal herself had encouraged to drop out of school. We made a little too much noise, and Mrs. Gilroy, who lives in the apartment below, went and called the police. They took our names, and I thought they would know I was violating curfew, or they would come arrest me the day after, but no one came.

Daddy found out about it and looked very glum when I came home from school the next day. Mama still hadn't come home, and the reality of her never coming home was beginning to settle in me like a glob of fresh cement. He was sitting at the kitchen table, nursing a cup of coffee between his hands and coming up out of an ocean of thought like someone who had been deep-sea diving for ideas all day.

"I realize I can't do this, Phoebe. I can't look after you, and this can't continue. You're just going to go from bad to worse," he said. He shook his head and drummed his fingertips on the tablecloth, looking like he had spent his last dollar.

His conclusion was that since there was no doubt now that Mama had left us for good, he had decided to deposit me with my aunt Mae

Louise, Mama's older sister. He told me he had already had a preliminary conversation with her and my uncle Buster about it.

"What are you talking about, Daddy? I ain't gonna live with no Aunt Mae Louise," I said after he told me. I wagged my head and put my hand on my hip. Usually, I could get him to ease up on any of his restrictions and punishments, but he looked very determined this time.

"This is no life for you here, Phoebe. Not the way things are now. It won't be forever, but it's a way to save you. Maybe the only way."

"I don't need to be saved."

"People who need to be saved usually don't know it," he replied. "Put on something nice. We're going to talk to Aunt Mae Louise and Uncle Buster tonight."

"No," I said.

"You do what I tell you, Phoebe," he said firmly. "If you don't, the law is going to come around and take you off one of these days anyway. They'll go and put you in some foster home with strangers, like the judge said, and I know you wouldn't like that."

"Uncle Buster and Aunt Mae Louise are no better than strangers," I whined.

"Stop it," he snapped, and pounded the table with uncharacteristically intense anger. I actually jumped back. "Now go get dressed, and don't put on any of those blouses so short your belly button peeps out. Go!" he ordered, his finger stiffly pointing toward my room.

I sauntered off reluctantly and changed into something that I knew would make him happy, but I wasn't smiling. All the way out to Aunt Mae Louise's house, I sat sulking in the car. Daddy went on and on about how this was my biggest and best opportunity to escape trouble and grow into a decent young woman, maybe even go off to a college and become something. He said he couldn't be expected to make a living and raise a teenage girl who had already been in enough trouble to bring a grown man to tears. He said bringing a girl like me up in the heart of Atlanta's toughest neighborhood was like planting a rose in a pigsty.

"Not that I'm saying you're any rose, Phoebe, not by a long shot," Daddy added. "I'm not one to be blind to my child's problems and my own. People who do that end up wishing they was born a few minutes earlier or later."

"Maybe Mama will come back," I offered as a last resort when we drew closer to Stone Mountain. "At least we should wait a week or so to see."

Daddy looked at me with those coldly realistic eyes of his, the sort of eyes that would clear fantasies off your own like windshield wipers cleared off rain.

"I don't fool myself about your mama, Phoebe. She was never satisfied with our life, and you know it. She's into bad stuff now. And anyway, I don't want her coming back," he added with more rage in his voice toward her than I had ever heard. "Not after what she's done this time."

I used to think nothing could make him really mad. He seemed to take every insult Mama threw his way. She complained he didn't put up enough of a fuss when his boss made him work harder and cover more territory.

"You sure you got a spine in there, Horace?" she would taunt him.

The most he would do is shake his head and saunter off, but I could see there was no way I was going to talk him out of this. My only hope was that after all was said and done, my aunt and uncle wouldn't want me. If I were them, I wouldn't want me, I thought. I don't even want me now, and probably Daddy didn't, either, and was just using everything as an excuse to pawn me off. Part of me was sick over it, and part of me was understanding.

Aunt Mae Louise and Uncle Buster Howard, who was a civil engineer, whatever that meant, had recently bought a nice home in Stone Mountain, a suburb community of Atlanta. It had two stories, a front yard and a backyard, an attached garage, and enough land between it and the houses beside it so that you couldn't reach out the window and steal bread off someone else's dinner table like you could in the run-down tenement we occupied in downtown Atlanta.

In other words, they had a home that would nourish a rose, even a weed. It was in a safe neighborhood. There were no gangs, and drugs if they came had to come subtly, through back doors, and not be sold in kiosks in the street outside your front door like they did where we lived. I could attend a better school, and, most importantly, Daddy emphasized, help my aunt and uncle with their two children, Jake, age five, and Barbara Ann, age eight.

Daddy, who had been a salesman of some sort or another most of his adult life, put all his skill and logic into his selling of me. There was just no other way to view it. He was there to convince my aunt and my uncle they should take me in, just like they would take in a new vacuum cleaner.

I really hated the idea of living in Stone Mountain, away from my friends and stuck with my snobby relatives, especially my mother's older sister, who was fond of lecturing her about how an African-American woman and man today could make themselves successful if they just had a mind to and had real ambition. Everything they had was real; everything we had was just a temporary fix.

"You know that most of the time my work takes me on the road, Mae," Daddy continued, directing his plea mainly at her. "These days I have to expand my territory to make expenses. She'd be left alone for longer and longer periods of time. It won't be long before the authorities come and take her off."

We were all in the living room of their Stone Mountain home. It was in a housing development that was at least eighty-five percent black. After they had bought the home, Mama told Aunt Mae she just traded one ghetto for another, but even I had to admit that was just envy talking. This was no ghetto. Close your eyes and then open them when no one was in the street in front of his or her house and you would think you were in the finest suburbs, built for middle- and upper-class white people.

"That's why Charlene went bad," Aunt Mae Louise piped up, those black green eyes of hers narrow, dark, and angry. To me she always looked like an alley cat poised to pounce. "She needed looking after, Horace. Charlene was never one to be on her own. My folks only had to leave her in the house by herself an hour for her to do something to add gray hairs to their heads. You should have known that from the day you met her," she told him. "I don't know why you went ahead and married her. Men sure don't think with their heads when they see a pretty thing. I won't deny she was always pretty, but I'll never claim she was anything but selfish and spoiled."

Aunt Mae Louise wasn't ever going to take her sister's side just because she was her sister, I thought. She probably never had, even when they were growing up.

She glared my way.

"You take after your mama too much in that regard, Phoebe. It's sad to have to say it, but she was a very bad influence on you. Lucky for the rest of us that she had only one child."

I knew Mama had almost had another but miscarried in the sixth month, probably because of the alcohol and cigarettes and her wild ways.

Even so, and even though I knew she had run off with a small-time con man named Sammy Bitters, I didn't like Aunt Mae dissin' her. I knew it was the same as criticizing me because, as she just said, in Aunt Mae Louise's eyes Mama and I were cut from the same cloth. She never hid the fact that she had doubts my father was my father, too. I knew it was like someone sticking a pin in his chest whenever she implied or even came out and as much as said it. Daddy was just too easygoing to ever show anger or pain, especially in front of her. Maybe he was just a pincushion after all. Mama got so she thought so. No wonder he didn't want her coming home now. Nothing would confirm that as much as placing me with my aunt and uncle. There was a finality to it, just like a period at the end of a long sentence. This is it; this is the way it will be, and that's that.

Everyone was quiet in the room because the heaviness of the conclusion hung in the air like stale cigarette smoke. They all wished I had never been born, and now there wasn't much choice about what to do.

"Of course," Daddy said softly, "I'd give you money every week for her room and board and whatnot."

He gave me a quick glance of deepest despair.

"We don't need you to pay for her food, Horace, but she will need decent clothes, shoes, and a little spending money," she said.

My uncle didn't look happy about it, but it was clear they were going to take me in. I felt my heart sink. I wanted to do something to stop it, but I was afraid Daddy might just give up on me and call some child protection agency or the court and say he gave up. Mama had left him. His work was getting harder and I was in too much trouble lately, trouble that deepened the lines in his face. He was tottering on the heels of his shoes.

"But first, I want some understandings set down right now, while your father is sitting here, Phoebe," Aunt Mae Louise began.

She stood up to continue, suddenly very full of herself. She was only about five feet two and weighed maybe one hundred and five. It gave her self-confidence to stand when she wanted to be firm and authoritative, I'm sure. Sitting, she looked like a little girl with those thin arms and tiny shoulders.

Unlike Mama, Aunt Mae Louise kept her hair straight and wore almost no makeup except some lipstick occasionally. Mama was five feet five, with a full figure. I had heard men say she radiated sex like a hunk of uranium or something. She could have a man eating out of her hand by just turning her shoulders, swinging her hips, and batting her eyelashes. Even though she drank too much and smoked too much and did drugs occasionally, she was obsessive about her teeth.

"Your smile is your billboard when it comes to men," she would tell me. "Make sure you take good care of your teeth, Phoebe."

As long as I could remember, Mama was giving me advice about men. She always made it sound like a war, like we had to prepare to do battle to defend our treasure. That was literally what she called our sexuality, our treasure.

"We don't need no dragon guardin' the door, but don't let 'em in unless there's more in it for you than some cheap thrill, girl. Otherwise, you'll end up bein' some sorry tramp like what hangs out at the club. I don't have no money to give you, just good advice, so you'd better take it and stuff it in your heart," Mama told me. It was usually after she had drunk too much and was feeling sorry for herself that she gave me these lectures. To me it seemed as if her sexuality had become more of a burden than an advantage.

Although she wasn't exactly a prude, Aunt Mae Louise was a great deal more self-conscious of her sexuality. Uncle Buster was a good-looking man, firmly built at six feet one. He had played football in college, but was never a hell-raiser. His father was a Baptist minister, and whenever Uncle Buster was around Mama, he always looked at her and treated her as if she was a saleslady for Satan. Mama told me that was because Uncle Buster wanted her so much he had to make her seem terrible. I knew she loved to tease him, which was something that made Aunt Mae Louise irate at every family gathering, not that we had all that many besides an occasional Christmas dinner, something we hadn't done for two years.

It was no surprise to anyone, least of all to me, that for me family was as fictional a concept as Oz. The lines between us, the linkage was so thin and fragile, I never felt anything special about it. My relationships with my cousins, my aunt, and my uncle weren't any warmer or tighter than the relationships I had with ordinary friends.

"First," Aunt Mae Louise said, "I want you coming straight home from school every day. You go right to the guest room, where you'll be, and you finish your homework," she said, turning and twisting like a traffic cop so she could point at each area of the house she made reference to. "Then, you come out and help me set the table for dinner. On weekends, we shake down the house. We vacuum every rug, polish furniture, and do the windows. On Sundays after church, we'll do all the ironing needs to be done.

"Uncle Buster and I play Bingo every Wednesday night at the church. We usually have a neighbor, Dorothy Wilson, baby-sit, but now that you're living here, you'll do it. That doesn't mean you can invite anyone to the house when we're gone. We'll tell you exactly how we want you and the children to behave, and you'll be responsible for them getting to bed on time, after they clean up and put away any of their toys, of course.

"Don't you think of accepting any invitations from anyone you meet until either Uncle Buster or I find out everything we need to know about the person. We see how young people today slip through the cracks because parents don't take enough interest in who their friends are and what they do," she said.

You're not my parents, I wanted to say, but kept my lips firmly glued shut.

Uncle Buster, still looking quite glum, nodded after every point she made as if he was in church listening to his father deliver a sermon. Any minute I expected him to let out with a "Hallelujah."

"Of course, it goes without saying that we won't tolerate any smoking or drinking, and if you do any drug, we'll turn you in to the police ourselves, won't we, Buster?"

"Without batting an eyelash," he confirmed, his eyes fixed on me like two laser beams that could burn through my face.

"Now, neither Jake nor Barbara Ann ever use any profanity, and I don't want to hear them start suddenly after you move in, Phoebe."

I sat there staring ahead.

"Well?" she asked.

I looked at her with a "Well, what?" expression.

"You understand and agree to everything I've said?"

I glanced at Daddy. He looked like he was ready to break into tears any moment, but I could see the fear in his face, too, fear I would say something nasty and end it all. His eyes were full of pleading.

"I understand," I said.

"Good." She turned to Daddy. "All right, Horace. We'll give it a try, but if she gives us any problem and doesn't listen . . ."

"Oh, she won't give you any problems," Daddy said quickly. "She's a good girl. She's just in with too many bad kids, and she doesn't have me around enough. I appreciate this, Mae. I know she'll do well in a home where there is love, responsibility, and supervision."

Aunt Mae Louise grunted skeptically and looked very self-important. I hated to see Daddy grovel like that, but I was afraid to raise my voice. I just continued to stare at nothing, like someone who could meditate herself right out of hell.

"When you bringing her things?" Buster asked. I saw that he kept his eyes on me instead of Daddy whenever he spoke about me.

"I thought tomorrow, Buster, if that's all right with you."

"It doesn't matter when she starts, Horace. It's how she behaves afterward," Uncle Buster said.

"Oh, right. Of course," Daddy said. "She knows that."

"The room's all ready. I always keep it clean and prepared for guests," Aunt Mae Louise said. "I'll just move some of my things out of the closet tonight so she has all the room she needs."

"What about the school?" Daddy asked.

"I'll get her registered and all," Aunt Mae Louise said. "I've already spoken to the principal, Mr. Wallop, about her, and he explained what has to be done. You sign a paper saying you give us temporary guardianship. We go to all the parent-teacher meetings so they know us well at the school. There was even talk about Buster being on the board," she said proudly.

"Maybe someday," he said, "but I'm a little too busy at the moment to give it the time it requires."

"There's a good lesson for you," Aunt Mae Louise told me. "Never take on any responsibility you can't give one hundred percent to."

I looked at her as if she was totally crazy. What did she think I was going to do, run for student government president?

"Then it's settled," Uncle Buster said. "How is your business going?" he asked Daddy, anxious to get off the topic of me.

They started to talk about the economy. Aunt Mae Louise brought me to the guest room and explained how she wanted things kept.

"You make sure you make the bed before you leave for school every morning, Phoebe. Fix it just like this, with the pillows fluffed and the comforter neatly folded. I don't want people coming to my home and seeing an unmade bed. And no clothes lying about on the floor or over chairs. Everything gets hung up properly. Nothing looks messier than discarded garments. I used to fight with your mother all the time about that. She was just too lazy and didn't care what people did or didn't see."

"I can keep the door closed," I said, "can't I?"

"It doesn't matter if a door is closed and everything behind it is a mess. It's still a mess. Now you be sure you don't drop any makeup or such on this rug. It's practically new," she pointed out.

"You'll be sharing a bathroom with Jake and Barbara Ann, of course. They know how to clean up after themselves. They even wash out the tub after they bathe. Jake does the best he can, and I come in after him and finish, but he's gotten into the good habits."

"I'm not a dirty person, Aunt Mae," I said.

"I never said you were. I'm just telling you how things are here in our home and how I want them to remain. I feel sorry for your daddy. I felt sorry for him two minutes after he said 'I do' to my sister. If you care about him, you'll be a good girl now. In a way," she said, "it might be the best thing that happened to the both of you, your mother running off like that. The Lord works in mysterious ways, and sometimes, something that seems bad really is good. You go to church with your daddy much?" she asked.

"Never," I said dryly.

She pulled up her shoulders.

"Well, we'll see about changing that."

I was going to protest, but Daddy came out and stood in the hallway with Uncle Buster, so I took a deep breath and looked away.

"Now, we'll talk to Jake and Barbara Ann," Aunt Mae Louise declared. "I asked them both to wait in Barbara Ann's room," she said, and led me two doors down the hallway.

Jake was sitting at a desk working on a puzzle. Dressed in a white shirt and a pair of black pants with his hair neatly trimmed and brushed, he looked older than five. Of course, he knew me well enough, but I also knew that both he and his sister had been warned about me often.

Barbara Ann was sitting and reading a book. They both looked up quickly when we entered.

"Children," Aunt Mae Louise said, "your cousin Phoebe is going to stay with us for a while."

Jake's eyebrows lifted.

"Where's she going to sleep?" Barbara Ann asked, probably afraid she would have to share her own room.

"She'll be in the guest room," Aunt Mae Louise told her, and she looked relieved. "Everyone is to behave and help everyone else. Everyone is to respect everyone else's property," she continued as if we were in a camp and not a home. "The same rules apply when it comes to watching television and to cleaning up after ourselves."

"Is she going to our school, too?" Barbara Ann asked. She was tall for her age and, unfortunately for her, looked more like her father than her mother. Her features weren't as dainty as her mother's, and she had big shoulders and plump cheeks. She looked a good twenty or so pounds overweight.

"Of course she is."

That seemed to interest her more.

"You can sit with me on the school bus," she said as if she was granting me a wonderful opportunity. "I'll save you a seat if I'm on first after school, and you can save it for me if you're first."

Great, a school bus, I thought, with a load of screaming children. That was just what I needed every morning.

"When is she coming to live here?" Jake asked.

It felt funny standing there and hearing everyone talk about me as if I wasn't there.

"Tomorrow. And that's that," Aunt Mae Louise said. "Get ready for bed, Jake. Barbara Ann, I want to see what you did for homework tonight."

We walked out and joined Daddy and Uncle Buster in the kitchen.

"You want something, tea or coffee, Horace?" Aunt Mae Louise offered.

"No, thank you, Mae. We'd better get back and start organizing."

"Good idea," she said. She turned to me. "You help your father now," she ordered. "This is not easy for him, and he's a good man just trying to do the best he can with his terrible burdens."

I flinched at being called a burden, but then I thought, what else am I really?

Daddy and I walked to the front door. Uncle Buster shook his hand, and we started out. As we walked down the sidewalk to the driveway, I gazed back and saw both Jake and Barbara Ann peering out the bedroom window, looking like two children kept prisoners in some high tower. That's how I'll feel for sure, I thought.

The night sky was so overcast I felt like I was moving through a tunnel, even with the streetlights in front of the other homes.

"This will be only for a little while," Daddy said after we got into the car.

I looked at him with eyes as coldly realistic as those eyes of his, and he turned away quickly.

Daddy wasn't good at lying to anyone, even to me. To my way of thinking, that was a weakness. I used to wonder how he could be a good salesman. Everyone lies to everyone about everything, I believed. If the story of Pinocchio were true, everyone in the whole world would have a long nose.

"I'm sorry I can't do more for you, Phoebe," he continued. "I don't like putting my responsibilities on someone else, but I've spent many a restless night worrying about you. At least I'll know you're safe. You understand all that now, right, Phoebe? You've got to be happy about that."

I didn't answer him. I stared out the window. This sleepy residential world looked like another planet. There were no bright lights, no music pouring out in the streets, and no one standing on any of the street corners. Everyone was locked safely behind his or her doors or gathered around television sets like cave people gathered around fires.

Then I thought that somewhere in the night, Mama was laughing. I was sure. She was listening to music and having a good old high time of it. Did she even pause once to think about me? Did she ever wonder about me? Or did she force herself to forget me? I had no doubt that she would probably say I was better off with her sister than I was with her. Mama never tried to pretend she was good.

"I'm born to raise hell," she would tell me, and she would laugh.

Am I born to raise hell, too? I would wonder.

"I hope you'll behave yourself, Phoebe," Daddy suddenly said as if he could read my thoughts.

He said it like a prayer.

And what are prayers, I thought, if not just little lies between yourself and God?

2

At Aunt Mae Louise and Uncle Buster's

I never really believed I was saying good-bye to anyone or saying good-bye to my home in the city. In my heart I truly believed I would be coming back sooner rather than later. Back at the apartment that night, Daddy hovered about like a nervous soon-to-be father, pacing in front of my door while I packed with little or no enthusiasm.

"Don't take any of those wild clothes of yours, Phoebe. You'll just steam up your aunt and uncle. Leave them here," he pleaded. "None of those rings in your nose and your belly button, and no cigarettes. For God's sake, no cigarettes. She becomes a banshee when she sees people smoking, a truly wild spirit warning people of impending death."

It irked me how afraid of Aunt Mae Louise he was.

"I don't have any cigarettes and I don't have any wild clothes, Daddy. I'm not wearing no old lady's clothes just to please her."

"You've got to make this work," he said. "Take it slowly, a day at a time. I'll come by as much as I can, and I promise I'll take you places on weekends."

"Where you going to take me, Daddy? Some kiddy fun park?" I threw back at him.

"I'm just trying to make it work," he protested. "We'll go to a movie or I'll take you to a nice restaurant, whatever, but I'm not bringing you back here to mingle with those juvenile delinquents, so don't ask."

"Right," I said, looked at a miniskirt I knew would set off Aunt Mae Louise, and then tossed it on the closet floor.

"Maybe I'm better off with some strange foster family," I muttered.

After I packed, I called Sylvia and told her what was happening.

"You're movin'?"

"It's temporary," I said. "Believe me."

"Right. You ain't that far away anyhow," she said. "You come in on weekends and stay with me."

That cheered me up until I considered that Aunt Mae Louise would probably not allow it, and Daddy had made it clear he wouldn't. I wasn't going to put up with it, I vowed. I don't know why I'm packing so much, I told myself. I'll be coming back so fast, it'll make Daddy's head spin. Either that or I'll just run off like Mama.

"Maybe you and Beneatha could come out there, too," I suggested to Sylvia.

"What's to do out there?" she asked.

"I don't know. When I find out, I'll tell you."

"Good luck with that," she said.

I was so depressed I couldn't sleep, so I went back out and saw Daddy was sitting in the living room staring at the television set. I could tell he didn't care what he watched. His eyes were glassy, and he didn't even realize I was standing beside him.

He can't be too happy about how his life was turning out, either, I thought, but I didn't feel sorry for him as much as I felt he should do something about it, prove he had that spine Mama said he didn't have. Why was he so defeated? Plenty of my friends lived with a single parent and got by.

"Why don't you just get a job here in the city, Daddy?" I asked him. "That way you wouldn't be away from home and no one could come take me off. Maybe we could move to a better apartment or something, too."

"Whaaa?" he said. He looked up at me.

"I asked you, why don't you get a different job?"

He shook his head and smiled like I was asking him to go to the moon.

"I've been doing this too long to change now, Phoebe. Soon I'll get better routes with better clients. Someone's retiring. Soon we'll have a better plan."

"Right. Better this, better that, soon," I said, disgusted, and went to bed hoping to bury my frustration and anger deep into the pillow.

Damn you, Mama, I thought. If you were running off, you could have at least taken me along. I fell asleep dreaming of it.

The next morning Daddy was up ahead of me and had my suitcase at the door.

"Can't wait to get rid of me, can you?" I told him bitterly.

"You know that's not so, Phoebe. You know what's going on as well as I do. Don't make this harder than it is for me. Or for yourself, for that matter," he said.

Sullenly, I drank some juice, smeared some jam on a piece of toast, and drank a cup of coffee. He sat there turning the spoon around and around in his cup, his eyes down. This might very well turn out to be the last breakfast we have together, I thought, and despite myself, I started to feel sorry for him, imagining him all alone in this dump. What would he do for fun? What would he look forward to in his life now?

"You gonna go out with someone new?" I asked, and he looked up sharply.

"What?"

"Someone new? Mama's gone for good, so why wouldn't you?" I pursued.

When I was very young, I saw him and Mama behave more like a husband and wife, kiss each other, hold hands, laugh, and even dance. I had no idea what had changed it all. It seemed almost to have happened overnight.

"I wouldn't go out with another woman while I was still married to your mother, Phoebe. That's adultery."

"Well, she's doing it."

"I'm not her," he said.

"But you're getting a divorce, aren't you?"

He nodded slowly, making it look hard to do, like someone who didn't want to face his troubles.

"So," I said, shrugging. "It's just a matter of paperwork before you can have some fun. Unless you're just going to join a monastery," I quipped. His eyes heated.

"That's enough of that," he said. "Contrary to what your mother might have drilled into your head, sex isn't the end-all of all things, Phoebe. It's a horse that pulls you along, maybe, but you gotta keep it from going wild. All you'll do is end up like she will someday, crying over a glass of cheap gin in some dump bar, deserted by men who found younger women and dumped her like yesterday's newspaper. Just keep that picture in your mind whenever you stop to think about her."

There was no doubt that was what he envisioned, or hoped.

"You really hate her now, don't you?" I asked.

"No," he said. "I really feel sorry for her, but the way I feel sorry for someone with a contagious disease. I don't want to get too close."

"You two weren't always like that, Daddy. What happened to change it?" I asked.

He raised his eyes in surprise again. I thought he was just going to tell me not to think about it or say something to pretend it wasn't so, but he nodded slowly instead.

"I guess you're old enough to know. This is hardly the first time she betrayed me with another man. I caught her with someone once before, someone I trusted, too, and in our own home!"

"Why didn't you throw her out?"

"It's not that easy, Phoebe. I was hoping it would be different," he said. "She seemed remorseful, and I thought if I forgave her, we'd get back to the way we were. That didn't happen, but there's no sense talking about all that now. Let's just think about the future."

"Right," I said, "the future. Like I have one waiting for me out there."

"It doesn't wait for you. You have to make it for yourself," he said.

It was on the tip of my tongue to say, "Like you did?" But I didn't feel that mean. Instead, I gazed around at our small apartment. I didn't have any real affection for where we were living. My room was a two-by-four and we had trouble with roaches all the time, but even a rat gets used to its hole, I thought, and for a moment or two when it was time to leave, I paused at the doorway as if I was saying good-bye to a real friend.

"You won't regret this," Daddy said, seeing my small hesitation.

I said nothing. I just followed him out and into the car. This time it felt like we were in a funeral procession all the way to Stone Mountain. When we arrived, Uncle Buster was at work, and Jake and Barbara Ann were at school. Aunt Mae Louise greeted us without a smile. I supposed that up until the last moment she was praying it wasn't going to happen.

Daddy brought in my suitcase, looking like some exhausted road salesman making his last stop. Afterward, he stood in the doorway with a face so sorrowful it made me sick to my stomach.

"Good-bye, Daddy," I said. He kissed me on the forehead and hurried back to his car, now looking as relieved as a mouse that had outrun a cat.

"Let's get to it," Aunt Mae Louise told me then, and followed me to my room so she could hover over me as I unpacked my things.

"Don't think they'll let you wear that to school," she said, pointing at my abbreviated blouse with spaghetti straps. "I don't know why you bothered packing such a thing and bringing it here. I won't let you go out of this house in such rags. You got to remember that everything you do now reflects on your uncle Buster and me. Every time you have to decide on something, no matter how large or small, you think of that."

I didn't say anything. When I was finished, she said we were going to the school so I could be registered. I was surprised at how much she had done in preparation for my coming. She had given the school guidance counselor information about me, and he had contacted my school in Atlanta. The new school already had my records. We met with the guidance counselor, Mr. VanVleet, a tall, red-headed man who smiled as if he had been waiting anxiously for me to finally arrive, as anxiously as he awaited some exchange student from another country.

"We want you to succeed here, Phoebe," he began. He tapped the folder on the desk. "I see you have had some difficulties at your previous school."

Aunt Mae Louise grunted and said, " 'Difficulties' is too nice a word." She squirmed in her seat, but Mr. VanVleet kept his smile.

Maybe it's a mask, I thought. Anyone would need a mask to keep smiling in Aunt Mae Louise's presence.

"What we'd like you to do is get you at the proper reading level as quickly as possible. We have a class designed to do just that, and for a while, that's where we want you to begin. Once you're at the proper reading level, we'll be able to schedule you into classes you should be in, but we don't want to do that until we're sure you'll succeed. You understand that, don't you?"

I shrugged. None of it mattered to me. I wasn't going to be here long.

"Whatever," I said.

"Well, look at it this way," he continued, "you wouldn't want a third-grade student put in an eleventh-grade class, now would you? How would he or she do? Not too well, right?"

"You saying I'm like a third grader?" I asked, not hiding my indignation.

His eyes shifted to Aunt Mae Louise for a second and then back to me.

"I'm afraid that's about your reading level, but don't you worry. We'll fix that fast if you give it some effort."

"You're going to put me with third graders?"

I'd be sitting in a classroom with Barbara Ann!

"No," he said, laughing. "But with other students who have some temporary reading difficulties. There are some who are older than you, in fact."

I felt a little relieved about that, but still suspicious.

"She'll do what she has to do to succeed," Aunt Mae Louise promised him. "She knows how important it is now," she added, stabbing me with her penetrating glare.

"That's good," he said. "Let me take Phoebe down the corridor to meet Mr. Cody, the remedial reading teacher. You'll find him to be a very good teacher, Phoebe. He has had lots of success."

"Go on," Aunt Mae Louise ordered, and I stood up and followed Mr. VanVleet out.

"I know how hard it is to start somewhere new," he said as we walked. "You don't hesitate to come to me with any problems first, okay?"

Here's my problem, I wanted to stop and say. My mother has run off with a cheap con man. My father is too weak to deal with anything and pawned me off on my ogre aunt and uncle. I feel like Cinderella without any hope of any prince and never a glass slipper. Do you have a pill or something that will make all that go away?

Instead, I was silent and walked along listening to him describe the school, some of its important rules and regulations, and why I could still turn my life around and be successful at something.

Teachers, I decided, live in a world of fantasy, a fantasy of their own making. If they blinked too hard, they would see their students for who and what they were and they would get so discouraged, they would run out the door. At least that was how I had seen the teachers in my school. Most of them looked defeated and taught to the one or two students who showed any promise at all. The rest were just a nagging reminder of how ineffective they were, and who wants to be reminded of failure?

But that was exactly what was happening to me at the moment. Failure was being rubbed in my face.

Mr. VanVleet opened the door, and I looked in at a dozen remedial reading students. There was an expression I had heard at my old school whenever teachers referred to students like this, I thought. They called them mentally challenged. We called them retards.

"This is a new student, Phoebe Elder," Mr. VanVleet announced to the group. Some looked as disinterested as they had been the moment before we came. Some brightened slightly with curiosity, and one girl with a caramel complexion and long, reddish brown hair broke into a wide, happy smile.

I looked at them all and felt as if I had been forced to look into a mirror that hid no blemishes. Was this really where I belonged?

Mr. VanVleet saw the expression on my face.

"You'll make fast progress here, I'm sure," he said, "and get back on track quickly."

The only thing that kept me from turning and running was the realization that I had no place to go. Mama hadn't left a forwarding address.

"Welcome, Phoebe," Mr. Cody said. He was a short, stout man with balding curly black hair, a thick nose, and soft, almost feminine lips. His chin cut in so sharply, it was practically nonexistent. "Sit right here," he said, pulling the chair out a bit at the desk near the girl with the wide smile. She was still smiling at me that way. Is her face stuck? I wondered.

Mr. VanVleet pulled Mr. Cody aside, spoke to him softly, and then handed him my file.

"Okay," Mr. Cody said. "While the rest of us work on these exercises, Phoebe, I'd like you to take this little test I've designed. It will help me understand how I can best help you, okay?"

Everyone is so eager to help me, I thought disdainfully. The truth was, they probably wished I never had come.

He handed me the test, and I reluctantly began to do it.

"You can't fail," Smiley whispered to me.

"What?"

"No one ever fails Mr. Cody's tests."

"I'll try to be the first one," I told her. Her smile finally faded.

"What?"

"Quiet, Lana," Mr. Cody told her. "Don't disturb Phoebe. Just work on your reading exercises."

She pulled back into her chair and squinted, looking like she was going to cry.

Because I had arrived late and all, there wasn't much time for me to do any more than take the test. I heard bells ring at the end of periods and heard students pass through the hallways, talking loudly, laughing, but none of the remedial reading students got up to go anywhere else. It was clear that all we left this room to do was go to the bathroom and to lunch. I hadn't understood.

"Don't I go to a science class or a history class?" I asked Mr. Cody after the first change of classes was over.

"For a while you'll have all that here," he said. "I divide the day into the subjects and work on the reading that applies to each subject. Everything involves reading, Phoebe."

"This is like grade school," I complained. "I guess they just dumped me somewhere."

"Oh, no, no," he assured me. "We give you and the others here very individualized treatment. You're very special."

"I don't want to be special," I muttered.

The others listened to my complaints with some interest. I was sure most of them felt like saying what I was saying.

"For now, it's the best way," Mr. Cody insisted.

How was I supposed to meet anyone or get to know anyone, locked up in here like this? I thought. And when I did get out, they would all know I was one of the mentally challenged. I remembered how those students were treated at my old school. They might as well have had leprosy.

All of this just added to my sense of entrapment. Daddy had thought I'd be like a mole coming up into a world of bright light and hope, but all I did was go deeper into the darkness. At least, that was how I saw it.

It took me hours to finish the evaluation test. Mr. Cody let me go to the bathroom once, and I left hoping to meet someone maybe smoking in a stall and borrow a cigarette, but there was no one else there and besides, I saw they had a teacher monitoring the hallways, checking passes, and making note of the time a student left a room and returned to a room. To my further surprise, the teacher already knew my name. What, was the whole school warned about me? I wondered.

When the bell rang at the end of the day, the teachers were out there herding the students into the buses to keep them from loitering in the hallways. Mr. Cody promised to have my test results first thing in the morning and then design a program for me.

"Every student gets his or her own program to fit his or her special needs," he explained after the others had left. "That way we can be sure we'll strengthen your weaknesses. Sound good?" he asked.

"Sounds like you think I'm sick," I retorted.

His lips held the friendly smile, but his eyes turned a little dark and cold. He was obviously someone who expected to be appreciated.

"Well, in a way that's what's happened. We take your mental temperature and treat your problems and make you a better student," he said, obviously proud of his answer.

I didn't say anything else. I left the room and followed directions to the exit where my bus was waiting. Barbara Ann was standing by the bus, looking for me.

"You gotta hurry so you don't miss the bus or don't get a good seat," she chastised.

That was just what I needed to finish my day—an eight-year-old bawling me out. She stomped onto the bus ahead of me, expecting I

would sit beside her. Instead, I slipped in next to a white boy with
curly light brown hair who was glaring out the window like he was
fixing to smash it with his fist. He didn't even notice I had sat beside
him until we were under way. Barbara Ann was sulking in the rear
with her friends. I supposed she had bragged how she was going to
boss around a high school girl.

Finally, the white boy turned and looked at me. His eyebrows rose
and then dipped in at each other.

"Who are you?" he asked.

"The Queen of England," I replied. He stared a moment and then
laughed.

"I wish I was in England," he said. "I wish I was anywhere but
here."

"That makes two of us."

"You just come to school here?"

"That's right, and not because I wanted to, either."

"Well, where you really from?"

"Atlanta. I'm living with my aunt and uncle for a while."

He nodded as if that was something very common.

"I know why I hate being here. What's your problem?" I asked him.

He looked out the window again and then turned back to reply.

"I just got thrown off the basketball team. My father's going to bust
an artery."

"Why'd you get thrown off?"

"Got caught with these," he said, and pulled a pack of cigarettes out
of his jacket pocket. "In the locker room. Didn't think the coach was
anywhere nearby so I went into a shower stall and lit up. No second
chances with Coach McDermott. I was on the starting five, too," he
added.

"What's your name?"

"Ashley Porter," he said. "Or it used to be. Now it's Mud."

"Can I have one of those?" I asked.

"Huh?"

"A cigarette. Can I have one?"

"You can't light up on the bus. You'll get me suspended on top of
everything else."

"It's for later," I said. "I couldn't bring any from Atlanta. My aunt
put me through a metal detector and a body search when I came to her
house."

"Did not," he said, smiling.

"Close to it."

"What's your name?"

"Phoebe Elder."

"What class are you in?"

"How to be a millionaire."

"What?" He laughed. "C'mon."

"They put me in some remedial reading class for the time being because I read like someone who just came from another country. I'm not staying here long, so I don't care."

"Where you going?"

"Back to my apartment in Atlanta, one way or another," I told him.

"Sure," he said. He turned away, and then he turned back and gave me a cigarette.

"Thanks."

"I should give you the whole pack. I wish you had asked me this morning and I had," he moaned.

"Maybe your daddy will get him to take you back on the team."

"My mother will try to get him to do that, but my father's a hard guy. He'll tell me I deserved worse and even call the coach and thank him for throwing me off the team. He was a marine."

"Your daddy was?"

"Yeah, and he never lets me forget it, so don't complain about your aunt."

"Who says she wasn't a marine, too?" I told him, and he laughed again.

I liked his smile. When he relaxed his lips, his eyes brightened like two candles of crystal blue light. He had a very small dimple in his left cheek, too. It flashed when he smiled.

"I get off here," he said as the bus came to its first stop. "Wish me luck."

"Good luck," I said as I stood to let him out. He brushed very close to me, pausing to look into my eyes, and then smiled again.

"How do I get into remedial reading class?" he teased.

"Flunk everything," I told him, and he laughed.

"See you tomorrow if I'm still alive."

"Same for me," I called after him. He waved as he went down the bus steps.

Then I flopped back into my seat. When I turned to look at Barbara Ann, I saw she was glaring at me, looking more like her mother now, her eyes full of suspicion and criticism, as if it came natural.

"How come you were talking to that boy?" she asked when we reached our stop and got off.

"Don't they let black girls talk to white boys here?"

"I don't mean that. He's on the basketball team. I saw him at the game. Shouldn't he be at practice?"

"You're awful nosy for an eight-year-old girl," I told her. "Watch you don't get it caught in a door."

"Huh?"

I hurried along until we reached the house. Aunt Mae Louise looked like she had been waiting at the doorway for quite a while to greet me.

"How was your first day at school?" she asked as soon as I entered behind Barbara Ann. Jake was still attending a preschool at a different location.

"Peachy," I said. "It's run like a prison."

"I'm not surprised to hear you say that. I'm sure you're not accustomed to a well-run school," she replied. "Never mind. Put your things away, change into something you can work in, and come to the kitchen. I'm rearranging the pantry and I want to clean it out first. Then we'll work on dinner, and you can set the table before you wash up and dress for dinner."

"Dress for dinner?"

"We always dress for dinner," she said. "The dinner table is a special place for a family and should be treated with respect."

I looked at her as if she had gone crazy, and she pulled those tiny shoulders back as she usually did when she didn't like something I said or did.

"Hurry up and do what I say," she snapped.

I wanted to say, "Aye, aye, sir," and salute, but I knew it would only make her more angry.

She had me take everything off the pantry shelves and dust and polish. Then, I had to put it all back in an organized manner, alphabetizing soups, pasta, rice, and vegetables and fruit in cans. Every once in a while, she would look in and tell me I had a *d* or a *g* in the wrong place and I had to take it all off and rearrange it.

"Concentrate on what you're doing," she said. "You know your alphabet at least, don't you?"

"What difference does it make if a soup starting with *c* comes after one starting with *t*?" I asked, referring to the chicken noodle and the tomato I had confused.

"I can tell instantly what I need. That's what. Being organized saves us money and time. I can just imagine what your mother's cabinets were like."

I shrugged.

"Most of the time, empty," I said, but she didn't think that was funny.

Finally, I finished it to her satisfaction, and she sent me off to clean up and dress for dinner. I had no idea what she considered proper, but I showered and put on a black dress Mama gave me last year when she remembered she had forgotten my birthday. It was one of hers when she was younger and much slimmer. I hadn't worn it since then, and when I put it on, I realized it was tight, especially around my breasts. It had a V-necked collar and because of the way it lifted and tucked, my cleavage deepened. I was going to change into something else when Barbara Ann opened my door to say, "Mama says it's time to come to dinner. Right now," she added. "Daddy's already sitting at the table and Mama says you got to help serve," she whined.

"Maybe I'll help her eat it, too," I said.

"What did you say?"

"Get your ears fixed," I muttered as I charged past her.

Uncle Buster looked up as soon as I entered the dining room. Jake was already seated and sitting like a proper marionette with his back straight and his hands folded in his lap. Aunt Mae Louise came out of the kitchen and stopped dead in her tracks, her mouth opening and closing.

"What's that you're wearing to my dinner?" she cried.

"You said to get dressed up, and this is the best I have," I told her.

Uncle Buster was just staring, a little wide-eyed.

"That's disgusting. You might as well have come in here naked," she spit back at me. "Where did you get such a dress? Does Horace know you have it?"

"Mama gave it to me for my birthday last year. It was one of hers."

"Well, that figures."

"You want me to go change or what?"

"No," she said. "We're not eating a cold supper because you don't dress properly. Get in here and bring out the string beans and then the mashed potatoes. Barbara Ann, you bring out the pitcher of cold water, and don't spill any of it."

She placed a roast chicken in front of Uncle Buster. He was still staring at me, now shaking his head slightly.

"Buster, you want to start carving the chicken?" Aunt Mae Louise asked him sharply.

"What? Oh, yeah," he said, and began.

After everything was brought out, we sat and Uncle Buster recited a prayer. Aunt Mae Louise kept her head bowed, but I could see her eyes were lifted enough to watch me.

"You use the smaller fork for your salad," she instructed.

"Why do we need two?" I asked, just curious.

"That's the way a proper table is set. I'm not surprised you haven't ever sat at one except the times you were here and obviously forgot."

"It's been a long time since we had dinner here," I remarked. I had to admit to myself that her cooking was good. She had done something to make the potatoes delicious, too.

"You were always invited for the holidays, but your mother had something better to do, like hang out at some sleazy gin palace, I suppose. Even though she was impossible, I did my best to help that girl, but when the devil gets a good grip on you and you don't care . . ."

"Amen to that," Uncle Buster said, chewing vigorously on his chicken leg.

"How come Mama fell to the devil and you didn't?" I asked. I was really curious about their upbringing, but she took it like a slap on the face.

"What's that supposed to mean? You think our mama and daddy were bad people? They did their best to show that girl the right ways. She was just born to be bad. Nothing they did worked, and they tried. We all tried, even after your daddy made a fool of himself and married her. Just look at you. Look at what she wrought."

Tears felt like little drops of burning acid under my lids, but I didn't let them out. I looked down and ate in silence. I am in hell, I thought. She didn't have to threaten me with it.

"Don't you take another tablespoon of those potatoes, Barbara Ann. You got weight to lose," Aunt Mae Louise snapped, and Barbara Ann's hand recoiled like a snake. She went into a pout. Aunt Mae Louise turned back to me.

"What's this I hear about you and some white boy on the bus?" she demanded.

"What?" I looked up at her and then at Barbara Ann, whose pout changed quickly to a smug smile on her lips.

"Not there five minutes and you make a scene?"

"I didn't make any scene. There was an empty seat beside him so I sat there. What did she tell you?"

"Never mind that. You be sure you don't bring any disgrace to our front door," she warned.

The mashed potatoes choked in my throat. I glanced at Uncle Buster, who still had a little of that look of surprise in his face from when I had come in wearing the dress. He ate and was silent like someone who was himself an invited guest at the table and had no right to speak.

"We'll clear the dishes and bring in the cups for your uncle Buster's and my cup of coffee."

"I don't get any?"

"Children don't need coffee," she remarked.

"I'm not a child."

"Girl," she said, standing and leaning toward me, "until you learn to behave like a proper young lady and not some urban alley cat, you're a child. You don't become an adult because you turn a certain age. That's the trouble with young people today, right, Buster?"

"Amen to that," he said, nodding and wiping his mouth.

"Last Sunday, the minister said we should issue licenses for adulthood and not let anyone drive a car, marry, or have children until they pass a test. We coddle and spoil our youngsters so much, we stop them from learning how to be responsible citizens."

"As ye sow, so shall ye reap," Uncle Buster recited.

"Amen," Aunt Mae Louise said.

"I guess the next thing we'll do is pass the plate for donations," I quipped, much louder than I intended.

Aunt Mae Louise looked like she was going to pop her eyes out onto the table. Uncle Buster dropped his jaw. Little Jake looked like he was going to laugh, and Barbara Ann bit down on her lower lip.

"You go right to your room," Aunt Mae Louise ordered. "No apple pie and ice cream for you tonight. Go on," she cried, her arm out and finger pointing.

No apple pie and ice cream? I guess I'll go and cry my eyes out, I thought, but said nothing. I turned and left them gaping after me. When I got to the room, I closed the door and sat on the bed, pouting. Maybe I should just run off tonight, I thought. I could go to Sylvia's for a day or so. Not having any real money made it all very hard, though. I barely had enough to pay for a bus ticket into the city.

Even though the door was closed, I could hear Barbara Ann moaning about her piece of pie being too small. Uncle Buster took her side, but Aunt Mae Louise was overpowering, and they all grew quiet again. Was this any more of a home than the apartment I had been forced to leave?

At this moment I really did feel like a trapped animal. It tore at my insides, making my nerve endings sing. I rose and went into the bathroom, locking the door. Then I took out the cigarette Ashley Porter had given me and lit up. Doing something as forbidden to me in this house as smoking made me feel a little free at least. I opened the window so the smoke would not be easily detected.

Just after I took one puff, Barbara Ann was at the door.

"I gotta go," she wailed.

"Just a minute," I said.

"I gotta go!" she cried louder.

"Damn it." I took another long puff, blew the smoke out the window, tossed the cigarette into the toilet and flushed. Then I waved the towel about.

"I gotta go now!"

"What's going on here?" I heard Aunt Mae Louise cry in the hallway.

I unlocked the door.

"I was just going to the bathroom. That's allowed, isn't it?" I asked.

"Go, but don't dawdle in there," she said.

Barbara Ann stood looking at me.

"I thought you had to go so bad," I told her.

She glanced at her mother and then rushed in and closed the door.

"Go back to your room. I'll tell you when to come out to wash the dishes," Aunt Mae Louise said.

I started away when the bathroom door opened.

"Come look at what's in the toilet, Mama," Barbara Ann said.

"What?" Aunt Mae Louise looked at me and then went in.

My heart began to pound. I started for the bedroom.

"Stop!" Aunt Mae Louise shouted. "Just stay right there," she ordered, her finger pointing to the floor. "Buster!"

Uncle Buster came around the corner.

"What?"

"You go into her room and tear everything apart. She brought in something she shouldn't and who knows what else?"

"I didn't bring in anything. I—"

"Go on, Buster," Aunt Mae Louise commanded.

"What she bring in?"

"A cigarette. A cigarette!"

He looked at me and marched past and into my room.

"God help you if he finds anything else," Aunt Mae Louise warned, her eyes on fire, "because He'll be the only one who can."

3

A Ravishing
Sexual Hunger

I was sure a correction officer looking for drugs in the most severe penitentiary didn't rip apart a prison cell as completely as Uncle Buster took apart my room. All the while I was made to stand in the hallway and wait outside while he went through my things. So miserable and unhappy, I was like an island with the sea eddying around me.

"If he finds any more or anything else, I swear I'll call the social services people and have them come and take you to be placed in a foster home this very minute," Aunt Mae Louise threatened.

I fought back the urge to turn and curse her, to shout that I didn't care and just run.

"You two get to your rooms now!" she snapped at Barbara Ann and Jake.

They hurried away.

"Smoking, and in my house, in my house! Don't you know how bad it is not only for you but for the people who smell your smoke, especially younger people like Barbara Ann and Jake? Don't you know that?"

"It was just two puffs of one cigarette with the window wide open," I said sullenly.

"Don't tell me that it was just this or just that. Just like you can't be a little pregnant, you can't be a little bad, girl. It's like a cancer. You don't cut it out right away, it will consume and destroy you. That's what the minister said last Sunday."

"That must have been a very long sermon last Sunday," I muttered.

Finally, Uncle Buster emerged and shook his head.

"Nothing else there," he said.

"You sure, Buster? You look good?"

"Go see for yourself, Mae Louise," he told her, and she stepped up to the bedroom door. Then she turned back to me.

"Get that room looking like it was and then you come out and do the dishes and don't dare drop anything. We'll talk about what this cigarette in the bathroom means tomorrow. Your daddy is going to be very disappointed if I tell him. Not here a day and you already break one of the rules. I'm not surprised."

She stepped back, and I looked in the room. The bed had been turned over, the mattress on the floor. The two pillowcases, the bed sheet, and the comforter had been stripped away and tossed about. All the drawers were emptied, my panties, bras, stockings thrown to the floor. Every garment I had brought was dangling over a chair or over the edge of the bed, especially my bras and my panties.

I shook my head.

"This is sick," I said. "What did he do, get excited over my clothes?"

"Don't you be disrespectful. Clean it up," Aunt Mae Louise ordered again.

I went in and began to put things back. Ten minutes later, she returned and handed me a pamphlet.

"What's this?"

"This is from the church. It tells young people why smoking is bad for them and why the devil himself wants you to light up. You read it and memorize it. Starting tomorrow night at dinner, I want to hear the first page."

"What?" I squinted. "That's—"

"You do what I tell you, Phoebe. I'm taking on my sister's responsibility and I intend to do it right. You read and memorize that. That's how you'll earn your right to eat," she declared, and left.

I looked at the pamphlet. Memorize? Right to eat? I'd rather starve, I thought, and tossed it to the floor.

Almost an hour later, she came by again and told me to look after the dishes.

"I'll be checking them so be sure there are no spots and smudges after you wipe them clean and put them back. There's polish and a rag on the counter. Do the dining room table after that, and I want the floor vacuumed."

"What are you going to do?" I asked.

She smiled at my quick comeback.

"Why, I'm going to pray for you, Phoebe, pray for you every night, and so will your Uncle Buster and your cousins."

"I don't know how to thank you all," I said.

She stood silent a moment and then in a cold, hard voice said, "I won't mention any of this to your father if you do everything I've told you to do. We expected a crisis or two with you. We just didn't expect it so soon, but I'm not about to give up on you. That is what you should be thankful for," she concluded, turned, and left again.

I wondered if Ashley Porter had it any worse when he got home today.

I did all she wanted me to do. While I was vacuuming, the phone rang and she came into the dining room to tell me my daddy was on the phone.

"I kept my promise," she said. "I didn't tell him what you did. He's waiting to talk to you. Go in the kitchen and pick up the phone."

I set aside the vacuum cleaner and did as she asked.

"Hey," Daddy said after I said hello. "How's it going?"

My throat closed up.

"Phoebe?"

"Fine," I managed. What was the point in complaining? He would only moan and groan about how helpless he was until things changed.

"It's a good school, isn't it?"

"Terrific," I said dryly.

"All well with Aunt Mae Louise? She seemed okay."

"Daddy," I said. "Don't call me or come here until you can get me home."

"What?"

"You heard me, Daddy. I am never going to be happy here. There's no sense pretending on the telephone."

"Now don't go and do anything stupid, Phoebe. You have a court record. Your mother's nothing more than a tramp, and I don't have the means to do what has to be done for you at the moment. You listening to me?"

"No," I said, tears finally rushing into my eyes, tears I had no time to trap beneath my lids. I flicked them off my cheeks as fast as they came.

"I'm working at this, Phoebe. I'll find a way. That's a promise," he said. "Be a good girl. Please," he begged.

"I gotta go, Daddy. I've got to finish my chores or I'll be locked in the basement."

"Phoebe?"

"Thanks for calling," I said, and hung up.

Aunt Mae Louise was standing right behind me in the doorway to the dining room. I knew she had been listening in.

"Didn't think you'd make it easy for him," she said. "Just go do whatever schoolwork you have. I'll finish up."

I walked out without saying a word. As I passed Barbara Ann's room, I looked in and saw her stuffing a chocolate bar in her mouth.

"I wonder what your mother would say if I told her about that," I said.

She stopped and looked terrified.

"That's the difference between us, Barbara Ann. I don't rat. I bet you don't have any friends, do you?"

"I do too."

"They would have to be fellow rats." I shook my head and went on to my room.

It wasn't too hard to fall asleep. The moment I crawled into bed, I realized how tired I was. I didn't want to think about my situation anymore so instead I looked forward to drifting off. The next thing I knew Barbara Ann was in my face to tell me Aunt Mae Louise wanted me up and about to help with breakfast, clear the table afterward, and take out the garbage.

"And Mama says you'd better have this room looking like it was before you go to school," she added, wagging her head.

"Get outta here before I turn your fat ears around," I warned her through clenched teeth.

Her eyes brightened with terror and she ran from my room. For a moment I just lay there wondering if I should simply refuse to do everything and get thrown out. Reluctantly, I rose, washed, and dressed in a pair of jeans and a blouse over which I put on a sweater I had lifted from the same department store I had been caught stealing from last month.

"Squeeze those oranges," Aunt Mae Louise ordered as soon as I appeared. "Your uncle Buster likes fresh juice every morning, and make sure you get out every drop. That's expensive."

Still half asleep, I did it, but she had to show me I had left some juice in every single orange.

"A penny wasted is a penny lost," she recited.

After I served Uncle Buster his juice, I got a lecture on how poorly I ate and why breakfast was the most important meal of the day. Aunt Mae Louise came to my room to inspect it after I had made my bed and went about criticizing everything: how I hung up my clothes, how loosely I had left the cover sheet, how I didn't fluff out the pillow correctly, on and on until I pointed out that I would miss the school bus.

"Don't forget to take out the garbage on the way out," she called after me.

I returned to the kitchen, got the bag, and dumped it in the can.

Barbara Ann was standing on the corner, embracing her books and talking to two other kids who looked about her age. They all turned as I approached, their eyes obviously brightened by the stories Barbara Ann had told them about me.

"Boo!" I said, and they jumped.

When I stepped up on the bus, I noticed immediately that Ashley Porter was sitting alone. He smiled and I slid in beside him.

"You survived, I see," he said.

"Barely. What about you?"

"My father took away my driving privileges, not that I had that much. Both he and my mother work and use their cars all day, six days a week. They let me use my mother's car Saturday nights and Sundays, but that's gone. I'm supposed to come right home after school, blah, blah," he said. "And you?"

"I gotta break a pile a rocks in the backyard with a sledgehammer."

He laughed and then asked me more about myself, about my school in the city and my friends. We talked so much, neither of us realized we were at the school until the driver opened the door.

"Maybe I'll see you at lunch," he said as we walked off the bus.

"I don't even know when that is. I came in after lunch yesterday and they keep us in that room."

He paused at the front door.

"Tell you what," he said. "Get sick about eleven-thirty. The nurse's name is Mrs. Fassbinder, and she's easy. You tell her you have cramps or something like girls have all the time and she'll let you lie down. I'll be there, too."

"What good's that?" I asked him.

"You'll see," he said with a twinkle in his eye, and left for his homeroom.

Armed with the results of my reading test from yesterday, Mr. Cody greeted me eagerly.

"I feel certain that you suffer from a learning disorder we call dyslexia, Phoebe."

I grimaced.

"What's that mean?"

"Well, the short explanation is that you confuse letters or words and write and read words or sentences in the wrong order. This doesn't have anything to do with your intelligence, which I believe is above average," he said.

Was that just to make me feel good? I wondered.

"It still sounds sick," I said.

"More people than you know suffer from dyslexia, Phoebe. Why, Tom Cruise was diagnosed with it, and he hasn't done so badly for himself, has he?"

I looked suspicious.

"Go read about him. You'll see. I don't want to get too technical with you. It's not necessary. You have a problem that affects your reading ability, and that has a big impact on your ability to learn, which would explain why you don't do well in subjects that require a lot of reading. No one wants to do something they keep failing at, so they avoid it, get discouraged. It explains a lot," he said in a voice a little above a whisper as if he and I were now sharing a very important secret.

"So?" I said.

"I'm surprised the teachers, evaluators in your previous school didn't concentrate on this problem for you."

"I'm not," I said.

If I told him how many days of school I had missed, especially when I was in grade school and Mama was either too tired or hungover to take me, he might understand, I thought. Later, in high school, my teachers were happy if I just didn't give them any trouble. They left me alone and I left them alone, when I was in class.

"Well, we're going to attack the problem and help you here," he vowed. "I know I can make progress with you very quickly," he said.

"You mean I'll get outta here, out of this classroom?"

"Sooner than you think, if you work hard at what I give you," he promised.

He put me on some reading machine that included a screen on which words were printed, a pair of earphones, and a microphone for me to read into. It also checked my understanding of what I read periodically. I noticed that the other students, including smiling Lana, seemed envious. When Lana asked Mr. Cody why she couldn't work on the machine too, he told her it wasn't for her. It was for someone with a different reading problem.

Instead of being happy about it, she looked disappointed. Mr. Cody winked at me, and I couldn't help believing he was telling me the truth. I was different from the other students. I really didn't belong in any class for the mentally challenged.

"That's better already," he said, looking over some of the work I had done the first hour.

Time passed faster than I thought it would, and I suddenly realized

it was nearly eleven-thirty. Remembering the plan Ashley had suggested, I stopped working and doubled over with pretended cramps. It
was something that always worked in classes where I had male teachers. Most of the time, they looked terrified and didn't hesitate to give
me permission to leave the room quickly. Mr. Cody was no different.
He told me where the nurse's office was, and I left the room.

Mrs. Fassbinder looked like she was close to eighty. Later, I found
out she was a retired nurse who needed to supplement her income. The
school had trouble finding anyone to fill the position. Her office was
much larger than the nurse's office in my last school. She had a desk
and a work area with scales and blood pressure cups, closets full of
bandages, disinfectants, and pairs of crutches, but off that office were
three rooms with cushioned cots, blankets, and pillows in them.

I told her my problem, and she assigned me a room.

"Just rest awhile," she suggested. "If you need something, it's right
here," she told me, and showed me where she kept tampons and sanitary napkins.

Now that I was in the room and lying on the cot, I wondered what
had happened to Ashley. I was beginning to feel silly about it when my
door opened slightly and he peered in, holding a cold wet cloth over
his forehead.

"Hey," he said, and I sat up.

He looked back toward Mrs. Fassbinder, and then he stepped into
my room and closed the door.

"Easy, wasn't it?"

"Yes."

"After a while she'll forget you're even in here," he said. "It's almost time for her to go to lunch. I'll be back as soon as she leaves," he
promised, and slipped out again.

A little more than five minutes later, he returned.

"She's gone," he said, sitting on the cot, "and when she leaves, she
locks the door and puts a sign up telling the students she's at lunch and
to go to the office for emergencies."

"I thought it would be harder to do something like this here," I said.
"You do it a lot?"

"Once in a while. When I have some good reason," he added with a
smile.

"What's your good reason now?" I asked him.

"You," he said, and leaned forward slowly to kiss me. I let him and
then leaned back on my pillow.

"How'd you know I'd let you do that?" I asked.

"I was hoping you would."

"You going to try to take advantage of me?" I asked him.

"No," he said, and smiled. "I'm hoping you'll take advantage of me."

We both laughed.

"I want you to know right now," he continued, dropping his smile, "that I'm not easy."

"Listen to you!" I said with some outrage. He shrugged.

"You're a very pretty girl, Phoebe. I don't know how long I can hold out."

"What?"

He leaned down and kissed me again, this time slipping his hands under my sweater and blouse. I held his arms for a moment and then he lifted his lips from mine, looked in my eyes, smiled again, and kissed me harder. It had been so long since I felt this good, I couldn't help but let my resistance slip away, especially when his fingers reached my breasts and his thumbs reached my nipples. I couldn't help moaning softly.

"I really like you," he whispered. "You're an exciting girl."

He lifted my sweater and I let him take it off, and then he unbuttoned my blouse and pressed his lips to my breasts, sliding them over to each nipple so slowly and gently, I tingled in anticipation.

"Man, you really are nice," he said. He surprised me by bringing his mouth down to my belly and then undoing my jeans to kiss me lower and lower.

Every few seconds I told myself, we're doing this in school, right in the nurse's office. It made it all seem more exciting—so exciting that my heart hammered at my chest and shortened my breath.

If I don't stop him soon, I'm actually going to give up my treasure, I told myself. He had his hands inside my jeans, moving around to cup my buttocks and lift me so he could kiss me lower, his lips now caressing the insides of my thighs.

"I've got what we need," he whispered. "Don't worry."

He backed away to prepare himself and in those seconds, I argued with myself, warning myself that this was my last chance to stop before it was too late. I knew what it was to reach a peak of excitement and then fall over like someone who had lost her footing on a cliff. I would be helpless, caught up in my own ravishing sexual hunger.

You're not here two days, Phoebe Elder, I lectured myself. How can you do this with the first boy you've met? You'll get a bad reputation so quickly it will be impossible to walk the halls. Stop him; stop him before it's too late.

It's all right, another side of me argued. He really likes you and you like him. When that happens, you don't need much time. It's magical. Go with it. Enjoy something in this miserable situation.

He stepped out of his pants and underwear and was between my legs. We were kissing harder now. I held on to his shoulders and waited, but before he could do anything, the door opened.

There was a moment of such deep silence, it was as if a nuclear bomb had gone off and it was just a split second before the explosion would sound. The silence made the situation seem more like a dream, like Ashley Porter and I were floating and would just fall to earth like two feathers.

Then we heard Mrs. Fassbinder's scream, and Ashley leaped back, scurrying for his clothing. I pulled up my jeans and turned away from the door.

"Get out! Get out!" she shouted at Ashley.

"I'm going. I'm going. Take it easy," he cried.

I got my blouse back on and buttoned it clumsily. Then I sat up and pulled my sweater over myself as Ashley rushed out the door. Mrs. Fassbinder stepped back with her hands still up and shaking.

"Oh, my God," she said, looking in at me. "Oh my, my."

She looked so confused and flustered, I half-expected her to suffer heart failure. Her pallid face was beet red, her lips twisting. Then, finally gathering her wits, she told me to stay where I was and rushed off. I finished fixing my clothes and walked out of the room. Ashley was nowhere to be seen, and neither was Mrs. Fassbinder. After I splashed some water on my face, I wiped it with a towel and returned to the remedial reading room.

"How are you?" Mr. Cody asked when I entered. "You look a little flustered yet."

"I'm all right," I said, and then noticed no one else was in the room. "What's going on?"

"It's your lunch hour, Phoebe." He pointed to the clock. "Be back at one-ten. You know where the cafeteria is and all, right?"

"I'm not hungry," I said.

"Well, you still have a long day ahead of you, Phoebe. You should get something in your stomach, unless the nurse has said otherwise, of course."

"That's right. She said otherwise," I told him.

"Well, I'm just off to lunch myself. You can sit here or go outside as long as you don't leave the school grounds, okay?"

I nodded, and he left. The truth was I was still shaking, the trembles rattling my very bones. I flopped into my seat and lowered my head to my folded arms. I think I fell asleep for a few minutes because when the door was opened and I heard my name, it was almost one o'clock.

A tall, dark-haired man wearing a tie and a shirt with no jacket stood in the doorway, holding the door open. His shirtsleeves were rolled up to his elbows. He had a firm mouth, a cleft chin, and two brown eyes under thick, dark brown eyebrows.

"Phoebe Elder?" he said again.

"Yes."

"Come with me," he said.

"Who are you?"

"Dean Cassidy," he said. "Let's go."

"Where am I going?"

"To my office, young lady. Move it. I don't intend to have a conversation with you in this doorway," he said sternly.

I rose and walked out.

"Keep going," he said, remaining a foot or so behind me. "Just past the guidance department," he added, and I turned into an office doorway.

The secretary turned from the filing cabinet and looked at us. She had short, auburn hair and was dumpy with a round face. Her eyes narrowed as she shook her head.

"Send for Ashley Porter," Dean Cassidy ordered, and she moved quickly to the phone on her desk.

"In here," he told me, holding a door open.

I entered his office, which wasn't much bigger than the outer office. On the paneled walls were all sorts of commendations, plaques, and awards from a variety of community organizations, congratulating Dean Cassidy for his work with the youth of the community, as well as his college degrees in gilded frames. I saw pictures of a pretty woman and two little girls on his desk.

"Sit," he commanded, pointing to a chair in front of his desk. He didn't go to his chair. Instead, he went to the window and looked out. He stood there without speaking so long, I assumed he was waiting for someone else, but finally he turned and glared down at me.

"I've been here for almost ten years now," he began. "I've dealt with many things, insubordination in class, truancy, theft, fighting, smoking, vandalism, but this is the first incident of something as sordid and disgusting as this.

"And then, on top of that, to have such a thing involve a student that hasn't been in my school two full days!"

I turned away from him and stared at the wall.

"I don't know whether to have you sent to a church, a mental institution, or a prison," he hollered so loudly it made my ears ring and shook my insides, but I didn't cry and I didn't cower.

Slowly, I turned my head back to him and looked up at him. He was frozen with his back bent, his face glaring, his arms out.

"Well, when you decide," I said softly, "let me know."

If a human being could explode and reform himself, he would have at that moment. His face got so red with blood, I thought the top of his head would blow off and stick to the ceiling. His throat undulated like the body of a snake, his Adam's apple bulging, and then he stammered and pointed at me.

"You . . . you show me some respect, young lady. Your life here is hanging on by a thread."

I turned away again, and there was a knock on the door.

"Come in!" he screamed.

The door opened, and his secretary told him Ashley was outside.

"Send him in here," he commanded.

I heard Ashley enter, but I didn't look back at him.

"Not only is the coach very, very disappointed in you, Ashley, I am absolutely disgusted with your behavior. What was going on in your head?"

I smiled to myself.

It wasn't exactly what was going on in his head that mattered, I thought.

"Wipe that grin off your lips, young lady, or I'll wipe it off for you," Dean Cassidy threatened.

"And how you going to do that?" I shot back up at him.

His eyes widened in surprise. I looked at Ashley, who was just as astounded. He shook his head gently as a warning.

Dean Cassidy got hold of himself and straightened up.

"I wanted the two of you in here together so I wouldn't get one story from one of you and another story from the other. You don't know how serious this is, Ashley. You could be in a lot more hot water than I cook up," Dean Cassidy told him, and nodded at me.

What was he implying? That I would accuse Ashley of trying to rape me?

Ashley looked sufficiently terrified now.

"I'm not going into detail about what Mrs. Fassbinder reported. You know what she saw. Do either of you want to deny it?" the dean asked.

"No, sir," Ashley said quickly.

"And you, young lady?"

"My name's Phoebe," I said.

"And you, Phoebe?"

I looked at Ashley.

"I guess what she told you is what it was, but I don't know what she told you, now do I?"

"Well, I'm not going to get into detail about it," Dean Cassidy said. He finally sat behind his desk.

"Okay, Phoebe, you wait outside. I want to speak with Ashley first."

I got up and walked out, closing the door hard behind me. I knew what he was going to say in there. I could have written his dialogue for him. He was going to tell Ashley Porter I was a very bad girl with a bad record from my other school and he had gotten himself into trouble because of me. He was going to tell him how devastated his parents were going to be when they heard about it all. He was going to tell him how he was a boy with a good future that he was tossing into the ash can. And then finally, he was going to try to get him to put as much blame on me as he could. By the time he was finished, it would be as Ashley had pretended: I had seduced him.

Ashley will probably do and say what the man wanted, I thought. What did I matter anyway? His parents lived here, and the dean would emphasize that he should be concerned about them.

"She doesn't care how her aunt Mae Louise and uncle Buster look in the community, or she wouldn't have gotten herself into so much trouble here so quickly. You have no reason to be loyal to a girl like that," he would say.

Maybe Ashley didn't need all that much convincing. The truth was, I hardly knew him. For all I knew, *loyalty* was a foreign word to him. He was certainly not very loyal to his teammates on the basketball squad, I thought.

Why didn't you think about all that before, stupid? I asked myself as I sat across from the secretary, who looked at me as though I were a serial killer. She avoided my eyes and worked on files.

After what seemed like thirty minutes, but was probably only ten, the dean's office door opened and Ashley, his head bowed, came out with the dean right behind him. He glanced at me and then quickly shifted his eyes guiltily away.

"Write him a pass back to class," the dean said with his hand on Ashley's shoulder.

"Phoebe," the dean said, and nodded at his opened door.

I stood up, looked at it, and shook my head.

"No, thanks," I said. "I been there, done that."

"What?"

Ashley spun around in surprise as I walked past him out of the office and started down the hallway.

"If you know what's good for you, young lady, you'll march right back in here!" Dean Cassidy called after me from the office doorway.

I know what's good for me, I thought.

That's why I'm not marching right back.

4

Daddy's Gone

I didn't know where I was going, of course. I just left the building and continued to walk down the street. I went about four blocks before a police car pulled up alongside me and sounded its siren. The policeman got out when I stopped and turned.

"Where do you think you're going?" he asked.

"Anywhere but here," I said.

"You can't do that, miss. The school is responsible for your well-being. Now get into the car," he ordered.

He wasn't that tall, but he looked like he could rip a tree out by its roots. His shoulders were wide, and he had a neck so thick, I thought it would look perfect on a bull. He stepped toward me threateningly.

I walked to the car and got in.

"Where do you live?" he asked, and I gave him Aunt Mae Louise and Uncle Buster's address.

"You're taking me home, then?"

"That's where the school wants you brought. Your mother's been called."

"She's not my mother," I said.

"Who is she?"

"My aunt."

"Whoever she is to you, she's been called. What did you do wrong, anyway?" he asked.

"Be born," I said, and stared out the window.

"Kids today," he mumbled. We drove without speaking the remainder of the trip.

I felt certain Aunt Mae Louise would get rid of me now. With all she was telling Daddy and me about how important she and Uncle Buster were in the school community, she would surely be too embarrassed to keep me around. In a way I felt relieved. Daddy would have to take me back, and we would have to find a way to make it work.

When we pulled into the driveway, the front door opened and she stood there with her hands on her hips, shaking her head. The policeman got out and approached her with me trailing behind.

"You her aunt?" he asked.

"Unfortunately, yes," she replied.

He asked her to sign some paper on his clipboard, which made me feel like a package being delivered.

"Good luck," he sang as he returned to his car.

"We'll need it," she called after him, and looked at me.

"Not here two days and you do something like this?" she asked.

"I want to go home," I said.

"Believe me, that's what I want, too. Get in and stay in your room until Buster calls. He's trying to locate your daddy right now."

"Good," I said, marching past her.

I went into my room and shut the door. All the while I hadn't noticed how gray the sky had become. The room grew darker and darker until I heard raindrops tapping on the window with a sound that made me think of tapping witch's fingers, long and bony with sharp, hard fingernails. It was something I heard and saw in recurrent nightmares all my life, only now the witch's face I imagined was Aunt Mae Louise's face.

More often than not, when I was younger and I had a bad dream, there was no one there to comfort me. I would put on my lights and catch my breath, but I distrusted every shadow, no matter how small. Nightmares hid themselves in shadows. They waited and watched until they were confident I was asleep, and then they crossed through the light and came into my head through my ears or my nose or my open mouth. That was what I used to believe and, although I never told a soul, still believed. Even when I was little, I sensed that if I told Mama, she would either ignore me, yell at me for being stupid, or maybe even laugh and tell one of her friends what I had said and embarrass me. She had done something like that often enough.

Now I sat here, unable to stop the trembling inside myself, despite the angry brave front I had put on in front of the dean, the policeman, and Aunt Mae Louise. It was one thing to be alone in a world where there were other girls like myself who were as alone or almost as alone as I was, but to feel like I felt here was harder.

This is all Mama's fault, I thought. If she hadn't been so selfish, she would have considered me and what would happen to me after she had run off. I hated Aunt Mae Louise, but she wasn't all wrong when it came to my mama, I admitted to myself. And she wasn't wrong about Daddy either, about him ignoring all the warnings and about him being too weak.

But he was all I had and I was all he had now. Lucky people had lots of choices for themselves. I had none. Wherever I was in my life, I thought, there would always be bars on the windows. There would always be shadows waiting to pounce on me. Lie back and take it, Phoebe, I told myself. Stop trying to go against the wind.

I closed my eyes and listened to the rain and fell asleep. The sounds that woke me were the sounds of Barbara Ann and Jake returning home. I heard Aunt Mae Louise chastise them for making too much noise, and I heard her warn them to stay away from me. The tone in her voice made me sound like I could contaminate them.

The drizzle turned into a heavy downpour. It went on and off for what seemed like hours and hours. I left the room only to go to the bathroom, and when I walked through the hall, I was struck by how quiet it was in the house. Both Jake's and Barbara Ann's doors were shut tight, and Aunt Mae Louise wasn't nearby. All I could do was wait. Finally, she came to my room.

"Your uncle Buster has not been able to locate your daddy yet. His company is trying to contact him for us, but he hasn't gotten to his scheduled stops, I guess. Anyway, you might as well come out and help me get the dinner ready. Uncle Buster is on his way home."

"Are you sure you want me touching things?" I asked sullenly.

She paused and furled her brow.

"No, I don't want you touching things, but I don't want you doing nothing either. Idle hands get into mischief."

I followed her out and set the table. The truth was, I was getting cabin fever in that tiny room anyway. Even her grouchy face and bitter comments brought some variety. When Barbara Ann came out of her room, she looked at me with different eyes, eyes not so full of herself as they were fearful of me. What did Aunt Mae Louise tell her, I wondered, or what had she heard from the other students on the bus?

As if she could read my thoughts, Aunt Mae Louise decided to tell me immediately why Barbara Ann was looking at me askance.

"The other kids made fun of her on the bus, I'll have you know. Seems the news about you and that boy spread like a bad rash through the school. All of our friends are going to hear about it now. Fine thing to do to us."

I didn't say anything. My tongue stayed glued to the roof of my mouth even though the words were scratching away at the base of my throat. I finished what I had to do and then, when Uncle Buster came in, I sat with my head down.

"Your daddy's going to be very disappointed to hear about this when I contact him," he said. Surprisingly, that was all he said. Aunt Mae Louise said grace, and then we ate in relative silence. Every once in a while, I looked up and saw Jake staring at me wide-eyed.

Finally, I couldn't take it any longer and I slapped my fork down on the table and stood up.

"I didn't kill anyone, you know," I screamed, and marched out of the dining room.

"Phoebe Elder!" Aunt Mae Louise called after me. "You don't get up from the table until you are excused. Do you hear what I said?"

"Let her go," Uncle Buster said.

I slammed the door behind me. What little I had eaten seemed to be caught in my throat. My stomach churned, and I went into the bathroom and threw up. They heard me, but no one came to see how I was. Now I was thinking that I wouldn't wait for them to contact Daddy. I would pack my things and just leave. I could hitchhike a ride back into Atlanta proper, and I knew where we kept our key outside the apartment. There was no sense in staying here a moment longer.

It was still raining very hard, however, so I thought I would at least wait for it to let up. In the meantime, I packed everything and then I sat on the bed with my arms folded, facing the door. To my surprise, it opened slowly and little Jake poked his head in.

"What do you want?" I asked him.

"Are you really going to hell?" he replied.

"Your mother tell you that?"

He nodded.

"No. I am not going to hell. I am in hell and so are you," I snapped back at him.

"No, I'm not. Only bad people go to hell," he said. Even at his young age, he had Aunt Mae Louise's scowl.

"Not just bad people," I said, "also unlucky people."

My answer put some confusion in his eyes. He shook his head and said, "No, they don't."

"You better not come too close to me," I warned, "or I'll take you with me. I'll wrap my arms around you so tightly you won't be able to get loose and we'll go down, down, down."

He started to shake his head and then I went, "Boo!" He backed out quickly and closed the door. I started to laugh, but stopped and suddenly felt more like I should cry.

Maybe Aunt Mae Louise was right to tell her children that. Maybe I am going to hell, I thought. I'm my mother's daughter, aren't I? What chance do I have to avoid it? The only thing I've accomplished in my short life is get myself deeper and deeper into trouble. It was a dark, descending road I traveled, and perhaps hell was at the end after all. I had no idea how or what would stop my fall. It seemed hopeless and useless to think of a way. I guess Mama had the right idea after all, I thought. Have a good time and don't worry about tomorrow.

The rain began to let up. I didn't hear it on the windowpane any longer, and when I looked out toward the street light, I saw the downpour had thinned to a slight drizzle. I decided I would wait until they were all asleep and then I would quietly slip out of the house and be out of their hair forever. Aunt Mae Louise would not have to worry about me corrupting her children, and she and Uncle Buster could make up any story they wanted and tell it to their friends in the community. Everyone but Daddy would be happier, including me.

It grew quieter and quieter in the house. I could hear only the muffled sounds of the television set, some water running in the kitchen, and then Aunt Mae Louise getting Barbara Ann and Jake to bed. Not much longer to wait, I thought. I felt like a racehorse champing at the bit. What lay ahead was not exactly a hike in the country. I had to carry my suitcase and get myself onto the more traveled highway before I could get any sort of ride. I didn't have enough money anymore to take a bus.

A little more than a half hour or so later, I heard the telephone ring. I was anticipating that they had finally contacted Daddy. I had made up my mind I wasn't going to talk to him on the phone. I had nothing to say now. This was his fault, too. He shouldn't have brought me here, and I shouldn't have come.

Why did I come? Did I hope this would work? Did I believe Daddy when he told me my life would change and I could have a future? I'm too poor and too cursed to afford a fairy tale, I thought. I should have known that only the rich and lucky become Cinderellas. Now, I would do what I had to do, and that was that.

Suddenly, I heard Aunt Mae Louise scream, "Lord, have mercy."

Uncle Buster called to her, and there was the sound of his heavy feet pounding the floor as he ran into the kitchen. I opened my door and listened. I heard him ask, "When?" and then, "How? Oh, Christ!"

Slowly, I made my way down the hall and stopped in the kitchen doorway. Uncle Buster had his back to me. He was still on the phone.

Aunt Mae Louise was collapsed in a chair, both her hands over her face.

"Yes," Uncle Buster said into the phone, "we understand. We'll take care of it. Give me that address again." He waved his hand toward Aunt Mae Louise, but she didn't see. She still had her hands over her face.

"What is it?" I demanded, and she lowered her hands and saw Uncle Buster's hand.

"Give me a pen and something to write on," he ordered. She jumped up and opened a drawer, found what he wanted, and gave it to him before turning to me.

"Terrible, terrible news," she said. Uncle Buster kept writing.

"What?"

"Your daddy, an accident. He's gone," she said.

I looked at her suspiciously, my head tilted.

"What do you mean, gone? Gone where?"

"To the lap of the Lord," she replied.

Uncle Buster thanked whomever he was speaking to and hung up the phone. With a long face, a face weighed down by gloom, he turned and looked at me. He shook his head, his huge eyes staring woefully back at me.

"What is she saying?" I asked him.

"Horace ran off the road sometime this afternoon. Luckily, some man sticking catfish in a stream came upon the car. It had gone down an embankment, through some woods before smashing into a tree and turning over and landing top down in the water."

"He always wears his seatbelt," I said, shaking my head.

"That didn't matter this time. Matter of fact, it may be why he didn't get out."

"Didn't get out? You mean Daddy drowned?"

"It's ugly," he replied.

What little food had remained in my stomach had long ago turned into a small pool of acid. It came rushing back up my throat. I stuffed my fist into my mouth.

"He was trying to cover too much territory in one day, I'm sure," Uncle Buster continued. "You get careless, go too fast around a turn, lose control."

"The Lord meant for it to be," Aunt Mae Louise muttered.

"What kind of Lord is that?" I shouted down at her.

"Don't blaspheme now, child. Your daddy needs to be with the angels and you will want to join him someday."

"No," I said. "This is all a lie. You're just trying to find another way to get rid of me."

"Boy, I wish that were true," Uncle Buster said.

"It is true. You're lying!"

"I got to make arrangements. We got to try to find your mother, Phoebe. No matter what she's done, she should know about this. You have any idea, any idea at all where she might have gone?"

I kept shaking my head.

"Well, I guess we'll have to get the police to help us," he told Aunt Mae Louise. She nodded.

"You're lying," I whispered.

"Now, you have to be a big girl, Phoebe. You have to be a good girl. This is a very hard time for all of us, and you don't know how hard it is going to be yet," Uncle Buster said. "I've got a lot to do here, and I can't be distracted by any unnecessary trouble, hear?"

I stared at him. My heart wasn't pounding. It felt more like it had stopped or melted. There was a deep, cold emptiness under my breast. I embraced myself.

"You see how hard life can be," he continued. "You see how important it is to be good, to be responsible and not be wasteful. Whatever blessings we have, we've got to cherish and appreciate."

He was going on and on like his father, the minister. I started to back away.

"It's all a lie," I muttered. "Another dirty lie. This is a house built on lies."

"That's it!" he screamed back at me. His voice bounced off the walls and I shuddered. "Stop that nasty talk now."

I couldn't stop trembling and I couldn't swallow. All I could do was shake my head.

"All right now, Phoebe," he said in a softer tone, "you go back to your room and get some sleep. We've got a lot to take care of tomorrow." He relaxed his shoulders. "You sure you can't help us find your mama?"

I shook my head harder.

"What's that man's name, the man she ran off with?" Aunt Mae Louise asked. "I didn't pay any attention to what your daddy told me. You know?"

"Speak up, Phoebe. This is not the time for any silly tantrums. Your aunt asked you something."

"Sammy Bitters," I said. It didn't sound like me talking. My voice was so deep.

"Name fits the situation," she told Uncle Buster. "Bitter."

He nodded.

"Go on, Phoebe. Get some rest," he said. "We'll take care of things. We'll take care of you and what has to be done."

Aunt Mae Louise looked up at him sharply. I could almost feel the new realization sinking into them both like a rock in soft mud: with my mother tramping about and not caring about me and my daddy dead and gone to the lap of God, they were all I had now. Like it or not, fate had more than just delivered me to their doorstep. It had put me smack into the middle of their lives. They couldn't send me back.

Aunt Mae Louise nodded.

"The Lord tests us," she said, more to herself than to Uncle Buster and me. "He gives us burdens to make us stronger and stronger."

First, I was a distraction, an annoyance, a responsibility my mama didn't want and finally denied, and now I had graduated to being a burden, but not just an ordinary burden, oh no. I was a blessed burden, a gift from God. The way she made it sound, I should be grateful. Think of all the young women my age who weren't a burden, who had a family that loved and cared for them, who were good students and behaved and said their prayers without being reminded to do so. Of what use were they for the struggle to reach the pearly gates Aunt Mae Louise saw parting for her celestial entrance? If there were no poor, there would be no charity, and how would my aunt get herself blessed?

I turned and walked back to my bedroom. When I got there, I closed the door and then I pressed my back to the wall and slid down slowly to the floor, where I sat next to my suitcase. I wanted to cry for Daddy, but I couldn't. None of this seemed real to me. Surely, Uncle Buster and Aunt Mae Louise would be coming to my door any moment to tell me that was all just meant to put the fear of God into me and make me behave.

"Now go to sleep and count your lucky stars that it isn't so," she would say.

Right? The little voice inside me, a voice I hadn't heard since I was no more than Jake's age, was asking.

Whether they felt sorry for me or what, I don't know, but a while later, there was a gentle knock on my door. I didn't open it or call out, but Uncle Buster opened it and peered in, confused at first when he didn't see me.

"What?" I asked him, looking up.

"What are you doing on the floor? Why is your suitcase out?" he asked quickly.

"I was going to leave," I said.

"No, no, no. You can't leave now, Phoebe. You're just confused and in shock," he told me. He didn't understand that I meant I was going to leave before the phone call. "Everything will be fine. You just get some sleep. I came by to see if you needed anything."

I stared up at him, and he looked uncomfortable.

"You should go to bed, Phoebe. It's going to be hard for the next few days. Go on. Get some sleep," he advised, and backed out, closing the door.

I lowered my head again and soon, I was feeling so tired I had to get up and go to bed. I was afraid of sleep, afraid of those shadows. They were closing in around me, encouraged by the news of Daddy's accident. Now there was definitely no one to come to help me chase them off. They would sink into my brain and make a home for themselves, swimming to the top of my thoughts whenever they pleased. Shout and scream, run and hide, I could do whatever I wanted and it would make no difference, not to them.

I kept my eyes slightly open as sleep crawled over me, slithering around my legs, my waist, and my breasts until it could tighten like a vise and close me in darkness. The shadows kept coming. I could almost hear them swishing over the walls and over the floor.

"Daddy!" I moaned, and then I closed my eyes completely and saw him again, rushing away, leaving me behind forever. It did no good to run after him. My nightmare diminished into a blob of darkness, and I woke with a start. For endless hours, I drifted fitfully on the rim of sleep, never finding the peaceful oblivion I desperately sought.

A cloud of silence came over my aunt and uncle the next morning. They kept Jake and Barbara Ann from making much noise and got them both off to their respective schools. When they spoke to each other in front of me, they practically whispered. Uncle Buster said he had to drive to where they had taken Daddy and make an identification. He never asked if I wanted to go along.

"I spoke with the police last night, and they are trying to locate your mama," he said. "Your aunt Mae Louise and I are making arrangements for your daddy's final resting place. We'll have a nice service for him here. My father will conduct it for us."

I listened to everything he said, but I didn't say anything.

"You better eat something," Aunt Mae Louise told me. "This isn't the time to get sick yourself."

I looked up at her. She almost sounded like she cared, but on second thought, I imagined her concern was that I might add some unnecessary complication. While Uncle Buster went to see about Daddy,

Aunt Mae Louise left to talk to her father-in-law and make the arrangements for the funeral. She didn't ask me to go along, either.

Not more than an hour after she left, the phone rang. I wasn't going to answer it, but it rang so long, I finally decided it might be Uncle Buster.

"Is this Mrs. Howard?" a man asked.

"No, it's her niece," I said.

"Well, is she home or is Mr. Howard home?"

"No."

"Well, this is Detective Morgan. I was able to track down Mrs. Elder," he said.

I held my breath.

"Where is she?"

"She's in the detox unit of a hospital outside of Macon," he said. "She was admitted two days ago after causing a disturbance in a nightclub and being taken to the emergency room. You can have the telephone number and address," he continued, and I jotted them down. "Have either of them call me if they would like," he concluded.

I didn't thank him. I hung up the phone and stared at the notepaper.

Then I crumpled it in my fist, but I didn't throw it away. I put it in my room.

But I never told either Uncle Buster or Aunt Mae Louise about the call.

Uncle Buster returned before Aunt Mae Louise. I saw from the look on his face that I would have had a hard time. It really wasn't until he walked into the house and stopped to look at me sitting there in their living room that the full impact and reality of Daddy's death hit me. For a while I was able to put it out of mind, pretend it never had occurred, that it was all one of those nasty dreams the shadows brought into my sleep. Most of the time Daddy was away from me, out there doing his selling. It wasn't hard imagining that he was doing that now, and that some day he would return or call, even though I had told him not to bother unless he was going to take me home. Now, he would never take me home; he would never call.

"Was it really my daddy?" I asked Uncle Buster, and his droopy eyes widened and even brightened.

"For a few seconds after they showed him to me, I had doubts," he replied. "Seems he didn't have his seat belt on after all, Phoebe. It must've slipped his mind. He was carrying a lot of worry. He hit the windshield pretty hard," he added, and immediately shut his lips, regretting that those words had somehow gotten out.

"Are you blaming it on me?" I asked in a voice much shriller than I had expected it to be.

"I'm not blaming nobody," he said. "That's the Lord's work. If you have a guilty conscience, you bring it with you to the church. Your mama should do likewise," he added, and then he thought a moment. "Where is that woman?"

He mumbled something I didn't understand and then went into the kitchen to use the phone. In the meantime I heard Aunt Mae Louise come in. She looked at me, shook her head, and sighed deeply.

"It's all arranged," she said. "Day after tomorrow, whether we find your mother or not."

"We found her," Uncle Buster announced, and returned from the kitchen. "Why didn't you tell me, Phoebe? Why didn't you tell me the police had called?"

"You knew and didn't tell?" Aunt Mae Louise exclaimed. "Why not?"

"What difference does it make? She's no good to anybody," I said, and left the room with both of them staring after me.

I should be feeling more pain, I kept telling myself. I shouldn't feel numb. I should feel sad. I should be crying hysterically, beating the walls, something. My daddy was killed. He's gone for good. My mama is in some nuthouse babbling helplessly. I had seen people lose their loved ones. A girlfriend of mine lost her five-year-old brother last year when he got caught in between two gang members shooting at each other. I never had seen so many tears, heard so many wails of agony. The pain in their hearts was so thick I could feel it in the air.

And then there was Rodney Marks's father, who had a heart attack playing basketball with Rodney and his friends. A tall, healthy-looking man who had something called an aneurysm and died right there on the court. I was watching them play and saw the look of disbelief on Rodney's face. I used to be jealous of his relationship with his father. They were together lots of times. He wasn't just losing a parent; he was losing a friend.

Maybe that was what was wrong with me and my parents. I never thought of them as friends, just as keepers of the cage. There was never much holding us together, but whatever there had been was now gone.

That's why I feel so numb and light all over, I told myself. I'm like a feather, floating. I have no interest in staying where I am and I have no idea where I should go. I'm in the hands of the wind.

That's how I felt over the next few days, like someone being carried along. Uncle Buster's father being the minister and all made it easier to arrange the funeral and burial. None of my friends back in the city came, and I was sure by now word had spread. Bad news had a way of working its way through walls. Maybe people were just happy to talk about terrible things happening to someone else and not to them. Maybe it made them feel safer.

Daddy's boss showed up with one of the other salesmen in the company. Some of Uncle Buster's and Aunt Mae Louise's church friends attended out of respect for them, or maybe out of pity for them being weighed down now with the responsibility of me. I could feel it in their eyes when they looked my way, and I saw it in the almost imperceptible shaking of their heads. They probably didn't realize themselves how clearly they were showing their thoughts and feelings. I didn't blame them. Like Uncle Buster had told me, there's no one we can blame. That's not our job.

I never looked upon Daddy in death. Because of how badly injured he had been in the accident, the coffin was kept closed and I didn't want any private visit. It was easier for me to keep pretending he wasn't dead, but just gone. I heard his name mentioned in the sermon, but I reacted with surprise every time.

Afterward, after Daddy's boss and fellow salesman and all of Aunt Mae Louise's and Uncle Buster's friends had left the house, she came to my room.

"Uncle Buster and I have been thinking about you," she said.

I kept my eyes down. I had found a comfortable, warm, and dark place inside myself, and for the time being, I didn't want to leave it.

"We decided we would give you another chance here, Phoebe. I had a long talk with Dean Cassidy and the school authorities. Your teacher thinks he can help you, too, and really make progress with your reading. It's going to be up to you entirely. If you behave, if you listen to people and you do your work, you can still save yourself.

"I don't hold up much hope of your mother ever straightening herself out, but who knows the will of the Lord? Maybe someday, she, too, will wake up and realize she can be a decent person, and the two of you can help each other."

I raised my eyes toward her. What enabled her to live in such a world of fantasy? I wondered. Her faith? Or was it just her ignorance of how hard it could be?

"All I ask of you is that you try, Phoebe, you really try. You going to do that for yourself? Well?"

I looked down again.

"I hope so, Phoebe. I really pray for it. You should go back to school tomorrow. It's not healthy for you to hang around here doing nothing but stare at four walls."

"What about my father's home?" I asked.

"All that's being handled by Uncle Buster. He's trying to get all he can to keep in trust for you so you'll have something out of all this misery, but I got to tell you, right now it doesn't look like there's much. That old furniture in that rented apartment isn't worth trucking out, and from what we can see so far, your daddy didn't keep up his payments on his term life insurance. I'm sure he needed every cent he could earn just to keep up ordinary expenses. And your mother, your mother is in the hands of welfare."

So I have nothing but Aunt Mae Louise's and Uncle Buster's charity, I thought, nothing but the few rags that hang in this closet.

"I'm sorry, child," she said. "But this is why you have to try harder to be good."

With that she left me.

Try harder to be good? She might as well have said try harder to fly like a bird.

What did being good mean? Doing everything they wanted me to do and never doing anything I wanted to do. That was the way I saw it. That was the way I always saw it.

And that was the way I always will, I thought.

Maybe I would go on the roof, wave my arms hard, and jump.

5

An Invitation to a Party

During the funeral and after, I saw that my cousins Barbara Ann and Jake looked at me with fear and expectation in their eyes. I felt they were waiting for me to go crazy, scream, and be wild, or maybe just explode as if a bomb of misery and sorrow had finally been ignited inside me. I understood they were expecting me to be as destroyed and distraught as they would be should something as horrible happen to Uncle Buster. I was at least smart enough to realize that for children their age, parents were their whole world, even if it had never been true for me. Parents brought sunshine and happiness, laid out their daily lives, and moved them about with godlike power. Nothing made you see that you could get sick or have an accident, whatever, and die too as much as the death of your daddy or mama. You look down into your own inevitable grave when you look down into theirs, and that puts the ice into your veins.

I suppose my lack of a real relationship with my daddy and with Mama helped me face a world without them. Maybe that was a good thing after all. I wasn't thinking all that much about them after I had been brought here, except in anger. In other words, we didn't miss each other the way parents and children should miss each other. They were almost completely gone when we lived together. This numb feeling that kept me from crying at the cemetery wasn't something I could explain or wanted to explain to Barbara Ann and Jake. They would eventually understand it themselves by just watching me go on, plodding through my day instead of crawling under my bed.

Barbara Ann didn't talk to me at all in the morning. Jake avoided my eyes. When it came time to go on the school bus, Barbara Ann hurried away to sit with her friends. Since my trouble at school and the death of my daddy and his funeral, it was easier for her to pretend she didn't know me. I didn't blame her for that. Actually, I thought, if I was her I would probably have acted the same.

Ashley was sitting with another boy when I got on behind Barbara Ann. He looked at me quickly, and then he and the other boy whispered something and laughed. I was disappointed, but not all that surprised. By now I was sure he'd had enough time to characterize me any way he wanted to and make himself look like some sort of victim. His parents were surely happier about that, and, from the way his friends gathered around him on the bus and in the halls, I could see he was something of a hero.

That's funny when you think about it, or just plain unfair. When a boy gets into trouble with a girl, his friends pat him on the back and he struts through the school corridors like some heroic war veteran. When a girl gets into trouble because of being with a boy, she's supposed to keep her eyes down in disgrace and be ashamed. Well, I wasn't going to keep my eyes down. I'd eyeball anyone who dared to look at me with disgust, not that I looked forward to it.

In fact, I didn't think I would be happy about being stuck in one classroom all day, but for now I was grateful. I didn't have to face the students here as much and see those crooked smiles on their faces and watch them whispering about me. The others in my class seemed unaware that anything had happened at all. Mr. Cody certainly treated me the same as he had when I first entered his classroom. He didn't mention anything except to tell me how sorry he was to have heard about my father's tragic death.

"You're lucky to have an aunt and uncle like the Howards," he added to make me feel better, I'm sure.

I didn't say thank you or anything. Suddenly silence had become a good and close friend. The quick comeback, smart remarks, sticking it to people I didn't like, none of that mattered. I was still moving in a very narrow, dark hallway of my own, and I had no interest in stepping back into the light of day. I buried myself in the work Mr. Cody gave me. I ate my lunch alone. I continued my work, and then I sat in the rear of the bus going home, my eyes looking blankly on the world outside, my ears shut to the gossip and laughter around me. I knew in my heart that, like a time bomb, sooner or later I would explode.

At least for a while at home, Aunt Mae Louise eased up on what she had described as my chores. She didn't call me out to set the table for dinner or help with any of the food preparations. I wanted to believe it was out of some kindness, some compassion, but it occurred to me that she wasn't all that eager to have more to do with me than necessary. At least for now, it was more comfortable for her to keep some distance and not have me at her side in the kitchen.

Death had brushed its hand over my face and left its dark shadow under my eyes. My mama was spinning about in her own lunacy, and I was an immigrant from that mad world. Like some unwanted foreigner who had to be tolerated, I was pushed off, driven by indifference into my own place. My room had become another ghetto. In fact, Aunt Mae Louise didn't even look in to check on how I was keeping it anymore.

I also noticed that at the dinner table, the conversation rarely, if ever, involved or included me. As if I was no longer there, they talked only about themselves. Aunt Mae Louise asked Barbara Ann and Jake about their school work, but never asked me anything. Uncle Buster talked about his job, a trip he planned for the family soon, and they both talked about things they wanted to do for the house.

I began to consider that I might really not be there. Maybe I was the one who had died in the car accident and this was my punishment, my hell, just as I had once told little Jake. Silly and wild imaginings like that kept occurring. Sometimes, they put a wide smile on my face, so wide and bright that Aunt Mae Louise was forced to ask me what I thought was humorous.

Interrupted, I looked at her as if I had just noticed she was there. It spooked her, I know, because she looked away or at Uncle Buster for help.

"Are you all right, Phoebe?" he would ask me softly.

"All right? Sure. I'm fine," I would tell him and return to eating.

I knew Aunt Mae Louise warned both Barbara Ann and Jake to keep their distance from me and be in my company only when it was absolutely necessary. Neither ever came to my room anymore, and when they passed me in the hallway going or coming from the bathroom, they kept their eyes down and their lips pulled tightly shut. Barbara Ann's puckered mouth was drawn up like a drawstring purse. She continued to ignore me completely on the school bus and walking to and from it. The two of them were keeping themselves in an invisible plastic bubble when it came to having anything to do with me. I didn't really care. It was just something curious because I wasn't quite sure if they had the bubble around them or I had it around me.

I continued to behave the same way in school, only vaguely aware of how many of the students were laughing at me until one afternoon, while I was eating my lunch at an outside table, two girls approached me.

They were both white, the taller one prettier, with hair like spun gold and turquoise eyes as bright as polished stones. She had a runway model's figure and a very confident air about her, telegraphed in her correct posture and the arrogant turn in her shoulders when she walked or spoke.

The other girl wasn't as pretty as she was voluptuous, with a fuller figure, dark brown hair, and hazel eyes. Her features weren't as dainty as the taller girl's, but her lips were thicker, sexier, like someone who had gotten those cosmetic shots to make them so. I had the feeling she was a work in progress and would probably have her nose redone.

"Hi," the taller girl said. "I'm Taylor Madison and this is Rae Landau. We heard about what happened with Ashley Porter," she added, and sat.

"Yeah," Rae said, sitting beside her. I looked at the two of them and smirked. Pride tightened my throat and lifted my shoulders back.

"Big deal. I guess you'd have to be deaf not to have heard," I said.

"Exactly," Taylor said.

"So what do you want? More details to spread?"

"No. We want to tell you we feel sorry for you," Rae said. "Ashley has been telling all sorts of stories about you, exaggerating and embellishing to make himself look better for sure."

"I don't care what he says," I replied. Then I paused to scan their faces, searching for their real intentions, since they said they weren't here to get more details. "Why would you two care so much, anyway?"

"He did something like this to me," Rae revealed. "And it was just as unpleasant for me afterward. I almost had a nervous breakdown."

I know I looked skeptical. I could see Ashley picking on a new girl, especially one like me who had no friends here, but not a girl who looked like she could buy and sell whatever she wanted, especially friends.

"A nervous breakdown?"

"She's telling the truth," Taylor said. "He tried to get me to go on a date with him after he dumped on Rae, but I wouldn't give him the time of day so he spread rumors about me, disgusting rumors."

"Like what? What do you think is disgusting around here?" I challenged.

"Saying I was more interested in girls and that was why Rae and I were such good friends."

I raised my eyebrows and wondered if there was a seed of truth to any of it.

"Someone like Ashley thinks that's the only reason a girl wouldn't be with him," Rae said. "He's too egotistical to believe anything else. He can never be wrong or the cause of any trouble."

"Yeah," I said with a deep sigh, "I can't deny I did agree to meet him in the nurse's office. I can't blame anyone else but myself for what happened."

"You certainly can and should blame him," Taylor cried, raising her voice. "You were here hardly forty-eight hours. He didn't care if he got caught. He knew he would get away with it. They didn't even suspend him, and guess what," she continued. "He's back on the basketball squad."

"He is?"

"As of this afternoon. There was a hearing or something and his parents came and pleaded and the school decided he had suffered enough being suspended from the team this long."

"I thought his daddy was a marine and was happy he was punished," I said.

They looked at each other and shook their heads.

"Ashley lies to people so much, he probably doesn't know himself what's true and what isn't anymore," Taylor said. "His father was in the army, not the marines, and he's an influential attorney who always finds a way to cover up his son's mistakes, especially speeding tickets."

"Of course, Ashley promised the school and the coach to be a good boy and never do anything like that again," Rae added.

"Believe that, and you'll believe in the tooth fairy," Taylor said, and they laughed.

"It doesn't matter to me. I couldn't care less who is on and off the basketball team. And I don't care if he gets away with murder around here," I said, and finished my sandwich.

"You should care. He got you into trouble and barely blinked," Rae said, her face scrunched in anger. "And on top of it, just as we told you, he hasn't stopped spreading nasty stories about you."

"Maybe they're true," I said.

"I hope for your sake they're not," Rae fired back without hesitation.

"They're even worse than the stories he spread about me," Taylor added.

I stopped smirking.

"What stories?"

"He said you were a professional, that you made money in the streets of Atlanta, and that your mother was one too and made you work with her," Taylor said. "He said that's why you were brought here, to get away from all that, and that's why he didn't get into as much trouble. He even said the dean took the money from you that you made Ashley give you."

"He said I took money from him to give him sex in the nurse's office?"

"Exactly," Rae replied. "Today he told everyone that your father was killed by your mother's pimp because he sent you to live with your aunt and uncle and took business from him. The kids believe him because they think his father has some in with the district attorney," she continued.

"It's not true, is it?" Taylor asked, her eyes somewhat narrowing with suspicion.

"No, and nobody better say it in front of me," I told her, "or it will be the last thing they say."

They looked at each other and then back at me.

"What?" I asked, seeing the hesitation in their faces.

"That's not the worst of it," Taylor said. "He's getting some of the boys to put money in a pot so they could buy sex from you. Someone's going to offer you money to come to a party, but there will be no doubt as to the reason why."

I bit down hard on my lower lip, trying to keep from showing my emotions. When you had no one in the world you could trust or believe in, you felt helpless, as helpless as an astronaut accidentally cut loose in space. Instead of coming to live in a better, safer community with a superior school, I felt like I had been forced to come to a den of poisonous snakes just waiting to pounce on someone like me.

"Thanks for warning me," I told them.

"What are you going to do about it?" Rae asked.

"About what?"

"She means, what are you going to do when the boys approach you?"

"Tell them where to get off," I said. The two of them just stared. "What else?"

"Taylor and I have a better idea," Rae said.

"What?"

"Agree to go to the party," Taylor said.

"What, are you crazy, girl?"

"Just listen," Rae said, moving closer. "We think the party's going to be at Ashley's house this weekend. His parents are going somewhere. Besides offering you money for sex, they'll have drugs. We know Ashley can get Ecstasy whenever he wants to. He's done it many times before."

"So?"

"Tell her who your father is, Rae," Taylor urged, and nudged her with her elbow. Rae smiled slyly.

"My father is a police detective. We're going to tell him what the boys are up to, and he'll be there with some other policemen and arrest them all."

"But what good is that to me? I'll look like I really am a whore," I said.

"No. Rae's father will know you are working with us and them," Taylor explained. "The police do things like this all the time. They call it a sting operation, right, Rae?"

"Exactly. Everyone will know how you cooperated with them. You'll look a lot smarter than those boys."

"Finally, we'll wipe that smug, arrogant smile off Ashley Porter's face and no one will believe anything he says about any girl anymore," Taylor said.

"You'll be doing us all a big, big favor," Rae continued.

"It'll be easy," Taylor said. "And just think how you'll feel watching them take those boys to the police station and calling all those parents, especially Ashley's, who will have to come home from their weekend holiday."

"Mr. Perfect goes in the toilet," Rae said, and Taylor nodded, both of them turning to me eagerly.

"Well, what do you think?" Taylor asked.

"I don't know," I said.

"You can do it," Rae urged.

"I know I can do it," I snapped back at her. I didn't need encouragement from this lollipop.

"So?" Taylor said. "What do you say? We'll be with you the whole time."

"Revenge is sweet," Rae sang, and beamed.

"There's no better way to put a cork in Ashley Porter's sewer mouth," Taylor emphasized.

"Why should I care if he talks garbage or not? It's not going into my ears," I muttered.

"Don't you have any self-respect?" Rae asked, pulling back.

No, I wanted to say. I don't even have a self anymore to respect. I don't know who I am, much less who I will be. I was living with relatives who really didn't want me. I had a learning disability and a court record. My father was dead and my mother in a madhouse detox unit. Nothing that happened to me or that I did seemed to matter.

"Everyone here, especially every girl, will see you as a heroine," Taylor said. "I bet your relatives will be proud of you, too."

"No one messes with Phoebe Elder," Rae declared as if she was writing a headline on a television news program.

"Will you do it?" Taylor pursued eagerly.

I took a deep breath. If I really didn't care, what difference did it make if I did it or not? I thought. I might as well do it. At least, it was something to do.

"Okay. What's first?"

"Wait to see if any of the boys approach you with the offer. Maybe it's all talk. If it isn't, however, Ashley will expect you to be indignant, angry about it, and chase the boy off. He's probably hoping for that and getting his explanation for that all ready, but you'll surprise him by accepting the offer. Now he'll have to put up or shut up, and he'll put up," Rae explained.

"He won't want to look stupid to his friends," Taylor added.

"Right. So you'll have a date and a place," Rae continued. "I'll tell my father and we'll plan out the trap."

"This is great," Taylor said. "I can't wait."

"One thing," Rae continued. "We don't want to spook them, so Taylor and I won't be friendly with you in school until afterward, okay?"

"They're not stupid," Taylor said. "If they see the three of us consorting, they'll back out or do something to ruin the sting."

"Just write down when and where and slip a note into my locker. It's number 103. You pass it every morning on the way to your classroom, okay?" Rae said.

"We'll call you the night you get the note into my locker and give you whatever instructions Rae's father wants you to have."

"What if he doesn't want to do it?"

"Are you kidding? My father is a very strict disciplinarian. He thinks kids are way too free today and would jump at a chance to make an arrest like this," Rae replied, "especially if there are any drugs involved, and especially with someone like Ashley, who thinks he's above the law. My father doesn't like his father either. He says he's helped too many criminals escape justice."

They both got up.

"Remember, locker 103."

I nodded and they walked away. At the door, Taylor turned and gave me a small wave good-bye.

Life in the perfect suburbs was turning out to be just as nasty as life in my neighborhood, I thought. One good thing that would come out of this would be my aunt Mae Louise would have to stop riding on her high horse and bragging about how much nicer and safer it was living here. That alone seemed reason enough to go through with it.

Nothing happened that afternoon, and no one approached me during lunch the next day. I was beginning to think it was all just a lot of talk, just as Rae thought it might be, something the boys bantered about to show how brave and sophisticated they were. And then, as I was walking back to class, two boys I had seen with Ashley came up beside me. One was about my height, with curly black hair and a pug nose. He was wide in the shoulders and wore a wrestling team jacket. The other boy was taller, with long straw-colored hair and a sharp, pointed nose over thin lips and a cleft chin.

"Hi," he said. "We heard how you got into trouble."

"Good for you," I said, and kept walking.

"We don't think it's right that all the other girls in the school are such snobs and don't have anything to do with you," the boy on my right said. "They should be welcoming you here, not ostracizing you."

I continued walking, keeping my gaze straight ahead, and they remained right alongside.

"Is that right?" I asked.

"Yes, it is. I'm Gerry Balwin. My friends call me Grog. And this is Skip Lester."

I stopped and turned to him.

"Okay, what do you want?" I demanded.

He smiled and looked at his friend.

"We just thought that maybe you'd like to come to a party we're having."

"What party?"

"A cool party," Skip said. "There'll be some other girls there, but three of us really want you to come. We thought, that is . . ."

"We'll give you three hundred dollars, that's a hundred apiece," Grog offered quickly. "That's what you got before, isn't it?"

A big part of me wanted to lash out and slap the side of his face so hard his head would spin around. My heart was thumping with anger I didn't expect, but I figured Taylor and Rae were right about how to get back at these boys. Just smacking them wouldn't do much and in the end, they would surely deny what they had said and I'd be the one getting in trouble again.

"Where's the party?"

"It's at Ashley's house. I wrote down the address for you," Grog said, "with the time. It's Saturday night." He handed me a slip of paper. "We'll have the money there and promise to give it to you as soon as you come. We'll keep it a secret, too."

"Most of the other girls in the school, the ones who look down on you, will be jealous you got invited and they didn't. We won't tell them why. You'll be invited to other things afterward," Skip assured me.

"What kind of a party is it going to be? I hope there's something else to do," I added.

"Oh, don't worry about that," Grog said, smiling. "Ashley's prepared. He'll have some good stuff."

I looked at the slip of paper and then from one boy to the other.

"Three hundred as soon as I get to the house?"

"Guaranteed."

"I want half tomorrow."

"Huh?"

"We got to trust each other, don't we?" I asked.

They looked at each other.

"Well?" I said, seeing the hesitation in their faces. "You want me there or not?"

"You'll have it at lunchtime," Grog assured me.

"Then I'll be there for sure," I said, smiling. "Now you go break open your piggy banks," I told them, and walked away.

I heard them laugh and saw them hurrying excitedly back to the cafeteria. When the police pounced on them, I would have sweet vengeance, but I'd also have one hundred and fifty dollars, and I had no intention of giving it up.

At the end of the day, I passed locker 103, paused, and dropped the slip of paper through the slot. That night, to my aunt's surprise, I had a phone call. She came to my room to tell me there was a girl on the line asking for me.

"She said her name is Rae," Aunt Mae Louise told me, her eyes full of suspicion. "Who is she?"

"Just some girl I met in school. Her father's a policeman," I added.

She relaxed.

"Oh. Well, we want you to have nice friends here, Phoebe. We're just going to always be concerned about your welfare," she explained.

She tried not to make it obvious, but I knew she was following me to the kitchen. She should be working as a spy for the government, I thought.

"What?" I said instead of a hello.

"I'm just calling you to confirm I have your note, and I've spoken to my father. He's very excited about this, and he wanted me to tell you thank you beforehand," she said quickly. "He says just pretend to be going along with everything, and he'll take it from there."

"What's that mean?" I asked, keeping my voice as low as I could. Although she wasn't in the kitchen, I was sure Aunt Mae Louise was just outside the door eavesdropping.

"You know, start like you're going to go through with it so they can't claim it wasn't what we know it is. You'll have to go into the bedroom with the first boy after they pay you. They'll do some Ecstasy first to build up their courage, and my father and his partners will be watching all the time. I know you're probably afraid, but . . ."

"I'm not afraid and I know what to do," I said. I didn't need my courage built up by the likes of them.

"Good. We'll have our own little celebration afterward. I promise," she told me, and hung up.

"Where's the party?" I pretended to ask after she hung up. "I'll have to ask my aunt and uncle. Thanks," I said, and hung up.

As I anticipated, Aunt Mae Louise was right outside the door.

"The girls are having a party this weekend and asked me. Is that all right with you?"

"Where is the party?"

"At Rae's house. Her mother and father will be there," I said. "It's like one of those pajama parties, girls getting to know each other and all."

"That sounds fine. I'll see about Uncle Buster taking you there."

"He doesn't have to," I said quickly. "Rae's going to pick me up."

"Oh. What's her name again?"

"Rae Landau," I said. "Her father's a detective."

She made a mental note of it and told Uncle Buster. I overheard them talking about it. He phoned someone to check on my story. They were being extra careful all right, I thought. However, when he returned and reported I was telling the truth that there was indeed a Detective Landau, I had to admit to myself I felt better about it, too.

Anticipating Saturday night and how sweet my revenge would be put some excitement into my life. I actually looked forward to going to school and seeing how the boys looked at me, Skip and Grog smiling and winking, and how excited both Taylor and Rae looked whenever I confronted them.

On Friday, right after I entered the cafeteria and got my lunch, Grog came up beside me and handed me an envelope.

"Just put it away quickly," he said, looking around nervously. "We can both get into lots of trouble for this."

I dropped it into my purse and later, in the girls' room, I took it out and counted seven twenties and one ten. I smiled with glee. Won't those rich arrogant boys be surprised? Just the thought of it put some pep into my steps and gave me new energy. I worked hard in class, so hard Mr. Cody gave me a compliment.

"You keep going like this, Phoebe, and you'll be on reading level and back where you belong before you know it."

The others looked at me with envy.

That's exactly where I'd like to be, I thought. Back where I belong.

That evening and all the next day, I tried to be Miss Perfect at home. I didn't want anything to happen that would interfere with our plans. I offered to help Aunt Mae Louise with the dishes before she asked. In the morning right after I rose and dressed, I started to vacuum, cleaning my room and then going into the halls and the living room.

Aunt Mae Louise smiled and nodded. Later, Uncle Buster asked if I would like to go with him, Barbara Ann, and Jake for some frozen custard. I thanked him and told him I had to get myself ready for my party. I chose the most conservative thing I had to wear and asked Aunt Mae Louise's opinion, something that took her by complete surprise.

"Yes," she said, "that's appropriate." She thought a moment and said, "Once your father's estate is straightened out, we'll use whatever there is to buy you some new clothes, Phoebe. A girl your age needs a nice wardrobe. Some day you'll go off to college or a business school and need nice things to wear."

I nodded. Me in a college, even a business school? Get real, I thought, and then, for a moment, I tried to imagine it. Every image seemed silly. I was sure I'd end up like Mama, a waitress in some restaurant. It made me angry and even more eager to go to this party and turn those rich boys and their friends upside down.

Rae and Taylor showed up exactly at seven o'clock. Aunt Mae Louise insisted I bring them into the house to meet her. They looked more nervous about it than I was.

"I think it's real nice of you girls to welcome someone new to the community like this," Aunt Mae Louise told them. "It shows a warm heart, a charitable and compassionate heart, and that's how we all walk in the light of the Lord."

They smiled at her and looked to me to get them out quickly. As soon as we left, Rae pounced.

"You didn't mention the sting operation to your uncle and aunt, did you?"

"No. You don't have to worry about that. I know what to say and what to do," I told her sharply.

These spoiled girls with their fancy clothes and cars weren't going to make me feel innocent and incapable of handling myself. They hadn't seen half the things I had. If they had, they'd be the ones hiding in a closet, I thought.

"Rae's father told us we're supposed to act like we don't know anything," Taylor explained. "The boys will be sitting around, drinking. There'll be music and then Ashley will bring out the Ecstasy. You should take it just to keep them from being suspicious. You ever do that before, take drugs?"

I raised my eyebrows.

"Where I come from, it's like candy," I said.

"I bet. After this is over, I want to have a real party at my house so the girls can get to know you. Some of them are so naive and simple, they'll think you're out of a movie or something."

"But not you, huh?" I said.

"Taylor and I are a lot more sophisticated than our friends," Rae explained, "mainly because of things I hear my father talk about, things he doesn't even know I've seen and heard."

"That's nothing. That's like watching it on television," I said.

They were both quiet. We traveled through another neighborhood where the houses looked bigger and more expensive than the ones in my aunt and uncle's development. It had been mostly cloudy all day and had grown darker and darker until the wind picked up and some drops of rain struck the windshield. By the time we drove up a long driveway lined with lanterns and beautiful cypress trees pruned to the exact same height all the way up to the circular driveway, the raindrops had become a steady drizzle.

I was impressed with the size of Ashley Porter's house, but I didn't want to gape and sound like I was. It was a two-story home with a steeply pitched roof and tall, narrow windows. I could see the chimney on the left side. The walls of the house were solid brick. I saw five other cars parked in front.

"Looks like everyone's here," Rae commented.

"Where's your father?" I asked, gazing around.

"They're either here already or right behind us," Rae said. "Don't worry about them. If we can see them, then the boys might be able to see them."

The moment we opened the car doors, I could hear the loud music within the house.

"They're starting early," Taylor said. "Good. They'll be too wasted to be careful."

The front door was slightly open, which explained why the music leaked out so loudly.

"Hey, we're here!" Taylor cried.

We heard a whoop from the room on the left. I tried not to gawk at all the artwork, the statues, expensive-looking rugs, and gilded mirrors. In the living room there were pieces of furniture that looked built for giants. The fireplace was the biggest I had ever seen, not that I had seen that many.

I recognized most of the boys and saw only one other girl. Some of the boys were sitting on the floor and some on the long sofa and over-sized chairs. What looked like two bottles of vodka were on the large, oval coffee table with soda water, juice, glasses, and a bucket of ice. Most everyone was smoking, and it didn't smell or look like plain cigarettes.

Ashley, who was in front of a stereo, turned and smiled. There was no doubt in my mind that something slippery and ugly was hidden beneath those laughing eyes.

"Hey, the party's here!" he cried. The boys cheered.

I had seen people my age wasted on drugs and drink. I had been at many a party where sex, booze, and drugs were common, but there was something about this scene, about being among so many rich kids that made me nervous, as well as our secret plan I had to make work. Maybe it was just the size of the house and all the expensive things. I was in unfamiliar territory, and even though I wasn't afraid of any of them, I couldn't help feeling like a fish out of water. Even a shark has trouble there, I thought.

"What would you like to drink?" Ashley asked. "Or do you just want to go right to the party?"

I looked at Rae and Taylor. Rae nodded slightly.

"Why waste time? Ain't time money?" I fired back at him, and the boys all whooped again.

"Well, enjoy an E," he said, and handed me some Ecstasy. "It's a fringe benefit."

"Thanks," I said, and pretended to take it, but kept it in between my fingers.

Grog jumped up.

"We already decided," he said. "I'm first."

"Lucky you," I said, and there was another cheer.

I looked at Rae, and again she nodded. I glanced at the windows.

Were the police watching? Were they already in the house? Could they hear everything?

"Right this way," Grog said, taking me by the right elbow.

"Hold on," I said, glancing at Rae. "Where's the rest of your money?"

"Oh, right, sorry," Grog said, and dug into his pocket to produce a fifty-dollar bill. He held it up.

The other boys seemed hypnotized, even Ashley. Soon, he would be choking on his nasty words, I thought.

Taylor and Rae watched me pluck the bill from Grog's fingers and stuff it into my purse. I tried to make the action as big as possible so Rae's father would be satisfied, wherever he was. Then I turned toward the door.

"He won't be long," Skip Lester called after us. There was another whoop of laughter.

We crossed the hallway and entered what looked like a big office.

"Right through here," Grog said, continuing to a door in the rear.

I walked slowly behind him, anticipating Rae's father's arrival any moment. Grog opened the door to what looked like a small bedroom that had been created out of a big closet.

"What is this?" I asked, surprised.

"Ashley's father's little hideaway. Perfect, huh?" he asked.

I shook my head. There wasn't a window. Behind me, the music got louder. Where were Rae's father and the other policemen?

"Well, let's get to it. Just pretend we're in the nurse's office in school," Grog said, unbuttoning his shirt quickly and then undoing his pants.

I looked back. Something was wrong. Something was very wrong. Silent screams stuck in my throat when my heart began to pound warnings.

"What's up?" Grog asked, standing there with his pants half down.

I turned without replying and headed back across the office, but when I reached the door, all the other boys were standing there.

"Where are you going, Phoebe?" Ashley asked. "He wasn't that fast, was he?"

I tried to look past them for Rae and Taylor.

"Where's Rae? Where's Taylor?" I demanded.

"Oh, they had another appointment," Skip said. "They told me to tell you, don't worry. They'll be back."

"What? Be back? What are you talking about? Where are they?" I demanded, and tried to look past them.

"Hey," I heard Grog call from the little room, "I'm ready!"

"He's ready," all the boys chorused.

"What's the matter, Phoebe?" Ashley asked, stepping closer. "Expecting someone else?"

"Let me outta here," I said, feeling I was snared in some spider's web that was partly my own making. I tried to push past them, but they held fast, not making any space for me.

"Don't tell me we didn't pay you enough," Ashley said. "You don't get this much on the street, plus benefits."

They were all looking lustfully at me, their eyes burning with pornographic fantasies. I backed up. This was really a trap, and I had walked right into it, arrogantly, confidently, stupidly. There were no policemen; there was no sting operation. What kind of girls would do this to me? The boys stepped forward, moving in a clump.

"Tell you what," Ashley said. "For another hundred, we'll all be able to watch. What do you say?"

I spun around. Grog was in the doorway behind me, his pants and shirt off.

"Bastards!" I screamed at them, scooped a small statue off the desk, and held it like a club.

"Put that down," Ashley ordered.

Panicked now, I swung it and hit Skip Lester, who was moving up on my right. I caught him on the side of his forehead, the small pedestal of the statue cutting deeply and quickly into his skull. Blood spurted instantly, and all the boys washed back like a wave at the sight of it. Skip staggered and fell toward them. I saw my opportunity and ran past them through the office doorway.

I heard them screaming after me, but I didn't hesitate. I went right to the front door and out, charging down the steps.

"Get her and bring her back here!" Ashley ordered the others from the open doorway.

I ran as fast as I could down the driveway, almost slipping on the slickness from the drizzle, and then I cut across the lawn and into some bushes and trees. I heard the boys' footsteps clacking behind me on the driveway. I continued to charge forward, bushes catching my dress and tearing it, but I didn't stop until I was out on the road. I could still hear them shouting after me. I kept running until I reached a street corner and paused to catch my breath and listen.

They had stopped chasing me. I no longer heard them. After a few minutes, I continued walking quickly until there was nothing behind me but the darkness and a bad memory.

6

The Best of Nothing

I walked for hours because I didn't know where I was going or how to get home. First fear and then rage filled me with energy, my fury carrying me along like some magic carpet on the wind. I couldn't wait to get my hands on that Rae and Taylor. Their meanness in conspiring with those boys was lower than anything I could remember. I had never been so betrayed. How could I have been so trusting, so gullible? I blamed myself for wanting to believe in them, for being desperate to have friends.

Despite the rage boiling inside me, I was a lot calmer because of the distance I had made between me and Ashley's house. Now, as I walked, I felt the ache in my calves and thighs and some sharp pain on my right side where a bush branch had slapped against me. I realized my feet were muddy and wet, too. The slight drizzle had stopped, but my hair was wet, soaked from the rain and my own sweat.

Finally, I stopped at a fast-food store and got some directions. I didn't realize just how far out of my way I had gone until the counter girl explained the directions back to my uncle and aunt's home. Grudgingly, I started out again, worried about every car I saw pass me by, half expecting some of those boys to jump out and attack me.

By the time I turned into my aunt and uncle's housing development, it was close to midnight. I was tired, damp, and dirty, and there was that long rip through my skirt. Aunt Mae Louise was surely going to raise the roof, I thought. How was I going to explain all this?

What caught me by surprise, however, was the sight of a police patrol car in our driveway. I stopped to think. Why would the police be here? Did it have something to do with what happened tonight, or did it have something to do with Mama? A part of me wanted to turn and run again, but my curiosity was strong, too. I had no reason to run, I told myself. I didn't do anything bad. Bad things were done to me.

Before I could decide which way to go, the front door opened and the policemen stepped out, with Uncle Buster beside them. They all saw me standing half in shadow, half in the light at the foot of the driveway.

"Phoebe?" Uncle Buster called. "That you, girl?"

"Yes," I said.

"You come right up here," he said sharply.

I walked up the driveway slowly. He turned and shouted into the house.

"She's home, Mae Louise!"

I heard her running up the hallway to the front door.

"Where have you been, Phoebe?" Uncle Buster asked me.

"I got lost," I said, looking from one policeman to the other.

"Everyone's been looking for you, girl," Uncle Buster said.

Aunt Mae Louise came up behind him.

"Where you been?" she shouted at me.

"She said she was lost," Uncle Buster said.

"Oh, she's lost all right, but unlike the prodigal son, she's not lost and found, no, sir. Not by a long shot. How could you do something like this now? With your daddy not even cold in his grave, how could you be so bad?"

"What did I do?" I moaned. I looked at the scowling policemen and realized they weren't here about Mama. They were here about me. Those boys had told some other lies. I began to babble. "They're the ones who deceived and trapped me. They're the ones who lied."

"What are you talking about? They lied? Talk about lies. You said you were going to that girl's house when you were going to a party with lots of boys instead," Aunt Mae Louise said sharply. "You don't know how to do anything else but lie and you're still doing it now."

"That's not true," I moaned.

"You hurt a boy real bad tonight," Uncle Buster said. "He's in the hospital. You know that?"

"He deserved it. They all deserve to be in the hospital."

"Oh, just listen to her," Aunt Mae declared to the policemen. "She's much too much for us to handle."

"You'll have to come with us to the police station," one of the policemen said. "Serious charges have been lodged against you, miss."

"Charges? What about what was done to me?"

"You'll have your chance to tell your side of it," he said.

"Oh, sure. I'll have lots of chances," I snapped back at him.

"Come along," he said, moving to take my arm.

"Uncle Buster, it's not what they say. I was fooled into believing something else was going to happen tonight. They were all out to get me."

"You better just go with them for now, Phoebe. I'll be along," he said in a tired, skeptical voice.

"But—"

"This is very, very serious. Just do what the police want you to do, Phoebe."

"Right. Just do what they want," I mimicked. A lot of good it was going to do me appealing to him for any help, I thought.

"Let's go," the policeman said, moving me more forcefully toward the police car. The other patrolman opened the door, and they practically pushed me into the car. Aunt Mae Louise stood on the stoop shaking her head at me and mumbling some prayer under her breath.

"It's not my fault! I'm not lying!" I screamed back at her.

The policemen got in, and we started out of the driveway. I looked back and saw Uncle Buster arguing with Aunt Mae Louise, and then we made a turn and headed out of the development. Fuming, I sat back and glared straight ahead. Daddy sure made my life more miserable bringing me here, I thought. I would have been better off living in the streets of Atlanta.

When we arrived at the police station, they put me in a room by myself. It was brightly lit, with bare walls and a mirror. They sat me at a long table, but no one came for so long, I fell asleep with my head down on the table. Then I felt someone nudge me, and I raised my head slowly and looked at a policewoman. She had short, dark hair, beady eyes, and a small mouth. There was a small bump in the bridge of her nose. I had seen policewomen before, but she looked too small and fragile to be one.

"All right," she said. "Let's hear your side of this."

I stared down at the table, my arms folded under my breasts.

I didn't want to talk to anyone. What good would it do? What good did it ever do?

"You had better start talking. That boy, Skip Lester, he has a concussion and fifty stitches. He'll have a scar. His parents are pretty angry," she said calmly. "They want us to charge you with more than just assault and battery. They think you tried to kill him."

"If I was trying to kill him, he'd be dead," I said.

"An inch or so to the right, and you would have hit him in the temple and done just that," she shot back at me. "I don't think you should be such a smartass, girl."

I pouted, still fuming too much to speak.

"Now, if you don't tell us your side of it, all we'll have is their side, and that doesn't look too good for you. There's an assistant district attorney coming here soon to decide how to charge you and what to do with you now. You don't have to be charged as a minor if it's a serious felony. You could go to adult court, Phoebe. That's your name, right, Phoebe?"

"Yeah, that's my name."

"Well?"

I took a deep breath and sat forward, wondering just where I should begin. Perhaps I should start with the day Mama left me alone when I was only four and I accidentally pulled a pot of boiling water off the stove, scalding my hand and wrist and screaming so loud, I brought neighbors to the door. Mama yelled at me and shook me so hard, I thought my teeth would fall out. From then on it always seemed to me it was me against the world. This was just another in a series of attacks, attacks that would never end until I did.

"I got into some trouble in school," I began, and told her the story from start to finish, right to the moment I walked up to my aunt and uncle's driveway. She listened, which was more than my uncle and aunt were willing to do. After I was finished, and actually as I was speaking, I had the sense other people were watching and listening. The mirror on the wall was probably a one-way window, I thought.

"Okay," she said when I stopped speaking. "You want something to drink?"

"Some water."

She got up and a few moments later, brought me a bottled water.

"Just relax awhile," she said.

"Am I going to jail?"

"We'll see what's what soon," she told me, and left again.

Nearly another hour went by before she returned.

"Okay. For now you've been released back to your uncle and aunt's supervision," she announced.

I looked up, surprised.

"I am?"

"Yes. It's not like you're on bail, but your uncle has vouched for you and promised he would make sure you came to the court when you have to come. He could get into trouble if you don't listen or try to run away. He's going to take you home now," she said.

"What about the charges against me and such?" I asked.

"They'll decide about all this in court later," she explained. "For now, go home, listen to your uncle and aunt, and keep your nose clean."

When I walked out, Uncle Buster was sitting with his head down in the lobby. He looked up at me and then rose.

"This wasn't all my fault," I told him in a hoarse voice.

"Let's just get home and get some sleep, Phoebe. It's been a long, long night," he said, looking almost as exhausted as I felt. "Your aunt's sick over worrying about you."

"I'll bet she's worrying about me," I said.

I followed him out to the car.

"You can't go anywhere but to school and back," he told me when we got in. "Otherwise, you could end up right back here and things will go very bad for you when we do go to court, Phoebe. It might be a lot different here than where you lived. They don't see as much of this sort of thing, and they might be a lot sterner."

"I don't know why I'm the one who has to go to court. They're the ones who tried to rape me!"

"Let's not talk about it anymore," he said.

"Let's not."

I fell asleep again with my head against the side of the car and woke up when we pulled into the driveway and then into the garage. Wrapping her bathrobe around herself, Aunt Mae Louise came out of her bedroom when we entered the house.

"Don't say anything more now, Mae," Uncle Buster begged her before she could begin. "Let's all just get some rest. You want to be up early for church and make those corn muffins for Dad."

"Seems we all oughta be up early for church," she muttered, her eyes fixed stone-coldly on me.

I didn't reply. I went into my room and without even taking off my clothes, went to sleep. Collapsed was more like it, because I didn't even take off my muddied shoes.

I heard my door opening in the morning, but I kept my eyes closed.

"She doesn't even have sense enough to get undressed for bed," Aunt Mae Louise said.

"Just let her rest, Mae," I heard Uncle Buster tell her. "She'd only fall asleep in church and embarrass us both and you'd be more upset."

"Ain't that the truth," she replied, and the door was closed.

I lay there listening to them move about the house, Aunt Mae Louise snapping orders at Barbara Ann and Jake and even Uncle Buster until they were ready to leave. When the door closed and the house grew silent and I was absolutely sure they were gone, I rose.

I took off my clothes and had a hot shower. Then I dressed in a pair of jeans, a blouse, and a light leather jacket. I slipped on some running shoes, ran a brush through my hair, and then packed my suitcase, taking only the things I absolutely wanted. I dug out the hundred and fifty dollars I had taken from Grog in school. I had buried it in a drawer under my panties. I scooped up my purse and put the money in it along with the fifty I had kept from the night before.

On the way out, I drank a glass of orange juice. I wasn't very hungry, but I thought I had better take a piece of bread anyway. I paused in the doorway.

"Good riddance to you all," I told the house. "I'm not hanging around here to see whether or not I get put in jail or something."

I closed the door and walked out of the housing development. First, I thought I would just go back to our apartment in Atlanta, hoping it was still ours and the landlord hadn't moved Daddy's things out yet. But as I rode the bus toward the city, another thought entered my mind. When we reached the bus station, I stood considering for a while before deciding to take the next bus to Macon.

I decided I was going to see Mama. Maybe if I went to see her, she would be encouraged and want to start her life anew. Maybe we could be together after all, just up and go somewhere we had never been and be a mother and a daughter for once and for all. She can't want to stay in a detox ward, and she might be disgusted enough with her choices to see the light and want to be with me.

For all I knew, she didn't know about Daddy, too. Perhaps that would affect her. She would realize I had no one now and she would care, especially when I complained about her sister, my aunt Mae Louise. Mama never liked her own sister. She'd understand why I was so determined to get away.

Sure she would. She would have to, I thought. The more I thought about it all, the more excited I became, so excited, I wished the bus would go faster. When we pulled into the station in Macon, I practically knocked people out of my way to get off. Then I found a taxi stand and had the driver take me to the place I knew Mama was being kept.

After I spoke with the receptionist, she made me wait in a small lobby, but I didn't wait long before a tall, thin African-American woman in a lab coat came out to see me. Her hair was a thin reddish brown, and she had freckles on her caramel cheeks, a long but nicely shaped nose, and lips that were almost orange.

"I'm Doctor Young," she said, extending her long arm and thin fingers at me.

I took her hand and stood.

"I want to see my mother," I replied.

"You're Charlene Elder's daughter?" she asked as if she didn't believe Mama had a daughter.

"Yes."

"We've been trying to locate her husband. Where is your father?"

"He's dead," I said. "He was killed in a car accident recently."

"Oh. I'm sorry to hear that. We actually tried contacting . . ." She paused to look at her clipboard. "Contacting a Mrs. Mae Louise Howard, but she hasn't returned any calls. That is your mother's sister, isn't it?"

"She's probably trying to forget she's related," I said dryly.

"Well, who do you live with?"

"Nobody," I said, not hiding my impatience. "I just want to see my mother. Can I see her?"

"Yes, yes. I think it might do some good. Come along," she said eagerly. "What do you know about your mother's condition?" she asked.

"Nothing," I said. What was I going to do, tell her my life story?

"Your mother has been suffering from serious substance abuse and is still in a period of withdrawal."

"How did she get here?" I asked as we continued down the corridor.

"As far as I know, she was dropped off at the emergency room, but whoever did that didn't hang around. It's quite common," she added quickly as if she thought I would get hysterical over it.

"Is she going to be all right?"

"These things take a lot of time," she replied. "They require a great deal of therapy and a willingness on the part of the patient."

She stopped and touched my arm.

"I don't know how much you know about what happened here."

"I don't know much. She left my daddy and me and ran off with someone."

"I see."

She hesitated and then, from the look I saw in her eyes, decided she had to be truthful, even to someone as young as I was.

"Your mother tried to commit suicide," she told me.

"Suicide? We didn't know that."

"I did leave a message for your aunt."

I shook my head.

"She never told me," I said more to myself than Doctor Young.

"It's not uncommon to see patients with problems like this get this depressed and try to take their own lives."

"What did she do?"

"She cut her wrists with a ballpoint pen, but fortunately, an attendant was nearby and we were able to prevent serious consequences. At the moment she's quite withdrawn. It's not uncommon, given the drugs, the alcohol."

"Nothing seems to be uncommon," I commented.

She stared at me a moment and then nodded.

"I'm just trying to prepare you. You don't look that old," she said as we continued. "With whom do you live now?"

"I was living with my aunt."

"Your aunt? But I thought . . . I mean, as I said, we've tried to get her to call us. Does she know you've come here?"

"I'm making other living arrangements," I said quickly, hoping she would stop asking so many questions.

She widened her eyes.

"I see. Okay. We have your mother under twenty-four-hour observation in here," she said, taking me through another door. We paused in the hallway. "She's in this room. Don't be alarmed about how stark it is. With cases like this, we have to limit the patient's ability to find ways to harm him- or herself."

A tall black man in an attendant's uniform peered out of a doorway, holding a cup of coffee.

"How is Mrs. Elder doing?" Doctor Young asked.

"No different. No problem," he said.

She reached into her pocket and produced a key chain. Then she unlocked the door of Mama's room and opened it. Mama, in a patient's light blue gown, was sitting on a bare bed looking at a bare wall. There was no other furniture, not even a chair.

"Charlene?" Doctor Young said. "I have a visitor for you. Someone's come to see you."

Mama didn't turn. She didn't look as if she had heard.

Doctor Young nodded to me, and I stepped forward.

"Hello, Mama," I said.

Mama's eyes fluttered, and then she turned and looked at me, but her expression didn't change. I saw the bandages on her wrists, but shifted my eyes away quickly. Just the sight of that made my heart thump hard and fast.

"Your daughter has come to see you, Charlene. Isn't that nice?"

Mama looked at Doctor Young.

"I want a cigarette," she said as if I came to see her every day and it was nothing unusual.

"Now you know you can't have cigarettes yet, Charlene. Why don't you just visit with your daughter now. Have a nice visit, and we'll be talking again this afternoon."

Mama pursed her lips the way I knew her to do when she had an angry or unpleasant thought. Then she grunted and turned back to the wall. I looked at Doctor Young, who nodded some encouragement.

"I'll be right outside," she said, and left the room, but leaving the door slightly open.

"Hi, Mama," I said.

"What are you doin' here?" she snapped back at me. "This ain't no place for you, girl."

"I came to see you. I had to see you, Mama. I was hoping you'd be better and—"

"You got any cigarettes?"

"No, Mama."

"They keep me from having cigarettes. I'm dying for a drink. It's like prison. I get outta here, I'm gonna get even with Sammy for dumpin' me like that."

"What happened?"

"I don't know," she said, and then looked at me sharply. "Your daddy send you here hopin' I'd come back?"

"Didn't anyone tell you about Daddy, Mama?"

"They don't tell me nothin' 'bout nobody. All they tell me is what I can eat and drink, when I should sleep, and how I should try to care more about myself. That doctor drives me crazy with all her talk. Makes my head spin. If you got a cigarette and you're not givin' it to me, Phoebe . . ."

"I don't have any cigarettes, Mama. Aunt Mae Louise won't let a cigarette ten feet near her."

"Mae Louise?" She blew some air between her lips. "She only let that man of hers near her twice, to have those brats, and that was that. I can see it in his face when he looks at me. Man's starving for some lovin'," she said, smiling. "Mae hates it when I'm around."

She looked at me again, angrily.

"Why didn't your daddy come here himself? Man has no spine, sending a girl to do his work."

"Daddy can't come here even if he wants to, Mama. Daddy's dead," I said.

She tilted her head a bit and narrowed her eyes.

"I don't know why no one has told you that. Maybe they have and you forgot," I added, more for my own thinking than hers.

"Dead? How's he dead?"

"He was killed in a car accident, Mama. I've been living with Aunt

Mae Louise and Uncle Buster since you ran away with Sammy Bitters. Daddy thought it was better than my being alone in the city, only it's been worse," I continued, since she looked like she was really listening to what I had to say now. "It's a snobby place and—"

"You say Horace is gone?"

"Yes, Mama. Daddy's gone."

She nodded and then rocked herself.

"He was like dead anyway," she told herself. Then she stopped rocking and looked at me.

"So who you living with now?"

"I just told you, Mama. I'm living with Aunt Mae Louise and Uncle Buster, but I can't stand it there so I ran away."

"Ran away?" She smiled and then chuckled. "I wasn't much older than you when I first ran away. Runnin' is in the blood, I guess."

"Mama, I want you to get better and come out of here. We could go off together, start a new life somewhere, far away from people like Aunt Mae Louise."

"You can't ever get away from people like your aunt Mae Louise. They're everywhere, like locusts," she said angrily, and started rocking herself again.

"We can, Mama. Just you and me."

She looked at me with a smirk.

"You and me? Girl, you don't even have a cigarette," she said. "You come here and you don't even have a cigarette for me."

"Mama, you can get all the cigarettes you want when you come out of here and we're together. We'll get jobs together, maybe even in the same restaurant or something, and we'll have a nice apartment and take care of each other."

"Who told you to say all that? Your daddy tell you? He'd try anything to get me to come back."

"No, Mama." I squinted at her. "Daddy's gone. I told you. He was killed in a car accident. Don't you understand? We don't have anyone but ourselves now."

She stared at me, looking like the things I was saying were finally taking hold.

"We can't go off, Phoebe. I gotta wait here for Sammy. We're goin' to California. His cousin owns a beauty parlor in Encino and there'll be a job for me. I always used to talk about goin' to California," she said, smiling. Then she stopped. "He shouldn't have left me here so long." She leaned toward me. "Those people, that doctor, they ain't nice at all. They want to keep you here because they get more money that way from the state." She smiled and nodded. "They don't think I know about such things, but I do."

"You can get out of here, Mama. You can get out of here and be with me. We'll go to California. I promise," I said. "I'll just get some part-time work and raise the money for our trip. I can do that."

"Can you go out and come back here?" she asked.

"Yes, certainly. I'll find some place to stay and I'll find some work."

"Well, go on and buy some cigarettes and come back," she said, and waved her hand as if I was dismissed.

"Mama, why are you talking about cigarettes? I'm talking about starting a life together, a whole new life."

"I started a new life," she said. She rocked herself again. "I don't know where my clothes are or anything." She stopped and looked at me. "You know what I've been thinking, Phoebe? I've been thinking your daddy did this. Somehow, he did this, got me in here. Well, you go home and you tell him it's not going to work. I'm not going back there, you hear me, girl? That's my message and make sure he understands it's firm and final."

I stood there staring at her, watching her rock herself, start to say something, stop, and then rock on.

"Mama," I said softly. I reached out and touched her shoulder. She didn't turn to me. She kept staring ahead.

Whatever it was that you had to reach back into to find yourself was still quite buried under confusion in her, I thought. I had been too optimistic, even arrogant, to think that I merely had to appear and all sorts of good thoughts and dreams would be revived, the mother in her would come rising to the surface like some corpse dead and under water for too long. The sunshine would resurrect it. The new hope would renew all that naturally binds a mother to her child and a child to her mother. Memories of the umbilical cord would be vivid and startle her and she and I would walk out of here like mother and daughter should.

When do you stop believing in fairy tales? I wondered. Or is it that you never stop? Even on the day you die, you think about doorways to paradise, to places without pain and sorrow where the only shadows that hover alongside you are the ones that want to dance with you.

Well, you don't dance, Phoebe, I told myself. You walk out of here alone.

I lowered my head.

Doctor Young appeared in the doorway and opened it a bit more. I shook my head at her, and she beckoned me to come out.

"I'm going now, Mama."

She didn't turn to me. I drew closer and I kissed her on the cheek.

She felt my tears, tears that moved to her skin, and she brought her hand to it.

"Am I crying?" she asked me.

"No, Mama, I am," I said.

She nodded.

"Doesn't surprise me," she said.

"Me neither, Mama. It never does anymore. Good-bye," I said, and walked out.

"You shouldn't be discouraged," Doctor Young said. "We've only just begun to work with her. Give it time."

I smiled at her. Another one who believes in fairy tales, I thought.

"Where are you going now, Phoebe?" she asked.

"I'm not sure," I admitted.

"Come to my office and rest awhile. We'll talk some more about your mother's condition and maybe I can help you understand," she suggested. "Are you hungry?"

I hadn't realized it, but I was now that she mentioned it.

"Yes, I am."

"Good, let's get you something to eat first."

She took me to a cafeteria and told the cashier to charge everything to her. She told me how to get to her office and left me. I had a small salad, some macaroni and cheese, and a piece of chocolate cake, much more than I thought I would eat.

Afterward, I walked to her office. She said she had to attend to a patient, but she would be right back and told me to make myself comfortable. There was a very soft leather sofa, and I sat on it and glanced at some magazines. My eyelids grew heavier and heavier. I wasn't aware of how tired I was from the strain of traveling here and the emotional tension I had just experienced with Mama.

I'll close my eyes for a little while, I thought, and leaned back and to the side on the sofa. I guess I fell asleep quickly. I woke up when I sensed someone looking down at me. My eyelids fluttered like the wings of a newly hatched baby bird, and I focused on a pair of gray pants. My eyes traveled up until I confronted a state policeman.

Doctor Young stood right beside him. I sat up quickly.

"You weren't supposed to leave your aunt and uncle's home," the state policeman said gruffly.

I looked at Doctor Young.

"They say you ran away, Phoebe. Is that true?" she asked softly.

"I wanted to see my mother."

"But you didn't tell your uncle and aunt you were coming here," she said. "Everyone was worried about you."

"Sure they were. Just sick with worry," I said. Then I narrowed my eyes. "I thought you couldn't reach her. I thought she wasn't interested."

"Your uncle spoke to me when I told him you were here. They have the police looking for you. You don't want to be on the road alone, Phoebe. You'll only get yourself into more trouble."

"Thanks a lot," I said.

"We have to do what's best for you, Phoebe. You won't help your mother's situation by getting yourself into trouble. I'll keep your uncle and aunt informed about your mother's condition," she promised.

"Don't waste your time," I said.

"Let's go," the state policeman told me, and shook his head at Doctor Young, who stepped back.

"I wish you the best," she called after us.

"Best of what?" I muttered.

I already had the best of nothing.

What else was there for someone like me?

7

Waiting for the Music

I was surprised when the state policeman did not bring me straight back to Uncle Buster and Aunt Mae Louise's home. I wasn't even sure we were going in the right direction. Most of the roadside looked unfamiliar to me. The late afternoon sun played peekaboo through trees and around houses, putting me in a daze. I dozed on and off. After about two hours on a main highway, the policeman pulled off and into the parking lot of a roadside diner. It was one of those silvery-sided ones shaped like a railroad car that looked like it had been built fifty years ago. It wasn't very busy. There were only four cars in the dimly lit parking lot.

"I'm not hungry," I said immediately.

"I'm not bringing you here to eat," he replied. "Get out."

Confused, I got out of the vehicle.

"Take your suitcase, too," he ordered.

"My suitcase?"

"Your uncle is waiting for you in there," he said, nodding at the diner.

I looked at the other cars and realized one of them was my uncle Buster's. I could see he was sitting in a booth by a window and looking out at us. I gazed back at the state policeman, who was standing by his car door, and I shrugged. Then I reached in, took my suitcase, and shut the door.

Thanks for nothing, I thought, and strolled up to the diner's entrance. As I opened the door, the state policeman drove off. I entered the diner. The sound of some country-western female singer with a very heavy twang in her voice came through the small speakers on the wall behind the counter. Two elderly ladies sitting at the farthest booth on my left turned to look at me and then went back to their conversation like two swimmers who had raised their heads for a breath.

I walked down to Uncle Buster's booth and stood there. Where is Aunt Mae Louise? I wondered. Why would she miss an opportunity to tear into me as soon as it was possible for her to do so?

"What's going on, Uncle Buster?" I asked. "Why did that policeman bring me here?"

"Sit down, Phoebe," he ordered gruffly through his clenched teeth. His eyes burned up at me like two small candles flickering in a hot breeze. Rage tightened his lips at the corners. Here we go again, I thought.

"Before you start," I said after I put down my suitcase and sat, "I wanted to see my mother. I should be able to see my mother if I want."

"You don't pack a suitcase to go visit someone, Phoebe. Don't you ever stop lying? Even when you're caught with your hand in the cookie jar, you claim you didn't do it."

"I took my suitcase because I thought . . ."

"Thought what, Phoebe? Huh?"

"I was hoping Mama would want me to live with her again," I said quickly.

He lifted his eyes toward the ceiling and pressed his lower lip up into his upper, scrunching his chin.

"You thought she would want to live with you again? Come on, Phoebe. The woman ran out on you and your daddy. If she was so worried about you and wanted you with her, she wouldn't have done that, now would she?"

"People change. I was hoping—"

He slapped his palm on the table.

"None of this is the point," he said sharply. "You were released from police custody into our care, and in order for that to happen, I guaranteed the district attorney and the judge that you would not run off and you would be there to answer the charges. How did you get down to Macon?"

"Bus."

"Where did you get the money?"

"I had some money."

He straightened his back and peered at me.

"I kept some of the money those boys gave me."

"What boys?"

"You wouldn't listen to my side of the story," I said, "so you don't know."

"Listen to me, Phoebe. It's one thing to slap someone, to kick someone, even to punch him, but when you hit someone with a statue and so hard you hurt him seriously and put him in the hospital, you are always going to come out looking like the bad one, so whatever your story is, you better first face up to that."

"If I hadn't done it, they would have jumped me, Uncle Buster. That's what they got me over there to do that night. That's what I've been trying to tell you."

The waitress came to the table.

"Just some more coffee," Uncle Buster said. "You want something, Phoebe?"

"Coffee's fine," I said.

"What were you doing over at the house with all those boys anyway, Phoebe?"

"We were there to . . ."

"To what?"

"Get revenge. But they lied to me."

"Who lied to you?"

"Those girls, Rae and Taylor. They said her father was going to arrest the boys for having drugs and for paying for sex."

"Paying for sex? Is that why you went there?"

"Not to really do it. Just to pretend and get them in trouble."

"And that's the money you have?"

"Yes."

He shook his head. The waitress brought the coffee.

"Anything else?" she asked sullenly.

"No, thanks."

She ripped off the check and dropped it on the table like a policeman giving someone a parking ticket.

"Trouble just seems to know your name, Phoebe. All the times you were in trouble in Atlanta, being arrested, going to court, we worried for you and for your daddy. I knew your mother wasn't going to be much help in that area, being she was in trouble a lot herself most of the time. Mae Louise doesn't know it, but your daddy called me first, called me at work and pleaded with me to get your aunt to agree to taking you into our home."

I kept my eyes down and stirred my coffee.

"He was desperate, Phoebe. At one point he sounded like he was crying."

Hearing that brought tears to my eyes, but I held them back for fear that if I didn't, I would cry forever.

"He said he had no doubt in his heart and mind that you were headed for big trouble, that you were mixing with the worst sort of people. He said we'd be saving your life by letting you live with us."

I looked up, but not at Uncle Buster. Instead, I gazed out the window and watched a white ambulance pull up and park. No one got out. All that was written on the ambulance were the words Emergency Transport.

"Mae Louise was very worried about Barbara Ann and Jake, but I turned her around so she would at least consider taking you in with us. We even spoke to my father, who helped convince her it would be the charitable thing to do."

"I'm no one's charity," I muttered, still without looking at him.

"We're all someone's charity, one way or another," he said. "Anyway, you can imagine how she feels now. First, you smoke in the house. Then you get into serious trouble in school after less than two days there and then get arrested and charged with a felony crime. On top of that, you violate the agreement I made with the authorities, and we look very bad in the community."

"I get the idea, Uncle Buster. I'll just get up and walk out of here and you won't hear from me again," I said defiantly.

"I can't let you do that, Phoebe. Aunt Mae Louise wouldn't take you in without your father assigning full guardianship to us, remember? She didn't want any arguments down the road as to whether we had the right to do this or that. You know your daddy agreed to do that," he said.

The tears were burning under my eyelids now. For some silly reason, a memory returned, the memory of Daddy and me going to a fun park together. I couldn't remember exactly how old I was, but I wasn't more than seven or eight at the most. He won a doll for me at the baseball game by knocking over milk containers and I carried that doll everywhere, clutching it as if it was a real baby sister. We rode a modified roller coaster and screamed and held on to each other. I thought we'd never let go of each other.

Now I was in that car alone, and I was going down very fast.

"Your mother deserted you, and she's not capable of taking care of herself, much less a teenage girl like you."

I looked at him sharply.

"Like me? I guess I'm just a curse on everyone I meet, right?"

He sighed deeply and looked down at his cup of coffee.

"You're not a curse, Phoebe, but it's not much of an exaggeration to say you're a handful. Mae Louise is right about that, and she's right that we just don't have the time and the ability to change you."

"So?"

"So," he said, "we don't want to see you go to women's prison, either. Young girls your age don't come out of there any better. Most come out worse."

"I'm not going to any prison," I said.

"Keeping you out of places like that means hiring expensive lawyers, Phoebe. That's not something we can do. Mae Louise is right. It's just a matter of when, not if, you'll be put in with hardened criminals and become more like them. We both feel we'd be letting your poor daddy down something terrible if we let it happen."

"Daddy's dead," I said sharply.

"When someone dies, you don't lose or forget your obligations to him or her. If anything, what you promised becomes more important because it's really all up to you. That's a lesson I guess you were never taught, but then there are many lessons you were never taught and should have been. That's why we're sitting here like this right now."

I squinted at him.

"Why are we sitting here, Uncle Buster?"

I didn't think he was going to answer because it took him so long. Finally, he looked up at me.

"When we came home from church and realized you had run off, I had to call the police, Phoebe. Your aunt Mae Louise was hysterical about it, too. The police sent that policewoman over to speak with us. She was concerned, and she told us about a school that might be able to help you."

"What school?"

"A school for girls who get themselves into too much trouble, much more trouble than most parents or guardians can handle themselves. We know you've got a history with the devil. This time you almost killed someone. Next time, you might do that or something almost as serious. Then what, Phoebe? We would be to blame, too."

"I don't see how another school makes any difference, especially any school around here. The girls and the boys here are just too stuck-up and fancy."

"This school's not around here, Phoebe. You won't be living with us anymore."

I raised my eyebrows. That should have sounded good to me, but something in his voice made me hold back my glee.

"Where is it then?" I asked.

"That boy you hurt, his father has a lot of influence in the community, Phoebe," he replied instead of answering my question. "This situation isn't going to disappear, especially now that they know you broke the agreement and ran off. They'll expect you to do it again. I can't chain you to the bed in your room, can I? And your aunt doesn't want to stand guard outside your door, and I can't be called away from my work to go looking for you or to solve some new crisis."

"I get the point, Uncle Buster. I never wanted to live with you and Aunt Mae Louise. You know that."

"Right. Right," he said. He sounded too relieved.

"But I don't understand about this school."

"It's a school that's run by people who know how to help you, to save you from yourself."

"What is it, some Bible-thumping, hymn-singing camp? Because if it is . . ."

"Now you listen to me," he said, pointing his thick right forefinger at me. "This is precisely your last chance. After this, no one's going to take your side or be bothered with you, Phoebe. You'd be left out there with the sharks and you wouldn't last long, no, ma'am."

He nodded after his own thoughts.

"You be grateful you have this opportunity, and you don't fail at it, understand?"

"Whatever you say, Uncle Buster," I told him.

He lowered his hand.

"Your aunt's right about you, girl. You do need this."

"Yeah, everybody has always been right about me, except me." I pushed the coffee cup away, spilling some coffee on the table.

He took out his wallet and put down some money.

"We're going now, Phoebe," he said. "You want to use the bathroom? You have a trip ahead of you."

"What do you mean, a trip? Aren't we going back to the house first?" I asked, a small sense of panic balling into a lump in my throat.

"No. Your aunt would rather she didn't see you right now. You need the bathroom?"

I slid out of the booth and headed for the ladies' room without answering him. After I went, I stood by the sink and looked at myself in the mirror. I was tired, very tired. I could see it in my eyes, eyes that had seen too much sadness and too much disappointment. They wanted to just close and remain closed forever and ever. For a moment I understood why Mama had tried to cut her wrists. Sometimes, it all gets to be too much, even for someone as young as I was.

I ran the cold water and splashed it on my face. Then I ran a brush through my hair. I stood there staring at myself and didn't realize how long I was there until I heard a voice behind me and turned to see a tall woman with very short hair. She wore a blue jacket and a pair of dark blue slacks.

"Your uncle sent me in here to see what was keeping you," she said.

Now he was asking strangers to help. I grimaced and picked up my purse.

"Nothing's keeping me. That's the point," I told her, and walked past her and out the door.

I returned to the booth, but Uncle Buster wasn't there. And neither was my suitcase!

I looked around the diner. The woman from the bathroom came up beside me.

"Just keep going out the door," she said.

"Who are you?" I asked, pulling myself back.

"Your escort," she replied.

"My escort?" I didn't know whether to laugh at her or tell her to get lost. "Where's my uncle?" I cried, and headed for the diner entrance.

She followed right behind me, spooking me with how closely she kept to me. I stepped out and looked over the parking lot. I didn't see him or his car anywhere.

"We're here to escort you to your new school," the woman said, stepping up beside me.

"You're taking me to a school?" I pulled my head back. "Where's my uncle? What happened to my suitcase?"

"He took it and he's gone," she said. "You just come with us now."

"Why would he take my suitcase? My uncle didn't say anything about any escort."

"Trust me," she said. "That's who we are."

The lack of any emotion and the firmness with which she stood facing me actually frightened me. That surprised me because I had seen things and been confronted by people who looked a great deal more threatening than she did, but there was something so cold about her calmness.

"I'm going back in there and call my aunt," I said.

"That would be a waste of time. Just get into the vehicle and we'll get started," she said, blocking my path back to the front entrance of the diner.

"What vehicle?" I looked in the direction she nodded. "I only see an ambulance there."

"That ambulance is for you," the woman said.

"What?"

She nodded again at the white ambulance I had seen pull up. A man sat behind the wheel staring at us.

"This is really stupid. Where's my uncle?" I asked again. I could feel my chest tightening.

"I told you. He's gone," the woman said. "You don't see his car anymore, do you?"

She was right about that, which only increased my anxiety. A state policeman had brought me here to meet him, and now Uncle Buster had just disappeared without saying good-bye? And he had taken my suitcase! This didn't make any sense at all.

"Why would he just leave me? What is this?"

"Your last chance," she said through tight lips. "Go on," she urged, her hand now on my shoulder. She pushed me a few steps toward the ambulance.

I turned out of her grasp sharply and then heard the ambulance door open and close. The driver came walking toward us. He was wearing what looked like a pair of construction man's overalls with deep pockets and a T-shirt that his firm and thick muscularity was stretching to the limits of its seams. He had a shock of black hair and sleepy brown eyes.

"Trouble?" he asked.

"No, not yet," the woman said. "She's just a bit tired. You're tired, aren't you, Phoebe?"

"I'm not tired. I want to see my uncle," I said, sounding a lot more frightened than I had wanted to sound. It was just hard to put up a brave front under such weird circumstances.

"We don't have time for this," the man said to the woman.

"I know what time it is and what we have and have not time for," she told him irritably.

He lifted his hands as if he was going to have nothing to do with any of it anymore and stepped back.

I turned in a circle. Where was Uncle Buster? How could he just leave me? Why would I be going anywhere in an ambulance? And how could they call that an escort service?

"I gotta get out of here," I moaned.

"Now you just relax," the woman said, and before I could take another step, she put her arm around my shoulders. I tried to pull away, but she was amazingly strong and had my arms pinned against my sides.

"Let go!" I screamed. An elderly couple who had just pulled up and parked looked at us, but the sight of the woman holding me just made them walk away faster.

"Okay," she told the driver. "You'd better give her the first-class ticket."

"Glad to be of service," he said, smiling. He stepped up and pulled a syringe out of his deep pocket. I felt the needle go into my arm, and again I tried to pull free, even kick her. Then he stepped back and walked quickly to the rear of the ambulance. She held on to me as I continued to squirm and cry out.

Suddenly, though, I felt so numb. I wasn't even sure I was making any sound even though my mouth was opening and closing. The whole parking lot went into a spin.

"Hurry up, will you!" I heard her shout at the driver.

"I'm coming, I'm coming. Man, you're getting to be a slave driver."

A stretcher was wheeled toward me, and I felt myself being lowered to it. First, I sat and then, despite willing myself to put up resistance, I was easily made to lie back. Straps were pulled over my legs and across my chest under my breasts. A pillow was shoved down beneath my head.

I heard someone ask what happened and the woman say, "Epileptic fit."

"Oh, poor thing."

"She'll be all right," the woman said.

I vaguely felt myself being lifted. I had no pain. It was actually a pleasant sort of feeling that came over me. I wasn't exactly asleep either, but I wasn't fully awake. I was caught somewhere in between and I was drifting. I heard the door shut after I was moved farther into the ambulance.

Then another door opened and shut. The woman was beside me. I sensed her, but I didn't see her. My eyes were closing.

"I never like it like this," the driver said.

"Shut up and drive," the woman told him.

I was sinking farther down now. I thought I was falling through the stretcher. It was like my whole body was melting, too, and seeping into it. Was this death?

I began to hear music. The driver started to sing along with a song.

And then I heard other music, a tune coming from a black marble pedestal upon which two ballerinas twirled. I remembered it well. It was at my bedside, a birthday present. I was hypnotized with it, with their graceful movements as the male dancer twirled and swung the female.

How wonderful it must be to dance like that, I thought, to be airy and unafraid of your body failing you. How I wished I could be a dancer.

"It's pretty," I heard myself say.

"The moment I saw it, I knew I had to get it for you, Phoebe," Daddy said.

There he was, standing at my bedside, smiling down at me. Then he lost his smile and put his hand on my forehead.

"Still got some fever," he muttered, and straightened up quickly, concern on his face. "She still has some fever, Charlene," he called behind him.

"It's nothing," Mama shouted back. "Kids get fevers all the time."

"Maybe we should take her to the doctor. She's been sniveling and coughing for days."

"She'll be all right. Everything scares you, Horace. I swear you were brought up a mama's boy, frightened by the sound of your own footsteps. You going with me or not?"

"Going? We can't leave her, Charlene. The girl's sick. What, you crazy?"

"Suit yourself," she said. "You know where I'll be."

Daddy wound up the music box again and I watched the dancers.

"I'll get you some hot tea and honey to drink, Phoebe. You feeling all right?"

I nodded, unable to take my eyes off the dancers.

Daddy left, but he didn't come back. The dancers stopped and the music ended.

I wanted it all to start again.

"Daddy," I called. "Daddy."

He didn't reply. I struggled so hard to get to that music box, but I couldn't reach it.

The dancers waited. This was all they were created to do, dance, but it was enough to give them purpose and beauty. Silence and neglect were the two sides of the same cruel sword cutting their lifeline. And they weren't just waiting for any music. They needed the music that belonged to them, the music they were born with, the music that had become a part of them. They looked so helpless, waiting there, so full of disappointment, too.

They started to disappear.

I felt myself drifting pleasantly again, but I kept thinking about the dancers.

And then it came to me.

I'm just like them, I thought.

Waiting for the music that belonged to me.

MIDNIGHT FLIGHT

Contents

MIDNIGHT FLIGHT

	Prologue	327
1	Orientation	335
2	Dr. Foreman's Funny Farm	349
3	Three New Squaws	366
4	Betrayal	382
5	Catfight	398
6	Group Therapy	415
7	Posy's Story	430
8	Confession	444
9	Dr. Foreman's Spy	460
10	Good-bye, Posy	478
11	Inward Journey	490
12	Pajama Party	503
13	Marooned	520

14   Natani's Lesson   535

15   Posy Returns   550

16   Fly Away Home   563

       Epilogue   575

Prologue

Just like someone rising to the surface of a pool filled with ink, I slowly awoke from what felt like a month-long coma. My eyelids flickered, but they were two tiny lead curtains slamming closed repeatedly until I managed with determined effort to keep them open. Shadows swirled and wavered and then gradually came into focus. However, the shapes they began to form made no immediate sense to me.

Something was roaring in my ears. For a moment I thought I was right beside a waterfall, and then as my eyes focused, I read the instructions on the back of the seat in front of me: KEEP YOUR SEAT BELT BUCKLED WHEN IN FLIGHT.

In flight?

I lifted my head and looked about. I was in a small airplane that had room for what looked like twenty or so people, and I wasn't just buckled in the seat. A thick, black leather strap was around my upper body, tightened just below my elbows, keeping my arms so close to my sides I could barely move my hands.

No one else was in the plane!

I had been in an airplane only once before in my life when Daddy and Mama took me to see Daddy's father in an old-age home in Richmond just before he died. I was only five at the time, but I never forgot being on a plane. Mama wouldn't let me sit by the window. She wanted me between her and Daddy so I wouldn't really think about being up in an airplane. Daddy thought she should let me sit by the window, but she wouldn't have it.

"I don't want no kid screamin' and cryin' 'bout being afraid. It's enough I agreed to go on this depressing trip," she declared.

Mama never cared about raising her voice in public, and the only way Daddy could stop it was by looking away and stopping the argument.

I wasn't afraid of being in a plane. Actually, I was fascinated with everything, especially the feeling of being lifted into the sky. When my heart started to pound, I closed my eyes and smiled to myself. It was better than the time Daddy had taken me on the Ferris wheel. However, when it came to my getting up to go to the bathroom, I was nervous. Daddy wanted Mama to take me and she was annoyed.

"She can go to the bathroom herself at home. She can go in a plane," she told him.

I went myself, and when I came back to my seat, I curled up and fell asleep. The next thing I knew we were getting off the plane in Richmond. Because I'd behaved well, Mama let me sit by the window on the way back. I couldn't stop looking at the clouds and the earth below where houses looked like toys. I thought to myself that this was the way God saw the world every day. He rode inside a cloud or on the back of the wind.

But this plane ride was different, so different. I felt I was being transported from one dream to another. Was this real? Or would I wake up any moment and realize it had all been a terrible nightmare?

I was so busy looking around that I didn't realize immediately how I was dressed. Gone were my clothes. Instead, I wore what looked like a thick, faded white nightgown created from an old potato sack. It was that coarse. Whatever was on beneath it didn't feel like my panties either. Where were my jeans and blouse? And my watch? Even the ruby ring Daddy had brought back for me from one of his sales trips was gone.

I squirmed in the seat and glanced down at my feet. I was wearing white stockings, the sort of stockings I saw nurses wear, and instead of my pink and white sneakers, I wore a pair of the ugliest-looking black shoes with thick heels I think I had ever seen.

What was going on?

"Hello!" I screamed.

The only response was the continually monotonous roar of the engines. Whoever was in the cockpit might not be able to hear me, I thought.

I looked around the plane again. How had I gotten here? Who had strapped me into this seat?

I struggled through the maze of blurred memories, desperately trying to understand, to remember, and then, as if a dam in my brain had broken, it all came rushing back over me, and as soon as it had, I wished it hadn't.

After Mama had left Daddy and me and I had been in trouble too often in Atlanta, Daddy had convinced Mama's sister and brother-in-law, my aunt Mae Louise and uncle Buster Howard, to take me into their suburban home in Stone Mountain and enroll me into a better school. Daddy was on the road too much to keep an eye on me. Unfortunately, I got into trouble quickly with a boy there named Ashley Porter, who came from a wealthy white family, and then after Daddy had been killed in the car accident, I had decided to run off.

I had learned that Mama had been left in a clinic where she was being treated for substance abuse , and I was headed there. I was hoping she would be well enough to get out and go somewhere where she and I could start a new life. I was hoping she would be as excited about that as I was, but when I arrived at the clinic and went to see her, she was so confused. She just couldn't or wouldn't understand what I was telling her about Daddy being killed in a car accident and me being forced to live with her sister, Mae Louise.

Unbeknownst to me, while I was visiting Mama, the doctor at the clinic had called my uncle and aunt and my aunt called the police. The state police were sent to bring me back. I wasn't supposed to leave Stone Mountain for any trips since I was to go to court for hitting a boy named Skip Lester with a small desktop statue when he, Ashley, and the other boys had all ganged up on me. Girls from my new school tricked me into joining what they called a sting operation to permit the police to arrest Ashley, who had been spreading stories about them and me. He was going to be arrested for selling and using drugs. Of course, the girls were in cahoots with Ashley and his friends to trap me and have fun with me. I still couldn't explain why I was so stupid and gullible enough to believe them. That's how you get when you're so desperate to have friends. You can have only one friend, I concluded, yourself.

The state policeman who picked me up at Mama's clinic dropped me off at a roadside diner to meet my uncle Buster. I thought my uncle was just going to bawl me out without my aunt being present and then he was going to take me home. Instead, he left me there to be taken to what he called some special school for troubled teenagers like me, girls whose parents and guardians could no longer contend with them and their problems.

No one wanted to listen to my side of things, especially my aunt and my uncle. My uncle didn't even have the courage to tell me what he had secretly arranged to take place at the diner. He tricked and betrayed me. I went to the bathroom and when I came out, he was gone and so was my suitcase.

A man and a woman came for me in an ambulance, and when I resisted, they stuck a needle in my arm and gave me something that made me dizzy and confused. I passed out as I was being loaded into the ambulance. That was the last thing I remembered.

And that was what my aunt and uncle had done to me, and I was supposed to be the bad one in the family?

Now, here I was alone in this strange plane. Had I died? Had they given me something to kill me? Was this how people were really transported to the other world?

"Hey! Anyone! Please," I screamed. "Someone, help me!"

I twisted and pulled and tried to kick the seat. Frustrated and frightened, I went numb inside and the tears in my brain flooded and washed my screams onto my face.

Still, no one responded. I gazed out the window at the wing and the engine. It was twilight, that time when the earth became a giant sponge and absorbed all the light around it. The dark sky lying in wait came rushing in behind like a black velvet ocean. I saw some stars appear. Their growing brightness comforted me until we flew into a wall of puffy, gray clouds that whirled about like so much smoke.

Every nerve in my body grew tighter and tighter, threatening to snap. My throat was so dry and my shoulders ached, the fingers of pain stretching down from the base of my neck. I continued to struggle against the straps, but they were too thick and too securely fastened. All I was doing by struggling was irritating my skin. Helpless, I relaxed and closed my eyes, trying to keep a lid on my boiling rage. Whoever had done this to me was going to be sorry, I vowed. As soon as they unfastened these belts, they'd see. How dare they take my clothing and put me in this rag and these ugly stockings and shoes!

As best as I could, I wiggled my fingers and explored what I was wearing beneath. It felt like . . . like a diaper, firm as plastic on the outside like one of those special undergarments women who have bladder trouble wear.

What was going on? Who dared to undress me? Was someone playing some sick joke on me? How long have I been on this plane? Where was I being taken? I thought I was going to some school. Why wasn't there anyone else with me? What if something terrible had happened to me? What if I was being kidnapped to become someone's slave? Who would know? Would that satisfy my uncle and aunt? All they cared about was getting rid of me. Whatever happened to me wasn't important.

As I thought of these things, the rage began to boil over again. I tried to turn and press my body against the straps in hope of breaking loose, but nothing helped. They felt woven of steel thread. Beads of sweat popped out on the back of my neck and my forehead because of my efforts. It was another futile attempt. I was just wasting my energy, energy I might need the moment I was finally released.

Inside, my stomach was churning, grinding rocks of frustration into sand. I closed my eyes and, taking deep breaths, again tried desperately to calm myself.

"Get hold of yourself, Phoebe Elder," I muttered. "Easy. You'll get out of this soon. You've been in worse places."

No, I haven't, I thought.

I opened my eyes and looked at the closed cockpit door. Why wasn't anyone at least interested enough to see if I had regained consciousness?

"Damn you!" I screamed. I could feel the veins in my neck becoming embossed in my skin. I shouted and then just released a long, animal cry of pain.

As if my scream affected the plane, it bounced and then dropped. I balled my fingers into fists and pressed them against my sides, gasping. What was happening now? Were we crashing? The plane bounced again and again and then rattled. Looking out the window, I saw how we dropped lower and lower until we were out of the clouds. Way off in the distance, I could see the lights of some small city, but other than that, the landscape was dark, just like that pool of ink out of which I had imagined myself rising.

The plane continued to descend. Finally, I heard wheels being lowered and locked into place and then the plane touched down with a small bounce. It slowed and taxied until it turned. Wherever we were wasn't much of an airport. Maybe because of the angle I was at, I couldn't see any lights or people or cars. I heard the engines being shut down and the propellers slowing. When it all stopped, I waited in anticipation to see who would come out of the cockpit. The door did not open for so long, I began to think no one was flying the plane.

Then, the two pilots emerged. They looked so young to me, too young to be in charge of an airplane, but they had wings on their white shirts and gold-threaded bars on their shoulders.

"Where am I? Who did this to me? Why am I tied down?" I fired my questions at them in machine-gun fashion.

They looked at me, but neither spoke, making me feel as if I weren't really there. Instead, one of them undid the door and lowered the steps. I heard a woman outside ask if everything was all right.

"Just peachy keen," one of the pilots said, and the two left the plane. No one else had emerged from the cockpit. Who was in charge here?

"What about me? What is going on?" I shouted after them. I watched the doorway and then tried to kick at the seat in front of me. "What's going on, damn it!"

Finally, a young woman with short, dark brown hair appeared. She was as tall as I was, about five feet ten or so, and she was wearing a dark blue uniform jacket with brass buttons and a pair of blue slacks. I thought she wasn't much more than nineteen or twenty years old. She was wide in the hips and small on top with narrow shoulders, making it look like two different bodies had been slapped together when God was busy attending to other matters.

"Who are you? What's going on?" I demanded.

"Keep your voice down," she said sharply, and approached. When she drew closer, I saw she had a pudgy face with thick lips and wide nostrils. A streak of freckles burst down the bridge of her nose on both sides and over the crests of her puffy cheeks. She wore no makeup, not even lipstick, and a small, thin scar was on the left side of her chin.

"Where am I?" I asked as softly and as calmly as I could. First, I had to have some answers. Then I could take some action, I told myself.

"You'll see," she replied, and began to unfasten the straps.

"Who are you? Am I at some school? Where is this school that I had to be flown here?"

"You're wasting your breath asking me questions," she said, stepping back. "Get up and get out."

"What happened to my clothes? Why am I wearing this rag dress?"

Her untrimmed eyebrows lifted and I thought she smiled, although it was hard to tell because her lips were so stiff. She seized my right arm and tugged to get me to stand. When I did, I wavered for a moment and she had to grab my shoulders to keep me from falling.

"I'm so dizzy," I said. "They put me to sleep. Maybe they gave me something poisonous."

"Oh, you poor little thing," she said with exaggerated sympathy and sweetness. Then she snapped, "Walk!" She poked me at the base of my spine with her thick, right forefinger, which felt like the barrel of a gun.

I scowled back at her and made my way down the small aisle to the door. For a moment I was dizzy and nauseated again. Then I caught my breath and navigated the half dozen metal steps. The outside area was well lit, but all I saw was what looked like a building made of concrete. It had bland gray walls and a metal door with no windows on it. The front of the building had no windows either.

The first thing I noticed when I started down the steps was how hot it was. It was dark, but it felt like the middle of a summer day in Atlanta, especially in the poorer part of the city where we had lived. It wasn't true that people of African descent didn't notice the oppressive heat and humidity as much as white people.

"Where is this? It's so hot."

"Hell," I heard her say behind me. "Keep walking toward the building before I have you carried there," she threatened, and I continued slowly. Where had the two young pilots gone? Why wasn't anyone else around? I stopped to look and she gave me another shove to move me toward the building.

"Where are we going?"

"Just walk to the building and keep your mouth shut," she ordered.

Every time I turned my head to look around, she pushed me.

"Keep your hands off me," I warned.

"We've got a long night ahead of us. Move it," she commanded.

When we reached the door, she stepped ahead and opened it. The hinges squeaked as if it hadn't been opened for a hundred years. It was like opening a tomb. How could this be a school? Why was I being brought here?

"Go in," she said.

I hesitated and she reached out, seized my wrist, and pulled me forward, driving me into the building with such force, I nearly stumbled and fell.

The inside was poorly lit by some weak overhead neon lights, but I could see it was just a dusty, empty warehouse or something. At first I didn't realize anyone else was there. They were both so quiet and so still. Then I saw a petite, rust-color-haired girl sitting on a stool in front of a desk on my right. Her hands were folded, the fingers gripping like the fingers of someone in pain. Her knuckles looked as if little white buttons had been sewn onto them. She was dressed in the same sort of one-piece rag I was wearing, and I could also see she had the same style shoes.

Sitting off on my left was another girl with styled pecan brown hair. Even though she, too, was dressed like me and the other girl, she held her head with a more arrogant air, her posture firm, but her arms folded under her breasts. I thought I could even make out a small smirk of impatience on her lips. Who were they? Was this concrete building supposed to serve as a classroom? Why was it so poorly lit then? A hailstorm of questions peppered my brain.

"Sit," my escort ordered, and pushed me toward the empty stool and desk at the center.

"What is going on? Why am I in here? This isn't any school. I'm supposed to be taken to a school. I want to know where I am," I demanded more loudly, my hands on my hips. My voice echoed in the tomblike building.

"Just sit and shut up," my escort blared. "The longer you act stupid, the longer this is going to take."

I looked at the other two, who glared back at me with an expression of annoyance that suggested I was making things harder for them as well. Reluctantly, I did what she said.

"Now what?" I snapped back at her.

She did finally smile.

"Now, it begins," she said, turned, and walked out of the building, closing the door behind her.

I was right about that door. It sounded like a lid being shut on a coffin.

1

Orientation

The moment we were alone, I turned to the girl on my left.

"What is this? Where are we? Why are we in this place?" I asked.

"Why are you asking me? How would I know?" she shot back at me. "What do I look like, information please?"

"Well, you were here before me so I thought you might know more," I threw back at her with just as unfriendly a tone.

"We got here only a little while before you did," the second girl said, somewhat softer. I turned to her. "So we don't know any more than you do. I'm Teal Sommers. That's Robin Lyn Taylor. She didn't tell me her name," Teal added with a smirk. "I heard one of those girls call her that." She leaned forward to glare past me at Robin Lyn.

"I'm not exactly in a party mood, you know, and I told you, I don't like to be called Robin Lyn. Just call me Robin. You, too," she ordered me.

"Yes, Your Majesty," I said, and Teal laughed.

Robin folded her arms and turned away. "Well, we're here together so I guess we'll have to talk to each other decently. Where y'all from?"

"Where y'all from?" Teal laughed. "I'm from Albany, New York. I was flown in here just a little before y'all were, I think. I'm very un- sure about the time. They took my watch."

"Mine, too," I said, rubbing my wrist. "And my ring. Why did they do that?"

"Maybe they're jewel thieves. They took Robin's watch, too, right, Robin?"

"Big deal. I stole it. I'll steal another first chance I get," she said defiantly, looking at the closed door. "I'm supposed to be at a school, a special school. That's what the judge said," she shouted at the door. "Not some dumpy, smelly building."

"Judge?" I asked.

She spun her head around to me so fast, I thought it would just keep going in circles on her neck.

"What are you, a scholarship winner or something? Is that why you're here?"

I stared, confused.

"Hardly," I finally replied. "My uncle and aunt arranged all this without telling me anything about it. I was drugged, kidnapped, and brought here."

Robin started to laugh and stopped. "Did you say drugged and kidnapped?"

"I know exactly what she means. That's how I felt," Teal said. "My father arranged for me to be transported here. He was nice enough to tell me I was going to a special school, but my parents didn't even let me take a change of clothing. Daddy had a hired goon bring me to the airport and to the plane. Next thing I knew, I was flying away and no one told me where I was going. They kept the windows shut, too. They gave me something to drink, and before I knew it, I was asleep, so I was drugged, too. When I woke up, I was here and dressed in this rag and these stupid clodhoppers as well as this . . . diaper."

"I guess I shouldn't have expected anything better from my aunt, but why did your father do that to you?" I asked. Even though I had had some of my things when Daddy brought me to live with Aunt Mae Louise and Uncle Buster, I didn't feel much different except I knew why they'd got rid of me. There was no surprise for me there.

"He was, I guess I can safely say, at the end of his patience with me. I was an embarrassment to my mother, who sits at the head of the social table of high society."

"What did you do?"

"I robbed a bank," Teal muttered.

"What?"

"I stole money from Daddy's secret safe, his and my brother Carson's."

"And your own father sent you away for that?"

"Well, it was a little more, I guess," Teal admitted.

"I bet," Robin muttered. "Don't be fooled by her sweet little face."

I turned to her. "What about you?"

"I didn't rob a bank, but I was part of an armed robbery of a supermarket where I worked," Robin said, looking ahead. It was as if she were reminding herself and not telling us. "This is supposed to be an alternative to going to a real jail. My mother darling talked me into it, and like both of you, I was eventually put in a plane and the same things happened to me. I fell asleep and they took my clothing and brought me here."

She smiled and shook her head and then shouted at the closed door, "They're just trying to frighten us with all this . . . this horror-hotel stuff, but it doesn't scare me! Y'all just wasting your time! You might as well give me back my clothes!"

"What brought you here?" Teal asked me after Robin's screams died down.

"I ran away from my uncle and aunt where I was supposed to stay."

"So, big deal," Robin said. "I bet we've all done that one time or another."

"I was supposed to be in court for hitting this boy with a little brass statue."

"Did you kill him?" Teal asked, her eyes widening with interest.

"No, but I put him in the hospital. He was part of a group of boys trying to rape me."

"So why would they put you in jail for that?" Robin asked skeptically. "It just sounds like self-defense to me."

"There's more to it."

"I bet."

"Look," I said, turning on her, "I don't have to defend myself to you. In fact—"

Before I could say anything else, we heard the door squeal open, followed by the machine-gun *rat-ta-tat-tat* of stiletto high heels on the concrete floor.

Out of the dark shadows came a tall, elegant-looking woman, statuesque with a firm figure in a ruby-red skirt suit. She had highlighted golden brown hair, about the base of her neck in length, neatly styled. As she moved more into the light and drew closer, I saw she was an attractive woman with high cheekbones and a perfect nose. She was wearing a soft red lipstick, very understated. A girlfriend of mine, Louella Mason, who was determined to become a beautician, had told me when a woman wants to emphasize her eyes, she de-emphasizes her lips, but this woman looked like she didn't need anything special to make her eyes prominent. They weren't big as much as they were striking and intense.

She paused, looked at the three of us, and smiled so warmly, I felt like getting up and rushing into her arms. It was a smile that brought a ray of sunshine to a rainy day, and, boy, did I need some sugar now.

"Hello, girls," she said. "I'm Dr. Foreman. Welcome to my school."

"This is a school?" Teal piped up immediately. "It's more like someone's filthy basement."

Dr. Foreman turned to her and, holding her smile, said, "No, this isn't the actual school." She looked about and smiled as if she didn't see what we saw. She saw a beautiful lobby or something instead. "This is my orientation center. The school is some distance from here, but I like to meet my girls as soon as they are brought and introduce them to the way things will be as soon as possible. That way, if they don't accept what I say and don't do what I say, I can put them right back on the plane and ship them somewhere else where a far worse fate awaits them. Is this plan all right with you, Teal?"

I could see Teal was both impressed and intimidated that Dr. Foreman already knew which of us she was. Teal didn't answer. She just sat looking at her, her mouth slightly open. Dr. Foreman did not turn away immediately either. She held Teal's gaze, froze that now cold smile on her lips, and only after a few beats, slowly turned back to Robin and me.

"Now then, as I was saying, welcome to my school," she continued.

As if that was their cue, three young women, the one who had escorted me from the plane to the concrete building, and two others dressed similarly with their hair cut identically short, entered and took position just behind Dr. Foreman. They stood with military posture, their arms behind them, hands clasped, and looked forward, not at us, just forward and poised like guard dogs ready to pounce upon command. Foreman's rottweilers, all teeth and muscle, I thought.

"I created my school only five years ago, but I have, shall we say, graduated dozens of girls like you, releasing them back into society as productive young women, all of whom have kept out of any trouble with their families or with the law. Three are in fact law officers now themselves," Dr. Foreman said, smiling wider with pride. "Two are correction officers and one is a policewoman in a big city."

"Something for us to look forward to," Robin muttered. "A career as a policewoman."

Dr. Foreman looked straight ahead, but her body began to turn as if it were robotic, slowly, stiffly, her shoulders firm and straight.

"Right now, Robin Lyn Taylor, all you have to look forward to is getting yourself into more trouble and so deeply that you are eventually put away in a room without any hope of getting out. In effect, you have no future. The reason you have been sent here is to help you regain one. Until that happens, you, all of you," Dr. Foreman said, looking at Teal and me as well now, "are nonentities. You don't exist for your families. You don't exist for yourselves. All you've accomplished up until now is sharpened yourselves as thorns in the side of civilized society. With me, under my care, you will either develop the ability to have a future or you will be pulled out of the side of the civilized world and discarded like any nuisance. The choice is ultimately yours to make, but," she said, smiling warmly again, "we will do our best here to help you make the right choice. In the past, whenever you were given the opportunity to do what was right and decent, you all made other choices. We expect to correct that. We will help you.

"Someone, thanks to the mercy of our court system, has decided to give you this one last chance. Rather than sit here sulking and trying to think of wisecracks, you should begin to show some appreciation.

"But," she continued in a sweet, melodic tone, "I am the first to recognize that you are all here because you are all filled with defiance, anger, and most of all fear."

"Fear?" I muttered. I couldn't help it. It just slipped out between my lips. How could fear have brought us here?

"Yes, my dear Phoebe, fear. Antisocial behavior stems from a well of fear. You act out because you are defensive, slightly paranoid, I'm afraid. In your present way of thinking, the world around you threatens you. You believe everyone is against you and you're just naturally antagonistic to everything."

I guess she saw the lack of understanding in my face. She smiled, again so softly, I felt I could relax and listen to her for hours.

"Don't worry about any of that yet, my dear. You'll see. You'll all see. That's what's so wonderful about my work," she said excitedly, "at least to me, especially the way it opens the eyes of my girls. For me," she said, her voice rising an octave, "there is nothing as satisfying as seeing one of my girls suddenly come to the realization she can be as good as anyone else out there, she can be productive and worthwhile. She can make friends and be liked and like others. Her heart can hold sunshine, even on rainy days."

She did make it sound wonderful. For a moment she paused with her face so radiant and full of happiness, I felt some hope seep into my hardened and crusty surface. She looked at me as if she could sense it and gave me a special nod, a little more of her smile.

"People are always asking me, 'Dr. Foreman, you were a successful and renowned college professor. Why did you throw away your classroom work, your publications, your lectures, put all your fortune into this school, and go off and surround yourself with the hardest sort of challenge: girls whom everyone has given up on, girls who would easily end up in penal institutions?'

"Well, the answer is you, my dears," she declared with her arms out as though she were about to embrace all three of us at once, "you and your awakening. Nothing is more satisfying to me than to bring someone back from the dead," she continued, her right hand over her heart, "for that is where you are now, in some cemetery of your own making, burying yourselves in your disgust, your fears, your dysfunction."

She grew stern looking again and took another step toward the three of us.

"Within the next twenty-four hours, fourteen hundred teenagers like yourselves will attempt suicide, twenty-eight hundred will get pregnant, fifteen thousand will try alcohol for the first time, and thirty-five hundred will run away from home."

She let those facts linger in the air between us for a moment. I glanced at Robin and then Teal. Neither seemed impressed nor seemed to care.

"But not you. No, not my girls. To me," Dr. Foreman said, looking up at the ceiling as if she could look right through to the heavens, "you will all be like Lazarus, rising from the grave."

"Does that mean you're God?" Teal asked, her mouth dripping with sarcasm.

I thought I was brave and tough, but this soft, pretty white girl who sounded like she had been born with a silver spoon in her mouth was sure nasty and unafraid, even after all that had been done to her, to us.

Dr. Foreman's eyelids fluttered. She had what seemed unflappable poise. That smile never faltered as she lowered her gaze at Teal like someone lowering the barrel of a cannon at a new target.

"For you and for the others, dear Teal, as long as you are here, that is exactly who I will be."

She waited a moment for her words to settle. Teal shook her head and looked away.

"Now," Dr. Foreman said, turning back to speak to all of us, "let me begin by explaining that you're not going to a school any way like the ones you have attended. First, my school is at my ranch. It's a working ranch and you will all participate in the daily chores."

"Oh, so we're really a form of cheap labor, is that it?" Robin complained.

"Hardly cheap, Robin. For your work, you will be given full room and board."

"Isn't my father paying you?" Teal fired at her. "I shouldn't have to do any daily chores," she declared staunchly, her eyes burning with arrogance.

"Yes, in your case, the family is paying, but there is much more that will be given to you than you would get anywhere else for that amount of money," Dr. Foreman said calmly. The arrows and darts Teal shot at her with those fiery eyes seemed to bounce off an invisible wall of protection that surrounded her.

"Like what?" Teal demanded, refusing to step back. I saw how the girls behind Dr. Foreman glared at Teal. They all looked eager to get their hands around her neck and shake her head off her body.

"Like my expert treatment, my therapy sessions, my proven techniques," Dr. Foreman said to all of us and not just Teal. "It's off the charts when you start computing the costs, and even Teal here, who points out that her parents are paying the tuition, couldn't really afford the tuition if it were equated with the value you will all receive."

"Why are you so nice and generous to us?" Teal muttered, the corners of her mouth folding in.

"Why? I do this because I want to give back to the science that has been so good to me, as well as my deep desire to help young women in desperate need, to help them find what is spiritually good in them."

"Oh, brother," Teal muttered. "We're in a nunnery."

Dr. Foreman's rottweilers moved restlessly. She glanced at them and turned back to us.

"To continue"—Dr. Foreman glared at Teal—"at my school you will not find a staff of teachers to coddle and prod you into doing your homework, studying properly, and achieving. I will assign you all your work and you will have to master it all yourselves."

"Huh?" Robin said. "Did you say ourselves?"

"What are we going to study, basket weaving?" Teal asked with a crooked smile.

"You will be studying regular academic subjects, of course. We want you to qualify for high school graduation, to be able to pass exams, even be good enough to be admitted to institutions of higher learning, but you will be in a different sort of classroom. Life itself, you will see, will become the chief subject. You're all failing at that right now, and for now, that is far more important a subject than anything else."

"I don't get it. How are we supposed to learn anything without a teacher?" Robin asked. "It was hard enough to learn with one."

"Oh, you'll be surprised at what you can accomplish when you are left to your own initiative, Robin Lyn. Of course, you will all help each other. Cooperation in that regard is very important. I will want you all to fully understand how important it is to get along with each other, with others of different backgrounds. Out there, that's what you must do to be a contributing member of society.

"But, self-reliance is essential, too. We can cooperate with each other, but we can't become totally dependent upon others or we become a burden, don't we? That is truly what the three of you are right now, a burden. You'll either be cast off or you'll learn to walk on your own. Sink or swim," she said, her face now turning cool. When she called for it, that iciness seemed to emerge from within her, rise to the surface of her face, penetrate her eyes, tighten her lips, and make her look taller, more intimidating.

I glanced again at the other two. Despite the brave fronts they were putting on, I sensed they were just as anxious about all this as I was. I noticed as well that the three young women behind Dr. Foreman had grown still again, had barely moved a muscle since she had looked at them. How could they be so disciplined? They were three statues.

How much longer would we be kept here? I wondered. It was dank and musty, the air so stale my throat ached. Why did we have to begin in such a place anyway? The stool was uncomfortable. The lighting was dull. What was the point of having us sit at old grade-school desks? I was still tired and achy from my unpleasant trip. I couldn't wait to go to sleep in a bed and I had to go to the bathroom, but I was afraid to mention it yet. I didn't want to be the first one.

"To be sure you are making the right amount of effort at your schoolwork, you will be tested from time to time on your academic subjects, and if you don't pass, you will be given demerits," Dr. Foreman explained.

"Demerits?" Teal said, smirking. "What does that mean, we won't get our Girl Scout patches and medals?"

"No, my dear," Dr. Foreman responded. "Nothing that important. You are all as of now under my merit system. Since you have all been brought here as a last resort because of your antisocial behavior, you will all be beginning with a minus ten and have to work your way back up to zero before you can even hope to achieve rights and privileges."

That did sound threatening.

"What rights and privileges?" I asked.

"Well, for one thing, you will have to wear what you're wearing until you achieve the points to wear my school uniforms."

"What are we wearing? This is disgusting," Teal complained. "Not only are these . . . these rags irritating my skin, they smell, and why do we have to wear diapers, for Christ sakes? I want my clothes back."

"Yes, I'm sorry about these transitional outfits. They do have that unpleasant odor." Dr. Foreman sounded sympathetic. She also made it sound as if there were no other choice. I finally saw the three rottweilers soften their lips into a smile.

"But why are we wearing diapers?" Robin asked.

"Because, my dear, you are being reborn. Unfortunately, none of you have shown enough maturity to be considered anything but infants, and until you do, that's how you will be treated," Dr. Foreman said firmly, losing the smile. Then she blossomed into another to add, "Believe me, my dear, you'll be grateful you have them on."

The slight smiles on the three young women behind her widened almost into laughter when she said that.

"That's cold," Teal said. "And disgusting. I feel like some old lady with bladder trouble. I want my clothing back. They were expensive, especially the designer jeans. You have no right to take them away from me. Why can't we all have our clothes back?" she whined, now sounding more like a spoiled child than a defiant teenager.

"I've already given that answer. One thing you will learn and learn very quickly here, Teal, is if I or anyone else has to repeat something to you, it's because you don't or won't listen, and that will result in a demerit."

"I don't care about any demerits. I want my clothing!" Teal shouted back. Her voice echoed off the cement walls and then died as if her words were smashed to bits, the letters splattered and then raining down to the dank concrete floor.

Dr. Foreman took a step toward her. "Oh, but you will care, my dear. That will be one of the significant changes in you very soon," she said slowly, her voice so full of chill, I imagined the words turning to ice in the air between them. Even the cold smile disappeared.

"I want to go home," Teal cried back at her. "Right now."

"Do you? Unfortunately for you, for all of you, no one wants you back, Teal. In fact, I'm the only one who wants you."

"How long do I have to stay here, live on your ranch, and milk cows or whatever?" Teal was definitely someone who couldn't stand being bossed around.

"That's entirely up to you," Dr. Foreman replied. "Now then, there will be no more questions." She turned to Robin and me. "No more questions from any of you. You will all just listen and you will do what you are told to do. Listen well, girls," she added, her cold smile returning to those lips. "Be keen, girls, be keen. Your comfort and happiness depend on it like they never have before."

She stepped back, glanced at the young women behind her, who looked excited about her firmness. I wouldn't admit it, of course, but

they frightened me. I wondered if Robin's and Teal's hearts were pounding as hard as mine was now, despite the brave face masks they wore.

We were all brought here more or less against our will. Dr. Foreman was probably not wrong about that. We had no one out there to help us, no one to call, no one to come for us. I couldn't help feeling that I was dangling in space, holding on to a thin piece of spidery web that this strange woman, sometimes sounding nice, sometimes sounding scary, held at the other end. If she decided to let go, I, as well as Robin and Teal, would fall into some darker place. What else could we do but listen?

"Now, so there are no misunderstandings and no whining like we're hearing," Dr. Foreman said, glaring at Teal again, "let me be clear about what you should expect after you leave here. At my home you will find there are no radios, no magazines, no CDs, and especially no television for anyone until she has earned the right to leisure time. The only books permitted are the books related to your subjects, not that any of you look like you read very much," she added with a tightening at the right corner of her mouth.

"No one will have any phone privileges until she earns twenty merit plus points. That means no one can call you as well—not, from what I know of each of your histories, that anyone would want to call you."

"We really are like prisoners," Teal complained, and quickly looked down.

"Since that wasn't put in the form of a question, I will let it pass without penalizing you another demerit. If you are like prisoners, as you say, it's because you have imprisoned yourselves. You have put bars on your own windows and built the walls between yourselves and the rest of humanity. I am your best hope to remove those bars, to crumble those walls. Right now, you see me only as a disciplinarian, but in time, very soon, you will learn to appreciate what I have to offer you.

"It's a lot like Annie Sullivan and Helen Keller," she said, looking off. She smiled at some image of herself, and even that smile was disturbing enough to make my stomach feel as if I had just drunk a gallon of sour milk. "For in truth, you all can't really speak, can't really hear, can't really see. You're locked up inside your own troubled bodies, and I will free you. Yes, I will."

There was a long silence. My throat was dry. My stomach continued to churn and I felt the growing pressure of having to go to the bathroom. I trembled, but I had to ask. I raised my hand, hoping she would permit it.

"I said no questions," she declared.

"But . . ."

She raised her head and the very air seemed to freeze around us. If I uttered another sound, lightning might sizzle my brain, I thought. I bit down on my lower lip. She smiled again.

"I don't want to leave you thinking that all that awaits you is hard work, rules, and restrictions. We will have wonderful sessions together, my group therapy, during which time you will all have this, this terribly dark curtain of pain and anger lifted from your eyes. Believe me, girls, that will happen and you will be grateful. I've seen it so many times before on the faces of my girls. My girls," she repeated, her eyes glossing over as if she could see them all parading before her, hugging her like high school graduates at their diploma ceremony.

She was quiet again. We could hear a drip, drip, drip of something in the plumbing above and behind us. Her eyes slowly brightened, the gloss changing to a thin layer of ice. She stared at us so long, I felt uncomfortable and saw both Teal and Robin squirming a bit on their stools as well.

"Part of your work and your life at my school will be your confronting your own fears. One of the best ways to do that is to be out in nature. Nature has a way of tearing away all the conflicting, confusing things that have distorted our vision of ourselves. In nature you can make no rationalizations, no excuses, fall upon your knees and beg for mercy. You either become strong or perish. Everything out there teaches us that lesson and it's a wonderful lesson, one that we tend to forget in the world we call civilized. We'll help you regain that wisdom. Or, I should say, nature will."

Nature? I thought. What was she talking about, camping trips? Sleeping in a tent? Maybe Teal wasn't so off. Maybe this was like the Girl Scouts.

"Now then," Dr. Foreman said, pulling herself up and stepping back. "Unfortunately, I must conclude our little talk with a severe warning. Any signs of insubordination, even nasty looks and evidence of an attitude, will result in demerits. Profanity will be punished severely. If any of you get two demerits in one day, or fall two points or more below the minus ten I have generously given you, or finally do something so terrible that it is off the charts, she will be sent to our Ice Room to chill out, as you kids like to say these days."

Ice Room? What was that?

She looked around the cement room, once again as if she could hear my thoughts. "This place is a first-class hotel room compared to our Ice Room." She didn't make it sound like a threat either, but it clearly put the shivers into Teal and Robin as quickly as it did in me. Not describing it any further left it to each of our imaginations, and I was sure we each came up with our worst fears.

"And now, my dears," she said again, sounding as if we were all at a grand tea party, "it's time for you to be introduced to your buddies. They are three of my graduates, three of whom I am very, very proud. They have earned the right to assist me."

The girls beamed with joy at her compliments and gazed at her adoringly. I didn't know why yet, but it made my nerve endings sizzle to see the way they all looked up to her. I had the feeling she could ask one or all of them to open their wrists, and they would instantly obey.

As Dr. Foreman continued, she looked at them with a mother's pride. "I call them your buddies because they are here to give you the benefit of their experience. They will be in charge of your daily life, your daily development, and since they have experienced my school firsthand, they have real insight into what goes on in a new girl's mind. Depend on them, listen to them, and most of all, obey them."

She turned back to us. "Even though they are your buddies, you are to treat them as respectfully and obediently as you would me. In order to establish that, and to help you understand how far they have grown and what they have become now, you are to address them only as *m'lady,* for that is truly who they are, ladies."

Teal couldn't help a guffaw, her laughter spurting out of her lips like something she was unable to keep from coming up. It was like a small explosion.

"If you don't tighten your lips this instant," Dr. Foreman snarled at her, "you'll be starting at a minus fifteen with the Ice Room as your initiation to my school."

Teal's smile evaporated.

After a long silence, Dr. Foreman stepped to the side and introduced M'Lady One, who was the young woman who had escorted me off the plane. She stepped forward and waited, still at attention. M'Lady Two, who stepped up beside her, was a far more attractive woman with light brown hair, a perfect nose, and a far more feminine mouth. She wasn't as tall, perhaps only five feet five, but because of her firm military posture, she didn't look much shorter. She had a nice figure, well proportioned, that couldn't be disguised even in the blah uniform.

M'Lady Three was the stoutest and shortest. I thought she was barely five feet tall. She had shoulders like a football player and hard, sharply cut facial features. Her dark eyes were too far apart and her short, dull brown hair was trimmed farther back on her forehead than that of the other two. When she opened her mouth, I saw she had crooked teeth, especially on the bottom.

"A new student does nothing without permission until she is told she may do so," M'Lady One recited.

M'Lady Two continued, "That means even going to the bathroom. A new student does not speak unless given permission to do so."

M'Lady Three picked up immediately when M'Lady Two stopped. She had the deepest, coarsest voice. "A new student learns that in the real world nothing comes to you because it's supposed to come to you. You earn everything; you are entitled to nothing. This is reality. Therefore, we will have reality checks periodically to determine whether or not you have earned what you want, what you have."

"This means everything," they all recited. They spoke like some chorus that had performed these speeches many, many times, all speaking without much emotion, except for the underlying and continuous threat.

"A new student knows that complaints earn demerits. Cheating, laziness, slacking off, any of that earns demerits," M'Lady Two said.

"And demerits put you in the Ice Room," they all chorused.

"Thank you, m'ladies," Dr. Foreman said. They looked at her as if they were desperate for approval, then they stepped back.

I raised my hand and she looked at me so long, I thought she was going to simply ignore it. Finally, she asked me what I wanted.

"I need to go to the bathroom," I said.

The three buddies smiled simultaneously as if they were of one face.

"After all this, that is what you ask? Have you heard nothing?"

"But I need to go," I cried, now unashamed to admit it.

"Your needs are no longer what is of primary importance. We are now going to think first of the group's needs."

"But . . ."

"You're here because you are selfish, and that will be the first demon we will destroy. I promise you that," Dr. Foreman said. "Now then, I have one more request of you all that you must fulfill before we can go any further."

She turned to the buddies and each stepped forward, M'Lady One coming to me, M'Lady Two going to Robin, and M'Lady Three to Teal. They handed each of us a small composition notebook and a pen.

"What is this?" Teal muttered. "Homework, already?"

"That's a demerit," Dr. Foreman said, pointing at her with a long, thin finger. "You didn't have permission to speak. One more and you're in the Ice Room."

Teal looked away. I could see, however, that she was fighting back tears, tears of rage and fear.

"Now then," Dr. Foreman said, "as a second part of your orientation, I want each of you to write her story. Tell me everything you can about yourself, what you remember as a child, where you lived, the friends you had or thought you had, the teachers you remember. I am very interested in how you see yourself, what you expect you will eventually do with your life. I want the notebooks filled with details, exact details of every thing you remember as important to you. I am particularly interested in your fears, so I want you to give lots of thought to that. All of us, including me, have something we fear. It's natural or, perhaps, it's something we have inherited or developed because of who we are, where we have lived, whom we have known. Don't dare leave that out.

"If you lie and I find out you have lied in this introductory history, you will be fined ten full demerit points. Remember, I know much about you. This is both a test of your veracity and a chance for you to think about yourselves."

We looked at each other in disbelief. Write our histories? Surely, this was a joke.

"I see you are not taking me seriously," Dr. Foreman said. "I assure you that you will all remain here until you are all finished. Until then, no one will get anything to drink or eat, nor will anyone"—she centered on me—"use the bathroom. That's academic anyway since there is no bathroom," she added dryly.

I felt my face flush. No bathroom? Reminding me I had to go built the pressure inside me. I felt myself breaking out into a sweat, my heart pounding. Didn't the other two have to go? If they did, they didn't show it.

"Finally, let me remind you that no one is to speak to anyone during this exercise. One of your buddies will monitor you, and should anyone speak, you will all remain here one hour longer for every word uttered."

Then, as suddenly as she finished speaking, she smiled warmly at us and in loving tones said, "Welcome, girls. Welcome to my school. I truly hope this will be a lifesaving experience for you all."

With that she turned and walked out, her heels clicking and echoing around us until she was gone and it was deadly silent.

It was as if all clocks had stopped. Nothing beat anymore.

Not even our own hearts.

2

Dr. Foreman's
Funny Farm

Two of the so-called buddies left with Dr. Foreman, but M'Lady Three remained behind, her arms folded, her back against the door, glaring at us, the corners of her mouth dipped with annoyance at what I was sure she considered baby-sitting duty.

"This is so stupid," Teal muttered.

"Did someone speak?" M'Lady Three chimed. Like a hungry cat she was so eager to pounce.

We all looked down ashamed of our fear. That was when I saw that someone probably feeling as desperate as we did had carved the word *help* into my old desk. I felt like adding my own cry of rage. I would carve in *betrayed.* When I looked up again, I saw Robin open her composition notebook and begin writing. She shrugged at me as if to say, what else can we do? Humor her. Teal, on the other hand, remained stubborn, her head in her hands, the notebook still closed. I opened mine.

My life story?

Where do I begin? I was born in Atlanta. My daddy was an auto garage tool salesman and my mama worked as a waitress in one dump after another, drinking up most of what she made and sometimes not coming home until morning. It was one thing to remember it all, to think about it, but another to actually put it in writing. It made me more angry than ashamed to see it in black and white. Perhaps that was Dr. Foreman's purpose: to get us to hate who we were, who we are. I suppose I couldn't blame her. Why else would we work on changing ourselves?

It was funny though how tears came into my eyes after I began to describe our apartment in that rat-infested building, described my room, the crippled kitchen with the stove that worked when it was in the mood, and the living room with the threadbare rug where Daddy sat and watched television alone so many nights. Why would I cry over and long for a return to the life I used to hate? Why would I want to be back in that two-by-four room of mine where I could hear pipes groaning at night like someone with a bellyache, and people in other apartments yelling at each other and clawing the walls the way prisoners going mad might?

I wasn't in a good place to grow up. Even as a little girl, I knew bad things happened in our building. Someone I only knew as Mr. Rotter died of a drug overdose in the apartment directly below ours. It was the first time I saw a dead person. I stood on the stairway and watched them taking him out on a stretcher, the sheet over his whole body. The police said the apartment stank. He had been dead for nearly a week, but he had no relatives in Atlanta. Only in his midthirties, he was already dead.

That was when I first understood what Daddy meant when he said we were living in a cemetery. The doors of the apartments should look more like tombstones and read their names and *born in 19__; died in 20__. Rest in peace because that's the only peace you'll have.*

No wonder I didn't want to come home nights or stay there on weekends. No wonder I took advantage of Mama being at work and staying out to all hours and Daddy being on the road, away from home. I shouldn't have been blamed for that. Anyone living like I was living, seeing the things I saw, would have done the same thing.

The only excitement and happiness I had were what I had with my friends. So we smoked and shoplifted and drank at parties. So what? We didn't hurt people badly, did we? Well, maybe we hurt ourselves somewhat, but we weren't on anyone's Most Wanted list. Teachers barely tolerated us, were happy when we didn't bother them, and swept us along like so much dust from one room to another, one teacher to another, as if everyone was to share the burden.

Yes, I wrote in the notebook, it's true I did get arrested more than once. I was put on probation. I did violate it and I was in danger of going to a real prison. Yes, I knew why Daddy felt he had to place me with my uncle and aunt after Mama ran off with someone and deserted us, but I also knew my aunt and uncle never wanted me and were surely relieved when I got myself in new trouble and ran away. My aunt could claim she was right about me: I was hopeless and now she had a good excuse for getting rid of me forever.

I described it all, how I was cornered into hurting that boy, how I was arrested for it and decided to run off, how disappointed I was in Mama when I found her in that clinic, and how betrayed I felt when my uncle tricked me and got me taken here. I was never as mean to anyone as they were to me, I wrote. I don't deserve this.

As to my fears, I couldn't come up with much except what I had feared when I was a little girl and could actually hear the rats scratching their way through the walls, visiting different apartments as if the whole place were a mall for rats who could shop in this one's kitchen cabinets and then another and pass the news on to the world of rats out there: *Come to Phoebe Elder's home. Her mother is a slob. Lots to eat on the floor and counters, and she's so out of it nights in a drunken coma, she won't even know we're there.*

I used to curl up in my bed, wrapping the blanket so tightly around myself it was a wonder I didn't smother to death. Some nights I sobbed myself to sleep. Some nights I woke up positive a rat had crawled over my legs or sniffed my hair. I would throw off my blanket and turn on the lamp, but thankfully, I never saw one in my room. That didn't mean I didn't believe they had been there, however. I imagined their tiny footprints everywhere, and sometimes, I was sure I saw a pair of beady little eyes watching me from some crack in the wall.

I had no idea how much I had written in the notebook when I raised my head. I saw Teal had given in, and she and Robin were still reluctantly at it themselves. Then I heard the door open and saw M'Lady Two hand M'Lady Three a tumbler of ice water. Teal and Robin also watched her drinking it. She seemed to take longer and slurp it for our benefit. She spilled what she hadn't finished on the floor and looked at us with a smile so spiteful it made anger simmer my blood into a rolling boil.

I squirmed in my seat. My need to pee had become impossible to ignore. Soon there would be no way to keep it from happening. It brought new tears to my eyes, tears that escaped my lids. I embraced myself and rocked as I moaned.

M'Lady Three got up and walked toward me. "What's wrong with you?"

"I have to pee, badly."

"So pee. You're wearing a diaper. We'll change you afterward."

I looked up at her in shock. I could see she was serious. It put me into a small panic, and when I looked at Teal, she seemed angrier about it than I could be. Then she nodded at me, her eyes small, urging me to call her bluff. Only I knew it wasn't a bluff. Robin looked down, ashamed for me.

M'Lady Three turned back to the door and then I let it go. It dripped off the chair. She looked back, smiling. Then she opened the door and shouted, "Get up a diaper. Baby One had an accident."

I heard some laughter outside.

I was crying harder now, the tears of shame and rage sliding off my cheeks as if my skin had turned to ice, my fists at my sides, my nails digging into my palms.

"Bitch," Teal shouted at M'Lady Three.

Her smile faded. "One word without specific permission. One extra hour for all of you to spend in here," she pronounced like a judge laying the death sentence on some convicted murderer.

M'Lady One returned with a new diaper for me. Teal and Robin watched with disgust and rage. Then Teal stood up and just let go. Robin smiled and did the same. M'Lady One and M'Lady Three looked at each other, then M'Lady Three smiled back at Teal and Robin.

"Gee, girls, sorry," she moaned as if she really cared, "but we had only one extra diaper." Her phony smile vanished. "Now sit down and shut up," she snapped at them. Their faces of defiance quickly changed into faces of disgust and panic. "Sit down or we'll keep you here two more hours for every minute you're standing."

Without any other choice, they did what they were told, both grimacing with discomfort. I returned to my seat and held up my completely filled composition book. M'Lady One took it and flipped through the pages. Then she took the pen and left.

Robin and Teal started to write faster, the need to get out of here that much greater.

M'Lady Three shook her head and smiled at them gleefully. "That's better, girls. The faster you all learn that obeying orders makes things easier for you, the better off you'll be."

When Robin and Teal were finished, they lifted their notebooks and M'Lady Three took them, checked them, and went to the door. She handed them to M'Lady Two and looked at us.

"After your hour's punishment, we'll be learning the school prayer," she said, and left.

"I'm taking this off," Robin said, standing immediately and removing the wet diaper. Teal did the same.

"They're crazy. That doctor's crazy. I'm not staying here," Teal vowed.

"Really? What do you intend to do? Catch a cab home?" Robin asked.

"I don't know. Something."

"You better not let them hear you talking or they'll tack on more time," I warned them.

"Don't tell me what to do! I don't give a damn! I won't . . ." Teal stopped and slammed her lips shut when she heard the door opening.

M'Lady Three returned. "Lucky for you two, we found two extra diapers," she sang. She gave one to Robin and one to Teal. "Put them on and keep quiet," she ordered, and left again.

I watched them change. We all walked about like caged animals, looking at each other as if one word would set us clawing ourselves as well as the walls, then we glared at the door. Teal tried it and of course it was locked.

"What if they just leave us here forever? Who would even know?" Robin queried. "There's no other way out."

Teal and I looked at each other.

"My parents would eventually find out. They can't do that. They wouldn't dare. My mother would sue the panties off that Dr. Foreplay or whatever she calls herself," Teal said.

"Right, your parents are worried sick over you. That's why they had you sent here."

"Shut up. You don't know anything about me or my family."

"Who wants to?" Robin mumbled.

All I could think about was getting out of here. Soon we'd be at each other's throat, but the hands of whatever clock we were on were arthritic or something. It seemed like much longer than another hour before the door opened and the three so-called buddies returned.

"Everyone stand in front of her desk," M'Lady One ordered. We did so, all of us thinking the same thing: we'll do anything to get out of here. "Okay, here is the school prayer. You are to recite it every morning and you are to recite it until you get it perfect. We'll stay here as long as we have to until all three of you have it memorized."

M'Lady Two came forward. "Repeat after me. 'I am nothing. I am less than nothing. I am a burden to my family and to my country. I must hate myself to death and I must change. I must thank Dr. Foreman for every punishment I receive.' "

Teal grimaced. "That's a prayer?"

"It's stupid," Robin agreed.

"Suit yourselves, girls. We're comfortable," M'Lady Two said, and started out.

"Wait a minute!" I cried.

She paused.

"I can't stand it in here anymore."

She looked at Robin and Teal.

"All right. How does it go again?" Teal asked.

M'Lady Two smiled and repeated it for us. None of us got it right the first time, so she repeated it and again we mumbled it as accurately as we could. They demanded we speak louder. Teal made an error and we were stopped and told to start again. I thought she wasn't going to do it, but she did and, of course, made a small mistake. All three of us were tired and groggy and uncomfortable. It was so hard to concentrate on words we hated anyway. Finally, we had it right almost to the end, when I left out a word and they jumped on me. Again we recited it and again one of us made a small error. Eventually, we had it perfect and they agreed we had done so.

"Orientation is over," M'Lady Three declared, slapping her hands together. "We can move out and take you to Dr. Foreman's School. Remember," she added before we started, "no talking without permission."

We marched out of the room. I don't think I was ever happier to leave a place than I was leaving there. Even the hot evening air seemed a relief. A dirty, white, windowless van was parked in front of the building. The rear doors were opened and we were told to climb in. There was nothing to sit on, just the metal floor of the van. A solid wall separated the back of the van from the driver. All three of us hesitated. It smelled like some farm animals had been transported in it only minutes ago. The odor of animal manure was strong.

Teal raised her hand.

"What?" M'Lady Three asked. We understood now that M'Lady Three was assigned to Teal; M'Lady Two to Robin, and of course, M'Lady One to me.

"There are no windows in there. How long is the trip? We'll suffocate."

"The trip is as long as it takes to get to the school. Get in. It will be longer if you waste time. We might," M'Lady Three said, smiling at the other two, "take you on a detour if you don't behave."

Teal looked at the two of us and then gazed around and into the darkness. Would she try to bolt and run? I think she realized she had no idea in which direction to go and the chances of her outrunning them were slim. Defeated, she climbed into the van and sat with her back to the side, her arms folded. I did the same, sitting across from her, and Robin got in and sat next to her. They closed the doors on us and we were in total darkness.

That wasn't the only problem. Teal was right. Once the doors were closed, we had little fresh air, the odor was nauseating, and the van walls felt like the walls of an oven.

"We'll die in here if we have to stay in here long," Teal moaned.

"Keep your voice down," Robin said. "Whisper. Who knows what else those sadistic creatures will do to us if they hear us talking."

"If I wasn't so tired, I'd choke one of them," Teal claimed.

"They don't look like they're afraid of that, especially your buddy," I told her. "I think she's a former football player or bouncer from some bar."

Robin grunted her agreement. We heard the van's engine start, then the van pulled away. It was smooth for a while, but not five minutes into the ride, it suddenly became quite bumpy, and for us to bounce sitting on this metal floor was not easy. It was at times painful. We all screamed and shouted complaints, but whoever was driving didn't hear us or care. The van jostled and shook us as it went along. At times, the driver turned so hard and sharply, we were thrown from side to side. Finally, the ride became a lot smoother.

"I'm going to strangle my mother darling when I get away from here," Robin vowed. "She just wanted to get me out of her hair while she tries to become a famous country singing star. She didn't care where I was sent. Just go, she told me. I'm better off. What she really meant was *she* was better off. She could party and carry on without worrying about me."

"What did your father have to say about it?" Teal asked.

"I don't have a father. Mother darling got pregnant when she was a teenager and my grandparents made her have me as a punishment. They are very religious and we had to live with them. Mother darling's not sure who my father is. The best she can remember is she was at a party where she had sex with three guys."

"Three in one night?" I asked.

"That's what she claimed."

"Some mother," Teal said.

"I didn't exactly have a choice, you know. From the sound of things, you're not that much better off."

"Yeah, well, at least I'm sure who my father is," Teal said.

"Doesn't sound like he wants to be your father," Robin batted back.

"How come you don't get along with your parents?" I asked Teal. Talking at least passed the time and stopped me from thinking about the horrible ride.

"They had me late in their marriage. I was an accident for sure," she replied bitterly. "I have a brother who's much older and he's by far the favorite. He works with my father in his business. No one had any patience for me. I'm sure they're just as happy to get rid of me as Robin's mother was to get rid of her."

"She'll be sorry," Robin swore. "If she ever does become famous, I'll tell the world how Mother darling treated me."

"Why do you call her 'Mother darling'?" Teal asked.

"Just to annoy her. You've heard of *Mommie Dearest,* right?"

"Yeah," Teal said so vaguely I was sure she hadn't. I hadn't but I didn't say so. What difference did it make? I thought.

"My daddy wouldn't have put up with this," I told them. "He was hoping to take me back as soon as he got himself a position where he didn't have to be on the road all the time."

"Sure he was," Teal said.

"He was!" I insisted. "If he didn't get himself killed, my aunt and uncle would never dare to do something like this to me."

"What about your mother?" Robin asked.

I told her about how she had deserted us in Atlanta and how I had gone looking for her in hopes of our starting a new life.

"Get real, girl," Teal said. "Those kinds of dreams are for girls who still believe in the tooth fairy."

"I'll choose my own dreams, thank you," I said, but not with a great deal of confidence.

They were both quiet for a while, thinking. I guess in our secret heart of hearts, we were all longing for someone who would care enough about us to keep such cruel things from happening to us. Those kinds of people were just impossible to find for the three of us, I thought.

The van continued to ride over smoother roads. After a while, especially because of all we had already been through, the monotonous sound of the engine and the squeaks and moans in the metal were hypnotizing. We were all having a hard time keeping ourselves awake.

"I'm tired," Robin said. "I can't believe how tired I am. I feel like I just went through a torture chamber."

"I hate to think what awaits us at Dr. Foreman's funny farm," Teal said.

We were all silent again, each of us thinking about that, I'm sure. I know I managed to drift off for a while, but when I woke, I was sore and achy all over. I heard the other two rustling about. Finally, we felt the van turn sharply, speed up, bounce hard, then come to a stop. I didn't know about the other two, but I was sweating so much, I thought I would slide out of the van.

The door was opened and we saw a pole light shedding illumination on what looked like a gravel driveway. M'Lady One was there at the opened doors.

"Get out," she ordered.

We crawled to the doorway and climbed out of the van. Across from us was a long, two-story, pitch-roofed, pink-stucco Spanish colonial house with an upper-level, full-length porch. The railings looked quite fancy. I could see the six doors that opened onto the porch. I imagined each one opened onto a room, and I hoped each of us was to have one of those rooms. All I could think of was dropping my head on a pillow and curling up on a soft mattress.

"All right, follow us," M'Lady One ordered. "This way." She started around the van.

Why weren't we going directly into the house? I wondered. We were all so tired. Surely they were tired, too. There just couldn't be more to this orientation. The three of us stumbled after them. Robin kept looking from side to side like someone who wanted to break loose and run, but all I could see through the darkness was a corral, another barn, and a large shed. There was no road and there were definitely no other houses anywhere nearby. There were no cars going past and no sign of any road. Just a mountain range in the distance, silhouetted against the blue black sky, now dazzling with stars.

Where were we exactly? I had no sense of direction, but because of how long it had taken me to get here by plane and van, I was sure I was at least halfway across the country. It was a frightening thought, to realize I was so far from anywhere and anyone I knew. Vaguely, I wondered what my old friends were doing at this moment. I envied them for being asleep in their own beds. I even envied the ones I knew shared beds with younger brothers or sisters.

We were directed off to the right and brought to what was outside showers. There were no stalls, just three showerheads over a concrete floor.

"Get undressed and take your showers," M'Lady Three commanded.

"This is a shower?" Teal muttered.

If M'Lady One heard her, she chose not to acknowledge it. "You take a shower every night before going to bed at Dr. Foreman's School."

We were each handed a bar of coarse soap, a stiff brush, a towel, and a small kit that included our toothbrush, toothpaste, and a supply of tampons.

None of us moved to undress, however.

"Well?" my buddy said, glaring into my face. "Let's get started. We don't have all night."

"Right out here, like this?" I asked, looking around. It seemed deserted, but it was still getting naked in full view of anyone.

"Always ask before speaking," she reminded me. "Yes, right out here like this. Do it! You all stink and the stench will keep you awake and bother others."

Others? I thought. What others?

Robin began to take off her sack, then undo her shoes and lower her socks. I followed, but Teal looked like she was going to be defiant.

"You won't go to sleep until you do this," her buddy told her.

She started to undress.

The water was a shock. It wasn't just cold; it was freezing. Every time we tried to get out from under, they pushed us back and shouted, "Scrub!"

I did it as fast as I could. Eventually, the other two did the same, but it wasn't good enough for our buddies. They told us to do it again and scrub harder. The bristles of the brush were stiff and painful. Finally, we were told to step out and turn off the water. Even in the darkness, I could see how red and irritated Robin's and Teal's skin were. We dried off quickly and put the degrading outfits on to keep ourselves warm again, despite that the sacks stank and would defeat the purpose of the shower. I was afraid to point it out, however.

"Let's move it," M'Lady Three commanded. She still did not lead us toward the house, however. Instead we were taken to an area off to our right where the three of us saw our clothing piled, shoes and all.

A sweet feeling of relief settled in me, as well as the other two.

"Finally," I heard Teal whisper.

"No speaking," M'Lady Two screamed.

We stood there obediently, waiting for the order to fetch our clothes. To our surprise, M'Lady Three went instead to a large open barrel beside them. She lit a match and dropped it into the barrel. Instantly, a flame shot up. Something very flammable was in the barrel.

"Okay, girls," M'Lady One said. "Take those clothes and throw them into the barrel."

"What?" Teal couldn't contain herself. "Burn my clothes? Why?"

Out of the shadows as if she were formed from darkness came Dr. Foreman.

"I know this seems hard to you, girls, but it is a very, very important first step. What we are doing here tonight is burning away the old you and beginning your rebirths. This isn't just symbolic. It has a great deal of psychological importance."

The fire crackled in the barrel.

"But that's not the old me. That's my clothing, my designer clothing!" Teal exclaimed.

For a long moment, no one spoke. Then Dr. Foreman stepped a little closer.

"We'll stand here all night if we have to," she warned. "It is essential to my system, my process, that you all participate in your own rebirths."

"This is really crazy," Teal muttered.

"I'm so tired, I don't care about anything anymore," Robin declared, and went to the clothes.

"Don't throw mine in there," Teal screamed at her.

Robin picked out her own things and began to toss them into the barrel. I followed after her and did the same. Finally, Teal, standing alone, went to the remaining garments. Then, like someone giving up the most precious jewels, dropped them into the barrel.

"Good," Dr. Foreman said. "You're all beginning well. I'm proud of you girls, and to show you my appreciation, I'm giving you all plus five points. You're now that much closer to receiving comforts and privileges. M'ladies," she said, turning to the buddies. "Show them to their sleeping quarters."

Thank God, I thought. I followed along, my head down, not realizing where we were going until Teal moaned. We were standing at the barn.

M'Lady Two opened the door. We could see it was well lit within.

"Home sweet home, girls," she said, standing back.

"Home! What are you talking about? This is a barn," Teal moaned.

"Demerit," M'Lady Three said. "Even though Dr. Foreman rewarded you with five plus points, you have one demerit from before and now a second. Two demerits in one day qualify you for the Ice Room. Dr. Foreman must be immediately informed. You could go right to the Ice Room."

I raised my hand.

"Very good, Phoebe. Permission to speak. Speak," M'Lady One said.

"Can't you be a little bit understanding? We're confused and tired and this looks like a barn."

"It is a barn and we're not here to be understanding. You were given the rules and you must obey them. It's what we had to do and what we did." M'Lady One looked at M'Lady Three. "It's up to you," she told her. "What do you want to do about Teal?"

"I'll let this one slip, but consider it the one and only time I will," M'Lady Three told Teal.

We were then ordered to enter.

Before us were five wooden cots lined up beside each other. Two had mattresses, pillows, and blankets on them. The other three were just bare.

"Those three are yours," M'Lady One said, pointing to the bare ones.

Robin raised her hand.

"Permission to speak," M'Lady Two said.

"There are no mattresses or anything on them."

"You have to earn that," her buddy replied.

"But . . . how . . . ?"

"Reality checks, remember? You earn the points and then you are rewarded with comforts. It's how it works. Here we earn everything we have, even every morsel of food we eat. Whoever doesn't do her share, doesn't share. That includes water as well as food."

We all looked about despondently. The floor literally had straw over it. The place smelled like a real barn. The four windows had no curtains over them. The walls were bare and there wasn't much of an interior or any other furniture. Only by the two beds that had mattresses, we saw what looked like two small wooden chests.

Teal raised her hand.

"What?"

"Who sleeps on those?" she asked.

"Those are Gia Carson's and Mindy Levine's beds. They've earned enough points to have an hour's recreation time in the library where they can read approved books and listen to approved music. They will be back here momentarily. I now advise the three of you to go to sleep."

"I'm sure my father didn't pay all that money for me to sleep in a stinking barn," Teal declared.

M'Lady Three stepped up so closely to her, their noses almost collided. "Okay, you're not sleeping in the barn. I'm sick of your whining. You've just lost the privilege."

"Privilege?" Teal started to laugh. "You call sleeping in a barn a privilege?"

M'Lady Three nodded at the other two buddies, who then picked up a bunk and carried it out the door.

"Follow them," Teal was told. She looked to us desperately for some help, but neither Robin nor I had the courage to say a word. With her head down like a flag of surrender, she walked out of the barn. I would never have thought sleeping in a barn was so great, but it had to be to be better than being out there, I thought.

At the door, M'Lady Three turned to Robin and me. "Go to sleep. You'll need every moment of rest you can get, believe me."

She left, closing the door behind her.

"Any moment I'm going to wake up. Tell me that's true. Tell me I'm in a dream, a nightmare, and it's coming to an end," Robin muttered in the tone of a prayer.

I just shook my head and sat on the first bare wooden cot. The surface was hard, but I didn't care.

"I'm so tired," I whispered.

The lights in the barn flickered in warning that they would soon be out, then the door opened and two girls entered. The first was a diminutive girl with a mop of hair the color of black licorice. She had large, dark, haunted eyes with a small, delicate nose and thin lips turned down in the corners. Each girl was dressed in a pair of blue coveralls with a faded white short-sleeve shirt that looked more like a man's shirt than a woman's. They wore the same ugly shoes, too.

The second girl was tall and thin with hair so pale yellow it looked almost white. It hung down like dead straw over her ears, the bangs nearly over her eyes. My immediate thought was she was anorexic. Her wrists were slim and bony. I imagined that a strong handshake could shatter them. Her cheeks were sunken. The skin on her face was so taut it was transparent. Once, she must have had a pretty face, I decided. She had high cheekbones and a nearly perfect nose, but when she glanced our way, she never changed expression or in any way showed that she saw us. She looked more like someone dazed, moving in her sleep.

Both girls diverted their eyes to the floor and moved so softly, I had the sense they were floating in, gliding toward their bunks. They said nothing to each other, did nothing to indicate they were aware of each other.

Robin looked at me with quizzical eyes and shrugged.

The girls, still ignoring us, began to take off their coveralls and their ugly shoes, caked with mud. They did everything with great care as if they were performing a delicate lifesaving operation: folding their coveralls neatly and placing them in the chests beside their bunks, rolling their white stockings down and then again taking great pains to fold them perfectly as well and placing them in the trunks, all the while moving like two people in a hypnotic state.

Neither girl wore what we called diapers. They had ordinary-looking panties and both had bras over what looked to me like quite underdeveloped breasts. How could two such fragile-looking girls have gotten in the sort of trouble that would send them to a place like this? I wondered.

Because the door of the barn was still wide-open, neither Robin nor

I risked speaking to them. They didn't seem to care anyway. They still showed absolutely no interest in us. We watched them with fascination, however, as they both got under their blankets and lowered their heads to their pillows.

I felt like someone in a desert watching someone drinking a glass of cold, sparkling freshwater. Those bunks looked so comfortable. How rich they were to have an actual pillow, a soft mattress. When I glanced at Robin, I saw a similar covetous expression on her face.

M'Lady Two stood in the doorway.

"Lights out, girls," she announced, and although I didn't see her throw any switch, the lights snapped off. It took a few moments to get used to the darkness. The starlight coming in through the four windows helped.

"Hey!" I chanced, calling to what I thought now were lucky girls. "Who are you? How long have you been here? Is this the only place for us to sleep?"

Neither responded.

"I'm Robin and that's Phoebe," Robin added. "What are your names?"

Silence remained.

"What's wrong with you?" I asked. "No one's here. Can't you talk?"

"We're not going to bite you," Robin said. They didn't budge. "You believe this?" she asked me.

"No. They're just being brats. What's your damn name?" I asked sharply, raising my voice a bit too loudly.

Suddenly, the door of the barn swung open and the lights went on.

M'Lady One was standing there.

"Who's talking?" she demanded. "Well, who is it? Confess or I'll hold you all accountable."

The smaller girl sat up and pointed at me.

"She talked," she accused.

My mouth dropped. How could she do that, squeal on me?

"Sure. It just had to be my girl," M'Lady One muttered unhappily, "and after I thought she was beginning to do well." She entered the barn and approached me.

I turned away and looked down, but she kept coming.

"When lights are out, you go to sleep," she said, hovering right over me. I kept my head down. "Are you just stupid? Or are you just a hard case? What do you need to convince you we're serious about the rules here? Well, which is it, stupid or defiant? Answer immediately when you are asked a question," she bellowed.

I turned slowly. I was tired. I ached and I was afraid, but I couldn't help myself. I looked up and into her face as bravely as I could manage.

"I'm not stupid. This place is stupid."

She raised her eyebrows and then smiled. "Really? What do you find stupid? Surely, not your buddies," she said, and M'Lady Two entered the barn. She walked up beside M'Lady One and put her hands on her hips.

"What's the problem now?" she asked.

"My little sister here says this is all stupid. I'm trying to find out what exactly is stupid."

I looked at Robin, who immediately looked down at the floor when they turned to her as well.

M'Lady Three entered. "What's going on? I'd think everyone would be quite tired by now."

"We're about to hear a critique on Dr. Foreman's School," M'Lady Two told her.

"Well, Phoebe bird, what's your answer? What exactly do you find stupid?" my buddy repeated.

"The whole thing," I said. "Making us sleep on a hard wooden cot and making us earn food and water and wear these, these stupid sacks with diapers."

"She doesn't like her clothes," M'Lady One told M'Lady Two as if that were an amazing thing to hear me say.

"Well then," M'Lady Two said, "she shouldn't have to wear them."

"Exactly my thoughts," my buddy replied.

Before I could respond or move away, they seized my wrists. M'Lady Three stepped up. I screamed and struggled, but they were so strong. They got me down on the wooden bunk and M'Lady Three took hold of my sack and drew it up and over my head. In moments they had it off me and I was naked, but for the diaper, socks, and shoes. I knew how ridiculous I looked. I cried and screamed and they released me and stepped back. Immediately, I covered my breasts with my arms and sat up.

"Now, are you happier?" my buddy asked.

"No. Give it back to me," I cried.

"This . . . what did you call it . . . stupid sack? We don't want you to feel stupid."

She turned and the three started out.

"Wait!" I cried. "I'm sorry. Please. Give it back. I can't lie here like this."

They paused and looked at each other.

"Think she's sorry?" my buddy asked the other two.

"It's hard to tell. She looks sorry, but she looked sorry from the moment I set eyes on her," M'Lady Two said.

"Okay, let's see how sorry she is. Step outside," my buddy said.

I looked at Robin. She wore an expression of abject terror and avoided looking back at me. The other two girls remarkably were as they had been, their eyes closed, still on their backs. They hadn't turned or budged to witness any of it.

"Why?" I asked.

"Yours is not to question why," my buddy said.

"Yours is but to do and die," the other two recited.

I walked slowly behind them out of the barn. The first thing I saw was Teal lying on her side on her bunk. She must have tried to run off or something because I saw her feet were shackled to the cot. She was folded in a fetal position, her eyes closed, but her body shaking. It wasn't warm anymore. In fact, it was cold. I shuddered as well.

"Over here," my buddy ordered, placing me in the pool of illumination thrown down by a pole light.

I did as she said.

"Arms at your sides, face forward. Do it!" she screamed at me, and I did. I felt myself shaking harder and harder. "Okay, now recite the school prayer. Go on. Recite it and do it loud enough for them to hear inside. Do it!"

I started, trying desperately to remember it, but stumbling over words. Each time I did, one of them stepped close to me and shouted in my ear, "Wrong! Start again. Wrong!"

I don't know if I ever got it completely right, but eventually, I did recite it close enough to satisfy them. My buddy, M'Lady One, handed me the sack.

"Okay, put it back on."

I took it.

"Don't we get a thank you?" M'Lady Two asked.

"Thank you," I mumbled.

"We didn't hear you," my buddy said.

"Thank you!" I cried. I dressed quickly before they could change their minds and put me through something equally terrible.

"Get back inside and go to sleep. Another infraction of the rules and you'll go to the Ice Room," my buddy added.

I glanced at Teal. She hadn't dared turn to look at me. She was still shivering, but not as much. Sleep was overtaking fear and anger, I thought.

As I started toward the door of the barn, I glanced to my left because I saw something moving in the shadows. The silhouette became clearer and I realized it was Dr. Foreman. I cringed inside. She had been standing there all the while, watching them torture me. How could she let them do these things to us? A part of me wanted to call out to her, call out to that sweet smile of welcome she had first given us in orientation and ask her what had happened to that, but I was too afraid to do it. In a moment her silhouette seemed to merge with the shadows anyway and she was gone. I wasn't even sure she had really been there.

I entered the barn and went quickly to my bunk. The two girls were still asleep and Robin was on her side with her back to me. I lay down with my back to her. The lights went out again and the door was closed. I heard it being locked and it occurred to me that they had never told us where the bathroom was. What if we have to get up and go? I wondered. Were we supposed to just do it in our diaper again?

"Robin?" I whispered.

I listened, but heard nothing from her. Perhaps she had finally fallen asleep out of the same exhaustion I felt, or perhaps she was simply too terrified to utter a sound. I couldn't blame her.

Suddenly I heard the cry of something wild, a coyote, I thought. There was another, then another. It sounded like a whole pack of them out there in the darkness. They sounded like a pack of vampires. I wondered how Teal was doing and shuddered thinking about it. Sleep would be a hard-won prize tonight.

The long journey that had begun with a disappointment and a betrayal was finally over, I thought.

I was here.

This was my first night at Dr. Foreman's School for Girls.

And all I could think was I was right about that plane ride I took. Surely it must be the way the dead are taken to their afterlife.

I'm in hell.

What else could it possibly be?

3

Three New Squaws

Even if our buddies weren't there to whip us with their screams in the morning, the blazing sunlight pouring through the unblocked windows lit up the inside of the barn so brightly, it burned through our thick walls of sleep and dreams, melting away any determination and resistance we had to awakening. There was no question either of us wanted to wake up in a place like this. Teal, who I imagined was used to sleeping into the midafternoon when she didn't attend school, was probably in utter shock out there.

Almost simultaneous with the glaring light exploding around us came the shouts of the m'ladies to rise. I groaned and looked at Robin. She was awake, but she just lay there staring up. I turned and saw that the other two girls, Gia and Mindy, were already dressed and outside. When did they do that? Did they dress and leave in the dark?

As soon as I sat up, my back felt as if all the muscles in it were tearing away from the bones.

"Stand up!" M'Lady Two screamed at Robin.

M'Lady Three lifted her bunk at the foot of it, then dropped it hard to the floor.

Robin cried out with pain. Reluctantly, she rose, groaning like someone in her eighties or nineties.

"What time is it?" she asked, rubbing her lower back.

"Did you speak? Did you say something without permission? I didn't hear anything, did I? Well?" M'Lady Two demanded, her nose so close to Robin's, I thought they would touch.

Robin shook her head.

"All right then," M'Lady Two said, standing straight. She turned so she was addressing me as well. "This morning you will be introduced to your chores first and then you will be taken to breakfast."

"This first breakfast is a gift since you have done little to earn the food," M'Lady One said. "Consequently, from this time on, whenever you approach a m'lady or any other student at this school, you are to say, 'Excuse me. I'm sorry.' Should you forget to do it, you will be given a demerit on the spot. Is that understood? Is it?" she screamed at me.

"Yes," I said. Robin nodded.

"March out," M'Lady Two ordered, and we did so.

The sunlight made me squint. I covered my eyes and gradually got accustomed to what I was seeing. How could it be so hot so early? I wondered.

I looked for Teal. She was standing by her bunk, wavering as if drunk, her head down. The shackles were off her feet, but still attached to the cot. I looked around. The other two girls were nowhere in sight.

"Okay, let's have it," M'Lady One ordered. Robin looked at me. Teal raised her head. None of us knew what she wanted. "The prayer!" she screamed. "Our morning prayer. Are you all as stupid as you are incorrigible? Recite."

We began.

"No mumbling. Loud," she commanded.

Teal, who now looked terrified of making any mistakes, did the best. Robin and I spoke a split second behind her, correcting ourselves.

"Not absolutely perfect, but passable," M'Lady One decided, just as M'Lady Three came toward us. She was carrying three shovels over her shoulder.

"Good morning, girls," she sang with exaggerated glee. "Isn't it a beautiful morning? This is one of your tools." She distributed the three shovels to us. Teal took hers as if the handle were made of steel wool, holding it as softly as possible with just the tips of her fingers.

"From now on, you are responsible for it," M'Lady Three continued. "We will show you where the tool shed is. You will put them away neatly with every other tool. When you open the tool shed door, wait a moment or two since rattlesnakes seem to find it comfortable in there and I know we're low on antirattlesnake venom."

Teal looked up sharply and then at the two of us. I saw Robin was having trouble swallowing. She looked like she would topple any moment. My heart was pounding like a jungle drum, sending warnings to every part of my body. My blood was in a panic, rushing through my veins as if it were looking for a place to hide.

"This morning you will join Natani. He is a Navajo Indian and the farm manager. You are to give him the same respect and obedience you give to any of us. He will explain your work to you and you will work for two hours before we go to breakfast. As you have been told, you haven't done enough to earn it, but you will be given this first meal anyway. However, I assure you, anyone who doesn't do her job adequately will not be given breakfast and will remain out there working until she does."

Robin raised her hand.

"Yes, you may speak," M'Lady Two said.

"Can I go to the bathroom first?"

"You all can go to the bathroom one at a time." She turned to her right to point at a narrow shack.

"What's that?" Teal asked. "I mean, permission to speak."

M'Lady Three nodded.

"What's that?"

"That's your outhouse."

"What's an outhouse?"

"It's your bathroom, stupid. Once again, I advise you to hesitate a moment or two after you open the door as rattlesnakes like to curl up and sleep around the toilet at night."

Robin froze, her eyes widening.

"We're not going to wait all day for you to go to the bathroom, girls. If you don't go now, you pee or whatever in your diapers. Move!" M'Lady Three screamed.

With great hesitation, Robin started for the outhouse and Teal and I followed behind. As we did, I started to look around more at our surroundings. Obviously we were somewhere deep in some desert. I could see cactus and brush, but outside of the immediate property, which was fenced in, there was no grass, just long, rolling, brown, crusty dirt in every direction. The sunlight wavered over it, making it look even hotter and drier. Mountains were way off in the distance.

To our right we could see dozens of pigs bumping and pushing at each other to get at feed. They slobbered through mud and their own excrement, their heads down, consuming themselves in eating. Farther to the right were four horses nibbling on hay. The gardens were on our left and from the looks of them were bigger than any other garden I had seen. I recognized cornstalks, but nothing else, not being much of a farmer or around farms ever.

Robin opened the outhouse door and jumped back. "Who wants to go first?" she asked Teal and me.

Both of us looked in. Toilet? There was nothing but what looked like a big pipe with a crude wooden seat around it. Instead of toilet paper, sheets of what looked like wrapping paper were beside it.

"Let's go, girls," M'Lady Three called. "Every minute you waste here, you have to make up at the garden, and that's how much longer it will be before you have any food."

Teal stepped in timidly. She started to close the door behind her and then screamed and jumped out.

"Something's crawling in there. I saw it!" she cried.

"It's more afraid of you than you are of it, whatever it is," M'Lady Three said, stepping up. "Either pee in your pants or go in and do it now."

"Oh, God!" Teal screamed, her hands pressed to her temples. "I can't stand this. I can't stand it!"

Her whole body started to shake. I looked at the three buddies to see what they would do, but they just stared at her, watching her cry and pound herself. She raged for a few more moments, then sank to the ground, sitting and sobbing with gasps like someone who couldn't catch her breath.

"I want to go home!" she cried. "I'll do anything, say anything, promise anything. Let me go home. Please."

M'Lady Two turned to Robin. "Are you going to the bathroom or not?" she asked as if seeing Teal's tantrum and fit was nothing out of the ordinary for any of them.

Robin nodded and went into the outhouse.

Teal fell on her side and closed her eyes. "I want to go home," she whispered. "I want to go home." She said it louder: "Please, let me go home."

"What happened to the tough rich girl whose father would be angry at us? I have news for you, girl. Listen to this headline. You've got a long way to go before you go home," M'Lady Three told her. "And all you're doing this morning by throwing this stupid tantrum is making that journey longer yet."

The door opened and Robin came out. She looked pale, but said nothing. I stepped in, quivering all over, and did my business. When I came out, Teal was sitting up and wiping her cheeks.

"It's all right," I told her. "There's nothing in there but some bugs and ants."

She grimaced, got up, and went in. When she came out, we were marched toward the gardens. I couldn't imagine working in this sun for two hours before we could get something to eat. Surely, this was cruel and these people would be held responsible for whatever happened to us. They would be sorry, I thought, and that thought of them all getting into big trouble gave me enough strength to walk on.

As we approached a new field, we saw Gia and Mindy hard at work turning over the earth. Now that we were outside with them, I could see how tan their faces were. It amazed me that Mindy was able to do any work being as thin as she was, but she seemed unstoppable, digging, turning, digging, without looking up. Gia worked the same way.

At first none of us saw the man we were told was called Natani. He seemed to rise up from the ground where he was squatting, emerging like an instantly growing, dark brown tree trunk. He looked our way, then he wiped his hands on the sides of his overalls and walked toward us. As he drew closer, I thought he was at least a hundred years old. Although his hair was black with barely a sign of gray, his face was a dried prune. He had a small build and was surely not more than five feet four inches tall.

"Here are your three new squaws," M'Lady Three told him, and laughed. "They are very delicate flowers so you will have your hands full keeping them alive."

He said nothing, but looked at us and nodded not to agree with her, but more to acknowledge us. He wore a pair of white muslin trousers, a calico shirt, a pair of buckskin moccasins, and a bandanna twisted and tied around his head. On his right wrist was a leather band fastened with buckskin lacing and decorated with silver and turquoise.

"I am Natani," he said to us. "I will show you how we grow what we eat, how we care for the animals that care for us and give of themselves to us, and how we must live side by side with what is wild and true."

He looked at the buddies to see if they had any more to say or any other instructions.

"If any of them give you any trouble, let us know," M'Lady One said in as threatening a tone as she could produce. Natani looked at her without expression, then turned and beckoned for us to follow him.

I watched Gia and Mindy working. They still seemed to have little or no interest in the three of us. To me they were like people who had suffered a lobotomy or something. Were we doomed to become like them?

"This is good ground," Natani explained, and waved his hand over the earth before us like a priest blessing it. "It can bring all our seeds and plants to blossom and feed them what they need. It has sun all day and there are no big rocks, just little ones to remove. Here we have little wind. We must turn the earth on its back and then again to soften it and make it welcome our seeds and the roots of the plants we introduce to it."

He nodded at three wheelbarrows full of plants.

"It is the same for us, for we want to be welcomed wherever we go to live and grow. There is much to learn from the earth and the wind, the sky, and even the rocks. Never turn your back on anything and never stop listening."

"Oh, brother," Teal said. "We're in the hands of some crazy Tonto. Next we'll see the Lone Ranger."

Natani did not look like he heard or understood, but something in his aged face told me he had.

"Let's just get this over with," I muttered. "I'm starving and thirsty."

"We will turn over the ground and then we will with trowels dig holes for our tomato plants."

"Just what I always wanted to do," Robin said. "Plant tomatoes. Like I didn't work hard enough on my grandparents' farm. They raised sheep, and talk about stinks," she said, holding her nose.

"Here we have goats," Natani said. "And we make cheese with the milk."

"Goats? I thought those were pigs," I said.

"Pigs, too."

He smiled wider and we could see he was missing some teeth. He spread us out and showed each of us how we should use the shovels and how to turn the earth. We started to do it, and Teal immediately cried about her hands.

"This is hard. I'll get blisters!"

Robin and I worked quietly, glancing every once in a while at Mindy and Gia, who stopped working and left the garden.

"Where are they going?" Robin asked jealously. "I didn't hear any bells ringing."

We worked on, Teal moaning the loudest, but soon all three of us were muttering to ourselves. I didn't think it was possible to get this tired and sore. Every once in a while, Natani would take the shovel from one of us and again demonstrate how to use it efficiently. He seemed to have magical hands, making it all look so easy.

At one point he knelt by Robin and picked up a rock. It glistened.

"She has waited a long time to see the sun again," he said.

Robin looked at me and shook her head. "She?"

Teal groaned and cried, "I'm going crazy. How is this a school? I nearly froze to death out there last night."

"What choice do we have at the moment?" Robin asked dryly. "It doesn't look like there's a bus station nearby."

"I don't care. The whole thing, this idea of this being a school, all of it is someone's idea of a sick joke. My parents probably arranged for all this just to scare me to death. Well, I'm not ashamed to admit they have. I just want to go home."

"Big deal what you want, what any of us want," Robin said.

Teal looked at her with a mixture of disgust and anger. "You might be willing to hang around and take all this crap, but I'm not."

"Yeah?" Robin rested on her shovel. "And what are you going to do, call your daddy?"

"I might just do that and wave good-bye to you when they take me home."

Robin laughed.

Teal looked like she would go at her, but for the fact that M'Lady Two appeared and announced we could go to breakfast. My mouth was so dry from the heat and the dust, I couldn't swallow. We laid our shovels down, and like truly obedient puppy dogs, we followed her back to the main house. Outside the door, we were told to take off our clodhopper shoes and wash our hands in the springwater coming out of a pipe in an outside wall. We were also permitted to take a drink. Water had never tasted as good or as refreshing.

Suddenly, Dr. Foreman appeared in the doorway. She looked as elegant and composed as she had the first time we had met her. One thing was for sure—she never did any chores on this farm, I thought, not with those fingernails.

"Good morning, girls," she said. "I understand you've had a good beginning. There will be merit points waiting for you at the day's end if you continue to behave and follow our rules."

Robin raised her hand and Dr. Foreman nodded at her.

"Will they get us mattresses, pillows, and blankets?"

"They could. Let's wait and see, but you're thinking on the right track, Robin. That's good. That's reality. Now come in, take from the food table, and sit at the dining room table. One of Natani's nephews is our cook and he's very good."

We walked into the entryway and looked to our right where a table of fruits, juices, breads, cereals, and hard-boiled eggs were displayed. At the long dining-room table, Mindy and Gia ate quietly, neither looking up at us nor at each other for that matter.

M'Lady Two came up behind us. "Remember, when you meet each

other, when you meet one of us, you say, 'Excuse me. I'm sorry,' " she instructed. "We'll be listening for it."

We were herded to the food table.

"Do not make a pig of yourself or you will sleep with the pigs," M'Lady Two warned.

All of us timidly filled our plates and poured ourselves some juice. Then we approached the table and Mindy and Gia looked up.

Robin said it first: "Excuse me. I'm sorry."

Teal and I recited it as well and we sat.

"After breakfast, you will return to the garden. There is no lunch. You will go from the garden and be oriented to your chores on the farm, and then you will be brought back here for your first therapy session. The initial one will be a group session. I like to think of them as get-well sessions," Dr. Foreman told us, wearing that friendly smile.

"Following all that, we will have a reality check and your buddies will give me their evaluations of your behavior. We will assign merit points as they were earned and you will be rewarded accordingly. Eat slowly, girls. Waste not, want not," she sang, and walked away. The buddies followed her out of the dining room and we were all finally alone and together.

"Why did you tell on me last night?" I demanded immediately of Gia.

She didn't look up, but Mindy did and said, "She received two plus points for that. She's close to being able to make a phone call or receiving one."

"Golly gee, how lucky can a girl get," Teal muttered. "A phone call."

"You'll see how lucky that is after a while," Mindy told her confidently.

"How long have you two been here?" I asked.

"I've been here four months. Gia's been here seven," Mindy said.

"Seven!" Teal exclaimed. She looked at Gia. "How could you last here that long?"

"We manage. Like Natani says, a branch that doesn't bend, breaks. You learn how to bend," Mindy said. "It's that simple."

"Doesn't she talk, say anything except point out who has broken a rule?" Robin asked, nodding at Gia.

Gia looked up at us. Her eyes looked more ebony than mine perhaps because they were shining with such anger. However, it didn't look like anger directed just at us. She looked as though she was in a habitual rage, hated everyone and everything. A tiny, cold smile flowed into her small mouth that seemed to have forgotten how to smile.

"Oh, you're so smug and so smart now," she said. "You still think you're stronger than they are, or someone will come charging in here and save you and tell you it's all a big mistake. They can't do these things to you. You don't have to be here. You have rights. How dare they take away your rights? You'll get so you pray for it, but all you will hear in return are the yelping coyotes or Natani's drums when he is talking to the wind and the stars.

"You see this piece of bread?" she said, holding it up. "It's more important to me than your friendship. Think you'll never get that way yourself?"

She laughed a maddening, shrill laugh that put icicles under my breasts. Then she lost her energy again, and like a weakening lightbulb paled and lowered her head to continue eating.

None of us spoke. I saw that Mindy was staring at me curiously, waiting to see my reaction.

"I hope I never get like that," I said.

Gia nodded her head but kept it down and kept eating. "You're eating on our plates and out of our bowls," she muttered.

"What?" Teal asked.

Mindy turned to her. "Later today, they will take you to the pottery room in the cow barn and Natani will show you how to make dishes and bowls. They will be what you'll eat upon, and if you don't make it right, you'll eat off the table until you do. Remember, reality checks. Everything you have, you have because you've earned it, made it, provided for yourself."

"Oh, I hated doing that in school," Teal said. "Arts and crafts class. I never did any of it right. It's disgusting and so messy."

Mindy smiled at her. "Wait until you clean a pigpen or shovel cow manure and then tell me pottery work is disgusting."

Teal's lips began to tremble again. She looked as if she were going to go catatonic.

"Just eat. We don't eat again until dinner. You heard her," I advised her.

Robin nodded. "Phoebe's right, Teal. Stop worrying about it all. You'll make it bigger and bigger in your mind and only bring pain to yourself." Robin ate faster.

Teal did the same and we were all quiet again.

"Where you from?" Robin asked Mindy.

I thought she wasn't going to answer, but she finally lifted her head as if it were made of stone and gazed at Robin across the table. "Nowhere. I'm from nowhere."

Before Robin or I could respond, M'Lady Two entered.

"Time to go back to work, girls. Take your dirty dishes to the sink. Mindy, you and Gia remain behind and wash them today. Tonight, Robin, Teal, and Phoebe will do the dinner dishes and silverware. Make sure the table is clean before you return to your farm chores.

"You three will return to the garden now and work until Natani says it's time to go to clean out the pigpen."

Mindy smiled at Teal, who glared back at her.

"Get up now!" M'Lady Two commanded.

We did so and Gia and Mindy began to clear the table.

"It's proper to thank each other for the food," M'Lady Two declared. "Do so."

Everyone mumbled a thank-you to everyone else.

"And don't forget to add, 'God bless Dr. Foreman,' " we were told.

We did so. Then we were marched out to put on our shoes and return to the garden.

Natani wheeled over the tomato plants, handling them as if they were babies.

Teal mumbled just that and he stopped and looked at her.

"They are babies," he said. "Everything is born, begins, matures, and grows old in the world. I'm sure you have heard, 'As ye sow, so shall ye reap,' have you not?"

"I have," Robin said. "My grandparents practically told that to my mother every day, and my grandfather told my grandmother the same thing every time my mother did something he didn't like, which was about always."

"Well, I haven't," Teal said. "I haven't heard anything that has to do with plants."

"Oh, it has more to do with people," Natani said.

Teal smirked at him.

"I know you are not happy," he said. "But you must remember that life's sorrows often bring great joys."

"Here?" I said. "What joys could we possibly find here?"

Natani looked out toward the sprawling desert. "Many years ago the Great Spirit made the sky and the earth and he put the animals on the earth. One day he decided to move the vulture bird to the desert to live. The vulture took one look about and said, 'What a forsaken, miserable place is this. It is hot and dry and full of poisonous creatures. What joy could I possibly find here? Why did the Great Spirit move me here?' And then he saw a dead desert rat and swooped down to gobble it up. After that he saw a coyote that had died when it had disturbed a rattlesnake, and he feasted on that. Then, he smiled as well as vultures could smile. He was full of joy because what better place is there for a vulture than the desert?"

"I'll remember that next time I come upon a dead desert rat," Teal muttered.

"Yes," Natani said. "I'm sure you will."

He began to show us how to plant the tomato plants and we worked at it until all were in the ground.

"When you eat your first tomato from the plant you have put in the ground, you will understand what joy is here," Natani declared. "Now we go to clean the pigpen."

"What difference does it make to a pig if his pen is clean or not?" Teal asked.

"Maybe nothing to the pig, but much to us," he said. "First, we will use what they drop as fertilizer. Second, we will keep them clean so they don't get diseases and smell bad."

"I can't believe I'm doing this," Teal moaned. "We had maids. I never cleaned my room. I never ironed or washed clothes in my life, and now I'm cleaning a pigpen." She looked around. "How far is the nearest city?"

"A lifetime," Natani replied.

"What's that mean?"

"It probably means if you ran off in any direction, you'd die," I said. "Is that what it means, Natani?"

He smiled. "One must learn to live within a small circle before he or she tries to cross the world."

"I just want to get home," Teal moaned. "Not cross the world."

"To go home is to cross the world," Natani told her.

We paused at the pen. Natani opened the gate and shooed the pigs away. Then he stood back.

"I'm going to vomit on the spot. I mean it," Teal warned.

"If you do, you'll clean it up," we heard, and saw M'Lady Three standing nearby. "Start shoveling. You have to go to the pottery barn before therapy today."

"Therapy? We'll need more than therapy at the end of this day," I muttered.

The three of us began to shovel the pig manure into a wheelbarrow. Natani would then take it around to the side of the garden and dump it in a pile while we filled another wheelbarrow. The stench made me dry heave so hard I thought my stomach would crack open, but we didn't stop because every time we tried to back away, we heard one of the m'ladies warning us about the Ice Room.

Where were Gia and Mindy? How come they didn't have to do this? I wondered.

A good hour or so later we found out. They were in with Dr. Foreman. We saw them leave the house and head toward the barn, both walking with heads down.

"What's with Tweedledum and Tweedledee?" Robin asked.

I shook my head. "Maybe they're finished with their chores and have free time."

"Free time? What good is it? What could you do here but twiddle your thumbs?" Teal asked.

"Don't worry about it. Free time is something you won't see for a long time," M'Lady Two replied, coming around the corner of the pigpen. "Pottery time," she declared, and led us to another barn where we passed cows in stalls and entered a room where there was a kiln, tables, and clay.

Natani was already at work at a table. We were told to sit around and listen to his instructions. He showed us how to mix the clay, how to keep it from being too wet, then how to shape our bowls and dishes. M'Lady Two stood back near the doorway watching us work. She wore a wry smile and seemed to enjoy Teal's discomfort. Natani was patient and focused. Once again, I thought he had magical hands. Everything seemed to come so easily to him.

"You must see the bowl and the dish here first," he said, pointing to his temple. "Then it will travel down into your fingers and it will be born through them."

Teal swung her eyes toward the ceiling, but said nothing. Every once in a while she moaned over the clay that was getting under her fingernails. Finally, we had each formed our bowl and our dish well enough to please Natani and he put them into the kiln.

"Let's go," M'Lady Two said. "Dr. Foreman is waiting for you."

Robin asked for permission to speak.

"What do you want now?"

"Can't we clean up, rest a moment?"

"Why? You're not going to a party, stupid. Follow me."

None of us moved with any energy. We dragged ourselves through the afternoon's hot sun and, once again, took off our shoes and washed our hands in the springwater. We gulped water until our buddy told us to move and we entered the hacienda. M'Lady One led us into the house and brought us to an office with a long, brown leather sofa, an oversize leather chair, and a coffee table between them.

On an oversize dark cherrywood desk, papers were neatly arranged, with a computer on the side, the monitor lit with a screen saver showing spiraling solar systems twirling. The walls had plaques and frames, some with degrees in them, some with letters of commendation. The windows were shaded with blackouts and the room was cool and comfortable, obviously well air-conditioned. A large oval area rug with desert colors was on the floor, between the sofa and the desk.

"Sit on the sofa," M'Lady One told us. "Remember, no one is to speak until asked to do so. We'll be listening."

We sat on the sofa; then she closed the door behind her as she left. For a moment, the three of us, so tired and exhausted, just sat quietly enjoying the cool air. Teal turned her hands over and looked at her palms. She grimaced sharply, looking like she might burst into tears. Robin closed her eyes and sat back. I lowered my head and stared at the floor.

"I'm running away from here tonight," I heard Teal whisper.

"You can't do that. You'll get lost and die out there," Robin said.

"I'll die here anyway," Teal replied, but not with as much conviction as someone who really believed she had no other choice.

We heard the door being opened and pressed our lips shut. Dr. Foreman walked in, smiled at us, and went first to her desk. She turned some pages of a document in front of her, then came around her desk and sat in the oversize chair, the document in her lap.

"So here we are," she said. "I thought it would be nice if our first session was together, the three of you and me, beginning as a group. How does everyone feel?"

For a moment none of us took the question seriously. How do we feel? How could we feel but miserable?

"I'm exhausted," Teal finally said. "I had a horrible night because I was forced to sleep outside chained to a cot, and it was cold, very cold. I don't know why I'm not sick with pneumonia or something, and I stink. We all stink. I want to go home. I'm sure my parents don't know what this place is like or they wouldn't have sent me here. When they find out, heads are going to roll."

Dr. Foreman had a face like a mask, I thought. Her eyelids barely blinked and those eyes of hers looked like they could bore holes into all three of us. Her lips remained firm, tight. Teal had to look away. She sucked in her tears and held her breath.

"Of course your parents, and your uncle and aunt in your case, Phoebe, know what this is like," Dr. Foreman began. "They were given our brochure and everything, every detail was explained to them. We don't take anyone here without all that being understood first. Agreements had to be signed. I can show you them, if you wish. Your parents want you here, Teal. Why do you suppose that is?"

Teal didn't reply. She kept her face turned away, her chin in her hand with her elbow braced on the arm of the sofa.

Dr. Foreman turned to Robin and me. "Anyone? Why do you suppose you were sent to me, to this school?"

"It isn't a school. It's a torture chamber," Teal snapped at her.

"Can you imagine what sort of torture you have put your families through?"

"Nothing as bad as this," Robin replied defiantly.

"That becomes a matter of opinion, doesn't it, Robin? The emotional and mental torture your families suffered was worse than anything to them or they wouldn't have turned to me in desperation, they and the courts that are frustrated with your behavior, that are ready to give up entirely on you. Tell me, any of you, why should your families have kept you? What did you give to them besides heartache? What do you give to anyone? What value are you to the world?

"Natani's cows give us milk, his pigs give us ham, his garden gives us vegetables, his pottery gives us dishes, his animals give us clothing. What do any of you do but take from the world around you, the world you spent your time damaging? Who will miss any of you?"

Maybe we were all just too tired, but when I shifted my tearful eyes toward Robin and Teal, I saw they were as pained and saddened.

"You were born, you hurt people, and you have been removed, just like some diseased rodent," Dr. Foreman continued, glancing at me. "You're going to lodge complaints? You dare to threaten? You don't know how ridiculous that sounds. Why should anyone listen to your complaints now? All your lives you never listened to anyone else's."

"What do you want from us?" Teal screamed, the tears streaming down her cheeks.

"What I want from you is what you should want from yourself. A rebirth, a complete change."

"I'll change. I promise," Teal followed.

"No. You can't promise that. You've promised it before and broken the promise. Now, you really have to do it, and to do it, you must truly come to hate who you are now and bury that person out there." Dr. Foreman nodded toward the windows.

"We might just do that if you keep torturing us like this," Teal shot back at her.

"Then that is what will be, but I don't think so. I think you'll change for the better. We're here to begin. Today, I want you each to tell me one thing that you did that you admit was shameful, something that in itself would almost justify your being here. I want to believe you when you tell me that, too, so don't just say anything. I know a great deal about each of you. I know what I would choose if I were any one of you." Dr. Foreman sat back. "Who wants to begin?"

Robin and I looked down. Teal turned away.

"No one is ready to begin her cleansing?"

"I didn't do anything bad enough to deserve this," Teal insisted.

Dr. Foreman looked at Robin.

"I'm here only because my mother darling wants to be free of me," she said.

Dr. Foreman turned to me.

"My aunt and my uncle hated having me. They jumped on the first opportunity to get me sent away."

Doctor Foreman nodded. "Okay. It's not unusual for you all to be like this right now, to not be ready. On rare occasion, one of my students will have insight immediately, but that's, as I said, rare."

"Students," Teal spit. "We're not students. How are we students? We're trapped here and tortured. We're prisoners in some madhouse."

"I'm sorry you feel that way." Dr. Foreman sounded so sincere, really sorry, as if Teal had insulted her. I raised my eyebrows. Could she be serious? How else did she expect we would feel? Did she really believe all she was telling us?

She rose from her chair and went to the door.

"Girls," she said, and stepped back. All three buddies entered the office and looked at us. "My new students are not ready for any rewards yet. Therefore I am rescinding any positive merit points that they earned today. They'll begin again tomorrow."

"Does that mean we're sleeping on those hard cots again and still wearing these . . . these things?" Robin asked.

"If you're lucky," Dr. Foreman said, her eyes small, threatening.

"That's not fair!" Teal moaned. "We've done everything we were told to do. Look at my hands!" She turned the palms up to show the redness and puffiness.

"Why is it all right for you never to be fair and not for the rest of us? That's the world you created around you. Welcome home," Dr. Foreman said. "Now get up and follow your buddies out. I don't like wasting my time," she said sternly.

"What did you want us to say?" I cried with desperation, my arms out like some street beggar's.

She paused, her lips relaxing, her eyes brightening with cold excitement. "I want you to tell me the truth and I want you to be truthful with yourself."

"What truth? I don't understand what you're talking about, what all this is," I said, shaking my head.

"Oh, but you will, Phoebe. Soon, you will," she said, smiling. "I have no doubt of that."

The buddies were all smiling, too, all of them confident we would fall into line. They were obviously enjoying this, enjoying seeing girls who were once like they were, girls who would be molded into whatever form Dr. Foreman had envisioned for us. Just as she had told Teal in that concrete building—she was playing God.

"Let's go, ladies," M'Lady Three sang.

With great reluctance, we rose and left that cool oasis, that comfort, and followed them back out to the still hot and glaring late-afternoon sun. When did it cool down?

We put on our shoes and followed our buddies away from the house, all of us shuffling along with exhaustion, looking like some ragtag, defeated army. The hot sun made the plains of the desert shimmer around us, the hot air wavering. I thought it wouldn't surprise me to see a mirage.

I looked back and saw Dr. Foreman standing in the doorway watching us.

She was smiling again and that smile was like a knife at my pounding heart.

And that was no mirage.

4

Betrayal

We were taken back to the garden and told to finish planting the tomatoes. M'Lady Two warned that if we didn't do our work well, we would be denied dinner. Sullen, but afraid to resist, the three of us began again. Natani had a way of appearing as if he just materialized out of thin air. None of us heard him approaching until he was there, standing behind us, observing, occasionally instructing again, and helping us get through it.

The sun was lower in the sky, now nearly completely behind a mountain in the distance. It was almost tolerable to be outside. As the glare lessened, I saw how badly burned both Robin and Teal were. Their cheeks were clown red, their upper arms especially looking raw. Neither realized it yet, I thought. When they turned their backs to me, I saw how crimson the backs of their necks were, too. They would surely be feeling miserable tonight, especially sleeping on those cots. When I looked at Natani, I saw him nod as if he could hear my thoughts.

"You must come with me now," he told Teal and Robin.

They looked at me. I shrugged as if to say, who knew what was next?

"I can't do anything else. I'm ready to die!" Teal moaned.

"You must come with me," Natani repeated.

None of the buddies were there to bully us, but we followed him around the far barn, carrying our tools. There we saw what looked like a dumpy old shack made out of logs and brush and mud. He pulled aside the blanket door and stepped back, urging us to enter.

"What is this?" Teal finally asked.

"This is my house," Natani said. "We call it a hogan."

We entered slowly. It wasn't much of a house. A thick blanket and a slim mattress were on the left. On the right was what looked like an ancient stove, the pipe up through the roof. We saw a drum and a pile of clothing beside it with two pairs of moccasins. Strings of beads hung on one wall.

"Where's the television set?" Robin joked.

Natani smiled. "My television set is out there." He indicated the door.

"Don't knock it," Teal muttered. "At least there are no commercials."

"Right now, I'd settle for commercials," Robin replied.

Maybe because we were all so tired and overwhelmed, we all became silly.

"And think of this: he doesn't need any cleaning lady," Teal said.

"And his electric bills must be very low," Robin added.

"He can't complain about the neighbors making too much noise. It won't do him any good," I said. "The neighbors are all animals."

Natani looked at us as if he had known us all our lives and expected us to be silly. He went to his stove where he had a pot of water simmering. Then he plucked a leather bag off the wall. The bag had fringes and a band of colorful beadwork on the bottom, as well as beads on its drawstrings. He opened it and produced handfuls of what looked like beans, which he dropped into the simmering water. He covered the pot and turned back to us.

"What are we doing here?" Teal asked. "Is that supposed to be our dinner tonight? Another sick joke of Dr. Foreman's, I bet," she said to Robin and me.

Could it be so? I wondered.

"No food, no. Soon, you will hear the sun," Natani said.

"Hear the sun?" Teal turned to me. "What the hell is he talking about now?"

"I think he means your sunburn."

As if speaking about it woke it, both she and Robin grimaced and then looked at their arms and felt the backs of their necks.

"Oh, Jesus," Robin moaned. "My skin feels like someone's holding a match to it."

"Mine feels like it was turned into cellophane. I think I can hear it crinkle," Teal added.

"You must sit," Natani said, indicating a place in his hogan. We did. Then he took his drum and sat with it between his legs.

"I'm in a tent with an old Indian man playing a drum. Am I going crazy or am I going crazy?" Teal muttered.

"We're beyond crazy," Robin said.

Very low at first, Natani began to beat a rhythm and chant something.

"I thought we weren't permitted entertainment until we earned it," Teal joked through her lips, now twisting with some agony. The sun was speaking, just as Natani had predicted.

"This is starting to really hurt," Robin complained as she touched the back of her neck again. "Now that we're indoors, I see what he means about the sun talking. It's not talking; it's shouting."

Natani raised his voice and we all jumped. His chant became stronger, his drumming louder.

"Should we just run out of here or what?" Teal asked.

"Wait," I said. "I have a feeling he knows what he's doing."

"And you have sunstroke, too," Robin told me.

Abruptly, Natani stopped chanting and put the drum aside. Then he rose and went to his stove and the pot. He took it off the flame and stirred the contents. He poured the remaining water on the ground, then squatted in front of us and set the pot between his legs.

"These are beans from mesquite," he said. "They will keep the sun quiet."

"You're kidding," Robin said. "Mesquite. Isn't that a bug?"

"No, it's a plant," Teal said. "I know that much."

Natani dipped his fingers into the pot and came up with the dark, muddy mix.

Teal grimaced. "Maybe that will make it worse. Who told you it works?"

Natani smiled. "Many, many years ago, the coyote told us."

"The coyote? What coyote?" Robin asked.

"The coyote," he repeated, and urged her to give him her arm.

"You should let him do it," I said. "He lives here. He should know what works and what doesn't. You can be sure Dr. Foreman and her buddies won't care about your sunburn. I didn't see a nurse's office at this school."

"Quit calling it a school. It's a hellhole," Teal said.

Robin grimaced and then timidly leaned toward Natani. He began to wipe the mix over her shoulder and arm. He did the same with the other arm, then turned his hand to indicate she should let him get to the back of her neck. She closed her eyes and did so.

"How does it feel?" Teal asked.

Robin thought a moment. "Better, I think."

"Damn, I have to put mud all over me. It's not enough I have it under my nails," Teal complained, but offered her arms and her neck to Natani, who applied the mix on her. Then he put the remaining dark mush in a can and handed it to me.

"For later," he said, and I took it.

"Look at my hands!" Teal moaned, turning her palms up and then showing the blisters to us.

Natani nodded and rose. He went to his bag again and brought back another salve, which he applied to her hands and then to Robin's and mine.

"Natani!" we heard M'Lady Three scream. "Are those delicate flowers in there with you?"

"Go," he said, nodding. "You did good work today. Every day it will get easier, like a stream starting in a new direction. Soon, it flows freely."

"Just what I wanted to be all my life," Teal said, "a stream."

"Thanks," I said. Robin and Teal thanked him, too, and we left his hogan.

M'Lady Three was standing there with her hands on her hips. "Oh, you poor babies. Natani felt sorry for your delicate skin, I see."

"Didn't he do the same for you or weren't you as delicate?" Robin shot back at her.

Her face reddened. "That," she said, pointing at Robin, "will cost you a demerit, smart-ass. One more and you're in the Ice Room. Now get back to your bunkhouse. It's time to clean house."

We looked at each other. Clean house? How could we clean that barn? It had floor of straw and no real furniture. When we arrived, we saw that Teal's cot was still outside. Our other two buddies were waiting at the door.

Teal raised her hand.

"Speak," M'Lady Three said.

"Am I going to sleep out here again tonight?"

"Let's have you all decide." M'Lady Three nodded and M'Lady Two called Mindy and Gia out. "Teal here wants to sleep in the barn tonight. We're going to let you all vote. Of course, she can't vote, so it's the four of you. A tie means no."

Teal looked hopelessly at Gia and Mindy.

"Would you like to tell the voters anything before they decide?" M'Lady Two asked Teal. "You did insult their house last night."

Teal glanced at us, lowered her head, and then nodded.

"And what would that be, pray tell?" M'Lady Two asked.

Teal raised her head. "I'm sorry. I didn't mean to insult the barn or any of you. Please let me sleep inside tonight," she begged.

The buddies looked self-satisfied. I, as well as Robin and Teal, I was sure, wished I could smother them.

"Okay, then," M'Lady Two said. "All in favor of Teal being permitted to return to the barn, raise your hands."

Robin and I lifted our arms quickly. Mindy and Gia looked as if they were still not going to vote for Teal, but after a second more, slowly lifted their arms.

"Well, then, Teal, you and your friends can bring your cot back inside. You all have an hour before dinner. You are to wash down your cots and wash the barn windows. Gia and Mindy have done their part. They brought the soap and water and the rags into the barn for you," M'Lady Three said.

Robin and I carried Teal's cot back into the barn and put it where it had been. Then, with the buddies watching us, we began to wash down our cots. We were all working like robots now, just moving thoughtlessly, doing what we had to do. When we finished the windows, we were told to bring the dirty water out and dump it. Then, we were rewarded with ten minutes of rest before dinner. I was afraid if I lay back and closed my eyes, I would fall right to sleep, even on the hard wooden surface of the cot.

"I mean it," Teal muttered. "I'm running away tonight. I'd rather die out there."

"You will," Mindy said. "You don't know anything about surviving in the desert. You would have to trek through miles and miles of brutal desert where there are scorpions, snakes, poisonous lizards, and devastating heat and dryness during the day, bone-chilling cold at night. You wouldn't know the first thing to do if you ran out of water or if you got bitten."

"Oh, and you do?" Robin snapped at her.

"I know some, but not enough to make me confident enough to try it."

"What about you?" Teal asked Gia. Gia looked up at us. "You want to run away? You want to get out of here? Give Dr. Foreman what she wants. That's your only escape."

"When are you getting out, smarty pants?" Robin asked.

"Soon."

We were all quiet. I knew I was thinking she might be right and she was lucky if it was soon. Robin looked defeated, too. Teal just looked angry.

"Okay, my little princesses," M'Lady One said from the doorway.

"It's time to go to dinner. You all go to the pottery room first and fetch your bowls and your plates. When we see them on the table, we'll decide if they're good enough to eat upon. Move it!" she ordered, and we rose and filed out.

As we crossed toward the bigger barn, I could hear Teal muttering under her breath. She was losing it faster than Robin and I were, I thought. Soon, not even Natani's mystical medicines would be enough to save her.

Our bowls and dishes were on the table. They didn't look bad to me. I couldn't imagine anyone not approving of them. We carried them back to the house, set them down, removed our shoes, and washed our hands. Then we were permitted inside. Our food was already on the table to be served family style from large plates and bowls. I saw what looked like steamed vegetables, as well as mashed potatoes and slices of chicken. There was water to drink, but no bread and certainly nothing for dessert.

We set our bowls and dishes down and greeted Mindy and Gia with the "Excuse me. I'm sorry." I had forgotten about it, but Robin remembered and we did it.

Dr. Foreman entered the dining room. She was wearing a pink and white blouse and a skirt. Her hair was the same, but I could see she wore some lipstick. She stood there for a moment looking us over.

"Natani took care of two of them, I see," she said to the buddies, who smiled. "I hope you thanked him properly. Tomorrow, after breakfast, I will be giving the three of you your school books and assignments. Every night after dinner, you will have two hours to work. You can work together or separately. That's a decision I leave up to you for now."

She nodded at the buddies, who then stepped forward to inspect our pottery, M'Lady One inspecting mine, M'Lady Two inspecting Robin's, and M'Lady Three looking at Teal's. They ran their fingers over the plates and around the bowls and then looked at each other and shook their heads.

"Bumps and crevices," M'Lady One said.

"Inferior work," M'Lady Two agreed.

M'Lady Three dropped Teal's bowl and plate and they shattered on the floor. The same was done to Robin's and mine.

"Eat off the table tonight and try again tomorrow," M'Lady Three told us.

"Before you leave, you will wash their bowls and dishes carefully and then clean up these broken inferior bowls and dishes," M'Lady Two said.

"There was nothing wrong with my bowl. That wasn't fair," Teal protested.

I looked up at Dr. Foreman.

She smiled at me.

Soon, she was surely thinking, soon you will be my girls and whatever I ask you to do, you will do.

The four of them left the dining room and Teal lowered her head to the table and started to sob.

"Don't do that," Gia said sharply.

Teal raised her head slowly and looked across the table at her. "Why not?"

"There's no point in trying to get them to feel sorry for you or any of us for that matter. We can't do much, if anything, to help you. And it doesn't do you any good here to feel sorry for yourself."

"Oh, you're so damn smart," Teal said, flicking the tears from her cheeks.

"No, not smart. Desperate," Gia replied with no emotion.

"Why are you here?" I asked her.

Mindy began to serve herself food.

"Lots of reasons, I suppose." Gia began to serve herself as she spoke. "They called me an arsonist."

"Arsonist? What did you set fire to?" Robin asked.

Gia paused. "My own house." Then, in the coldest, most matter-of-fact tone I could imagine, she added, "Almost killing my baby brother."

The three of us sat staring across at her.

"You'd better eat," Mindy urged. "They'll be back very soon and whatever you've eaten will be it."

Robin dipped the serving spoon into the mashed potatoes and dropped a glob on the table. Then she took some vegetables and some chicken and did the same.

My stomach churned both with disgust and with hunger. I quickly copied her. Reluctantly, Teal followed and the three of us ate like dogs over a table, gobbling the food, drinking some water, and staring blankly ahead. All the food tasted bland. The chicken had been boiled until it fell apart when touched, and there was no salt or pepper or any seasoning on anything.

"The chef has to be a reject from some fast-food joint," Teal said.

Sooner than we expected, the buddies entered and announced dinner was over. Mindy and Gia rose immediately and left the table.

"The kitchen sink is right through that door," M'Lady One told me, and pointed.

I gathered Gia's dishes and Robin picked up the silverware and Mindy's bowl and dish. Teal stood there watching us.

"That table better be gleaming when we return," M'Lady Three told her.

Teal followed us into the kitchen and found the sponges and cleaning liquids. "I never cleaned anything," she moaned.

"Oh, give me that already," Robin snapped, and took everything out of her hands. "You just dry the dishes Phoebe washes. I'm tired and I want to get out of here."

She returned to the dining room and Teal stood beside me while I washed off the pottery.

"Don't you want to try to run away with me? You can't want to stay here a moment longer than you have to," Teal urged.

"I do, but I'm afraid. I've lived in the city all my life. I wouldn't know a poisonous anything and I'm so tired, I don't think I'd get far anyway."

"Maybe we just have to follow the dirt road out. Maybe they're lying to us and we're not that far from a town?"

"You see any lights out there at night? And what if they're not lying? You have any doubt that they wouldn't bother to come rescue us? I don't."

"I won't make it through another day like this," she moaned.

"You'll make it."

"I don't deserve this. My parents were just very upset. My father and mother will take me back if they know I'm sorry. I've just got to be able to call them and tell them," she said, nodding at her plan. "Maybe, maybe I can sneak in here during the night and use the phone in Dr. Foreman's office."

I raised my eyebrows and looked at her. "And if you get caught? That's the Ice Room for sure, I bet."

"And I bet there isn't even such a thing. It's just something they say to keep us terrified."

I tilted my head and looked at her. "Do you want to be the first one to find out if there is or isn't?"

She started to shake her head and raised her hand too quickly, knocking Gia's dish out of mine. I was just about to give it to her to dry. It flew up and away, shattering on impact with the floor, the pieces exploding in every direction. For a moment we both stared in disbelief. I felt the blood draining from my face. Teal's eyes bulged and her mouth dropped open. She looked at me.

"Why didn't you wait until I saw you were handing it to me?" she cried.

"Wait until you saw? Why didn't you watch how you were swinging your hands wildly?"

"I wasn't. I . . ."

We both turned to the doorway. M'Lady Three was standing there, her arms folded under her small bosom, her shoulders back.

"Who did that?" she asked, nodding at the pieces of ceramic dish splattered over the floor. "Who threw that plate?"

"Nobody threw the plate," I said. "It was an accident."

"There are no accidents at Dr. Foreman's School. You did that deliberately."

"We didn't," I insisted. "You weren't here to see it."

She smiled coldly. "I was here as a student just like you two, remember? I know what you're thinking, feeling. You're angry because you had to eat off the table. This is just your way of showing it."

"That's not true," Teal wailed.

M'Lady Two came up beside M'Lady Three and looked at the shattered dish. "I remember doing that."

They both nodded.

"We didn't do it on purpose," I shouted. "Just because it's something you two might have done doesn't mean we did. Stop saying we did."

"You won't make any progress here until you admit to your guilt, to your meanness and selfishness, and you hog-tie that anger," M'Lady Two said. "Now, finish up here, clean every piece off the floor, and come outside immediately."

They left.

"Nice work," I told Teal.

I turned back to the sink and washed the remaining silverware and pottery. Teal dried everything carefully and placed the remaining pottery so softly on the counter, I could barely hear it touching. We both picked up the pieces and put them into the garbage bin.

"What are they going to do to us now?" Teal muttered. "Put us in a scaffold?"

It sounded silly, but my eyes widened. Anything was possible in this place.

Robin was already outside, her shoes on when we walked to the front door.

"What did y'all do?" she whispered. "I heard them talking about y'all. Your buddy"—she nodded at me—"sounded as though you let her down. I get the feeling they'll be punished if we don't do exactly as they expect and rewarded if we do. Maybe they're still under obligations of some sort to Dr. Foreman."

"I don't believe it. I think they're just sadists," Teal said. "They enjoy doing this."

"Well, what did y'all do in there?" Robin asked.

"We broke Gia's dish, but it wasn't our fault," Teal moaned. "It was just an accident."

"Okay," M'Lady Three said, coming out of the house. "Robin, you return to the barracks and go to bed. You two, follow me."

Robin looked at us with sympathy, but also with relief that she wasn't being included in whatever new punishment we were to suffer. We were led around to the rear of the cow barn where we saw M'Ladies One and Two waiting, each holding a blanket. Behind them were what looked like coffins.

"What is this?" Teal asked, stopping.

"This is the death of evil. Dr. Foreman wrote an interesting paper on the concept," M'Lady One said. She approached me and started to wrap the blanket around me.

I pushed it away and stepped to the side. "What are you doing?"

"You will want this blanket, believe me. It gets very cold in the desert before it gets warm again."

I shook my head. Teal turned to run, but her buddy was right there to seize her and hold her, screaming and kicking.

"If you cooperate, it will be so much easier," my buddy told me. She smiled. "We're doing it for your own good. You'll thank us someday, just the way we thanked our buddies and Dr. Foreman."

"You're all sick, crazy," I cried, and continued to back up. But M'Lady Two was behind me and wrapped her pincerlike arms around mine, also practically lifting me off the ground. M'Lady One wrapped the blanket around me quickly, then ran wide tape around that while I kicked and struggled. It was as good as a straitjacket.

All the while Teal was screaming at the top of her voice. When they were finished with me, they let me stumble and topple to the ground while they went to M'Lady Three and assisted her in doing the same thing to Teal. After both of us were snugly wrapped in the blankets, they took the lids off the coffins.

Teal's voice was so shrill, it seemed far off to me. I was shaking my head, my eyes closed, and mumbling my pleas. They can't be doing this to us, I thought. This can't be happening.

"It was an accident," I said. "Really, it was just an accident."

I felt myself being lifted and opened my eyes to see myself being lowered into the coffin.

"Please don't do this," I begged. "I'll do anything. Please. Let me talk to Dr. Foreman. Please."

"Dr. Foreman knows all about it," M'Lady One said.

The lid was put over me. I could see a number of holes drilled in it to permit air, but it was still a coffin and a lid and I couldn't move.

I could hear Teal's hysterical screams go hoarse and finally muffled, so I assumed she was in her coffin and the lid put over her as well.

"There are no accidents at this school," we heard the m'ladies chant.

I closed my eyes. Teal was struggling madly, twisting and turning her body in the coffin. It went on and on, and finally she grew quiet.

"Teal?" I called. "Teal, can you hear me? Are you all right?"

There was just silence and then the cry of a coyote. It grew closer, then there was another and another. It sounded as if they were right near us. My heart was thumping and I was sweating now. I managed to get some more space inside the blanket. The tape stretched a bit, but I could do little more.

Suddenly, I heard the distinct sound of Natani's drum. The slow, rhythmic beating was accompanied by a soft, melodic chant. It was truly like a lullaby. Thankfully my eyes grew heavier and I either fell asleep out of exhaustion and fear or simply passed out.

The next thing I knew the lid was being removed and the sunlight was blaring down on me. I felt myself being lifted out of the coffin and stood. I was confused and groggy, barely aware of what was happening. The tape was removed and the blanket unwrapped. The air, not yet heated to the temperatures of midday, felt soothing. I opened my eyes and focused on Dr. Foreman, who stood there smiling at me.

"Good morning, Phoebe," she said. "You have come through this well. I'm proud of you. Something rotten in you was buried forever last night, I'm sure. I want you to shower and come directly to breakfast. Then we'll talk before you start your daily chores today, okay?"

"I'm thirsty," I muttered. "Very thirsty."

"You'll feel better soon, a lot better. We always feel better when we peel off a miserable part of ourselves."

I looked at the other coffin. The buddies were removing the lid and reaching in to lift Teal out. Her head drooped. She did not regain consciousness.

"What have you done to her?" I asked under my breath. The buddies were holding her upright and her head still dangled loosely.

Dr. Foreman approached her, took something out of her pocket, and put it under Teal's nose. Teal's head snapped up and she shook it sharply before opening her eyes.

"Good morning, Teal," Dr. Foreman sang. "You look like you've buried something rotten and miserable, too. I just know the both of you will be so much better for it."

The buddies unwrapped Teal, but she was so wobbly, they had to hold on to her. They looked to Dr. Foreman, who seemed unhappy about that.

"Walk her about for a while. She'll get her legs back. I want them both showered and then brought to me," she said.

"Will do, Doctor," M'Lady Three said.

While she and M'Lady Two walked Teal about, my buddy directed me to the shower. Slowly, my arms and legs aching, I got undressed and went under the freezing water. I lifted my head to drink and swallow as much as I could. It did revive me. M'Lady One had a towel ready for me. While I was drying myself, I saw Robin, Gia, and Mindy leaving the house and heading for the fields where Natani was waiting for them. Robin looked like she was afraid to look my way. Just like the other two, she kept her head down, her eyes to the ground with only a passing glance my way when she walked by.

We are becoming like them, I thought. Robin is first. I'll surely be next.

"Let's go. We don't have all day to pamper you," M'Lady One told me.

Pamper?

I saw Teal walking on her own now, but her face was so empty of any feeling, any awareness, she truly looked like someone in a hypnotic state. Mechanically, she began to undress and then stumbled under the showerhead and stood there stupidly. M'Lady Three turned it on, and she jumped and screamed.

"Wash!" they all shouted at her.

She looked my way and began to scrub. Because of her sunburn, it hurt far more. I felt sorry for her, but as Gia had so coldly pointed out at dinner the night before, there was little we could really do to help each other. It was everyone for herself here in the end.

Afterward we were brought to the house and left in Dr. Foreman's office to wait for her. Neither of us had said one word to the other.

"Are you all right, Teal?" I asked her.

She lifted her head slowly and turned her droopy eyes toward me. "My throat aches."

"You were screaming so much."

"I dreamed I heard a drum all night."

"There was a drum and chanting. Natani must have been there. It helped me."

"Yes." She turned her head slowly to look forward again, her eyelids barely open.

Dr. Foreman entered with two glasses of orange juice in her hands.

"Here you two are," she said as if she had really been looking everywhere for us. "Drink some juice first."

We both took a glass and drank.

"Slowly, girls, slowly. You don't want to give yourselves bellyaches."

She sat in her chair and watched us for a moment, that same happy smile on her face. She was the crazy one, I decided, but I dared not say it.

"Now where were we? Oh, yes, you were both about to apologize for your misbehavior last night, I believe."

"It's not fair," I was about to say. I was going to describe just how the plate had come to be broken, but Teal lifted her head quickly.

"I'm sorry," she said. "I'm really sorry. I won't do anything like that again. I swear."

"Oh, that's so good to hear, Teal, dear. You don't know how words like that please me. They fill my heart with so much joy and make every ounce of effort I spend on you girls worthwhile whenever I hear a sincere apology."

She turned to me expectantly.

I glanced at Teal and nodded. "Yes. I'm sorry, too. It was wrong and we won't let it happen again."

"That is just wonderful. Something terrible did die last night. We buried it together. We have so much more to bury before we're through, but I know we're going to succeed. Now, Teal, what do you think we should bury next?"

Teal looked up, terrified.

Dr. Foreman laughed. "Oh, I don't mean in the coffin. Hopefully, neither of you will sleep there again." Teal's face immediately softened with relief. "But we have other ways to bury bad things. I'm hoping now that the two of you, the three of you, all of you, in fact, will be doing it yourselves. So, let's get back to where we left off the first time we all met here. What is one thing you did that you know contributed to your being brought here? Teal? Why don't you be first."

Teal tilted her head, her eyes full of defeat. "I vandalized the girl's bathroom in my public school. I broke the mirrors and clogged up the toilets and turned on all the faucets to flood the place. My father had to pay for the damages."

"And how do you feel about that now?"

"I wish I hadn't done it," she said readily.

"Why?"

"It upset my parents."

"Is that the only reason?" Dr. Foreman pursued.

Teal looked at me frantically. I could see it in her eyes: What was the right answer? What was the answer Dr. Foreman wanted, the answer that would free her, get her out of the limelight and danger?

"No," Teal said. "It was wrong. It made it impossible for anyone to use the bathroom for a while and it was a juvenile thing to do."

"Yes, that's true. Why did you do it?"

"I was angry."

"At whom, Teal? At whom were you angry?" Dr. Foreman leaned toward her with excitement in her face. "Well?"

"I don't know. Everyone, I guess."

"No, not everyone. Someone. Who, Teal? Whom were you trying to hurt the most? Tell me."

"My father," Teal cried back at her, the tears streaming from her eyes. "My father!" she shouted.

Dr. Foreman smiled and sat back. "That's good, Teal. That's a wonderful start. I know you're hungry and you need something in your stomach before you go to your chores, so I'm excusing you now. Go to the dining room and have some breakfast and then report to Natani in the field. Go on."

Teal looked at me and lowered her eyes with some shame before leaving the office. I watched her and then turned back to Dr. Foreman.

She had her fingers pressed together at the tips and sat there staring at me.

"We're gong to become good friends, you and I," she said. "You're going to help me with the others, and someday, I believe, you will serve a tour of duty as a buddy here." She smiled. "I know you will," she said with cold confidence, so cold it put a chill in my heart and washed ice water over my resistance. I tried to swallow, but couldn't. Her eyes were burning into me. "I am good at predicting that sort of thing, Phoebe. You'll see."

"What do you want from me?" I asked, barely holding on to my dwindling pride.

"I want your loyalty, Phoebe. I want your complete and utter loyalty." She leaned forward. I thought she was going to reach out to touch my hand, but she didn't. She just continued to stare a moment, then said, "And I'm sure you will give it to me eventually. The faster you realize that, the better it will be for everyone."

She sat back again. My heart wasn't racing now. It was more like it had actually stopped. I couldn't feel my pulse. My blood seemed to have frozen in place.

"Now tell me," she said, "which one of you, all of you, has spoken about running away?"

I raised my eyebrows.

She smiled. "I know it wasn't you, Phoebe. I know my girls. You're too realistic to contemplate such a thing. You're street savvy. You know what it means to survive out there. There are all sorts of jungles and deserts in the world. You don't have to come here to know that, not you. So who was it? Someone is trying to get the rest of you, or the three of you, to try it. I know. It's typical. Is it Robin or is it Teal, or has one of my other two been clever enough to lie to me? Did Mindy or Gia propose the idea?"

"It's not right to tell on someone," I said.

"Of course it is if telling on them will help them. What if this person actually attempts to run away? She'll die, Phoebe, and you"—she stabbed the air between us with her long, thin right forefinger—"will be very, very responsible for that death. I will hold you fully accountable and that will mean a very long, long time here as a student. Maybe you'd never leave."

Student? I thought. How could she get away with calling any of us that? Teal was right, of course. We were victims, prisoners.

"Well? Am I wrong about you? Will you be loyal to me and become one of my girls or not?" Her voice was full of dark threats.

"She just said it because she's frustrated and afraid and tired," I said.

"Who?"

"She didn't mean it. You can't punish her any more."

"Who?"

I took a deep breath. I was tired and hungry and afraid. I felt lower than the low.

Any one of them would turn me in, I told myself. Any one of them would make a deal with the devil to avoid any more punishment, and maybe Dr. Foreman was right about it: I would be helping her, saving her. Maybe she would try to run away now. I would be responsible in a sense, wouldn't I?

"Teal," I muttered.

"Who?" She wanted me to say it loudly and clearly and firmly. She wasn't going to accept a little bit of victory. She wanted a full, complete, and unquestionable victory.

"Teal," I said louder.

She nodded. "I knew it was Teal, Phoebe. You did the right thing in being honest with me. I'm proud of you. You're going to succeed here. You're going to become something. I want you to come to me or to one of the buddies if she continues to talk about this. If she does and you don't, I won't appreciate it and you will be hurting her more. Do you understand? Do you?"

I nodded.

"Good. Now go have yourself some breakfast. We'll talk again soon," she said, standing.

I rose. My head lowered itself with shame as I walked to the door.

"It's always hard to do the right things after doing the wrong things for so long," Dr. Foreman called after me as I left her office.

You're the one who doesn't know the difference, I thought.

But that was a sentence I would not utter aloud, even to the others.

I had something worse to keep locked in my heart now. Rationalize all that I might, make any excuse that I could think of, it was still the same thing, a betrayal. That was what I had committed in there, under Dr. Foreman's threatening eyes. I was afraid, more afraid than I had ever remembered being. Even the rats hadn't frightened me as much. Now nothing was clearer to me than this secret pain I had to carry and not show—none of us could be trusted. Not if I was the one who betrayed one of us so easily. I had thought I was stronger than the others. What a laugh, I thought. I might be the weakest of us all.

The cloud of depression darkened and fell over me as I walked on. We were all running down a street that would eventually become a dead end. The result of all this was never clearer to me.

She will win, I thought. Eventually, Dr. Foreman will get everything from us that she wants, and the most horrible thing of all will be that we will willingly give it to her.

5

Catfight

Even though I knew no one, especially not Robin or Teal, would suspect I was a snitch, I had difficulty looking either of them in the eye. Robin was intrigued about everything that had happened to us. It frustrated her that while we worked in the field this time, the buddies hung around seemingly just to make sure we didn't speak to each other. Finally, they grew bored and left. Robin nearly leaped out of her clodhoppers to get at us.

"What happened to you guys? Why didn't you come back to the barn to sleep?"

"We had to bury our evil," Teal said dryly.

"Huh?" Robin looked to me for a more sensible reply. Was there one? I wondered.

"They put us in these coffins they keep for a little extra persuasion," I told her, then described it. She paled, even through her darkening tan, as I spoke. Even her lips turned pale white. While I spoke, Teal kept her head down and leaned on her shovel.

"They can't do these terrible things to us," Robin exclaimed.

Mindy, who had been working on the other side and had been listening, laughed.

"They can't! It's illegal for sure," Robin insisted.

"So call the cops," Mindy taunted.

"I can't stand her," Robin muttered, glaring at Mindy. Her eyes suddenly grew smaller with a new suspicion. "You want to know something? I don't think she did anything wrong."

"What are you talking about?" Teal asked, looking up quickly.

"I think Mindy is here just to aggravate and annoy us to death. She's like one of these plants. She works for Dr. Foreman. She's a spy or something. I'm going to make her admit it," Robin said, throwing her shovel to the ground.

"Don't do anything stupid," I warned, and looked around. "They hear everything we say, I think. Even when they're not around."

"What do you mean they hear everything we say?" Robin asked. Teal looked at me with new fears in her face.

"Just that. I don't know. Maybe this place is bugged with microphones or something. I get the feeling sometimes that when Dr. Foreman asks us a question, she already knows the answer," I said.

The two of them looked at me. Out of the corner of my eye, I saw Mindy cross the field toward us. Gia finished what she was doing and sat back on the ground, embracing her legs and lowering her head.

"What did she ask you?" Mindy fired at me, still crossing.

"What?"

"What was the question that she already knew the answer to?"

"Who's talking to you?" Robin snapped at her.

"What was the question?" Mindy repeated, ignoring her.

"I didn't say there was any specific question. It's just a feeling I have about her, that's all," I said quickly, maybe too quickly.

"Yeah, well, it's a good feeling, a true feeling, so watch your mouth," Mindy advised. "And watch what you say about any of us."

"Who are you to tell any of us what to do and not to do?" Robin demanded. "Maybe you should be the one who should watch her mouth."

"What? What's that mean?"

"How come you know so damn much about this place?" Robin stepped toward her. "What did you do to be brought here anyway?"

"I don't think it's any of your business," Mindy said, and turned to walk back.

Robin shot forward and grabbed her arm, spinning her around. "That's a lot of bull. You seem to know about everyone else and everything else. We should know something about you. Unless there isn't anything to know. Is that it? Well?"

"Leave me alone." Mindy turned to walk away again, but Robin seized her arm again, this time more firmly.

Mindy tried to break free, grimaced with pain, and screamed. They both struggled in the middle of the new field of tomatoes. Natani came hurrying out from behind the barn and the buddies were crossing the yard, M'Lady Three leading the charge. Neither Mindy nor Robin appeared to notice. Robin wouldn't let go of her. She was turning and twisting her as if she were a big rag doll. They continued to wrestle until Robin threw Mindy to the ground. She fell over a few newly planted tomato plants. Robin reached down to pull her up again.

"Stop it!" M'Lady Three shouted. The three buddies ran forward and M'Lady Two wrapped her arms around Robin and lifted her up and away from the sprawling Mindy.

"It's her fault!" Robin screamed, kicking and squirming. "She's been taunting and teasing us ever since we got here."

Mindy stood up and brushed herself off. Three of the new plants were smashed. Natani knelt beside them and handled them gently.

"Nice work, stupid," M'Lady Two told Robin. "That's a capital crime at Dr. Foreman's School for Girls, destroying food, food we all need."

Robin relaxed with fear and M'Lady Two released her.

"I didn't destroy food. I . . . she . . ."

"Blaming someone else for things you do is worthy of five demerits," M'Lady Two said.

"All right, both of you, march back to the house," M'Lady Three ordered. "The rest of you keep working."

We watched Robin and Mindy walk ahead of the buddies. M'Lady One looked back at Teal and me so we started to dig again. Gia returned to work and finished placing another plant. All the while I noticed how little interest she had taken in what had occurred. She hadn't come to Mindy's aid when Mindy and Robin were struggling and she offered no help afterward, didn't try to defend her. They really had no friendship. The realization that the two of them could be here so long together and not become significant to each other depressed me further. Was that how it would soon be for the three of us? We would just slide down this tunnel of anger and fear until we hit bottom and sank into some swamp of disgust?

Two of the smashed plants were too damaged to remain in the ground. Natani dug them up and carried them away. He returned with new ones and planted them himself. About a half hour later, Mindy came back to the field. She glanced at us and returned to work. Gia didn't speak to her at all.

"Where's Robin?" Teal asked nervously, looking back.

The ranch house was ominously quiet. We could hear bees buzzing at the corner of the cow barn and the pigs slushing about their pen, grunting. About midday, M'Ladies One and Three came out to tell us to report to the pottery barn.

"You're not only going to try to make your own bowl and dish again, you're going to make a new dish for Gia and you're going to stay there and do it until you do it right, even if you have to stay there all day and all night. And Dr. Foreman, remember, is giving you all your schoolwork to start today," M'Lady Three told us. "So you better not waste a second moaning and groaning about how hard your life is."

"Permission to speak?" I asked.

"What do you want?"

"Where's Robin?"

"She's where you go if you do something Dr. Foreman considers way over the line."

"Where's that?" Teal asked. M'Lady Three glared at her. "Permission to speak?"

"That, Teal, is the Ice Room."

"Where is the Ice Room?" she asked.

"Wherever you keep your worst nightmares," M'Lady Three replied. "Now get moving. You're wasting precious time."

"I can't imagine anything worse than what was done to us last night," Teal muttered. "She is stupid. After what we told her, she goes and loses her temper. She could have gotten me into trouble again, somehow."

"I'm sure she's sorry now," I said.

Teal looked hatefully at Mindy. "I don't trust her either. I don't trust anyone." She glanced at me and I shifted my eyes away guiltily. "Anyone."

We marched back to the pottery room. Natani wasn't there, but we knew how to proceed. It took us the remainder of the day to produce five pieces of pottery our buddies approved. Just before they returned to inspect, Natani came in and without speaking helped us. Actually, he was the one who produced the finished products. He left before the inspection.

"All right," M'Lady One told us. "Return to the barracks. You have your schoolwork waiting. You have an hour to make use of before dinner. Every minute of time here is to be productive. Laziness is just as bad as anything else and is rewarded with demerits."

We found textbooks on our cots and sheets of assignments alongside them. There was work to be done in literature, science, math, and social studies. Everything had a specific deadline, the first being tomorrow.

"When do they expect we'll be able to do all this?" I moaned.

Teal shook her head. "This is crazy. She's giving us impossible things to do just so she can punish us with these sadistic things for not doing them. I don't care if I die out there. Tonight, I'm going to sneak some food away from the dinner, even if it's just a piece of chicken or something, and I'll find something to put water in. I'm leaving this place," she vowed. "I'll get someplace where there is a phone and I'll call home. Once my parents find out how gruesome this is, they'll come get me. You can come with me or not," she concluded with a heavy note of definiteness.

"You can't sneak enough food out of there, Teal. And you'll need more than a can of water. You don't know what direction to go in. At night you won't see anything. You could get terribly lost. It won't work."

She didn't reply. She sat on her cot with her back to me and then lowered herself to her side. I looked at her and thought, Was there any hope to an attempted escape? Could she be right? Should I go with her?

Mindy and Gia came in, glanced our way, then went to work on their academic assignments. I opened my math book and looked at the explanations and the problems. It might as well have been written in Greek, I thought. Maybe it was. I closed the book and walked to the doorway. Mindy glanced at me, then looked at her books. Gia never looked my way. Teal was still lying still. She had probably fallen asleep, exhausted. I didn't know what was keeping me awake and moving me.

I saw Natani come out of the cow barn carrying a pail of water that he dumped. Then he went back inside. None of the buddies were in sight. We knew that they lived in the hacienda, probably in the very rooms I had first thought would be ours. What a wishful dream that was, I thought now, and laughed at my naive optimism and innocence. We hadn't been here long, but to me at the moment, it seemed like months.

I gazed back at Teal once more, then left the barracks and crossed to the cow barn. Natani was adjusting the flow of water into the troughs. He looked up as I approached, then looked at the faucet again.

"I'm sorry my friend broke your plants," I told him.

"They are not my plants," he said. "They are yours. It is from these plants, from everything we do here, that you have what to eat and drink. Very little comes from anyplace else."

I jumped on what he said. "How far away is anyplace else, Natani? Really. How far away are we from anywhere?"

He stood up and wiped his hands on a cloth. "Many days, walking."

"But doesn't Dr. Foreman leave occasionally? There's a van, of course. The van they used to bring us here. There has to be a road that leads to places, a place to get gas, whatever. Where is this place?"

"The van comes once a month with food and other supplies. We have a big gas tank here for the van and the tractor. A truck comes and fills it once a month, and we run our electric generators on natural gas. That comes regularly, too.

"When the doctor leaves, she goes to a place where a small plane waits for her and takes her quickly to where she wants to be and brings her back. She doesn't go very often."

I looked around. Perhaps microphones really were secretly placed everywhere. Would Natani tell them whatever I asked him or said? Was he someone to trust? Did he fool us by helping us? I had to know as much as I could. I had to risk asking him questions. Teal sounded so determined. What if I did decide to go with her? Would it be madness?

"Do you like working for Dr. Foreman?"

"I don't work for Dr. Foreman," he replied.

"What do you mean you don't?"

"I work for what grows. I work for the animals. I work for the sun and the moon and the stars. My people were here long before Dr. Foreman or anyone else. Signs, houses, papers, don't change the way things grow, the sun's rising and falling. I do what I have always done."

"She doesn't pay you?"

"The earth pays me."

Maybe he's just crazy, I thought. Maybe the sun fried his brain.

"What if someone ran off, Natani? Just left one night and walked away in the right direction? People can walk for days and days, right?"

He smiled. "Once, a vulture picked up a squirrel at the edge of the desert and flew off with him. The squirrel awoke and screamed, 'I am not dead. How dare you take me?' The vulture, shocked himself that the squirrel wasn't dead, opened his mouth and the squirrel fell to the desert floor. The squirrel brushed himself off. He was insulted. Imagine, he thought, being thought to be dead. He started to strut in one direction and then stopped, scratched his head, and started in the opposite direction. Once again, he stopped and scratched his head. Where were the trees, the rivers he knew? What sort of place was this with ground so dry even rocks looked unhappy?

"Nervous and worried now, he walked faster, again stopped, and turned to go in another direction. Each time, he walked faster. He grew very tired, very thirsty. Nothing made any sense to him. He could not understand the way and he saw no creatures who could give him any information. The lizards and the snakes were afraid of him. He didn't belong there so they did not trust him enough to wait to hear his questions.

"Night came and he didn't like where he had to sleep. Something crawled over him and made him jump and he was awake so long, he barely had any rest before the sun came up. He scurried up a small hill and looked around. As far as he could see, there were no trees, no streams, no place to gather food and no one he knew.

"He walked on, desperate now. He tried to keep himself in one direction, but every once in a while he leaned too far to one side or another, and soon he realized he had been walking in a great circle. Everything looked the same. Very thirsty, very weak, he finally stopped and fell to the dry earth. His eyes closed and opened, closed and opened, and then closed.

"And lo and behold, the same vulture appeared and strutted up to him. He opened his eyes and looked at the vulture, who seemed to be smiling.

" 'I thought you said you weren't dead,' the vulture said.

"The squirrel tried to move, but couldn't and did die. The vulture picked him up and carried him off again.

"The vulture knows. He or she who doesn't belong out there will soon belong to him. Patience rewards him. He will wait, and to those who scream back at him, 'I am not dead,' he will say, 'You are dead. You just don't know it yet.' "

Natani turned back to pour some feed in the trough.

"But people cross the desert. You do, I bet, or did, didn't you?" I insisted.

"People who know how to speak with the desert can live with it, but there is little forgiveness there. A mistake, a misunderstanding, and soon, the patient vulture, the desert's undertaker, appears."

"If we had food and water . . ."

"You cannot carry enough. You must know how to get the desert to give it to you."

"You could show someone how to do that, couldn't you, Natani?"

He didn't reply.

"You could show someone enough to help her get across the desert to where people live, couldn't you?"

"When it comes time, I will teach you what I know."

"When is that?"

"When it comes time. It's not for me to decide. It's the doctor who decides."

"What do you mean? She lets us try to escape?"

"It's her way. I do not understand all her ways, but it's her way. She is a very wise woman."

What was he talking about? How did he know how wise she was and wasn't? Where did she find him? Was he just here when she arrived as he said? He couldn't like what he saw happening to the girls. He must despise the buddies. I saw the way he just looked at them when they spoke to us or even to him. It was as if he could look through them or put himself in a different place when he wanted to, but why did he bother? Why did he stay here? Surely there was another farm, another place unlike this where he could be happy.

None of it made any sense to me. I felt like I was spinning in a nightmare.

"Why are you here? Why don't you work on a happier place without all this?" I asked, waving my arms. "Are you really part owner or something?"

He smiled and shook his head. "No, nothing but what I have made myself belongs to me."

"Then why are you here? Of all places, Natani, why Dr. Foreman's School?"

He looked like he wasn't going to answer anymore, and I thought I was probably wasting my breath, but suddenly, he looked at the hacienda and then at me.

"The doctor helped my daughter's daughter, and I have made her promises that are as strong as the sun. I do not understand all her ways, but she does not understand mine. The birds do not understand the lizards but they live side by side. Each has its own way. This is how it is," he added, and returned to his work.

I left the barn and returned to the barracks. Teal still had her back to Gia and Mindy and me.

Gia looked up. "You shouldn't have let her sleep."

"She's exhausted. We're both exhausted."

"You've got to start your work, show Dr. Foreman you're making an effort."

"I don't understand that math. I couldn't even begin to do it."

"You can do it," Gia insisted. "Let me see what she gave you as your first math assignment."

I brought the book and the assignment sheet to her and she nodded. "It's the same one we had to do. Okay, sit." She patted her cot.

I sat and she started to read and explain it to me. Mindy glanced at us every once in a while, but said nothing. Before we were summoned to dinner, I did understand the first lesson.

"Thanks," I said.

"You can show Teal how to do it now," Gia told me.

I woke Teal up but she was too groggy and cranky to listen to anything. She still mumbled about running off as soon as it was dark enough to escape. Dr. Foreman's words returned to me. I'd be responsible if Teal went off and died out there, and Dr. Foreman would be displeased with me. Who knew what that meant?

M'Lady Two came to our door and summoned us to dinner. I was hoping we would find Robin at the house when we got there, but she was nowhere in sight. We took off our shoes, washed our hands, and went in to have our dinner. Just a simple thing like having our own bowl and plate had now become a wonderful thing. We went through our ritual of thanking each other and begging each other for forgiveness, then ate what seemed to be a more tasty food that Mindy described as polenta, a mush of cornmeal, black beans, and a beef in some sort of sweet sauce.

Dr. Foreman arrived and declared she was rewarding all of us for putting in a decent day's work. We were given a plate of cookies for dessert. Mindy, Gia, and Teal were assigned to washing dishes and silverware, and I was told to clean the dining room afterward. While I worked, Dr. Foreman reappeared. She watched me for a few moments. I had the sense she was waiting for me to say something.

I stopped working, thought about Natani's tale of the squirrel, and then turned to her.

"What is it, Phoebe?"

"I'm afraid for Teal."

"Tonight?"

"Maybe."

"You've done a very good thing, Phoebe." Dr. Foreman stepped up to me and took my hands, turning them to look at my palms.

"Follow me." She led me out of the dining room, down the corridor, to a bedroom. It was surprisingly bland and unfeminine. There were no pictures on the walls, no pretty curtains or rugs, nor any photographs of family or friends. What kind of a family did she have? I wondered. Had she ever been married? Did she have a boyfriend, children of her own, parents still alive?

The king-size, four-poster bed looked so comfortable and luscious with its oversize cream-colored, fluffy pillows and comforter, I longed to crawl into it and sleep for a week.

She smiled at the covetous expression on my face. "All good things will come to those who earn them, Phoebe. Reality checks, remember?"

I nodded and she took me into her bathroom, opened a medicine cabinet, and plucked out a jar of some skin cream. She rubbed it into my hands.

"Natani isn't the only one with miracle medicines here," she said, smiling. "You don't want your skin to get too soft when you work a ranch, but you don't want to irritate anything and get infections either."

"Thank you."

She put her hands on my shoulders and looked into my face. "You're going to be one of my girls. I'm confident of that. Now return to your barracks and do your schoolwork."

I thought I heard what sounded like someone sobbing and thought about Robin. Where could she be? Was she sent away? Wherever she was sent, it would be a blessing, I thought.

"Where's Robin?" I asked, and Dr. Foreman's smile faded.

"Robin is defeating a very bad part of herself. She will be better tomorrow. Go on."

I left, went out, put on my shoes, and crossed the yard to the barracks, wondering if I had heard someone crying and if it was Robin. What horrible thing was being done to her? Could it be worse than being in one of the coffins?

As soon as I entered the barn, I stopped with surprise.

On my cot was a mattress, a pillow, and a blanket, and on the blanket was a pair of blue coveralls, the same white, short-sleeve shirt Mindy and Gia wore, and a pair of panties. I was being rewarded. I was pleased, of course, but at the same time I felt a dark sense of foreboding and guilt as I took off the coarse sack dress and the oversize diaper.

When Teal, Mindy, and Gia returned, they stopped and looked at me sitting on my cot and reading.

"Why did you get all that?" Teal asked.

I shrugged. "It was just here when I returned."

Mindy smiled coolly, her eyes small. "Sure it was. It just grew there."

"Leave her alone," Gia snapped. Mindy turned with surprise. "You're no angel. You have no right to judge her or any of us."

"I didn't say that I did."

"What does all that mean?" Teal asked. "Why are you arguing?"

"Around here, the fewer questions you ask, the better off you are," Gia told her. "Get your work done or you'll soon be where your friend Robin is."

"Where is she?" I asked quickly. "I think I heard her crying when I was with Dr. Foreman before. Is that where the Ice Room is? In that house."

"You didn't hear her crying," Gia insisted.

"I did."

She was quiet.

"If I didn't hear her crying, who did I hear crying?"

"Forget about it. You don't want to know," Gia told me.

"Is she in the Ice Room?"

Gia didn't reply. Instead, she turned to Teal and said, "If you want to do your friend some good, just keep your mouth shut."

"She's not my friend. We only met when we were brought here. We hardly know each other. I probably know just as much about you as I do her, or you," Teal said, nodding at Mindy, "or Phoebe."

"You're better off," Mindy said dryly, and went to her books. Gia did the same.

Teal walked slowly to her hard cot, her eyes on me. We were all like a bunch of alley cats, scratching and hissing at each other, I thought. It made me feel sick inside. If I followed Gia's advice, I would walk around with a head full of air. Teal looked like she was going to burst into tears again and have another tantrum. It wouldn't do anyone any good, least of all her.

"I can show you how to do the math assignment," I said. "Gia showed it to me earlier."

"I don't care. I'm not doing any of this," Teal said, and kicked her books.

Mindy and Gia looked up and then went back to their work.

A deep sense of dread passed through me.

Where was Robin? I wondered, looking at the doorway. Why wouldn't Gia talk about her? What was happening to her?

What would happen to Teal?

And then to me?

I worked until lights out. Teal went to sleep before, her back to me.

When I crawled under my blanket, I luxuriated in the softness of my mattress and pillow. My fatigue seemed to seep down through my legs and into the bed. I drifted into my first comfortable night's sleep in a long time, and I was so deeply asleep, I didn't hear anything around me. When I opened my eyes, I didn't resent the morning light as much as I had the day before. Mindy and Gia were just rising, too. I sat up and turned to Teal.

Cold shock began at the base of my stomach and shot up to my heart.

Her cot was empty. She was gone!

I turned to the others. "Where's Teal?"

They both looked as if first noticing she wasn't there themselves.

"Maybe she's so eager to get to work and start on the new vegetables, she got up and left before dawn," Mindy said.

I looked at Robin's empty bunk. "Why isn't Robin back?" I muttered. "What have they done to her?"

"Didn't you hear what Gia told Teal last night? You're better off not asking questions." Mindy smirked at me. "But you've already learned how to be better off."

"What's that supposed to mean?" I shouted at her. She turned her back on me, pulled on her shoes, and started for the door. "If you hadn't opened your big mouth, Robin wouldn't have gotten into trouble," I screamed.

Mindy turned slowly. "How did she get sent here if she wasn't in trouble?" she retorted, and walked out.

Gia looked at me. "Just get to work. It's the only way to get out of this place."

She left. I sat there fuming, but I wasn't sure if I was fuming at Mindy for being right about me or just fuming at myself for doing what I had done.

Had Teal run off? Was she out there in the desert, dying like Natani's squirrel? Surely, since I had told Dr. Foreman what Teal was thinking about doing, she wouldn't have let her do it.

I hurried out, hoping to find her beside Natani, planting cucumbers and carrots in the section of land he had irrigated. I saw Mindy and Gia joining him, but no sign of Teal or Robin. M'Lady One, looking like she was dragging herself out and about herself, came strolling toward me. She smiled when she drew closer. "Don't you look and feel better in those clothes?"

I didn't say anything.

She stopped in front of me. "You're a quick learner, Phoebe. That's good, and since you're my assignment, it helps me, too. Don't screw up and we'll both be happier people." Then she nodded at the planting. "Get to work."

"Where's Teal? Don't start with that permission to speak. Just tell me what happened to her," I demanded.

Her smile faded. "Maybe you're not so smart after all." She started to turn away and I reached out and touched her arm.

"Did she run off? Does Dr. Foreman know? Is she sending someone out there to bring her back?"

She spun on me and poked me hard with her thick, right forefinger in the chest between my breasts. It threw me off-balance and I fell back, sitting on my rear and looking up at her. My chest smarted. She might as well have poked me with a pipe, I thought.

"Don't you ever touch me again, understand? Don't you put your paws on me, girl," she fired down at me. "No one touches me. The last one who touched me was a sorry rat."

She looked insane, beyond rage, like someone who had slipped into a second personality and was capable of great violence. It occurred to me that all the buddies were former Foreman wards, which meant each of them had done terrible enough things to cause them to be sent here. What were my buddy's crimes and sins? Was she really cured or was she still quite capable of whatever acts of savagery had brought her to Dr. Foreman's School for Girls?

I rose quickly and turned away from her, heading out to the field.

"Don't you dare touch me again, understand?" she screamed after me.

I kept walking, my shoulders hunched up. In my neighborhood in Atlanta, I had seen people under the influence of drugs and alcohol. I had seen hard kids practically brought up in the streets, but something in my buddy's eyes I had not seen. It was as dark as death.

I stopped next to Mindy and Gia and listened to Natani's instructions about how to plant the different vegetables, trying hard to keep my attention and concentrate. Every once in a while, I looked back at the house, but I didn't see my buddy or anyone else. Instead, I started to work and desperately worked at keeping myself from thinking about any of it.

Just after we finished our morning chores and were heading toward the house for breakfast, we saw a lot of dust down the dirt road and heard the van approaching. All three of us hesitated at the fountain and watched as the van pulled up. M'Lady Three stepped out of the van. A dark-skinned man was driving. He looked like an Indian, too. He stepped out and went to the rear. They opened the door and pulled out a stretcher. Teal was lying on it, her face looking swollen and red. I saw what looked like a large circle of red on her right calf, which also looked swollen. She was grimacing with pain and looked like she had screamed herself hoarse. She didn't open her eyes.

"What happened to her?" I cried, hurrying toward them.

"Get back," M'Lady Three ordered. They carried her toward a corner of the hacienda. The three of us watched until they disappeared. Then we heard the door open and looked up to see Dr. Foreman.

For a long moment, she and I fixed our gazes on each other like two combatants locked in an unrelenting grasp. Then she smiled.

"Breakfast, girls," she sang, turned, and went inside.

Mindy and Gia were looking at me. They knew what I had done. They knew why I was so shocked.

"Don't ask about Teal," Gia warned.

"Just keep giving Dr. Foreman what she wants and get out," Mindy added.

They both walked into the house. I stood there for a moment. If I could cry, I would, I thought.

But shock, fear, and exhaustion had stolen all my tears.

It made sense I was in the desert. Even my well of sorrow was dry.

My second shock came when I entered the dining room and found Robin sitting at the table. She was hunched over her plate eating and drinking ravenously. Her body trembled and she looked like she had been rolling around in a coal bin. Her hands, however, were clean. She looked up at me and quickly looked down at her food.

"Robin. What happened to you? How are you?" I asked.

Mindy and Gia paused in dishing themselves some scrambled eggs and looked at me, their eyes full of warning. I didn't care. I had to know.

Before I could say another word, however, M'Lady Two was at the door.

"Girls, Dr. Foreman wanted me to tell you that she wants you all to devote this afternoon to academic studies. This is actually a reward. We're easing the restriction on talking. You're free to speak to each other at all times in the barracks and on the grounds, but don't forget to excuse yourselves and thank each other."

My first thought was this confirmed for me that the barracks was bugged. Dr. Foreman wanted us talking now. She wanted to hear what we said and thought.

"You're to spend the day in your barracks doing your lessons and homework," M'Lady Two continued. "If you do all your work properly and you have a satisfying session, you will have free time after dinner."

"Free time? What can we do with free time here?" I asked.

"Breathe," she replied, and laughed.

After she left, I turned back to Robin, hoping she would tell me something about what had been done to her.

"Stop looking at me," she snapped. It took me by such surprise, I turned to Mindy and Gia.

They both looked at me with I-told-you-so expressions. I served myself some breakfast and ate with my eyes straight ahead. I couldn't remember ever feeling more alone and lost, more helpless than I felt at that moment.

Afterward, on our way back to the barracks, Gia stepped up beside me.

"Even though they're easing up on the no-talking restrictions, don't keep asking Robin about the Ice Room," she said. "She's been told it's forbidden to talk about it, and if she does, she can end up back there. Basically, she's ashamed of herself."

"Why would she be ashamed of herself?" What did Gia know?

"Because of what happened there and what she promised or said to get out."

"How do you know?"

Gia stopped. She didn't look at me. She just gazed ahead, her eyes growing small, dark. "Because I was there, too." Then she walked on, leaving me behind, staring after her.

I looked back at the house and thought about Teal. I really couldn't blame her for running off, but what was the point of Dr. Foreman forcing me to tell on her if she let her go off like that? Nothing made any sense to me. Nothing I did seemed to help. Whenever I thought things might be getting better, they were actually getting worse. I was afraid to make any more decisions. We could talk, but I was afraid to talk. What if I said the wrong things? What were the right things?

Standing there under the glaring sun, I felt suddenly like I couldn't move. Any direction I took, anything I said or did, would not help me. I was filled with a sense of dread and terror of any decision I might make. Even walking to the barracks seemed like it might be wrong.

Suddenly a cold wave of panic nailed my feet to the desert floor. I couldn't even swallow. My heart was pounding as if I had been running for miles, though. It was getting harder and harder to breathe. I was caught in some sort of invisible web. My arms and legs were stuck. I could almost see the spider approaching. I've got to do something, something . . .

I didn't realize I was being watched, and not by any of the buddies or Dr. Foreman. Natani stood so still and so quiet, I could have walked past him and not realized it. Finally, after looking at me for some time, I guess, he came forward, materializing out of thin air.

"The rabbit," he said, "grows so afraid, he cannot move. He trembles in place and the fox has a pleasing time of it. Your eyes are clouded with fear, daughter of the sun. Open them wider, look beyond. Go where the sun goes." He pointed to the western horizon. "See yourself outside and you will not tremble in your footsteps."

I looked where he pointed. See yourself outside? Yes, think about anyplace else but here. I thought of Atlanta, of being with my old friends, of laughter and freedom and the neon lights, the music, the noise. Envisioning it seemed to wash a cool relief over my body.

"See yourself outside," I muttered, driving the lesson home to my heart.

"Yes," he said, and put a turquoise stone in my hand. "Keep this close. It is a piece of the sky that fell many, many years ago and it will remind you to look up and see yourself outside." Then he walked off.

I turned the stone in my fingers, then looked up at the sky. Who knows, I thought, maybe it was a piece of the sky. I put it in my pocket and felt myself regain my strength. My breathing eased and I started across the yard again. When I stepped into the barn, I saw Robin was sitting with Mindy on her cot and working with her on the math assignment. Gia was nearby, her books opened.

"It's better for each of us if we work together," Gia said. "We can break up the assignments and each take something we're each good at."

"I'm not a great reader," I admitted.

"Well, we already know you're not great at math either. What are you good at?"

"Making excuses for not being good at anything," I replied, and Gia actually laughed. It was as if a thin wall of ice had shattered between us.

"Okay," she said. "I'll partner up with you. Come on, we'll start on the social studies assignment."

I picked up my book to join her, then noticed Robin's cot. It had a mattress on it, a pillow, and a blanket, and Robin was wearing the same coveralls and shirt.

"You were rewarded," I said excitedly. "How come?"

She looked at me with joyless eyes and then looked down at the math text.

"Let's just get this done," Gia said, urging me to drop the subject.

She didn't need to. Robin's quick, subdued looks were enough. I understood. Whatever she was being rewarded for was not something she was happy to describe. What terrible things had been done to Robin and what had she given Dr. Foreman as a result? Was it something about me, something I had said? I ran back whatever I could remember saying, drawing in my thoughts and words like a fisherman reeling in fish. Many things would have angered Dr. Foreman, I thought, but from the way Robin looked, she wouldn't tell me even if she wanted to tell me. She looked the way I had felt right after I had given up Teal. I felt sure I was not the only one who betrayed.

And more important, perhaps, was what Dr. Foreman had been after right from the beginning. She would find ways to turn us against each other until all each of us had was herself and Dr. Foreman. She was the spider I had envisioned out there. I and the others were trapped in her web now.

I quickly put my hand into my pocket to feel the stone.

Natani's words returned.

Think of the sky. See myself outside.

Yes, that would be my chant.

That was what would get me home, I thought, wherever home might be.

6

Group Therapy

Teal didn't return to the barracks for nearly four days. Every time I started to talk about her and wonder aloud what was happening to her, Gia came at me, telling me to stop asking and to mind my own business. I wanted to suggest that Teal was my business and should be hers, too. We should all be each other's business. Whom else did any of us have here? But neither Robin nor Mindy spoke up in support of me. They avoided my eyes, looked away, went about their work. Teal could be gone for good and none of them would have asked after her. It would be as if she had never existed, the same if I had never existed.

I began to wonder if Teal hadn't been sent away, maybe placed in a formal detention center or even a prison. I told myself she would be better off. We all would.

I mumbled this idea loud enough for Gia to hear, and finally she fixed her dark, steely eyes on me and said, "Don't ever believe Dr. Foreman when she threatens to send us back. No one gets sent back. Dr. Foreman does not fail, does not give up. If one way doesn't work for her, she tries another and another. You either change to her liking or . . ."

"Or what?" I quickly countered.

"Or you don't, but you don't leave unless it's on her terms."

"The buddies left."

"Did they?" Gia tossed back at me. "They're still here, aren't they?"

"Because they want to be."

She smiled at me as though I were a child.

"Well? Why else would they stay? What's here for them? Even if they enjoy torturing us, it's not enough. Don't they have boyfriends or want them?"

Gia was thoughtful for a moment. I could see that was something she had thought about, too.

"She has ways we don't even know exist," she said. "She has ways of changing your head. Don't try to understand the buddies, why they are like they are. I don't want to even think about it. I just think about . . ."

"About what, Gia?"

"Nothing," she said quickly. "I don't think about anything anymore."

"Why not?"

"Why not? It's like being in a prison cell with a window that looks out on the most beautiful place, a place you can't go to, but only see from behind bars. That's why. Do you understand me? Do you?" she shouted.

I just stared at her.

"You and your damn questions. Making us think," she said, making it sound as if I were responsible for all her pain. Before I could protest, she walked away quickly.

Finally, one night after dinner, we returned and Teal was there, lying on her cot, which now, like the rest of ours, had a mattress, a pillow, and a blanket. She was in what I called our school uniform, too, only her hair, her hair had been cut down to where she was nearly bald, her beautiful hair was gone. She lay there with her eyes wide open, staring up at the ceiling and looking even more drained and in shock than Robin had when she had been released from the Ice Room.

"Teal!" I cried, and hurried to her side. "How are you? What did she do to you?"

The others watched and listened but remained behind me.

"Are you okay? What happened to you? Where have you been all this time? What happened to your hair?"

She didn't answer for so long, I thought she wasn't going to say anything, but then she turned her head slowly and looked at me with eyes so cold and empty, they put a chill in my heart.

"My hair," she said, "escaped."

"What?"

"That's how we do it." She propped herself up on her elbows so she could look past me at the others. She looked like the idea was exciting to her. "We escape in pieces. Maybe my teeth will be next or my ears. Right, Gia? Mindy? That's how it's done, isn't it?"

Neither replied. They ignored her and went to their own bunks.

"What are you talking about? You're not making any sense. Did you get far? What did you do?"

She stared at them a moment longer, then turned to me, her eyes as angry and dark as Gia's. "I would have made it. I know I would have made it. I saw light in the distance, but I got stung by a scorpion."

"A scorpion!" I stepped back as if it were still there and could sting me as well.

"That's what they said. It made me pretty sick and it hurt so much, I thought I would die. My leg swelled up. All I did was stop to rest awhile and I guess I stopped right beside one, but you don't have to go out there to find them. They're here, too, you know." She looked around the barn as if that information made her happy. "You could get stung just as easily sleeping in this filthy barn."

I looked at Gia and Mindy. They continued to undress and get themselves ready for bed.

"That's not true, is it?" I asked.

"Of course it's true," Mindy replied.

"Gia?" I asked.

She paused and thought a moment before turning to me. "You know what a minefield is? How they put bombs in the ground to blow up enemy soldiers who might step on the wrong spot?"

"Yes, so?"

"Well, that's what it's like being here. You're always walking through a minefield. If it's not one thing, it's another, and Dr. Foreman doesn't do much to make it any safer for us either. In fact, she plants the mines."

"You don't mean she puts things in here, do you?"

"What do you think?"

"That's crazy. That's . . . we could be killed or something."

"Hello. Welcome to your nightmare," Gia said, smiling.

She seemed to take such pleasure in telling me all these horrible things.

"Yeah, well, if it can happen to me, it can happen to you," I threw back at her.

She shrugged. "It's already happened to me."

"What? What's that supposed to mean? What are you saying, Gia?"

She ignored me. Robin got into bed without speaking and Teal continued to stare up at the ceiling.

"Well, it hasn't happened to me!" I screamed.

The door opened. M'Lady Three was standing there.

"What's going on in here?"

My heart was pounding. I half expected either Mindy or Gia would point a finger at me to earn more of those precious positive merit points, but this time no one spoke.

"You had better get some rest, my little princesses," M'Lady Three said. "You'll need it. Tomorrow, we're whitewashing the cow barn and it will take all day."

She closed the door and the lights went out. All I could think of now was something creepy crawling over me. I felt as if I were back in my Atlanta apartment, waiting to feel a rat scurry over my feet.

"They can't do this to us," I muttered. I was thinking aloud. "If we die, they'll be responsible. They'll get into trouble."

"No, they won't. They'll just make up a good story," I heard Mindy mumble. "I'm sure she's done it before. I'm sure she's made up a whopper about Posy."

"Who? What did you say?"

"Shut up and go to sleep," Gia commanded sharply. "Keep your mouth shut, Mindy."

"What did she say? Who's Posy? Gia?"

"If you don't shut up, we'll all get into trouble and it's going to be hard enough tomorrow. You heard her. Believe me, we know what it's like when they pile it on," Gia said.

"I won't let her cut my hair like that," I vowed.

"Of course not," Mindy said, laughter in her voice. "Teal didn't let her either. You heard her. Her hair ran off."

"Maybe that's what happens when you get bitten by a scorpion. Your hair falls off," Robin offered, and the two of them laughed.

"I'll give you a maybe," Mindy said, propping herself up on her elbows. "Maybe Teal wasn't stung by accident."

"What?"

"Maybe someone followed Teal and when she lay down to rest . . ."

"I'm warning you, Mindy," Gia said.

"Okay, okay. Good night, ladies," Mindy sang.

That couldn't be true, I thought, could it? Dr. Foreman had her stung by a scorpion to teach her a lesson?

I lay there with my eyes open, listening. Was it possible to hear something crawling over the straw-covered floor? After a few moments, I could hear Teal's breathing get low and regular. Robin whimpered and then went silent. Maybe it was my imagination, but I thought I heard someone crying just as I had when I was with Dr. Foreman in the house.

This time I knew it wasn't my imagination. I did hear someone crying.

It was me.

I cried myself to sleep just as I used to when I was a little girl and no one came to my bedside when I had nightmares or fears. It made me think I was going backward, getting younger and younger. One morning I would wake up in here and I would be an infant.

I had no idea how or when I fell asleep, but I did. The morning light was like an alarm bell. Everyone groaned and rose before M'Lady Two opened the door to announce we were to line up outside like troops. When we dressed and stepped into the unrelenting sunshine, we were made to recite our prayer as usual, then told to march over to the barn for our individual assignments for whitewashing the cow barn. Each of us would be responsible for a specific section. Cans of paint were open and ready with the rollers. Ladders had been set up as well.

"Try not to make a mess of things," M'Lady Three said. "Breakfast in two hours. Get started."

We began our halfhearted attack on the sides of the barn. Teal was the first to wail complaints. She splattered herself with some paint and moaned about its getting into what was left of her hair. The mess wasn't what made it terrible, however. I think they deliberately chose to have us begin on the east side of the barn. That way the rising sun would be sending its hot darts into us the whole time. In a matter of minutes, everyone looked drained and defeated; even Mindy and Gia were feeling it more than usual. Mindy trembled so badly on her ladder, it rattled.

At one point she turned and looked at Robin, Teal, and me angrily. The fury in her face made me uneasy. I couldn't stand being stared at so hatefully.

"What is your problem, Mindy?" I asked.

"I'll tell you my problem. They're only making us do this because of you three and the stupid things you do. Robin starts a fight with me and Teal tries to run off. You break plates, talk back. I know Dr. Foreman believes we should all share the punishment. I know how she thinks. It applies to everyone, anyone, no matter who she is and what she has or has not done. So thanks."

"Stop it," Gia told her. "You know you're not going to make it any better for any of us by bitching. No one here knows it better than you, Mindy."

Mindy was quiet again, but she didn't like it. Her strokes were harder, her anger pouring down through her arm.

"I don't care how you think," Teal told Mindy. "Or you, Gia. I'm not sorry I ran off. I almost made it."

"Oh, really. You almost made it, Teal? Made it to what?" Gia asked.

"To a phone. My father would have come for me."

"Your father?" Mindy said, laughing. "I heard your story. Your father put you here, just like mine put me here."

Teal looked at me and Robin and then turned back to Mindy. "Your father did this to you also?"

"Just work and shut up," Mindy said. "You've made enough trouble for us."

"What did you do? What's the big secret, Mindy? You know everything we did, why we're here." Teal turned to Gia. "What did she do that's so much worse than what you did or what I did?"

Gia paused and looked at Mindy as if she had never considered it from that viewpoint before.

"Yes, Mindy, what did you do?" she teased.

"Shut up, Gia. Just keep your mouth shut."

"She did a lot of things with a lot of boys."

"Shut up, I said." Mindy's anger made her wobble again on her ladder.

"And a baby."

"Shut up!" she screamed so hard and so loudly, her face turned crimson.

We heard a door slam and M'Lady Two came out of the house. Gia turned quickly and began working again. We all did the same. Mindy, still fuming, stared needles and pins at Gia and then shot them at us.

"What's going on here? More talk than work? Well? You should have had more done by now, Teal."

"I'm still weak and tired from being sick. I shouldn't have to do this."

"You'll be sicker yet if you don't do your fair share," M'Lady Two warned. "I want to see you all double what you've done by the time I return, understand? Otherwise, plans for the day might be changed, radically changed, and you won't like it, believe me."

She stood there watching us for a moment, then walked back to the house.

"Thanks, Gia," Mindy muttered.

Gia said nothing. None of us did. Her words had left our imaginations to run loose and I could see it on the faces of Teal and Robin; they weren't just running loose, they were galloping through every possible horrifying scenario involving a baby.

Finally, we were told to put everything aside to go to breakfast. No one even attempted to speak to anyone else. Mindy was sullen and Gia avoided her bee-stinging eyes. Robin, Teal, and I said nothing to each other or either of them. The air about us felt as if it were laced with

TNT. Someone rubbing her hands together too vigorously could set off an explosion.

We washed up and entered the house. At the table everyone mumbled the forced thank-yous to everyone else, then we ate like five mutes. Silverware clanked against bowls and dishes. I could hear everyone chewing, swallowing, drinking, each of us keeping her eyes forward, looking into her own dark and troubled thoughts.

"Good morning, girls," Dr. Foreman cried from the dining room doorway. She practically sang it. "What a glorious day and I see you've all gotten off to a productive start. How wonderful. This afternoon, around noon, I want you all showered, cleaned up, and brought back here for some refreshment, after which we will hold one of my famous group sessions. Mindy and Gia are well acquainted with them, aren't you, girls?"

"Yes, Doctor," Gia said quickly. Mindy nodded. Both of them looked so frightened, it frightened me.

"Good. Well eat up, girls, waste not, want not." Then Dr. Foreman was gone as quickly as she had appeared.

Mindy and Gia looked after her and then looked at each other, the air between them still heavy and flammable. Gia began to eat again.

"Why is she making us part of their group session, Gia?"

"How would I know?"

"We're not going to get through this," Mindy muttered. "We're never going home."

"Shut up," Gia told her.

"She's going to stop us."

"Quiet, Mindy."

"She doesn't want anyone to be free. Not since Posy. You know I'm right, Gia. You've said it yourself many times."

"Stop it!" Gia snapped.

M'Lady One appeared in the doorway. Both girls quickly returned to eating.

My buddy glared at them for a long moment. "Something wrong?" she asked, her eyes small with suspicion. "Someone planning something nasty?"

No one responded.

"All right, let's get moving, girls. You have a lot to accomplish by noon. Robin and Teal, you clear the dishes and wash down the table. The rest of you, start back to the barn and your work."

Gia gulped the rest of her juice and stuffed another piece of bread into her mouth as she stood up. I followed her and Mindy out to put on our shoes and start for the barn. When M'Lady One was far enough away, I stepped up beside Mindy and whispered, "Who was Posy?"

She looked at me as if she was going to reply but then glanced at Gia and walked faster, pulling away from me and closer to M'Lady One. Gia dropped back.

"Stop asking questions or you will be sorrier than you could ever think possible, and it might not be only because of what they do to you," she threatened sharply.

We returned to work. From time to time, I saw Natani pause in his own work and look our way. I thought I saw him smile at me, but it was hard to tell as the sun rose higher in the sky and made even the dirt gleam. At noon we were told to stop, clean up in the shower, and return to the house. We had just about completed the east wall of the barn. Everyone had spots of paint on her face, hands, and arms, as well as in her hair. Teal was the most depressed about it.

"I used to go to a beauty parlor once a week," she said, running her fingers through her stubs.

"Lucky you," Gia said.

"At least I had a reason to go."

"Keep your mouths shut," M'Lady Two called. "Just walk to the showers."

We were given soap, brushes, and towels and made to scrub until every spot of paint was off our bodies. Then we dressed and started for the house.

At the house we were treated to wonderful ice-cold lemonade. No one was ashamed to show how much she enjoyed it and coveted every drop. After the cold shower and this refreshment, I did feel better.

"Is it going to get easier?" I asked Mindy.

She tilted her head. "What?" She batted her eyelashes. "What was your question?"

"Are things going to get better now?" It seemed like a fair question to ask. We had all been through fire, punished, beaten down to where we were all obedient.

"Better?" She smiled. "Things are only going to get worse," she predicted with a smile that was so cold, I thought her teeth had turned to stone.

We were marched into Dr. Foreman's office and told to sit. Gia and Mindy kept looking at each other as if they knew exactly what was coming and it wasn't good. Teal had her head back, her eyes closed, and Robin sat staring forward, her eyes like sockets without bulbs.

Dr. Foreman entered smiling warmly and sat in her chair with a notebook in her hand. For a long beat of silence, she just sat there looking at all of us like a proud parent might contemplate her children. Was I right in thinking that we had reached a point where she was pleased?

"Okay, girls," she began, "we can finally get down to why you've all been sent here. We can finally go after your recuperation and get you all set on the right road. Everyone here has done something to lead me to believe she can change, she can improve, but you all have a ways to go yet, and now that you have spent quality time together and gotten to know each other better . . ."

I was expecting her to compliment us about it, but she surprised me when she continued, "You all know who among you has the least chance of achieving immediate success. Unfortunately, whoever that is will only hold the rest of you back." She panned us slowly, her eyes pausing on each of our faces, then moving on to the next and the next, spending a little more time on mine. "You've all got to think of what's best for everyone and not for yourself. That's the only way to help yourself.

"Now, the most important thing to achieve is honesty. I'm sure you'll all agree. Honesty requires trust, and you girls are the best to decide who among you can and cannot be trusted. Am I right?"

There was a deep thump in my chest. In the back of my mind I wondered if she would tell everyone how I had betrayed Teal, use me as an example.

"I want you all here to hear each other because I do not like it when one girl goes behind someone else's back. That's deceit. We've all got to face the blunt truth about ourselves. I know how hard this is to do. For most of you, if not all of you, deception, dishonesty, conniving, have been the order of the day. How refreshing it will finally be for you to throw all that off and be truthful." She smiled as if she were offering us a party.

She rose, scooped up five pencils from the top of her desk, and handed each of us one. Then she gave each of us a piece of paper.

"Let's begin, however, with a secret vote. That's the best way to break the ice."

I glanced at Mindy. She looked absolutely terrified.

Gia looked angry. "We've done this before, Dr. Foreman. Can't we be excused?"

Dr. Foreman's face hardened even though she kept the smile on her lips. "Yes, Gia, you have done something similar before, but not satisfactorily. Not yet. And besides"—Dr. Foreman's eyes gleamed as she nodded at Robin, Teal, and me—"you have new companions now. Things can't be the same. Every situation is different and you've got to be able to adjust to new situations all the time, adjust to different personalities. That's what it's going to be like out there, right?"

Gia looked like she was going to say something more, but then stopped and looked down.

"Right?" Dr. Foreman insisted.

Gia looked up. "Yes."

"Good. All right. Now let's begin. I want you each to write the name of the girl you think will take the longest to improve and leave the school."

I was stunned. Vote on who among us was the worst?

"What if we don't know enough yet about everyone else?" I asked.

"Oh, I think you do by now."

"We weren't permitted to speak to each other much and . . ."

"You've seen and spoken to each other enough to make the decision I expect," Dr. Foreman said sharply. Then she smiled. "If you can't choose, then write your own name down, and of course write your own name if you believe you are the weakest one."

Was this really some kind of a serious vote? What would happen to the girl who won this vote? Would she be treated more harshly? Isolated from the rest of us? I looked at everyone else. No one was going to write her own name. Why should I write mine?

"But . . ."

"Quickly. We have a lot to do and you're all going to be sent back to the barracks afterward to complete your schoolwork. There are due dates for all your assignments, remember, tomorrow being one."

I looked at the others. Robin was writing and so was Teal. Mindy stared down at the floor like she was giving it all real thought, but Gia wrote a name quickly on her paper. Whom was I to choose? There was no doubt in my mind. It would be Teal because she was the one who whined the most and she had tried to run away. I felt so guilty about having betrayed her, but from the way Dr. Foreman was looking at me, those eyes of hers so full of awareness, I was afraid if I didn't write Teal's name, she would know I wasn't being honest.

"Fold your papers and hand them to me."

We did so and Dr. Foreman sat with them all in her lap.

"Okay, let's begin." She opened the first paper. "Teal," she read. She looked at Teal, who glanced at all of us and then looked away with fear.

Dr. Foreman unfolded another. "Teal."

The third was the same.

Opening the fourth, she said, "Teal."

Then she opened the fifth and smiled. "Robin? I guess we can safely conclude you wrote Robin, Teal."

Teal looked terrified and shook her head.

"I don't imagine Robin would have written her own name, and you wouldn't have written yours, dear. There's no point in denying it now. Instead, we'll ask you to tell us why you think Robin is the weakest in the group. You seem to be the only one who thinks so." She still made it all sound so harmless and friendly.

Teal looked at Robin, who was glaring at her hatefully now. She glanced toward me as well, and I thought from the way she looked at me that she had expected I would have written Robin's name and not hers.

"She . . ."

"Yes? We're all ears. Go on, Teal."

"She hates her own mother. She couldn't care less if she goes home or not," Teal offered weakly.

"Oh, and you just love your parents, especially your father, who you said doesn't love you. She stole money from her own father," Robin reminded us. "That's why he sent her here. They can't stand each other."

"That's not the whole reason why and you know it," Teal countered. "Anyway, you're always going to get into trouble because you're stupid. You let a boy talk you into being part of an armed robbery. That's a serious crime."

"Oh, I'm stupid? You're the one who runs off into the desert not knowing where she's going or anything, and I'm stupid. Besides, everyone else voted for you, didn't they? I'm not the only one who doesn't trust you."

"That's true, Teal," Dr. Foreman said. "Everyone else did vote you as the weakest in the group. Why do you think that is?" she asked as if she really didn't know the answer.

Teal opened and closed her mouth. She looked like a deer caught in the headlights of a car.

"Well? Think, my dear. I need to know what you think," Dr. Foreman said.

"I don't know. They're all jealous of me, maybe," Teal muttered.

"Jealous of you?" Robin said, and laughed. She looked at me, her eyes asking me why I wasn't speaking up. Gia and Mindy were both looking straight ahead, clearly showing that they wanted to be somewhere else, anywhere but here.

"Well, let's get some opinions about that," Dr. Foreman said. "Mindy, are you jealous of Teal? Is that why you voted for her?"

"You know that's not true, Dr. Foreman."

"I know it's not true, but how would anyone else, Mindy? Go on, tell them why you're not jealous of Teal."

"I'm not." She looked at Gia.

"Gia's not going to speak for you, Mindy. You speak for yourself," Dr. Foreman ordered.

"My family is probably as wealthy as hers, but I'm not a selfish brat, and I don't think she's prettier than I am. She's weak and complains and moans all the time. She's spoiled silly and can't stand any discomfort. I've seen her tantrums. That's why I picked her," Mindy exclaimed, the words rushing out of her like someone finally giving up a secret.

Dr. Foreman nodded, satisfied, and then looked at me.

"Why did you choose Teal, Phoebe?"

"She tried to run away," I replied quickly, hoping she wouldn't make me say anything else or ask me anything else.

"I would have thought that showed strength, determination, courage," Dr. Foreman said. Robin's eyebrows lifted with surprise. "Wouldn't you, Phoebe?"

"Well, no, not if you're doing something impossible. I mean, I told her what Natani had said. I told her how easy it is to die out there and she still went."

"At least I tried to do something for myself. I didn't just whine and complain like they do," Teal said.

"Is that what they do?"

"Yes. And don't say you don't, Robin. She was the one who got into a fight, wasn't she?" Teal accused. "She thinks Mindy is your spy," she revealed, snapping her lips shut as soon as she had.

A heavy silence fell over us for a moment.

"Oh?" Dr. Foreman asked.

Robin seemed to wilt in her chair when Dr. Foreman turned toward her. She shook her head.

"Is that what you thought, Robin? Mindy here was my spy, someone I planted in the barracks?"

"No, I mean . . ." She looked toward me for some help, but I looked away.

With a look of great patience, Dr. Foreman turned to Mindy, who was smiling gleefully at Robin's discomfort.

"Why would Robin think you were my spy, Mindy?"

Mindy's smile wilted. "I don't know," she muttered.

"Well, you said something that gave them this ridiculous idea, didn't you? What sort of things were you telling them?"

"I didn't tell them anything," she cried defensively. Then she pointed at me. "Phoebe was telling them that you had microphones secretly placed all over the place."

"Microphones?" Dr. Foreman smiled. "You really believe that, Phoebe?"

"Sometimes it seems like it. Gia's always saying I shouldn't be asking questions."

"Oh. You didn't tell them I have microphones all over the place, did you, Gia?"

"No. She's exaggerating. She's just a big mouth and I was trying to tell her she would get herself and someone else, maybe all of us, into trouble if she didn't keep that mouth shut." Gia fixed her eyes angrily on me.

"So why didn't you write her name on the paper?" Dr. Foreman shot back at her like a prosecutor in a courtroom.

"I should have," Gia replied without hesitation, glaring at me. "I'd like to change my vote in fact, from Teal to Phoebe."

"Phoebe, what do you say to all this?"

"Gia's just being vicious and spiteful. I know she thinks Teal is the weakest."

"Maybe she's not. Maybe it was courageous to try to escape like that," Robin muttered like someone thinking aloud.

I spun on her. "You don't believe that. You're just trying to kiss up."

"Don't tell me what I believe and what I don't believe, and I don't kiss up." Robin smiled at me, her lips twisting toward the right corner of her mouth. "I'll tell you what I don't believe. I don't believe you when you say you only hurt that boy with a statue. I bet you weren't really just defending yourself. I even think you killed him."

"What?"

"What are you saying, Robin?" Dr. Foreman asked.

"She told us she's here because she hit someone and supposedly put him in the hospital, but I'm beginning to wonder if that was all that really happened and if it really happened the way she said it did. She makes herself seem like such a goody-goody while the rest of us admit to doing bad things. That's not honest, is it, Dr. Foreman?"

All of them were looking at me.

"Is that true, girls? Does Phoebe make herself out to be a victim?"

"Yes," Teal said. "She does."

"What do you think, Mindy? Could Phoebe have been the right choice?"

"Maybe."

"Is that right? You're the one who's always warning everyone.

You're the one who might be the most afraid and weak here," I practically shouted at her. "You're the one who talks about this Posy."

I immediately felt the heat rise up in the room. Mindy sank in her chair and looked quickly at Dr. Foreman. Gia, who never looked afraid, suddenly had eyes filled with terror.

"Is that so, Mindy? You talk about Posy?" Dr. Foreman looked more at Gia, who quickly shifted her eyes away guiltily.

"No," Mindy said. "I don't."

"How would she know her name if you hadn't talked about her?" Dr. Foreman leaned toward her, grasping the pencil the way I have seen boys grasp switchblades.

"It . . . I didn't say anything. I just mentioned her."

"How did you mention her, Mindy? What did you say about her?"

"Nothing. Really," she wailed.

"I thought you weren't going to talk about Posy anymore," Dr. Foreman said to Gia.

"I don't!" she exclaimed. "She does!"

Dr. Foreman sat back. Mindy looked down. Gia was biting down hard on her lower lip, so hard I could feel the pain in my own. Silence seemed to fall like an iron curtain between us.

"Okay, girls," Dr. Foreman finally said. "These sessions are what I call purges. We get some of the hateful, spiteful, evil things out of our system. We don't have to be deceitful about any of it anymore. You all have much to do to repair yourselves, and this has been a beginning."

She held up the slips of paper. "We'll take this vote again sometime soon, perhaps, and it will be interesting to compare the results. For now, I want you all to return to the barracks and do your schoolwork." She stood and opened her office door.

We rose and filed out. The m'ladies were waiting for us in the hallway.

"Be sure they go directly to the barracks and get to their schoolwork," Dr. Foreman told them. Then she reached out and touched Mindy's shoulder. "I'm not angry at you, Mindy. I have great faith in you. I know you're going to continue to do well for me, for yourself, right?"

Mindy nodded, and Dr. Foreman lifted her hand from Mindy's shoulder.

No one said anything. We put on our shoes and in a silent parade marched across the yard. I heard Natani on his drum in his hogan. No one else seemed to notice or care. After we entered the barracks, the door was closed and we all went to our respective bunks.

The silence and heaviness in the air was so thick, I could have molded it into a dark plate to put into the kiln.

"Are we going to work together or what?" I asked.

No one said anything.

We might as well all have been in separate buildings, I thought. I started to read the chapter in science, but my eyes drifted off the page.

Mindy was staring at the floor. Suddenly, she started to tremble.

"Stop it," Gia told her.

She didn't. She grew worse, shaking harder.

"What's wrong with her?" Robin asked.

Teal stood up. Drool was running down the sides of Mindy's mouth and she was making a small but deep moan.

"Maybe you should call for someone," Teal said.

"No, leave her alone." Gia got up and seized Mindy's shoulders, shaking her. "Stop it, Mindy. Stop it. You know what will happen if you don't."

She shook her head. "It . . . doesn't . . . matter. She's mad at me, really mad at me this time," Mindy gasped. Her eyes were wide with such terror, it took my own breath away.

I turned to Gia, pleading with my eyes for her to do something.

She smirked and took a deep breath. "She's not mad at you, Mindy." Then Gia shouted at me, "Damn you. Did you have to tell about Posy?"

"I didn't tell anything. I don't even know who Posy is!" I cried. "She's the one who mentioned her. How were we supposed to know we shouldn't say the name?"

"Who is she?" Robin asked. "What's all the damn mystery about that y'all know and we don't?"

"Yes," Teal followed. "Who is she?"

"Why can't we mention her name?" I demanded more firmly.

Gia rose and looked at us while she kept a hand on Mindy's shoulder. Mindy continued to tremble and held on to her.

"Well?" I said. "Who was Posy?"

"She was Dr. Foreman's daughter," Gia said.

7

Posy's Story

"What do you mean, her daughter?" I asked. "Dr. Foreman is married? Where is her husband?"

"I don't know if she's married or not," Gia said.

"You don't know?"

"We don't know. Is there something wrong with your hearing?" she shouted at me.

"Well, how do you know she has a daughter?" I came right back at her.

"We know." Gia paused and looked at Mindy before turning back to us. "Whether she was married or not isn't the point. Posy wasn't her actual daughter. She was adopted and you don't necessarily have to be married to adopt someone."

"Adopted?"

"Adopted?" Mindy turned to mimic me. "Yes, adopted. You ever hear of it?"

"Mindy was adopted, too," Gia revealed.

"Oh. Well, I still don't understand it all. What was Dr. Foreman's daughter doing here?"

"What's good for the goose is good for the gander," Mindy sang.

"What?" Teal asked, stepping forward. "What are you saying?"

"It's what Posy used to say after Gia found out she was Dr. Foreman's daughter. Right, Gia? It means whatever was good to do to anyone else here was good to do to her. Right, Gia?"

I looked at Gia, who wasn't answering.

"So she was here as a . . . a student or whatever we are?" I asked.

"Yes, one of us lost souls," Gia said. "Posy was, shall we say, a bit of a disappointment to her brilliant mother."

"Sort of what all of us are to our respective mothers, real or otherwise," Mindy added, her words dripping out of the corners of her mouth.

"This is still very confusing," Robin said. "Why would Dr. Foreman have her own daughter, adopted or otherwise, in this place?"

"You are thick," Gia said sharply.

I saw Robin's face show crimson, even through her now deep tan. "I'm thick?" She started toward Gia, her hands clenched into fists. "You want to see how thick I am?"

"Stop it!" I cried at Robin. "Look, I'm not as smart as you are, Gia, but I can see that ripping us apart is what Dr. Foreman wants."

Gia relaxed her shoulders and looked at me and then at Mindy. Then she sat on her cot.

"Probably," she admitted.

"Why?" Teal asked. The three of us were around Gia and Mindy now.

"I don't know everything either, but I know she doesn't want us to be strong, and if we all got along and protected each other, it would be us against her."

"Exactly," I said. Gia looked up at me. "She had us tearing each other apart pretty good in there. It's exactly what policemen like to do when they arrest you and start to question you. They get you fighting among yourselves and pretty soon someone gives someone else away and it all falls apart."

"How come you know so much about all that? How often have you been arrested?" Mindy asked me, her face scrunched up with both disgust and curiosity.

"Enough," I said.

"Where is this Posy now?" Teal asked, still thinking about her. "And what kind of a name is Posy? I can't see Dr. Foreman naming a daughter Posy, can you?" she asked me. "I would have expected something more like Hortense."

"Posy named herself Posy, I think," Mindy said. "Isn't that what you said, Gia?"

"Yes. I can't remember Dr. Foreman calling her anything but 'young lady.' "

"You never met this Posy, Mindy?" I asked.

"No. She was already gone by the time I arrived. Gia told me all about her."

"Well, what happened to her? Where is she? Did she graduate or something?" Teal asked Gia.

Gia's laugh was thin and maddening. "Graduate? Yes, I guess it is a sort of graduation when someone gets out of here, if she gets out of here." She was silent a moment; then, after glancing at Mindy, she turned back to Teal and said, "I don't know."

"Why not?" Robin asked.

"We can't be sure, right, Gia?" Mindy said.

"What does that mean? Did Posy tell you something?" I asked Gia.

"It wouldn't have mattered if she had. When she was first brought here, she told Gia so many different things, it was obvious she was a habitual liar."

"Really?"

Gia nodded. "For the longest time, I didn't know she had any relationship to Dr. Foreman at all, much less being her daughter. She never called her or referred to her as anything but 'Dr. Foreman,' and I never saw anything warm between them, anything even to suggest they had once lived in the same house."

"Tell them what she did say, Gia," Mindy urged.

Gia looked at her and then turned to us. "Posy would talk about her parents as if they were the most wonderful people. They had everything imaginable and they loved her and were just heartbroken over the fact that she was here. In the beginning I didn't know she was lying. She made it all sound believable. I mean, she had it down to the smallest details, the colors of her bedspread, the dolls her father had bought her, her secret magical place in their beautiful big home that she shared with an adorable little sister, I think she called Tamatha."

"Amazing," Teal muttered.

"All of it was her fantasy," Gia said. "Nothing more than her long wish list."

"Gia says she was a habitual liar or something. We're not even sure about the bad things she had done, exactly why she was here, right, Gia?"

Gia nodded. "Sometimes it seemed to me she was here only because she couldn't tell the truth."

"Well, then how do you know she was telling the truth when she told you she was Dr. Foreman's adopted daughter?" Teal questioned.

"She never actually told me she was," Gia said. "I told her and she finally admitted it."

"Tell them what she said then, Gia," Mindy urged. It was weird to me how she enjoyed hearing about it all so much, as if she really enjoyed reliving Gia's experience.

Gia laughed. "She said she didn't tell me because she didn't want me to think she was getting any special treatment. That was a good laugh. If anything, I was getting special treatment, not her, but she always had to have a rosy excuse for everything," Gia said bitterly. "Rosy lies, I should say."

"I don't get it," Robin said. "If she didn't tell you herself first and neither of them showed how they were related, how would you know?" She looked poised to hear Gia insult her again, but instead, Gia looked at Mindy, who shook her head.

"What difference will it make now if they know," Gia asked her.

"One of them is sure to betray you. You know that."

"I always thought she knew anyway, Mindy. Was I wrong?" Gia asked, her eyes small and fixed on Mindy.

"What's that supposed to mean?"

"You know what it means."

"No, I don't," Mindy said, looking around as if searching for a way out.

"Sure you don't," Gia said, twisting her lips.

"What's going on?" Teal asked me. "What are they talking about now?"

I shook my head. "What is going on, Gia?"

She thought for a long moment, then shrugged. "Oh, what difference does it make anymore?" she muttered. "It was my idea to do it. I'll admit to that. I was bored," she offered as a defense. "I wasn't here all that long, but it was obvious to me it was going to be a drag. The early nights, lights out, no television or radios or anything, just work and studies and those damn therapy sessions, those questions, prodding, making me think of things I didn't want to ever remember. On and on until . . ."

"Until what?"

"I was curious and, like I said, bored."

"So?" Teal asked, impatient. "You were bored. Big deal. A news flash. She was bored. What did you do about it?"

"I decided to spy on Posy and Dr. Foreman when Posy was in there alone."

"How could you do that?" I asked.

"I found a way. There's a basement to the house. The door is on the other side and it was opened late one afternoon when I had some free time. I just wandered down the steps and in, almost as a way to escape the sun and heat as anything else. I heard voices and followed the sounds down to my right. There's a floor grate in Dr. Foreman's office. As soon as I knew what it was and where I was, I ran out. I was terrified of being discovered listening in. I didn't even know who was in there with her."

"It couldn't have been me," Mindy said quickly.

"No, it wasn't Mindy because she wasn't here yet. I didn't tell her anything about Posy for a while after she had arrived."

"Almost a month after," Mindy moaned.

"I'm not exactly used to trusting people," Gia said.

"Wow," Robin said. "Imagine, putting your own daughter through all this."

"Your mother is putting you through it, isn't she?" Gia fired at her. She could be so mean and angry sometimes. It made me feel that if I brushed against her, she might explode and blow me up with her.

Robin was about to snap back at her, but hesitated, thought a moment, then relaxed her shoulders. "Yes, she is. Mother darling is doing exactly that."

"Well, then it shouldn't surprise you. It shouldn't surprise any of us. Dr. Foreman believes in everything she does to us. She has this grand plan, this collection of theories. Every one of us is another case study for her. I once glimpsed at some papers on her desk and saw it."

"Saw what?" I asked.

"She's writing about each of us all the time. We'll be collected in some book and she'll probably win some prize. And all at our expense!"

"Tell us more about Posy," I said, folding my legs and squatting on the floor like a little girl who had asked to be told a story.

"I didn't get to know her all that well. Like Mindy says, she was always lying to me anyway. She was here a little over a month or so. One day she arrived with Dr. Foreman when she returned from one of her periodic trips away from the ranch. I came in from work and found her sitting right there." Gia nodded at my bunk.

"She smiled at me and said, 'Hi, my name's Posy. Don't call me anything else, please.' You would never know she was sent here as any sort of punishment. Nothing bothered her. Everything was interesting to her. I got so I hated hearing the word. *Interesting*. 'Isn't this interesting?' 'Isn't that interesting?' "

"What did she look like?" Teal asked, sitting beside me.

"She wasn't much bigger than I am," Gia said. "I thought she was about twelve, but she swore she was sixteen, dark haired, pretty with soft brown eyes and a dimple in her right cheek. She liked to walk on her toes and said she was once taking ballet lessons."

"Another lie, no doubt," Mindy muttered.

"She swore it was true of course, like her swearing to anything meant anything," Gia said, "but I had no other way to determine anything about her, not even her age."

"Didn't you ask her why she was here? What she had done?" Robin asked.

"No."

"No?"

"I didn't have to ask. She told me right away. She said she was here because she had trouble following rules. She claimed she just forgot all the time. She made it sound so innocent."

"What rules?" I asked.

"Any rules. She said she just forgot and didn't mean to hurt anyone's feelings. She proved that by ignoring the rules here. She talked without permission when she first arrived and it did them no good to scream at her or punish her.

"She just looked at them with that same sweet smile on her face, making the buddies feel like they were the ones who were to be pitied.

"She never blamed anyone for anything no matter how cruel they were to her, including her monster of a mother."

"Did you try to get her to stop thinking like that?" Teal asked.

"Of course. I tried to get her to see how stupid she was being by forgiving them or understanding them or calling them interesting. She would just say, 'They can't help it. They just like me so much they can't help trying to help me.' For three days they wouldn't let her eat anything, and all she could say about that was she was a little too heavy anyway."

"It doesn't sound like she belonged here," I said. "Sounds like she belonged in some mental institution."

"Don't we all," Mindy muttered.

Everyone was silent, contemplating what she had said.

"Dr. Foreman believes she can change anyone. That's the point," Gia finally piped up. "Don't you get it yet? No behavior, not even mental illness, can't be changed or cured. She thinks we're all Skinner pigeons."

"Skinner pigeons? What's that?" Robin asked.

I looked at Teal to see if she knew. She shook her head and shrugged. "I wasn't exactly a good student," she said. "What is it, Gia?"

"Didn't anyone tell you guys anything about this place and Dr. Foreman before you were sent here?" she asked.

"Not much more than this is your last chance," Teal said, smirking.

"Same for me," I said.

"Me, too," Robin chimed.

"Dr. Foreman is a behavioral modification scientist. They believe they can change the way people act and think by using certain techniques like carrot and stick, positive and negative reinforcers. Do this and there's a reward; do that and there's a punishment. If it's repeated and repeated, it gets so carved into you, you behave accordingly."

"But why did you call us all Skinner pigeons?" I asked.

"This scientist, Skinner, is famous for getting people to believe in these things. He did it with pigeons in a box. If they pressed a lever, they got fed. They soon understood that if they did this, they were rewarded. If they didn't, they weren't. That's what Dr. Foreman means by her stupid reality checks. We get rewarded for doing what she wants us to do, and when we do something she doesn't . . . we suffer. That's reality. That's the way it is out there," Gia said, waving toward the door.

"Dr. Foreman," she concluded, "believes those theories apply to everything. She can change anyone. We're not here just to be good little girls. Just like she said the first day, we're here to be changed, completely and utterly remade."

"Posy had to be very frustrating for her," Robin said. "Here she was a so-called expert on all this and her own daughter was a problem."

"Exactly," Gia said. "She has success with strangers, like our buddies and like us. Her methods do work most of the time. You're not going to get into any fights so quickly now, are you, Robin? You don't want to go back to the Ice Room."

Robin looked at me and then looked down.

"And you, Teal. You going to run away again?" Gia taunted.

"Maybe."

"You won't. Anyway, the difference with Posy was no matter what they did to her, what negative reinforcement they applied, she smiled at them. And then she would go and make up a story about it like she had to clean the pigpen all by herself because we were too busy or she was good at it. They would just get angrier and angrier at her. She never let them make her face reality. You know she never had a mattress, pillow, and blanket the whole time she was here."

"How could she stand that so long?" Teal asked.

Gia shrugged. I began to wonder if she didn't admire Posy as much as she pitied her.

"She told me she was used to sleeping on hard surfaces. She liked to go camping, and mattresses and sheets and pillows made her itch and sneeze. I actually believed her for a while. She was really good at it, at telling tales. I can just imagine the stories she had people believing. It must have driven our Dr. Foreman bonkers.

"But . . . Natani liked her," Gia said wistfully. "He favored her, talked to her all the time, taught her stuff, like how to meditate and step out of pain. That's the way she put it. I know the good doctor wasn't happy about that and eventually told him to stay away from her."

"Why does he obey her, work for her?" Teal asked.

"His granddaughter was a drug addict. She managed to get her on the straight and narrow. At least, that's what I think," Gia said.

"It's true. He told me something similar," I said, "just not in as much detail."

"Whatever. He must owe her big time to put up with all this," Robin said.

"He doesn't see it that way," I told her.

"Then he really is a crazy Indian," Teal quipped.

"Well, how did Posy end up? I mean, why don't you know what happened to her?" I asked Gia.

"No one would talk about her. I quickly saw it was forbidden to mention her name. One morning she was just gone, and when she didn't return for days, I knew she was gone for good. At first I assumed she was sent home or somewhere else."

"So, then that's what happened," I said, shrugging. "What's the big mystery?" From the way Mindy and Gia glanced at each other, I saw they had other ideas. "What?"

"I'm sure I saw her from time to time, but only at night," Gia said.

"And then you stopped seeing her altogether, right, Gia?" Mindy said.

"You never saw her at night or otherwise?" Robin asked Mindy.

"Never."

"So, then she is gone," I concluded. They didn't look convinced. "Is there something else?"

"The one thing I think Posy needed more than anything was company, friends. She tried so hard to get us to be her friends. I could tell she was making up story after story about all the best friends she had. She often contradicted herself or forgot a name or a story," Gia explained.

"So?"

"So Gia thinks Dr. Foreman decided her best way to change her was to isolate her from people. She hated being alone most of all," Mindy said.

"So much so that she invented people to talk to, just like a little girl or little boy might."

"I often heard her talking to someone, and then if I asked her who she was talking to, she would say no one, but she would smile at the air as if someone invisible to me was standing there. It was weird, eerie. Sometimes, I got so I thought I saw someone standing there myself," Gia explained.

"Maybe you're just as crazy as she is," Robin told her.

Gia shrugged. "Maybe I am."

"So if Dr. Foreman wanted to keep her away from people, what did she do?" I asked.

"It's just a guess. We have no real proof of anything and we would never say it loud enough for anyone to hear it," Gia offered.

No one spoke for fear she would stop.

"That door I told you about? The one going down to the basement?"

"Yes?" I said.

"It has a lock on it now."

"Maybe she just didn't want you sneaking down there anymore," I said quickly.

"I thought that was it, too." Gia eyed Mindy. "Especially after she seemed to know I had been there."

"I never said anything!" Mindy exclaimed. Gia shot her a skeptical look. "I didn't. I swear!"

"Well, what changed your mind?" Teal asked her, ignoring Mindy.

"Occasionally, I've heard crying, coming from the basement," Gia said. "Mindy thinks she has as well, right, Mindy?"

"Well, I wasn't exactly sure about that," Mindy said cautiously.

"What are y'all saying?" Robin asked, looking like her heart had stopped. "Dr. Foreman is keeping her daughter in the basement, like a prisoner in solitary confinement?"

"Maybe," Gia said.

"To this day?" I asked.

"What are we if not prisoners? But don't ever say it or suggest it in front of one of the buddies. Actually, never mention this again ever."

"How long has it been since you stopped seeing her, even at night?" I questioned.

"About a week or so before Mindy arrived," Gia said. "That's about four months, right?"

Mindy nodded.

I turned to Robin. "Locked in a basement to be kept away from people for more than four months? That would be worse than the Ice Room, wouldn't it?"

"No," Robin said.

"Why not?"

She stared at me.

"Because you're not put into the Ice Room," Gia answered for her. "The Ice Room is put into you."

"Put into you?" I looked at Robin. She was nodding. "I don't understand."

"Leave it that way, Phoebe. Sometimes, it's good here to not understand. You're better off," Robin said.

But I was a moth drawn to fire. I couldn't stop thinking about it.

Like some fatalist who knew she was headed for disaster no matter what road she took, I had no doubt in my mind that I would understand what they meant someday.

"Since Natani favored her, maybe he knows something. Have you ever asked him?" I inquired.

Gia raised her eyebrows. "Have you ever asked Natani a question about anything yet?"

"Yes."

"So you know how he answers. He doesn't give straight answers. Instead, he tells you some Indian folk tale about animals and you're supposed to get the point."

"Maybe that's his way to avoid reality," Mindy suggested.

"Or maybe it's his way not to," I said.

No one spoke again for a long moment.

"Let's do our homework. At least it's something to do and it keeps her from blaming us for something else," Gia said in a tired voice.

Everyone returned to the books and we were soon working together, each of us every once in a while pausing to think about that locked basement door. I know that's what was on their minds. It was on mine and I could see the fear, like some sheet of thin ice sliding over their eyes.

Of all the things they told us about Posy, the story about her inventing friends and speaking to invisible people lingered in my mind more than anything else for some reason. In the working silence, our subdued voices, the turning of pages, I could imagine a sweet, petite girl like Posy sitting beside us, cheering us up with her unyielding smile, her vision of everything through rose-colored glasses, and her stories, her fantasies. Who cared if they were true or not? They gave us all hope and made us feel better about ourselves.

Then she was plucked from our midst, stolen away because she helped us resist. Even though we had never met her, hearing about her like this put her into all our minds. I could sense it, and despite Gia's and Mindy's attempts to forget her, she was still here with them as well. In the end, hearing about her, listening to Gia's obvious affection for her and fear about what might have happened or be happening to her, appeared to mend the rift among us. Just a little while ago, we were at each other's throat in that room with Dr. Foreman. Now we sensed that we really didn't have anyone else but each other. Posy, even without Robin, Teal, and me ever having met her, gave us that, I thought. It was truly as if an invisible person stood with us, comforted us.

After we completed our work, we were permitted some free time before dinner. M'Lady Two took our homework and test papers and in a threatening tone told us she was taking it all to Dr. Foreman, who would grade everything herself. Failure, we were to remember, meant demerits. No one said anything, but I could hear the same thoughts in a chorus. Piling threat after threat on us, waving fingers and sentencing us repeatedly to hard labor, lost its impact when it was done so often and so much. What's new? I thought, and so did the others. M'Lady Two must have remembered herself at our stage. I could see it in the disappointment she expressed in her smirk when we didn't look like we were shaking in our shoes.

"Don't go anywhere you're not supposed to go," she warned, and left.

Where could we go? I thought. There were some shady places, and the breeze this late afternoon didn't feel as if it had been born in a furnace. Mindy, Gia, and Teal sat on what little grass there was under a tree. Robin and I went to look at the horses. We were told that it wouldn't be long before we would be brushing them down, cleaning their stalls, and feeding them, too. One of them, which Robin identified as a dark brown stallion, looked like he was dreaming of jumping the corral and galloping off toward those mountains in the distance.

"We had two horses on my grandfather's farm," Robin said. "He called them Buck and Babe. They weren't really riding horses, but when I was little, he would put me on either one and, holding the reins, lead me about. It was practically the only fun I had on that farm and one of the few times he acted like a real grandfather instead of a soldier in the army of God or something. I remember that sometimes I would catch him looking at me as if he expected to see Satan's face emerging out of mine. He expected me to do bad things. After all, I was mother darling's daughter. I guess he's happy now that he was right. It probably has made him even more of a fanatic. I pity my grandmother."

"What would happen if we got on the backs of some horses and rode out of here? You think we could ride to somewhere?"

"Horses aren't camels," Robin said. "They need water, too, and we wouldn't know which way to go."

"We're so damn trapped," I muttered. "Maybe no better off than Posy if she is in that basement." I glanced at the hacienda. The very thought of being a prisoner in the darkness below for so long put a chill through me, even in this heat.

Natani emerged from the barn, saw us, but kept walking toward a water trough. Using a hose, he filled it. I glanced at Robin and then approached him.

"Hello, Natani," I said. He nodded. "I bet you have seen many girls like us come and go."

He nodded again, turned off the water, and began to wrap the hose neatly around its holder.

"Are there any other girls here now?" I asked, eyeing Robin. "Besides the five of us, I mean?"

He didn't answer. He tightened the faucet, then stood and looked out at the horses, who had lifted their heads and started toward the water trough.

"I see only what I see. You must see only what you see, too," he finally replied, and went back into the barn.

"What's that mean? I see only what I see?" Robin asked.

"I think he's afraid to say anything," I said, nodding. I looked back at the house. "I don't know about you, but I'd like to find out if she's locked up down there."

"What for?" Robin folded her arms under her breasts. "What could we do about it anyway? We can't do anything for ourselves, much less for someone else. Forget about it. That's what he meant when he said see only what you see. Don't go looking for things you can't see. He didn't live as long as he's lived poking his nose into someone else's business." She started away to join the other girls.

I watched the horses drinking a moment, then followed Robin. Gia looked up when I sat. I could see Robin had told her I had spoken to Natani.

"You're not playing with fire," Gia said. "You're playing with TNT and I'm telling you now, we're not going to get blown up with you."

"Oh, let's stop talking about her. Let's just relax," Teal said.

It was difficult to let ourselves relax. I could see everyone had nerves as taut as tight guitar strings. The breeze, playing through us, sounded the same high-pitched note. Gia lay with her eyes closed. Teal stared at the horizon, dreaming of floating out there, I'm sure. Robin had her head down, and Mindy played with blades of grass like a little girl, forming shapes. No one spoke. A door slammed and we all looked toward the house. The three buddies laughed at something, then got into the van and started away.

"Where are they going?" I asked.

"Wherever it is," Teal said with some excitement seeping into her voice, "it's close enough for them to get there and back quickly enough. I knew there was someplace. I knew I wasn't imagining those lights."

"Forget it," Gia said.

"Why?" Teal asked.

"It's nothing. It's an Indian trading post off the reservation. They can get magazines, candy, cigarettes, but not much else. There's nothing to do there and it's miles and miles this side of nowhere. This is the Mojave Desert."

"They have more than cigarettes," Mindy said, her lips twisting.

"How do you know?" I asked.

She didn't reply.

"Gia?"

"We know. We heard them talking about it."

I stared at her and she looked away. "How did you hear them talking about it, Gia? Was that something you heard when you were in the basement?"

"No."

"Then how?"

"We just heard."

Mindy laughed and Gia threw her an angry look. She smiled and shook her head.

"What else haven't you told us?" Robin asked.

"Nothing."

"Oh, tell them," Mindy said.

"So now you want me to talk, is that it, Mindy? You're no longer worried about being betrayed?"

"It doesn't matter anymore, Gia. What else can they do to us that they haven't already done?"

"They'll think of something." After a moment Gia turned back to me. "One night, we went spying on them. We went around the rear of the hacienda and climbed up on the lower roof. We could look into their windows. We just wanted to see how well they lived, how nice their bedrooms were compared to our barn."

"And?"

"We saw them partying."

Mindy laughed. "Partying?"

"That's what it was," Gia snapped. "They had some weed. Probably got it from some Indian or something. They were laughing and enjoying themselves."

"And they had a magazine with pictures of naked men."

"You're kidding!" Teal said, coming to life.

"Does Dr. Foreman know?" Robin asked.

"What do you think?" Gia replied.

"You could tell on them," Teal said quickly. "Or threaten to tell on them."

"Oh, that would be terrific. Get them in trouble and that way they won't be as hard on us," Gia mocked.

"Well, I just thought . . . what do you think, Phoebe?"

"I think I'd like to make friends with them and be invited to their bedrooms," I quipped, and held my serious expression just long enough for them all to think I wasn't kidding. Then Gia laughed and the rest of them joined her.

We were all quiet again.

Teal stared down the gravel road. "I don't care if it only goes to an Indian store. It goes somewhere," she said in a loud whisper.

None of us disagreed. The shadows grew longer as the sun slid down toward the mountain. Everything that lived and spent its time in the daylight here surely gave thanks for the mountains, I thought. Funny, I realized, how I had never once thought to be grateful for anything in nature.

Maybe I was not grateful for anything at all.

Maybe that was why I was here.

8

Confession

In the days that followed, we were given new chores, which included learning how to milk cows. We were then made to do that first thing in the morning instead of working in the garden, after we recited our morning chant, of course. Added to the milking of cows came the caring and feeding of the horses. Once again it was Teal who moaned and groaned the most, complaining about her callused hands, the odors, and the hard work. We were truly exhausted when the sun set, but we knew that didn't mean the end of our responsibilities.

Dr. Foreman had given us all passing grades on our schoolwork, but then she added more and more to our assignments as if she was trying to see how much we could accomplish before crying "Uncle!" A new and more efficient and effective spirit of cooperation had been born among us, however, and Gia was smart. Robin commented that she was actually learning faster under Gia's tutoring and better than she had in regular school and I couldn't disagree. To our buddies' chagrin, we actually enjoyed working together. M'Lady One couldn't resist commenting, "Aren't you all turning into nerdy little goody-goodies."

No one responded. We just kept working. I was afraid this new spirit of cooperation would be torn apart at the next group therapy session, but we didn't have another like that. Instead, Dr. Foreman began what she described as a new and more personal round of analysis and healing. She called us in one at a time, me being the last. When one of the previous four returned, I looked at her and waited in anticipation, hoping to hear something that might help me when I was summoned to see Dr. Foreman.

However, whoever talked with Dr. Foreman returned in a cocoon built out of painful memories or fears and didn't want to speak. Gia was like that for days afterward, as was Mindy. Teal seemed sadder, more defeated, and Robin angrier. It was as if the invisible bonds that had grown among us were cut again. When it came my turn, I was truly frightened. What powers did she have? What would she do to me?

The afternoon of my appointment, Natani was showing me how to groom a horse he called Wind Song. A quarter horse, he had a short back, muscular chest, and muscular hindquarters. The other girls weren't as interested as I was in horses, and I could see Natani liked that I was. The only time I had ever been close to a real horse before was when I had watched a parade in Atlanta.

Natani was demonstrating how to use the hoof pick and telling me why it was important to remove the buildup of dirt and debris. Long-time exposure to bacteria could cause infections, he said, and stones could eventually cause bruising.

Wind Song was patient and cooperative as though the horse understood what Natani was telling me and doing. When I commented about that, he nodded and said, "He does understand. Not words, but actions. That's how animals speak to each other and how we speak to them, by what we do, not by what we say."

"There can be no lies between us then," I muttered.

He smiled at me. "Yes, daughter of the sun, yes."

I was afraid when he handed me the pick, but soon I was doing it and Wind Song was just as calm as he was when Natani worked on him. Before I could finish, M'Lady One was at the door of the horse barn.

"Dr. Foreman wants you," she said. "Now!"

"Can't I finish this first?"

"No. It's time for your therapy."

Wind Song turned toward her as if he could feel my nervousness. He bared his teeth, snorted, and shook his head. Natani looked at me hard, but I'm sure it wasn't difficult to see the anxiety in my eyes.

"In here," he said, holding his hand over his heart, "is your hogan. No one can come in there unless you say yes."

"Move it, girl," M'Lady One shouted.

I handed the pick back to Natani and started out.

"He's a crazy old loon," M'Lady One muttered as we walked toward the house. "All that peyote has gone to his head and turned his brain into mashed potatoes. I don't know why Dr. Foreman keeps him here."

"Why are you here? Why do you want to do this rather than be out there with people, having fun, getting on with your life?" I dared ask her.

"Why am I here? It's the least I can do for Dr. Foreman. She's done so much for me. If you don't appreciate her yet, it's because you haven't improved enough. But don't worry," she said, smiling, "you will. She has never failed yet with one of her wards."

"Never?"

"Never. It's just a matter of time. Longer for some than others maybe, but just a matter of time, so don't think you're anything special."

"You're improved?" I fired back at her. The smile flew off her face like a frightened bird lifting off a branch.

"Yes, I am." Her eyes were small and cold. "If you think I'm mean now, just imagine what I was and what I can be again if I have to be."

"If that's true," I said, pausing to take off my shoes, "then you've really not changed, have you?"

"Oh, you're so arrogant and smug. You're lucky you're going in there to therapy or I'd have you digging in the cesspool for that remark."

"Is that what you had to do?"

I thought she would get angrier, maybe even come at me, but instead, she smiled. "Worse. Which is what you can look forward to, Phoebe bird. Now get in there, and if you're smart, which you're probably not, you'll keep your wisecracks to yourself and be very, very cooperative."

Holding that cold smile on her lips, she watched me go into the house.

"Go into the office, Phoebe," Dr. Foreman called from the dining room. She was speaking with the cook.

I entered the office, but I didn't sit. Curious about what Gia had told us Dr. Foreman was doing with our case studies, I looked at some of the papers on her desk. That was a mistake, but not because she came in behind me and caught me doing it. It was a mistake because of what I saw.

It was a letter faxed to my uncle Buster and aunt Mae Louise. The letter was from the doctor at the clinic where Mama was being treated.

It began with the words, *I'm sorry to inform you . . .*

I should have stopped reading. I should have backed away from the desk and pretended I had not seen the fax, but I didn't. I drew closer and picked it up and read . . . *that Mrs. Elder passed away last night. We believe her last visitor brought her some bad crack cocaine, not that there is any good crack cocaine, and it had a dramatic and fatal effect on her heart. We have turned the information over to the police. Please accept our condolences and contact us concerning Mrs. Elder's remains as soon as possible.*

The letter seemed to float out of my fingers. It struck the edge of the desk and fell to the floor.

"Pick that up immediately," I heard Dr. Foreman say. She was standing behind me in the doorway.

I looked at her, then did what she said.

"Who do you think you are searching through papers on my desk?" she asked as she entered.

"I didn't search through papers. I just saw . . ." I glanced at the paper again. I had a right to look at this anyway, I thought. This is about my mother, I told myself, and then it hit me harder, sharper, like a slap across my face. My father is gone and my mother is dead now, too. Even though Dr. Foreman hovered just behind me, I had to read it again to be sure I hadn't imagined it. Remains? It made it sound like leftovers. Send a doggie bag for what was left of Mrs. Elder.

"Put that down and sit," she commanded. I didn't move. "Sit!" she shouted, pointing at the chair. "Right now."

I put the letter on the desk, went to the hardwood chair she had facing her desk, and sat. She sat behind her desk and looked down at the letter from the clinic. She seemed to be reading it for the first time.

"I was going to tell you about this myself, break it to you in a far more charitable and considerate fashion when I thought you were ready," she said, her voice a little softer.

I wondered if she was telling the truth. The paper had been at the center of her desk and turned so that anyone approaching from the doorway would see it immediately. According to the date on the letter, it had been sent out almost a week ago. How long had she had it? Did she get it the same day my aunt and uncle had? Why hadn't she told me immediately? Was she worried about what the news would do to me? Was she worried it would interfere with her efforts to change me? At the moment I was more curious about that than I was angry.

"How does this information make you feel?" she asked, and sat forward as if any syllable I uttered would be earth-shattering in importance.

I shrugged and looked away. Why did she always keep the window curtains closed in this office? Was she afraid we would find something far more interesting to look at out there? My eyes drifted to the floor. Where was that grate Gia had described? Was anyone listening in on this conversation? Was Posy down there? I heard nothing, not a peep.

"When you've been apart from someone like you have been apart from your mother, news like this"—she held the paper up—"doesn't seem real. Long-distance death loses its impact. You have to be close up, right there sometimes, to believe it at all.

"But despite the face you're trying to put on, I can see you believe it, Phoebe. Holding it all bottled up inside you won't help and it doesn't make you stronger. It eats at you from within. If anything, it makes you weaker. I'm always telling my clients that, because it's one of the truest things about human nature, you know. Shutting your emotions up, never expressing your feelings, just causes it all to fester and sour, and that ugly degeneration comes out in how they look, how they think, and what they do. It's poison. It's truly as if you were poisoning your own blood."

She sat back, relaxed. "What was the nicest thing, the happiest thing, you remember about your mother?"

"I don't remember anything nice or happy."

"Sure you do. You're just afraid to recall it now, afraid to mention it because that will make you feel sad, and believe me, Phoebe, you're afraid of being sad, afraid of it more than any of the other girls here," she assured me with a wave of her hand toward the door. I said nothing, just stared at the floor. My head felt as if it were full of angry bees.

She rose and walked slowly to the front of her desk, then leaned back against it.

"Think back," she coaxed. "Surely you have good memories of when you were just a little girl. Think, remember. I want you to try, Phoebe."

"Why? Why do you want me to do that?"

"I want you to feel, to see and understand the most basic human needs in you."

"You're right. I don't want to be afraid and I don't want to be sad. Okay? You're right." Hot tears bubbled under my lower eyelids. "Satisfied?"

"I'm not worried about being right, Phoebe," she said slowly, and smiled. "I have nothing to prove."

I raised my eyebrows skeptically at that and I could see she didn't like it. She stopped smiling, stepped away from the desk, and stood as firmly as a steel pole, her eyes sharp, angry, bearing down on me.

"I'm already a success at what I do. I have the respect of my peers. I have been awarded many honors, and courts, judges, counselors, and other psychiatrists have given me the trust and the responsibility to reshape and save girls like you, so this is not about ego."

"What's it about then?"

"Right now? It's about you. Do you realize"—she reached back for the letter from the clinic—"that you are really all alone in the world now?"

I tightened the embrace of myself and looked at the closed window curtains.

"Oh, I know you have an uncle and aunt, but I also know you're not fond of them and you do not believe they are very fond of you. You believe they would rather you disappeared. Am I right?"

I didn't answer.

"I said, am I right? Wasn't that in the autobiography you wrote for me on orientation day? Well?"

"Yes."

She nodded, satisfied. "You were correct in your analysis of them. They haven't even called to see how you reacted to the news. I've heard nothing," she said with such vehemence, I thought she was enjoying the pain her words imposed on me. They were like whiplashes, slicing and stinging my weakened wall of protection.

"In this world," she continued, returning to that teacher voice of hers, "someone without any family, without any friends, loses any sense of herself and any reason to go on and do anything with her life. Like it or not, this is your new home, Phoebe," she said, holding her arms out widely apart.

"We are your new family. I want you to believe that and I want you to trust me, trust that I have your best interests at heart, no matter how hard and severe I might seem to be. We have demons to drive out of you, important changes to make. Just like a surgeon has to cut out a cancer, I have to cut all that out of you. Oh, not with a knife, a scalpel, of course, but with every available technique at my disposal. All I ask is you cooperate and try to help yourself.

"Is that asking for too much?" she followed in a tone so reasonable, all I could do was shake my head.

"Good. I think you're different from the others, Phoebe, and I don't mean the color of your skin or your background or anything like that. I think you have potential. There's more to you and a lot more to save."

She stood there looking at me. I kept my eyes directed at the floor, then I sniffed back my tears and closed my eyes and took a deep breath.

Of course she was right about what I was feeling and what I was desperate to avoid. Good memories, happy memories, of Mama were trying to rush in and I was holding the door closed, but I could hear Mama's laughter, catch a glimpse of her in the mirror as she fixed my hair or talked to me about how to make up my eyes like hers. The images were leaking in under the door. These memories weren't memories of the woman I had seen at the clinic after I had run away from my uncle and aunt. These were memories of my mama of long ago when I was still young enough to forgive her for her weaknesses and her failures, when I was still young enough to believe things would be better for us all.

"You want to cry, Phoebe. I can see it. Go on. Have a good cry. There's no shame in that."

I wiped away a fugitive tear quickly and shook my head. She approached me and touched my shoulder. I looked up at her. Should I trust her with my tears? I wondered. Was she sincere? So many cruel things were done to us here. Was she right in doing them? Did we need that? Was it the only thing that would change a girl like Robin or like Teal, Mindy, and Gia? Or me? What terrible thing had Mindy done with a baby? And Gia, I was sure, setting fire to her own home, among other things, surely made her a lost cause out there. Suddenly, I began to wonder if Dr. Foreman wasn't the last and best hope for girls like us after all.

"Poor Phoebe. You didn't deserve the life you had. You don't have evil in your heart. You never really intended to hurt anyone, did you?"

"No."

"Of course not. All sorts of events, social and psychological experiences, have put you in a place you don't want to be in."

"What's going to happen to me?" I asked, flicking off another errant tear.

She smiled. "You're going to get out of that terribly dark place. You're going to grow and improve and become one of my girls, a Foreman girl, proud and strong and capable."

She returned to her chair behind her desk, folded the letter, and inserted it into an envelope. I watched her put it into a drawer.

"The funeral was yesterday," she said.

"Yesterday?"

"Yes, I wish I could have sent you back for that, but it wasn't possible. Your uncle and aunt understood. I finally decided to call them. Actually, they weren't at all disappointed about your not attending the services," she added dryly, sounding like she was on my side against them. "That's why I said what I said before, but none of that is important now. Forget about them. Someday when you're more confident of yourself, when you're better, you'll visit the cemetery and you'll be strong enough to bury all the ugly and nasty feelings right there alongside your mother's coffin."

She smiled as though that was a wonderful dream, a dream I should pursue.

"Now, let's make good use of this session and talk about other things, okay?"

I nodded and sucked back the remaining tears.

"Good." She folded her hands and leaned forward. "When you were all here in group therapy, I was somewhat amused to hear Mindy being accused of being my spy. The truth is I don't find Mindy making much progress. I would never solicit her help for anything just yet. Actually, Phoebe, I expect her to be here long after you leave."

"Really?"

"I'm afraid so. She's a very, very troubled girl. She tries to convince me she's better. She even tries to be my little spy and tells me about the others, about you. I know she's simply attempting to ingratiate herself with me, win my favor. She's very transparent, albeit a very sneaky person, our Mindy. I bet you have no idea that she told me about Teal's intention to run off before you told me, do you?"

I shook my head.

"She heard her talking about it and she told me. When I asked you about Teal, I wanted to see if you were capable of being honest. You were and you are and you're going to do well here. So," she said, sitting back, "I've decided to make you my confidant."

"What do you mean?"

"I mean you're going to be special to me, Phoebe. Would you like that?"

I was afraid to say no, so I nodded.

"I thought you might, but if I am to trust you more and more, you have to trust me more and more. That's understandable and fair, isn't it?"

"I guess so."

How unexpected all this was, I thought. I had come trembling into this office, expecting her to do something more to me, something that would send me out of here all bottled up and wounded inside just like the others. I half expected to end up in one of those Skinner boxes Gia had described, but here she was making me feel special.

"What did Mindy do before? I mean, why is she here?" I dared ask. I was anticipating the usual sort of response to this. It was none of my business. I should be concerned only with my own problems, but again, she surprised me.

"She gave birth to a baby and left it in the rear seat of a broken-down vehicle. A passerby luckily heard the infant's wail and brought the police. Someone had seen her go into the vehicle and she was arrested. It wasn't her first experience with police and courts."

"What about her parents? Didn't they know she was pregnant and wonder about the baby?"

"I am always amazed at how much parents do not know about their own children, Phoebe. What about your mother? Did she know much about you, what you were doing?"

"No. She wasn't around enough to ask or care, and my daddy was on the road too much."

"And even if they were there more, would they know everything?" she asked, tilting her head a bit.

"No."

"Exactly."

Her small smile grew softer. Then she stopped smiling and sat firmly again.

"What do you think of Gia?" she asked in a sharper tone. "She troubles me. She's very smart, I know, but I'm afraid I'm not really making enough progress with her."

"I don't know." I didn't. I had no idea how to look for progress here or even what she meant by it.

"She's still very volatile," Dr. Foreman continued as if she and I were two psychiatrists conferring about one of our patients. "Without warning, she can become a very violent person. I bet you've sensed that, haven't you, Phoebe? You come from a world full of violence. It's not a stranger to you."

"No. It isn't."

She nodded, happy at my answers, I could see.

"Gia's parents are better off financially than yours were, but they were just as much into themselves. Besides, Gia has always been good at fooling people, lying. She's one of the best I've seen, actually. And very clever. She did something no one else I've treated for similar problems ever did."

"What?" I could see she wanted me to ask, and for some reason, that set off alarm bells inside me.

"She made up a person and blamed everything she could on her. She was so good about it that many people believed the person actually existed. At one point," she said, almost laughing, "the police were looking for Gia's imaginary person, sent out one of those all-points bulletins."

She paused and looked even more serious and concerned. "I have come to the conclusion she herself now believes this person exists. I'm working very hard at curing that, and I am going to need your help with it from time to time."

"Made up a person?"

"Yes," she said, smiling. "With amazing details, too. Clever in a way, isn't it? But she is very smart, our Gia. I know from our last talk here with everyone that Mindy has mentioned Gia's imaginary person to you and the others, and I'm sure Gia's spoken about her as well since. I just don't know how much she has said and if she continues to talk about her since the group therapy session."

"About who?" I asked, my heart now pounding and reverberating through my bones like the beat of a steel drum.

Dr. Foreman smiled. "You know, Phoebe. Posy."

I tried to swallow, but a lump in my throat felt like a small rock.

"Well?" she asked.

"Well, what?"

"Is she talking about her? What did she tell you about her?" she demanded.

I shook my head. "Nothing. I mean, nothing much."

She held me in her eyes so firmly, I thought I couldn't turn my head to the right or to the left. I couldn't even lower my gaze to the floor again.

"Haven't you heard anything I've said here today, Phoebe? Didn't you hear about all the responsibility and trust I have decided to place in you? Are you going to disappoint me now, now that I have determined you are worth all my effort and energy? Are you going to have me throw you back into the water as if you were some sick fish? Well?" she said, raising her voice and widening her eyes with fury.

I was frightened. I was very frightened, but I was more terrified of telling her that Gia claimed Posy was her daughter, and not only that, that her daughter might be locked up in the basement right below us. What would she do to Gia and then to the others and what would they think of me?

In the back of my mind a little voice whispered, "What if Gia was the one telling the truth?"

I gathered all my ability to slip away, an ability I had employed many times before to escape from the chains and shackles adults in authority could throw over me. Too often in my life, I'd found myself having to avoid punishments and blame. The trick was never showing I was afraid and guilty. I would go on the offense and usually that worked.

But Dr. Foreman was the expert in all this. I had no doubt she had dealt with girls as good at it as I was, if not better. Still, I chose that route.

"I don't listen to their garbage talk," I said with as much anger as I could muster. "Sure, I heard her mention someone named Posy, but it wasn't anything I cared to hear about. I have my own troubles."

She didn't change expression. She continued to hold that gaze, fix those eyes on me. I tried not to blink, not to look shifty, but she didn't nod or smile or in any way look satisfied.

"You're making a big mistake here today, Phoebe. It will bring you even more pain than this," she said, opening the drawer, taking out the envelope that contained the letter about Mama and snapping it in the air. "You'll be out there alone. The other girls won't help you. You should hear the bad things they say about you, Gia, especially. I know she's lying, they're all lying about you, but it doesn't matter. None of them would be friends with you on the outside anyway, would they? You'll go back to your world and they'll return to theirs, right? Why protect anyone but yourself now?

"Besides, if you care about them, if you have some sensitivity and conscience about it, then assure yourself this is the best way to help them. Just like you tried to help Teal."

"But you let her run off anyway," I said as sharply as I could.

"Of course, I did. So she would learn something, but thanks to you, she was under surveillance the entire time and luckily, too. After she was stung, she might have wandered into worse places because she can't tolerate pain. She has a very low boiling point, being spoiled so much. No, you did a good thing then. You did save her life. Do a good thing now.

"Tell me exactly, in as much detail as you can, what Gia said about Posy."

She leaned forward expectantly.

"She didn't tell me anything specifically. She was talking to everyone."

"That's what I mean, Phoebe," she snapped, her eyes flickering with heat and ill temper. "Don't play with words with me. We're not in court. Well?"

"I just heard her say something about a girl who was here before."

"Are you going to have me pull every word out of you? What did she say about the girl?"

"That she was a liar," I said. "Made up stories."

"And?"

"That was it. Now she's gone. I didn't think it was anything to talk about."

She snapped back as if her body were wrapped in rubber bands attached to the chair.

"I was mistaken about you, Phoebe. You're not ready for what I want to do for you. You need more time." She put on that cold smile again. "That's all right. Time is something we have at our disposal here. I'm going to give you time to think about today. Perhaps you'll come back to me on your own, perhaps not. It doesn't matter. In the end, Phoebe, you will return.

"You're free to resume your chores." She waved her hand at the door.

I rose quickly.

"Wait," she said when I reached the door.

I turned and saw her open the desk drawer.

"Take this with you. It's all she left you, apparently, the news of her unnecessary death."

"I don't want it."

It was as if I had refused a valuable gift, insulted her, and disrespected her ancestors all at once. She whipped her head back, tore the envelope in two and threw it in the black metal wastebasket beside her desk.

"Consider that your attendance at your mother's funeral," she said, and turned her back on me.

It was as if my feet were turning to balloons. I walked out, but it seemed more like I floated along. M'Lady One wasn't there waiting. No one was there. My heart was still thumping as I sat and put on my clodhopper shoes. Almost the second I put on my left shoe, I felt it, and it was like no pain I had ever felt before. I screamed and threw off the shoe.

The pink insect with its back end curled up fell out, partly crushed. I looked up in a panic. My foot seemed to be swelling up right before my eyes.

"Help!" I screamed. Where was everyone?

M'Lady One appeared in the doorway. She had to have been standing right there all the while, I thought.

"What seems to be the trouble?" she asked sweetly and calmly despite my cry.

"I've been bitten by that!" I cried, pointing to the dying insect.

M'Lady One came down the steps casually and looked at the insect. "What'dya know about that, you've been stung by a scorpion, too."

"A scorpion?"

"Big deal. Put your shoe on and get back to work."

"But shouldn't I be given some medicine?"

"No. Now get moving or I'll assign you that cesspool digging instead of permitting you to return to the horses."

I looked in the shoe and shook it out and did the same with the other. The pain started to increase in my foot. It was traveling up my ankle. I felt it rising in wave after wave, the tide of it already reaching into my stomach.

"It hurts a lot!" I moaned when I stood up.

"You'll get over it. You're tough, a girl of the streets with a big mouth. What's a mere scorpion sting to you?"

"I want to see Dr. Foreman."

"I'm warning you to get moving and get moving now."

"She should know what happened to me."

I started for the stairway and she blocked me. M'Lady Three appeared in the doorway, a bottle of Coke in her hands. She sipped from it, her cheeks going in and out as she sucked on the bottle. Then she stepped down.

"What's going on?"

"She's refusing to return to her work detail," M'Lady One said.

"I was stung by a scorpion. There it is." I pointed to the ground.

M'Lady Three continued down the steps, picked up the dead scorpion, put it in her pocket, and turned back to me. "Refusing to return to her work detail after you told her to do it?"

"Yes."

"That's insubordination."

"I'm not trying to be insubordinate. I want to see Dr. Foreman. I've been stung I tell you! My foot is on fire."

M'Lady Three put the bottle of Coke down on the ground and stepped beside M'Lady One. They were like a wall now between me and the steps to the house.

"Start walking," M'Lady One said, pointing to my right.

"I can't walk. It hurts too much," I cried.

"Stop your whining. No one cares about your little pain. You're insubordinate. That's a ten-point demerit. You're not going back to your soft chores. You're going to the Ice Room."

"No!" I screamed.

Dr. Foreman finally appeared in the doorway. "What's going on, girls?"

"Phoebe refuses to return to her work detail," M'Lady One said.

"I was stung by a scorpion. It was in my shoe." I looked at M'Lady One. "I bet she put it there."

Dr. Foreman didn't move. "Where is it?"

"She put it in her pocket." I pointed to M'Lady Three.

"Is that true?"

"Of course not, Dr. Foreman."

"Make her empty her pocket," I cried.

"We don't lie to each other here," Dr. Foreman said. "My girls and I have an unbreakable chain of trust among us. If she says it's not in her pocket, it's not."

"But . . . it is. Wait, look at my foot." I took off the shoe and my stocking. Then I lifted my foot so she could clearly see the swelling.

"I don't see anything unusual," she said dryly.

"What?"

"I'm like you, Phoebe. I see and I hear what I want. Insubordination means a session in the Ice Room. M'ladies, do your duty."

"Yes, Dr. Foreman," M'Lady One said.

Dr. Foreman glared at me a moment. I was frozen, my foot still dangling before her. She turned and went back into the house.

"Get the shoe back on and move," M'Lady Three ordered.

I shook my head.

M'Lady Two came walking across the yard. "Trouble?"

"Not much. Phoebe here was insubordinate and is to be spending a session in the Ice Room. She's continuing to be insubordinate, which means that session will be longer," M'Lady One explained calmly. She could have been reporting the weather.

I turned away. I couldn't run from them, not with the pain in my foot. I was unable to put any weight on it, and where would I run to?

"You know what one of these is?" M'Lady Two asked, bringing a small, black metal thing out of her pocket. It looked like a man's electric razor. "It's called a stun gun. Ever see one used?"

I had. Willie Sturges had bought one and as a joke used it on Dennis Hampton, a fat boy in our tenth-grade class who was always the butt of jokes. I couldn't believe how fast he went down and how he writhed in pain. The sight made me sick and I ran. I really thought Willie had killed him. Afterward, I saw Dennis, still looking stunned, his pants showing where he peed on himself, stumbling along home. Everyone but me thought it was pretty funny.

"Please," I said. "I really did get stung."

"And you're about to be stung again, only this will be far worse," M'Lady Two warned.

"Move," M'Lady Three said, pointing.

"I can't walk," I cried.

"Hop," M'Lady One said. "Now."

They closed in on me. I started to walk, but merely putting my toe to the ground increased the pain. The tears were streaming down my cheeks. I could feel my shortened breath straining my lungs. My stomach churned.

"I'm getting sick," I moaned.

"Poor little Phoebe bird," M'Lady One chimed, and they all laughed. "What's happening to the tough girl we all knew and loved?"

"Where are we going?" I screamed, or at least I thought I had.

When we rounded the corner, M'Lady Two rushed ahead and opened a door. I hesitated and looked back. Where were the other girls? Where was Natani?

The room inside looked dark. All I could think about was the way Robin had been after she had been put in the Ice Room and the things Gia had said about it, too.

"Listen to me," I pleaded. "I just found out that my mother died. I don't mean to be insubordinate. I'm upset."

M'Lady One pretended she was playing a violin.

"I'm sorry. I'll go back to my work. I promise I won't say anything nasty to any of you."

"It's too late for promises, Phoebe," M'Lady Three said. "Weren't you told that? When you came here, you left all your promises and excuses behind you. You're naked here. It's reality. You are rewarded for good and punished for bad. It's simple and it never changes."

I looked through the door. All I saw from where I was standing was the foot of a bunk. What was the room, just a solitary confinement? I'll get through it, I thought. I'll show them.

The sting was singing louder, however, and the churning that had begun in my stomach turned into nausea. I faltered and M'Lady One came to my side and kept me from falling.

"This is going to be good," she said. "The Ice Room on top of it all. I tell you, Phoebe, I couldn't do it."

"Me neither," M'Lady Two said. "Glad it's you and not me."

"You're all a bunch of wimps," M'Lady Three said. "Phoebe's going to show you up. Aren't you, Phoebe? Girl of the streets, tough."

"I think I'm going to throw up," I said.

"Get her in there before she does. I hate the smell," M'Lady Two said stepping back.

M'Lady One twisted my arm and pushed me through the doorway. There was a bunk, but at the head of it, there was what looked like a helmet with wires attached.

"What is this?"

"We've told you before. It's your worst nightmare," M'Lady One said.

I tried to resist, but her hold was so firm, I thought her fingers would break through my skin and flesh. She turned me into the room, and together she and M'Lady Three forced me to lie down.

"I'm sick!" I screamed. "I need a doctor, medicine!"

They put the helmet over my head and strapped it on tightly. I resisted but I couldn't keep my arms from being straightened and then a strap was fixed over my chest, just under my breasts. It was just as it had been when I'd woken up in the plane that had brought me to this hell.

A visorlike part of the helmet was lowered over my face. It was dark and their voices grew more muffled because of the earphones over my ears.

"Enjoy," I heard, and heard them leave the room, closing the door behind them. Their voices drifted away and there was only silence.

What was this? A helmet over my head with a visor to keep me in the dark and in the quiet? It was stupid. The coffin was worse, I thought. This isn't so bad except I felt so sick and the pain was still as sharp as ever in my foot. I was getting hot, too, and it wasn't just from the stuffiness in the room. I knew I was developing a fever. The nausea built up until I started to vomit, but I could only turn my head a little to spit to the side. Finally, that stopped, but it left me feeling so tired, so weak.

I'll just sleep, I thought.

I'll beat them. I'll sleep and get better and beat them. This wasn't so terrible.

Ice Room?

There was nothing icy about the Ice Room. It was just as I had suspected, a lot of intimidation, a lot of scary talk and nothing else. Robin just couldn't take being locked up and strapped down and forced to be in darkness. I'm stronger than she is. I can wait it out. I'm stronger than the whole lot of them, even the buddies, I told myself. I am special. Dr. Foreman was right about that.

I'll sleep, I assured myself. I'll sleep and I'll get better. Keep telling yourself that, Phoebe, I chanted. You'll get better. You'll beat them. Think about something good. Think about Wind Song and Natani and the beautiful desert sky and the horizon and tomorrow. Tomorrow, yes, getting out of here, getting away from here. Remember what he said about the hogan. Don't let them into your house. I wouldn't.

I can do this. I can win, I thought.

And then.

It began.

9

Dr. Foreman's Spy

At some point your screaming becomes so high-pitched it seems to be coming from someplace else. It's like someone else is screaming in the distance and you can barely hear it, but that sensation doesn't happen immediately. First, you practically blow out your lungs with the effort and your vocal cords strain and you grow hoarse.

It all began with the sound I heard through the earphones in the strange helmet, an all too familiar squeaky sound that quickly built into a horrific chorus. First, I could hear only one, then another and another until I knew there was a pack of them.

Rats.

I don't know what the helmet and the visor were, but what I saw and heard was truly lifelike. I soon realized it was something I understood to be called virtual reality, but to me no virtual was involved. They were all over me, crawling, sniffing, nibbling. It was reality. I could actually feel their cold noses, their tiny teeth, their slimy tails, and their little claw feet.

They didn't just run over my body. They gathered and began to explore every part of me, going up the leggings of the coveralls and over my thighs, between my legs, under my panties, then under my shirt, pushing themselves under my breasts, sniveling around my nipples and climbing up my throat to my mouth, pushing between my lips, shoving their heads into my mouth. They were at my ears as well, worming their way into my head. Their fur was wet, their tails long and slimy, the tiny nails in their claws painful.

I could even smell them, smell this putrid, stale odor that they picked up from wallowing through piles of garbage and dead animals. Waves of revulsion traveled up and down my entire body to add to the nausea I was experiencing from the scorpion sting.

And I could do nothing to drive them off. Because of how tightly I was strapped onto the cot, I could barely wiggle, not that it would have helped, of course, since they weren't actually on me.

It was no good closing my eyes. The images were projected through my lids, and in these images, the rats were at the lids, forcing them open. I screamed and screamed.

And then suddenly, as quickly as they had come, they were gone. I don't know how long they were there, but they were gone and there was just darkness, the relief of total darkness.

Moments later Dr. Foreman's voice began softly.

"Phoebe, my poor Phoebe. I'm here to help you. You believe that now, don't you?"

All I could do now was whisper and I was afraid she wouldn't hear me.

"Yes," I said, my throat straining with the effort. "I do. I believe it."

"That's good, Phoebe. We need trust between us. It's what I have been telling you ever since you were brought here. You can trust me and I can trust you now, can't I?"

"Yes, Doctor, yes."

"That's good, Phoebe, so good."

Her voice was so soothing. I was actually afraid she would stop talking.

"I was so worried about you, worried about your bad behavior."

"I'm sorry, Dr. Foreman. I'm sorry."

"Sure you are, Phoebe. You never mean to hurt anyone. You're a good girl. Let's get back to our little talk, okay? You were going to tell me about Gia and Posy. Remember?"

"Yes, yes."

"What exactly did Gia say about Posy, Phoebe?"

"She said she was your daughter and that you couldn't stop her from lying and breaking rules and inventing imaginary people, and she was an embarrassment to you so you locked her up in the basement," I rattled off.

"I see. Anything else?"

"That she was adopted."

"Adopted. Yes, that makes sense. This is very good, Phoebe. This is a real breakthrough. You and I are going to depend upon each other a great deal more now. Would you like that?"

"Oh, yes, Dr. Foreman, yes."

"We can't have you ever being insubordinate again, Phoebe."

"I won't be. I promise. I know promises are not considered important anymore, but I do. I really do."

"I believe you, Phoebe, but as you've seen already, only action means anything."

"I feel so sick, Dr. Foreman. I'm so sick. I'm nauseous and I threw up. I was really stung by that scorpion. I'm not lying."

"I know. You'll be fine, Phoebe. Don't be concerned. I want you to sleep now."

"I'm nauseous again."

"I said I want you to sleep."

"Okay, I'll sleep."

It was quiet enough for me to hear the rhythm of my beating heart thumping in my ears. I held my breath. Was that the sound of squeaking again? Were they returning?

Despite my terror, I did fall asleep, but right before I did, I told myself I had been so stupid. I had put my fear in that biography I wrote in the orientation room. I had given myself up before I had even arrived here. She's too smart, I thought. She will get what she wants. M'Lady One was right. Dr. Foreman doesn't fail. There was no Posy. There couldn't be anyone she didn't change or mold into the person Dr. Foreman wanted her to be.

I didn't realize it until much later, but before the door was opened again, I had slept all day and through the night, waking and then becoming nearly comatose repeatedly. The helmet was unfastened and light burned through the shadows. It was so painful. I grimaced and closed my eyes, but the light was too strong.

"What a mess she is," I heard M'Lady Two say.

"Let's get her to the showers."

"You're disgusting, Phoebe bird. You've spoiled your coveralls and you stink so badly, I don't think the buzzards would even bother with your remains," M'Lady One said.

I was weak. I couldn't lift my head, but they pulled me up. My legs gave out immediately. They scooped their arms under mine and dragged me out of the Ice Room. M'Lady Three was there with a wheelbarrow.

"I thought we would need it," she said triumphantly. They all laughed.

They lifted me and dropped me in the wheelbarrow, my legs twisted, my head hitting the metal sharply. I moaned and tried to get more comfortable, but they were rolling me along and bouncing me over the dirt and gravel so hard, I did all I could to keep my head from repeatedly smacking the inside of the wheelbarrow. When we reached the showers, they began to tear off my clothes. Then they put me under the shower and ran the cold water. I screamed, but I had lost my voice the night before, and all I actually did was open my mouth. I welcomed the water in my throat.

They stood by watching me squirm.

When they decided I had had enough, they shut off the water and tossed me a towel. I was given new panties and a new pair of coveralls and a new shirt. They barked their displeasure at me. It was taking me too long to dress, but I had no energy. My foot still looked quite swollen. I put my clodhopper shoe on as carefully as I could and they scooped me up again.

"You'll walk on your own now," M'Lady One charged. "Dr. Foreman wants you fed, so head for the house."

I limped forward. I didn't see any of the others, but I thought I caught a glimpse of Natani watching from a corner of the barn. The buddies kept chiding me for moving too slowly, poking me in the ribs and back. I shuddered but kept moving, accepting the pain every time I put my foot down, swallowing it back and moving ahead, driven now by my need for something more to drink. My mouth still felt as if it had been turned into sand and my tongue into one long razor blade. I touched my lips to see if there was any blood, but they were so dry, it was like touching wood.

They had to help me up the stairs and then direct me to the table where I was given juice, some soft-boiled eggs, toast, and jam. I was still too nauseated to eat much, but I knew I would need something to build my strength, so I made as much of an effort as I could. Only M'Lady One remained behind to watch. When Dr. Foreman appeared, I felt myself flinch. Every cell in my body, every part of me, was afraid of her now.

She smiled. "How's my girl? Those spider bites can be so devastating."

I wanted to ask why she didn't believe me when I told her then, but I didn't even move my lips.

"You're going to need a little TLC now. Just like Teal did, only Teal thinks the world owes her TLC." Dr. Foreman told M'Lady One, "Take her to the guest bedroom. Give her two Tylenol and the ice pack for her foot." She turned back to me. "You'll be a lot better by this evening. I need you to be strong for me, Phoebe. We have a lot of work to do together now, you and I, right?"

I nodded.

"Good." She looked at M'Lady One. "Send me Gia after you see to Phoebe," she ordered sharply.

"Okay, Doctor."

I was too tired and too numb to think about anything, but I felt vaguely sorry for Gia and wondered how she and the others were going to treat me now.

M'Lady One helped me to a bedroom. The mere sight of a real bed made me relax. I couldn't believe how wonderful it felt to lie down on a thick mattress. She gave me the pills and some water and brought me the ice pack.

"Keep it on your foot," she said, pulling me up so I could hold it there myself.

"You put that scorpion into my shoe, didn't you?" I managed to ask her in a hoarse voice.

She smiled. "Now how could I do a terrible thing like that? Remember? I'm a different person now. I don't do mean things to people anymore," she replied, and left.

I kept the ice pack on my foot, but the pain there was receding anyway. I was so tired, I couldn't stay upright and eventually just gave up on the ice pack and fell asleep. It was probably the best sleep I'd had since I'd arrived at this ranch. I didn't wake up feeling energetic, but I felt a great deal stronger. The nausea was gone and I didn't think I had a fever any longer either. I saw that the sun was low, falling behind the mountains in the west. I had slept through the day.

"Well," I heard from the doorway, and looked up at Dr. Foreman. "You've woken just in time for dinner. That's good. I want you to eat well tonight, Phoebe. You have to get stronger, okay?"

"Yes, Dr. Foreman."

"Good. Go on to the dining room then."

I slipped my feet into my shoes cautiously. I couldn't help it. Memory of that sting was still so vivid, I thought my foot would rebel and refuse to go into the shoe. Dr. Foreman watched me and then stepped back as I started out of the room.

"It's a comfortable room, isn't it, Phoebe?"

"Yes."

I hadn't looked at anything but the bed, but now I saw a dresser and a mirror, a small desk and chair, and a vanity table with another mirror. The floor was done in a blue-and-white tile with an oval, cream area rug next to the bed. Beside the bed was a pole lamp with a shade that looked to be made of seashells. There was even a radio on the nightstand.

"This could be your room, Phoebe." I glanced at her a little too hopefully. "We'll see." She indicated I should walk ahead of her to the dining room.

The others were already there eating. They all looked up when I appeared, all except Gia. She kept her eyes on her food.

"As you all heard, Phoebe hasn't been well. She is therefore excused from any kitchen chores tonight," Dr. Foreman announced.

Mindy smirked. Robin and Teal stared at me enviously.

Dr. Foreman put her hand on my shoulder. "Get something to eat and then return to your bunk and get some rest, Phoebe. You don't have to work on any school assignments either."

The more favors and privileges she placed upon me, the more embarrassed and ashamed I felt. The others sensed it and were now all looking down at the food. I went to my place and began to fill my plate with food. I was hungry and thirsty. Dr. Foreman stood there watching for a few moments, then left.

No one spoke for a while.

Finally, Teal broke the silence. "You were in the Ice Room, weren't you?"

I nodded.

"What was it like? What happened? What did they do?" she asked, her eyes wide with expectation. "Robin won't tell me anything about her experience," she added, glaring at her.

I just shook my head.

"Talking about something like that causes you to relive it," Gia mumbled. "So shut up."

"Don't keep giving me orders," Teal shot back at her. She looked at me again. "What did she mean you weren't well?" she asked, refusing to be quiet even though Robin and Mindy and not just Gia were now glaring at her so hard, anyone else would have been intimidated.

"I was stung like you, by a scorpion, and this was right after Dr. Foreman gave me the news that my mother died last week."

"What?" Robin asked. "Your mother died?"

"Some drug she took affected her heart and she died in the clinic she was in."

"Why did she wait so long to tell you?" Teal asked.

"I don't know." I know I sounded like it, but I couldn't help it: I was searching for sympathy, and understanding.

"Oh. This is all so terrible," Teal said. "And then to be stung by a scorpion. Where were you stung?"

"It was in my shoe."

"How could it be in your shoe?" Robin asked, grimacing.

"Spiders can get into shoes when they're left outside. It's not a big deal," Gia said dryly.

"Well, it got under my overalls, so I guess it could get into a shoe," Teal added.

Robin smirked and stared at her. "You know, now that I think about it, Teal, how come you didn't get put in the Ice Room for trying to run off?"

"I don't know," Teal said quickly. "I was too sick, I guess. They put me in one of the bedrooms here. Maybe she was afraid I would die and she would get investigated and then go to jail."

"Phoebe's sitting here after one day. How come it took you so long to get well enough to be returned to the barracks?" Mindy questioned, her eyes now also full of suspicion.

"I had a worse reaction obviously. Maybe it was a bigger spider or a more poisonous one or something, and don't forget I had been out in the desert a long, long time walking. I was two miles past total exhaustion and my feet were sore and I was very dehydrated. I should have been sent to a hospital, not kept here," Teal whined loud enough for someone outside the dining room to hear.

"The way we're being treated, we'll all end up in a hospital soon," Robin offered.

"Exactly." Teal nodded and turned to Gia. "Maybe that's where Posy is. In a hospital."

Gia looked up sharply and glanced at me. Then she dropped her fork so hard, she almost cracked her dish. "Why don't you all shut up? All this whining and moaning, day in and day out. That's what she wants you to do. I'll tell you who's going to end up in a hospital here, me. I'm going to get sick as hell listening to all this groaning and crying."

"Is that right?" Teal retorted, her eyes filling with indignation. "You never cry? You never moan or complain? You're little Miss Perfection."

"Stop it!" I cried, slapping my hand on the table. "Gia's right. Just stop it. Everyone just shut up."

Teal folded her arms under her breasts and turned to me.

"Please," I added.

The rage drained out of her face. She looked at Mindy, Robin, and Gia and went back to her food.

We ate in funereal silence, all of us staring out as if our eyes had been turned around and we were looking in at our own dark thoughts. I was sure we resembled inmates on death row contemplating their end.

Afterward, I returned to barracks alone and went to bed. The others marched in slowly when they were finished with the kitchen chores. Teal announced that thanks to having to pick up my load, she was too tired to do any schoolwork. No one said anything different, even though the expectation was they would all receive a demerit for turning in the work late. Someone turned off the light before the buddies could.

The door opened and M'Lady Two looked in. "Tired girls?" She laughed. "I'll let everyone know you went to bed early. Maybe we'll get you up earlier."

I heard the door close and then I heard Robin say, "And let them know you should drop dead, too."

Teal laughed and Mindy giggled. Gia was quiet. Dr. Foreman's warnings about how volatile she could be returned. Was she planning some sort of revenge? Was it safe to fall asleep with her only a few feet away? I wanted to apologize, to explain, and to get her to see I had no choice, but I was afraid to do it. Instead, I lay awake for as long as I could. Finally, my eyelids refused to be open and sleep came sweeping over me like a cool breeze.

The way the morning began, I thought the silence that had fallen among us would continue all day. No one spoke. With little more than a grunt, everyone rose, dressed, washed, and went to the bathroom. Reciting the morning chant was the most words any of us uttered for hours, even at breakfast. While the others milked the cows, picked chicken eggs, fed the pigs, and did some weeding in the garden, I was assigned to feed and brush down all four horses, as well as clean out the stalls. I worked almost mindlessly, moving as if I were a robot or someone in a drugged stupor.

Once in a while, I would pause and think about Mama. Had she died in her sleep or did she get an attack and panic and die while they were trying to help her? Was she sorry in the end? Did she think at all of me? Think of my daddy? I couldn't imagine anything more lonely than to die among strangers, to have no one around you who would shed tears over your passing, no one who was more than just professionally interested in what was happening to you. You would know that when it was over, they would shake their heads and most likely within the same hour, maybe the same minute, return to their normal daily lives. Some who witnessed your passing might not even remember to mention it to anyone afterward. You were, after all, just a statistic.

What did the doctor ask in that letter? What she should do with Mama's remains? How do you write such a question? Surely the doctor was thinking, we've got to get her out of here. She's one of our screwups. Come get her, sweep up this mess, remove it from our sight.

Did Mama deserve it? Was she so wicked that she was being punished?

Is that what was happening to all of us now? We were bad; we had all done illegal things, some of us worse than the others. Both Mindy and Gia were nearly responsible for killing another human being, and Teal and Robin were thieves. Should anyone feel sorry for us? Should we be upset at the cruelty of the buddies? Was Dr. Foreman right? Could she cure us of evil, turn us into good people? Should we resist? Should I blame myself for surrendering completely?

These questions circled in my brain like mayflies. The more I tried to swipe them away, the more they came. They were relentless. I had to stop working and hold on to something to keep myself from spinning and fainting. I caught my breath and started to brush down one of the horses; then I saw Gia in the doorway. She had a small garden spade in her hand. With the sunlight behind her, her face was in total darkness. She looked more like a ghost or a shadow coming to life as she slowly walked into the horse barn toward me.

I stepped to my right and took hold of the handle of the shovel we used to clean out the horse stalls. I wasn't going to let her hurt me. She stopped about halfway.

"You think you told her something about me that she didn't already know?" Gia began.

"She made me. She put me in the Ice Room and you know what she can do to you. You were the one who said you're not in the Ice Room. The Ice Room is in you. Now I know what you meant. That helmet thing . . . there were rats all over me and she knew how much I hated them."

"She didn't have to do that to you to get information. She just wanted to break you, Phoebe. She already had Mindy tell her everything I said about Posy. Mindy denies it, but I know she did. She pretends to believe me, but she doesn't. Dr. Foreman has her thinking otherwise."

"Is it true, Gia? Are you making up Posy?"

"What do you think?"

"I think you are," I said, my eyes on the hand that held that spade like a switchblade.

She smiled coldly, her small mouth stretching and curling in the corners with disgust. "You're going to be a Foreman girl then, are you? You're going to stay here or come back here and become a buddy someday so you can torment and torture someone like you?"

"No."

She crossed over to a bale of hay and sat, digging her spade into it.

"She told me what Mindy did with her baby," I said.

"Did she?" Gia smiled and shook her head. "Dr. Foreman used the same technique on me, telling me what Posy had done. This was afterward, of course."

"After what?"

"After the imaginary Posy disappeared, but that's what imaginary people do, don't they? They disappear."

"What did she tell you Posy had done?" I asked.

"Why do you want to know if you don't believe there ever was a Posy?"

I didn't say anything and she looked at the horse behind her. "Posy liked the horses, too. She would have slept with them if they had let her. I told you Natani took a liking to her just as he has taken to you. He taught her many things, but the most valuable was how to escape."

"Are you saying she escaped? I thought you believed she was put into the basement and might even still be there."

"From time to time, Posy escaped, and maybe in the end, forever."

"I don't understand, Gia."

"Do you know anything about meditation?"

"No. I mean, it's a religion or something, isn't it?"

"It's not a religion, but it's part of some religions. It's part of what Natani believes."

"What does that have to do with Posy?"

"He taught her how to meditate, to leave this world and enter some spiritual place, and when she was there, no one could touch her, hurt her. It got so she would rather be there than here all the time, and it wasn't long after that when she disappeared." Gia looked like she was crying now. I thought I saw a tear glistening on her cheek.

I stepped closer to her. "It doesn't make any sense to me. I don't know what any of that means."

"Maybe you can get Natani to show you."

"I want to believe you, Gia. I really do, and I don't want to hurt you. I'm sorry I betrayed you in there."

"You didn't betray me in there, but you are betraying me out here," she said, standing. She took her spade out of the hay.

"What does that mean?"

"You don't believe me. That's more important to me."

"I said I want to believe you."

"Do you?"

"Yes."

"Okay, we'll see. I'll give you the chance to prove that." She started out.

"When?" I called after her.

She turned back. "Maybe tonight."

"How?"

"We'll get into the basement."

"I thought you said the door had a lock on it. How can we get in?"

"Leave it to me. We'll get in and then we'll see if Posy is there or if she was," she said, and walked out of the horse barn.

Wind Song reached over the stall door and poked me in the back of my head.

I looked at him.

Was that meant to be a warning? Did he see something in Gia's actions?

Was I as crazy as Gia? Now I believed what Natani had told me . . . horses and people could talk to each other.

Meditation? Escape? What was she talking about? How was I supposed to understand any of this? More important, how had I fallen into this whirlpool of pain and confusion?

Every time Gia saw me the remainder of the day, she looked at me weirdly. She said nothing else to me about the basement and Posy, so I thought it was just something that had flown in and out of her mind as quickly as a hummingbird. However, just before we started to the house for dinner, she stepped up beside me and whispered, "Don't tell the others anything about this. It will just be you and me, understand?"

I nodded, but it all made me nervous. The one thing I didn't want to do was get into any more trouble here, but I didn't want to anger Gia any more than I already had either. I was so anxious about it all that I didn't eat well, and sure enough, before the dinner ended, Dr. Foreman came into the dining room.

"How are my girls doing tonight?" she asked, her eyes fixed mainly on me.

We all muttered all right and thank you.

"You should make sure you eat well, Phoebe. You have to keep up your strength for the challenges that lie ahead, and believe me," she said, looking at everyone now, "there are challenges. I would like to speak with you before you return to the barracks to do your homework, Phoebe. Come to the office when you're finished with your kitchen duties."

I nodded and returned to eating, but the other girls, especially Gia, looked at me and then each other.

"What's that about, I wonder?" Mindy asked.

"I don't know," I said.

"What I don't know is why she is so worried about you eating and you getting stronger," Teal said. "She didn't watch over me like that after my horrendous episode."

"Well, then," Mindy said, "maybe your episode wasn't as horrendous as you make it out to be."

"What are you talking about? You were there when they brought me back. You saw."

Mindy shrugged. "I know how to put it on, too."

"Put it on? Listen to that. Phoebe, tell her what it's like to be stung by one of those . . . things."

I looked up. "It's painful, makes you nauseous. I think I even had a fever."

"See?" Teal jumped on the end of my words.

"That's Phoebe, not you," Mindy said, barely looking at her.

"I wish it happens to you, that's all. Then we'll see how horrendous it is and isn't."

"And I wish you get bitten by a rattlesnake in the bathroom in your you know what," Mindy countered.

Teal flung a glob of her mashed potatoes at her, hitting her in the cheek.

"Bitch!" Mindy screamed. She was about to toss her glass of cranberry juice at her when M'Lady Three appeared in the doorway.

"Problem?" she asked.

"No," Mindy said quickly.

"You're a bit of a messy eater, aren't you, Mindy? Why don't you do all the dishes, silverware, and clean off the table yourself tonight? Maybe that will make you neater. You have any problem with that?" she asked quickly.

"No," Mindy said, shaking her head. Some of the mashed potato fell to her plate. She wiped her chin and looked away quickly.

"Good. The rest of you, except for Phoebe bird, return to the barracks. Let's go."

Teal, Robin, and Gia rose. Mindy lowered her head, but I could see the tips of her ears were so red, they looked like tiny candle flames. She didn't lift her head until they were gone.

"She'll be sorry," she muttered. "Just wait and see."

"Don't get into a fight again, Mindy. They're just hoping you will," I advised her. "And then you'll know what it's like in the Ice Room."

She looked at me with surprise, not expecting anything nice or kind from anyone, I think, especially one of us.

"Right," she said. "Thanks." She began to gather the dirty plates and bowls. I thought about helping her, but something told me Dr. Foreman watched us in this room. Maybe there really were microphones or secret cameras all over this place.

"See you later," I said, and went out and down to Dr. Foreman's office.

To my surprise she wasn't sitting behind her desk, but on the sofa instead. She was reading a magazine and looked up and smiled.

"Hi. Come on in."

I did and she indicated I should sit on the sofa.

"I can't believe some of the fashions young people your age are wearing these days. Look at this, for example." She turned the magazine to show me an actress wearing what looked like nothing more than two large Band-Aids over her breasts and a flimsy skirt. She had what resembled a dog collar around her neck. "And she's about to enter some award show. Would you wear that?"

I shook my head.

"I didn't think so. Mindy might. She probably wore things like this. She was a classic nymphomaniac, you know. You know what that is, of course."

"A nympho? Someone who has a lot of sex."

"Yes. Only she had those tendencies ever since junior high school, even sixth grade. To me a girl who is so wild and loose with her body has no respect for herself. I know your mother was very loose, right?"

I nodded. What could I do, deny it? She obviously knew a lot about all of us, and I did write about some of Mama's sexual escapades when I wrote my autobiography for Dr. Foreman.

"I'm impressed that you don't have those tendencies, Phoebe, but you did get yourself into trouble because of sex in your new school, didn't you?"

"I guess so." I had met a boy in the nurse's office as he had preplanned and the nurse caught us. It wasn't something I had done often before. In fact, I had never done anything that serious in school. I wanted to explain it, of course, describe how I had been desperate and angry and didn't care. However, she didn't need my explanation.

"You were most likely getting at your aunt. You wanted to embarrass her and your uncle, didn't you? You didn't want to be there and you were hoping you would be sent home, back to Atlanta, where you could be with your father, right?"

"Yes."

"Only he wasn't home very much. You would have ended up even worse than you did, Phoebe. In a way you were lucky to get into so much trouble so quickly and be sent here. I can't imagine what would have become of you had you not been picked up at the clinic. Strike that. I can imagine. I've seen girls who had to live in the streets. It's not a pretty sight, and their life expectancy isn't any better than the life expectancy of young women in some third world countries.

"Sometimes"—she sighed and looked toward the window, which had the curtains drawn open for a change—"I feel as if I have been chosen for my work, given all this responsibility by a higher power." She looked pensive for a moment, then shook her head and smiled. "Here." She handed me the magazine. "I'm sure you're interested in all this nonsense anyway."

I looked at the magazine. I did want it, but if I took that and brought it back to the barracks, I would have some explaining to do.

On the other hand, I saw that if I didn't take it, she would be angry, suspicious, and I was more afraid of that than anything.

"Thank you," I said.

"You're welcome, Phoebe. So, tell me, how did Gia treat you today?" she asked, holding her soft, friendly smile.

There was little question in my mind that she already knew.

"She was angry because I told you what she had said about Posy."

"Her Posy," Dr. Foreman muttered. "Yes. You told her you had no choice, of course."

I nodded.

"You're free to tell the other girls about it. If Gia sees no one believes her, it will help. Should Gia get violent or physical, I want to know immediately, understand?"

"Yes, Dr. Foreman."

"Good. How did she defend herself? Did she tell you anything else about her Posy? Claim she did anything?"

"She said she worked on the horses like I am." The more I told her that was true, the less I might have to tell her what I feared to tell her, I hoped.

"Yes, well, of course it was Gia who worked on the horses. You believe that, don't you?" she said quickly.

"Yes, I do."

"Good. As I mentioned before, Mindy troubles me more and more these days," she suddenly said, changing the subject. "She's really regressing."

"Regressing?"

"She's becoming more and more like she was when she first arrived here. She's too aloof, too distant most of the time. I think she's actually getting worse in some ways. I'm getting bad vibes these last few days. I want you to keep an eye on her, too, for me. Keep track of what she says, does, whenever you're around her."

"Everything she says?"

"You'll know what I want. Enjoy the magazine, but be sure to get your homework done first, understand?"

"Yes, Dr. Foreman."

"And no one else is permitted to read it, not even over your shoulder."

"But . . ."

"I don't want to hear that they have," she added, her eyes full of threat.

I nodded.

"You're excused."

I rose and started for the door.

"Phoebe."

"Yes, Dr. Foreman?"

"I think you could look a lot prettier than that so-called actress, even in those ridiculous clothes. I can see you in a modeling career someday. Would you like that?"

I nodded.

"Good. I'll see what I can do about finding you a good modeling school when the time comes."

Every time she offered to do something good for me or said something nice to me, I felt worse.

Why was that?

Why should I care about anyone else anymore? She was right after all. They would all forget me and have nothing to do with me once we all left this place, especially if I returned to my neighborhood in Atlanta or someplace like it. I was tempted to reveal the rest of it, describe exactly what Gia was planning to do tonight.

"Was there something else you wanted to tell me, Phoebe?"

Did she know already? Was she expecting me to tell? Was this another test and was I failing it?

What kept me from telling her, I do not know, but I couldn't do it.

"Yes," I said. "Thank you."

She smiled. "You're welcome, Phoebe. Most welcome," she said, nodding slowly.

I turned and left the house.

On the way back to the barracks, I was tempted to throw away the magazine, but I worried that she might ask me to return it. I know I was becoming what Gia called paranoid, too. I couldn't help looking around, searching for hidden cameras, microphones, or perhaps one of the buddies watching me from a hidden place.

Robin, Teal, and Gia looked up when I entered. They were already working on math problems. I noticed Mindy was still not back.

"Where did you get that?" Teal asked quickly, eyeing the magazine.

There was no point in lying about it. "Dr. Foreman gave it to me, but she warned me not to let anyone else look at it."

Teal immediately recoiled, pulling her head down and her arms back. "Oh, we can't look at it. Only the special Phoebe can look at it. Big deal. Who cares about some stupid magazine anyway?" She returned to her homework.

Robin stared at me with an expression of disappointment.

"I didn't ask for it. She gave it to me."

"Of course she did," Gia said. "She did the same thing with Mindy soon after I arrived. It's another one of her little ways to set us against each other and depend on her."

I wanted to warn her not to say so many terrible things about Dr. Foreman aloud. Surely a hidden microphone or two were in the barracks, but if I warned her, Dr. Foreman could hear the warning as well.

I said nothing and they returned to the homework. Gia asked me to join them and helped me with my assignments. I put the magazine under my cot and got my books and notebook. After a while, we all wondered what was keeping Mindy. Even alone, she should have finished by now, we thought. Of course we had no way to tell how much time actually went by since none of us had a watch and there were no clocks, but Robin estimated it was nearly a good two hours.

M'Lady Two appeared in the doorway and told us to prepare for bed.

"Where's Mindy?" Teal asked.

"It's none of your business where Mindy is. Your business is where you are."

I thought Teal was going to say something else, but she looked at me and then turned to her cot. Before we were all actually ready to go to bed, M'Lady Two shut off the lights.

"My business," Teal muttered. "My business is getting out of here."

No one said anything more. The air felt so heavy, even the starlight streaming through the windows looked droopy. I closed my eyes and hoped I would fall asleep quickly, but I didn't. I saw from the way Teal was lying that she had, and Robin had turned her back to me and looked very still as well.

When Gia poked me, I nearly jumped and screamed. She had moved so quietly to my bedside.

"I don't like it," she whispered. "If Mindy's not back by now, Dr. Foreman has her, and there's no telling what will happen to her. Did she indicate she was unhappy with her in any way?"

I hesitated. Should I report what Dr. Foreman had said to me?

"Yes," I whispered. "You should be careful about what you say, Gia. I really do believe there are microphones hidden around us."

"It doesn't matter. She knows what we think. Okay, let's go."

"Go?"

"To the basement, like I said we would."

"But, with Mindy gone and all, don't you think it would be more dangerous?"

"That makes no difference. Don't worry. The buddies are already into their own thing by now. They're not going to stand guard over this place. Get up, put on your clothes quietly."

"But . . ."

"Either you want to know the truth or you don't, Phoebe, but you better not call me a liar and let the others believe it. Make up your mind." Gia's face was so close to mine, I could feel her breath. "Okay. I'll go with you."

In the back of my mind I thought that if we were caught, I would tell Dr. Foreman I was going to tell her what Gia wanted to do and went along because she was going to do it with or without me. It was a weak excuse that she would probably see right through, but it was all I could come up with quickly.

Hopefully, we would find an empty basement and that would end it.

Maybe Dr. Foreman would even congratulate me. Was I terrible in hoping for that, hoping for another reward, perhaps less work, sleeping in that comfortable bed in her house, and going to a school for modeling? Was it terrible to want things for yourself, even at the expense of the others?

Natani knew how to survive out there in the raw desert world, but I had to learn how to survive here and in the world I would eventually return to, for as Dr. Foreman had made clear, I had no one but myself now. I almost never did. That was true, but at least I had had a place to call home.

That was gone forever. I guess I really did have nowhere to run to.

Did any of us? Really?

I saw Gia was already dressed and waiting.

Everyone has her own way to survive, I thought.

Maybe this was just hers and maybe I had no right to ruin that for her.

But one thing I had learned and learned painfully, choice was a privilege. Here we did what we were told or what was expected of us. Now I was Dr. Foreman's little spy.

And I had almost nothing to do with the decision to be so.

10

Good-bye, Posy

When you grow up in a city where there are always some lights on and almost always noise and traffic, your nervous system has a hard time adjusting to a world of pitch darkness and silence. For one thing, you suddenly realize the majestic starlight. Almost always, even during the short time I lived with Uncle Buster and Aunt Mae Louise in the suburban community of Stone Mountain, there were streetlights or other lights that washed out the stars and there was some traffic, people walking, music from cars.

Out here in the desert, especially late at night, the uninterrupted sky was peppered with pinholes of light, some of them so big and bright, I waited to see if they were planes. They weren't. They were simply unblocked, crystal-clear, dazzling beads of illumination. I thought to myself that if I ever wondered how God could see so much, this could be the answer. The stars are His eyes and He has so many of them.

Here on the ranch, the darkness was so different from the darkness I had known in Atlanta. This darkness was like the darkness in a dream. All of the structures, even the hacienda, were now inky silhouettes. The stillness made me conscious of my heavier, anxious breathing and the crunch of our footsteps over the gravel as we walked toward the back of the big house. There wasn't a light on anywhere inside, which meant the buddies were asleep, too.

I looked toward Natani's hogan. He wasn't anywhere in sight. He could be outside, cloaked in a shadow. Most of the time, he was just there, appearing as if he formed out of thin air, walking so softly on those moccasins that even birds didn't realize he was atop them. However, this late I imagined he was within his little house, asleep on his blanket. Even the farm animals were deathly quiet. If they weren't asleep, they were like me, listening. I did think I heard a horse snort. It was probably Wind Song, I thought. He could sense that I was out here and he wanted to know why.

"Move it," Gia whispered, and beckoned for me to catch up with her.

Suddenly she turned and headed quickly toward the tool shack.

"Where are we going?"

"I need something," she said. "You'll see."

When we reached the shack, she opened the door an inch at a time, moving the hinges as softly and as quietly as she could. Apparently, she knew exactly where what she wanted was located, because it was so dark inside, I couldn't tell a rake from a hoe. I was always thinking about snakes, although Natani had told me that snakes would look for a rock warmed by the day's sunshine and curl up on it at night. Gia didn't seem to have an ounce of fear about them. She was in and out quickly, a screwdriver in her hand.

She nodded toward the house again and we walked around the corner to the metal doors that opened on steps leading down to the door of the basement. When we were there, she indicated we should be as quiet as could be. My eyes were used to the darkness now, as were hers. Nevertheless, she surprised me by digging into her coverall pocket to produce a cigarette lighter.

"Where did you get that?" I whispered.

I could see her smiling. "I stole it from the buddies. When I was in there with Dr. Foreman one day, she left me alone and I wandered through, popped into the buddies' quarters, and found it on a desk. I got back to her office before she knew I had been about the house. I thought it would come in handy one of these days. It has.

"Here." She handed me the lighter. "Flick it on when I say. I just need to see where the hinges are screwed in. Go on, flick."

I did so and the small flame threw a lot more light on the doors than I thought it might. She started the screwdriver and had me turn off the light. I crouched and watched as she worked, moving with such care, I barely heard anything. She put each screw she took out into her pocket.

"We'll fix it when we leave," she whispered. "That way no one but you and me will know we were down there."

I nodded.

When all the screws were out, she lifted the hinge carefully and folded it over with great care, barely making a sound.

Then she stepped back. "Ready?"

I wasn't, of course. I could never be ready for this, but then, I thought, we'll go down there and look around. There'll be nothing there and she'll change on the spot, maybe even admit she had made up Posy. The whole thing would finally be over and done. It will be better for both of us. Dr. Foreman will stop questioning me about it and surely congratulate me on helping her cure Gia.

She lifted the door ever so gently and held it open just enough for me to slip in and under.

"Go ahead," she said. "Flick the lighter so you can watch your step. When you're down far enough to make room for me, I'll come in and close the door softly after us."

I hesitated and looked up at the dark windows. They were more like mirrors now, reflecting starlight. On the stucco walls, shadows danced almost like savages gleefully watching me do something stupid.

"Go on before someone hears us," Gia urged. "Go."

I took a deep breath and snapped the lighter on again. In the glow I could see that the stone steps were chipped and cracked. I saw spiderwebs in every corner, but fortunately, no sign of any snakes. Gia put her hand on my shoulder, pressing me downward. I lowered my head and stepped onto the first step, then turned and slipped under the opened metal door, backing down carefully. I held the lighter up in front of me. My arm was trembling so much that the little flame wavered, but stayed lit.

"Okay," I said.

"Wait."

"What?" My heart seemed to thump and come to a stop in anticipation. "Gia? What is it?"

"I think I hear something. Just keep still."

To my surprise and shock, she lowered the metal door. I didn't move a muscle. The light went out so I had to flick it on again. Then I heard a strange new sound, like a tiny grinding. What was that?

"Gia?"

I stepped up until my head was an inch or so from the metal door.

"Gia, what's happening?"

The grinding continued and then stopped.

"Gia?"

I heard nothing. I waited and listened.

"Gia?" I called more frantically. I pressed on the metal door, but it didn't lift. "What's happening?"

At last I heard her whisper through the crack, "I can't face her. Go on inside yourself and talk to her."

"What?"

I listened and heard nothing.

"What did you say, Gia? Gia!"

I pushed on the metal door. It moved, but this time the hasp and the lock stopped it from going any farther.

That grinding.

She had put the hinge back, screwed it in. I was locked within. My heart pounded until the blood filled my face and the pounding echoed in my ears. I pushed and pushed, but the metal door didn't budge. It was heavy, too.

I thought about screaming for help, then stopped before I started and thought, how would I explain this to Dr. Foreman now? I hadn't done anything but violated rules. The buddies were sure to pounce on me.

"Gia, please. Let me out. Please," I begged. "We'll both get into so much trouble if you don't. Please. Hurry."

I thought I felt something on my ankle and spun around, losing my balance. Fortunately I caught myself on the side of the concrete before I fell down the remaining steps, but in doing that, I dropped the lighter. I heard it bounce down the steps. Now, in the pitch darkness, I was sweating more from panic than heat. I heard myself whimper.

Slowly, using my foot, I searched each step until I felt something move. I hesitated, waiting to see if it would move again, but under its own power. I touched it, and then, confident it was the lighter, I knelt down in careful increments and felt for it. When I had my hands around it, I permitted myself to breathe again.

I flicked it on.

I had the lighter, but what was I going to do?

I looked at the door at the bottom of the stairs. Maybe it was unlocked and maybe I could make my way through the basement and then upstairs and out the front door of the hacienda without anyone hearing or knowing. It was worth a try. Certainly, I couldn't stay here all night and I didn't want to shout for help if I didn't have to.

I continued down the stairs and turned the door handle, pushing gently on it. The door groaned so I stopped and waited, listening to see if anyone moved about above. There was no sound so I pushed again and the door opened enough for me to slip through. I thought about it again, looked back up the stairs, realized I had no choice, and went into the basement.

It wasn't much of a basement, just a single, long room. I lifted the lighter as if I were imitating the Statue of Liberty or something and turned slowly. There was furniture, a small bed and a dresser. The bed had a light blue pillow and a blanket. Someone had obviously slept there. The pillow was still indented with the shape of her head.

Over to the right of the bed was a small desk, resembling the desks we had sat at when first brought to the orientation room. Instead of a stool, there was a wooden chair. I saw a small lamp on the desk and approached slowly, gazing into the dark depth of the basement. What frightened me the most, of course, was the possibility of rats.

But the basement floor was bone dry and actually looked as if it had recently been swept and vacuumed. I didn't see any spiderwebs either. I lifted the lighter a little higher and the darkness retreated a bit more. I could make out a short stairway at the far end. I didn't see into every dark corner yet, but I didn't think anyone was there.

I walked down a bit farther and held the light high enough so I could find the floor grate Gia had spoken about. I didn't, but I thought I did hear voices, so I turned quickly and retreated.

I approached the desk and found the switch for the lamp. To my joy, it lit, and with that illumination I could clearly see the whole room. Except for this little bit of furniture, there was nothing and, I concluded, releasing the hot breath I had bottled up in my lungs, no one in the basement.

I gazed at the desk and saw an envelope. The envelope wasn't addressed, but when I picked it up, I realized something was in it. I took out the paper and unfolded it. This was a letter and it began with *Dear Mom and Dad . . .*

I sat on the chair and began to read the letter.

First, I want to tell you I'm all right. It was very, very hard at first. Dr. Foreman made it seem as if this was going to be a fun place with strict rules, but nevertheless, not an unpleasant experience. She and I had a wonderful talk when I first arrived. She explained how her first concern would always be my well-being, but she wanted me to understand that sometimes, she would appear very cruel and unreasonable to me. She compared herself to a dentist.

"I've got to drill away the rot in you," she said, "the decay that's poisoning the healthy part of you."

I thought that was very reasonable and I promised her I would always try to see things from her point of view. We got started on a good note.

Here at her school, she has older girls to assist her. She told me those girls were former students. At first, I couldn't believe it. She had given them so much responsibility. How could they have been in enough trouble to be sent here and then become trusted assistants?

Dr. Foreman said that when I improved, I would probably make for a great assistant, who she calls buddies because they help the new students. They acted tough and hard, but I knew they were only trying to help me.

Anyway, I have another reason for writing this letter. Dr. Foreman has gotten me to understand that I can't improve until I admit to my problems and weaknesses. She says girls like me have to go through a process not unlike the process alcoholics experience. We have to stand up and confess first. We have to say, "I am an alcoholic."

Of course, I'm not an alcoholic. I have to say I'm a liar and a deceitful person. So, first, let me say that. I have lied and deceived you both many times. I'm sorry about it, but I'm most sorry for what I did right before I was sent here. I know it was a horrible thing to do to make Tamatha sick by putting that insect poison in her food. I was so angry, but that didn't justify it. As Dr. Foreman says, I have got to learn how to channel my anger into other, more productive activities and learn how to talk about the things that bother me. I can tell you I worked hard at hiding everything and it wasn't your fault that you never knew half the terrible things I had done. You didn't deserve to have a daughter like me.

Thanks to Dr. Foreman and her treatments, I can now do all that she suggested I should do. I'm ashamed, of course, and I'm sorry, too. We don't promise things here. Promises are like soap bubbles. They look really beautiful, but when you touch them, they pop and fall to earth and are gone. Dr. Foreman says, "They're not worth the air they're written on." She has a wonderful way of putting things sometimes.

So I won't make promises about the future and how I will behave. I'll just do the right thing.

I don't want you to believe that all this has happened overnight. It took a long time and I had to do many, many things that I know would be unpleasant to any-one else, especially some of my so-called friends. Dr. Foreman has shown me how none of them were really my friends.

There is only one other girl here at the moment. Dr. Foreman says the new girl and I are sort of between scheduling periods, and new girls will be arriving soon. Dr. Foreman just doesn't take anyone that people want to send here. She spends a lot of time analyzing and thinking about the girl and her problems first.

This other girl who is here is a lot like me in so many ways, but she is very unhappy and still very angry at the world and everyone in it. She hates me for being happy about anything. She calls me Pollyan-

naish and says my eyes are blinded by stars. She's very intelligent, but very bitter.

Dr. Foreman decided recently that she was not a good influence on me and we, therefore, had to be separated. She gave me a new place to stay. At first, it was a very lonely place and then, one day, a man, an Indian man who is in charge of the ranch animals and farming, told me that the world is really inside you and not outside you. His name is Natani and I did not understand what he meant, of course.

But he showed me how to look inside myself and find the world I needed. That's really where I go now. In the beginning, I was there for very short periods. Those periods grew longer and longer until I realized I could go there forever, if I wanted. I told Natani and he didn't say I should or shouldn't. He said I would know myself how long I should be away.

This is probably confusing you. I know it's hard for anyone who hasn't done it to understand.

But, I can't explain it any more than to say, I'm happy, happy enough to want to stay here forever.

So, Mom and Dad, I wanted to write this last letter to you and tell you good-bye, but not a sad good-bye. Oh, no. This is a happy good-bye for I am not leaving you. In my world we are always together and, Mom, you are as beautiful as you were when you were a young woman, and, Daddy, you are as handsome as you were when you were a young man, and do you know what else? You don't get old in this world. You are young forever and ever, and you are always laughing and smiling. We're together the way we should be, the way we once were, and you always have time for me.

So be happy for me, Mom.

Be happy for me, Dad.

I love you more now.

Forever,

Posy

I stared at the name and then I reread the letter.

Something creaked behind me and I spun around, half expecting now to see a fragile, diminutive, young girl smiling. There was no one and it was deadly silent.

I folded the letter and put it back into the envelope and left it on the desk. I wanted to get out of here as quickly as I could. I switched off the small lamp and flicked my lighter. Moving slowly to keep the flame from going out, I headed toward the short stairway.

When I reached the foot of it, another light went on and every breath in my body flew out of my body like a flock of sparrows abruptly frightened. Every bone turned to marshmallow. I felt as if I had stepped into a pool of ice water, the cold racing up my legs into my stomach and over my breasts, pushing my blood into my head.

There, in a tiny circle of illumination created by a large flashlight pointing up just under her chin, was Dr. Foreman. Her face absorbed the light and emerged from the darkness as if it were made of some luminescent substance, her eyes dark and gaunt, her teeth incandescent. Actually, she looked more like a skeleton resurrected.

"Careful, Phoebe," she said. "Watch your step, dear."

I didn't know what to say, what to do. I was still too frozen to move.

"Don't be afraid. First, I want you to return to the desk and get that letter. Go on." She pointed the flashlight to create a lighted pathway for me. "Go!"

I moved quickly, snapped up the envelope, and returned to the stairway.

"Come up now." She directed the beam of light to the wooden steps. "The lighting down here doesn't work. It hasn't for as long as I've had the place, but it never mattered. I don't use the basement that often. We clean it from time to time and check our plumbing, but that's about it," she explained, as if it were important for me to know the most insignificant details about the house.

I started up the stairs and she turned and opened the door that led into the downstairs hallway.

"Come along."

I followed her down the hall to her office. The house was as quiet and as dark as the basement had been. She flipped the light switch and entered, turning to encourage me to follow. I know I was moving, but I was so frightened, I didn't think about it. I floated in behind her and sat on the sofa.

She pulled a chair up and sat right in front of me, smiling at me. I still held on to the letter, expecting she would take it, but she didn't ask for it or pluck it from my fingers.

"Look at you. You look like you've actually seen a ghost."

"I'm sorry, Dr. Foreman. I thought that if I did what Gia wanted, she would change. I would tell her there was no Posy and then she would stop talking about her, but she tricked me and locked me in and . . ."

Dr. Foreman actually laughed. "Cure Gia? That's what you hoped to do in one evening? I only wish it had been that easy, Phoebe. Gia has been here almost a year."

"A year? But Mindy told us she was here four months and Gia was here seven."

"That's what Gia told her, I'm sure. Actually, that makes sense. It was about five months ago that Posy left. In her bizarre counting, that's how she sees it."

"What do you mean since Posy left? I thought there wasn't any Posy? That letter downstairs? Was that written by the real Posy?"

"No," she said, still laughing. "That was Gia, but that was when Posy left. It's all as I told you."

"I don't understand," I said, shaking my head.

"You will." She looked very pleased.

"You're not mad at me for going down there?"

"No, Phoebe. It was my idea. When I spoke with Gia after you told me what she was saying, I convinced her to do exactly what she has done."

"What?"

"I told Gia she had to do it, she had to get you into the basement so you could see for yourself that Posy was gone. Actually, she went about it cleverly. I didn't think about the details, unscrewing the hinge, screwing it back on, all that. I expected to find her down there with you. See how bright she can be? If some of the girls sent to me would put their energy and ingenuity into worthwhile and good things . . ."

She shook her head and contemplated me again. "I knew you didn't believe me completely. I thought that this would be the best way for you to see for yourself and understand. You do now, don't you?"

"No, not really." I didn't know whom to feel sorrier for, myself or Gia.

Dr. Foreman looked impatient and annoyed for a moment, then softened.

"All right. I'll spell it all out for you. Gia was the one in the basement. I put her there as part of a therapy program I designed. She had cleverly invented this fictional character so as to avoid any hardship, any pain inflicted on her. As long as she had Posy, she could deny her own problems. They were Posy's problems, understand?

"Making Posy my daughter was her way of getting back at me."

"Why didn't you just send her away to a clinic or something?" I asked.

"She wasn't crazy. She was clever and still is. I knew I would eventually help her if I kept trying and utilizing some of my own methods. They worked. She wrote that letter as a way of saying good-bye, which was also quite clever I thought."

"What is all that about Natani?"

"Natani." She shook her head. "He's delightful with his Indian ways. He has no idea how often he has helped me with my girls.

That's why I keep him on, actually. He's a calming factor. Sort of a release valve. This place is a pressure cooker at times."

"But, Gia told me I'd find Posy down there so she still believes in her. She's still not cured, right?"

"Well, it doesn't matter that she still believes there was a Posy. The most important thing now is after you tell her and show her everything, she won't be using Posy ever again as a scapegoat. That's my first goal in treating her. Anything she does now, she knows is her own fault. Unless, of course, she creates someone else, but I don't think she will. I think she's finally past all that and on her way."

"What do you want me to do?"

"Specifically, you will return to the barracks and you will tell her there was no one there, and you'll give her that letter. You'll tell her you read it. You know it was a letter to Posy's parents and you know she's gone for good. And you know Posy lied when she said she was my daughter.

"So," she continued, leaning over to pat my knees, "you see, you really will have helped me. Unwittingly, perhaps, but nevertheless, you will have."

I shook my head. It was all still so confusing, so off-the-wall for me, the way she had used me and was still using me. If anything, it made me want to get out of here even more. I think she saw that in my face.

"For now, I don't want any of the other girls to know about any of this. It's our little secret, our problem to solve. I expect you to carry out this order, Phoebe," she said sternly. "You understand what I want?"

"Yes."

"You've made some nice strides these past few days, Phoebe. I can see you growing and changing and becoming someone who can be trusted with responsibilities. You're going to be fine, despite the unfortunate hand you've been dealt in your life."

She stared at me with that soft smile on her face again, the smile that deceives, that gives girls like me so much hope. I remember seeing a mean boy tormenting a stray dog once in Atlanta. He spoke to it softly, kindly, and the dog wagged its tail and filled its heart with trust as it drew closer, and when it was close enough, the boy swung the stick he had behind his back and struck the animal so hard, it lost its balance, scraping its paws over the road to get its bearing and get away, but it wasn't fast enough to avoid a second cruel blow. It managed to run off then, the boy's evil cackle following it like some flame of hate and rage. The boy turned and looked at me. He had a face full of anger, but also satisfaction. He had hurt something and taken revenge on a world that rained pain on him, I thought.

And then I thought what great pain was showered down on Dr. Foreman to make her the way she was?

If she knew I even thought such a thing, she would lose that smile so quickly, my head would spin.

"Okay, Phoebe. Go on back to the barracks. Take the letter and do as I said."

I rose and walked out of her office, down the dark hallway and out the front door. The grounds that had been dreamy with a ceiling filled with stars now just looked dark. I felt as if I were walking through a tunnel at the end of which was only a deep hole.

When I reached the barn, I paused and looked back. I thought I could make out a tall, darker shadow on the steps of the hacienda.

Doesn't she sleep? I wondered, and entered the barn.

Gia was in her cot and looked to be asleep. Everyone else was.

I approached her quietly and knelt at her side, poking her gently.

Her eyes opened and she looked at me, but she didn't sit up.

"I'm sorry," she said. "I had to do it that way."

"I know."

"Did you see her?"

"No, but I found this letter she wrote. She's gone. It's a letter to her parents telling them good-bye. I read it and I know she's gone, and I also know she was lying about being Dr. Foreman's daughter. Whatever you heard her say to Dr. Foreman wasn't true. Dr. Foreman probably just humored her until she could help her. Read it all and you'll see."

She glanced at the letter, but she didn't move.

"Take it and read it in the morning," I said, offering it.

She started to shake her head.

"You have to take it." I shoved it under her pillow.

I stood up and only then realized that Mindy was back and in her cot. She was lying there, her eyes wide-open, staring at me.

"Where were you?" I asked.

"I had a special session with Dr. Foreman. Where were you?" The silvery starlight through the windows put an evil glow on her smile.

I didn't reply. I went to my cot and fell asleep almost a second after I closed my eyes. I was so deeply asleep so quickly, I thought the poke in my ribs was part of my dream. Finally, I realized it wasn't and awoke.

Gia was at my bedside, her face close to mine. "At least now you know I wasn't lying. There was a Posy."

She returned to her cot. Mindy watched her and looked at me.

I don't think I had ever really prayed properly in my life. Daddy did his best to teach me religion and took me to church whenever he had an opportunity, but I always had trouble talking to an entity that never spoke back. I used to sit in the church and wait anxiously to hear some great, booming voice come down from the ceiling or out of the altar. When it didn't, I just thought everyone was pretending.

I asked Mama about it once and she told me I was a fool, but my daddy was a bigger fool.

"God talks only to the rich," she said. "Why you think they're so damn lucky?"

I didn't know what that meant either.

I still didn't really know what it all meant.

But what I did know as I lay there was I was going to find a way to ask God to help me and get me out of this place.

I wasn't rich, but I had confidence that He would find a way.

But what it would take me a long time to understand was why He chose the way out for me He chose.

11

Inward Journey

Gia was certainly different after my basement experience. She seemed less angry, but more depressed. The defiance we had sensed within her when we three had first arrived was gone. She no longer snapped at Teal or Robin, and especially not at me. In fact, I saw her avoiding me. All I had to do was turn her way and she would quickly shift her eyes or look down to avoid mine. It was almost as if she were ashamed of what I knew.

She had less energy, too, worked slower, ate slower, and ate less. Mindy could babble in her ear and she wouldn't turn on her and whip her with any words, any warnings, as she had usually done since the day we had arrived. It was almost as if she were truly shrinking inside herself, disappearing the way her precious Posy had disappeared.

Dr. Foreman looked pleased about all this. I saw the smile of satisfaction on her lips when she looked at Gia now. It soaked me in a new downpour of rage to know I had been manipulated and used to help bring this about. I was the one who felt guilty now. I felt responsible for the changes in Gia, even though Gia had trapped me in that basement.

No one does anything she really wants to do here, I concluded. It might take some time, more time for one of us than another, but eventually, Dr. Foreman pulls our strings. We move like puppets on a stage she creates.

I think she caught these thoughts in my eyes when she glanced at me and saw how hatefully I was glaring back at her. She didn't cut her face with the sharp, cold smile I expected. Instead, she fixed her gaze on me thoughtfully for a few moments, then turned away slowly and walked off. I can't say I wasn't frightened by that, but my anger disguised it well.

These dark realizations should have left me as depressed and defeated as Gia now was, but instead, it restored my inner fury and strengthened my defiance. Certainly I was afraid of being returned to the Ice Room and having the rats, real or not, running all over me. So, I worked at my chores. I obeyed all the rules. I recited the morning prayer in which we gave thanks to Dr. Foreman. I recited the apologies we were supposed to make to the buddies and to ourselves. I did all I was told to do obediently, but a fire was building inside me. I could feel the heat around my heart. It made me toss and turn at night. It put a little more strength in my walk and it made those mountains in the distance look closer.

Like the cornered rats that filled me with terror, I bared my teeth. I raised my back and I looked for an opportunity to strike out.

Despite what I was sure Dr. Foreman saw in me, she continued to be pleasant, to offer me new privileges, to drive a wedge between me and the others. I knew I couldn't refuse anything, but I believed in my heart that she knew she hadn't defeated me yet. Of course, that frightened me more than anything. She was not going to give up. She had so many other techniques and plans yet to employ. Something new could come from any direction at any time. The expression *you're walking on thin ice* never had more meaning for me than it did here. I knew I would in time fall through and she would have me wrapped in something so terrible I would lose my name. I would be erased and recreated in her image. It gave new meaning to the word *clones* that Gia had used when she used to talk more angrily about our buddies.

As Dr. Foreman had warned us that first day in the orientation room, she did have godlike powers in her world and we were surely in her world. Her voice cracked like a whip above our heads, even, I noticed, when she spoke to the buddies. They were her girls, but they were almost as afraid of her as we were when they were in her presence.

Only Natani seemed to have a sense of well-being and peacefulness here. He moved through all this as if he were truly in his own world, isolated from the loud shouting, the biting sarcasm, the punishments inflicted on us, and the clouds of depression that hovered above our heads. How could he do that? I wondered. It was like a man walking through a raging fire, never singed, not even sweating.

I studied him with more interest, especially now that I had read the letter written by the imaginary Posy. Was that all part of Gia's madness or was there really such a thing as escaping into yourself? Was there a way to fortify yourself, to do something that would protect you from Dr. Foreman's bullets and arrows? And if there was, would Natani, who supposedly owed her so much, be willing to show it to me? Was that what he was trying to do when he had told me to keep my hogan closed inside me?

I was still the one he favored to work with the horses. Gia had said that Posy had loved working with the horses, and Gia said Natani had taken a special liking to her. Of course, now I knew that she meant herself. She just couldn't believe anyone would or could like her, and if they did, they had to be liking her imaginary second self.

A little over a week after my experience in the basement, I was brushing Wind Song when Natani came into the barn and began to repair a stall door.

I took a deep breath and turned to him. "Natani, can you show me how to escape from unhappiness, to travel to another world, a world inside you?"

He paused and looked at me without saying no or saying yes.

"I'm afraid that if they put me back in that place, the Ice Room, or do something equally terrible, I'll crack up completely. I need someplace else to go."

He nodded and sat back on the barn floor.

"There is a story," he began, "about a desert rat pacing back and forth in front of a tortoise and pausing once in a while to look at the tortoise, who had a smile of contentment on his face.

" 'What do you have to be contented about?' the rat asked him. 'It's one hundred and twenty degrees. Ravens and buzzards are circling around us all day. Who knows when it rained last?'

" 'I am contented,' the tortoise replied, 'because when something unpleasant happens, I just return to my shell. In here I can cross over to a world where it is cool, where there are no ravens and buzzards, and where there is always a cool and refreshing stream.'

" 'How can you have all that in there?' the rat asked, amazed. 'Your shell is far too small.'

" 'No,' the tortoise said, 'this world in which you pace and worry is too small. In here, there are no horizons, no bottoms to streams, and no roof to the sky, because in here, I make my dreams.'

" 'How do you make dreams?' the rat asked.

" 'Ah,' the tortoise said, 'if you knew that, you would be a tortoise, too.'

"And with that, he pulled into his shell and the rat went on pacing and worrying until he wore himself out and a buzzard had him for breakfast."

Natani turned to go back to fixing the stall door.

"I don't understand your story, Natani," I said. "What does that have to do with me and my problem?"

He paused again. "First, you must become the tortoise, daughter of the sun. First, you must make yourself a shell."

"But how?"

"You must find a place where you can make your dreams safely. But, there is another story I must tell you. It is the story of a tortoise who grew so contented and so satisfied with his dreams, he never came out of his shell. He starved to death."

"Yeah, well, I might be better off," I muttered.

He thought for a moment and then nodded. "Tonight, when the clouds are asleep, too, you come to my hogan and I will help you find your shell."

A part of me was afraid, not of what Natani might do and say, but afraid that he might be doing something Dr. Foreman wanted him to do. She had told me she tolerated him and that he served a purpose. She seemed so powerful. It was hard to imagine any place or anyone on this ranch of hers that wasn't in some way under her control.

What if she had expected I would ask Natani for some sort of help now? What if she assumed I would because of what I had read in Posy's letter? She might even have told Natani to expect me to ask. How much in debt to her was he? Were the animals the only ones to trust on this ranch? The only ones who didn't lie?

I didn't say anything about all this to either Teal or Robin, and certainly I wouldn't have said anything to Mindy or Gia. It saddened me to realize that no one could be trusted even after all this time together, that we were all so beaten down and defeated that they might betray me as quickly as I might betray them. In the end we will have no place to go and no one else to turn to but Dr. Foreman, I thought. It was almost as if I could feel two large hands molding us into forms the way we had molded our ceramic dishes and bowls.

There was truly no other escape but Natani's tortoise shell, whatever that was. I would either get up the courage to sneak out of the barn tonight and go to his hogan, or I would continue to be the desert rat and pace and worry until Dr. Foreman, like the buzzard, plucked the soul out of me and turned me into one of her famous Foreman girls. That had been Gia's prediction for me, but ironically, it was turning out to be a prediction she should have made for herself. We were all closing up, but not in the sort of shell Natani had described. We had met as strangers and we were returning to being strangers.

These days the buddies didn't have to enforce the no-talking rule when they wanted it to be enforced. We all ate quietly at dinner after mumbling thank-yous to each other, chewing mindlessly, staring at nothing. Mindy was the occasional exception. She had the most nervous energy, I thought. The silence appeared to heighten it. Her eyes darted about as if she was expecting something terrible to occur or someone to yell at her. She nearly dropped a plate during cleanup and turned white with fear for a moment. Was Dr. Foreman right about her? Was she regressing, becoming worse instead of better each day?

After we ate dinner, we did at least help each other with the school assignments, but that was still for selfish reasons. No one wanted to earn any more demerits. Our grades were all passing and even the buddies had to admit we were doing well on that score. This was still Gia's doing. She seemed alive actually only when it came to schoolwork, and I began to feel sorry for her, sorry that she wasn't at a real school because she seemed to enjoy studying, reading. It was the only time now that we heard any excitement in her voice, saw any brightness in her eyes. She might even make a good teacher someday, I thought, a real teacher with students who were interested and cared.

Funny how memories of school suddenly became desirable. I had hated it so much when I was there, or at least, I thought I had. Now when I recalled the chatter, the excitement, even the classes, I felt a longing I hadn't thought I would ever feel. This was in no way like the school I had known and abused.

This particular evening, after dinner, we had only a little schoolwork in comparison to what we had been given beforehand nightly. It left us with some free time, and to the surprise of us all, M'Lady Two showed up with a half dozen relatively recent magazines popular with teenagers.

"Dr. Foreman says you all deserve some foolish and wasteful reading. You can share these among you." She dropped the magazines at her feet.

Teal started eagerly for the pile, moving like a starving person toward food, but Gia stopped her with "Don't touch them!" She said it with such hysteria, Teal practically jumped back.

"What? Why not?" She looked at the pile. "What's on them?"

"In them," Gia whispered. "It's what's in them." She stared at them, then looked up at all of us. "Subliminal messages," she muttered.

"Huh?" Robin said, scrunching her nose. "What's that?"

"It's a secret way to get you to think what she wants you to think," Gia said.

Robin pulled her head back and looked at Teal, who shook hers and shrugged. Mindy didn't move, didn't speak.

"We don't understand, Gia," I said. "How can she put something in a magazine secretly?"

"She can! It's like you go to the movies and they stick a few frames of popcorn in the movie. It flashes by too fast for you to realize it, but you suddenly want to get up and get popcorn."

"You're crazy," Robin said.

"It's a proven thing. I read about it," Gia said.

"So she gets me to eat popcorn. Big deal," Robin told her, moving to the magazines.

"That's just an example. She'll get you to do something else. She never does anything, gives you anything, unless it helps her control you, change you."

"You're a paranoid." Robin picked up the magazine she wanted and looked at Gia. "When are you going to learn? Adults always get us to do what they want one way or another. You're the one who taught me that." Robin looked at Teal, who moved to the magazines next. Mindy shrugged and did the same. Gia looked at me and shook her head in pity. Her warning got me thinking.

Dr. Foreman had given me a magazine and told me I wasn't permitted to let any of them read it. Was there something in it specifically for me, something that made me do what she wanted? Maybe there was. Maybe Gia wasn't as crazy as they thought, at least when it came to this.

I turned away from the pile without taking any magazine.

"You're not taking a magazine? You believe her nonsense?" Robin cried, amazed.

"I'm just not interested in any of the magazines."

"That's bull. You took one from her already. Now, because of what Gia's saying, you're afraid," Robin said, smiling. "Gia has you afraid."

"So, I'm afraid. Think what you like. I stopped caring about what any of you think about me," I said. "Just like you stopped caring about what any of us think about you."

I went to my cot to lie down. Robin and Teal thumbed through the magazines excitedly, talking about the clothing styles, the new television shows, the movies they were missing. They moaned over this dreamy young male actor or that. They did it all with exaggeration to make me jealous.

Teal began to describe some of the wonderful things she had at home and Robin talked about her music, admitting she even wished she could listen to her mother darling's singing and playing. Both wondered aloud what was the latest hit record, and suddenly, I realized what Gia was saying.

I sat up and exclaimed, "That's it!" They all looked at me.

"What's it?" Teal said, smiling.

"Gia's right."

"She's right?"

"Only it's not sub whatever she called it. It's right there in front of you, in front of us. Just listen to you talking. She wants you to see what you're missing, to moan and cry about it all."

"Why?"

"So you'll be sorrier about what you're missing, and more obedient and hope more that you'll go home," I said.

"Yes," Gia said, nodding and whispering. "Yes. You understand, Phoebe. Good. These magazines, anything like that, are a form of subtle torture, torment." She turned to the others. "Don't you understand what we're saying? Look at yourselves, what you're wearing, your hands, your hair, and then look at the girls in the magazines. What would you do, would you give, to be like they are?"

The three of them looked at the magazines and then at me.

Robin was the first to understand. I could see it spread through her face, brighten her eyes. She flung her magazine across the barn as if it were poison. Teal stared sadly for a moment, then dropped hers where M'Lady Two had put the pile. Mindy looked wistfully at her magazine and then flipped it.

"I hate her," she said in a loud, hoarse whisper. She slammed her folded arms against herself so hard, I thought she might have cracked a rib. Then she went to her cot.

Moments later, they were all on their cots and back to being enveloped in a coat of depression. Gia and I exchanged looks of satisfaction, but also sadness. Who wanted to be right about such a thing?

The girls said nothing more. They were all asleep before the lights were out in fact, but I couldn't fall asleep.

I could think only of Natani's shell.

When I felt it was safe, I crawled out of bed, quietly put on my shoes, and tiptoed out of the barn. I stood for a few moments outside and studied the yard. Lights were on in the hacienda, especially upstairs where the buddies stayed, but everywhere else was in darkness and thick shadows because the sky was partly overcast with a thin, long sheet of clouds sliding over the stars.

As I started across, I heard a coyote howl, then a bird that seemed to be on fire flew from the roof of the horse barn into some high brush. I tried to keep within the shadows until I turned the corner and headed directly for Natani's hogan. There was no way to tell if he was awake. There was no light. I knocked softly on the frame of the doorway, and when I heard his voice, I slipped into his home. He was sitting in a lotus position and in front of him was what looked like a pile of ordinary rocks.

"Sit, daughter of the sun," he said, indicating I should take the place before him.

I hesitated for a moment, then did it, folding my legs like his. He reached back and cupped a jug.

"Drink this first," he said, offering it to me.

I wasn't particularly crazy about the smell, and again I thought, what if this was all arranged by the good Dr. Foreman?

"What is it?" I asked.

"It is something that will start you on the path, help you find your way. Just this once. You won't need it after this. I promise."

"How can this drink do that?" I looked at the tea.

"You will see things as they really are, and when you do, you will be in your shell."

Skeptical and still afraid, I nevertheless began to drink the tea. While I did, Natani began a soft, low chant and tapped on a small drum. As I continued to drink the tea, I couldn't help but think about some of my friends back in Atlanta and how they would laugh and ridicule me for being with this old Indian man. But of course, they were there and I was here.

I wasn't put off by the taste, and I think that even if I were, I would have forced myself to drink it all. I was that desperate. I waited for more instructions, but Natani just continued to chant and play his drum. I was beginning to feel more disappointment than anything else. Here I was sitting in an old Indian man's shack, listening to him play a drum and sing some song I couldn't understand. I couldn't help feeling ridiculous. Maybe that was Dr. Foreman's intention. I was a fool after all.

Natani knew some things, but he was still an old, nutty man. Everything in Posy's letter was part of an imagination gone wild. It all started to make more sense to me. Dr. Foreman didn't care if we talked to Natani or asked him for his mystical help. He was a big joke, a dead-end road that didn't lead out of here after all.

Suddenly though, I became aware of a slow dance of golden lights rising out of the pile of stones between us. They turned red and moved in rhythm to Natani's drum. I rubbed my eyes, but they were still there so I closed my eyes, but the shapes continued. They went from yellow to red to gray and then blue. They looked like jellyfish, but became small balls that elongated and turned to ribbons of light. Finally, they all became bubbles and rose quickly, popping and disappearing.

Natani's drum seemed to be beating inside me now. When I looked at him, I focused on a crease in his shirt, and for some reason it looked beautiful. The shape of it, the way it flowed along and softened, was all fantastic to me. It made me feel good to make such a discovery.

I gazed around the hogan and stared for a while at a feather he had on the wall. My eyes were like magnifying glasses because every part of the feather stood out, its shape, its color, its texture. Again I thought, how beautiful it is and how wonderful that I have made the discovery.

I felt myself smiling, and although I couldn't explain why it should be, I was content, happy. For a moment I thought of Natani's story and the rat's question to the tortoise: Why are you so content?

The drum stopped and Natani reached for my hand and guided me to my feet. "Go look at the world you have come to hate."

I turned and stepped out of the hogan.

The darkness was lifting like a curtain. I looked at the hacienda, the horse barn, the pigpen, the barn in which we slept, and it all just seemed to come together, but in a lovely way. Each shape was unique and yet I could feel the way everything flowed into everything else and flowed into me.

Suddenly, I wanted to embrace all of it, the weeds that grew at the sides of the buildings, the railings on the hacienda, which were so amazing in the way they were the same and yet different, each with something unique about it that I had not seen before, the garden with plants that were like ocean waves in the breeze. I loved everything.

"What do you see?" Natani asked me.

"Everything." I held out my arm and I felt myself touch the railing, touch the weeds, touch the plants. I could reach the very stars that pulsated, each resembling a tiny heart beating. It made me spin around and laugh. "It's all beautiful!" I cried. Even the ground looked beautiful, spreading before me like a soft carpet, the grains of sand dazzling.

"If you see the world as it is, you will see you are a part of it and none of it will make you unhappy," he said. "The world itself is a great shell. There is no other to seek.

"First, be at peace with your surroundings. See how you are a part of all that there is and how all that there is becomes you. All else will follow, daughter of the sun. I have given you only a small window. You must understand how you should not hate the wind for being the wind or the sun for being the sun. Soon, you will not hate yourself for being who you are either. If you do this, you will need nothing more. You will find your way in and out of your shell and nothing will harm you."

A moment later he was gone. He had stepped back into his hogan.

I don't know how long I remained there looking at everything as if for the first time. I don't remember returning to the barn and getting back to my cot, but then I was there, and for a long moment I wondered if I had ever left the barn. Had it all been a dream?

I fell asleep and did dream. I saw my daddy beckoning to me. He wanted me to come with him, to go somewhere with him. I was very little. My hand was lost in his. He lifted me into his arms. I could feel him carrying me along. Where was he taking me? What did he want to show me?

Outside our window on a ledge, a sparrow had built a nest and the eggs had cracked open. Tiny baby birds were crying and their mother was rushing to and fro with insects for them to eat.

"They're like you," Daddy said. "This is your nest."

I was fascinated.

I had forgotten that time, those birds. The way Daddy had held my hand and watched them with me. How could I have forgotten all that?

My daddy closed the window softly and carried me back to bed, where I fell asleep with a smile of contentment on my face that would make the desert rat and even the tortoise envious.

In the days following my visit to Natani's hogan, I wasn't able to tell anyone what he had taught me. I wasn't sure what it was myself exactly. All I knew was, whenever I felt overwhelmed, annoyed, or angry, I would stop, take a deep breath, and concentrate on something beautiful around me. The bad feeling would lose its grip on me, and after a while whatever it was that had caused it no longer seemed important.

The buddies, especially M'Lady One, took my behavior to mean I had lost all resistance and defiance. They had me where they wanted me. At least, that was what they believed. I could see it in their satisfied faces and even heard them say things like "I knew it was just a matter of time with her. They think they're all so tough until they get here."

Even hearing that sort of thing didn't bother me. If it was so important to them to win, let them win, I thought. What was it they actually won anyway? I guess it was the satisfaction in knowing no one was better than they were, no one could resist and fight what they couldn't resist and fight. That made them comfortable with who and what they were now. Whether they were uncomfortable wasn't important. It was a waste of energy to hate them. Someday, they would be gone forever from my life.

None of the other girls seemed to have what I now had, especially Teal. Of all of us, even after what we had each experienced in one way or another, Teal was still the most impatient, upset, and annoyed. Being terrified of any new punishment kept her from being too loud or ever openly refusing to do anything. She never muttered anything within the hearing of any of the buddies and was always subdued and as submissive as a puppy in Dr. Foreman's presence, but when she could, when it was safe, she moaned and groaned.

She hated the wind for what it was doing to her skin and she hated the sun for the same reasons. This was a filthy, dirty place. We were all going to die of some disease. We might as well just run off and die in the desert as she had almost died. What was the point of waiting for a release that would never come?

I was tempted to send her to Natani. I even started to talk to her about it, but she shook her head and said, "He's as crazy as the rest of them here. Why would he stay here? Why would anyone choose this place?"

It did no good to tell her that this was his world and he was happy in it. She could never understand how anyone would be happy in a world without television, movies, cars, parties, clothes, and jewelry.

Perhaps it was the rhythm of our lives here, the sameness of our chores, our schedule, the ordinary meals, the continuous schoolwork, and the dreaded therapy sessions with Dr. Foreman that tore at Teal more, but I could see she was growing worse with every passing day. Like Gia, she ate less and less. She was soon almost as thin as Mindy.

And she returned to her chant: "I'm going crazy here. I can't stand it much longer. I've got to get out of here. I've got to try to escape again. Why would those damn buddies enjoy this? Why did they come back? If I ever got the opportunity to get away, you wouldn't see me within a hundred miles of this place."

She recited it all one morning when it was just she, Robin, and me out there working in the garden. Mindy and Gia had been given orders to straighten up and clean out the shed.

"It could be they're having more fun than we think," Robin offered. "And I don't mean just tormenting and lording it over us. Remember what Gia and Mindy told us about spying on their partying."

Teal nodded. "Yes, at least they have that, don't they? Why don't we spy on them one night, too, and see just what it is they do have?"

Neither Robin nor I replied. Stepping out of the prescribed order of things had become frightening.

"Well, what's wrong with that idea? At least it will be something fun to do. Robin?" Teal continued, her voice building with enthusiasm.

"I'd be afraid of getting caught," Robin simply admitted.

"We won't get caught. Phoebe?"

"I'm not interested in them."

"Me neither. There couldn't be more uninteresting people on the face of the earth. It's just something to do, something that we weren't told we have to do," Teal moaned. When neither Robin nor I replied, she said, "Oh, forget it. I'll do it myself. I don't need you."

Robin and I still said nothing. Sometimes, I thought, it was better not to talk, to be like the animals, to listen and see and react only to actions.

Teal realized her threat wasn't getting her anywhere with us and she returned to whining. "Come on, Robin, don't be such a wimp. It's something to do and who knows what we'll see. Maybe we'll learn something. Come on. Do it with me. Please. What's the big deal? We'll peep in a window, that's all, but I'd like to see them with their panties down. I'd like to have something on them. It will make us feel better. You'll see. Please."

Robin looked at me and shrugged. "I guess it might be worth a smile, and if we were very careful about it . . ."

I shook my head. "It's not worth anything to me."

"We'll sneak out tonight," Teal said excitedly, building on Robin's weak moment. "Okay?"

"Yeah, maybe," Robin told her.

"Good. Come on, Phoebe. One for all and all for one. We came here together," Teal reminded me as if that solidified us for life and we owed each other.

I had to laugh. It seemed years ago when we'd first met in that concrete room. "Yeah, we're about as loyal to each other as people in the same chain gang." I laughed again. They laughed, too.

The sound was so rare, it was alien to me for a few moments. Laughter, fun, excitement. How far back had I left them? Was it possible to regain any part of myself or was it all being buried for good out here?

How long had it been since I had done anything that was in the slightest way fun? Parties, boys, pizza, my desire for it all seemed to have gone into hibernation, and that really bothered me. The only thing that made my heart pound now was fear.

"All right," I said. "Maybe."

"Should we tell Mindy and Gia?" Teal asked.

"I don't think so," I said.

Subtly, I had begun to feel the division that had existed when we had first arrived. It had all returned.

"Phoebe's right. They've already done it anyway," Robin reminded us. "It won't be as interesting to them. We'll just have to be very quiet about sneaking out."

"Okay," Teal said. Nothing could discourage her now. She was on a roll.

In fact, she was so cheered by the idea of such an adventure she worked harder, and that night she ate better than she had all week. I thought one of the buddies or Gia would be suspicious and realize something was up, but no one seemed to notice, especially not Mindy, who was spinning someplace deep in her own thoughts. She was doing it more and more now, sometimes actually talking aloud to herself.

What was happening to her? Was it something Dr. Foreman actually saw or actually caused?

Against this cloud that both Gia and Mindy kept around them was the light of Teal's brightened eyes. It was infectious. Robin looked excited and happier, too.

Perhaps something good had already come of the idea, I thought.

I just hoped nothing bad would.

12

Pajama Party

Just above the metal doors that opened on the stairway down to the basement, there was a slanted roof that looked like it was part of a recent addition to the main section of the hacienda. The roof was different, even though the walls were the same shade of stucco. We didn't go back there much, but I had seen it when I was with Gia and could see it from the cornfield when we worked there. Above the roof was the line of windows that we assumed, from what Gia and Mindy had described, were in the rooms occupied by the buddies, rooms we had once hoped would be ours.

Teal, now emboldened by her excitement, went behind the hacienda right before showering for the night and returned to report what she had seen. We had decided not to ask Gia or Mindy about how they had spied on the buddies. That would tip them off that we were going to do it now, too.

Teal said a metal drum was rolled over in the yard right behind the hacienda. She said we could stand the drum up, then stand on it to boost ourselves onto the short roof.

"It was probably the way Gia and Mindy did it," Teal said. "It's easy."

Pretending to go sleep was hard. Now that I had committed to the spying, I was filled with anxiety that made me feel as if I had swallowed a dozen live butterflies. They were flapping their silky wings against the inside of my stomach. I couldn't stay in the same position on my cot for more than a minute or so, and I was afraid my tossing and turning would stir Mindy's or Gia's curiosity.

Neither she nor Mindy said anything to indicate they heard or were still awake, but I still thought Teal was getting up too early. She squatted and tapped Robin on her shoulder. I watched them, and for a moment I seriously considered not going along. They hesitated and beckoned. I took a deep breath, glanced at Mindy and Gia, who looked dead to the world, and then I rose, picked up my shoes, and carried them as I walked as softly as I could over the straw. We said nothing to each other. At the door, Teal smiled. She looked as excited as a young girl on her birthday.

Maybe she had gone nuts, I thought. Maybe I was letting a crazy person lead me into disaster. If I had any real weakness, it was not thinking things out carefully and long enough before doing them. Look how easily I had been led to the slaughter back at Stone Mountain when I lived with my uncle and aunt. If I had been more cautious and skeptical, I wouldn't be here now.

Or would I?

Was this my inevitable fate, a destiny I could prevent as much as I could prevent the sun from coming up every morning?

Teal opened the door softly and slipped out. Robin and I looked at each other to see who would go out next. It was on the tip of my tongue to say, "Let's just go back to bed, Robin," but I didn't and I feared that I would later regret it.

She went out and I followed.

For a long moment, the three of us just stood there in the darkness listening and waiting to see if anyone was outside watching us. It was quiet. Not even a coyote was howling tonight. Teal nodded at the house and we made our way through a tunnel of shadows, winding from the barn toward the rear of the hacienda. Once there, we looked up and saw the lights were on in one of the buddies' rooms. We could hear music leaking out from under an opened window. Silhouetted behind a sheer curtain, figures moved like in a puppet show and there were short rolls of laughter, happy thunder.

For a while we stood looking up at the window, none of us speaking. Maybe they, like me, were trying to remember when they had had as good a time.

"What could they possibly be doing that's so much fun here in this disgusting place?" Teal asked, now gazing up with both jealousy and anger.

"Pajama party?" Robin offered, her voice dripping with sarcasm.

"I'm sure whatever it is, it's not going to be worth our coming out here and risking getting in trouble for," I said, hoping Robin would agree at last.

"Let's find out," Teal insisted, and led us to the overturned barrel.

We rolled it close to the house, then stood it up. Because of the slant of the roof, only another three feet or so remained to the edge of it.

"See? This will work," Teal said, and climbed up on it.

She began by getting most of her arms over the roof and then jumping up and pushing. I was surprised she had the strength to lift herself and swing her leg over the edge of the roof so easily. She looked so thin and fragile to me these days, but she was determined and hoisted herself completely onto the roof. She sat in a pool of self-satisfaction and smiled down at us.

"See? Piece of cake. If I can do it, you two can do it," she challenged.

Robin was next. Teal helped pull her along and they were both up there. I hesitated and looked around, half expecting Dr. Foreman herself to step out of a shadow from which she had been observing.

"C'mon already," Teal whispered.

I got up on the barrel. For me it shook, probably because of my nervousness and hesitation, and that panicked me. I caught hold of the edge of the roof and the two of them grabbed my arms, but when I lifted my feet, the barrel toppled and I dangled there.

"Great!" Teal moaned. She and Robin then struggled to pull me up.

Finally, scraping my left forearm, I got most of my body up and over the edge. I swung my feet around and lay there, panting.

"How are we going to get off now?" Robin moaned, looking at the barrel on its side.

"We'll just lower ourselves slowly and jump. We're not that high up," Teal said, refusing to be discouraged. "Ready?"

Robin nodded and the three of us, kneeling to stay low and out of the light that poured from the window of the hacienda, walked slowly over the roof toward the illuminated window. As we drew closer, we heard both the music and the laughter get louder.

We hesitated.

Teal indicated we should lower our bodies to keep out of sight. Practically on our stomachs, we inched toward the window. A loud peal of laughter from all three buddies stopped us for a moment. My heart was thumping. My forearm burned where I had scraped it, and I felt so weak in my stomach, I thought I might lose my balance and go rolling down and over the edge of the roof.

Teal wiggled like a snake under the window to the other side. She beckoned to Robin, who rose a bit and pressed her back to the wall. Moving on only her heels, she drew closer to the window, then they both waited for me. Another loud roar of laughter came from the buddies and the sound of someone clapping.

Robin reached down for my hand. I clasped hers and crawled closer to the window. Then Robin leaned in small increments until she was looking into the room. What she saw made her jaw drop. She looked at Teal, who peered in and then pulled back quickly, her head against the wall.

Stepping back to make room for me, Robin tugged at my hand and I rose to look through the window.

M'Lady Three wore a pair of jeans and a bra. She had her thick arms around M'Lady Two, who was in her uniform, and they were dancing. M'Lady One was on the bed to the right, dressed only in her bra and panties, smoking what looked like a joint and laughing as the two danced.

M'Lady Three had no rhythm. She was like a tree trunk, unmoving. M'Lady Two turned out and moved well to the beat. Then M'Lady Three let go of her hand and reached for the joint M'Lady One was smoking. She lay beside M'Lady One. M'Lady Two kept dancing while the other two shared their joint, watched, and laughed.

How could they do this without Dr. Foreman knowing and approving? Was it some way of rewarding them? Or were they just confident she wouldn't hear them or bother with them?

Suddenly, M'Lady One clapped her hands and cried, "Take it off, take it off," at M'Lady Two, who was still dancing. She laughed and turned to them and began a striptease.

Robin leaned in to look over my shoulder, and Teal lowered herself and peered in now through the opening in the window. We watched in awe as they cheered on M'Lady Two. She dropped her jacket and undid her blouse, turning and swaying to the music as she disrobed. When she stepped out of her skirt, the other two stopped cheering and watched with fascination.

"This is stupid and disgusting," Teal whispered.

Robin shook her head and put her finger to her lips.

The striptease continued. M'Lady Two unfastened her bra and held it up and then flung it at them. They laughed and sat up watching as M'Lady Two slowly took off her panties. Then she bent over and wagged her rear end at them and they laughed. When she turned and straightened up, she looked toward the window and we didn't get our faces back fast enough. That was clear from the expression on hers.

Teal scampered on all fours under the window and we rushed to return to the place where we had boosted ourselves up on the roof. We could hear the window being opened wider.

"Who's out there?" M'Lady Three cried.

The three of us stopped and dropped on our stomachs, hoping we weren't seen. We held our breath, but our hearts were pounding like three jungle drums.

"I see them," I heard.

"Let's get them!"

Teal rushed to get to the edge of the roof, lost her grip, and rolled over with a short scream. I heard her hit the barrel below.

Robin and I swung our legs over the roof and, as gracefully and carefully as we could, lowered ourselves and dropped. We fell on our rumps, but neither of us got hurt. Teal was squirming on the ground, holding her ankle and crying.

"I smashed it against the barrel," she moaned. "It feels like it's bleeding!"

"No time to look," Robin said.

Without delay, we got her up and had her put her arms around our shoulders. Then we moved as quickly as we could, staying within the darkest shadows, Teal limping along. We were practically carrying her most of the way. When we heard a door close behind us, we tried to go faster. Teal moaned and nearly fell, even with us doing most of the work. Neither Robin nor I looked back.

When we reached the barn, we opened the door and hurried in, setting Teal on her cot.

"My ankle feels like it's on fire."

"You'll have to put up with it and keep quiet, Teal," I said. I helped her get her shoes off and then we got her under her blanket and made it to our cots and under our blankets just as the door was opened. Incredibly, neither Gia nor Mindy had awoken, or if they had, they pretended to be asleep.

I thought the buddies would put on the lights and start screaming at us, but it was quiet. I had my back to the door and looked at Robin, who had hers to the door as well. Finally, I did hear footsteps over the straw and, moments later, jumped when a stiff forefinger was poked sharply into my side.

I spun around.

M'Lady One was kneeling at my cot. In the moonlight that poured through the barn windows, I could see her dropping her cold smile over me. "Been flying about, Phoebe bird? You and your new friends?"

I started to shake my head, but M'Lady Two pulled the blanket off Teal, who screamed. M'Lady Three approached her. Mindy and Gia finally turned and sat up.

"What's going on?" Mindy asked.

"We're doing a bed check. Shut up and go to sleep," M'Lady Three ordered.

Mindy lay back and practically pulled her blanket over her head. Gia remained sitting up and stared silently.

"Get up," M'Lady Three ordered Teal. She looked at me helplessly and struggled to her feet, swallowing as much of her pain as she could.

M'Lady Three saw the blood leaking through Teal's white sock. "Hurt yourself running about, did you?" she asked in a mock sweet voice.

Teal nodded. "I need to go to a doctor. I need an X ray. I might have broken my ankle."

"Oh, sure. We'll just bring the limousine right up and get you into it. Move!" M'Lady Three ordered, pushing her toward the door.

Teal started to cry. "I can't walk on it!" she moaned.

"Move," M'Lady Three repeated, poking her sharply in the ribs.

Teal limped toward the door. "What do you want? Why do I have to go outside? It's late," she pleaded.

"I want you to enjoy the cool evening air."

I started to get up to protest, but M'Lady One put her forefinger between my breasts and pushed so hard, I lay back down.

She hovered over me. "Just relax, girl. You're not going anywhere."

"Leave her alone. She's really hurt," I pleaded.

She smiled. "Suddenly, you care about each other? How sweet."

I looked at Robin who was back on her side, shivering in fear that she would be next, I was sure.

"If you don't bring Teal back in here . . . ," I started to threaten.

"You'll do what, Phoebe bird? Huh?"

"I want to see Dr. Foreman," I said, starting to sit up again.

"Oh, you'll be seeing her. Don't worry about that. You want to spend some time in the Ice Room first?"

"You're disgusting. You're all disgusting."

M'Lady Two drew closer. "You better shut your mouth, or we'll shut it for you for good."

She had as mad and as wild a look on her face as I had ever seen on anyone. I swallowed hard and looked at Gia, who was staring at me without any feeling, any expression, not even slight interest.

I folded my arms under my breasts and lay back again.

The two buddies turned and followed Teal and M'Lady Three out of the barn, closing the door behind her.

"What are they going to do to her?" Robin wailed.

"What did you do, spy on them?" Gia asked us, speaking as if she were in a dream.

"Yes," Robin said. "Teal remembered your telling us about it, about their partying."

"You went up on the roof and looked in their windows?"

"We did and we saw worse than you saw. They weren't just listening to music and smoking pot. They were dancing and striping for each other. They're sick and disgusting. Wait until we tell Dr. Foreman what we saw. Right, Phoebe?"

I didn't respond.

Her words died like hollow threats in the dark. Gia went back to sleep and Robin turned on her side, but I sat up for awhile and listened for Teal. I heard nothing, not a cry, not a loud voice, nothing. Finally, I couldn't keep my eyes open any longer and lay back.

Teal wasn't there in the morning. The first thing I did after my eyes opened was sit up and look for her, but her cot was empty. Gia and Mindy were dressing silently. Robin was still asleep. I woke her.

"They never brought Teal back," I said. I wondered why they had chosen her out of the three of us. Why hadn't they taken Robin and me, too?

Robin looked worried, but said nothing. We dressed and stepped outside and the buddies were there as usual, waiting to hear us recite our prayer.

"Where's Teal?" I demanded.

"The prayer," M'Lady One said, stepping up to me.

We did it and then I asked after Teal again.

"That girl," M'Lady Two said, shaking her head, "keeps getting hurt. She shouldn't have walked so much on that injured ankle, but we couldn't stop her from going around and around. Now she's in the infirmary again, but she'll pay for it. As you know, there are no excuses for not doing your work. Dr. Foreman will give her five demerits for this."

"What will she give you when she finds out what you did?" I muttered.

"What did you say?" She stepped up to me again, her nose touching mine. I stepped back. "Well? Did you say something? Did you threaten something, Phoebe bird?"

"No."

"Very wise reply for a stupid girl. Get to work, all of you."

I looked at Robin, whose head was down the whole time. Mindy was muttering to herself and Gia was staring ahead, her eyes so dark.

I took a deep breath and turned to go into my shell, chanting to myself.

From the confident way they acted, I was sure that the buddies had told Dr. Foreman what we had done, but they had given her selected information, of course, leaving out what they had been doing. To my surprise Dr. Foreman didn't ask Robin or me anything specific about it. Teal was kept in the infirmary and apparently not questioned either. Dr. Foreman didn't come charging out of the house, her eyes blazing with anger.

However, the silence made me more nervous. It was like the moments before a bomb would explode. Our days weren't any different, except Teal wasn't with us. One afternoon we saw Dr. Foreman leave in the van and I didn't see her return that day. She wasn't there at dinner either. What does all this mean? I wondered.

The next morning, I did see the van out front again, and later in the day Dr. Foreman sent M'Lady One to call Robin and me in from the garden work.

"This is it," Robin said.

We hurried to her office, expecting now to hear her anger over our spying on the buddies. She was sitting at her desk, filling out some papers. When we entered, she looked up.

"Oh, Phoebe, Robin," she said in a friendly voice, "I want you girls to take some lessons from Natani."

"Lessons?" I asked. Was she going to make fun of his idea of the shell?

"Yes. I usually start the girls on these lessons earlier, but we've had so much orientation and setting up to do, it's just all taken a second seat. I find it more effective for Natani to work with no more than one or two at a time. He's expecting the two of you in his hogan after dinner tonight. You're excused from any other schoolwork for now. I'll ask you to be polite and give him your full attention. We'll talk about it all afterward. That's all. You can return to the gardening." She returned to her paperwork. "Oh," she added as we were leaving. "Don't discuss it with the others. I hate these petty jealousies that develop. They'll have their turn when it is their turn."

We left in a daze.

"I thought for sure we had bought it," Robin said as we walked down the steps. "What is this about, lessons from Natani? He gives us lessons in farming as it is. What else could he possibly teach us?"

"I'm not sure," I said. "The way she talked, it sounded like some sort of reward or privilege, but yet, I can't help being very suspicious."

"Oh, well. No homework. I'll take whatever little gifts I get here. That's for sure."

We returned to work and, as Dr. Foreman had ordered, said nothing about Natani and the lessons. All day I waited to see if Teal was being released. I listened when the buddies talked to each other, too, to see if they would mention her and anything that had been done to her, but it was as if she had never been here. Not a word about her was spoken.

Once again, she wasn't at dinner, and once again, neither Gia nor Mindy seemed to care or be interested. What did interest and surprise them was our not returning to the barn to do our schoolwork.

"How come you're excused from that?" Mindy asked irritably.

"We have some other chore to attend to," I said.

"Ah," Mindy said, nodding. "You're finally being punished, aren't you?"

"We'll let you know," I said.

Gia made her eyes small, studied me for a moment, then walked off silently.

Robin and I headed for Natani's hogan. When we got there, he had us sit on the floor. The rocks were gone but he had animal skins in a small pile. Both of us eyed them timidly as we sat, especially the snakeskin.

"What are we here to learn?" Robin asked him.

"The desert."

He said he wanted to begin first with the desert's poisonous creatures. He reached into his pile and plucked out the snakeskin, which was so long and real the two of us gasped and sat back when he held it up.

"Sidewinder," he announced as if he were introducing us to one of his pets, and moved his body to show us how it moved and from what it got its name. "In the sand, it makes this shape." With a stick he drew parallel J-shaped marks. "Tells you it's been here. If the mark is very fresh, you take another path."

"I would take another path if it was months old," Robin muttered.

"Snakes come out at night. Sleep in burrows or under brush. They don't try to hurt you if you leave them be," he said. "That's a good lesson about most things in nature."

"I would have no trouble leaving it be," I said. Robin nodded in vivid agreement.

"Sometimes, foolish person blindly invades its safe place and it will strike." He held up his healing pouch. "Inside is rattlesnake weed." He dipped his hand in to take it out and show it to us. "If someone is bitten, cut the wound immediately, suck out poison, and squeeze juice of the plant into cut. Chew plant and swallow juice. Make you vomit."

"Ugh," Robin said. "Do you have to tell it all in such detail?"

"Person who has been bitten is very sick, sweating. Bind the wound with plant after it is boiled. It will save the person's life maybe or keep him from being very, very sick."

"Why is he telling us all this now?" Robin muttered, squinting. "We should have learned it all the first day we arrived at this hellhole."

He put the pouch down and reached into the pile of skins to show us a lizard with brightly colored, beadlike scales on its back.

"Gila monster," he said, holding it up. "Poisonous bite." He shook his head. "Let it be and it let you be."

"It will have no problems from me ever," I said, inching back when he brought it closer.

He then showed us four other lizards, the chuckwalla, the desert night lizard, the thorny devil, and the armadillo lizard, just so we would know them and not be afraid of them. He held up another skin he called a blind snake and told us it was harmless.

"It doesn't look harmless to me," Robin muttered. "A snake's a snake."

Natani stared at her a moment. "Once the night lizard asked the rattlesnake why he ran from men and got so angry if they came too close. The rattlesnake replied, 'A man's a man.' "

"Very funny," Robin said. I smiled and she looked like she saw the point, too.

"Scorpions you know," Natani continued, but showed us dried scorpions anyway so we could tell the difference between the poisonous and nonpoisonous, and then he held out a dead poisonous black widow. One creature I didn't anticipate was a centipede he said had venomous pincers and could give a painful bite.

"Always shake out clothes and blankets good when in the desert," he warned. "You can have a bad surprise putting on shirt with one of these inside."

One final creature was the velvet ant. Natani said the wingless females could inflict a painful sting and he called them "cow killers."

I could see Robin was getting paler and paler. "All of these creatures are around us, some right under our noses?"

Natani nodded and she looked like she might heave any moment or maybe faint. She was swallowing hard and shaking her head. "If I knew all that was here, I would have chosen a maximum security prison."

Why had Dr. Foreman decided to have Natani do this now? I won-

dered. Was this our punishment? To be confronted by all these frightening creatures and insects so we would dream about them at night or
tiptoe about this place? Was it meant to keep us confined and discourage us from wandering about the ranch? If so, it was working. Robin
looked like she would roll herself up into a ball and stay that way, and
my stomach was so tight and twisted inside, I thought I would donate
my dinner soon to the ants and spiders and snakes.

Natani pushed all the skins and creatures aside and sat across from
us.

"Traveling in the desert is harder during the day, but the poisonous
creatures I show you come out only at night. Animals in desert know
to burrow and sleep during day."

"Sounds like a peachy keen life," Robin said dryly. "What is all
this?" She turned to me. "Are we going for a hike or something?"

"Maybe," I said.

"Not me," Robin said. "They'd have to drag me screaming and
clawing. That can't be on the agenda, can it?" She looked from Natani
to me for some assurances, but all I could do was shake my head.

"Let's wait and see," I said.

"Always cover your head in desert," Natani continued, ignoring our
conversation. "Shorts, less clothes, are not good. Sun can be like a
knife. You already know," he said, looking at Robin. "But I will teach
you now how to make fire in the desert."

"Fire in the desert? That's like bringing ice cubes to Eskimos,"
Robin said, grimacing. "Why would anyone need a fire in the desert?"

"Fire is a way to signal, cook food, make water good. You know it
can be very cold at night, too."

Natani showed us how to use a stick with a piece of dried wood or
the thick branch of a bush to generate enough friction. Once the smoke
started, he bore down harder, then fed the area with some dried twigs,
constantly blowing on the tiny embers. They flamed up and he sat
back.

"You try." He gave both of us the means to work a friction fire.
Robin and I got the smoke started, but both of us failed to get the
flame going until Natani demonstrated again. Finally, we both got a
flame. It felt like a major accomplishment.

"Isn't it easier to just carry a pack of matches?" Robin muttered.

Natani's eyes darkened, then brightened again when he looked at
me. "Natani can't teach in one day what it takes a lifetime to learn,
and what you learn here is good forever. Everywhere there are deserts,
even in the middle of your cities."

"What is that supposed to mean? Don't worry about it, Natani,"

Robin said, nodding, "I'm not exactly going to need to know all this when I get out of here. I promise you, I won't even look at a desert on television."

M'Lady Three poked her head into the doorway of Natani's hogan and we all turned when she asked, "Are you finished in here?"

"No," he said.

"Well, that's too bad. Dr. Foreman wants to see them now."

I looked at Natani. Something in his otherwise impossible to read face frightened me. He wasn't happy for us.

"Now," M'Lady Three snapped.

We rose and emerged from the hogan to walk to the house.

"How was your lesson from the chief, girls? Think you could survive a day in the desert without your makeup?"

"You survived, didn't you?" I fired back at her.

"Are you saying if I did it, you could do it?"

"Maybe."

She laughed.

"And then again, maybe you didn't survive," I said.

She stopped smiling and reached out to grab my shoulder and turn me around to face her. "What's that supposed to mean?"

I didn't reply. She kept her eyes fixed on me, the fury so hot between us, Natani could make a fire with a stick he held up in front of our faces.

"Get moving. You haven't changed," M'Lady Three muttered as we walked. "You haven't improved one bit despite your act. You might have fooled some people around here, Phoebe bird, but not me. Remember that."

I wanted to turn around and just charge at her and scratch those hateful eyes out, but I kept walking.

To our surprise, Teal was alone in Dr. Foreman's office. She had a crutch and was seated on the sofa. She didn't look up at us but, instead, kept her eyes fixed on the floor. I thought she looked a little thinner and paler, but other than that, not much different.

"Teal!" Robin cried. "How are you? Where have you been?"

"Here," she said quickly. "Where else?"

"Well, what happened?" Robin asked, sitting beside her.

"Nothing. Dr. Foreman determined that I had a sprained ankle and kept me in one of the rooms."

"The room with the big bed and canopy?" I asked, slowly lowering myself to the sofa.

She looked at me with small eyes and nodded.

"Didn't she ask you how you sprained it?" Robin questioned.

"She already knew all about it," Teal said.

"But . . ." Robin looked at me. "She never said anything about it to us. Things haven't changed much, right, Phoebe?"

"I don't know. Have things changed, Teal?" I asked, my eyes drilling into her. She shifted hers away quickly and shrugged.

"What . . ." Robin buttoned her lip as Dr. Foreman marched into the office and sat behind her desk. Suddenly, she looked more like a judge in a courtroom to me.

"Periodically," she began, "I review the progress my newest girls are making and I send this report to the courts, to the families, so everyone will know what to expect and when to expect it.

"In some ways, many ways," she continued, looking mainly at me, "you have made great strides in a positive direction. You have learned how to obey rules and you have become somewhat less self-centered.

"Now we are at what I like to call the first of many crossroads. How much faster and further you go in a positive direction will soon be understood, and after that, I will be able to evaluate you and make my report.

"To get right to the point today, the three of you know that I have been very disappointed in your behavior lately. I have waited to see which of you would come forward to tell me about it, which of you has grown in moral capacity to know enough to come to me and confess, to relieve yourself of the guilt you must be carrying.

"I can't tell you how disappointed I am, especially in one of you." She again looked more at me than she looked at Robin or Teal. "I waited and waited and hoped, but, alas, I realize we have a way yet to go.

"So," she said, leaning against the desk and folding her arms under her breasts, "let's begin.

"Teal has told me that it was Robin's idea to commit this stupid night foray to spy on your buddies, to climb on a roof and endanger yourselves."

"What?" Robin cried, practically leaping up.

I looked at Teal, who kept her face turned away from us.

"She's a big liar. She's the one who came up with the idea," Robin shouted. She poked Teal in the shoulder. "How could you tell her that?"

"None of that," Dr. Foreman said sharply.

"Well, she's lying, Dr. Foreman."

"Phoebe," Dr. Foreman said, "is she lying? Was it her idea?"

Teal turned sharply and looked at me, her face so full of fear, I couldn't help but feel sorry for her. I also thought of myself and how I had betrayed her. I wasn't any better than she was, and neither was Robin.

"As a rule I don't like any behind-the-back tattle-tales," Dr. Foreman said, now firmly fixing her gaze on me. "That's sneaky and it doesn't show me any real growth. You have probably all done something like that in the past, and you know very well that you can put on one face with the authorities and another for your friends. It's deceitful and not the sign of someone who has truly found herself and her moral way.

"Either I hear a confession and an agreement about that from the other two, or one of you or two of you reveal to me this instant whose idea it was.

"Well?" she snapped, rising to her full height and glaring down at us. "Whose idea was it?"

"It wasn't Teal," I said.

"What?" Robin screamed, spinning on me now.

"It was Gia's idea," I said quickly. Why it came to me to do that, I couldn't say for sure. I think it was a combination of things. First, it was truly Gia who had put the idea into our heads, and second, assigning blame to someone who was already condemned in Dr. Foreman's mind didn't seem such a terrible thing to do. It was like blaming a murderer on death row for another murder. What difference could it possibly make to him?

Dr. Foreman's eyes grew smaller, darker. "Gia?"

"Yes," I said without hesitation.

"Then why did Teal assign blame to Robin?"

I looked at Teal. "She's more afraid of Gia than she is of Robin. We all are."

Dr. Foreman held those scrutinizing eyes on me for a long moment. She walked to the front of the desk, folding her arms under her breasts and nodding slightly. I thought she was just going to start screaming at me for being a liar, but something kept her from it.

"Are you saying Gia accompanied the three of you as well that night?"

"Oh, no."

"Then what are you saying, Phoebe? Gia did this before or she just came up with the idea?"

Robin and Teal were looking at me with faces of hope, both counting on me to come up with the right answers to get us out from under the hot lights of Dr. Foreman's eyes.

"I don't know, Dr. Foreman."

"You don't know?"

"I can't be sure of anything Gia tells me." This time I held my gaze and met her perceptive eyes. She knew what I meant.

"Don't make me sound like a prosecutor, Phoebe."

"I'm not," I whined.

"Did Gia tell you that she spied on my girls? Yes or no?"

"Not exactly."

"What?"

"She said Posy had done it," I told her.

Teal and Robin looked even more shocked at my mention of Posy's name. They turned quickly to see what Dr. Foreman's reaction would be. She looked thoughtful, but not enraged. She turned to Teal and Robin.

"She told you two this as well?"

"Yes, Dr. Foreman," Teal said quickly. "I'm sorry I didn't tell you. Phoebe's right. We were all together when she spoke about it and what she said Posy saw. We were just bored and we were told how much fun the buddies were having at their so-called parties, so—"

"I'm not interested in that," Dr. Foreman snapped, thought again, and walked back to her desk chair. "I'm disappointed." Then, after a beat of silence during which she looked as troubled as I had ever seen her look, she added, "In all of you."

After another quiet moment, she looked up sharply at us, wearing a face of utter disgust, and said, "You're dismissed. Return to your quarters until I call for you."

"You mean, stay in the barn?" Robin asked.

"Are you deaf? Yes. Now go." Dr. Foreman waved at the door.

The three of us got up slowly and walked out, each of us holding her breath.

Had we escaped a terrible punishment? Dr. Foreman had so wanted to divide the three of us again. I could almost see her tasting the new victory. Surely that was what had disappointed her, but when she was disappointed, she was so depressed and angry, it made Mama's tantrums look like child's play, I thought.

None of us spoke until we were far enough away from the front of the hacienda not to be overheard.

"How could you do that?" Robin began, grabbing Teal so hard, she almost pulled the crutch out from under her. "How could you say I was the one?"

"I didn't know what to say. She had me trapped in that room and it was terrifying. First she was so nice, so thoughtful and concerned, and then she was so angry, I thought she was going to boil me in a big pot, and I was very frightened whenever the buddies came around. I was stuck in that bed and the door was always locked and—"

"Forget about it, Robin," I said. "You would have given up your mother."

"Big deal. I'd give her up for a piece of apple pie right now," she said, still fuming. Then she relaxed and looked at me and smiled. "That was good thinking in there, Phoebe. I didn't remember Gia saying it was Posy who did it, but that was a good idea. It stopped her cold. I could see that."

"Yeah, thanks for getting me off the hook," Teal said, limping along. "I'm surprised she let us go so easily. I guess Gia might be right after all. I guess Posy was her daughter."

I stopped walking. "There was no Posy. She has no daughter. Posy was just someone Gia made up."

They both stared at me.

"How do you know that for sure?"

"Gia wanted to prove to me that there was a Posy and that she was in the basement."

"How?"

"I went there with her one night and she tricked me and trapped me below. But it wasn't her fault. Dr. Foreman had her do it."

"Why?" Teal asked.

I told them about my experience in the basement and the letter.

"You've kept that all to yourself?" Teal complained.

"It wasn't anyone else's business," I said, "and those were Dr. Foreman's orders."

"You could have told us anyway."

"Oh, suddenly you're my new best friends? C'mon, if she told you to keep quiet about something that involved me, you would become a total mute. Don't put on any airs or try to make me feel bad, Teal."

"She's right," Robin said, still unforgiving. "You gave me up and I don't care what they did to you."

"And she's right about what you would have done, too."

"Okay, so we're not exactly loving friends. What's the difference whether or not Phoebe told us about Gia and the imaginary Posy?" Robin said. "She's right. It had nothing to do with us."

"Oh, how I hate this place," Teal moaned.

Robin turned back to me and smiled. "You were even more clever than I first thought, Phoebe. Blaming an imaginary person that Dr. Foreman wanted you to keep secret. What was she going to do? Call you a liar? And in front of us?"

I looked back at the hacienda. "I don't know. Maybe it was smart.

Maybe it was the dumbest thing I've done since I was brought here. Whichever it was," I said, starting along again, "I have the feeling I'm gonna find out soon.

"Maybe sooner than I imagine."

We continued along, silence like a big black sheet falling over us with just the sound of Teal's crutch poking the dried earth accompanying us back to our barracks.

None of us looked forward to sleeping tonight.

We'd all see those eyes.

Dr. Foreman's eyes at the end of our session, full of the most utter disgust and contempt I had ever seen in the eyes of an adult who was looking at me.

What would cause such rage? I wondered.

And then I thought, perhaps we . . . or maybe just I was the first candidate she had ever had that she thought she might fail to make into a Foreman girl after all.

Something told me she would never permit a failure to leave this place.

Even Posy, imagined and unreal, had to be made to disappear.

13

Marooned

To our surprise, not only didn't we hear a second shoe drop, but in the morning we were greeted with unexpected gifts. M'Lady One entered with her arms full of clothing. She distributed prettier white blouses and khaki walking shorts as well as new socks and pairs of light brown sneakers. Teal was depressed because we were also provided with new hairbrushes and she had no hair to brush.

"Is this some sort of a reward for work or something?" I asked M'Lady One.

"No, stupid," she said. "It's a punishment."

"I almost feel like a human being again," Robin cried after she put on a blouse and brushed her hair. "These shorts aren't too bad either."

Teal checked for a label and saw where they were made in China. "Probably fall apart in a day or two," she muttered, still pining over her shortened hair. "The sneakers aren't bad though."

I was cautiously happy. Only Gia looked upset about it. She stared at everything as if one of those centipedes Natani had shown us might be lodged in something. All of us were changed and dressed and she hadn't changed into anything yet.

"What's wrong, Gia?" I asked.

"I don't know. This is not like her. I don't know."

"She probably had the clothes lying around or maybe it's like those prisoner of war camps where someone comes to inspect and she's just getting us ready for it," Robin suggested. "What do you think, Phoebe?"

I stared at Gia. "I don't know what to think. Maybe it's like the magazines, huh, Gia?"

"Maybe," she said finally, putting on a blouse. "Maybe it's something more."

"Maybe it's something more, maybe it's not like her, maybe it's maybe. You can drive someone nuts," Teal shouted at her. "Why don't you just take it and be grateful and get yourself out of here already? Or don't you want to go home?"

Gia looked at her as if it were a good question. "Maybe I don't." She turned her back and put on the shorts.

Mindy watched her and then gazed at me with concern.

"Well, I know I do. I'd crawl out on my hands and knees if I had to. Almost did," Teal reminded us.

"It's not over yet," Gia said, looking up as she buttoned her shorts. "You may be on your hands and knees yet."

Teal smirked, shook her head, and sat to put on her new sneakers. "I have about fifty pairs at home, every color you can imagine, every new style." She sat quietly, remembering.

"Let's go, ladies," M'Lady Three said from the door. "This morning you're going directly to breakfast. No morning work detail."

Again, we looked at each other. I began to really wonder if Robin wasn't right. We were going to be inspected by some agency and Dr. Foreman was putting on a shiny new look.

"Was this place ever inspected since you've been here, Gia?" I asked.

"No. Or at least not that I know of."

"Then, I'm right," Robin decided. "It's obviously time for an inspection."

"Well, I can tell you this," Teal said, "if someone pulls me aside to ask me how things are going, he or she is going to get an ear so full, his head will tilt to one side."

"Just remember," Mindy cautioned, "if you're not shipped out soon after you spill your guts, one of the buddies might spill them for you."

"I don't care! I'm sick of all this and I want the world to know it!" Teal screamed at her.

Mindy just smiled at her, which irritated Teal even more.

"You're sick," she said. "You're all sick," she continued, looking mostly at Gia.

"Shut up, Teal," I said.

"I want to go home. I'll do anything to go home," she moaned, and hobbled along.

We did have a more elaborate breakfast, even some Danish pastries, which reinforced our theory that we were about to be observed and evaluated by some government agency. Gia ate tentatively, looking

everything over twice to be sure rat poison wasn't over it or something. She made me nervous, but Robin and Teal weren't in any way
intimidated. They ate as much as they could, as did Mindy, who reminded me of a starving dog, gazing around her after almost every
bite to be sure no one was nearby to take it away.

Toward the end of breakfast, M'Lady Three came into the dining
room to announce the day's chores and assignments.

"Mindy and Gia are to report to the garden as usual. Teal, Robin,
and Phoebe are going on an off-grounds work detail and, after they
clean up in here and put everything neatly away, are to report outside
to get into the van."

"Off-grounds?" Teal asked first. "What's that?"

"That is off-grounds, an outside area. You still speak English, don't
you?" M'Lady Three quipped.

Teal looked at me, but I was staring at Gia, who was staring back at
me, and what I saw in her eyes, I did not like.

"Move it!" M'Lady Three ordered, and Gia and Mindy left the
room quickly, neither looking back at us. "Clean up. Ten minutes to
departure," she shouted at us.

"What's this mean, working off-grounds?" Teal asked me as soon
as M'Lady Three was gone.

"I don't know, but I don't like it."

"I guess we really are like prisoners on a chain gang," Robin said.
"We're probably volunteered by Dr. Foreman to work on a road or
something just like inmates."

"How can I work on a road? I'm injured," Teal protested.

"I'm sure they'll find something you can do," Robin said, taking
dishes off the table.

I helped her and Teal was left to clean the table off. Robin and I
washed and dried the dishes and silverware, neither of us talking much
at all.

"Stop looking so worried, Phoebe," she finally told me. "At least
we're getting out of here and can see some new scenery."

"I hope you're right," I said without confidence.

When we were finished, we joined Teal and all walked out front to
where the van was parked. M'Lady One was there with three small
bags, the kind of backpacks you could wear over your shoulders.

"These are your off-grounds kits," she explained, and opened one
up to take out its contents. "First, a canteen full of cold water. Drink it
sparingly. Second, bars of nutritional food. Each of you has three. A
towel to wipe your ugly faces, some tampons just in case, a vial of

cyanide just in case you're captured." She laughed. "Just kidding, of course. Who would want to capture you?

"All right," she said, opening the van doors, "get in. There's work to be done."

"How far away are we going?" Teal asked.

"We were thinking of your sweeping streets in New York. How far are you going? Just get in and shut up."

Robin got in first and I followed, then we helped Teal in with her crutch. M'Lady One shut the door immediately.

"This brings back fond memories," Robin said.

"If there is even the slightest chance of getting away once we get to wherever we get," Teal said, "I'm going for it."

"On a crutch?" I asked.

"I said I'd crawl if I had to and I will."

"Maybe I would, too," Robin added.

A tiny bit of light came through the crack in the door so at least we weren't in total darkness as we had been the first time we were in this van. I sat back and tried to relax when I heard the engine start and felt us pulling away. Then I glanced to my right.

Something was there.

"What's this?" I muttered, reaching for it. It looked familiar.

I held it up.

"What is it?" Teal asked.

"Phoebe?" Robin followed.

I looked at the two of them. "It's from Natani. It's his healing bag."

"What's that for? I mean, what does it mean that he left it in here?" Teal asked, whining.

"It means, we're in bigger trouble than we imagined. Dr. Foreman is finally punishing us."

"I don't understand," Teal said.

"I think I do," Robin said.

"Well, tell me, big shot."

"Maybe we should just wait to see," I said. "Let's not panic until we have to panic."

"Oh, great. And here I thought we were going on a picnic," Teal moaned.

We were all quiet, listening to see if we could hear anything that would give us even a slight hint as to where we were going and what we would be doing. The roughness of the ride, however, began to reinforce my worries. I couldn't see Robin's face clearly, but I was sure the same was occurring to her as well.

"How far away are they taking us?" Teal cried after what was surely a good hour. "I'm so nauseous, I'm sorry I ate anything this morning."

Finally, the van stopped. We heard a door slam and then the back doors were opened. The brightness made us all squint for a few moments.

"Ladies," M'Lady Two said, standing there and looking in at us. She wore a wide-brimmed hat.

Robin crawled out first and I followed with Natani's medicine bag around my shoulder. I reached back to get Teal's crutch, then Robin and I helped her down. We stood there looking around. We were, as I had feared, in the middle of the desert. The mountains, in fact, looked farther away than they did when we were at the ranch.

"Where are we?" Teal asked first.

"That's top-secret information," M'Lady One said.

"We're going for a long walk in the desert, aren't we?" I asked. "This isn't a work detail."

"Believe me, Phoebe girl, a walk in the desert is a work detail," M'Lady Two replied, smiling.

"How can I walk in the desert? I can't walk back at the ranch that well," Teal complained.

"You can walk just like the rest of us. You've been using that sprain as an excuse from work long enough," M'Lady Two said. "Ready?"

"I'm not going," Teal declared, and folded her legs to sit on the ground.

M'Lady One looked at M'Lady Two.

"I'll meet you at the designated spot," M'Lady One said, and got into the van. We watched her start the engine and drive away.

"This way, girls," M'Lady Two said, and began to trek forward.

No one moved. She stopped and looked at us. Teal tried to keep her mask of defiance over her face of fear.

"I'm walking and meeting that van," M'Lady Two said, pointing at the van, which was disappearing over a hill. "If you girls want to remain here, you can," she said, shading her eyes to gaze up at the noonday sun burning down on us. "However, I wouldn't advise it."

She started away. I looked at Robin.

"We've got no choice," I said, and began to follow.

"No," Teal moaned.

"Come on," Robin said, helping her to her feet.

We started behind M'Lady Two, who moved at a steady, quick pace over the sand and rolling small hills. I quickly envied her wide-brimmed hat and remembered Natani's advice to always have our heads covered in the desert. He had also advised against us wearing shorts, and suddenly I realized these sneakers were not proper shoes for this as well. So Dr. Foreman's apparent gifts were not gifts after all. We would have been better off dressed in the outfits we had. She had set us up to suffer out here. M'Lady One's sarcastic reply to my question wasn't sarcastic after all. Punishment had a new meaning and certainly a capital *P*.

I looked back and saw how Robin and Teal were already struggling. The crutch looked to be more trouble than it was worth, especially over this kind of terrain.

"I can't walk this fast!" Teal screamed.

M'Lady Two didn't turn around. She kept her pace and kept her direction.

Robin caught up with me. "What's going on? Why are they doing this to us?"

"It's the punishment. Remember what Natani said about clothing, covering our heads, all that? She gave us all this before putting us out here, and these are exactly the wrong things to be wearing."

"Damn her."

"Yeah, well, it's too late for that." I was breathing heavily already. How could M'Lady Two walk so fast and so steadily? I wondered. She was probably the best at this and that was why she had been chosen to lead us.

"I'm burning up," Teal moaned, catching up to us and wiping her forehead.

I thought a moment, then reached into my bag and took out the towel. "Wrap it around your head. At least you'll get some protection from the sun this way."

"I need sunglasses. My eyes ache!" Teal complained.

"Mine, too," Robin said.

"Walk with them closed half the time," I advised. M'Lady Two was pulling farther and farther away. "Come on, we can't lose her out here." I quickened my steps.

Teal kept complaining and struggling. Finally, out of disgust, she threw her crutch down and hobbled. Before long, she was putting weight on the ankle and enduring the pain just so she wouldn't be left too far behind. From the way the sun moved in the sky, I was sure we had already walked a good hour.

"Can't we rest for a while?" I called to M'Lady Two. She kept walking, not even turning her head.

"Why isn't she tired, too?" Robin asked. "I was going to drink some water, but I didn't want to do it until she stopped and did it."

"That's a good idea," I said.

"I've already drunk some of mine," Teal admitted.

"Don't drink any more," I warned.

"Why not? We can't be going too much longer before we reach the van, can we?"

"Look out there," I said. "Any sign of a van for miles and miles?"

Teal paused and panned the scene before us. The cacti stood like sentinels over the sand, rocks, and bushes. There wasn't a house or a road, or any sign of civilization, for as far as we could see in any direction. Heat seemed to be steaming up from the earth. Nothing moved that we could see. It was as if the whole world had come to a complete stop.

"Where are we?" Robin asked.

"What is this? Stop!" Teal screamed, the panic settling in her throat like a lump of coal and turning her scream into more of a desperate screech, but I was sure her voice didn't even reach M'Lady Two.

"Just keep going," I advised.

At one point M'Lady Two was so far ahead, she disappeared over the top of a knoll. We all walked faster. I even broke into a run because I saw how we had lost too much distance and how long it would otherwise take to catch up to her. When I reached the top, I stopped and the other two caught up with me.

"What is it?" Teal asked. "Why are you stopping?"

Robin and I turned our heads and put our hands on our foreheads to shade our eyes. Sweat was running down my forehead, under the towel. I had to wipe it away to keep my eyes open.

"I don't understand," Robin said.

"What?" Teal moaned. "What is it now?"

"I don't see her," I said angrily. "Do you?"

"Huh?" Teal shaded her eyes and looked as well. "Where could she be?"

The knoll slanted down on our left. I thought she might have gone that way and then back around to the other side to lose us and frighten us a bit, so I walked quickly and than ran to the end and went around it. Robin followed.

We both stood there looking for her.

"Do you see her?"

"No," I said.

"Maybe the other side or maybe . . ." Robin looked ahead. "Maybe she reached that hill before you had gotten to the top."

"That's pretty far away, but I hope so," I said. "She's not heading back from what I can see, although I'm not sure if that's back or not anymore," I added, pointing.

"Well, the sun is going west and it was . . ."

"Directly overhead. I can't remember. Let's get going. She must be over that far hill just as you say."

We started in that direction and Teal met us in the middle.

"Did you see her? Is that where she went?" she asked, nodding in front of us.

"We think so, but we're not sure."

"This is crazy."

"No. It's part of a plan, I'm sure," I said. "They want us to be frightened, to suffer, to cry and to panic."

"Well, I have news for them," Teal said. "We are doing all that so they can stop it. Stop it!" she screamed.

"Keep walking," Robin said. "You're just acting like an idiot."

"I'm acting like an idiot? My feet are burning. These sneakers are too thin and the sand is so hot it's like walking over the top of a stove."

"Maybe we can catch a bus over the next hill," Robin told her.

"Funny. Boy, are you funny."

"You're wasting your energy, both of you," I chastised, and I walked harder and faster, leaving them a good twenty or thirty yards behind me, their bickering sounding like a dozen chipmunks. When I reached the far hill, I stood and looked around again, and again I saw no sign of M'Lady Two. Where could she possibly be? The cacti were too narrow for her to be hiding behind one and the bushes were too low, I thought. I would see her.

While I waited for Robin and Teal to catch up, I took my first drink of water. Then I sat on the sand, near some brush. One of Natani's thorny devil lizards peered out at me curiously. I watched it and was amazed at how still it could be. As soon as the other two came up, it pulled itself back into the darker areas of the brush.

"What?" Robin asked.

"She's gone," I said.

"Gone?" Teal said.

"How can she be gone?" Robin wondered, and lowered herself to the ground. She saw I had taken a drink from my canteen and took out her own.

"It's like she just disappeared into thin air," I said.

I stared at the vast stretch of desert sand and brush in all directions. Still, nothing large enough to be M'Lady Two moved. The heat wavered over the ground, making it all look unreal. Above us, there wasn't a cloud in the sky. It seemed all sun, one gigantic ball of fire bearing down and over us.

I watched another lizard, a chuckwalla, burrow itself deeper into the sand and I nodded.

"What?" Robin asked, seeing a smile on my face. "What's so funny? We're lost in hell."

"I think I know what she did. She had time to bury herself in the sand before we reached the top of that first big hill back there. In our panic and excitement, we might have walked right past her."

"You're crazy," Teal said. "She couldn't do that."

"It wouldn't take all that long to do, and who would have expected it? We were looking out there, searching for the sight of someone walking."

"I can't believe it," Teal insisted.

"I can," Robin said. "I think Phoebe's right."

"Well . . . well, why would she?" Teal asked, the dread and the fear slipping into her voice.

"She waited until we were far enough away and then she came out of the sand and probably walked back to where the van dropped us off," I said, imagining what their plan might have been.

"You mean, they've left us out here?"

"See that, Teal," Robin said, "when you're left to your own, you can think and reach conclusions."

"Very funny. They wouldn't, couldn't do that. Why, look at this?" Teal said, waving her arms at the desert around us. "This is the desert."

"You ran off into it before, didn't you?" Robin said.

"I didn't get half as far as we've already walked. I followed a road that just disappeared on me, but it wasn't like this. There was . . ."

"What?"

"That road. I thought about going back to it. I just got too tired. This is different. This is really the desert."

"You sure made it sound like you almost got away," Robin reminded her. "What are you saying now, you went only a little ways from the ranch before you had to take a rest?"

Teal was silent.

"You probably didn't get half a mile away. How pathetic."

"At least I tried," she whined.

"Can't you two shut up?" I said.

"What do you really think is happening, Phoebe?" Robin asked.

"It all makes sense now . . . Dr. Foreman ordering Natani to give us desert lessons, giving us these clothes . . . we're in another one of her tests, I suppose. If we survive, we'll be better for it. Something stupid like that."

"Then she knows where we are?" Teal asked hopefully.

"In a very general way, maybe."

"A general way? What if we die out here?"

"So, we tried to run away and we died," Robin said. "Right?"

I nodded.

"Well, what should we do?" Teal practically screamed.

I stood up and brushed off my legs.

They both looked up at me.

"Yeah," Robin said, "what should we do?"

"Survive." I started to walk again.

"Wait," Robin said, rising.

I paused and looked back. "What?"

"Why are we going in that direction? Shouldn't we try to get back to where we were?"

I thought a moment and shrugged. "Can you remember the way back?"

"Yes," Robin said. "Or we could just follow our steps or look for something familiar."

"You have to be kidding. Familiar?" Teal said. "It all looks the same."

"We'll look for our steps. We'll get back there to that place, I'm sure," Robin insisted. "And then we could follow whatever road they took, or hopefully whatever is left of the tire tracks."

"Okay," I said. "Let's try."

We began to walk back. For a while we did see signs of our steps, but the wind had come up and the sand was beginning to flow like waves in the sea. Soon, it was as if we had dropped a tablespoon of water in the ocean and then tried to find it again. Teal was screaming and complaining constantly, but the wind took her voice off as well.

At a particularly large clump of bushes and near some cacti, I paused to give us a rest, then took a second swig of my canteen. We hovered around each other.

"Are you sure we're not going too far on the right?" Robin asked me.

"No, I'm not sure. I'm not sure of anything anymore."

"What does that mean?" Teal cried. "You don't know where you're going now?"

"I'm not your desert guide, you know. I'm no better at finding my way around here than you are."

"But you're leading us and we're following."

"So you lead," I said.

"I'm so tired," Teal replied instead of arguing. "Can we take a longer rest?"

"We're going to burn up out here," Robin reminded her. "Look at your legs. Look at mine."

I nodded and reached into Natani's healing bag to come out with the ointment he had once used on them. They recognized it immediately and began to smear it on their legs and arms and each other's neck, neither complaining about how it made them look now.

"Do your faces, too," I advised. I took some and put it on my own.

"Why are you doing that? Natani calls you daughter of the sun because you're black, doesn't he?" Teal asked, sounding jealous.

It made me smile. "Yes. I have an advantage out here, but black people do get sunburn and do get skin cancers. My daddy told me that and I never forgot it."

Teal looked skeptical.

"You know . . ." Robin said, looking around and watching the wind roll dried brush over the sand. It bounced and flew with such ease. "Maybe we should follow Natani's advice about traveling in the desert and wait until the sun goes down."

"What are you talking about?" Teal said sharply. "If we don't get back to the van, they might think we're lost and leave without us or something and then we'll really be lost."

"If they were really worrying about that, Teal, they wouldn't have left us out here like this," I said. "I doubt very much that they're sitting in some hot van waiting to see if we'll make it back. Robin's right. It's harder to travel in the desert now."

"Well, what are we going to do?"

"Have lunch," I said, "and then burrow under the sand and take a nap."

"What? I'm not burrowing under any sand. That's disgusting, and who knows what sort of things will be crawling all over us."

"Suit yourself." I opened one of the nutritional bars.

Robin did the same. Petulantly, Teal followed. She reached for her canteen again, and I held out my hand.

"You're drinking too much too fast."

"So?"

"Look around. I don't see any restaurants. If you run out of water way ahead of us, we'll have to give you some of our own and then we'll all suffer more."

Teal looked at Robin, then tightened the cap on her canteen and stuffed it back into her bag.

Using the bag, I began to dig myself a ditch in the sand. Robin did the same, and soon we were low enough to cover ourselves with sand and keep the sun off our exposed legs and arms especially. Teal watched, still stubborn. I put the bag over my face and closed my eyes. The wind continued to blow around us.

"This is insane!" Teal screamed.

However, it wasn't long before we heard her start to dig, mumbling and complaining all the while.

"You're listening to a crazy old Indian. Maybe this is wrong," she said.

Neither Robin nor I answered.

We heard her scream in frustration and then she was quiet. Soon, I did feel cooler, not cool, but cooler, and it was enough to permit me to close my eyes and seek some rest. Soon I surprised myself and actually fell asleep.

I woke first and not because I was fully rested before Robin and Teal. I felt something on my stomach and then on my chest. When I opened my eyes, the sun was almost completely down behind the mountains in the distance, but it was light enough for me to realize I was looking at the side of the head of a Gila monster, the poisonous lizard. I did not move a muscle. Eyeing me, it didn't move. My heart began to pound so hard, I was sure that would frighten it.

But it was Teal's scream that did that. She had woken and sat up and saw it on me. The creature scurried off and disappeared quickly.

"What was that?" she asked. Robin sat up and wiped her face.

"Gila monster," I said, amazed at how casual I sounded about it. "Okay, we each take another drink of water and then we continue."

As we started walking again, the sun continued to descend. Soon night began to slide over the desert sky and stars popped out brightly. There was no moonlight, but the sky was so clear that the starlight was enough to illuminate the desert. The sand glistened and the silhouetted cacti seemed to look even more like soldiers at attention.

Robin was the first to hear the coyotes. I was too deep in thought and Teal's ears were full of her own stream of constant moans and complaints, curses and cries.

"Look," Robin shouted, pointing to her right.

We stopped. A pack of coyotes was moving rapidly parallel to us, but not coming at us.

"Oh, my God," Teal said. "Do you think they want to eat us?"

"Probably, but as I understand from what Natani told me, they are cowards," I said.

"Cowards in a pack create their own courage," Robin said wisely, "but as long as we look strong, they'll keep their distance, I'm sure."

"I'm glad you're sure. How do we show them we're strong and unafraid of them?" Teal asked.

We all thought a moment.

"Let's start singing," I said. "What do we all know?"

"Singing? Are you crazy?"

"No, she's right," Robin said. "How about the national anthem? We all know that. We've heard it enough at school."

"The anthem? You're kidding," Teal said.

"No, no, look. See how the cacti are already standing at attention."

"Huh?"

"Good idea," I said.

We started walking again and Robin began to sing as loudly as she could.

"Oh, say can you see by the dawn's early light . . ."

Teal reluctantly joined in and soon our voices carried over the desert. None of us could reach the high notes and our sad attempts brought some laughter.

"Let's play ball," Robin shouted when we finished.

We walked on and soon lost sight of the coyotes.

"See, it worked," I told Teal.

"They weren't afraid of us. They just couldn't stand our singing," she said.

We laughed again, and then, when we reached the top of a knoll, I decided we should rest and eat another nutritional bar.

"It's time for dinner," I declared, and folded my legs. They did the same.

"Wait, wait," Teal cried, holding her hand out. "No one eats without thanking everyone else and saying I'm sorry."

"Exactly," Robin said, and did it. I did the same and then Teal did and we laughed again.

"Do you think Mindy and Gia are sick with worry over us by now?" Teal asked.

"No. I think they're sick about having to do all the dishes and clean the table and whatever else we did together," Robin told her.

"I didn't mind the work so much. I just mind someone telling me I have to do it or I don't get to eat," Teal said.

"Come on," I said. "You minded the work. When did you ever really work? You told us about your maids and your servants."

"Well . . . okay, I hated the work."

"I can't understand you," Robin said. "You had so much. Why did you get yourself into so much trouble all the time?"

"I had a big house and my family has lots of money, but I just didn't feel like I belonged. It's hard to describe."

"No, it's not," I said. "Blood doesn't make family."

"What does?" Teal asked me.

I shook my head. "I don't know."

"Love," Robin said. "As corny as it sounds, real love, someone who cares about you as much as, if not more than, he or she cares about himself. That's what a mother's supposed to be," she said bitterly.

"But," she added after chewing some of her bar, "I guess she was brought up without love so she didn't know how to give it to me. Anyway, I'm tired of hating her. Hate is exhausting."

We were all quiet. Her words seemed to settle the same way in us all.

"I don't think there was anything I wanted more than my mother and father and my brother to love me," Teal said.

"Why is it that the one thing we all need more than anything, we all have a hard time giving to each other?" Robin asked.

I had no answer.

I finished my bar and lay back with my head on my hands and looked up at the sky blazing with stars.

"If you lie back like this," I said, "and concentrate on the stars, you can feel like you're falling into them and not looking up. Try it."

They did and agreed.

I told them about Natani and the shell. I had told Teal but she had mocked it back on the ranch. Now she listened as attentively as Robin did.

"I guess you have to be out here to understand what he meant," Teal admitted.

"It gives you some power, some control over yourself, something they can't take from you," I told them.

"I'd like to learn more about that," Robin said.

"Maybe we are, right now," Teal commented, and again we were all silent.

It was funny, I thought, but out here, with our lives really still in some great danger, we had suddenly grown closer to each other than we had back at the ranch where we suffered so many of the same fears and punishments. Here, at least for a little while, we were unable to be too selfish. What happened to one of us happened to all of us.

"We're going to make it out of here," I suddenly declared.

"Yes," Robin agreed. "We will."

"We will," Teal repeated.

"Everyone ready?"

"Aye, aye, Captain," Robin said, saluting. Teal started to struggle with her surely painful ankle, and Robin reached out to help her.

"Thanks," she said.

We stood up, fixed our packs, and started to walk again.

"We need a new song," Robin declared. "I've got one. It's one of my mother's, one she wrote herself. She'd never believe I remember it and would sing it, because I used to make so much fun of it, but here I go.

My heart is a prison and you've got the key,
But darlin' there's no prisoner I'd rather be.
So build up those walls and chain me to your heart,
For darlin', oh darlin', we can never be apart.

"That's corny," Teal screamed. "But I like it. Keep singing. It'll keep the vultures away."

I laughed.

Robin continued to sing. She had a good voice and she put real feeling into the words, too, I thought, and then suddenly I was jealous.

She was reaching back, thinking of her mother, connecting with her, even this far away.

That was something at least.

I wished I had a song in my heart. I wished for it more than I even wished to get out of this desert trap.

For I knew, if I had a song like that, there wasn't a desert hot enough or long enough to defeat me.

We walked on.

The stars following us.

The night circling with all the creatures that had fled the heat emerging and I'm sure wondering who we were.

It was a question on our own lips.

Who are we?

Would we ever really know?

Perhaps if we do get out of here, I thought, perhaps then, we would.

With every step I took, with the heat fleeing and the cold descending, I longed for the comfort of Natani's drum, for I knew in my heart dangers were lurking in the patches of new darkness around and in front of us.

However, I really wasn't a stranger to all this.

I had known poisonous creatures all my life. Just like here, they lurked in the shadows, waiting to strike.

The shadows that hid them on the street were cut from the same blood-hungry darkness.

And just like in my city, we couldn't get home without walking through them.

14

Natani's Lesson

The later it became out in the desert night, the brighter it grew because more and more stars seemed to appear, and those that had appeared were bigger and seemed closer. At one point when we reached the top of a hill, I looked up and felt as if something, some power, could lift me at any moment and send me flying into space as if I had become a rocket.

I was tired, and my throat was dry. My legs ached, especially in the calf muscles, but at that moment, I had a wonderful sense of pleasure. I was truly in Natani's shell. I felt part of all that was around me. There was still no sign of anyone, no lights in the distance, no sounds, no reason to be hopeful, but I had gone beyond panic and anger and found some other place to rest my emotions. It was truly as if I was rising above the hardship and misery.

"Why in hell are you standing there and smiling?" Teal asked as Robin helped her up and beside me.

I turned to her.

I had become the desert tortoise and she had become the desert rat. It was truly as though Natani were standing there beside me.

"I know we're in trouble, but look at how beautiful it is out here," I said.

"Oh, brother. I'll take you to Disneyland as soon as we get home," Teal said. "All expenses paid. You'll stay at the best hotel they have."

"Somehow, I don't think it will be the same thing."

"No. It won't because we'll have the biggest, softest king-size beds, a plush bathroom, and lobster and steak and big fat rich desserts for dinner, and we'll swim in a magnificent large pool and in our skimpy bikinis drive boys mad with lust and desire."

"Is that what you like to do?" Robin asked

"So do you, so don't put on any goody-goody acts," Teal told her.

I thought they would begin another one of their chatty arguments, but instead, Robin smiled and shrugged.

"Sometimes," she admitted. "Phoebe?"

"I don't even own a bathing suit," I said. "Where would I have used it?"

"As soon as we're out of here, I'm buying you one," Teal vowed.

"And where are you getting all this money for five-star vacations and clothes and travel?" Robin asked.

"I'll blackmail my brother or something, but I'll get it."

"You know if you keep talking like that, Dr. Foreman is going to think you're not cured," Robin said.

We all laughed, but then, as we continued to look out into the desert darkness where pockets of thick shadows disguised what lay ahead, our laughter wound down into smiles that faded.

"I don't think we're heading in the right direction," Robin said. "From this perspective, we should be able to see something out there, don't you think?"

"I don't know. Maybe in the morning."

"Are we going to stop and sleep now?" Teal asked. I heard the hope in her voice.

"The more we walk now, the less we'll have to do in the heat," I said. "We'll stop midday tomorrow and take another long rest. Maybe we'll find some real shade."

"Or water."

"Yeah," Robin said. "I'm sure there's a fountain out there somewhere just waiting for us."

I started down the hill. Teal groaned with disappointment, but followed Robin. For a while we trekked in silence. I wasn't watching Teal and didn't realize she was not only falling behind, but because she was closing her eyes too often, she was wandering too far to the right, practically walking in her sleep. Robin, like me, was plodding along, lost in thought and not paying attention to Teal either.

Suddenly, we heard a frightening rattle sound and then Teal's scream. When we turned around to look, she was five yards or so off our trail and she had walked right into a low bush under which a sidewinder rattlesnake was concealed. It had given a warning, but she had either snapped to attention too late or lost her bearing and stepped too closely to it.

Robin and I saw it whipping from side to side in its flight, its body gleaming until it disappeared under a rock almost as if it was ashamed of the damage it had caused. For a moment neither of us could move. A cold wave of panic turned our feet into fifty-pound dead weights. Teal had fallen to her side and was screaming in such a high-pitched voice, it seemed to be coming from inside my own ears. She had her hands around her leg and was rocking.

Both Robin and I got hold of ourselves and charged at her.

"What happened?" Robin screamed.

"It just bit me. I'm going to die! A rattlesnake bit me. I'm dying, I'm dying!"

I fought back the panic that was trying to climb up my legs as if I had stepped into a pool of ice water. Then, Natani's instructions came back to me. I turned in a new panic. What could I use to lance a wound? We had no knives.

Teal's screams were vibrating my very bones.

"Calm her down!" I screamed at Robin, and reached into the bush under which the snake had been resting. I broke off the thickest branch I could, then took it to a rock and worked on sharpening the edge.

"I'm going to die."

"If you don't settle down, you will," I screamed back at her as I worked. "You're making your heart race and that's sending the poison out over your body faster. Stop it!"

She paused and looked at me and then at Robin.

"She's right, Teal. Calm yourself."

"What are we going to do? We'll never get me to a hospital in time," she moaned, tears streaming down her cheeks.

"Natani taught us how to handle a snake bite. He put something in his bag," I said, bringing the sharpened branch back to her. "Straighten her leg out and let's see the bite."

I saw the holes made by the snake's teeth clearly.

"I've got to lance it, Teal. It's going to hurt. Just bite your teeth together and try not to think about it."

"How am I not going to think about it?" she screamed back at me.

"Think about the boys you're going to tease at the pool," Robin told her.

I held her leg with one hand, then brought the sharpened edge to the teeth marks and pressed. She screamed and I hesitated, my own heart probably pounding as hard and as fast as her heart was pounding.

"Can you do it?" Robin asked me.

I swallowed, or thought I had, and nodded.

I brought the branch back and pressed harder and faster until the skin broke and I could tear down through the wound. Blood seeped out around the incision.

"Do you remember his instructions?" Robin asked.

"I think so."

"You think so?" Teal asked through her cries.

I placed the bag on the ground and carefully looked at the contents until I located the rattlesnake weed. Then I looked at Robin.

"Got to suck it out now," I said.

"I've already had dinner. Okay, I'll do it," Robin said, which surprised me. She looked at Teal. "This doesn't mean we're in love," she told her, and brought her mouth to the wound. She sucked and spit, sucked and spit. When I thought it was enough, I tapped her on the shoulder and she sat back. Then, again following Natani's instructions, I squeezed the juice of the weed into the wound.

"What is that? It looks like some weed," Teal said.

"It is, but it has medical powers," I said. "Natani told us."

"Maybe it's just in his imagination."

"We'll know soon," Robin said.

"Thanks a lot."

"You're going to have to chew this now, Teal, and swallow the juice. Swallow as much as you can."

I gave it to her and she grimaced. "It tastes horrible."

"Chew it!" Robin and I screamed at her simultaneously.

She closed her eyes and chewed.

"We have to make a fire, Robin, and boil the leaves in water."

"What water?" she asked.

I smirked and lifted my canteen. "What choice do we have?"

We broke another thick branch, and I sifted through the sand and rocks under the brush until I found the thickest dead twig I could. I beat it open with a rock and brought the first branch to it. Robin gathered some dry moss and we took turns rubbing and rubbing, spinning the branch just the way Natani had shown us. It seemed to take forever, but finally there was some smoke. Encouraged, we both worked harder and harder, bearing down as he had instructed until, finally, a tiny flame was born.

Cheered, we fed it the dry moss carefully until we had a good flame.

"I can't believe you two did that," Teal said, watching calmly, her eyes opening and closing. Suddenly, as if the sight of the fire was too much, she began to heave. She vomited hard and fast, moaning and groaning.

"He said whoever was bitten would be very sick," I reminded Robin.

"Oh, I'm going to die," Teal moaned, embracing herself.

Using more branches and thin vines, I devised a way to hold the canteen over the flame. Into it, I stuffed the remaining snake weed. When I thought the water was boiling, I fished out the leaves, and then, using the thin vines of the bush, we wrapped them around Teal's wound, again as Natani had instructed. Teal vomited again, but now she was just dry heaving and really suffering.

"What do we do now?" Robin asked.

"Looks like we take our rest earlier than I had hoped," I said.

Using the backpack to fix a pillow for Teal, we urged her to try to sleep. She was shivering now. The desert night had dropped the temperature to where it was actually cold. Robin fed the fire, building it until we had some decent flames.

"Make it gigantic," Teal muttered. "Maybe someone will see it and come help us."

"Maybe," Robin said, and started to forage for more wood.

"Be careful, Robin. I used all the snake weed in the bag on Teal."

She walked on tiptoe, gently moving brush, avoiding big rocks, and gathering twigs and branches as quickly as she could. Teal watched with a dazed look on her face.

"Will I be all right?" she asked me.

"Sure," I said.

Of course, I had no idea if she would be all right. How poisonous was the snake? How much poison was in her body? How effective was Natani's weed medicine? Was it crazy to believe in him? The treatments he had given Robin and Teal for their sunburn seemed to help, and the ointment he had given them for their hands helped. The Indians lived side by side with all this danger, these creatures. What they had to help themselves must work or they wouldn't use it, I thought.

Teal's eyes closed and opened. She shivered and moaned. If she died out here, it would be so horrible, I thought. It made me rage against Dr. Foreman, but I did so silently, for I didn't want to stir Teal up and worry her any more.

Robin returned again and we fed the fire. It did provide warmth. The embers rose with the smoke and traveled out and away with the wind.

"Anyone looking for us would see this," Robin said.

I nodded.

We both looked at Teal. She seemed to have fallen asleep, but every now and then she would shudder and moan and cry.

"Maybe we didn't get the poison out fast enough or all of it," Robin said.

I shook my head. Her guess was as good as mine. We continued to sit on both sides of Teal, our knees up, looking at the fire. Coyotes howled around us, the wood crackled.

"Once, when I was very little, I went on a picnic with my mother," Robin said. "She had some boyfriend with us, but I can't remember his name. I remember we made a fire and they roasted marshmallows for me, and then we had hot dogs and my mother sang and played her guitar. I fell asleep on the blanket, and when I woke up, there was no one there. They were off in the bushes or something."

"Weren't you afraid?"

"I was for a while and then I watched some birds and got intrigued with how hard they worked at feeding themselves. It was a particularly beautiful day, too. I remember that, and I remember really enjoying myself. Finally, my mother and her boyfriend came from wherever they were and her boyfriend carried me on his shoulders all the way back to our farm. I can't remember his name, but I remember his hair. It was a reddish yellow and I had clumps of it in my small fists, holding it like the reins of a horse. Sometimes, he cried out because I was pulling on his hair too hard, but I remember feeling as if I was on the top of the world, seeing everything from an adult's height.

"I never went on another picnic, and I never saw that boyfriend again. Sometimes, I used to think of it as a dream I had when I was very young. If I mentioned it to my mother, she would look as if she didn't remember it at all. I don't think it was a special or important day for her.

"After a while, it slipped out of my memory, but just now, as we were staring at the fire, it returned and I recalled my fists full of reddish yellow hair. That's silly, isn't it? The only thing I really remember vividly, that hair."

"No. Maybe you remember it so well because it made you feel safe to hold on to it."

She turned and looked at me. "Maybe." She smiled. "Maybe that's what I was looking for through the fire, a way to feel safe again."

We were quiet.

Teal moaned.

I lay back and Robin did the same. Before we fell asleep, we each had our arms around Teal, and that was how we were when the sun woke us with its stinging good morning.

Teal looked groggy, her cheeks stained with lines her tears had made zigzagging their way off her face. Robin and I sat up and watched her wipe her eyes. She looked at us and blinked as if she had forgotten everything. Then she spoke and sent new chills of fear down my back and Robin's, even in this desert heat.

"Where's my mother?" she asked.

"What?"

She sat up and looked at us and then around us, shaking her head. "I've got to get home."

"What is she talking about?" Robin asked.

I shook my head and reached out to feel her forehead. It was so hot, I had to take my hand away.

"She's burning up."

"If I don't get home quickly, my father will be very angry and he'll ground me again," Teal said. "Who's driving me home?"

"We have to walk first," I told her.

"Walk? To where? Can't you call a cab?"

"Can't you see where you are?" Robin asked.

Teal turned to her, her eyes blinking. "Who are you?"

"Great," Robin said. "What do we do now?"

"It'll pass," I said. I stood up and looked out to my right and to my left. Had we gone too far off the trail back? Nothing suggested we were heading in the right direction. It all looked so similar, the same hills, the same cacti and bushes. I glanced at the sun.

"We should probably go more to our left," I said.

"You don't understand," Teal muttered. "I can't stay any longer. I'm already well past my curfew."

"Me, too," Robin told her.

Teal touched her lips and looked at her fingers and then at us.

"I'm very thirsty. I'd like a Coke or something, please."

"I'll call the butler," Robin told her, and looked at me.

I checked Teal's canteen. It was bone-dry.

"We better get some water in her," I said, and gave her my canteen. I didn't see how the boiling would have harmed the water. It was just very warm.

The moment it touched her lips, she complained, "Isn't there any ice?"

"Gee, we're all out. Here, try this." Robin gave Teal her canteen. The water was cooler. Teal gulped at it.

"Easy," I said, and lowered the canteen. "You can get yourself sick drinking that too fast now."

"I am sick. I want to go home this instant. Where's the phone?"

"Gee, we forgot to pay the bill so they turned off our service," Robin said.

"You're not very funny." Teal's eyes grew small as she scrutinized Robin's face. "Are you Jeff's cousin?"

"No. Jeff's my cousin," Robin said. For a moment that did confuse Teal and I actually smiled, although I couldn't see what we had to laugh about now.

"Let's get her up," I told Robin, and we helped Teal to her feet.

"Ow!" she screamed, and looked down at her leg wrapped with the leaves. "What happened to me?"

"You hurt yourself dancing last night," Robin said. "It's the best we can do for now. We've got to walk on."

"I can't walk."

Robin tried to pull her forward but she resisted.

"Oh, great. What do we do?"

"Come on, Teal. You have to try or you won't get home," I said. I took her other arm, and together Robin and I forced her to take some steps. She cried with every one taken, putting as little weight on the bitten leg as she could. Finally, Robin put Teal's arm over her shoulder and that way we were able to get her to move forward a little faster, but I knew Robin couldn't carry her for long.

We took turns, resting every hundred yards or so.

"We're not going to get very far this way," I said.

Teal's eyes were closed and she was rocking softly from side to side.

"You better put the top up. It's too hot," she muttered. "And stop to get me a drink. Anything. Even a beer."

"Yes, it is too hot," Robin said. "Phoebe, can you raise the top on the convertible, please?"

"She's delirious."

"I wish I were. Who wants to realize what's really happening and where we really are," Robin said. "What are we going to do, Phoebe? We can't carry her all the way out of here. We don't even know if we're heading in the right direction, and we've just about run out of water."

I shook my head. I was out of ideas. Gazing around, I spotted something on a branch.

"What's that?" I asked Robin.

She shaded her eyes and squinted. "What?"

"Looks like . . . something tied to that bush." I rose and walked ahead to my left. It was a ribbon. Something was wrapped on the end of it, tied so it wouldn't fall out. I undid the knot and a small turquoise stone fell into my palm. An electric surge of hope shot through my body.

"Natani!" I screamed.

"What?" Robin shouted back, standing.

"I think this was left here by Natani." I looked farther ahead and saw what was definitely another ribbon. "C'mon," I said, hurrying back. "He's showing us the way."

"Why didn't he just show himself and help us?" Robin asked.

"Maybe he's afraid of what Dr. Foreman would do or say. I don't know. Let's go."

We got Teal standing again and again took turns helping her walk. She mumbled gibberish, phrases and sentences from memories, about people she knew, things she had done, words she had exchanged with her mother, her father, and her brother. Most of the time, her eyes were closed.

On the ground under the third ribbon, we found a basket. I uncovered it and pulled out leather canteens filled with water, packs of dried food, and a pot with matches in it.

"What's that for?" Robin asked.

I unwrapped another packet and found some more snake weed. "He wants us to boil this and change her bandage, I'm sure."

"It would help if he would just send for a helicopter."

"Somehow, I don't think he can do that, Robin. Come on, let's not waste time now. Gather some wood."

She did and we built a fire quickly. Once again, we boiled the leaves, then I changed Teal's bandage, this time using some tape Natani had left as well. We were able to give Teal a good drink of water, then wipe her down. She seemed to become more comfortable.

It was becoming scorching again. We had a hard time making it to the next hill, but when we got there, following another set of ribbons, we looked out and saw what was clearly the ranch.

"I never thought I'd be glad to see that place again," Robin said.

"Me neither."

"I'd like my breakfast now," Teal declared.

"Oh, sure, miss. What would you like this morning?"

"Just some scrambled eggs, orange juice, cinnamon toast, and coffee."

"Is that all? We'll have it for you in a jiffy," Robin told her.

Teal nodded, her eyes still closed.

"Let's take a good rest before this last piece." It looked like a good mile or so to me. We sat and ate what Natani had left.

"I have no idea what I'm eating," Robin said, feeding Teal as well. Teal ate as if she were really having what she had ordered.

"Me neither, but it feels good in my stomach."

Whatever it was, it seemed to renew our energy. After some more water, we fixed our towels on our heads, smeared some more of the sun protection on our skin, and started toward the ranch.

When we were about four or five hundred yards from the corral in which the horses were kept, Wind Song trotted to the railing and whinnied, raising his head. The other horses gathered beside him and looked out at us.

"At least someone is happy to see us," Robin muttered.

Like three soldiers home from battle, we limped along, Teal still relying on our shoulders and keeping most of her weight off her right leg. As we drew closer, the buddies began to appear, coming around the corner of the horse barn. None of them rushed forward to give us any assistance. They stood watching us limp home until we were close enough to hear them.

Then, they began a silly cheer.

"Come on, girls. You can make it. Keep coming. Two, four, six, eight, who do we appreciate? Phoebe bird, Phoebe bird."

They laughed and clapped.

"She was bitten by a rattlesnake," I said when we were standing right in front of them.

"Did it die?" M'Lady Two asked, and the three of them laughed.

"If she does or gets sicker, you'll be sorry as hell," Robin said, her eyes blazing at them.

"Whoa," M'Lady Three cried. "Listen to her. A couple of days in the desert and she thinks she's tough or something. I'll tell you, girls, I'm really impressed. How did you manage to find your way back?"

"How could you leave us out there like that?" I countered.

"It broke our hearts to do it," M'Lady One said. "But we have to do what we have to do. Go shower up and wait in the bunkhouse for Dr. Foreman," she followed curtly.

"What about Teal?" Robin asked.

"She'll live, although I can't say the same for the snake."

"She can't walk on her own," I said.

"We'll take care of her. Move it."

Slowly, we lowered Teal to a sitting position.

"I'm sorry, Mother," Teal said. "It couldn't be helped. Our car broke down."

"Oh, did it?" M'Lady Two asked. They all laughed again.

"She still has a high fever. She's delirious. She needs medical help," Robin said.

"She was always delirious," M'Lady Two said. "Will you two get moving or do we move you?"

"We're not leaving her," I declared, reaching a firm, quick decision. I reached down to help Teal up. Robin did the same.

"I told you we would take care of her," M'Lady Two said.

"Like you've been taking care of us?"

She stepped forward threateningly, but I didn't flinch.

"Go on," I said. "I have just enough strength to fight one more battle."

"Me, too," Robin said.

Maybe it was the ordeal in the desert. Maybe it was the wild, determined look on both our faces, or maybe it was just the sight of us, standing fast despite all that we had endured, Teal wavering between us, whatever, but M'Lady Two hesitated, then relaxed and backed up.

"Take her to the house yourselves then," she ordered, and stepped aside.

We walked on, struggling because Teal was doing less and less to move herself now. Despite the effort, both Robin and I reached down into some reservoir of energy, fueled by our anger, our hate, our indignation, by years and years of our pain and suffering. We stumbled and nearly fell. The buddies roared with laughter, then, suddenly, I could hear Natani's drum. Robin heard it, too. We looked at each other and found the strength to cross that yard to the front of the hacienda.

As we continued, I kept my eyes forward, never wavering, so I didn't see or know if Gia and Mindy were watching us. When we stood at the steps, the front door opened, and Dr. Foreman, dressed in a cool, mint green skirt suit, her face freshly made up with a brighter lipstick and even some eye shadow, looked down at us and smiled.

"Oh, I just knew you would do well. I just knew you had it in you to be cooperative, unselfish, and resilient. My girls, my Foreman girls, always come through for me, for themselves. What a wonderful day," she cried.

Was she blind? Could she not see that Teal was practically comatose and we were standing on legs held up only by sheer determination?

"Teal was bitten by a sidewinder," I said. "She's delirious."

"And you knew what to do, I see," Dr. Foreman replied, still not moving to help us. "Natani's lessons. How fortunate that you paid attention. Imagine if you paid attention in regular school as well. Maybe now you will. See?" she asked as if in that simple question she justified this whole experience, her techniques and theories and all that was done to us in the name of recovery.

"Teal is very sick," I replied in a dry, stiff voice.

She blinked rapidly, but held that cold, egotistical smile I had come to hate, to have dreams about shattering.

"She'll recover," she said, "and she'll be better for it."

"Have you been bitten by a sidewinder?" I fired back at her.

"Don't be insubordinate." She nodded at the buddies. "Take Teal to the infirmary immediately."

M'Ladies One and Two moved forward and lifted Teal from our shoulders. Then they scooped her under her legs and carried her up the stairway. Dr. Foreman stepped aside and opened the door for them.

"Are we home?" I heard Teal ask.

"Yes," M'Lady One said, and laughed.

The door closed behind them and Dr. Foreman turned back to us. "I want the two of you to shower and change back into your coveralls and wait for further instructions in your bunkhouse. You may rest while you wait." She turned and walked into the house before either Robin or I could say another thing to her.

"Let's go, girls," M'Lady Three said.

We turned and crossed the yard to the showers. Both of us were actually looking forward to the cold shower. We couldn't swallow enough water and it felt wonderful on our bodies. Soaping up, scrubbing our hair, revived us both.

"Enough, girls. Move it," M'Lady Three shouted.

I looked for Mindy and Gia and didn't see either of them in the gardens or the pigpen. We slipped on our shorts and blouses and battered sneakers before going to the barn bunkhouse. Both of us stopped dead on entering.

Our three cots had been stripped of their mattresses, blankets, and pillows. Our coveralls and old blouses were on them and our clodhopper shoes beside them.

"Why?" I asked, turning to M'Lady Three.

She shrugged. "You had demerits. You have to earn what you get, remember?"

"This stinks. It's unfair!" Robin cried.

"Welcome to the real world. You have to learn how to deal with unfairness. Not that this was unfair. Rest up, girls. You'll need it, believe me," she said, and left.

"Look," Robin said, nodding at Gia's and Mindy's bunks. Mindy's was stripped down as well. "I wonder what she did to deserve her unfairness."

"I don't care anymore," I said. "I'm too tired to care about anything, even this."

I went to my bunk and swept the coveralls and blouse off. Then I thought again and rolled them up to use as a pillow. Robin nodded and did the same.

In minutes, we were both dead to the world, asleep. Soon after, however, we were poked and prodded until we woke up. M'Ladies Two and One were there with notebooks in their hands, the same sort we had been given at orientation.

"You've slept enough, girls. Dr. Foreman wants you both to start on your journals. She wants you both to write about your experience out there and what you have learned from it. She expects details and honesty," M'Lady One said, and handed me a notebook with a pen.

Robin was handed hers as well. We both just stared blankly at the notebooks.

The buddies smiled, then left.

"She must be kidding," Robin said.

"I strongly doubt it," I said.

"I can't keep my eyes open, much less write something."

We looked at each other and came up with the same cry: "What more can she do to us?"

I put the notebook down and sprawled out again. Robin did the same and we were asleep almost as quickly as we were the first time. We slept well into the late afternoon and woke this time when we heard the door open.

Gia stood there looking at us. I sat up quickly.

"Gia. Where's Mindy?" I asked, seeing she was alone.

"Mindy's gone."

"Gone?" Robin asked, sitting up. "You mean she was sent home?"

"No, I mean gone." Gia walked to her cot. She sat, staring down at the floor. I looked at Robin and then rose and walked over to Gia.

"What happened to her, Gia?"

She looked up at me. "I couldn't stop her. She used the scythe Natani had us use to cut the high grass. I was working and suddenly realized she was no longer in the field. She had been strange all morning after a session with Dr. Foreman. She wouldn't tell me anything about it, but I could see she was very upset, more upset than ever. I kept asking her about it, trying to find out something, some reason for her deep depression.

"Finally, she muttered something about never going home and how it was her fault.

"I tried to get more information to help her, but she clammed up and just went to work with me in the field. As I said, I was working and thinking and not paying attention to anything and then suddenly realized she was no longer there.

"So, I went looking for her and found her in the barn, sitting on the floor. She had taken the sharpest scythe and she had cut both her wrists very deeply. There was so much blood already, but she was smiling at me. I shouted for help, of course. No one was around, so I ran to find Natani, but he wasn't there either."

"That's because he was out there helping us," I said, looking at Robin. She nodded. "What happened then?"

"I tried to stop the bleeding, but that was impossible. She said, 'Leave me be. I was wrong. I'm going home.'

"So I ran out again and went to the house where I found Dr. Foreman lecturing our buddies in her office. She demanded to know why I had entered the house without permission. She stood there screaming at me. Finally, I managed to tell them about Mindy and they ran out to the barn.

"I saw them carry her off, but I knew it was too late. Later, the van took her away. I saw them carrying her out of the house. This afternoon," she continued after a long beat of silence, "I think Dr. Foreman was to meet with the police. Did you see how nice she looked?" she asked as if that really mattered to any of us. "She'll make it look like an accident."

"How horrible," Robin said.

"You know what was done to us, how we were left out there in the desert?" I asked.

"I know." She looked up at us. "I didn't expect you would make it back."

"Natani helped us. That's why he wasn't here when you needed him," I said.

"She's going to get away with it," Gia said. "She got away with Posy. She'll get away with all this, too."

"Maybe the police are still here or someone from the social service agency. Maybe we can talk to them," Robin suggested excitedly.

"No," Gia said. "They're gone. She did her good job on them, I'm sure. We're high-risk girls, you see. Anything can happen and it's not going to be her fault. Look at all the girls she's helped, the ones she's released back into society to be productive citizens. Once in a while, she loses one. It can't be helped. The girl was beyond redemption. I know her whole speech. I've heard it before. I've heard it all my life, that speech. How terrible I am. How beyond help. How selfish. How downright no good.

"Sound familiar?" she asked us.

"Not as much maybe, but I've heard it, yes," Robin admitted.

I thought about my uncle and aunt and how they saw me. "Me, too."

"Won't Mindy's family be upset, angry, demand answers?" Robin wondered.

"The family that failed, that gave up? Please," Gia said. "They'll feel sorrier for Dr. Foreman. They'll even apologize for giving her a girl she couldn't cure."

"She's more dangerous than we'll ever be," I said, "because she gets them to believe she does it all out of some desire to be good."

"Exactly." Gia looked past me at the cot. "I see you were given the notebook to fill. I have one, too." She reached under her pillow to show it to us. "I'm to write about what I learned from Mindy's failure."

Gia put it aside and looked at us again, finally realizing Teal wasn't there.

"Where is Teal?"

I told her what had happened and where she was.

"She'll take good care of her," Gia said. "She might even have her transported to a real hospital or something. She can't afford to lose another girl so quickly."

"She almost lost all three of us out there."

"That's different. You ran off. You were beyond her help, her ability to do anything. If you didn't show up, she would have called the police and covered her rear end. Don't worry about Dr. Foreman. She's invincible," Gia said.

She lay back and looked up at the ceiling, her hands folded on her stomach.

"What do we do?" I asked. Robin shook her head.

"Nothing," Gia said. "Go write in your notebooks. I have mine half-filled."

"I'll write something. What I write will make her ears burn," Robin threatened.

Gia smiled. "Good idea. That's what I'm doing."

We had no idea what she meant.

But we would.

Soon.

We would.

15

Posy Returns

Teal wasn't sent to any real hospital. Natani's Indian medicine worked well. After another two days, she appeared at the barracks, weakened, but essentially well enough to be on her own again with just a little limp in her walk. The snake bite and the events afterward appeared to have erased most of her memories of our desert ordeal. Robin and I had to describe it all to her, and as we did, she kept shaking her head and saying, "I did that? We did that?"

Apparently she had been in more of a daze and in more confusion than we'd realized after she had been bitten by the sidewinder.

Apparently because of her condition, Dr. Foreman did not give her a notebook to fill with thoughts and lessons learned. Neither Robin nor I had really done much in ours, but we were told we would not be given back our mattresses, blankets, and pillows until we had completed the notebooks.

I was afraid of writing anything truthful, afraid that somehow Dr. Foreman would find a way to use it against me, use it as a weapon to tear me down, just as she had done with my revelation about my fear of rats. Gia was writing in hers, but we had no idea what she wrote. She wouldn't reveal it. She just kept mumbling, "I'll remind her. I'll remind her."

One of the first things I did when I had free time was to thank Natani. He said nothing, admitting to nothing until I described how I had found my shell and used it to help get me through the ordeal.

"So now I shall no longer call you daughter of the sun. You are daughter of the tortoise," he said, and came the closest to laughing with me.

"You shouldn't stay here, Natani. This is a mean and ugly place. You don't belong here."

"I must stay with my plants, my animals, my trees. We look after each other. Someday, daughter of the tortoise, you will learn that the Earth Mother is your true friend and the only home you will have."

"I think I learned that already, Natani. Thanks again for what you did for us."

He nodded and smiled. "You did well with what you learned."

Because of our near exhaustion and what we had endured, we weren't given heavy, long labor during the first few days after our return. Most of my day was spent helping Natani with the horses, work I had come to love. One afternoon, Natani asked me if I would like to learn how to ride Wind Song. I was terrified of the idea, but he told me I was ready and Wind Song approved. I had little doubt that he could speak to horses.

Natani showed me how to ride bareback. His first instruction was to mount Wind Song from the left side. Even at his age, he was nimble enough to leap and swing his leg over Wind Song's back. I tried it and failed miserably, probably because I was too frightened. Finally, he boosted me up and I swung my leg over. It was not exactly the most comfortable place to be, but Natani said I needed to relax and believe in myself, and if I did, it would be like riding on a cloud.

"Be one with Wind Song. He will know if you feel like a stranger. He will not expect it or like it if you don't join with him," Natani advised.

I put my hand on Wind Song's powerful neck and he shook his head and then tapped the ground with his right hoof.

"He says hello," Natani told me.

"Hello, Wind Song," I replied.

Natani handed me the reins, which he wanted me to take in my left hand first.

"Never let go of the reins," he said. "It is how you talk to Wind Song, to tell him which way to turn and when to stop. He is rein trained." Natani showed me how to lay the reins on Wind Song's left side to turn him right and vice versa.

"Do not pull back when you are standing still. He will think you want to go back. Hold the reins like a bird: too tight and you will choke it, too loose and it will fly away, daughter of the tortoise.

"Wind Song likes you, but he will want to ride you and not you ride him. It is natural to him. He is a proud animal, full of spirit, so be firm with your movements. You must feel his moves, and when he starts to turn where you don't want him to turn, stop him, because once he is into it, it will be hard to make him change his mind."

"Do I say giddap?" I asked.

Natani smiled and shook his head. "You watch too many cowboy-and-Indian movies. You press firmly with your heels into his sides when you want him to go forward. Don't worry about hurting him. You won't, but he will know you are serious if you press firmly. Bounce with him, daughter of the tortoise." Natani then slapped Wind Song on the rump and he started around the corral.

Bounce I did and I came down too hard and fast. Natani told me I was being too stiff. I knew I had to hide my fear, but it was hard. Finally, I discovered that Natani was right: If I relaxed, it was less difficult and I didn't bounce as hard. I softened and I could feel I was riding better and better. After a few more trots, Wind Song stopped as if he was testing me, and Natani urged me to move him ahead. I did so, firmly kicking with my heels. He began to trot again and Natani shouted for me to practice turning him.

"Firmly, firmly," Natani called to me. "Do everything to show him you mean it."

It was easier than I had expected, and soon I began to enjoy it. I even turned him sharply, then started around again just to see if I could make him do that. My courage was building with every minute I rode.

Look at me, I thought. Look at me. Who on the street in Atlanta would believe Phoebe Elder would be riding a horse bareback?

On my next turn, I saw M'Lady One standing next to the fence. She was smiling, but it wasn't a friendly, happy-for-me smile. It was impish. I looked to Natani, but he didn't see her.

As we drew closer, she leaned over the fence. "Having a good time, Phoebe bird?"

I was about to say yes when she flicked a cigarette lighter, one of those that had a knob permitting you to increase the flame. Wind Song caught sight of it and reared sharply to his left, whipping into a gallop. I tried holding him back, but he was excited and afraid. I thought he was actually going to try to leap over the fence, but he stopped short and raised his forelegs. I lost my grip and slid off his back, splashing down into the horse manure.

M'Lady One, now joined by the other two buddies, roared with laughter. Wind Song trotted away and stared at me, snorting, brushing the ground with his right hoof like a bull about to charge. Then Natani entered the corral and walked toward him. He held out his hand and placed it on the horse's head. For a moment Wind Song looked like he would throw it off, but he didn't. He calmed down and stood still, his tail slapping at flies again.

"I guess she's a born rider, huh, Natani?" M'Lady One called.

Natani said nothing. He helped me up and I started to brush off.

"It's lonesome in the saddle since my horse died," M'Lady Two sang, and the three of them walked away laughing.

Natani stared after them, his eyes dark. Then he tilted his head as if he heard something and looked off to the right where some clouds slid beside each other, the bellies of them all dark.

"She flicked a lighter, Natani. She frightened Wind Song."

He nodded. "I saw." He continued to stare out at the clouds. "The wind is angry. There will be thunder inside us. That will be enough for today."

What does that mean? I wondered. I stood there and watched as he led Wind Song back to the stables. I was so angry and frustrated. Maybe that was what he meant by the thunder inside us. There was enough inside me to cause a flood, but all I did was mumble curses under my breath as I went to the showers to clean off the manure as best I could.

Afterward, I told Robin and Teal what I had done and what had happened. I also told them what Natani had said as he looked off at some dark clouds in the distance. Gia was nearby and listened, but these days she was more introverted than ever. She kept her distance, kept to herself as if she was afraid we would do or say something that interfered with her thoughts. Sometimes, I would catch her pausing in her work, staring at the hacienda, her lips moving, but no sounds coming from her. After a while she would realize I was watching her and she would return to work.

At dinner she was no less quiet and to herself. She ate, did her chores, spoke only when she had to speak, then returned to the barn barracks where she read over what she had written in her notebook, did some homework, and went to sleep. She was going to sleep earlier and earlier each night. Robin asked me about her. She and Teal had noticed the dramatic changes, too, but whenever I asked Gia if she wanted us to do anything, she shook her head and said nothing. Once she did say, "Not now."

Did she mean she wanted nothing now or nothing was wrong now?

I assumed her behavior might have a lot to do with Mindy and how much she missed her. Despite the way she used to snap at her and criticize her, Mindy was still closer to her than we were. It made sense. She had spent more time with her. Occasionally, I would see her staring at Mindy's cot, but even her staring was different now. She seemed to be seeing things. Her eyes would grow larger and smaller, her lips would move, and sometimes she would shake her head or nod slightly. She was so intense about it, she was lost in it. The barn could fall down around us, and she would still be standing there, looking at that empty cot, I thought. She heard nothing, would respond to no one, and then, when she was finished, just turn and curl up on her cot.

Didn't Dr. Foreman see these changes in her? I wondered.

Every day after we had returned from our desert ordeal, I anticipated some sort of therapy session with Dr. Foreman, either with the three of us or one at a time, but she wasn't around as much. We didn't see her at dinner for three nights in a row, but we did see the van coming and going with her.

"She's probably working on replacements, not that I have any high hopes about us being released any too soon," Robin said.

I imagined she was right. There did seem to be a new stirring about the ranch. The buddies were on our backs less and more to themselves, one day going off on a so-called R-and-R trip and returning laden with lots of goodies, I was sure. They were too happy and lighthearted. We didn't dare go to the back of the house to spy on them, but we had little doubt they were partying.

And then, a little more than two weeks after our return, it happened.

We would spend many hours reviewing the details, trying to make some sense of it. We would also spend a lot of our energy trying to forget it. It would be the stuff from which nightmares were made. Every scream I heard thereafter would nudge the memories and fill me with cold shudders. The same would be true for Robin and Teal, maybe even more so, especially for Teal. There was never a question about her being the weakest of the three of us, the most thin-skinned, although by the time this was over, she was probably as hard as a turtle shell compared to the friends she had and the friends she would make.

Natani once told me that life, time, experiences, spin more and more of the cocoon around you, insulating you against more of the same in the future or anything that can hurt you.

"We are truly like trees," he said. "As their bark thickens and they grow taller, wider, so do we."

I suppose it was his way of telling me not to be afraid of life, but to profit from it, to always be a student, to never turn my back on anything. One of the first things he had told us when we had first arrived was "I know you are not happy. But you must remember that life's sorrows often bring great joys." With that attitude, he would never be depressed, never be sad very long. It made him as strong as the tree trunk he sometimes resembled.

It's no exaggeration to say that sometimes a series of events or even a single event would make you feel as if you had passed through a lifetime. That night was one of those times. It seemed to last forever, and for a while it was as if nothing had come before and nothing could come after.

I woke with a start. My cheek felt like a cold hand had been on it, a very cold hand, the hand of death itself. I listened and thought I was still sleeping, dreaming, because what I heard seemed so far off, seemed like something coming from deep down inside me, a voice echoing up from a well or out of a tunnel, a long, thin cry.

I sat up.

The stars were blazing, but there was more light than usual and it wasn't from what Natani called "the pregnant moon." I scrubbed my cheeks with my palms and swung myself around. Gia's cot was empty.

Curious and also confused now, I slipped on my coveralls, shoved my arms through my shirt, and put on my clodhoppers. I stood up and looked at Robin and Teal, who were both asleep, their backs to me.

The scream I had heard in my dream grew louder and became a chorus.

"Robin!" I cried. "Robin, Teal."

Robin turned and groaned. Teal did not wake up.

"Whaaa?" Robin groaned.

"Listen. What is that? Listen."

She ground her eyes with her fists as if she heard through them and then sat up slowly.

"What do you think that is?"

"I don't know," she said.

I went to Teal's cot and poked her in the shoulder. She spun around angrily and looked up at me.

"What do you want? It's not morning already, is it?"

"Listen," I said.

"What?"

Robin was getting dressed, too. "Shut up and listen," she ordered.

Teal sat up, groaning. Then her eyes widened. "What is it?"

"We don't know. Come on," I said. "Get dressed."

Reluctantly, she did and the three of us went to the door. I hesitated. The screaming was louder now, much louder. I opened the door and it looked as if the whole world was on fire. The blaze that came from our right had flames that seemed to be scorching the very stars. The three of us stepped out, astounded, our faces caught in a ghoulish yellow glow.

Natani and his nephew were rushing about.

The hacienda was consumed in flames. The screaming we heard came from the rear.

"Someone's trapped," I said, and we hurried across the yard and toward the rear of the house. When we got there, we stared up in shock.

The slanted roof upon which we had climbed to spy on the buddies was streaked with flames. Part of the center of it had fallen in. In the windows we could see the buddies, all three of them looking out at us, their faces so illuminated by the flames that licked and traveled along the edges of the main house that they looked as if the fire was already burning within them, making them glow like lightbulbs.

The front of the hacienda was consumed in even bigger flames so that the fire had sandwiched them inside the house. M'Lady Three tried to step out of the window, but the roof in front of her became a bed of fire almost the same instant. The fire seemed truly to counter every move they made, every idea they had for escaping.

Behind us, Natani and his nephew were struggling to get a ladder up against one yet-to-be-consumed section of the roof. We watched as Natani's nephew climbed up the ladder as quickly as he could, smacking at the flames with a wet sack to see if he could make a pathway for the buddies.

We could see the fire inside the house eating away the walls behind them. M'Lady Two, stepped out of the window and turned toward Natani's nephew, who was now at the top of the ladder, beating at the flames. She lifted her left arm protectively and edged forward in his direction, but the roof, weakening all around that window, gave way and in the same instant we saw her fall into the belly of the fire. She went down without a sound. It was a sight so unreal, I had to convince myself I wasn't still asleep on my cot in the barn.

The flames as if in a march of victory rose to heights above the windows. Through them, I could see M'Ladies One and Three. They were screaming, but we couldn't hear them. It was a silent movie in vivid color. The roof above them caved in and the house seemed to crumble and fall into itself. Natani's nephew leaped from the ladder as it, too, fell forward. He hit the ground nimbly and Natani helped him up.

All of us stepped back farther and farther. The waves of heat were burning our faces.

"Get back," Natani shouted at us. "Back, back."

We retreated to the center of the yard, where we stood and watched the house burning. Off in the distance, like lanterns in the night, two revolving lights appeared. Someone was coming, but far too late, I thought.

Behind us, the horses were neighing in fear and kicking at their stall doors. Natani rushed back, his arm extended upward, his hand tracing the embers that were being carried in the smoke. I realized his concern immediately. They were moving toward the barn and the barn was dry, especially the roof.

I joined his nephew and him and we got the horses out of the barn and into the corral.

"They'll still be very frightened," Natani said.

He ordered his nephew to open the corral so the horses could go as far as they needed. Then he turned his attention to the other animals. I worked at his side for what I later realized was hours. Robin and Teal began to help as well. Natani's foresight proved correct. A section of the horse barn caught fire. His nephew tried to contain it with their water hoses, but it was too little and had limited reach. It wasn't long before the horse barn was too far gone to save.

The lights I had seen belonged to a fire truck and an ambulance with two paramedics. There wasn't much for them to do but stand by like us and watch the hacienda burn to the ground. Soon after they had arrived, a sheriff's patrol car drove up and then another.

Exhausted from our efforts to save all the animals, Robin, Teal, and I sat in front of our barn barracks, which had escaped the embers because of the wind's direction. We watched the police, firemen, and paramedics conferring with Natani. It all remained unreal to me. Their faces glowing, the flames, the crackle of the fire, the tower of smoke that the wind carried into the desert. Through it, the stars twinkled as if the heavens approved of it all.

"Where's Gia?" Teal asked, and Robin and I looked at each other.

During all the excitement, our frantic activity and terror, none of us had thought about her.

"I haven't seen Dr. Foreman either," Robin said.

We turned back to the dwindling conflagration and stared at the flames like three hypnotized people, no one speaking, no one moving. Finally, Teal leaned against me. I put my arm around her and Robin put her arm around me. It was the way the police and the woman from the social service agency found us. We were like three girls frozen, discovered at the top of some very, very high mountain. I'm sure we looked as if it would take a crowbar to pry us apart.

We had sat there together throughout the night and into the first morning light. The fire had burned the house to its foundation. It still smoldered enough to send up a significant tower of smoke I was sure could be seen for miles and miles.

Strangely, other Indians appeared out of the desert as though they had always been out there. I couldn't imagine from where they had all come, but at least a few dozen men and women and some children were on the property. I saw from the way they circled Natani and spoke to him that they respected him greatly. Later, I would learn that he was actually a descendant of a famous Navajo medicine man, and the Indians had high regard for inherited powers.

The woman from the social service agency introduced herself as Mrs. Alexia Patterson, but insisted we call her Alex. All three of us had been through enough layers of the juvenile system to understand it was her way to get us to see her as a friend and not a bureaucrat. A sheriff's officer was with her when she first approached us. I could see that he knew exactly what the ranch was used for and who we were. He wore a hard look of accusation and suspicion and wanted to talk to us first.

"Let them clean themselves up," Alex told him. "They've worked hard helping with the animals and everything, Lieutenant."

He grunted a reluctant okay and we walked in a daze to an outside sink where we washed our faces and hands, our necks and arms. The stench of smoke and burned wood was so thick it was deeply embedded in our very skin. It would take more than a rinsing to get it off our bodies. It would never wash off our souls and hearts.

While we cleaned up, Alex and the sheriff's deputy stood off to the side talking and watching us. The terror and shock we had experienced leveled off, but rushing in to replace it were waves of anxiety. What would happen to us? What had happened to Gia? What did the authorities think about us?

"How are you doing, girls?" Alex asked, walking over to us.

"Ginger peachy," Teal told her.

Alex didn't blink. She smiled and nodded. "That, um, barn or building over there?" She pointed to our barracks. "That's where you girls slept?"

"Yes," Robin said. "It's the first-class accommodations here."

"I think," the sheriff's deputy said, stepping up beside Alex, "that the time for smart talk is well over." He glared at us and no one spoke.

"This is Lieutenant Rowling, girls. He and I have to ask you questions. Why don't we all go into that building then and have a talk," Alex said in as sweet a voice as she could muster. Lieutenant Rowling nodded his approval, but kept his eyes fixed on us with the accuracy of a pair of well-aimed pistols.

We all walked to the barracks.

After we entered, Alex stopped and looked around the Spartan quarters. She was truly surprised that the floor was covered in straw and all the cots but one were without mattresses, pillows, or blankets.

"I don't understand," she muttered, and looked at the sheriff's deputy, who just shrugged. "Let's sit here," she said, nodding at my cot, which was the closest.

We sat on it and Lieutenant Rowling pulled another one closer. Alex sat on that, but he stood glaring down at us.

"How many of you are there at present?" she asked.

"There were five of us when we three came. There were four of us last night. Mindy's dead. She committed suicide," I told her.

Alex looked at Lieutenant Rowling, who smirked. "Who committed suicide?" he asked.

"Mindy."

"Mindy Levine," Robin said.

"You saw her commit suicide?" he asked.

"No, Gia told us that happened. We were out in the desert," I said.

"Who's this Gia?" he asked, looking from me to Robin and Teal.

"She was the other girl, the fourth girl," Robin told him.

"You said you were out in the desert. What does that mean?" Alex asked.

"We were being punished. We were taken out there and left to find our way back," I explained. "Teal got bitten by a rattlesnake. Natani saved our lives." I felt like I was repeating a recording, speaking with little or no emotion, just reporting facts.

Again Alex's eyebrows hoisted and she looked at Lieutenant Rowling.

He shrugged again. "You guys should know more about this place than we do," he said defensively.

Alex nodded. "We should. But, we obviously don't."

"Yeah, well, that's for later. Right now," he continued, bearing down on me especially, "what do you know about this fire?"

I shook my head and the other two did the same.

"We woke up and saw the whole place illuminated, so we dressed and stepped out and saw the house was in flames. We ran around back and watched Natani and his nephew, the cook, try to save the buddies."

"Buddies?"

"Assistants, I suppose you would call them," Teal said dryly. "We had better names for them."

"Do you know anything about Gia?" I asked.

"What about Dr. Foreman? Was she in the house or what?" Teal followed, her arrogant, demanding tone making her sound more like the Teal I knew.

"We're asking the questions here," Lieutenant Rowling said so sharply it was as if his tongue were made of razor blades.

"Okay, girls," Alex said, giving him a stern look and then turning back to us. "For now, I want you to rest. We'll get you something to drink and eat. I'll return soon."

She and the lieutenant left the barracks.

"How come they didn't know about Mindy?" Teal asked. "If someone dies, especially like that, wouldn't the police know?"

"It's all very weird," Robin said.

I agreed and then my eyes went to Gia's cot. The edge of her notebook could be seen just under her pillow. I went to it and pulled it out. I opened the cover and sat on her cot to read.

"What?" Robin asked when I shook my head.

"I guess she returned to being Posy. She starts this off with a 'Dear Mother.' "

I started to read on. "No, wait. Maybe not."

"Read it aloud," Teal said.

I looked up at them, then did what she asked.

"Dear Mother,

"Did I ever tell you about the first day I saw you, when I was ten and they brought me to you? How does a girl get over the fact that her real mother and her real father gave up on her completely and agreed to give her away, give her to you, let you adopt her and make her your daughter?"

"What an imagination she had," Teal said, shaking her head. Robin nodded.

I continued reading.

"I never understood it all, of course. I always expected I would go home someday, no matter how you explained it. You told me you wanted to be my mother now. I would be a shining example of your powers, your abilities. You would be sitting out there on my high school graduation day and my college graduation day and you would be so proud of me.

"I'm very smart, you said. You said you could tell that and you were sure I was going to be an excellent student once I was cured.

"I must tell you I never thought of myself as sick so I never understood why you called it being cured. Sick to me was sneezing and coughing, bellyaches and headaches, but not being angry and afraid and alone. How is that being sick? From what I have seen of other kids my age, and especially the ones who were brought to you, being angry, afraid, and alone is more normal these days than being sick.

"There you go, I'm sure, shaking your head and pursing your lips. More proof that I'm sick, more proof that I'm sick. That's what you're

saying and what you've been saying since the day I was brought to your home.

"*I understand my parents being afraid of having me in the house after the fire, but I never stopped believing they would come back for me someday. Not until now. Now I know they won't. You wouldn't want them to. You wouldn't want to give up your prize patient, would you?*

"*You made fun of my Posy. You did everything you could to kill her, to crush her like some insect, but she got away, just like Mindy. We can get away from you, but not all of us. Not all of us can stand up to you and your little army of so-called buddies.*

"*You know what frightens me the most today, Mother? That I'm finally calling you Mother. That you got your way with that, but now I'm terrified that you will win, that you really will be sitting out there on my graduation days and I will be your little protégé, your shining example, and you will use me to get rid of every Posy who is out there and every Mindy.*

"*I was thinking I would give you this to read, but then I thought, if I do, you will find a way to overcome. You always do. You're the best at what you do, Mother. You will always win. You will always have your way with us.*

"*Guess who has come back tonight?*" I read, and looked up at Robin and Teal, who were sitting there mesmerized. I looked back at the notebook. "*That's right, Posy. And guess why? She has a plan. I don't know why I didn't think of it on my own. You've had me spinning in circles, I guess. Anyway, she's here to help. She hasn't forgotten me. She couldn't leave me behind after all.*

"*We're on our way to activate our plan, Mother. You'll know it all very soon.*

"*I wonder if my real mother and father ever really asked after me. You said they didn't, but maybe, maybe you were lying to me. Maybe they haven't forgotten me completely. Maybe they'll think about me now. Posy says they will.*

"*And Posy knows.*

"*Posy always knew.*"

I closed the notebook.

"I feel so sick inside," Teal said. "So sick and tired."

"What's new about that?" Robin muttered, then quickly added, "So do I."

We all looked up when the door opened and a female sheriff's deputy entered carrying some sodas and a bag of sandwiches and candy bars.

"Hi, girls," she said. "Brought you something to eat and drink."

She set it all down.

"Chocolate bars?" Teal said, opening the bag. "And subs. They look like they have everything on them!"

"They do," the deputy said. "I didn't know what you liked, of course, so I got the works. Enjoy. Mrs. Patterson and Lieutenant Rowling will be back to speak with you all soon."

She left and Robin dug into the bag. "Roast beef. And a Coke. I think I forgot what that tastes like. Look." She held up a bag. "Potato chips!"

Teal was already eating and closing her eyes with pleasure. I was the most surprised of us all that I had an appetite after what we had just been through, but nervousness burned calories, I guess. I ate as fast as they did and enjoyed what I was eating just as much.

When we were finished, we went to the doorway because we heard a loud roaring sound. We saw a helicopter landing. Two men in suits and a uniformed policeman who looked like a general emerged, bent over to avoid the propellers, and ran toward the ruins of the house. Many more patrol cars, another ambulance, firemen and police were moving about the grounds and around the smoldering hacienda. Off to the left, I saw Natani and his nephew surrounded by policemen, who were listening to them answer questions.

"Who's that in the helicopter, the president?" Teal wondered aloud.

"What's going to happen to us now?" Robin asked.

Both Teal and I turned and looked at her. Funny, I thought, how I had never even considered it until she had just mentioned it. What would be done with us?

"Whatever it is, it'll be a vacation compared to this," Teal replied.

Somehow, I didn't believe a vacation was what was ahead for us.

16

Fly Away Home

The two men in suits whom we had seen come in the helicopter joined Alex and Lieutenant Rowling when they returned to the barn barracks. Once again, Alex told us to sit on a cot. She sat on the one brought closer to us, and the three men stood around and stared down at us as if we were extraterrestrials or something that had just been found in the desert.

"We need your help to understand what exactly happened here," Alex began in a soft, friendly tone.

None of the men smiled. I had the feeling that if she weren't there, they would beat every answer out of us.

"All three of you were sent here as part of the juvenile recovery program, correct?" she asked, thumbing through some pages in a file she carried.

"Was that what they called it?" Teal asked, looking at Robin and me as if we had kept it a secret from her.

"I never heard that term, Teal," I said.

"I thought it was part of the garbage recycle program," Robin muttered.

"Maybe we should conduct this interrogation someplace else," Lieutenant Rowling growled, "like the state's maximum security prison."

Alex held up her right hand without turning to him. She kept her eyes on us.

"Listen to me, girls. People are dead. This is an obvious case of felonious arson."

"*Murder* is a better word," Lieutenant Rowling corrected.

Alex closed and opened her eyes, again without looking up at him. "Before we can take you to more comfortable surroundings and see about your futures, we need to know as much as possible about what transpired here. How long have you girls been here?" she asked, flipping through those pages again.

We looked at each other, and then, after a moment, when no one replied, we all just laughed.

The men again looked ready to pounce and pound us.

"We're not being disrespectful, Alex," I said. "We've all lost track of time. It seems like a very long time, but I imagine it's not."

"When you arrived here, these other girls, Mindy and Gia, were already here, however?"

"Yes," Robin said.

"Is Mindy dead?" I asked. I looked up quickly at Lieutenant Rowling, anticipating his saying again that they were the ones who asked the questions, not us. "We're worried about her. We don't know what to believe."

Alex nodded. "We understand she did attempt suicide. She's at a clinic. A mental clinic, and she is in treatment."

"She didn't die?" Teal asked, then looked at me.

"Why did she get to go to a clinic and not Gia?" I wondered aloud. "Maybe none of this would have happened then."

"Why do you say that? Was Gia angry about Mindy?" Alex asked.

"She told us she was dead. I don't think she was lying. I think she really believed it, so, yes, she was upset about her. When we returned from our picnic in the desert, we found her to be very different. She didn't talk to us very much. She slept a lot," I said.

"What did she actually do?" Teal asked.

Robin and I looked up in anticipation of hearing the gruesome details.

"Did she talk to you girls about doing anything?" Alex replied instead of answering directly.

"No," I said.

"All she did was work, eat, and write in her notebook," Robin offered. "Like us."

"Notebook?"

"Dr. Foreman made us write in notebooks," Teal said. "If we didn't do it, we lost privileges or were punished. After we had done so this time, we were supposed to get our mattresses, pillows, and blankets back," she added with indignation, as if she were lodging a complaint with a hotel manager. "We handed them in and never heard a word."

"Did Gia hand in her notebook, too?" Alex asked.

"No. It's right there, under the pillow." I nodded at Gia's cot.

Lieutenant Rowling, probably frustrated with just standing and listening and not applying some sort of electric torture, lunged at the cot and found the notebook. He opened it, then smirked with disappointment and handed it to Alex. I don't know what he was expecting to find between the covers. Maybe a confession.

Alex read some of it quickly, nodded, and handed it to the shorter of the two well-dressed men. He began to read it with the other man looking over his shoulder.

Alex turned back to us. "Just give me a quick understanding of what went on here."

"Went on?" Teal asked, tilting her head as if she were talking to a complete idiot.

"You had classes you attended. You talked about good and bad behavior. You had therapy sessions with Dr. Foreman, who tried to help you understand why you were getting into more and more trouble. I imagine you had your chores every day, helped with the management of the ranch, the preparations for your meals, am I not correct?"

None of us replied. We all stared at her again.

Then Teal leaned forward, holding her head with that superior air as only she could and looked Alex in the face. "Your understandings are somewhat misdirected," she said in perfect, teacherlike tones.

Alex lost her smile. "Then help me understand correctly."

Teal looked at us. "Shall we help her, girls?"

"Look, Mrs. . . . Alex, whatever," Robin said. "Y'all been given a lot of hogwash it seems. We didn't have any real classes. She threw books and assignments at us and we were left on our own to do them, and if we failed, she gave us demerits, and if we got too many demerits, we lost privileges, and if we got even more demerits, we were sent to the Ice Room."

"Ice Room?"

The two men in suits closed Gia's notebook and turned to listen to us.

Neither Robin nor I was anxious to describe the Ice Room. In fact, Robin just wouldn't say much at all. I explained how I had revealed my fear of rats and how that had been used to torture me into obedience.

"Virtual reality," one of the men in suits said. He nodded at the other. "Pretty sophisticated equipment. Look into that as they sift through the ruins. See what you can find."

The man nodded and left the barracks.

"Tell me about this desert trip," Alex asked.

Robin did describe that. When she reached the point when Teal got bitten, Teal started to cry silently. It was almost as if she didn't know she was crying. She sat there staring and the tears started to emerge from under her lids and trickle down her cheeks.

"I'm sorry, girls. I don't want to force you to relive painful experiences," Alex said, "but we're just trying to understand how all this came about."

"Did you help this Gia with the gasoline?" Lieutenant Rowling demanded, raising his voice with impatience and stepping closer to us.

"Gasoline?" Robin responded.

"No." I looked at Alex. "What did she do exactly? Please tell us already."

"This is ridiculous," Lieutenant Rowling complained. "This girl, Gia, went out and did all this and you three are sitting there and telling us you knew nothing about it. Is that it?"

"Y'all don't have to believe it, but that's true," Robin told him, her eyes just as fiery.

The stronger my friend was, the prouder I was of her, and the stronger I felt myself become.

"Gia was smarter than any of us," I said. "She helped us all get through the schoolwork. Whatever she came up with to do, she didn't need any of us to help her do it or think it up. What did she do?" I repeated with more firmness.

"It looks like she poured gasoline strategically around the hacienda so that the fire and the flames would entrap the inhabitants. She poured it on the roof, around windows, everywhere. The lieutenant believes she might have spread this gasoline over a significant period of time and not have just come up with the idea and done it all at once. That's why he and some others are so suspicious about no one else noticing anything," Alex explained calmly.

"If she was carrying that much gasoline to that house, she would be marching back and forth a number of times from the barn where the tractor was housed," Lieutenant Rowling continued. "Someone would have to see her doing it and ask what she was doing. She would smell from gasoline, too."

"We all smelled from one thing or another around here," Teal said. "You ever clean out a pigpen?" She wiped away a tear.

"Maybe there was some gasoline closer to the house," I suggested. "Besides being in the barn with the tractor."

Teal looked at me. "That big tin drum," she said.

"What drum?" Lieutenant Rowling asked.

"There was a big drum behind the house." I then described how we had spied on the buddies. Confessing about something so innocent compared with what had just happened here and what had been done to us over time didn't seem risky. I told how we had gotten the idea from Gia in the first place.

"So she knew the drum was there," Robin said.

"I don't think there was anything in it then. I didn't smell any gasoline," Robin said, "and it fell over, remember? We would have seen gasoline spill out."

"It just wasn't in it then," I said.

Robin shrugged.

"She might have been sneaking gasoline from time to time and spilling it into the drum until she thought she had enough," Teal suggested.

"I guess that makes sense. That way she wouldn't have to be running back and forth with pails all day and night to spill it all around the house," Robin added. "I guess she did have it all well planned out."

Her look of appreciation for Gia's ingenuity only made Lieutenant Rowling more enraged. "And you are sitting there and telling us you didn't help her and you didn't know anything about it?"

"See that?" Teal said, looking at me. "And you said he wouldn't be able to figure it out."

If the top of Lieutenant Rowling's head hadn't been securely attached to the rest of his skull, it would surely have blown off from the explosion of anger inside his brain.

"Girls, please," Alex said. "I'm trying to get this all over with quickly for you and get you out of here."

"I guess they did belong here," Lieutenant Rowling said. "I guess no matter what was done to them, it wasn't enough to change them."

"Oh, we're changed, sir," I said. "We're changed. We used to be nice people."

Robin laughed and Teal smiled widely.

"I'm sorry," I said to Alex, "but we're tired and we have seen terrible things and terrible things have been done to us, whether we deserved them or not." I glared up at the policeman. "Won't you please tell us what happened to Gia? What happened to Dr. Foreman? Was she in the house?"

"Five people were killed. Figure it out," Lieutenant Rowling snapped. "You're smart enough to add."

"Please, Lieutenant. You have enough information to go forward, don't you?" Alex asked, directing herself mostly at the man in the suit.

He nodded. "Okay. We'll talk to them after you've gathered the information you need and made what arrangements you need to make," he said softly. He nodded at Lieutenant Rowling, who turned reluctantly and followed him out of the barracks.

"Gia and Dr. Foreman are dead, girls," Alex said as soon as they were gone. "And so are the girls assisting Dr. Foreman."

"Gia got trapped in her own fire," I said, realizing.

"No, she went into the building after she began the fire."

"Why did she go into the building after she started the fire?" Teal asked.

"To spread it inside as well, probably," I said.

"No, not only for that. It looks like she went in to prevent Dr. Foreman from getting out."

"How can you tell that?" I asked, grimacing.

"They found a chain around Gia's waist. The chain was around Dr. Foreman's waist, too, and there was a lock on it preventing her from just slipping out of it. She was caught in bed, sleeping apparently. There was a struggle of some sort, but dragging Gia out along with her was too difficult, and by then the fire must have been consuming the hallways, the rooms, and all the exits."

"You're saying Gia wanted to die with her? She sacrificed herself to be sure Dr. Foreman couldn't escape?"

Alex nodded. "It certainly looks that way, I'm afraid. You girls are telling the truth? You knew nothing of this, nothing of her intentions? You didn't know she hated Dr. Foreman that much, enough to be responsible for her death?"

"No, ma'am," I said.

"We all got so we hated Dr. Foreman," Teal told her, "but maybe Gia had reason to hate her more."

"No maybe about that," Robin said. "I guess Mindy was the breaking point."

"Gia wasn't right from the start, was she, Phoebe? She was living in her imagination, creating a girl named Posy. I guess for a while that was her escape," Teal said.

I watched Alex Patterson's face as they spoke, then I leaned forward. "Was it all her imagination, ma'am? I mean, everything in that notebook?"

For a long moment, I didn't think she would reply, but then she shook her head. "No. What she wrote in that notebook was true. It's all very sad." She stood up.

"All of it was true? She was Dr. Foreman's adopted daughter?" I asked.

"Exactly," Alex said. "You're right," she told Teal. "This Posy she created was her way of dealing with all that, her escape I imagine."

"How desperate she must have finally become," Teal thought aloud.

Alex nodded. "I'm going to arrange for the three of you to be taken to a facility in Phoenix. You'll be questioned further there and I'll be on the phone with the various justice agencies you've all been involved with and that have had stipulations as to your dispositions. There is a lot to do, so we'll have to get started soon. I don't imagine you have anything much to gather up and take with you."

We shook our heads, our voices trapped inside our thoughts.

"I should have a car here within the hour. Don't wander too far," she advised.

We watched her leave.

"Wander too far?" Robin muttered.

"We could run away," I said, looking at Teal.

She started to laugh, her shoulders shaking, and then that laugh turned into a sob. We joined her like a chorus, all three of us crying for so many reasons it was impossible to center on one in particular.

Afterward, before the car arrived for us, I left the barracks and went to find Natani. He and his nephew had rounded up the horses and gotten them back into the corral. They were still nervous, the stench of the fires filling their nostrils and rekindling their recent traumatic horror. Wind Song looked at me as I approached the railing. He snorted and patted the ground, but he didn't walk over as he usually did. I didn't blame him for distrusting humans who were supposed to protect him.

I saw Natani's nephew filling the water trough and was about to ask him where Natani was when I heard the drumbeats coming from Natani's hogan. I hurried over to it, knocked on the frame of the door, and peered in. He was squatting on the floor, the drum before him, those magical rocks spread around it. He said nothing, but I saw him greet me with his eyes so I entered and sat across from him.

"What do you have in your healing bag that can fix all this, Natani? Who knows where we're going to end up now?"

He closed his eyes and stopped his drumbeating.

"Once, when I was a young boy, my mother took me by the hand and made me sit and watch a mother wren care for her newborn babies. She brought me back day after day and I watched how hard the mother worked to feed and care for the newborns, who never stopped demanding.

"They grew quickly. I was surprised at how quickly, and soon they became more adventurous and began to explore the world outside their nest. Everything frightened them though and they returned, hovering beside each other and waiting to be fed and protected.

"And soon they were too big to be in the nest, but they tried to stay. I saw that. I saw the mother drive them out of the nest. She refused to permit them to return. They looked very lost and afraid to me, but after a while, they flew off and my mother had me bring the empty nest down and keep it and think about it until I could answer for myself why the mother wren drove her own babies away.

"I had trouble with the answer for a long time. And then my grandmother died, my mother's mother, and after she was gone, my mother came into our hogan and sat beside me. I was very, very sad. I was my grandmother's favorite.

" 'What has this taught you about the birds?' my mother asked me.

"I looked at her with great confusion at first. How could my grandmother's death teach me anything about a nest of baby birds and how their mother had cared so devotedly for them and then driven them away? My mother waited and waited. I soon realized I knew the answer, daughter of the tortoise. I knew it but I didn't want to know it."

"What is the answer, Natani?"

"The mother bird knew she was much older and there would be a time, not far off in the earth's life, when she would be no longer and her babies would die with her if they didn't go out and become strong and independent. To turn your own from your door is hard, but it is nature's way.

"I used to wonder if the mother bird ever saw her babies again, and if she saw them and they saw her, would they show it or were the babies so angry at her that they would no longer acknowledge her or care for her?"

"Did they?"

"You never see a bird die, do you, daughter of the tortoise? They die in the dark, alone. You don't look up and suddenly see one topple to the earth. In the morning you might find them, but they have died in the dark.

"It was my father who told me that in the dark the babies gather and thank their mother as they hope their babies will thank them. Before the sun is up, they are gone.

"*Hagoone* is our word for good-bye, daughter of the tortoise, but there is no word for good-bye for children and parents. You cannot say good-bye to that which is part of you or of which you are a part. It is forever with you and with those who come after you. It is the greatest gift of all, this truth, this never saying good-bye.

"What you think is gone, what you think you will never see or hear again, is still with you. Go away with that in your heart. Nothing here has changed that truth nor could it.

"They died in the dark," he said, nodding toward the demolished hacienda. "I saw their spirits go with the smoke to join what has come before them."

He lowered his head and I rose to leave.

"Thank you, Natani. *"Hagoone."*

He looked up at me and smiled. "Remember the tortoise that stayed too long in his shell. Do not stay too long in yours."

"I won't," I promised.

And I left him.

Afterward, the three of us rode away in silence, none of us looking back. All I took with me was the turquoise stone Natani had given me, a piece of the fallen sky. Alex had brought us some clothes to wear. Of course, Teal complained about them, how cheap and ugly they were, but I could see how grateful she was for them.

We dozed on and off. The landscape flowed like a continuous stream of sand, rocks, and desert plants. I saw some rabbits, but we were moving too fast to really see anything else. Alex sat up front with the driver and frequently asked us how we were doing, if we were thirsty or needed the bathroom. Most of the time, we just shook our heads. No one seemed to want to break the silence. Maybe we were all afraid that if we talked too much, we would stop this escape, for that was what it surely was to each of us, a rescue, a flight from someone else's private hell.

Eventually, we were brought to a government building where we were taken to a room and, once again, asked a series of questions about the final events at Dr. Foreman's School for Girls. The two men in suits back at the barracks turned out to be special agents of the FBI, the reason for that, we learned, being that the ranch was leased by Dr. Foreman. She actually leased it from Natani's people so he had more reason than she had for staying and caring for it. Any crime committed on Indian land came under the jurisdiction of the FBI, as well as the Indian agency and their own tribal police.

Teal joked that it was an accomplishment to be interrogated by FBI agents. We had all been arrested at one time or another by city police, local law enforcement, and now we had graduated to the head of the juvenile criminal class. We laughed, but we didn't really think it was funny. We laughed because we were still nervous about what would happen next.

We were fed, given cold drinks, and left to rest in a lounge. Funnily enough, having not had television for so long, we were all bored by

what was on and ignored it. Teal was the first to start looking at the
magazines. Robin joined her and I soon followed. It was as if we were
slowly emerging from a coma, which was what I had felt when I had
first been brought to the orientation room. It was all a sleep and an
awakening, after all.

Finally, Alex returned and we all looked up with great anticipation.

"I'm not going to go through all the details concerning the various
government agencies that have something to say about your futures,
girls," she began. "You all know you were sent to this school as a result of a legal decision with guardian approval. The bottom line is
you're all still on probation. I'm to make sure you all understand that.
Do you?"

"Alex," Teal said with her cute little smirk on her lips, "we've been
on probation since the day we were born."

"Yes, well, as long as you understand you still are." Then Alex
sighed so deeply I thought she would come apart right before our eyes.

"Teal, you are going home. You'll be on a flight that will take you to
Albany via Newark. There'll be an officer from the juvenile criminal
division greeting you at the Newark airport and seeing that you get on
the right flight for Albany, where your parents will take custody.
There, a division of juvenile justice will see to your counseling.

"Robin, you have a direct flight to Nashville."

"I do?"

"Your mother will meet you at the airport and the same will be true
for you."

"Mother darling wants to meet me at the airport? Y'all sure about
that?"

"Your families have all been told something about the events that
have just transpired, and some of what you have been going through at
the ranch."

"Mother darling will probably write a song about it," Robin told
me.

I smiled gently, but my eyes were on Alex, who was looking at me.

"Phoebe, your uncle and aunt have refused to accept custody and
responsibility for you. I'm sorry. Arrangements have been made for
you to be with foster parents in Atlanta. They'll be greeting you at the
airport and you will have a direct flight. The same counseling and
overseeing will take place there for you. Arrangements will be made
concerning your schooling. They are, I've been told, a very nice couple, whose children are all grown and out of the house. They're actually looking forward to taking you into their home. I hope you will respect that and it will work out for you.

"Well, then," she added, standing, "any questions I can answer for you?"

"Yeah," Teal said. "Why were we born?"

"That, I'm afraid, is a question you'll have to answer for yourself, dear. I wish you all the best of luck. There are cars outside waiting to transport you three to the different terminals and the different flights. Why don't you all freshen up, go to the bathroom, and come out in ten minutes or so, okay?"

She smiled and then left us just like anyone who had unloaded a burden would leave us, her shoulders relaxing, her body softening, her mind rushing to think about something pleasurable that awaited her when she returned home from work and could put us out of mind forever and ever. I envied her for being able to do that.

"Anyone want to go to the bathroom?" Teal asked.

"Not me," Robin said. "Phoebe?"

"I'm not used to bathrooms inside," I said, "without something crawling around the toilet."

They laughed.

"You're such an idiot," Teal said.

"And what are you?" Robin asked her. "Besides a spoiled brat, that is?"

Teal pretended to think. "Nothing else. That seems to be enough for now."

We laughed again.

"The first thing my mother is going to ask me," Teal said as we started out of the room, "is what did I do to my hair? It would never occur to her that someone else would have done it to me. I'll be kept locked up until she thinks I look good enough to be out in public again."

"Were you ever good enough?" Robin asked her.

"Oh, listen to her? I hope your mother does write a song about Dr. Foreman's School and sings it to you every night."

"I might write it for her," Robin said.

A man in a suit who looked like another FBI agent waited at the front door of the building. Alex, apparently, was already gone.

He opened the door and began assigning the cars. They were parked in a line at the sidewalk, and the drivers of each looked bored to death. We paused.

It was dark now. There were stars, but they weren't as bright or as numerous as the stars in the desert sky. Streetlights and other lights washed them out.

"You're probably going to be better off than both of us, Phoebe. You'll have people who actually want you," Teal said.

"My daddy wanted me. I think in her own way my mama tried to want me, did want me very much once," I said, smiling.

They looked at me, each of them thinking of times when they had felt the same way about their parents, I'm sure.

"Let's get moving, girls," the man behind us ordered.

Robin pressed her lips together. Her eyes watered.

Teal looked away quickly.

"You know," I said, "I almost feel like thanking Dr. Foreman."

"For what?" Teal said, turning back quickly.

"For ourselves," I said.

"Yeah, well, if either of you see me on a street in Beverly Hills or Worth Avenue in Palm Beach, pretend we never met, will you?" Teal said.

She took a step toward her car, then turned and hugged Robin. They held each other as if they thought when they let go they'd fall into a dark hole.

Teal did the same to me and I held her tightly, too. Then Robin and I hugged.

None of us spoke. We looked at each other as if for the first time ever, then they turned to their vehicles.

Hagoone, I thought as they got into their cars.

Just before I got into mine, a sparrow landed on its hood, tapped proudly in a small circle, then lifted into the wind, looking like it could fly to the stars.

I watched it.

And then I got into the car, embraced myself, and snuggled into a corner of the seat.

I looked out the window, but I saw nothing but my own face reflected in the glass.

Then I fingered the small turquoise stone and smiled.

Natani's drum followed me all the way to my new home.

Epilogue

Dear Freaks,

I guess you didn't expect to hear from me, especially in the form of a letter, but all that writing experience at Dr. Foreman's School has paid off. Ha! Ha!

Seriously, I actually received an A in English this quarter. I'm doing well in all my classes, even math. Every time I receive a good grade for anything in any class, I thank Gia.

I figured the only reason I haven't heard from either of you was you didn't know my address, especially since I didn't know it myself when we parted. Why else would you have ignored me all this time? Unless, of course, you're both doing time in some maximum security institution for continuing to violate every law possible.

I haven't so much as been reprimanded in class, and I haven't been late to school or to any class. No one is more shocked about that than I am.

You know what frightens me the most about all this? If Dr. Foreman were alive, she'd claim credit. She'd be telling everyone she did it, then more poor and pathetic girls like us would be sent to her school. Maybe that is really why Gia did what she did. She put a stop to it.

I don't know how it is for you these days with all the time that has passed. Sometimes, I wake up and look around as if I expect I'm back in the barn barracks, and I'm surprised I'm in a real bed in my own room, which is a very nice room, by the way. I'm sure it's not as nice as Teal's, so don't start describing your room again and cataloging all your valuable possessions, Teal. I acknowledge you're a spoiled rich kid.

Just kidding. I'm jealous as always.

Sometimes, often I should say, if I hear a thumping sound, maybe just the bass on a speaker in some guy's car, I think about Natani. I laugh to myself, remembering the looks on your faces when he told us his animal stories or spoke in his mystical way. The truth is I miss him and wish that someday I can go back to see him.

The only thing is, just like you two, I imagine, thoughts about returning to that place make me shudder as well.

I wonder about Mindy. There doesn't seem to be any way to find out about her. For all we know, she might still be locked up in some clinic. Maybe she's too far gone to be cured, ever. I hope not. You ever think about her?

And of course, I think a great deal about Gia, how she kept so much of herself hidden from us, disguised in imaginary people and events. When I think about it, my parents essentially gave me away, too, and I rate my uncle and aunt about the same in the horror factor as Dr. Foreman. You'd have to meet my aunt to see what I mean. The big difference was that my daddy really hoped to have me back.

Well, I guess I'll have to tell you. I've met someone nice. I'm talking about a boy. His name's Ralston Marks. He's on the football team. Actually, he's the quarterback. Teal, don't start bragging about your boyfriends.

Ralston is unlike any boy I have ever been with. He's polite, religious, but not overly so, and he's a very good student. He looks to be a shoo-in for scholarships to important colleges. I don't know why he wants to be with me all the time, but, be still my pitter-patter heart, he does. He says I'm one of the most mature girls for our age he's known.

I guess how I am now is a result of what we all went through. Everything other girls are doing seems to be so silly to me lately. I hate just hanging around malls anymore, and when I hear them gossiping in school, I really do think of Natani's chickens clucking. That's how Ralston first saw me, sitting there with this goofy smile on my face. He asked me what was so funny, and I told him and he laughed and we haven't stopped talking and being with each other since.

I should tell you that my foster parents are truly very nice people. My foster mother's name is Coco. She's French Canadian. Her parents emigrated there (How do you like the big word?) from a place called Cap Ferrat in southern France where they were in the service industry, a nice way to say butlers and maids. She met Andre in Quebec and they were married in Canada, then came to America and settled in Atlanta because of a business connection Andre had. They now own a big department store, and Coco is the clothes buyer.

So here's the best news of all . . . yours truly models clothes at the store on Sundays, the new fashions from Europe. It was Coco's idea. I almost refused to do it because I remembered Dr. Foreman telling me I could be a model and she would help arrange for that if I was just a good little Foreman girl. Why should we stop ourselves from doing things we like just because Dr. Foreman mentioned them, however?

I might actually continue doing this on a professional basis. A woman who runs a modeling agency stopped in last week. She said she had heard about me and she wants me to come see her. Coco approves. I really love her. She's so up and happy all the time and her and Andre's three children all like me, too.

All this happiness frightens me. I keep thinking someone from my past is going to appear on the doorstep and have reasons why I can't continue. Do you have any of those sorts of fears? When will they stop?

Last week, at Andre and Coco's insistence, I went to the cemetery and visited my daddy's and mama's graves. It didn't seem real to me. I had to keep rereading their names to convince myself that this was where they really were now.

Is there really any way to make peace with your past? I was tempted to crawl into one of Natani's shells, to avoid the tombstones, but I didn't. I couldn't.

And he was right, I couldn't stand there and say good-bye.

I knew I would be back many times and I would tell them good things.

And maybe someday even bring my own children along.

When I think of all this, I realize what it is we've achieved. Again, ironically, what we have achieved is something Dr. Foreman said we didn't have, a future.

We have a future, don't we?

We can hope, and most of all, we can dream.

Write me if you can, if you want, if it doesn't bring back too many painful memories.

I don't ever, ever want to be the cause of someone's painful memories again.

Love,
Phoebe bird

Dear Phoebe,
You won't believe this, but I have been after my big-shot brother to use his connections to find out where you are. He promised he would and bragged how easily he could do that. He knew this one in government and that one, and until your letter arrived yesterday, he has been able to find out zilch. That's a new word for your expanding vocabulary.

I am writing you this letter from my dorm. No, I'm not living at home. My parents, after many intense discussions, decided to put me into this new prep school. I hate to say it, but it's a very good school, and like you, I am doing well in my academic work, and again like you, I haven't been in any serious trouble. Maybe a little trouble. I was almost caught out after curfew, but, and I know you won't believe it, I wasn't doing anything terribly exciting. I wasn't out meeting a boy or carrying on with some other girls or smoking. I was just walking and lost track of the time.

I do a lot of walking alone and thinking. Everyone thinks I'm weird, but I don't care.

My mother has visited me a number of times, more than I expected she would actually. She usually spends the entire visitation talking about her new charity events and planned vacations. She'll interrupt herself to tell me about some fashions she thinks are nice and elegant for me, and then she goes on to talk about some rich people I never knew and couldn't care less about knowing. But I have a new tolerance for her and I smile and look like I'm listening, and you know what, she's starting to talk more to me and look at me. It's as if by not showing her how much I hate what she is, she will start to change. The last time we spoke, in fact, she talked about just her and me going someplace together and getting to know each other better. She wants to take me to places she enjoyed when she was my age. Once, I would make fun of the idea, but now I've decided I would do it.

I guess what I'm saying is nothing can change quickly, and most might not ever change, but it's learning how to live with that realization that makes happiness possible. Otherwise, I return to what I was, always angry, always frustrated, always self-destructive.

Surprised at my self-analysis?

I have this psych course and I'm learning more about myself than I wanted to learn. I've even come to understand things about Dr. Foreman, although I battle back the memories. It's like trying to keep air bubbles from rising in a glass or something.

I'm jealous of you, Phoebe. I haven't met anyone like your Ralston yet. We have these mixers with an all-boys prep school, but it's all too artificial for me. I love spontaneity and I daydream about meeting Mr. Right on some street corner or in a store or in the park, anywhere except a prearranged mixer approved by both schools.

Am I hopeless?

Maybe not. You know how sometimes you can feel something is really going to happen if you're just patient and you keep yourself up and happy? That's how I feel about Mr. Right. He's out there. We're going to meet.

Not that boys are all I think about anymore. I'm not going into modeling, but I have been told by my English teacher that I have a flare—that's the way he puts it, a flare—for writing. He says I capture people and events so well, I should think about working in film. So, I'm enrolling in a film study course next semester. It involves writing scripts. When I'm big and famous and important, I'll cast you in a movie.

I wish my life now was all and only what I described. I still have bad nights, Phoebe. I see snakes. I see the buddies in the fire. I hear the screams. I'm getting better, but it's all not buried deeply enough. It will be someday. Won't it?

I miss the both of you. All my new friends are afraid of me or are obvious about how much they'd like me to like them. I need you two. I need to be reminded I'm not a big shot.

So, here's what I've decided. I'm getting my mother to ask my father to sponsor a trip for both you and Robin for my birthday. You'll both come to my big, rich house and we'll sleep on the floor and go to the bathroom outside, and plant a garden and take ice-cold showers.

Just kidding. We'll have a big, fat time. Will you come? Please. Bring Ralston if you have to. I just think we need to look

*at each other's ugly face again just so we know we are really
here, we really matter. I'll work out the details.*

*Love,
Teal*

Dear Losers,

*I photocopied this letter so I would only have to write y'all
one. I did it at my mother's agent's office. I don't call her Mother
darling anymore. She went ahead and wrote a song called
"Mother Darling." She really did and it was a big hit in the
country music world.*

*The good thing is she left the creep she was with shortly after
I had been sent to Dr. Foreman's School. Then, she got a lucky
break when a really big agent heard her singing and he helped
her develop her style, got her a great backup group of musicians,
and began to find her some important bookings. She has two
recordings on the charts as we speak.*

*Now here's the news. One day I was practicing with her just
for the fun of it and her agent heard us singing together and decided we should do a song. We worked on it together. We really
had never done anything like that together before, but she liked
my suggestions.*

*I know y'all are going to think it's corny but here it is. It's
called "Mama, Let Me Be Me":*

Well, I've been growing up and I've been doing all you say,
I've learned all my schooling and I've worked hard every day,
You laid out directions and made me follow in your way,
But, Mama, oh, dear Mama, let me be myself today.
Let me be myself today,
Let me look a different way,
Let me find a voice that's me,
Let me try to be the woman I was always meant to be.
Say good-bye to your baby,
Say hello to someone new,
And maybe then, dear Mama,
You'll see I'm really you.

*We do the chorus again and we're adding more verses. The
agent likes it. You've got to hear it with music, but I think you get
the idea. Phoebe, you wipe off that smirk. I remember how you*

made fun of country music, but I also know in your heart of hearts, you liked it.

I'm hoping to bring a copy of the taping when I see you two at Teal's party.

Now as to boyfriends. I do have someone I'm sweet on. He's a guitar player, the younger brother of a more famous country guitar player, and his name is not Willie or Boone, Phoebe. His name happens to be Thomas, and not Tom either. He likes Thomas, Thomas Caton. His great-granddaddy fought in the Civil War and not for the Yankees.

Mama said if I marry him, I'll be living on the road or in trailers or whatever, but then I asked her where she's living and she laughed.

I thought you didn't want to be me, she said.

I guess she doesn't know I do in many ways. Maybe she's learning that and that's why we're closer than ever.

Yesterday, I was thinking, when we crossed that desert together and survived, we crossed a lot more than just sand and rocks.

We crossed from one world to another. Maybe someday I'll be able to write a song about it and sing it, with Mama or not. Then I'll know it's finally all put away. There are lots of ways to bury pain, but in my business, you make it work for you.

Don't I sound sophisticated for a country girl?

Stop laughing, Teal. Teal, Phoebe . . . how many, many times I've muttered your names like a prayer.

Can't wait to see y'all.

Love,
Robin

On a summer day Robin and I were flown into the Albany, New York, airport and Teal met us at the gate. We were all too excited to wait for the others to stop talking.

"Wait," Robin cried. "Y'all just got to learn how to take turns. Where's those manners I heard y'all bragging about?"

We laughed and hugged and hurried out to get in the stretch limousine. Teal made it clear we were going to be spoiled and we were to be impressed no matter what or her mother would leave the country.

We couldn't get enough of each other and I thought we would talk ourselves hoarse.

Finally, we were all quiet. Our smiles rested on our faces like tired birds lighting on a branch, and we stared ahead and the limousine continued to sail over the highway.

It really didn't matter where we were going.

We were there already. We were there the moment we all met. Together again.

Later, Robin sang her song and we locked it forever in our hearts along with all the promises we knew now we would fulfill to each other as well as to ourselves.